Stress City

A Big Book of Fiction by ~~50~~ 51 DC Guys

edited by
Richard Peabody

John Guernsey's novel excerpt first appeared in *A February Song* (2007); Matthew Kirkpatrick's "Metal Church" first appeared in *Barrelhouse* #1 (2005); Richard Morris's chapter first appeared in *Cologne No. 10 for Men* (iUniverse, 2007); Terence M. Mulligan's "Babysitting" first appeared in *The Baltimore Review* 2:1 (Winter 1998); Jim Reed's chapter first appeared in *The Only American Waiter* (reedtome.com, 2006); Lewis K. Schrager's story is forthcoming in *Cottonwood*.

ISBN-13: 978-0-931181-27-6
ISBN-10: 0-931181-27-5
First Edition
Published in the USA

Book design by Nita Congress.
Cover by G. Byron Peck.
Printed by Main Street Rag Publishing, Charlotte, NC.

Paycock Press
3819 North 13th Street
Arlington, VA 22201
www.gargoylemagazine.com

Acknowledgments

A big shout out to Kevin Downs and Wendi Kaufman for their help with this one; the usual tip of the hat to Nita Congress and M. Scott Douglass without whom this book never would have happened; and heartfelt thanks to Sunil Freeman, Margaret Grosh, David Minckler, Jeff Minerd, Zenon Stawinski, Ross Taylor, Johnny Temple, and Julie Wakeman-Linn. And lastly hats off to Byron Peck for the slinky-kinky oh-so-guys' cover.

"Another day older and deeper in debt."

—*Merle Travis*

In Memory

George Beveridge,
Mark Hannan,
Reg Ingram,
John Pomeroy,
and
Sidney Sulkin

Contents

Intro

Welcome to Stress City. I'm a Washington native, born and raised in the belly of the beast, ground zero, here where maybe nine out of ten men have bite blocks because their jaws are clenched so tight they remind one of David Lynch's great cartoon *The Angriest Dog in the World*. A dog so angry its jaws are clenched tightly in rigor. Now we're talking. That's what this city is really like most of the time. A place where the stress is so palpable you can see it hovering overhead as you drive into town from any direction. A place where writers are hard pressed to invent fiction when everyday reality is so zany, grim, surreal, and askew. And somehow this is one of the most beautiful cities in the world. Somehow this city has a hustling bustling educated and diverse population. And now that a new generation of local fictioneers—Ed Jones, George Pelecanos, and Keith Donohue—have put DC on the map as more than a genre writer sort of town, the time seems right to gather some of the fiction written by other local inhabitants. We've already published three volumes of local women's fiction with a fourth volume in the works, so why not a humongous collection of writing by DC guys? That's the ticket we thought.

So here you are. Writing from a city Kafka would have loved. We get high on stress here in Washington, D.C. Check it out for yourself.

RP
2008

Clinical Delicacies

R. R. ANGELL

Eola was my first, and I'll always remember that. She was on the heavy side, no great beauty, but I wasn't concerned with beauty right then. She was flat on her back. Gravity pulled at her jowls, stretched her face, and tugged her ample boobs down on her biceps. Those were the big brown eyes that grabbed my attention.

I was eighteen, a prep school senior, and on the varsity lacrosse team. My teammates boasted, but I had never seen a woman naked before.

Eola let me look all I wanted.

She was fifty-seven. My girlfriend, Cindy, was seventeen. So far, Cindy and I had kept the lights off and most of our clothes on. This was different. In those first few minutes, I got to know Eola far better than I'd ever get to know Cindy.

Eola's stark nakedness made me forget the antiseptic smell, the green tiled walls, and the bright, bright lights. Her body as cold as the stainless steel table on which she lay.

The shining workbench was rectangular and rimmed to contain fluids, with little channels like a giant serving platter that funneled to a drain. That big puff of nasty pubic hair was staring me down when Charles snuck up behind and slapped a pair of latex gloves over my shoulder. He proffered an apron like a waiter at our country club.

"Put these on, Thomas, we don't have all damn day," he said. "It's coming on lunchtime, and I never miss lunch. You understand what I'm saying?" He fixed me with those bulging yellow eyes of his, and then went on with his prep work.

1

Charles doused his black hands with white talc and rubbed them together until they looked gray and leathery, like elephant skin. Then he stretched on the latex gloves, the cuffs snapping into place.

His green scrubs made him look like a doctor. Well, almost. He was the head Diener, the guy who dissects the bodies for the pathologist. I was in training, the privilege of being a doctor's son considering a medical career. There was even talk about me becoming Charles's vacation replacement.

My regular summer job was up in the pathology supply room where I kept track of glassware, Vacuutainers, and other supplies. It was a good job, very educational.

I went to set the gloves down on the table next to Eola while I put on the coat, and changed my mind; I was close enough. I jammed them into my jeans. The lab coat was loose on me, but it was a welcome extra layer in the chilly morgue. I noticed her butt as I tried the gloves.

"May I have some powder, please?" Charles flipped the shaker to me. A little white puff floated in the air where it passed over her. "Hey Charles?"

"What you want now?"

"Why is her butt all flat and purple-edged like that?"

He considered her.

"By look of it, she died early last night. Been laying on her back ever since. After while, blood and fluids sink to the lowest spot when they ain't moving around." Charles stretched his shoulders and neck as he talked, warming up.

He reached over and hefted her up, exposing her backside. "See," he said, "just like the underside of a chicken been laying on its Styrofoam in the store."

Her entire back was purple, and where she hadn't contoured to the channels in the gravy pan she looked all smashed and flat. Especially her butt.

He let her go and she slapped back in place.

"Take this." Charles handed me a scalpel. "Now make a cut straight across the chest from shoulder to shoulder here, then right down the middle, then across from hipbone to hipbone," he said, watching me wince. "'Course, you can do it any order you want. I like the long stroke first when I'm feeling mean. You ought to go across the chest first, though; them ribs will stop you from going too deep."

The scalpel flashed cold and sharp in my hand. The weight of it felt good. The handle was just the right width, just the right length. It was a nice scalpel, with elegant lines and—

Charles cleared his throat.

"Any time now, Thomas."

I moved right up against the shining worktable and tried not to look at her face. Her eyes were open. Her lips were purple. I started above her left boob, making a small incision about half-an-inch long, and deeper than I intended. The scalpel was sharper than I expected. I waited for Eola to flinch, and looked her right in the eye.

"Son," Charles said. "Did I forget to mention she's dead?" He had the biggest grin, and when I started to answer, he pulled away, chuckling.

"Jesus, Charles. I don't know, it's—"

"Yeah, I know. You didn't want to hurt her. I felt the same way my first time. All nervous and gentle like. Not knowing what to do. Just like sex. Oh baby, can you feel this little prick?" He was laughing, leaning against the wall and sneaking teary-eyed glances at me.

"Try it again, Tom," he said, wiping his eyes on his sleeve. I held the scalpel so tight my fingertips went numb. Determined, I put blade against skin and started to cut.

"Ouch!"

I jumped and the scalpel went flying. I wanted to scream an apology, and then Charles fell against the wall again, howling with laughter.

Charles let me watch him cut so I could get the hang of it. He made the first incision from between her boobs on down, not at all what he had told me to do. The skin parted with the deep cut, pulling itself back from the incision. Bright bubbles of yellow and white fat folded up like flowers after a plow, exposing the dark earth of muscle underneath.

The smell hit me then, knocking me away from the table. A blood mold and rotting stench, so thick it could hold your puke aloft. A consuming stench of rotten eggs and sauerkraut, notes of bile and shit, and a disgustingly thin and appealing overlay of fresh-cut meat. Charles looked over the rim of his glasses at me with genuine concern.

"Tommy? You OK?"

I nodded and moved back toward the table, vowing to make it, to survive no matter what, to make my dad proud.

"I forgot about the smell," Charles said. "That other stuff, that was for fun. Go on," he waved toward the desk in the corner where he conducted other mysterious parts of his job. "There's a jar of VapoRub on it. Put a dab under your nose. It'll clear the smell some."

I blinked. My eyes were watering and my stomach was knotting up.

"Go on," he said, waving me away. "And don't touch nothing without taking your gloves off first."

The astringent VapoRub overwhelmed the smells but made my lip burn, a fair trade-off.

"I got hepatitis from a guy years ago," Charles said, poking at the incision while he talked. "Was fiddling around in there trying to undo his liver. Everything all slippery, and I cut myself right through the glove. Ain't nothing to do about it, you know? So you be mighty careful. Always know where you are in there. Where they stop, and where you begin."

I imagined the scalpel cutting my finger through to the bone. The skin flayed back. Dead blood leapt up from the corpse to slither into my open wound. It made me shiver.

Charles cut across her chest, just under her tits, then up each side to her shoulders. The flap of skin, tits and all, peeled up off the rib cage with a sticky, ripping sound. He flopped it back over her face.

"I hate it when they watch," he said, grinning. It kind of pissed me off, I don't know why. But I felt better not having her face right there.

He sawed through the rib cage with this thing that had a circular blade on one end. You'd think the blade was sharp and spun like a saw, but it just vibrated like crazy, cutting through bone, but not flesh. Charles demonstrated on his palm, and I thought he was going to cut himself again, but the blade didn't even dent his glove.

The saw went through bone like butter, and the next I knew, he was lifting out her ribs like the grate on a charcoal grill. I saw what you'd expect from dissecting frogs in tenth grade. Seemed almost, well, undignified. Like we should be more evolved than frogs, have some special system just for us.

It does kill your appetite for meat, being in there up to your elbows like that. Like some butcher. Dad said that we were at the top of the food chain, and real men were supposed to eat flesh and like it.

"Be a man," Dad said. "Where's your pride?"

I switched to baked potatoes and salads for dinner, and avoided Dad's frowns. After Eola, I felt connected to meat, and wanted no part of it. Mom's, "how was your day, sweetheart," soon meant, "what will you eat tonight?" She didn't mind making extra vegetables and grilled cheese sandwiches if it kept me from throwing up one of her meals.

|||

A few weeks later I was getting the hang of things. Since we didn't do that many autopsies, I spent most of my time in the Pathology supply room. One day I was down in the morgue's icebox, a cold storage room with formaldehyde in the air that smelled like a bio lab, only worse. It made your eyes sting.

Anyway, I was down there getting Petri dishes for the Bacteriology Lab, and there were three fresh ones in there on their gurneys.

The hospital morgue is a spooky place to be alone, but you should try going into the icebox when it was occupied. I turned on all the lights and left the door wide open.

Charles told me about some corpse who sat up once, right when they wheeled him in. Scared the hell out of the delivery boys.

"But that was years ago," Charles said, in that glittery way of his, winking those bulging yellow eyes. "Ain't nothing like that happen since, so don't make no mind. Weren't nothing but rigor mortis setting up a contraction or two. You'll be fine down there all alone with them. No body's going to heave up and chase you outta there." He chuckled as he left. "Maybe they just want one last hug."

I think about probabilities. The longer it goes without happening, the sooner it's due. I know it doesn't work that way, but it messes with your expectations. I wouldn't put it past Charles to take a nap in there under a sheet, just to scare me shitless when I walked in.

And there they were: a guy and two old ladies. I checked for toe tags first to make sure they were really dead. No clothes, no shoes, you know? Charles would have to wear something to keep him warm, so that's how I figured I'd know.

That said, there was something comforting about finding old, gnarly, and fungus-covered toes.

The guy? He had nice feet. He was thirty-one, and nothing like the old and overweight mounds of flesh we usually got. He was in great shape. You could almost see his stomach muscles defined by the way the thin white covering lay across him. Definitely a six-pack. He was shorter then me. That made him less threatening. So I peeled up the sheet and looked at his face.

Dark blond hair. Glassy eyes. Like he was too sleepy to get up. His tag said he died in the emergency room. So that's why we had him; we had to figure out why he died, and make sure we hadn't killed him. Charles told me about that rule.

The guy had a nice face. Friendly, like my best friend, Jeff. The kind of guy if you saw him on the street you'd say he was going places. Athletic too. Big shoulders, no chest hair that I could see.

The sheet was lying on him as if it were glued down, from this angle, anyway the light or whatever. Yeah, well. You check people out. Other guys. You know what I mean? You know what I mean.

I could see he was hung. The sheet should have contoured to the crease between his thighs. But, it didn't. I had to see so I tucked the sheet in to make it more outlined, or make it go away if it was just some bubble, a lost sock, or something.

You learn a lot working in a hospital. Everyone should get some comparative anatomy, see the differences between spongy pink lungs and the nasty cancerous ones, or tumors the size of grapefruit. After a while you get a feel for the general range of what folk can look like.

I'd never seen anything like that. I felt like a nervous twelve-year-old in the locker room, taking peeks, scared about what someone would say if I was caught. I took a deep breath of cold formaldehyde air and held the edge of the sheet, raising it little by little, expecting him to sit up and call me names like Billy Freshik did in fifth grade.

It wasn't a sock. Or a cucumber someone had left there as a joke. I just stared at it for I don't know how long. I was thinking how much fun it must have been for him, imagining it hanging from my groin like that.

He must have enjoyed holding it. Even to pee. You start to wonder what would it be like. It got me all frustrated, and right then I heard the outer door open, and voices, women, coming in. I covered him up in no time flat, and had a big bag of Petri dishes in front of me by the time they stuck their heads through the icebox door.

"Hi," a bleached blonde nurse said, and then went back to chewing her gum. She was flanked by two other nurses, one of them a guy. They all had hundred watt grins, and I knew why they had come.

"Uh, hi," I said, my dry throat making me sound suspicious. I knew I was blushing in the hard light. I also knew other things would be obvious, so I held the Petri dishes a little closer. "I'm just here to get these for the second floor," I said.

"He's here to get the Petri dishes," the brunette said, looking to her companions. "Why, I wish my man would get the dishes once in a while." She winked at me.

The male nurse just said, "Uh-huh!"

"Excuse us for interrupting you, honey, but we are on a tour. This is our break, and we don't have much time."

I tried to smile. What could I say?

"Well," she said, winking at me. "We heard from the staff in the ER that there was a rare specimen down here. We just thought we'd sneak in and take a peek." The blonde was doing that "little old me" thing that some women do when you know you're about to be bulldozed. The guy was biting his lip, and staring at my Petri dishes. "You don't mind, do you, honeybunch?"

I shook my head. "Do you want me to show you around?"

"That would be nice sometime, honey, but," she leaned back and looked me up and down. "Somehow I don't think you'd foot the bill." They broke into giggles like kids. What was it about this place? "We came to see little old John Doe Dillinger here, because all the girls are talking about him."

She pushed past me, and I backed out into the hall as the others squeezed through the door to surround the gurney. The sheet flew up. They began talking about it. Openly. With me still out in the hall.

Their investigation ricocheted around the hard tile walls as I stretched toward the exit. I can still hear her voice as I went out.

"Oh, and feel how heavy it is!"

That was the last thing I heard. Honest.

|||

Charles called me two hours later. We had to prep for Doctor P. It could take an hour and a half. He expected us to work right through lunch.

"Bring your lunch sack with you. Or eat before," Charles suggested.

I didn't do either one. When I walked in, Charles already had the gurney out by the shining steel workbench. It was the guy. The sheet lay on him crooked, and his legs were sticking out. Charles didn't seem to notice.

"Help me get him moved," he said. "Grab those feet."

My knees went weak, but I grabbed him around the ankles and heaved with Charles. The body lifted and we staggered sideways as the sheet slid off. There it was, pointed right at me. I let go with the shock of it, and his ankles banged loud on the table, like a steel drum.

"Heavy little sucker, ain't he?"

"Um. Yeah," I stammered.

And everywhere I looked, my eyes found their way back to that thing.

I opened for Charles. He held a sandwich in one hand, holding the odd flap of skin or pulling the ribs away with his other. All with no VapoRub. Seems that little gimmick was just for newcomers. He never used it.

"You know, Thomas," Charles said, "it's a shame these white boys have such small peckers."

I shot him a look, then at it. I could feel my ears get hot. He just laughed and reached into the chest and stroked the exposed liver, then lifted up a lobe and looked underneath.

"Hmm," he said.

"What?" I looked at the dark red lobes and the gray intestines slimed over with membranes.

"Color don't look right," he said. "Pull it, and lay it out for Doc on the buffet."

The buffet was this stainless steel tabletop that ran down the side of the room. It was big enough to lay out most of the organs side by side. All the pathologist had to do was sidestep down the line. It was twenty feet long, and designed like a sluice so you could turn on the water and wash everything away when the doc was done.

"Reminds me about these two guys peeing off a bridge," Charles said, as I pushed the liver aside to get at the feeding artery so I could cut it loose. Blood gushed out, still under pressure. It filled the chest cavity before seeping back into the organs.

"One guy says 'Man, this water be cold,'" Charles said, dropping a suction tube into the red pool, "and the other one says 'Yeah. And it deep too.'"

He shoved my shoulder as he cracked up, and I let go of the liver. It slid down into the mesentery muck. Then he pushed me again, and I stumbled against the table. My left hand landed next to it on the opposite thigh.

I could feel the penis on my thumb, and I stared, unable to move.

"And it deep too." Charles grabbed his stomach and laughed, until he started coughing. I pulled my hand away. I stepped on the suction pedal and it sounded like a dentist office in there.

"OK, Tom." He straightened up. "You go on and finish in here while I go to the john. If I ain't back in a bit, lay out the heart and lungs like I showed you. Then I'll help you with his intestines."

"You're gonna leave me here? All by myself? What if I screw up?"

"You'll do fine. There's nothing here you can't handle. Take it slow. He ain't in no rush, and neither are we, you hear?"

I tried to cradle the liver over to the buffet before he left the morgue. The door closed down the hall, and I was alone with the silence of liver slithering onto stainless steel with a final sticky plop.

The VapoRub got strong in that brilliant empty room, and I felt the little hairs prick up on the back of my neck. I half expected a tap on the shoulder, to turn, to finally meet the thing that lived in the dark basement when I was a kid.

I spun around. He was still laid out. Skin flopped back over his face, the yellow fat and veined side glistening under the bright lights. His chest lay open, the ribs cut away to reveal the slippery treasures, ruby red lumps, marine blue veins. The ends of sawed ribs shone marble white and gleaming, as if placed there on blood velvet for display.

I reached in for a lung. The whole pink thing fit neatly in my palm. It was surprisingly small for the job it had keeping us alive. Such an interesting liver texture, the weight of it. Then it hit me, and I glanced toward the door.

I was alone with the penis.

It lay in the channel of cold thighs after traversing the lumps of his testicles. It occurred to me that they should be all bunched up because it was chilly, but a tight and shrinking scrotum is a true sign of life. I felt mine underscoring the point, and my nerves went on high alert. I peeled the bloody gloves from my hands and slipped on fresh latex, thought about what I had to do, and stretched on a second pair of gloves.

We do things when we're kids that we try to forget. It helps if you think of them like science experiments. Curiosity for the sake of knowledge. Like all those games of strip poker. They're educational.

It's so much easier to think clinically about your youth. Especially if you're going to tell someone about it. How else do you explain this mad, opportunistic desire to pretend, just for a moment, that you are a god yourself?

I lowered my trembling hand, traced the puff of pubic hair until it ran out, and I was stroking the soft tube, feeling little wrinkles and burrs of stray curling hairs, the ridge of a vein, all the way down to where the foreskin swallowed the glans, leaving it in its throat behind a pouting pucker. The twelve-inch Gila monster slept on.

I looked for a reaction, anything, but of course, the heart lay still.

The lungs didn't inflate with a sudden gasp.

Neither did it.

So I grabbed it, pulled it upright, felt how nice and heavy and substantial it was. I held the business end so that I could look it square in the eye.

There are some things, once started, you just can't stop. You've committed yourself to knowledge. The investigation becomes your driving force. There's no governor to throttle you back, nothing to squash your curiosity. There is only you, and your obsession.

I tried to slide the foreskin back down the shaft, but it bunched up, so I pinched the skin on either side and pulled.

The skin had glued itself together with dried fluids, and it gave a little crusty smack as I stretched it out. It puckered back some, but was stretched enough for the purple-pink glans to peek out. Not enough. I wanted to see the whole thing.

It was the first and only monster cock I had ever seen. Also, the only up-close-and-personal experience with foreskin. This was an interesting moment.

I held the heavy tube, letting it lie over the four fingers of my right hand, my thumb pointing along the shaft, pretending I was taking a piss, the end flopping down. Then I was holding it with two hands, plenty left to dangle out, remembering my own with barely enough length for a full stroke. Let alone two-handed pogo. I thought about him taking a dump, and having to hold it up out of the water as he sat on the bowl.

I got hard immediately.

It's too bad the dead can't get erections.

I was an expert snake handler in my spare time, and I could get used to this much fun. I thought about cutting it off and taking it home, slipping it like a condom around my own, maybe wowing them in the locker room.

What if I cut it off, then cut off my own and make the switch, like that guy, John Bobbitt. A guy could dream, couldn't he? Feeling would come back sometime, wouldn't it?

What a feeling.

Then there was Cindy. Imagine her surprise when her hands wandered during our next makeout session?

I had grabbed the penis at its base and squeezed the clotting blood down toward the tip like Jell-O in a circus balloon. The head peeked out even more, and the snake seemed to grow longer. Encouraged, I added my other hand and squeezed, stretched, and compressed the shaft so that the glans popped right out. There was a glob building up behind my milking fists like a pig in a python.

Longer and longer. Skinnier and skinnier. I had it to almost sixteen inches. I got harder and harder against the table. I pulled the skin back, sliding my hand up and down. I felt connected, in sympathy with my friend, and this stuff oozed out the end and dribbled on his thigh.

I was glad for my underwear, and the lab coat. Then I was just embarrassed and sticky.

So I let it flop back on his chest, which wasn't there. The penis fell backward into the slick balloons of his intestines, splashing out little flecks of fat and coagulated blood onto my apron. The impressions made by my fingers didn't go away. In fact, as I cleaned the blood off with damp paper towels, I realized the rings and bruises made by my insistent fists were going to be permanent. The head refused to be stuffed back into its sock, no matter what I did. They say you can't push a rope; now I know why.

I was done for.

Charles would be coming back anytime, and when he did, he would see what had happened. What I had done. And then Doctor P would be down at 1:00. And he would tell my dad.

Maybe worse. He would drag Dad down there and show him what his son had done the very moment he was left alone with a giant penis, uh, corpse. "What did he do with the women?" they would ask. I almost wished this guy had been a woman, and it had happened that way; it seemed easier to explain, somehow more acceptable.

I thought about running. There were friends I could stay with until it made the papers and they kicked me out. Maybe Jeff would hide me in his basement?

I could deny it, say that I had stepped out, and someone came in while I wasn't there. A cover-up. Everybody did it, right?

I backed away from the corpse and his kielbasa, and bumped into the buffet. My hand landed on the liver, which squished a little like a bloody sponge.

The phone rang, exploding shards of noise into the hard room.

I spooked, sending the liver sliding down the buffet. It left a deep red trail down the bright scratches of stainless steel.

Charles was out by the soda machine. Did I want a Coke? "Yeah. Bring me two," I said. "Take all the time you want. Yeah, I'm fine down here. The phone scared me, that's all."

Shit.

His intestines snaked through whitish membranes, their colors shrouded like sausages in knotted little lumps. I sank my hands into the slop of intestines, cutting the membranes so they would unravel, then I pulled his intestines out and down over his groin to cover the mottled and crinkled penis. I cut the esophagus free of the stomach. Nasty globs oozed out, and I could smell the guts even over the VapoRub.

There was no time to waste. I reached in under his collarbones, and sliced through the windpipe and esophagus, then pulled the whole assembly, lungs, heart and all, up like a small Christmas tree on its gory trunk. Then with both hands, I hefted it across the room to the buffet.

Blood smeared down the front of my apron. Sweat trickled under my shirt, down my back. I laid the pulmonary tree down, and went back to the envelope of the man, to clean up any pools of blood. I waited, staring at the guy who'd spilled his guts out to me in more ways than one.

The outer door opened, and I heard voices. Charles and Doctor P were together.

"What's going on here?" Charles said, looking at old intestine-legs.

"I, I was just, trying to get ahead," I said, my hands around a slimy gut rope. "It slipped out before I could get the bucket."

"Jesus," Charles said, glancing at the doc, "can't leave you alone for a minute. Let me help you."

"Thomas," Doctor P said with a quick nod, all business and no comment. He walked right to the buffet while clipping the voice-activated microphone to his lapel, pausing to put on gloves.

"You should have waited for me," Charles hissed.

"I'm sorry," I said, under the dictating hum of Doctor P's voice.

I took a deep breath and grabbed a handful of intestine and penis with both hands, and pulled with all my might toward the bucket. Everything was slippery, and I pulled free of the penis and it fell back to rest with a loud sticky slap. Doctor P glanced over at the odd noise, and then resumed his drone.

The penis was slimed.

You could sort of tell it had been grabbed, and I wondered if Charles would remember if the foreskin had been in place or not. He grabbed the knob of it and pulled it straight up, grinning at me. I thought I would die.

"And it deep too," he whispered, looking at it for a long moment. "Lucky little stiff."

I held myself like a suppressed sneeze.

"Hose this down for the doc," Charles said, letting it fall and slap. Doctor P didn't look over this time.

I went to work squirting the blood and flecks down the drain on the table. All the while the suction hissed in his chest. My sympathetic connection was gone.

When the table shone, and the body was clean and laid out, we were ready. The penis draped easy between his legs, its head resting on the cold steel.

Doctor P had finished slicing and dicing, and came to examine the body. We moved to either side and watched Doctor P examine the arms, lift the flap up off the face, and go down the other side.

I eyed Charles as the doc got near it. Charles grinned at me, and made a face. The doc kept going, never missing a beat. He never paused in admiration. Never broke a smile.

When he reached into his pocket and pulled out his little tape measure, I thought for sure this was it. But he measured a scar just above the knee instead.

"Three-inch healed laceration just above the right knee," he said, the tape snapped back. He kept moving. "The corpse is unremarkable, comma," Doctor P said, and shot me a look. He returned to his dictation. "No signs of mishandling by the hospital staff in evidence, period. Death is consistent with grand mal scenario, period. Ruthie, please insert the results of the blood analysis, and leave it on my desk." He turned off the recorder.

"Thank you, Charles, Tom." Doctor P peeled off his gloves and tossed them across the room. They hit the outside of the trashcan with a limp splat, and fell to the floor in a pink-tinted heap. Without making a move to pick them up, he stretched a smile and left them to us.

While Charles put his feet up and leafed through an old *Penthouse,* I cleared the buffet, dumping the guts into a plastic bag that

I sewed back inside him like giblets. I closed the cavity with nothing more than brown twine and a carpet needle, just like Charles had showed me. He had gone out to the lounge by the time I put the body away.

I remember humming one of his absent-minded tunes as I turned a hose on the table and wondered what we were having for dinner, thinking about Cindy, and the weekend.

I left the clean gleaming steel bathed in the darkness of the red exit sign, finished out my day upstairs, and went home. We had steak that night, medium rare, and so tender it cut like butter.

In a workshop long ago, R. R. ANGELL shared an early version of "Clinical Delicacies" with his fellow writers, one of whom was a woman who believed strongly that everyone only writes from direct experience. It is true that Angell was trained as a Diener, and the ensuing probing conversations lasted for years. The fun part is that Angell also writes deep-space hard science fiction, and they could never reconcile that anomaly and so parted ways. You may have seen his work in Asimov's, Interzone, The Baltimore Review, Gargoyle, *and a bunch of anthologies including* Sex & Chocolate *edited by Richard Peabody and Lucinda Ebersole and* Best Date Ever *from Alyson Books edited by Lawrence Schimel. His novelette in the January 2006 issue of* Asimov's, *"In the Space of Nine Lives," was nominated for a Spectrum Award. Find out more at www.rrangell.com.*

The Birdman of Razzamatazz

Scott W. Berg

We're in our bed, my wife and I, each of us reading and drifting toward sleep, when a knock sounds downstairs at the door. It's nearly eleven, and we look at each other. Cars don't approach in our neighborhood without the loud grind of gravel under rubber, and we've heard nothing. A visitor in this absence is something of a mystery, and we finally shrug our shoulders in unison and smile for a moment at the maneuver.

Janet, still watching me, calls downstairs to Brian. He doesn't reply; instead, we hear the complaint of sofa springs and steps across the hardwood. Chances are best that this caller is for him, one of his friends, or a pack of his friends, having ridden their bicycles straight across our newly installed sod. Brian will shout upstairs and ask if he can go "just down to the Stop-n-Shop," *just* meaning more than two miles of narrow unlit roads to a twenty-four-hour convenience store where beer and adult magazines and smokeless tobacco are all, I assume, equally available to our fifteen-year-old. I'll go to the head of the stairs and ask a few questions, following which I'll dissemble and give in. You'd think such displays of magnanimity would be counted in my favor.

But surprise of surprises. It is not for Brian.

"Mom, Dad," he hollers. "This one is all yours."

"Item one," says our caller. "I'm not selling anything."

The man is the spitting image of Mickey Rooney. It's uncanny—same pug build, same cantankerous smiling face. He stands on the other side of the screen door, his fists raised and loose in front of

16

his chest, as though they hold an invisible wide-brimmed hat. Moths swarm our porch, batting at his eyes, but he doesn't flinch.

"I hope you'll hear me out," he says. "I've got no choice but to throw myself on your good graces."

I'm about to turn him away when Janet brushes past me and swings the door open wide. "Certainly," she says. The man is now standing in our foyer, and so here we are: a fool has walked inside our house. His uniform—baby blue button-down on top, khakis on the bottom—is the uniform reserved for the special brand of prisoner who inhabits the minimum-security penitentiary visible across a rolling half acre of scrub grass from the front of our house. This man, our sudden guest, must know that we know what he is. He's not supposed to be alone and here, now, three hours after the last whistle has blown and the view from our upstairs window has emptied of men dressed in this fashion.

All deference, he keeps his eyes lowered. His hands resist movement with a noticeable effort while his toe disobeys, tapping briskly without rhythm. He speaks to Janet, whom he has pegged as his only possible benefactor here.

"This is a complicated situation but I'll try to make it easy."

"This is a jailbreak," I say, just to try it on for size. Mickey Rooney looks at me now, for the first time, and smiles. One of his front teeth is capped in gold.

"*Break* isn't exactly right," he says. Then he touches his nose—touches his nose, good God—and points the finger at me. "But you've got the idea."

I can look at him more closely now and make a better guess: he's perhaps five years older than myself, just past fifty. His eyes are large and bear wrinkles. They are level with mine.

Even I could scale the fence around Dunwoody Correctional, though I'm slower and weaker and half a belly larger than I once was. (Plus, I'm what you would call unathletic, a trait I seem to have passed to our son.) Two or three guards are sometimes visible but they don't seem especially concerned with keeping track of their charges, who play volleyball and practice their golf swings—with real golf clubs— and even roust up games of touch football which end quickly; on the whole, they're not young men. Their long, narrow yard is distin-

guished most by its color: lambent, taxpayer green. A work detail of
sorts often involves men bending over to pick dandelions.

I know something about the history of the place, because I made
an effort to learn that history when we—when I—first hatched the
idea to move here. Dunwoody had once been anything but genteel,
a medium-security facility miles beyond the suburbs' outmost reach,
fitted with bars and barbed wire and guards with guns at the ready.
Then the state built a new complex thirty minutes farther down the
river, after which all of the hard cases were vacated and replaced with
this white-collar criminal's club. That's when we made our move, a
year and a half ago now. Timing is everything, and sure enough,
new construction sprouts everywhere you look, dense and winding
townhome developments and mile-wide discount stores, so much
sooner than even I, in my most optimistic scenarios, dared to suggest.
The cycle plays itself over and over in the view out of our bedroom
window: machines beget dust beget walls beget progress. And here
we are, out on the frontier, waiting for it on arrival.

Cliff-diving, Janet had called it, our signatures fresh on the loan,
our condominium ten minutes from downtown sold for a nonsensi-
cally high number to a computer programmer growing his first beard.
The leftover houses here, most of them old as-is bungalows like our
own, are now selling by the half dozen, and Janet has done much
of that selling. Here, where the former version of the prison kept
everything tamped down, she's found her professional footing. She's
got the pioneer impulse, along with a cherry-red company blazer,
and she's going to see it all the way through.

I do take satisfaction in having allowed my common sense to read
our future here, rather than letting the dust and the dirt, the sagging
porches and peeling paint, tell the tale. Dunwoody Correctional in its
new incarnation is hardly an eyesore, more like a well-groomed military base than a prison. Many of the men inside have held positions
I'd be relieved, if startled, to see Brian pursue. I've often watched the
prisoners from our bedroom, through a set of powerful binoculars
I'll admit I bought for just this purpose. Though Janet fidgets and
makes nervous fun when I do this, I trust my motives. She says my
observation feels to her like a kind of stealing. Not *their* kind of stealing, I respond. We've quarreled about it enough that I've learned to
be furtive, to wait until Janet is downstairs, or away, or asleep. Then I

lift the Nikons and play my game, watching the men for signs, telltale outward indications of their criminal inner selves.

"You must know," says my wife to our visitor—and somehow we've moved to the kitchen table now, for all appearances a tight knot of chatty neighbors—"that you're a dead ringer for Jimmy Cagney."

"Mickey Rooney," I say gently.

Behind me, Brian laughs. Cackles, actually. I hadn't been aware Brian was in the room.

"Funny you observe that. I used to make money on the weekends, being Jimmy Cagney," he says. "I'd do Jimmy the G-Man and Jimmy the Gangster and Jimmy the Doodle Dandy. When I was younger. But you can guess what they all wanted. They all wanted 'you dirty rat.'" He looks at Janet and laughs, his eyes full of mirth. "Over and over, 'You dirty rat.' But who knows who Jimmy Cagney is anymore?"

"Not Dad," says Brian, and now Janet laughs, all three of them laugh, and I smile, only to be polite. Why, I want to ask Brian, on this evening of all evenings, have you chosen to once again contribute to a dinner-table conversation?

"I'll cut to the chase," says our celebrity impersonator, who's made himself too comfortable, leaning forward with his elbows squared on our table and letting himself smile much too broadly. Here is the chase: He must go to Eau Claire, Wisconsin, where his wife has filed for divorce. There's a story. Eau Claire was their hometown. There they went to high school and college together, courted and married and had the first two of their four girls together before they moved out East, out here where he made his money. Now his wife has gone back to Wisconsin and he has no way to get in touch with her. A friend of his, an old high school teammate, saw her in town. Jimmy Cagney has been getting no sleep, wondering if she's located a former flame, if she's gone to live with one of her aunts, if their daughter in high school needs this move at of all times now. She's the last at home, he says, a senior, she loves to play lacrosse, she's *excellent*, and that's not something they do much of back in Wisconsin.

He returns Brian's stare and then, bending his head, he winks. A winker and a nose toucher—I watch him even more carefully.

"I'm going to be straight with you," he says, and turns his eyes to Janet. This I understand; if his story is to be believed—so far I'm an agnostic—he must be drawn to her, a wife unremorsefully cohabitating with her enfranchised husband. Janet sets her hand on top of mine with a little bit of pressure as he continues. "I just now walked away, on the spur of the moment, and I'm not going back. I need a place to stay for one night."

"Embezzlement," I say. "That's my bet." This interrupts his plea. It also has the side effect of removing Janet's hand from mine. So be it; he will not be here much longer.

"Insurance fraud, then." I'll play a guessing game. At Dunwoody Correctional, I know, the possibilities have limits.

"How long have you been married?" he asks Janet, though how he intends to win my shelter by ignoring me is beyond my understanding.

"Seventeen years," she says, I think proudly.

"I admire that, I admire that," he says. "You don't know how much I admire that. I'm just short of ten."

And I know it in my bones, here it comes, his gambit.

"Brian," I say, "go upstairs."

"*What?*" says Brian, in that way he has, his insistence on making assumptions, leaping to conclusions, that sort of thing. All the way from enigmatic silence to naked whining in the blink of an eye.

I motion with my finger. "Up. Stairs."

"*Why?*" he squeals.

Brian is now four months away from obtaining his driver's license and there are moments, however brief, when I believe that that day will be the last we ever see of him. His life has gone all foggy and out of focus to me. Each morning he eats breakfast wearing his headphones—pardon, *ear buds*—and each morning he leaves with as few words as possible. (What he usually says is "Later.") His grades, once A's peppered with B's, are now B's peppered with more B's and a different C each semester. If he's getting high, or having girl troubles, or whatever might draw a teenager inside himself, he's hiding it well; but if he's happy, he's hiding that just as well.

Janet, with frustrating assurance, dates the trouble to our decision to move here. It was the one bone of contention between us: "A boy isn't interested in what a place is going to be*come*," she said. "What does the future mean when you're fifteen?" There's no one *here*, is what she thinks, and I wonder if her burgeoning career has something to do with filling up Brian's world for him as fast as she can. As a young boy, he would introduce his playmates with a look-what-I-found beam, proudly reciting their little biographies, while now his friends are distant entities, voices on the phone, circling bicycles in the street, shadows on our porch. To any other theory I advance Janet says: some coincidence! It would help me refute her diagnosis if Brian—whose vocabulary is exceeded only by his reluctance to utter words in the first place—didn't refer to our neighborhood as either "the ragged edge of the world" or "development hell"—phrasings for which I have to give him credit even if I think he's talking about something else, some inscrutable interior dissatisfaction, because what fifteen-year-old has real opinions about development? Sometimes after dinner he stays at the table with Janet and tells her soft jokes about classmates or teachers, but just as quickly and far more often he'll vanish into his room, ear buds in place.

Janet's solution is that I bring it up with Brian, but: I don't want to. Or: I don't know how to. Something else that's new: Brian, who used to read comic books and play video games with religious patience, now watches television every night with a commitment that amazes me, three or four hours which always end after midnight. The fare varies: black-and-white movies one week, talk shows the next, something out of left field, like safari shows or the shopping channels, the next. Nights when I can't sleep, when I've stared out of the window enough, sometimes I creep to the head of the stairs like a burglar in my own home and watch him. I watch him stretched at adult length on the sofa, and I want to kneel at his feet and shut off the screen and tell him what a waste it is, that's he's such an intelligent young man and this is keeping that intelligence bottled up, out of view and out of practice. But of course it isn't the television at all. And it isn't only, I have to believe, the move. I don't know what it is, but I am working on it. And when I'm done working on it, I'll talk to him.

Our visitor seems to have an actor's confidence that the appearance of truth equals truth, and more strangely, that some paltry stab at truth should produce trust. He has presented to us a prepared slip of paper, on which he's handwritten his name, his prisoner number, and his previous address and phone number, all in a hand so precise and anonymous that I ask him if he has career experience in creating ransom notes.

"This can all be verified," he says, ignoring me again. He's left happy behind and has reached excitable, because each minute Janet has listened to him gives him hope. "One phone call can put me back in, and I won't stop you. I won't pull the phone cord or do anything crazy. There's no buses, there's no way to run out of here. No train to jump. Have you ever lived near a train? The *whistles*," he finishes, and then: he softly whistles!

Janet laughs again, enjoying herself. She's always been happiest about the surprises our neighborhood has produced, those features that didn't make it into my initial sales pitch: the startling quantity of lightning bugs on still summer nights, the still-operating pig farm at the end of the development, the grove of trees across the road that surprised us last fall with serviceable, if puny, McIntosh apples. And now this—escaped convicts.

"I've watched you," he continues. "Your house. You seem like a nice couple." My face must do something, because he holds out two hands, very small hands, and hurries along. "I haven't really been spying, don't worry, it's just that we don't have much of a view from over there." He gestures vaguely toward the front door, and shakes his head. "You notice things from inside a prison. Your boy seems nice. I would have liked a boy."

He has, in the space of just a few sentences, raised my drawbridge all the way up. I realize just how close I was to letting him stay the night.

"When was your sentence up?" I ask.

"My sentence?"

I nod. "Your period of incarceration."

He's silent.

"What I'm asking is how much time did you have left?"

"Five months." He says this softly, and we all know something now.

"Out of?"

"What do you mean?"

Janet says nothing. This interests her, as well.

"Five months out of how many, total?"

He is now absently rubbing his hands together. "Out of eleven."

Now it's my turn to whistle, and I make no attempt to do so softly. The matter is settled. For many of these prisoners, escaping may be the only way to deepen the scar on their record. These men aren't society's outcasts; many will return to comfortable seats still warm. This must embarrass him, but still he tries to put on a sanguine face, and I vaguely admire his concentration.

"What was your offense?" I ask. Information is all I'm after now, hard facts, because I want to leave the police no doubts, no loose ends, when I call them after he's left. I half expect a knock to come any moment now and save me the trouble. I look at a clock: after midnight. My eyes feel raw.

"I was foolish with money," he says, finally.

"Whose money and how foolish?"

"Very," he says. "And if it were my own money, I wouldn't be here."

"That's no answer," I say, because I'm tired and want some resolution. "That's an evasion, is what that is."

"You can stay here," says Janet, flatly, out of nowhere.

"Of course he can't stay here," I say. My voice, traitor, cracks.

"On the couch," says Janet, to the prisoner, her jaw set. And then an image comes to me, sure as the thick night: Brian is at the head of the stairs, listening. Like father, like son.

From our bedroom window, I can see the lamps, white dots lining the outer edge of the penitentiary grounds.

"You're working overtime on this," says Janet. "If they find him here, *if* they even bother to look, we can just say he broke in."

"Without a trace? No broken glass? Am I going to have to go downstairs and break down our own door?"

"We left the door unlocked."

Near a prison? I am about to ask, but I know how far to unspool that string. My own arguments, three years old now, mount against me.

"What if we take him in and then he's caught?" I ask her. I'm looking for a wedge, an inroad, and she knows it. We are, after all, married. "Then he tells them how he came to us, how we agreed to hide him away. We become accomplices to a crime of significance. I'm calling right now."

I say this but I don't move. Janet touches me on the shoulder, and then plants her chin in the same spot. The timbre of her late-night voice, little more than a murmur, vibrates along my neck. "Who are they going to believe? You tell a little lie now, or you tell one later. I'm convinced he's grateful."

"We lie for him?" I ask.

"He left in the morning before we were up. We found an unkempt sofa, there was some bologna missing from the refrigerator. Blah, blah." She sits up and gestures. "This is not a puzzle to solve. This is not the Birdman of Razzamatazz we're dealing with."

"Alcatraz. The Birdman of *Al*catraz."

Janet looks at me, her direct, undistracted gaze no less lovely and baffling than it was eighteen years ago, when I first found myself unable to look in any other direction. Her way, her particular concentration, is to invest her attention on the unexpected and make it normal by force of patience and good humor, a quality that explains her decisions to marry me, to move here, to maneuver gently through Brian's new personality, and now, to allow our stranger his one night of refuge.

"He wouldn't be in there if he wasn't a felon," I say.

"He doesn't look like a criminal to me," she says.

"What does a criminal look like?"

"Mickey Rooney?" she says, and covers her face.

"What if he decides to stay another night?" I ask. "What if his ride doesn't show? What if all of this mushrooms into a very serious situation? We have Brian to think of." I add this last with all the utter sincerity that my frustration will allow, but Janet cuts me a look and I feel ashamed. And shame pushes me onward.

"What if there are others? What if they want to use our house as some kind of way station?"

"How thorough of you."

"I'm calling the police," I say.

"If he's still here at high noon tomorrow, you can call. OK?"

I'm quiet.

"Promise?"

I'm still quiet.

"Don't you believe him?" she asks matter of factly. "You believe he'd make up a story about going to Wisconsin to talk his wife out of leaving him?"

"Let me ask you a question instead," I say.

"Fine," she sighs.

I take a breath and thereby concede. "What is this man doing inside our house?"

"Hiding," says Janet, and her eyes go wide. I catch the excitement there, a kind of thanks. Then, so soon—too soon—she's fast asleep.

It's been a long time, years upon years, since I've been awake so late at night. Out of the window, I see the prison yard lit up by the periphery lights and a blue August moon. There, I've thought more than once, spyglasses pressed to my eyes, are the world's safest people. I've never shared the thought with Janet, because it has never formed more than halfway. But some nights the thought runs away from me and I lose myself in my imagined version of their lives: a cot, a distant problem, a past, bars, and now, room to sort it all out. Reflection, repentance, a paradoxical kind of freedom. But just as soon I'll come out of it and tell myself that when it comes down to it, these are men in a pen. I've watched them with visitors, mostly women who walk with them around the yard, sometimes their heads bent and step slow, other times in animated conversation. I may have watched this one with his erstwhile wife, but I don't remember. I wouldn't have known it was him, of course, out of all of them. I couldn't have known to pay particular attention to the short, somewhat overweight one with the marked resemblance to an old movie star.

If I had ever told Janet, I know that she would have asked me to do better than to play games; she would have asked that I put myself entirely in their shoes, but now that it comes to one prisoner in the flesh, I can't. I can't imagine myself locked away, Janet making a decision to go it alone, Brian in tow. I give the scenario a solid effort, I close my eyes and play it through. But I am tripped up again and again by the fact that Janet is *here*, lying beside me, her breathing raspy thanks to her perennial grapple with oak pollen. Then, finally, a quality of light in the hallway changes, there are sounds downstairs, and I have something else to occupy my mind.

It's easy to move unheard to the top of our stairs; the carpet is thick and soft and the boards underneath have completed their settling in. I see that the television is off and that Brian is talking with our visitor, who sits on the edge of the easy chair, now pulled next to the sofa. Brian, underneath a blanket, has propped himself on one elbow, and is nodding enthusiastic agreement.

In my effort to make sense of my son's new incarnation, I've made a special study of his eyes. When I pause to ponder his lately arrived blankness of face—something I can't do when I'm looking straight at him, of course—his eyes, an ocean blue, are limned in my mental picture with a certain metallic quality, an artificial vacancy. Janet says that Cal Ripken Jr. has the very same eyes and he's one of the best-looking men in the whole world. It's called coming into your looks, she says, we all did it during high school. But I know: he grew into that look all at once, and the truth as I see it but can't admit to Janet is that it took our trip here, to the ragged edge of the universe, to make it happen.

Their conversation is animated, mirthful, in tones low enough that it seems they are guarding against an interruption. I am punchy enough, sleep-deprived enough, to wonder if Brian could be making arrangements to go along with this man. But it's not that wild thought that puts fear and a slow anger into my chest. What catches in me is this: Here I am, motionless and eavesdropping, hearing my own breath come faster now. Here I am, the one acting like an intruder.

They don't finish their conversation until the moon begins to set and the sky turns coral. I know they've finished because our visitor reaches over and tousles Brian's hair and then stands and stretches. I retreat and when I return to our bedroom I notice that it's five-thirty in the morning, nearly four hours since I left our bed. My T-shirt is damp and my legs are sore.

I pick up the phone, and look at Janet, who is still sleeping. She is always up by six, has been every single morning of our marriage; already she stirs and murmurs, coughing a little. With my back to her, I cup my hand over the phone and whisper to the county police dispatcher who I am, where I live. Good thing I got up for a glass of water, I say. Is he violent? I ask. I've done a good thing, the woman's unexcited graveyard-shift voice tells me, adding that matters would have been all so much more complicated if he'd gotten away. Her reassurance lifts something from me, and I take a quick shower, to make myself presentable for the authorities, who I'm told will be here in short order.

It is six o'clock, and the sun slants into our eyes over the shoulders of several uniformed officers standing on our porch. They have come for their prisoner, but much to my surprise, I have no prisoner for them. Janet hasn't told me straight out why there is no prisoner to hand over, but there's no mystery to it: As I walk my way through a set of befuddled answers for the police, I understand that Janet had not been asleep, after all, when I'd picked up the telephone. I understand now that while I softly sang "baby, you can drive my car" into the shower walls, she had been coming to her own conclusions and making her own decision.

I tell the police that he must have heard me call. Silly me. Janet stands beside me, my wife, her arm in mine, looking airheaded, infinitely less intelligent than she actually is. I can't believe this masquerade has the power to fool anyone, and I become annoyed at these men for taking every sentence we utter at face value. They ask if he spoke to us, and Janet says yes, he did, he was such a kind man but that she was still afraid of him and that she didn't know what to do. She spends fifteen more minutes providing information she knows they already have: a description, a chronology of the evening. Sometimes our back door stays unlocked, she says. Silly us. Then, finally, she tells them that he said something about heading West, heading for "Norman." Could he have meant Norman, Oklahoma? Now I look at her in amazement. Norman is Janet's place of birth, her college town, still her mother's home. She is an Okie and a Sooner, and proud of it.

The authorities thank us, and then one of them, a tall man with dark eyes and a prodigious blond mustache, pauses on our front step and speaks over his shoulder. "Truthfully," he says, "we wouldn't have known he was missing until lunch time." He laughs, and Janet laughs, and I join in.

Much later that afternoon I find our visitor's prison togs folded neatly in our bedroom closet, and my explanation is complete. With a shock of discomfort, I realize that we are close to identical in height and build, so alike that at a distance we could easily be mistaken for one another.

The next evening Brian comes home from school and pins a Xeroxed map of the United States to our refrigerator, a westward-pointing arrow drawn in red ink linking Maryland and Oklahoma. Next to this, Janet hangs one of her realtor's stat sheets, a printout of information about Norman: population, median income, schools, population density, family attractions, distance to major cities, all kinds of numbers devoted to property taxes and the rate of new construction. The next morning, they craft a new routine: "How's the weather?" Janet asks over the morning paper, and Brian ruffles to the appropriate page and reads the day's forecast for Oklahoma.

I'm not displeased, but still, some part of my fatherly duty, such as it is, feels unfinished. I make a trip to the county library, and after a short time I've found what I'm looking for: the *Wall Street Journal*, May of 2002. Fisheries on the west coast of Canada, bank loans made recklessly and in the end illegally, millions of dollars scattered into the wind. I wait until after dinner, and then I claim Brian's attention and lay out another perspective: what our visitor's self-proclaimed foolishness might have meant, and still mean, for the lives and livelihoods of a great many innocent bystanders. There were businesses, small struggling businesses in Vancouver and Seattle and Portland that lost everything, families thrown into crisis, their dreams dead and crushing bills due all at once. My methods, I know, are far too blunt to leave any lasting trace on Brian, and my voice has risen for reasons I don't seem to be able to control—or understand—but Janet doesn't interrupt.

"So you're saying he gave them the money they asked for and they lost all of it?" Brian asks. "And he goes to jail for it? He pays for their problems? For trying to help?" He doesn't know what he's talking about, but he is skeptical and smart, and he is paying attention; for the moment, at least, he's engaged. I can't see any way to successfully join the argument with him, not in any way that will make a difference. But I can't think of anything else, so I continue: No, we all pay for this kind of crime, we're all victims here. I say that someone has to come up with thirty million dollars and that this will be every person with a single cent in that bank or any other bank. I don't know, or even care, that this last point is true, but it sounds true and that's why I'm saying it, just to say something. Janet touches Brian on the arm, and I can see what it is, sympathy and permission to leave. Brian moves to get up, and my heart goes out to him—it does—and forces me into saying something I'd never expected I'd say.

First I tell him to sit back down. Then I say, if you want to know what *I've* done, what *I've* done for love, here it is. I sweep the room with one hand, meaning to encompass this place and all three of us, but for all I know the gesture looks like one of frustration or mere confusion.

Brian's eyes edge into panic. His father is headed for a weird place. In the hesitation, I press on: I tell my son that I don't know exactly what my goal was in moving our family, that I'm still trying to understand what it was about this abandoned place that seemed so important to me, but that I do know that the goal was not to *damage* anyone. I don't pretend to be naïve; I realize that by saying this to Brian I'm really speaking to Janet, and that whatever it is I want to communicate is at this moment, and every moment, just out of my reach. Sometimes you know how inadequate you are to the task. Brian knows, too; he doesn't answer, doesn't nod, and his face burns red, trapped in between. Finally, without a word from either of us, he gets up and heads upstairs.

"You want to know something you've done for love?" says Janet, after Brian is gone.

I watch her.

"You've lied to the *feds*."

Less than one week later, a postcard arrives. On its front, an aerial view of what seems to be a perfect American Main Street, and above, EAU CLAIRE, WISCONSIN: SAFEST CITY IN AMERICA. The card is addressed to the three of us, and I find that I'm grateful to be included. The message is short: *Flown home.* After supper, I see Brian detour to the kitchen counter, where he picks up the postcard and turns it over once, twice, before he slides it into his pocket and heads for his room.

That night, as Janet sleeps beside me, I pull the binoculars from our desk drawer. The moon is waning; the lights enclosing the prison float like bright buoys in a deep sea of darkness. No one has returned to our door, no one has called, and I take the silence as a good sign. I stretch my imagination and wish for the authorities to close the case, to call off the hunt, to let this man go his way.

SCOTT W. BERG is the author of Grand Avenues: The Story of Pierre Charles L'Enfant, the French Visionary Who Designed Washington, D.C., *published in hardcover by Pantheon Books and in paperback by Vintage Books. He holds a BA in architecture from the University of Minnesota, an MA from Miami University of Ohio, and an MFA in creative writing from George Mason University, where he now teaches nonfiction writing and literature in GMU's graduate and undergraduate creative writing programs. He has published frequently in the* Washington Post *and lives in Reston, Virginia.*

Box Kite

SEAN BRIJBASI

I hadn't given up. It just wasn't meant to be. The hippo syndrome
I believe. That's what it was called. A two-curtain fait accompli with
a written translation below the stage and an applause sign for the
symphony. It was la-la land laconic but I didn't fall for it. Oh, they
want you to. They want you to know that they have the answers.
Systems are bad they write. As if we didn't know. But they show you
in a concise, systematic way. Here is what went wrong. Here is what
went right. Here is the answer. And they try to keep you in your place
with a little praise because in praising you they want you to know
that they know what you know and they want you to know that they
know what you don't know. Some people listen because they can't
tolerate the ambiguity. Others because they need the validation. But
I don't listen because (a) I don't know my place and (f) unlike me,
they're full of shit.

I was only passing through anyway. On my way south. To one of
those places dim with promise. Where a man without a crucible could
find one. I'd been talking for a long time. On corners. In parks. In
theaters. In stores. On stages. In Cleveland. But no one listens. They
like their shit usual.

Two mustards, a bowl of fig, and pasty camel hump to go please.
Please.

For example, let's take Brad. They have to know that Brad has
sisters. That his mother was raped by his father whom he never knew.
That his older brother was killed for being in love with a black girl.
That he was molested by his stepfather. That when he was a teenager,
he was falsely accused of molesting his cousin. That he has brown

hair. That he has brown eyes. That he is left handed. That he is six feet two inches tall. That he talks with an Alabama twang. That despite the South's unsavory history, his Southern culture has relevance. That no matter what happens to him in the "past" he is capable of redemption in the "present." That's Brad. Thank you Brad. You may take your seat beside all the others now.

It's very important for them to know they say because it tells them with whom they are to empathize. But what does it tell us? It tells us that people have become intellectually and emotionally complacent. It tells us that regardless of any radical characterization or plot, the human mind is incapable of thinking beyond the same flimsy skin and limp spine it's grown accustomed to. Greatness is what it always has been. But we know this isn't true. Or so we hope. I had my hopes anyway and I carried them with me to the Foggy Bottom Metro stop on my way to Union Station where I planned to hold up signs in protest against dumbness.

Stop being dumb. Dumbness is dumb. I know I'm dumb but I'm not as dumb as you are.

This was the land of redemption, after all. America. People here can be saved from dumbness. It wasn't one of those smaller countries where people were stuck in dumb for the long haul. Through no fault of their own, mind you, but they're put into a box with their own illusions and they go about punching shadows in there while the guys casting those shadows laugh their asses off.

Did you see her jab? I'm counting my money. I've got a big cheese grater. He almost left a dent.

Not in America buddy. America is too big for a box. There will always be at least one asshole who figures it out and destroys the illusion for everyone else. Because that's what America is all about. Destroying its own illusions.

It began to rain [Maria stroked my hair] and I took out several items from my bag that I had gathered on my peripateticism. That's a big word and I bet many of you stumble on it. I bet many of you have to look it up. I didn't. I want you to know that I didn't because I'm smart. Because I know the meaning of big words and have my doctorate in philosophy and I can tell you where Hegel and Schopenhauer diverge, where Kant and Confucius converge, and how an analysis of these verges justifies evil as what is best in man. I can quote Marlowe much less Shakespeare. I draw conclusions from metaphors in the poems of Akhmatova and envisage the future of art. I deconstruct modern man simply by comparing the ebb and flow of history to the contrapuntal constructions in a Bach fugue. I am, in a word, remarkable and that, in turn, gives me the right to tell you what you need to know because you—you my friend—are dumb.

A question arose in the background (like this) as a gadfly and brought the juxtaposition of divergent normals (normalis ex-communicatis) into focus. Normal 1 is a function of self-explanation. I, being me, explain myself to me and unintentionally to you. Normal 2 is a function of self-delusion. I, being me, hide myself from me and unintentionally from you. The breaking apart of two agents. A factor of schism I.

I confess part of me felt pity for Brad. I mean, who wouldn't? That was the purpose of his entire story. At the same time, however, I knew Brad got around and I couldn't help but feel that he was being just a tad selfish. Nevertheless, I was polite to him. I nodded. I gave him a thumbs-up and motioned to him that I had it all under control. I took a deep breath and counted to ten because I didn't want to tell Brad he was dumb. *El dummo. Le grand dum dum.*

At one, the stream I fell into shaped my awareness.

At two, single matriarchs combined to serenade my bounty.

At three, I gave people frequencies to tune into.

At four, transitions disappeared.

At five, I wrote the question why? between my shoulder blades.

At six, *hiroshima father breastlespur* consumed himself.

At seven, I felt a parade moving around my throat.

At eight, I saw a poster advertising the National Theatre's production of *Hedda Gabler*, the first woman I ever truly loved. That she was a fiction was beside the point. What was important was that I fell in love with her character, her nobility, her personal vision of the world, her stoic rebellion. The poster distracted me from my protesting and I plotted to find my way into National Theatre to proclaim to Hedda my previous affection for her. That I no longer felt any affection for her was also beside the point. We must make a final accounting of our lives one day and any proclamation to her would be part of that final accounting.

I once imagined that Hedda dreamed of designing great cities in circular patterns with parks and canals and that she and I were a statue in the center of it all. There was plenty of time to get serious for the sake of our legacy. We were serious, but I mean even more serious: child soldiers, famines, the holocaust, pathogens. Hedda and I stayed on the outskirts of serious. Down by the hem, where there always existed the possibility that we could be cut right off and serious could keep on walking without catching cold.

How has the perception of the golden mean changed in the last two hundred years and was this change in perception a catalyst or consequence of the industrial age?

Then we would run off into the future where she would soften and ask me questions that made me pause. What about the suffering of children? *Pause.* What about overcoming the odds? *Pause.* What about taking up arms against injustice? *Pause.* What about renewing hope and fighting destiny? *Pause.*

And during one of my pauses, she'll take a long walk back to where we started and meet someone named Brad with whom she'll have a revealing conversation by the statue in the center of our great city. A conversation about ordinary people like grocery clerks and people who work in the service industry and how their lives have as much meaning as the lives of the greatest human beings who have ever lived. About small towns and how they are emotionally, if not demographically, as cosmopolitan as any city in the world. Like Tokyo. That's funny. I know a Brad. Will she really believe him though? He molested his cousin. But she'll tell me he's changed and she'll tell me she's changed and she'll leave a gun on my bedside table in great anticipation because she has a vision of a beautifully ordered world, only to find out later that I died of something common like natural causes just to spite her.

At nine, I heard feeble complaints about being condescending.

At ten, I wondered what they were looking at. I watched their dumb eyes. They leaned over me. All that time I thought they were following my hand as I pointed to their dumbness. I felt the sun shine on my jugular even as the rain fell around me. A gust of wind blew around my hair and a kite rose up from around my neck. I felt a pull on my skin. It was me and I ascended, choking myself, until I vanished through the clouds. I'd finally get my answer, I thought. All this time. It was the only question. I felt a scribbling on my back and when it stopped, I turned my head until I saw me coming back through the clouds. I gasped for air and I pulled but I was too eager. The string snapped and I disappeared from my view. And I thought, well yes, it wasn't meant to be. For who deserves an answer?

But someone—one of those dummies said: look at what's on your back.

And I said: what?

And he said: I don't know.

Just like a dummy, I thought. Maria, take us out of here.

SEAN BRIJBASI. *Discarded moments. Unfinished gestures. Lived in London. Resident of Sweden. Lives in Washington, D.C. In East Berlin before the wall fell. In Russia before glasnost. Jazz in Copenhagen. Switchblade in Paris. Lost in Helsinki. Bar fight in Auckland. Awake for three straight days in Reykjavik. Bored in Brussels. Green light in Amsterdam. Red light in Hamburg. And more...*

La Petite Mort

Peter Brown

Kitty can't catch her breath after climbing two flights. Years ago, she preferred stairs to elevators. She could get there quicker, even wearing three-inch platforms. The quicker she hit the room, the quicker she could turn a trick, pull up her pants, and go to the toilet for a snort. She'd be strolling down New York Avenue again in thirty minutes flat, already one trick ahead for the night. She could forget a trick a lot quicker back then. The key was to be seventeen, a hundred and twenty-five pounds, and smart, like she had been. Seventeen, when she still looked girlish, and johns weren't so rough with her. Smart, so she could work alone, and keep working for decades in D.C.

She knocks on the door of room 206. "Kitty? Ish open," the guy slurs. She slips in, swinging yellow hair behind her. Bottles crowd the night stand. He's under the bed sheet, and his knees and toes make peaks in the fabric. She wonders, what's that sharp thing poking up?

He wipes tears from his eyes, and says, "Howsh my Honey?"

She mocks him, *"'My Honey.'* I'm lousy. Don't wanna talk about it." She drops her jacket on the floor, and flicks her spaghetti straps off her shoulders.

"You came back. I knew you would. My B-Baby. No, not my Baby. Nooooo. Sh-She left me. You're my Honey." He looks her over, up and down.

She thinks of her own bowed legs and deflated breasts. "What's it gonna be?"

"You're b-better than your pics on the website—tons better. More assh. Ish been growing on me."

She shoves her hot pants to the floor, revealing a lavender thong strung across her pelvis.

"I'll never be a shucker for you, Hon," he says. "Not like I was for her—my Baby. Such a s-stooge for her—I'd still take her back, after everything." He makes a fist.

Stooping, she grabs his bed sheet and gives it a yank. It's a one-handed tug-of-war.

"Na, not yet," he says.

"What're you hidin'?" Kitty drops it.

"Not yet. Why do I hang onto h-her, after she left me and k-kidnaped the twins? Haven't sheen 'em in nine monsh. Nine whole monsh."

"C'mon Mister. What's it gonna be?"

"*Even she* says I sh-should forget her. But she'sh my type, goddamn it." He cups his hands on his chest, "Nice'n plump. Can't—But I'm gonna end it—end it now."

"Don't waste my time." She reaches for her hot pants and sticks one leg through.

"Wait Hon. Got Jack and C-Coke." He points at the bottles.

No reply.

"OK, lesh go," he says. "Shame as last night. Jush do your thing again, but this time shut your eyes."

"I'm warning—Don't waste my time," she says. "What was last night?"

"Blowjob, Hon. 'Member? 'Member? Shame thing."

She nods.

"Close your eyes thish time."

"Extra fifty dollars," she says.

"Sure Hon. Wh-whatever."

"OK Mister, how's this." She shuts her eyes, tapping her foot.

"Not Mister, I'm S-Sully, 'member?" No reply. "OK," he says, "shame as last night. I won't even t-touch you. I'm harmlesh, 'member?"

"A blow? That's all?" Her ankles bow.

"OK Hon. Ready?" No reply, so he continues, "When I come, you split. You'll be done, so split. I'll do the resh."

She peeks at him. "The rest? *What* rest?" With a hand on her hip, she points at the sheet. "What're you hiding, Mister?"

"Shut your eyes, Hon, and you'll shee. I'll get a little bloody. Jush me. You'll be gone by then."

"Bloody? Asshole. You guys're assholes." She pulls up her spaghetti straps, stoops to get her shorts, and turns to leave. She imagines a hundred-dollar bill down the toilet.

"OK, here. Here's the cash," he says. He snatches a wad from under his pillow and shakes it at her. "Cold cash, just for goin' along wish me."

She's already reaching for the doorknob. "You said 'Bloody.'"

"*My* blood, not yoursh. You'll be way gone." He taps his chest. "I'm harmlesh."

Staring at the doorjamb, she's sick. Needs a snort. She thinks of trudging down the Avenue sick.

He continues, "The whole wad for fifteen minutes of your time. Ten minutes, maybe. Pleash, Kitty Honey." She takes her hand off the doorknob and remains. He kisses the air. "Mmm, hank you, love you love you. Jush get naked and blow me. Then split while I blow myself."

"Kill yourself?"

"Yep. A double orgashm. One f-from you, another from my gun."

"A gun's under there?" She faces him.

"My solution, coming and going, all at once."

With her hand on her hip, she says, "No guns, Asshole. No way." She turns to leave.

"Here. Here, take it all." Another wad of bills comes out. He can barely hold them in one hand. "Double money. Double o-orgasm. See, dyin's like coming. Your mind goes out of b-body. Death's an orgasm, and o-orgasm's like death, they say."

She hardly hears him, while she imagines white powder lines to the horizon.

He continues, "That'sh what the F-French call it. La petite mort—the little death."

"Call what? No parlez vous," she says, glancing over her shoulder at him.

He sits up. "Orgashm—la petite mort—the little death. Sheems like your soul leaves your body."

"What do *you* know about dyin', Mister?" Speaking over her shoulder, she shakes a finger at him. "Dyin' hurts, especially from a gunshot wound. I know. I've been grazed." She rubs a spot on her arm. "Like a motherfucker."

"Who sh-shot you?"

She shrugs. "All I remember is the pain."

"But, when you're out of body, it's ec-ecshasty. Gonna have a double shot of ecshtasy. One from you, 'nother from my g-gun. A lot better than dyin' from cancer."

She turns on her heel. "'Out of body?' I'll show you out of body. Get a toot." She points to her temple. "With a toot, you'll be mellow. You won't remember a thing. I've forgotten every john I ever met."

His brow is pinched. "Forgot? You forgot me? Lash night?"

She shrugs. She used to forget, back when a buzz was a buzz. She didn't feel the trick in the first place.

"You 'member lash night," he whines. "Aw fug it. Come here." He reveals the pistol. She jumps. He jerks it away from her, and checks his trigger finger.

The gun fires into the mattress and she screams. The bed sheet billows. Kitty bangs her elbow on the wall, then squats in her tracks and cradles it. Her eardrums feel broken.

He sits up, bony as a skeleton, keeping the gun at arm's length from himself. "Fug me. Could'a killed her. Fug me," he cries and pounds his thigh with his fist.

She rubs her elbow and sobs, "I'm shot to hell. Dead. No more tricks. I'm totally shot."

"You're all right. It mished you." With gun in hand, he prays to her. "Shorry—didn' mean to. C-come on, Hon. Up."

She rages, *Shoot me, Asshole! Put me out.*

He rolls over and gathers the wads of bills. "You're fine. Now shut your eyes, like I told you."

She shuts them. "I'm totally shot. Dead. Thirty years of this, and you're totally dead, Mister. No more buzz. You survive, but it still sucks. Knives, bullets. *Bullets.* For what? To be pussy for another asshole." She sighs, "Survivin' sucks."

"Relash. You've sheen guns before. Maybe I'm an ashhole, but I'd n-never hurt a flea. Not even my esh-wife, who deserves it. N-Never shot *her.* Here. Take it." He flings both wads at her and the bills scatter.

She crawls around after the money, then slumps. "All ones. Three fives. The trick's over. Can't feel a buzz. I'm not even pussy anymore."

"You were pushy lash night, all right."

With her head hanging, she can't hear him.

"Tha's why I'm broke," he says, "You got it all lash night." He gazes at the ceiling. "You freed me from everything—my own shkin even. When I came, I losh touch. Left my body. I could see myself."

"You felt that, when you came?"

"I wash floating," he says. "I dreamed—daydreamed—I was awake. I shaw you, Kitty. You were there, glowing—during my org—"

"All right, maybe I was here last night, but—"

"I wash free, out of body." He makes room for her on the bed.

"Shut up." She grabs the bottle. Swigs twice, then winces. Hair slides across her face.

He points the gun away. "I was out—"

"Don't *out of body* me," she mumbles. "Shut up and be still." She stands over him, pulls her camisole over her head and her nipples settle on her ribs. She shoves her hot pants down again, and they ring her feet like a garland. Naked down to her thong, she kneels over him on the mattress, with her nipples pointing like icicles.

At the touch of her tongue, his eyes roll back and flutter. "Ohh. Hank you, Hon. Hank you. That's it. Shhhuck me outta here." He puts the gun to his own ear.

She spews him out. "Put that thing down."

He whines and points it at her.

She dodges. "Not in the eyes." She turns her temple to him, and jokes, "All right shoot me. Here—right here. Put me out."

"C'mon, c'mon." He prods her, then turns it back on himself.

She clears her throat and opens wide again. She rocks the whole mattress.

"Aww, almosh there. Come on, Hon. Almosh. Yeah, yeah." He cocks his head, and releases a grunt. He pulls the trigger.

Boom. His blood splats everywhere. She lands on the floor, and the smoking gun lands next to her. Her ears ring. Can't think.

Up on the bed, Sully's a bloody heap. He's gone—no fretting, no aching.

The whole room is dead, except for the warm gun that smells of fireworks. She snuggles against it. She strokes the round trigger guard. She thinks, I could be gone too. She grabs the whiskey and swigs twice. It warms her throat, but the floor's cold.

She shivers and her ears keep ringing after the gun has cooled. Keeping it at arm's length, she sticks the barrel under the mattress and fires. She bobbles the hot steel. Soon, it's in her lap again.

She knows she should scram like she used to. Running in heels never slowed her down, not even on cobblestones. She could disappear. Now she's dying, and her shoes aren't to blame. Nope, it's blame itself that's killing her. She's to blame for being a pig—a glutton for the white stuff. She gets no buzz anymore, though she snorts it all night. Heels never caused her such trouble. She's planning to wear four-inch heels to her grave.

She squeezes the gun with her thighs and rocks back. She ignores everything else—her throbbing elbow—the voices coming from outside—everything but the warmth. She hears pounding on the door.

"Open up, or we're comin' in."

"No," Kitty whispers.

"*Bash it.*" A man shouts. The top of the door breaks. "*Bash it.*"

Kitty tries to crawl under the night stand.

"*Heave.*" Outside, a woman grunts like a tennis player. Inside, splinters fly.

A man shouts, "Security. Drop your weapons." Kitty hugs the gun tighter.

The banging continues, and the doorjamb cracks apart.

"*Stop,*" Kitty screeches. She tries to gag herself with her hair. She's never panicked before, even around guns. Guns are everywhere these days.

"All right, Corky. Hold up," he says. "This is Security. Drop your guns." A service revolver is the first thing through the doorway. A white man looks in, then lunges, crushing splinters under his boot. "Hands up, Lady. You armed?" Towering over her, the man twiddles his revolver like a cigarette.

Corky, a woman with no neck, steps in wielding an axe. Her jacket says "Security." Her close haircut gives away her age, twenty-five at the oldest.

The man says, "Look at the scum in this place."

"Armed?" Corky says to Kitty. "What are you doing with that thing? It ain't a dildo."

"It's *his.*"

"You shot him?"

"No."

"Drop it, slut." Corky says, raising the axe.

"Pigs," Kitty sneers. "I'll shoot you, you pig." She squeezes her thighs tight. The warmth is all she's got, and she craves it like the white stuff. Her elbow throbs and her head aches.

Corky strikes at Kitty's gun, whacking her thighs. Kitty collapses, and the gun hits the floor.

The man shouts, "Murderin' slut."

"Slut *yourself.*"

"Let's see who's a slut," Corky says. Squatting between her legs, she tears off Kitty's thong.

"Do the nasty," the man shouts, and he restrains Kitty. She's been raped plenty, but she never used to feel much. Now she's scared. She keeps mocking them.

"With her own dildo!" Corky brandishes Kitty's gun, and starts raping her with it.

Kitty gasps, "Put me out, out of—" She grabs the gun in Corky's hands and fires it on herself.

Corky jumps and scrambles out the door. The man snatches Kitty's gun and runs.

Kitty's eyes roll all around.

PETER BROWN's novel, Ruthie Black *(Argonne House Press, 2006) was a Reviewer's Choice in the* Midwest Book Review *and was reviewed by Man Martin in* Pleiades. *It is based upon his short story that won first prize in the 2004 O. Henry Festival Competition. Brown was judge of the* MacGuffin *magazine's first annual fiction competition (2006). He is an associate editor of* Potomac Review *and an instructor at the Writer's Center in Bethesda, Maryland.*

Full Moon Episode

KENNETH CARROLL

"Why must I feel like that,
why must I chase the cat?
Must be the dog in me."
—George Clinton

"**B**ow wow wow, yippee yo yippee yeah," sang Andre, echoing the words to the player's post-modern national anthem, George Clinton's "Atomic Dog." The tune thumped loudly from the three-way speakers in his black BMW. Pulling into the driveway of the Crescent Tower condominiums where he lived with Sandra, his long-suffering girlfriend, Andre suddenly realized that he had forgotten to call her with a gift-wrapped lie to cover his all-night prowling. But Andre was a D.C. player whose defiant philandering was buoyed by the often-repeated statistic that single women in the city outnumbered men fifteen to one. Of course the actual statistics were something like two to one, but real players could not be expected to sweat such trivial matters as statistical accuracy or showing respect for the women who supported them. Andre thought back to his night of "ho hunting," as he called it, blowing kisses to his reflection in the car mirror, thanking himself for an almost perfect night.

The only blemish on the night had been Denise's request that he not return until he left Sandra. "If you want to be number one, you goin' have to up the ante, baby," Andre told Denise, reducing their relationship to crass economics. She promptly asked him to leave. Andre figured a week of missing his lovemaking and she'd be calling his pager like he was 007. Andre smoothed out the thin mustache that ran along his lip like an after-thought. He blinked his green-gray eyes and licked his full lips while admiring himself so intently in the car mirror that he almost barreled into the dumpster near his parking space. Andre, the color of two teaspoons of cream in black coffee, felt his muscles flex as he coolly straightened out the car. His stunning looks were the arsenal that caused some of D.C.'s finest women to lose money, sleep, and ultimately self-respect. "Ah man," said Andre, unable to resist admiring himself one last time in the car mirror, "when do they give you your monument on the Mall, you handsome prince."

> "*Some people call me a pimp and a gambler, I ain't neither one,*
> *I'm just a slick little playboy who likes to have my fun.*"
> —*Big Joe Turner*

Andre activated the alarm on the BMW Sandra had bought him and walked toward the condominium complex. He wondered why women like Denise and Sandra were so possessive. Just because they paid the rent and the car note didn't mean he was their slave. I'm providing a community service, thought Andre, inebriated with ego and zinfandel. There are women out here who wouldn't know what an orgasm was if I didn't spread the gospel of good loving, he thought, laughing aloud.

The silk shirt floated like a elegant bird, landing dreamily at Andre's feet. He looked up and thought he could almost see Sandra's voice, dropping like heavy rainfall upon his head. "Carry your ass back to where you stayed last night, you whoring dog…" The rest of Sandra's words were muffled by the sound of another armload of Andre's clothing and possessions being dropped from the fifth floor balcony. The walkway was littered with his belongings. Pure wool, double-breasted suits hung like weird foliage from the trees and lower balconies. Alligator Ballys and Italian loafers commingled with silk sweat suits and French-cut dress shirts, creating a multihued abstract fixture of designer clothing. "Must be a full moon," Andre reasoned, packing his clothes in the Hefty Bags that Sandra had conveniently tossed out along with his worldly goods. Andre's neighbors filled their balconies, their upper-middle-class faces gnarled with expressions of embarrassment and amusement.

"And take these damn disco albums with you," said Sandra. Andre barely avoided being crushed by a crate of disco-erogenous LPs, including his favorite, the Donna Summer classic, *Love to Love You Baby*. He stuffed his possessions in the backseat of his car and entered the condominium lobby, conjuring a lie so magnificent the devil's press agent would envy him. But before he could punch the button for the elevator, Mr. D'Angelo, the property manager, and a security officer appeared.

The officer informed Andre that Sandra had a restraining order forcing him to turn over his keys to D'Angelo and requiring him to stay away from Sandra's condo. A wet, fat, full moon, Andre thought as D'Angelo shook his balding head like a mourner. "Sorry Wilson, your name's not on the lease, what the hell can I do?" Andre had spent many a lazy afternoon entertaining D'Angelo in the condo office with ribald tales of his sexcapades while Sandra was at work. Andre handed over his keys to the manager with a smile. "Don't sweat it, D'Angelo, I'll be back here in less than a week 'cause I'm strictly mackadocious." D'Angelo, who had spent fifty years managing apartments and condominiums, knew that all the funny words in a player's vocabulary wouldn't get Sandra to take Andre back—he would need a miracle.

||||

"They call me the howling wolf baby,
and I'm howling around your door."
—Howling Wolf

Andre wolfed down four chili-cheese dogs in two bites each and practically inhaled his large strawberry soda. He hastily wiped the spicy chili from his face and headed for the pay phone located, as a practical joke, Andre thought, near the blaring jukebox. The late-night crowd in Ben's would have made Freddy Krueger nervous, but Andre was more concerned with his wallet, which looked like it was on a Slim-Fast diet. He decided to call Denise and beg like a wounded dog—until he could get another woman to pay for the gold wand he imagined his penis to be. Dogs specialize in two things, he remembered being told: poontanging and begging. "Hey baby, it's me," he said upon hearing Denise's voice. "Listen baby, before you hang up, and I wouldn't blame you if you did—I want to apologize." Andre subtracted octaves from his voice until he made Barry White sound like a first tenor. Bitches love this shit, he thought. "For whatever it means, and maybe it means nothing since I've hurt you, but I've left Sandra. Last night made me realize now baby, more than ever, how much I love you."

"Oh Andre," Denise said quietly.

Andre smiled, energized by the rush of power he felt when his game was on. There're players in the world, he thought, then there's me. "Tell me something baby—can this man who loves you get another chance," asked Andre, coolly swirling a piece of ice over his tongue.

"I think there's someone here who can answer that," said Denise. Before Andre could speak, he heard, "Hello Mr. Stray Dog, you looking for a new home to bury your bone?" Andre dropped his soda and momentarily choked on the piece of ice in his mouth. He gagged and gasped for air before speaking, "Goddamn it Sandra, what you doing there?"

"Me and Denise are making friends with all these women you got in this data bank of yours. I wonder if they realized I was playing when I said you had HIV." Andre dropped the receiver. He could hear Sandra laughing as the receiver swung back and forth while he turned his pockets inside out. He wondered how Sandra had gotten his Casio 9000 Data bank phone, his high-tech black book that actually had different sounds associated with his women. Sandra was a gong, Denise was a chime, and his freakiest women were sirens. He could do searches based on the notes that accompanied each woman's name. For instance, he could summon all the women between eighteen and twenty-one, or locate his yellow honeys, his chocolate browns, or his exotica of the world, as he described them. His database was so advanced he could search for a woman by her favorite sexual position. Andre was closer to his Casio Data Bank 9000 than to his parents. He grabbed the phone again, his eyebrows knitted in rage. "Sandra, I want my Casio."

"Yeah, and I wanted you to respect me—I guess we don't always get what we want, huh?" A full moon PMS episode, Andre thought, listening to Sandra's acidic laughter. "Don't make me come over there girl," threatened Andre.

"Mothafucka pleeese," Sandra replied sharply, "Don't think 'cause I got an advanced degree that I won't get stupid on your ass! The last person you wanta see right now is me." Sandra's voice sliced into Andre's bloated ego. He had to face facts—she had trumped him—from the restraining order right up to the theft of his address book. But she was a woman, he consoled, inferior in every measurable way. Andre composed himself and lowered his voice to a pimp octave. "Messing with me Sandra is just like shoplifting; it's dumb," he said quoting a '70s public service campaign. "You shoulda smothered your little broken heart in tears, but instead you stepped to me and now I'm about to rip shit." Andre, feeling pit bullish, unleashed his viciousness. "I've been making love to your desperate-ass girlfriends for the last year and a half—call them. Their names are in there also, just type in 'Sandra's friends.'" Andre was going for scorched-earth broke—and he enjoyed it. He had a smile on his face and a semi-erection. Sandra was quiet, but Andre could hear her angry breath stroking the receiver.

"Andre you just stay right where you are," said Sandra, "I'm on my way. I finally figured out how to put this clip in right."

"Oh so you goin' shoot me—bitch you don't even know where I am."

"Well have another chili dog and a strawberry soda on me until I get there," said Sandra. "You took three years of good life from me Andre, I intend to get them back from you—in blood."

Sandra's voice had a Norman Bates calmness to it that worried Andre. He hung up the phone and looked suspiciously around the restaurant. "Another chili dog?" asked Earletha, the waitress. Andre turned around quickly, startled by her voice. He knocked over the sugar dispenser and a bottle of ketchup. He stared at the waitress distrustfully and moved quickly toward the door.

"Goddamn it Sandra," Andre screamed, standing in the empty parking space where he had left his BMW. He checked his pager alarm as he ran frantically to both ends of U Street. He bolted back into Ben's Chili Bowl breathing like an asthmatic. Earletha was working a chili dog with cheese.

"Hey bitch, where's my car," he screamed, jumping to conspiratorial conclusions. The restaurant became quiet so quickly that Andre's ears rang. Without comment, Earletha silently put the barrel of a graveyard black .38 against his temple. Andre instinctively raised his hands while Earletha, greasy spatula in one hand, .38 in the other, led him without incident out the door. "A full fucking moon," he yelled, running up the block frantically. He stopped at a pay phone that smelled of urine and stale beer and called Denise's house. She warned him that Sandra was on the way to the Chili Bowl with a gun.

"Please let me stay with you Denise—just for the night. You know you still care for me. Sandra just had someone steal my car and this crazy hot dog–frying bitch just pulled a gun on me."

"If I was Sandra, I'd be looking for you too," said Denise, her voice a dejected whisper. "Goodbye and good luck Andre."

"A full fucking moon," he said, slamming the charred plastic receiver into its holder.

Andre had to get away from Ben's. He cursed himself for relying on the high-tech efficiency of his Casio 9000 and not memorizing any of his other women's numbers by heart. All the male friends Andre used to have deserted him after his best friend took out an ad in the *City Paper* that accused Andre of stealing his wife. The ad even ran with Andre's picture and a home phone number. Rather than being ashamed, Andre was proud of the notoriety—until now. Andre decided to walk over to Murphy's Supper Club. "Shit, I'm Andre Wilson, mack of the D.C. club scene, if I can't get a woman to take me home, Popeye's a punk."

His fear diminished by his megalomania, Andre straightened his clothes and headed toward Murph's, as the patrons affectionately called it, to do what a player does best. He was halfway across 14th Street, when he spotted Sandra's Lexus barreling southbound toward him at what he estimated to be a hundred miles per hour. Andre froze in the high beams of the car. "A full fucking moon," he screamed as the lights of the car approached like some alien spaceship. Turning the corner while running back toward Ben's, Andre's Gucci loafers failed him. He slipped and tumbled roughly to the pavement, his momentum rolling him into the middle of U Street. His cotton Dior slacks were ripped, exposing bloody knees that stung like first-degree burns as he struggled to get up. The tires of the Lexus squealed, fishtailing in the intersection and bathing the street in blue smoke. "Sandra, no," Andre screamed, eyeing the barrel of the gun that extended out the car window on the driver's side.

He did not see the tow truck coming up the block with his BMW hitched to it. But he heard the horn, the screeching tires, and a voice, "Eh, boy get your ass out the street!" Just as Andre turned toward the voice he heard a thud. Andre wondered why he felt no pain, though he was sure that the truck had hit him. He was in a wonderful dream, he thought, soaring through the darkness, Donna Summer singing "Love to love you baby," while he made love to two women in a fog-enshrouded nightclub.

"Ooohhh, Love to Love you bayybee."

The impact lifted Andre fifteen feet into the air. He regained consciousness about halfway down, hurtling toward the unyielding pavement like a pimped-out Wile E. Coyote. After the dull thud, he lay in a contorted heap directly in front of Ben's Chili Bowl. The light from the restaurant revealed his arm, twisted in an impossible angle before him. But the most intense pain was in his legs and upper chest.

The Lexus squealed to a halt, its smoking front tires resting on the curb next to Andre's crumpled body. He waited for the end. What a way for slick playboy like me to go out, he painfully mused. He had always seen himself going out in the glow of a fantastic orgasm with two young honeys, freaking him like they were auditioning for the second coming of Vanity 6. Instead he was lying in the gutter in front of a greasy soul food joint that would probably be taken over by Koreans or be turned into condos in the future. Andre imagined his funeral. His guilt-ridden parents would be wailing, finally realizing what a great son they had. There would be hundreds of fine women crying, drenching the 13th Street Baptist church in perfume-scented tears. There would be scattered catfights between women who still longed to claim his love for themselves even in death, elevating his already legendary mack status to mythical proportions. Yeah, going out like a player, Andre thought. Sure, he could have been like his father: hard working, faithful, respectable, but guys like his dad were hardly noticed in life and quickly forgotten in death. No, Andre was sure everyone would remember him as a testosterone-charged disciple of hedonism. He even imagined two or three attempts at suicide when the *Washington Post*, in a front-page story, printed the details of his untimely demise. Ignoring the shards of pain ricocheting through his spine, Andre thought, maybe they'll send my dick to the Smithsonian. I ain't going out like a sucka, Andre thought. I ain't crying or begging Sandra to spare my life. In true unrepentant, mack-daddy style, he decided, if his jaw still worked, to call Sandra a bitch before she shot him. Andre heard the car doors slamming and angry voices from two women. He tried to guess who was helping Sandra, almost laughing at the idea that she had recruited his mother as an accomplice.

"Dag girl, this ain't hardly no Pee Wee," one of the women said, the voice unfamiliar to Andre.

"Don't you think I know dat now Nay-Nay," the other woman responded.

The young women, outfitted in black nylon designer sweat suits, were brandishing Tec-9 semiautomatics.

"Shit, why he run if he wasn't Pee Wee," Nay-Nay asked.

"Fuck I care," responded her friend. "Somebody probably looking for his ass too."

"What you wanta do now, Boo-Boo," Nay-Nay asked.

"Oh, we goin' find Pee Wee," said Boo-Boo, "Mothafucka marry me and I have his children and he think he just goin' leave me for some dumb-ass, fat-butt bitch—oh no, I don't think so!" Boo-Boo punctuated her words by waving her arms, wielding the Tec-9 like a toy. "Girl hold that gun right, 'fore you shoot some damn body," said Nay-Nay. "Only person I'm shooting tonight is Pee Wee's dog ass," Boo-Boo said, rolling her eyes and swinging her extended braids.

"Somebody get this nigga an ambulance," Nay-Nay screamed to the patrons who had locked themselves inside of Ben's.

"Girlfrien' he look like he need a body bag," said Boo-Boo.

Both women giggled, their extensions shaking stiffly as they walked calmly back to their car, leaving the street smelling like burnt rubber and Obsession perfume. The hustlers in Ben's broke out and nonchalantly stepped over Andre's prone body. The rest of the people waited inside for the police.

> *"They say a dog is a man's best friend,*
> *but a canine can't be mine."*
> —War

Andre, slowly going into shock, heard the patter of what he in his delirium first believed was the Grim Reaper. He opened his eye and saw a mangy, emaciated dog moving slowly toward him. The dog, limping along with an injured paw, seemed intent on passing him by. A black man lying motionless on the city's pavement was not a new sight, but the dog stopped and limped toward Andre, sniffing cautiously around his face.

Andre would have never reopened his swollen eye, it hurt too much, but he felt the warm tongue of the dog lapping at his chin, his lips, and his cheeks. I guess this is why they say a dog is a man's best friend, thought Andre, almost managing to smile through his pain.

But what Andre took as a sign of compassion was actually and simply a hungry bitch lapping at the taste of the chili dogs that he had eaten. When she could no longer taste the chili or the cheese, the dog stepped over Andre and disappeared into an alley. Hearing sirens in the distance and wondering if they were coming for him, Andre opened his swollen eye and saw a full moon laughing at him as it made its way down 13th Street.

KENNETH CARROLL is a poet, writer, and playwright, whose writing has appeared in Icarus, In Search of Color Everywhere, Bum Rush the Page, Potomac Review, Worcester Review, *the* Washington Post, Words & Images Journal, Indiana Review, American Poetry: The Next Generation, Beyond the Frontier, Gargoyle, Children of the Dream, Spirit & Flame, *and* Penguin Academics Anthology of African American Poetry. *His book of poetry is entitled* So What: For the White Dude Who Said This Ain't Poetry *(Bunny & The Crocodile Press, 1997). He has had three of his plays produced,* The Mask, Walking to Be Free, *and* Make My Funk the P-Funk. *He has performed at the Kennedy Center, Nuyorican Café, Library of Congress, Beyond Baroque, Gala Hispanic Theater, and universities and cultural institutions around the country. He is executive director of the award-winning community service program DC WritersCorps, and teaches at the Writer's Center. He was nominated for a 2005 Pushcart Prize for poetry. He is married and the proud father of a daughter and two sons.*

I Used to Love Her

THEODORE CARTER

She saunters out through the bedroom doorway naked, stiff-legged, her neck bent to the side, moving in a series of jerks.

"Sara, you all right?" I ask. We've been fighting recently. I want to sound concerned.

"Yeah, OK," she says, but her voice is gravelly, barely comprehensible, filled with phlegm. I leave her alone as she squeezes past me into the bathroom and closes the door.

We left the bar at three a.m. bickering because some stranger had tried to kiss her and nibble on her neck. "Maybe I should have let him," she said, as we stumbled drunkenly into a taxi. "Maybe you did," I said. We spilled out of the cab in front of our townhouse and made it up the steps to our front door with the help of the sturdy handrail.

Behind the bathroom door, I hear her making a hacking sound. It could be a cough, vomiting, I'm not sure. She gets pretty uptight about me being around when she's like this. She has antiquated ideas about looking "fresh," so I leave her upstairs and go down to the kitchen to make breakfast. I hear the shower running.

She comes into the kitchen wearing my old blue T-shirt, and a pair of mesh shorts. An odd choice of clothing for her, but I like that she's wearing my shirt. Maybe we've made up. The neck hole of the shirt pulls to the right, the waistband on her shorts is askew, and her underwear sticks out on one side, but not at all in a sexy way. She looks haggard. Death warmed over. Her normally pale skin is almost blue, and dark, purple bags show under her eyes. I should say something kind, reassuring. I pull out a skillet from the cabinet. "Do you want some eggs?"

She grunts in affirmation and scratches her wet brown hair. It falls in front of her face. I turn my back to her and work at the stove, pretending to labor over my eggs. She really looks like hell, and though I know it's petty, I'm pretty disgusted. I try to push such immature thoughts away. Sara is my first long-term relationship, my first go at commitment, and I shouldn't fuck it up because she looks like crap when she's hung over. I'm past that. I think I'm even in love with her.

I push the eggs around in the pan, and get a whiff of something acrid. I take the pan off the heat and smell it. Maybe the eggs are bad. It isn't the eggs though, and after a moment I begrudgingly come to the conclusion that the smell is Sara. I turn and look at her over my shoulder. She's sitting on one of the bar stools at the counter swaying back and forth like Stevie Wonder. She looks at me and makes a slow, guttural grunt. I turn back to my eggs. Jesus, she's disgusting. If it wasn't for her wet hair, I'd find it hard to believe she actually got in the shower.

I know there are times when I come home looking like shit, or I go play hoops and don't shower right away, and Sara never says a word. It's really ridiculous for me to be so shallow. I start thinking about all the things she does that annoy me, how she leaves the peanut butter knife out after making a sandwich, how she picks at her toenail polish when we watch TV. Stuff like that.

"Here are your eggs," I say, and I slide the plate and a fork in front of her. She grabs hold of the fork with her fist and starts stabbing at her eggs. When I went to her parents' house for Thanksgiving, they had about four forks next to each table setting. I can't believe this is the same girl those people raised. I figure, you know, sometimes when you're hung over, your whole body feels weak. Your arms feel heavy. She wouldn't give me grief for it, so I leave her alone. I stand at the counter across from her and eat my eggs, but can't help watching her. She only stops momentarily to look at the gurgling coffee maker with quiet skepticism, then she's slurping down her eggs again like she's eating a bowl of soup. Half of the eggs aren't even going into her mouth. She's like Cookie Monster, her food dribbling down her chest onto the floor.

"So, how you feeling?" I say. She still hasn't really said anything to me since she woke up, and I wonder if she's still mad at me. She doesn't answer, only shifts her wary gaze back toward the brewing coffee.

The coffee machine beeps, signaling it's done. Sara pops out of her seat when she hears the noise. She only looks at me briefly before walking over, with that same laborious gait, to the coffeepot, swiping it off the burner with a back-handed bitch slap.

"RAAAAAAAAAAAARRR!!!"

"Jesus Christ, Sara!" But I sure as hell don't want to fuck around with her if this is how she's going to act, so I don't say anything else. She stumbles out of the kitchen and out the front door letting the screen door bang shut behind her.

I let her go. Maybe this is best, for her just to leave for a while. When she comes home, she'll look at me with those soft eyes, her head down, and give me an apologetic hug. Still, I have to get the mop out for the coffee and sweep up the glass shards. It's hard not be angry about that.

I hear her an hour later. She lets the screen door bang behind her again as she enters. Instead of the soft forgiving look I was expecting, she growls at me and walks past me into the kitchen. Her skin is a deeper blue-purple tone now, and I can see the outlines of her veins like spider webs on her cheeks. This has to be something more serious than a hangover.

"Sara, you feeling OK?" I say. She only grunts.

Her bare feet are muddy and I'm thinking it's good I haven't put the mop away, but I'm worried now, while she goes into the kitchen, as to whether I've cleaned up all the glass. If she cuts her foot, she's likely to bite my head off.

I look at the brown footprints she left on the carpet. The markings are tinged with red too. I look out the front door and see a dead cat on our front steps, its neck bent at an unnatural angle and there's a pool of blood underneath its carcass. A neighborhood dog or raccoon probably got to it, I think, though I can't be sure.

I go into the kitchen. Sara paces back and forth mindlessly. Drooling. Grunting. "We should take you to a doctor," I say, but it is Sunday, and there's no way in hell Sara is going to let me drag her to Urgent Care.

She doesn't respond, only moves toward me with that painful-looking walk of hers. She holds her arms out stiff in front of her, her head bent to the side. A strand of spittle runs from the corner of her mouth. I think maybe she's approaching me for the apologetic hug I predicted. I smile at her and reach out my arms, trying not to show my hesitation, my wincing at her deathly blue skin, her rotten smell, her uncontrolled drooling.

We embrace. I grab her around the back and squeeze. She feels sweaty, fleshy, rigid, like a piece of bony fish. As I hold her, I think, *that's it, I need to break up with her, if not today, then soon.* I've felt this way before, but then settled down.

She leans into my neck and tries to bite me.

"Sara, stop!" I say, but she does it again.

I push her away and she snaps at my finger with her teeth. She misses and her jaw smacks closed with a loud cracking sound. She snorts through her nose letting out horrid smelling breath, so foul I wonder if she bit that dead cat, broke its neck with her teeth.

"Stop!" I yell.

Sara can be pushy, really bossy. She's never acted this bad before, but she does have a temper. She stands in front of me, her face contorted into an ugly scowl. This is when I get fed up. I can be understanding up to a point, but the truth is, she's been in a foul mood a lot lately. I know relationships are about compromise, but she's a real drag.

I look at her in silence as she approaches. She's still grunting softly. Maybe I'm not in love with her anymore, just wanting to be in love with her. She never lets me pick the movie at Blockbuster, never wants to eat out at my restaurants, never wants to hang out with my friends. She's always making snide remarks about my clothes, saying things like, "let's go buy you some more nice pants." Like the pants I have are rags. The bars she likes to go to charge five-fifty for a Corona. Whenever she borrows my car, she takes my Guns N' Roses out of the CD player and leaves Tori Amos in there. It's comforting to finally realize her selfishness, but I can't ponder it too long because she's stumbling toward me.

"I need some time to think," I say, but she doesn't seem to hear me. I scamper past her, out the front door. The neighborhood is quiet, almost eerily so, but it helps me think. After a few blocks, I become even more certain about things. Sara's not right for me. Not anymore. Commitment is good. I can commit, but I shouldn't commit to Sara. I deserve someone kinder.

It feels good to come to this conclusion on my own. I think it helps me act with a clear head later when she starts eating the raw meat out of the fridge and going after small animals in the yard.

"Sara, I'm sorry," I say to her as she lumbers across our cement patio, knocking over a lawn chair in an attempt to swipe up a blue jay she's wounded. "I've got to call someone. You're out of control." She's focused on the elusive, fluttering jay.

The operator says all ambulances have already been dispatched. "A busy day," she says, and as she's saying it I realize I can hear multiple sirens in the distance. She promises to send the cops.

I'm on the front steps when the squad car screeches to a halt in our narrow driveway. A big mustachioed patrolman gets out of the car holding a shotgun.

"Where is she?" he asks.

I notice the right sleeve of his uniform is torn and there is a smattering of blood on his thigh. "Out back," I say pointing.

He pushes past me into the house. I follow as his heavy boots shake the floor. He stops while exiting the sliding glass back door and stands with one boot in the kitchen, the other on the top step like he's afraid of getting too close. "Stand back," he says, and he points his shotgun at her.

"Wait!" I yell, but he ignores me and lifts the shotgun, taking aim. Everything is happening so fast. I want to talk things through.

Sara takes a slow, but aggressive step toward the cop, bares her teeth, and hisses.

"Sara, please," I say.

The gun gives a monstrous roar, and Sara's head is nearly blown clean off. It's devastating to see. I scream out in horror as the blood spills over the patio. Still, at least I know it never would have worked between us anyhow.

THEODORE CARTER lives outside Washington, D.C., with his wife and son. He's appeared in several magazines and anthologies including The North American Review, From the Asylum, Yankee Pot Roast, *the* Potomac Review, Well Told Tales, *and* Kiss the Sky: Fiction and Poetry Starring Jimi Hendrix. *You can find him on the web at www.theodorecarter.com.*

The Big Bad Wolf

CHRISTOPHER COLSTON

The first time Luke turned into a werewolf, it scared the ever-lovin' *shit* out of him.

He felt a creeping nausea at first, just before fetal-position-inducing cramping. His head pounded, a migraine times ten, his chest thumped, and every nerve ending in his body sizzled and popped like chicken fat over a campfire.

Over time he learned that fighting it only made it worse. Now he knew to take a deep breath, wiggle his fingers, roll his shoulders, and just surrender to it. The transformation still stung his body like a thousand hornets, but at least it was quick.

Luke Garue, thirty-two, stood six-three and weighed two-forty and a decade earlier had played linebacker for North Carolina State. Now he lived in Ashburn, Virginia, and worked as a guard at the Smithsonian Museum of Natural History. He didn't walk, he swaggered; he didn't talk, he bellowed, and he had always been that way, even before that August night on the camping trip when he was taking a piss behind a sassafras tree and the goddamned wolf snuck up behind him and bit a chunk out of his ass. He had yelped and whipped around, pecker dangling, and for a beat the wolf stared at him. A guttural sound roiled up from deep inside the thing, and Luke knew he was a dead man. Then, from camp, came the stomping of footsteps—"who's out there!"—and the beast bounded into the woods.

Luke preferred hunting trips with his Capitol Hill buddies who worked in Dick Cheney's office. But his boss at the Smithsonian, a tree-hugging, merlot-sipping liberal, organized this hiking-and-birding deal. Luke went along, anticipating a romantic rendezvous of the highest order with a nubile docent. But the nubile docents retired early; the rest of the group huddled amongst themselves at the far end of the campfire. Luke sat across from them sipping Wild Turkey before heading to the edge of the clearing to take his piss, and then came the bite, the rush to the emergency room, an interminable wait, stitches, salve, bandages. He couldn't sit for weeks.

He had experienced three cycles now. The first one took him by surprise, and like a bad drunken binge, he remembers little of what happened the rest of the night: just a blurry montage of intense smells—rancid meat in particular—a great itching, like he was wearing full-length wool underwear, and bright, searing lights. He woke up at dawn face down on the kitchen floor.

The second cycle, he remembered a mad dash through the slip of woods behind his townhouse, not so much running as gliding. And he remembered a deer, chasing it down, feeling a deep warm tickle, and then an uncontrollable spasm of energy, the sound of snapping bones, and the coppery taste of wild blood.

It was weird shit for sure. But once he got over the initial shock, he realized he rather enjoyed it. He rented all the movies, from the 1941 Universal classic *The Wolf Man* to Joe Dante's 1981 semi-satire *The Howling*. He had to laugh, how much of this whole werewolf thing the moviemakers got wrong.

Because what they never told you was how becoming a wolf made you so fucking horny.

||||

He had concocted a vague plan, arriving at Clyde's with Peggy Jones, a high school friend with whom he sometimes shared a bed. They found a table; he ordered a pitcher of Dogfish Head for himself, a piña colada for Peggy, and scanned the barroom.

There, squeezing between the crowd: A Middle Eastern–looking thing in a purple sweater and matching hair band, her buttocks stretching the gray wool of her skirt. He felt a tingle and kept his eyes on her for the next two hours, all the time plying Peggy with a steady stream of piña coladas.

When Purple Sweater emerged from the ladies' room, he stood waiting in the alcove, the top two buttons of his spread-collar shirt unbuttoned. He peered over his shoulder; careful, very careful. He doesn't remember what he said to her—probably very little at all. It was just a look—a Tom-Cruise-in-*Risky Business*-smile, head cocked to one side, arms spread—and she scribbled her address on the back of her business card as a blonde woman brushed past him en route to the ladies' room. He shot a glimpse at the blonde; she wasn't a regular here but she looked somehow familiar...

Luke returned to his table and turned over his half-filled pitcher of Dogfish on Peggy. The waitress rushed over and he apologized profusely. *My bad, maybe it's time to go*—all that. He made a big show of it, waving goodbye heroically and the regulars hooted his victorious exit.

He suggested Peggy stay with him for the night. While she stumbled to the bathroom, he dropped a sedative into a glass of water and stirred. Then he tucked her into his bed, said, "Drink this, you'll thank me in the morning," and in minutes she drifted off to sleep.

Now it was time to have some fun.

||||

Purple Sweater had been so easy. When she had asked him if he wanted a beer, he said, "Anything but a Coors Light," an inside joke she couldn't understand. In less than a half hour they had disrobed, and now he found himself licking her breasts: big, jiggling things, vein crossed, with a wide round sweep of dark brown aureole.

"Mmmm—white meat," he said, and she giggled, "All natural!"

He flipped her onto her belly and he nibbled at her rump. "Mmmm—hammmm," he said, and she laughed again, until he nibbled a bit too hard and she jerked away and said, "Oh, you beast!"

He apologized and worked his way down her thigh, licking, licking, licking down over the meat of her calf, and he fought the urge to bite again. Now he had her toes, oh so dainty ones, toenails gleaming pink, and he thought, "Dessert..."

He never transformed until orgasm. They were in a good rocking rhythm when he told her to stick out her tongue, and when it rolled out of her mouth he took it in his mouth, sucking gently at first. He felt the tingle coming, and WHAM the orgasm hit him like an anvil this time. He sunk his fangs into her tongue and jerked his head, in a flash clamping his paws over her mouth. He swallowed her tongue in a giant gulp, then with machine-like force locked his jaws on her neck and…well, she wouldn't be making any noises now, and he could take his time with her, which he did, until that final sound of the night, his dessert, the crunching of delicate bones.

He secured his alibi in the morning, when Peggy thanked him for not taking advantage of her while she slept.

||||

It had been a month since the unsolved death of Lina Shakarnaz, a grotesque cannibalistic murder that had dominated the front page of the *Washington Post*. Now the moon was full again, clear in the October sky. Clyde's was three-quarters full and Peggy had her hand on his thigh as he scanned the barroom.

Oh, there was a nice one. Where had he seen her before? From the neck up she resembled Hillary Clinton, only twenty-something. But she had muscled thighs and thin, tapered ankles that made her legs look almost coltish. He liked his girls a little plumper—not fat, of course, but something he could sink his teeth into. But those fine legs were meaty enough.

She caught him staring at her and smiled. She drained her drink and nodded to the door, walking out with a damn seductive hip-swaying walk, her haunches rustling beneath her red-polka-dotted skirt. He saw that she wore matching red sandals, and her toenails were long and painted a deep red.

Blood red.

He joined her outside where she leaned on the rail, smoking a cigarette. They traded names; hers was Flo.

She rubbed his chest. "I like hairy men," Flo said. "Are you the outdoorsy type?"

"You might say that," Luke said.

She tossed her cigarette, blowing smoke from the corner of her mouth. "Why don't you tell me a little about yourself, Tiger."

Luke smiled. He could have some fun with this one. He could talk about his favorite song (Duran Duran's "Hungry Like the Wolf"), or his favorite composer (Wolfgang Mozart), his favorite musician (Howlin' Wolf), favorite author (Thomas Wolfe), media personality (Wolf Blitzer), favorite *Great Gatsby* character (Meyer Wolfsheim), or his favorite NFL player (Warren Moon). Instead, he looked at his watch and figured, what the fuck.

"Well, Flo—it's Flo, right? If you really want to know—I'm a werewolf."

She laughed. "What are you saying—that you're a dog, you like to play the field, that you can't be monogamous?"

He just grinned and shrugged and shot a glance at her exotic feet and thought he might have to have dessert first tonight.

"This is rich," she said. "Well, look up in the sky, Luke. What do you see? Oh, that's right—a full moon! So where's the hair? The fangs? The claws?"

"It's not the moonlight. It's the lunar tug that sets the stage; something else…triggers it."

"Wait a minute—I've heard of your kind. Fancy yourselves lycan-thropes, do you? Oh, I know, there is no transformation per se; it's just an excuse to act all weird on people. You're all wack jobs, if you ask me." She pulled her sweater, a red knit one, over her shoulders.

She was mocking him, but that was fine. He would enjoy eating her even more now. He said evenly, "No, there is a transformation."

"Riiight. OK, so, do you, like, turn completely into a wolf, or are you one of those half-man, half-wolf things?"

"I've never actually looked at myself in the mirror. But I don't recall ever running around on all fours."

"What a pity! Isn't that the goal—to go whole hog? I mean, wolf?"

They never believed you until you took that first big bite, usually from their haunches, the nice fleshy hammy part of the buttocks. "I do notice that the hornier I am, the greater the transformation," he said.

"Well now," she said, playing along with him now, scratching his chin with her forefinger. "Maybe I can help you go whole wolf tonight."

||||

Midnight now, and Flo had finally succumbed, stretched out on her satin bed sheets and now he was licking her pale white body, working his way down to the blood-red toenails, his penis throbbing, and he knew this one would be especially messy. He started to feel the tingle coming, but before he could enter her, she said, "No. Me first."

Half-blind, Luke blinked at her.

"Eat me," she said, and Luke almost laughed out loud.

So he went to work between her thighs, flicking his tongue, working his way through the alphabet, and her groans grew louder, and he heard her begin to moan…

"Luke," she said between breaths, "I need…to tell…you…something…"

Lawd, what could this be? She's married? Has the clap? That's one good thing about this werewolf business, Luke thought. It seemed to make him impervious to STDs.

"My last name is Wami," she groaned. "Oh, yes. That's it. Right there. Good…"

Wami? Flo Wami? What the fuck kind of name is that? And why are you telling me this now? "And…we've met…before…God, yes, yes, just like *that*…and I knew… I had to have you…ever since…"

Luke popped his head up. He *had* seen her somewhere before! But where? She was too young to have gone to State with him…

She pushed him back down, her breath coming in bursts. She sounded close now. Come on you left-wing bitch! You can do it! Get it over with so I can get MINE…

"It was on a camping trip," she said. "I've been waiting…for this moment ever since I…Yesss!…I wanted your swinging cock so bad, but then the others came running…Oooooh GAWD YESSSSSSSSSSSS!!"

Luke gagged, his mouth full of something dry, like straw, and his nostrils filled with a rancid stench, something like vomited pork.

He looked straight into her eyes, now tiny red things flanking a black snout dripping with snot. They stared at each other and he knew then where he had seen her before, and he froze with the revelation. When she lunged at his cock he heard a sound like a dry twig snapping, and the last thing he saw was his blood splattering across her bed sheets.

CHRISTOPHER COLSTON is the author of an as-yet-unsold novel, "The Popsicle Lounge," a spiritual quest that features no horny werewolves per se. But it does include lots of sex, alcohol, fart jokes, a 1967 Bonneville convertible, and just about the coolest damn beach bar in world history. When he's not writing messed-up junk like this, he covers the NBA for USA Today. He lives in Herndon, Virginia, with his wife and two children.

Let Me Do the Talking

RICHARD CURREY

Bob? Yo, Bobbo, one moment, OK? Give me a moment here, because we must have a misunderstanding. I never said I'd do any such thing. What I proposed, right from the start, was an entirely different kind of enterprise. Let's get in sync here. Let's put our asses on the same fucking page: There's a job to do, something I think must be done, something I have to do if I'm gonna live with myself. And I'm doing you the honor of having you along, Bobby. You're my wingman, Bob. You're my right hand, my sidekick. I mean, Bob, let's be real, just for a minute here: I handpicked you to accompany me on a mission. Otherwise you'd be right where I found you, microwaving the quarter pounders at the McDonald's up on the highway. And—excuse me? I was working there, too? Well, yes, I was, Bob, yes—running the fryers, putting up them French fries, yes sir. But here's the difference, Bob: I am a man of vision. Yeah, you heard me. *Vision.* You think I was working Mickey D's because I, what, saw the future in the business? Because I want to take over the franchise? No, Bob, I was working toward a goal. A personal goal. And if you ever read any of the gurus—the gurus, Bob. *Goo-roos*, the dudes that know what there is to know and're writin' the books—if you read any of those guys, Bob, you'd know that the first step toward anything at all, anything that matters, is establishing a personal goal. And I'll tell you, Bobby, after I lost my little brother, I had me a motherfucking goal. Right after we got the news sitting there in the front room over on High Street and I watched my mother listen to that motherfucker from the sorry-ass Pentagon go through his little song and dance, I knew where I was headed, man. I mean, shit, man, my mom might as well've dived into the fuckin' bottle after that, I mean she—what? Did I hear you right, Bob?—She already lived in the bottle anyway? Well, hey, maybe she took a snort from time to time, maybe you'd catch her a little on the high side of things from time to time, but, Bob, after we lost my brother it was different, Bob. *Different*—OK? So don't give me any shit here. Hey, I'm the guy who lost a brother, Bob. And I'm the guy who has hereby done you the motherfucking honor of including you in my plan to make things right. To talk back.

Talk back to *who*? Jesus, Bob…are you ready to go? Well, then, get in the car. Throw your shit in the back and get in the car. We're wasting precious time sitting here shooting the shit. Get in the car and let's get this show on the road. OK. There you go. You settled? Christ, Bob, sometimes you're like a damned girl. Got your seat belt fastened? That's a good boy. So now that we're rolling let us communicate on one central point: I am in fucking charge here. Do not for one solitary moment in time imagine that your brain—which, Roberto, let's not fool each other, would weigh in at the general mass and girth of a bag of lettuce—do not imagine that you are going to mar this beautiful partnership. In fact, Bobbo—and I'm happy to say this—a beautiful friendship, but don't let that put you on any sort of high horse about who is the business manager in this relationship. I mean, you talk about *the job*, you know, like it was something we invented together, like it was an idea in what you might call tandem, two great minds come together and all that shit. No. No, Bob. *Please*. Definitely not. Yeah, right, I know we got high down in your basement and talked about it that first time but who was it brought the idea to you? Who brought the idea to the table, Bob? Bob? Will you just shut up for a second and listen to what I'm telling you here? Do not try and take credit when you have no motherfucking credit coming. I mean, Bobbo, you disappoint me when you do this. Do not let yourself be swept away by some notion, some extravagant notion that when it comes to ideas, when it comes to strategies, that we are equals. Oh, my, no. But here's the thing, Bob: I've said it all before and I'll say it again: I have honored you by inviting you into this arrangement. So don't get me wrong, my friend—I'm happy to have you along. You are my wingman. My goddamned sidekick. My *ramrod*. My main man.

You have the time, Bob? Yes, that's what I said. The time. That's correct, Bob, I'm asking you what time it is. What? Not wearing a watch—well, there we go, Bob. Just one more example of what I've been trying to say for, what? Twenty miles now? Thirty miles? The larger point I've been trying to make. The reason I'm the mastermind and you're the second frigging banana on this little road trip. I mean, not even a wristwatch and once more we see that you are not prepared, not even on the most basic level. What? Well, yes, Bob, time is important. Of course it's goddamn important. Time has a certain significance in the work we're about to do. I would surely hope that point is not lost on you. Time guides us, my man. Wouldn't you say that's the case? It certainly guides us in the proper execution of this plan I'm trying to see through, yet here I am with a partner who has somehow managed to show up for work without a functional timepiece. Shit, man, without any timepiece at all. So you might understand my irritation, just a little. Just a little, Bob. Hey, look, let me give you a small lesson on the subject of preparedness. Let me show you something in the way of coming prepared, showing up with the right tool for the job. Pop the glove compartment. Yeah, that's right, just pop it open. Hey now! What do we have here? What do you rest your eyes on, my friend? That's right, Bob, that's exactly what it is. It is a *gun.* You are very observant, Roberto—it is a gun, a pistol, a Glock 9 as the bad boys like to say. What? What do we need with a gun? Bob! My God, man, don't make me keep wondering why I brought you along on this expedition. It's for…well, hey, man, self-protection, right? And to, how should I say, cement the impression of strength, you know? Oh, for Chrissake, Bob, don't start with the freaking whining, man. Just don't do it. I can't stand it. I mean, Bobby-man, have we not been communicating these last many weeks? Or for that matter these last many miles? Has there been some lapse in our communication? We are hardly going to achieve our ends without the gun. And no, I do *not* plan to shoot anybody. Haven't I made that completely clear at every step of our planning process? But, by the same token, Mr. Bob, we've got to drive our message home. We've got to carry the impression of strength. Of resolve. It's got to look like we mean what we say. And here's the thing, Bob: We *do* mean what we say, right? Christ, my little brother bites the dust in some rag-ass desert about a million miles from here where they're fighting over…what? Who gets to cross the fucking road somewhere nobody gives a rat's ass about, and my little brother has to disappear because of that? Here's the thing, Bob, and I know I've said it before but it bears repeating: my little brother is a damned hero, Bob. He was the best thing that ever happened to our family. He was the one that kept my old man from beating up my mom and he's the one that kept my mom from killing my old man with a butcher knife. He was the one that bailed me outta jail that time I got into a little dust-up out at the strip joint. He was the one that came out and collected me when I totaled his Malibu. I mean, that damn car was my brother's pride and fucking joy, man. And I went and threw it into a ditch and it was still my brother that came out and got me. I mean, Christ, Bob, he got there before the ambulance did. Yeah, I *know* I've told you all this, but it doesn't hurt you one bit to hear it all again, Bob. I mean, it's the reason we're on this trip. My little brother is the reason we have undertaken this mission. I even kind of named it after him. Whenever I worked it all through in my head, sketched out the plan, how we could do it, I thought: this is Operation Hale Bodley. *Operation Hale Bodley.* Named after an American hero. And Operation Hale Bodley is all about one thing: Getting an apology from the man who killed my brother. The man who killed Hale Bodley as sure as if he pointed a rifle at him and pulled the trigger. I mean, Christ, Bob, the way I see it anyway is that the whole damned country ought to get an apology. Those motherfuckers in Washington ought to get down on their knees and beg our forgiveness. On TV. But they won't, will they, Bob. So that's why it's gonna take a couple dudes with vision and courage to make them apologize. And that be us, my friend. That be us.

Yeah, I saw the sign, too. Washington—sixteen miles. We're already hitting the traffic. Won't be long now. Which brings me to another vital point, Bob. *Let me do the talking.* You heard me. I'm the point man here. I've got a speech memorized. I know what it is that has to be said. Right, Bob, yes, I know, I hear you. Your point is taken. And don't get me wrong, I appreciate your contributions here, I really do. But women's stockings over our faces? For starters, Bob, that is so fucking ancient. It's completely, like, over, and don't tell me it isn't. It's like some kind of shit you're gonna see in a movie from, I don't know, 1974 or something. You know, the bad guys pour out of a van with these stupid-ass nylons pulled down over their faces, like they're wearing rubbers on their heads for Chrissake. You ever put a stocking over your head? You can't breathe, you can't see, you can't talk—what? How do I know? From experience, my friend. Well, OK, yeah, I know I just said it was a stupid thing to do, but this is how I *know* it's a stupid thing to do. This is science at work, Bob. This is what they call experimentation. And it was a long time ago I did this. It's not, like, a recent thing, you understand. It was a while ago. But I remember and that's why I'm here to tell you the stocking thing is out. Just listen up and you'll see why I'm running the show. Why I'm the motherfucking boss-man: We're going with *masks*. Yep. You heard right. Masks. But not just any masks. Oh no. We're going with Bush and Cheney. Georgie-boy and Big Dick. Absolutely, my friend. Oh yes, yes indeed, I have the masks, of course I *have* the masks, would I miss that piece? They're in the trunk right now. Ready to wear. All ready and waiting. Yeah, I know, you thought, being second fiddle and all that you'd be Cheney, but here's the thing, man: You're gonna be the President himself. Shrub is you, Bobbo. I'm gonna be Dick Cheney. And you know why? Because ol' Dick is *The Man*. He's the power behind the throne—I read that in a book, man, and it all came together for me. *The power behind the throne.* I was reading this book, all about how Cheney invented the damn war and came up with a bunch of lies to tell us about why we needed to send guys like my brother over there, and that's when I really understood that it's Cheney who killed Hale and ruined my mother's life and now there's nothing—nothing whatsoever, Bob, nothing at all—that Cheney will ever do to make it right. I mean, you think he's gonna give my mom a call and, what, express his regrets? Bob, this is one serious mean-ass son of a bitch we're talking about here. You ever see that dude on TV, man? He's mean. I shit you not, he's got that *stare*. And he's always staring like he hates you and every goddamn thing you stand for and every thought you're having or ever will have in your miserable life that he could care less about. I mean, Bob, it's almost admirable, that face of hatred, the way he keeps it in place like that, the way we never see him any other way. Dick ain't brooking no shit, I'm telling you. But here's the thing, Bob: Cheney might not brook no shit, but he's all wrong, man. He's living on the dark side. He's Bush's goddamn Darth Vader. And that's why I know it's Cheney who's got to apologize. To us. To the whole goddamn country. And that's what we're gonna make him do, Bob. I mean, can you imagine it, man? Can you just see it? When we ambush Cheney's motorcade and put him on his knees right there on the street, and make him apologize? But before he does we'll have every news outfit on the face of the damned planet right there with us. That's where you come in, Bob, you make the call—OK, OK, just checking, just making sure you know what you're doing and when you're doing it. I mean, TV news is our safety net, that's why all that Secret Service won't try anything weird. Trust me on this, Bob: They won't just shoot us down in the street because it'll all be on TV and no matter what, the Secret Service will draw the line at doing anything rash with all those cameras. Besides, by that time I'll have made it completely clear that all we want is an apology. I'll tell the world about my brother, and about how all my parents got was a folded-up flag and a medal in a box and how that's supposed to be enough to take care of…I don't know, man, everything they lost? And then I make it clear that as soon as Dick Cheney apologizes he can be on his way. And that, my friend, is why I will be wearing the Cheney mask when we execute Operation Hale Bodley on the streets of our glorious capital.

What happens next? Oh boy, you make me nervous asking that. Oh boy. Bob, Bob…we've been over the getaway, right? The *plan*? You know what you'll be doing, right? OK, all right, but, I mean, shit, you scare me when you ask questions like that. I mean, you're a key element in all this, Bob. We've been over it. Many times. I wrote a damned *script*, man. You're my ramrod. You're my *driver*, Bob. OK, right, I'll calm down. But turn the damn radio down, willya, Bob? That music's making me feel hazy, and I gotta be—No, I said *hazy*, not crazy. Yeah, I know your old man thinks I'm crazy. Hey, what if I am? Won't be the first time somebody said that about me. I mean, even little brother Hale said it, my own little hero of a brother, even he said that about me sometimes. He and my mom, one time they tried to get me to…shit, how did they put it? Go get some help. That was it: *Get some help.* They meant well and all, but you know what, Bob? In those books I read by the gurus? There's a whole shitload of examples in there about how the guys who did the most in their lives were called crazy. Really. I shit you not. This is the burden of having a vision, my friend. This is what having a goal and a plan and working your plan is all about. Anybody wants to go out and try and make a difference in this world you gotta—shit, what the hell is this? Fucking cops on our tail, man. Pulling us over. Christ. *Fuck.* We probably got a damn light out or something. Because I was definitely *not* speeding. Was I, Bob? I mean, I was *not* speeding. The last thing I'd do is get us into this sort of situation. Not on the mission. OK. Stay cool, Bob. Hand me over the Glock. What? You're throwing it out the window? Are you absolutely bugfuck, Bob? You think the cop won't see that? Just...shut the fuck up and hand me over that peacemaker. *No*, I'm not going to shoot a damn cop. What, you think I'm crazy? I'll keep it down here out of sight. OK, Mr. Police Man, I'm slowing down, I'm pulling over, I'm being a good boy. WILL YOU GIVE ME THE DAMN GUN, BOB. Don't want that cannon in the glove compartment do we?—I mean, the cop's liable to look in there, maybe. OK, I'm stopping. I'll just keep the gun down here, out of sight. We can't afford to get waylaid, Bob, you know what I'm saying? We have a mission, we got to think about the mission. That's what Hale used to say about the Army: They always kept the mission in mind. OK, here comes the cop. Rolling down my window here. Hey, remember what I told you, Bob: Let me do the talking. Just let me do the talking.

RICHARD CURREY's short fiction has appeared in many magazines, has received both O. Henry and Pushcart Prizes, and has been widely anthologized, including appearances in Best American Short Stories, New American Short Stories, Writers Harvest, *and* D.C. Noir. *His classic war novel,* Fatal Light, *will be released in a twentieth anniversary edition in 2008. A long-time Washingtonian, Currey lives in the Takoma Park area of the city.*

Harry Krishna

Kevin Downs

"Harry Krishna, Harry Krishna, Krishna Krishna, Harry Harry," I chanted, dancing around in rush-hour traffic, done up in my orange robes and shaved skull with a gob of goop that looked like day-old bird crap smeared on my forehead.

It all seemed so joyous, so blissful, so free—and so very far from home. Not just in distance. Hell, Daddy's hog farm was just a stone's throw across the Potomac. But in every other way I might as well have been a million miles away.

"Sneak up and grab her from behind nice and tight," Daddy'd used to say when we was back on the farm.

And with those words of advice I'd fix my eye on the fattest sow I could find, light out across the pig pen like a rabid hound, and shove it squealin' headfirst inside a holding stall. Next thing, Daddy'd let fly with the sledgehammer, stick 'em in the neck with a butcher knife, and we'd be knee deep in bacon for a month or more.

Later I came to philosophize about killing all creatures large and small. But, at the time, there weren't no need. My daddy was a pig farmer and I was duty bound to honor his wishes. I coveted no other existence and sought no other way of life, up until the day Daddy pointed his sledge out in the direction of Little Pork Chop, that is.

"Harry Rama, Harry Rama, Rama Rama, Harry Harry," I stood on the street corner, singing out loud, trying my darnedest to block out the memory.

"Be reminded there is more to chanting than reaching a state of pure negation," Brother Baba, our head honcho used to say. See, according to him, even a cornfed farmboy like me could become enlightened from calling out the names of the Old Blue One.

In case you don't know, the Old Blue One is the Lord Harry Krishna himself. And I guess I identified with the man for two reasons. First he was blue and according to Mama, I came into this world with my belly button cord wrapped around my neck, which nearly choked me to death, so I was also born blue. Second, like me, he grew up in the livestock business.

But that's where the similarities ended. The Old Blue One was a cattle rancher, but he weren't interested in them cows for beefsteak and hamburger. No, sir. The Old Blue One loved them cows like his own flesh and blood. So he forbade his people to butcher them even if they was starvin' to death.

"Tend your flock," he'd say whenever they was hankerin' for a good side of beef. In other words, "Do unto others as you would have them do unto you, cows included." And truth be known that's the same way I came to feel about Little Pork Chop.

How'd I come to hold one particular pig in such high regard? Well, Little Pork Chop had been born the runt of the litter, and no matter how hard he tried to suckle off his mama's tits, them other piglets would squeeze him out of the action. Knowin' he'd soon starve to death, I borrowed my brother Ricky's baby bottle every now and again and started nursing Little Pork Chop.

Later, as I watched him add on about two hundred pounds, I couldn't help but feel a sense of pride. So Daddy layin' the sledge to him was more than I could bear. My heart shot up inside my gullet and I tried hard to think of some way out of this mess. Desperate, I threw myself on the ground and faked one of my seizures.

"Mama! The boy's fixin' to swallow his tongue ag'in!" Daddy let out a holler and took off runnin' up the hill to fetch her. It was then that I unhitched the main gate and, with Little Pork Chop by my side, lit out toward them bright city lights.

The first time I'd ever laid eyes on them Harry Krishnas was about a year ago. Daddy and I'd driven into D.C. to auction off some hogs.

On our way back home, we stopped at a traffic light in the fancy part of the city that bordered the river, and there they was out on the corner done up in those fancy orange robes—hoopin' and hollerin' like it was the second comin' of Jesus.

"Look at them faggots," Daddy pointed and snorted.

The light turned green but the traffic stayed stuck. Daddy finished off a Pabst Blue Ribbon and jerked the flatbed over to the side.

"I gotta pee like a goddamned racehorse," he said as he climbed outside and made his way to a nearby burger joint. The Harry Krishnas swarmed around like flies on pigshit.

"Harry Krishna, Harry Krishna," they sang, holding out their hands for spare change and offering Daddy flowers and incense in return.

"Back off," he snapped. "I killed a dozen of your kind in Korea and I won't hesitate to do it ag'in!" He shoved his way inside but them people didn't even flinch.

I was duly impressed. Usually, when Daddy broke bad like that, it'd scare piss out of you. Instead, they just kept raisin' a ruckus, happy as the day they was born. I watched 'em carryin' on for a minute or two more, then kicked back with a big wad of Red Man Chewing Tobacco.

"Hold this book," a sweet-soundin' voice interrupted. "George Harrison reads this book."

I turned around to see the prettiest damn Harry Krishna girl you can imagine. Cute as a bug's ear, I tell you. I didn't know George Harrison from a hole in the ground but when a girl that good lookin' is shootin' the breeze with you, you gotta play along.

"You got a name," I said all calm and cool-like.

"Sister Saffron," she replied, handing me the biggest damn book I ever did see.

"You folks aren't from around here, are you?" I said, trying to engage her in some sweet talk.

"We're Harry Krishas," she chirped. "We chant Harry Krishna all day long. What do you do?"

"I raise pigs with my daddy," I answered.

"You don't eat them, do you?" she said all concerned-like.

"What the hell else do you do with a pig?" I puzzled.

"You love them!" she said.

Up until that time I figured I was the only misguided soul on earth who could love a pig. So I took another look at the book I was holdin' and figured I should find out more about these folks.

"How much?" I asked.

"As much or as little as you like," she replied.

I opened my wallet to find it empty 'cept for my lucky silver certificate, the one Daddy gave me when I slaughtered my first hog. I was fixin' to ask for most of it back in change but I never got the chance.

"Harry Krishna!" Sister Saffron chirped as soon as the bill hit her hand. Then off she skipped, singin' and dancin' back to the rest of her people.

I almost took after her but then Daddy came stompin' back outside. Knowin' he'd tear into me somethin' fierce if he knew what happened, I crammed that Harry Krishna book under the front seat and kept my mouth shut.

Later that night I finally got a chance to take a good look. Talk about a freak show. There was people with elephant heads on one page and monkey heads on the next. 'Twixt them all was pictures of the Old Blue One perched up on one foot like a chicken playin' his flute to the oddest lookin' herd of cattle you ever did see. I kept on lookin', hoping to find some sign of some pigs, but to no avail.

I didn't reflect too much more on them Harry Krishnas after that night. Until that day Daddy sought to lay the sledge to Little Pork Chop, and I unhitched that main gate, that is.

Now pigs ain't the fastest walkers in the world nor are they the best hitchhikin' companions, but somehow we made it across the Potomac into D.C. I guess we made for a pretty odd-lookin' sight, that pig and me, but no more than anyone else.

I mean you couldn't tell the menfolk from the womenfolk back in those days. And with so many of them millin' around done up in headbands, beads, and crazy-colored hand-me-downs, you could have sworn the circus was in town.

"It's Richard Nixon and Spiro Agnew," this one fella who looked just like Jesus Christ called out, "play 'Hail to the Chief'!"

His guitar-totin' friend pulled out a harmonica and started playin' a marchin' tune. Then the whole lot of them started cheerin' and salutin'. How I'd find them Harry Krishnas in the midst of all this hubbub, I had no clue. Then lo and behold there they was, singin' and dancin' right up on the street corner right where I left 'em.

"Sister Saffron!" I hollered and ran over with Little Pork Chop trotting along behind me. "We come to join up!"

"All who chant Harry Krishna are welcome," she said, grabbing me by the hands and jumping up and down like a Mexican jumping bean.

I nearly broke down bawlin'. These people didn't know me from Adam but here they was with arms wide open. Little Pork Chop weren't just no common slab of fatback to these folks. And I weren't just the son of some no good pig farmer, neither.

"This is yours, my child," Brother Baba interrupted, stuffing a tambourine in my hand. "Chant the names of the Lord and you'll be free!"

Overcome with joy, I started dancin' up a storm and shoutin' Harry Krishna with the best of 'em. And believe it or not, that's all it took. Just show up ready to raise a ruckus and you too can become official Harry Krishna.

My world changed overnight. The Harry Krishna Temple was located in an old warehouse by the banks of the Potomac. There we slept, worshipped and bedded down in the basement along with twenty-five other of the faithful.

Every mornin' around sunup I'd wolf down a bowl of free oatmeal while Little Pork Chop rooted around in a garbage dump next door. Then off we'd go, chantin' Harry Krishna for the next ten hours or so. Later we'd help Mr. Habib, the owner of our warehouse, unload truckloads of teas, herbs, and other exotic merchandise from around the world.

But it weren't all business 24-7. As you know, I'd been sweet on Sister Saffron since day one and before too long I decided to let her know.

"You want to meet up at the Temple later and dip some incense, just me and you?" I asked, less than a day after I got that first dab of bird crap smeared on my forehead.

"Keep thy thoughts with Lord Krishna," she scolded me.

"Ain't no Lord Krishna around here that I can see," I answered, refusing to take no for an answer.

"The Lord Krishna is with us always," she laughed, pointing to Brother Baba who was panhandling change from a visiting group of schoolchildren. "Seek out those who embody his pure Krishna consciousness and he will reveal himself."

I tried hard not to act too disappointed. I still had Little Pork Chop, I figured. Hell, a girl like that was out of my league anyway. So I sucked it up, thinking in due time she might reconsider. Till then I could do nothing but hang tough.

But a few nights later, as I lay fantasizing about what would happen if the Old Blue One ever did reveal himself to me, I realized what a long way I had to go. Next door was Brother Baba's private chambers and I could hear him and Sister Saffron commence their nightly meditation.

"Harry Krishna, Harry Krishna, Krishna Krishna, Harry Harry," they began all nice and slow-like. Then they picked up speed, huffin' and puffin', chantin' faster and faster like a stoked-up coal train. Then just when you thought they couldn't go no faster, "Harry Krishna! Harry Krishna! Krishna Krishna! Harry Harry!" they hollered out loud.

Talk about righteous. They sounded as if they was about as close to Harry Krishna heaven as two people could get. It was intimidatin' to say the least. I stroked Little Pork Chop who lay sleeping snoring and snorting on the floor by my side. A few minutes later, Sister Saffron waltzed into the room lookin' all calm and peaceful.

"That sure was some fierce chantin' you two been doin' in there," I said

"You can sing the praises of Lord Krishna in many ways," she said, "standing, kneeling, or bending down on all fours like the cows in Lord Krishna's field."

"Like this?" I said, rising from my cot to demonstrate.

"Follow the path Brother Baba lays before you," she interrupted, patiently guiding me back to bed. "He and he alone will tell you when that path has changed."

She stooped to give Pork Chop a gentle pat good night and headed off to the cots behind the water heater where the womenfolk slept.

I lay there in the dark reflectin' on this strange new life of mine. Sure it was confusin', but Brother Baba knew what he was doin'. All I had to do was have a little faith in the man and the Old Blue One would do the rest.

In the weeks that followed I applied myself to Harry Krishna'n like never before. I worked overtime unloading trucks and making deliveries for Mr. Habib. I bummed more change and sold more George Harrison books than the rest of the congregation combined. Every other free moment I spent out on the corner chantin' the Harry Krishna theme song.

I even got Pork Chop into the act, dressin' him up in a flower necklace and paintin' sacred signs all over his snout and belly. And with him smellin' the way he did, we must have sold a thousand sticks of incense or more.

"Lord Krishna is smiling on you and our fat little friend," Brother Baba said, singling us out as we made our way back to the Temple one day. I felt so damn proud I nearly busted a gasket.

"Brother Baba," I said, trying to make the most of the moment, "I was chewin' if you could tell me a little bit more about this path you got me on?"

"Why, your path is your path," he said, giving a shake of his tambourine to a bum passed out in a nearby doorway. "You chant Harry Krishna and seek to become enlightened."

"Fair enough," I answered. "But I done chanted Harry Krishna a gazillion times and I don't feel no different than the day I first packed it in with you folks."

"Be patient and calm like the river," he said. "Your way is infinite, your path is never ending, and you can only find its end when you understand it has no end."

You can only find its end when you realize it has no end? I thought. What in the name of Jesus H. Christ was that supposed to mean?

I tossed it around my brain for an hour or more looking for an answer but nothing came. I started to ask the man but he took off dancin' down the street 'fore I got the chance. Determined not to be left behind, me and Pork Chop ran after him, tryin' to catch up.

I chanted for days on end tryin' to cipher out a meaning behind that damn riddle, thinkin' it held some magic power or top secret information. Still, I came up with nothing. I grew so damn frustrated I thought about packin' it in.

Then I remembered something Daddy used to say when times got hard, "You got to wade through a mountain of pigshit if you want to have a nice slab of scrapple on Sunday."

So I decided to bide my time. The answer would come to me in the by and by. "Change is the one constant law of the universe," is the way Brother Baba woulda put it.

But as much as things can change for the better, they can also change for the worse, and soon us Harry Krishnas would know how true such words could be.

Her name was Moon Pie. And if Sister Saffron was a cute as a bug's ear, Moon Pie was a cute as a button on a bug's ear. She and her boyfriend had just been in town for a few days when he got in trouble with the law for shopliftin' a roll of bologna. I was out on the street corner chantin' and shakin' my tambourine when she walked up and introduced herself.

"The pigs just busted my old man," was the first thing I recall her sayin'. "You know where a girl can find some work in this town?"

I was shocked to find out Little Pork Chop wasn't the only pig in these parts and even more surprised to find out they was holdin' some kind of grudge against her boyfriend. Still I decided to play it cool.

"What kind of work you lookin' for?" I said.

"Dancin'," she said. "Topless, bottomless, full frontal, don't make no difference to me."

"See that man over there," I pointed to Brother Baba only a few feet away. "I was in your shoes only a few months ago and look at me now. If he can't help you, no one can."

"Far out," she said as she started to walk over.

I thought about calling after her, trying to introduce myself in a more formal manner. But that's when Little Pork Chop trotted over and stuck his nose up her private parts. So I thought it best to act like I didn't notice.

Now Brother Baba always did exhibit a kindness to strangers and Moon Pie proved no exception. In no time flat she was out chantin' and dancin' with the best of them. And when I say dancin', I mean dancin'. The collection plate damn near overflowed when she took center stage. We was all duly impressed—all of us but Sister Saffron, that is.

I first became aware of the bad blood the very next week. I was kicking back on my cot ponderin' what life would be like if the Old Blue One ever revealed himself to me. Maybe I'd become enlightened like Brother Baba. Maybe I'd get a promotion and start my own Temple or something.

It was usually about this time Brother Baba and Sister Saffron would begin with their special chantin', but tonight was different.

"Harry Krishna, Harry Krishna, Krishna Krishna, Harry Harry," I heard Brother Baba commence to huffin' and puffin'.

Then as I lay there listenin', gettin' all spiritual, I could barely believe it.

"Harry Krishna, Harry Krishna, Krishna Krishna, Harry Harry," a voice chimed in, panting right along.

But that weren't Sister Saffron callin' out the names of the Lord. It was Moon Pie. Confused and bewildered, I sat bolt upright. It didn't make sense. I'd been Harry Krishna'n' for a month or more before that girl got on board. How'd she get to chant on all fours before me?

Even Pork Chop looked confused. Then we noticed something rustlin' behind us. Seems like we weren't the only ones who'd heard what was going on. Sister Saffron was standing in the back of the room looking about as mean and ornery as an overworked plow mule.

"That son of a bitch," she muttered.

She turned and stormed out of the room. Considering the girl had always been as calm and peaceful as a clear blue stream, it came as quite a shock. First she tells me Brother Baba is my rightful Harry Krishna role model. Then she's cussin' him out like a sailor. Life was a lot simpler back on the pig farm.

I decided not to let such thoughts get the best of me. Things would look better in the morning. And even if they didn't, I still had Pork Chop, and a good friend is all you can ask for in this world anyway. We bedded down and drifted off to sleep with Brother Baba and Moon Pie chantin' themselves into a religious frenzy next door.

Bright and early the next day we was out on the street corner just like always. The only person missing was Sister Saffron. A few of the faithful was worried, but Brother Baba told us she was making a barefoot pilgrimage to some mountaintop of India. So none of us paid it no mind.

We continued dancin' and chantin' like always but our joy didn't last long. It was right around lunchtime. Moon Pie was shakin' it down like her pants were on fire and George Harrison books was selling like hotcakes.

"Go, Harry Krishna girl, go!" some cop in the crowd was a-shoutin'.

But then this circus girl yelled, "The bitch has a gun!" And that's all it took. The crowd cleared in a heartbeat and I got the shock of my life.

Standing smack dab in the middle of the sidewalk was Sister Saffron, a .357 Magnum in one hand and a bottle of Mad Dog 20/20 in the other.

"You no good piece of lying horseshit," she slurred her words to Brother Baba and aimed at his head.

"Darlene," he begged. "Remember your vow of nonviolence!"

"Gave it up, Ray Bob!" she snorted back.

Considering the girl had once spent an entire week meditating over the soul of a fruit fly it was an amazing turn of events. But what happened was even more of a surprise.

Moon Pie hit the ground in a three-point stance. "Drop it, lady!" she shouted, pulling out a police-issue .38 from under her robes. She fanned the gun over the entire congregation. "You're all under arrest."

"You've got nothing on me," Brother Baba shouted.

"Your buddy Habib just turned state's evidence," Moon Pie barked. "How about five kilos of hash smuggled through customs in a crate of George Harrison books?"

Unimpressed, Sister Saffron swayed drunkenly from side to side and cocked back on her .357. "I don't know which I hate worse, a narc or a whore!" she growled.

BAM! Moon Pie fell on her side, clutching her kneecap and screaming in pain. "Officer down!" she shouted into a tiny walkie-talkie she had tucked away.

Harry Krishnas, shopkeepers, circus folk, everybody ran for cover. Pork Chop commenced to squealin' like he was havin' a nervous breakdown. I tried dragging him away, but he dug his little hooves in and wouldn't budge. Sirens was wailin' in the distance. Sister Saffron stood there cool as a cucumber and took aim at Brother Baba.

"I should have left your ass in jail when they busted you on those fraud charges in Tampa!" BAM! She blasted a hole through his robes, missing his behind by maybe an inch.

Brother Baba dove for cover behind a nearby VW. "Name your price!" he yelled. "I'll give you half of what we bilked from these suckers and more."

"Ain't no sum of money can buy back the years I wasted on you!" BAM! Sister Saffron fired again.

The bullet cut through the VW like butter. Brother Baba leapt out from behind it, once again unharmed. Desperate, thinking she wouldn't shoot at a shield of flesh and blood he took cover behind me and Little Pork Chop.

"Chant Harry Krishna," I said. "Maybe she'll stop."

"Fuck off, hick!" he said, shoving me to the side. "It's just me and Porky Pig now," he called to Sister Saffron. "You know how you feel about cruelty to animals."

His begging was all in vain. "Burn in hell!" was all she said, too full of rage and cheap wine to give a damn.

"Duck!" I yelled, too late to make any difference.

The bullet ripped a hole through Pork Chop, clean through his side right where I'd painted one of his sacred symbols. He let out a painful howl and hit the ground like a ton of bricks, pig blood spurtin' everywhere.

Brother Baba took off running. Sister Saffron fired a few more shots in his direction, but he escaped down a nearby alley never to be seen again.

Blind to the commotion around me, I cradled Little Pork Chop in my arms. He let out one last gurgle and grunt and gently slipped away. Through my tears I vaguely recall Sister Saffron being thrown to the ground and handcuffed and Moon Pie being loaded into the back of an ambulance. Police was everywhere and one of 'em promised to return with the fire department and cart off the carcass of Little Pork Chop.

Knowing I owed that pig a decent burial, I told him to leave us be. For a moment I thought about setting him on fire and sending him out of this world Harry Krishna-style. But then I had a better idea.

With the help of a few locals I dragged him to the banks of the Potomac. There we placed him in the filth and the muck where the river meets the shoreline and watched him sink into its depths. Knowin' how much he always used to enjoy a good mud bath, it was a funeral fit for a king.

I folded my legs up like a pretzel, and sat there for hours in what the Harry Krishnas call the Lettuce position, chantin' and hopin' the Old Blue One would drop down from the skies and make everything OK. If there ever was a time for him to make his presence known, it was now, but my chantin' was all in vain. I never saw hide nor hair of the Old Blue One. Such things only happen to the high and mighty, I suppose.

I unwrapped my legs and wandered back up to M Street. It was Friday night and the circus folk were out in full force but their guitar playin' and singin' held no joy for me. Depressed and downtrodden, with no place else to go, I tucked my tail between my legs and headed back to Daddy's pig farm.

Given the choice between partnerin' with or without a pig for a hitch-hikin' companion, thumbin' solo is definitely the way to go. I made it back to the wilds of Virginia in only a few hours. And I would have made it even quicker if'n I hadn't been covered in pig blood.

Comin' up that gravel road, seein' that farmhouse in the distance was a welcome sight. Unlike life in the big city, there were no big questions, no never-ending paths, no high mucky-mucks here. Sure I was gonna have to eat some crow but I was willin'.

I reached the front porch, hesitated, and knocked. Daddy opened the door. He eyeballed me like he didn't know me from Adam. Then under the blood, robes, and bird crap, he fixed a bead on me.

"Looks like the chickens done come home to roost," he mumbled, spitting out a thick stream of tobacco juice.

"I made a fool of myself. I'll be the first to admit," I extended my hand, hopin' he'd let bygones be bygones.

But forgivin' ain't ever been Daddy's strong suit. So's he drug me inside, laid into me with the barber strap for an hour or more, and sent me down to sleep with the pigs for the night.

It was a cold November night and the mud and pigshit crunched beneath my feet as I made my way through the sty. I spotted some old razorback snorin' by the feed trough, so I rested my head up against his belly and bedded down. Lyin' there starin' up at the sky, I was comforted by the sound of that snorin' old hog beneath me and I started to drift off.

Then I heard this peculiar sound, somethin' distant and musical-like. I opened my eyes to take a look. Lo and behold, in the midst of all them pigs stood this odd-lookin' fella playin' a flute, perched up on one leg like a chicken, with skin the color of a light blue robin's egg.

Yep, there was no mistaking it. Like Moses and the burning bush, I was smack dab in the middle of a full-blown religious visitation.

"Old Blue One," I said, not the least bit afraid. "What are you doin' out here with me and the pigs?"

"I have come to tell you about your path, my son," he said, putting down his flute and standing on two feet.

"You came all this way down here from heaven just for me?" I said, so honored I could barely believe it.

He continued as if I hadn't said a word. "You remember those cows I used to herd in the hills of my homeland?"

"Damn straight," I said. "Your respect for cows is damn near as strong as my respect for pigs."

"I was wrong to deny the fruits of their flesh to the people of my village," he said. "They were starving then and they're starving now. The false prophets have led my followers astray. And that is why I have come to you in this form to personally instruct you in the mystic ways of your path."

Talk about changing rowboats in the middle of the stream, I thought. Still, I kept my mouth shut.

He raised his hand like a preacher at a Baptist tent revival meeting and addressed both me and the entire pigpen. "Be it known from this day forward that cattle were given to this earth to provide man with beef, swine were given to this earth to provide man with pork, and you were given to this earth to ask for no more than what this world can provide."

"But what about my path?" I pondered out loud.

"Your path is to follow dutifully in the footsteps of your father," he said, "to do his bidding and to question your reason for being no more."

"You mean there ain't no way out of this place no matter how hard I try?" I said, pointing to the mix of hogs, slop, and shit that surrounded me.

"Not in this life," he said.

He placed his flute to his lips and played a mournful jig as he turned to walk away. Several pigs tried to follow, but when he got to the pen's rickety gate he just melted right through it. He then floated up into the heavens, his faint image expanding larger and larger until it disappeared in the nighttime sky.

So that's it, I thought. You could chant Harry Krishna from now until doomsday and none of it would do no good. I pondered the injustice of it all, but my ruminatin' got broke by this timid little squeal.

This old sow was nursin' a pack of newborns and one of 'em was flailin' away somethin' awful. It was the runt of the litter and he couldn't grab a suck off his mama no matter how hard he tried—a sorrowful thing to see. So I shoved his brothers and sisters away, set him down next to his mama and let him suckle to his heart's content.

Sittin' there watching, I was reminded of Little Pork Chop. This weren't no kind of life here on the pig farm for that tiny pig. Nothing to eat but three-day-old slop, nowhere to sleep but in the mud and the shit, soon as he weighed in at 250, Daddy'd take the sledge to him.

The runt finally unhinged himself from his mama. I tucked him up under my coat and bedded back down. He was a trustin' soul and would no doubt make for a loyal and trusting friend. What else can you ask for in this world anyway?

I stated to doze off and thought about the Old Blue One with his flute and what he'd come down from heaven on high to tell me. Still I held that little pig close to my chest and said, "We'll get out of this shithole someday."

KEVIN DOWNS is the director-producer of several award-winning films and music videos. He teaches documentary screenwriting at George Washington University and narrative screenwriting at Georgetown University. His other fiction writing appears in It's Only Rock 'n' Roll *(David R. Godine),* Chick for a Day *(Simon and Schuster),* Alice Redux *(Paycock Press), and* Kiss the Sky *(Paycock Press).*

Trilogy: The Thirty-Seventh President of the U.F.S.

David Everett

Prologue: Researching My Fiction

His voice was coarsened, like a grifter forced to make too many pitches from sidewalk pay phones. The timbre was often more rutty than deep, especially when he said "shit" or "fuck" while sinking into his oak-armed chair. He sometimes leaned back and lifted both legs off the floor to press the soles of his wingtips on the edge of the desk in that flawed circle of an office. His knees would bend higher than his scrunched head. I know this because photographs exist, but I haven't confirmed the wingtips or even the socks. I am only supposing he wore the thin, shiny ones, where pale skin bleeds through. Who gave him permission to put his feet on the furniture?

Imagine this: Him, in the presidential tub upstairs, his thighs wet against his chest, scrubbing the scumfilm of grime from under the protruding bones on his ankles. You take the washcloth to that, too, don't you? His bony, mottled ankles.

His voice was corrugated and peckish and never full enough; it was complex and inappropriately soily for his role in our lives. It wasn't as deep as you remember. On the tapes, it easily could become one octave too high, like what we are surprised to hear in a recording of ourselves, or when we try to explain something horrid, not our fault. I remember him declaring, "I will resign the office of the president of the United States" and so on—I haven't checked the precise quotation—and I thought, "Is he telling me now, face to face, or is he blaming someone else again?"

For my maiden fiction draft, I made plans to avoid those famous words. Instead, I wanted his final ones on earth, so I begin walking in the misting rain to the great library in my town, which is the same town from which he sleeve-wiped and coptered away in 1975. My research will permit me to know what last words he said, to whom he said them, and how he said them; fiction must be truer. (You know that.) But the rain gets fat and harmful, and I scurry from the perilously wet sidewalk into my favorite café for a jumbo cup. For him, a minor pants legs splash is reason enough to delay.

I order black, so I can add my own sweetener and whitener, but I can't make out what the counter guy is saying. It's his accent, Eastern European maybe? He shrugs and yells more unintelligible lingo toward another counter person, and I get what I want. The coffee is from a half-empty pot, so it isn't scalding. This café isn't a franchise.

When the weather is pleasant, I sometimes do my office work on the roped-off patio outside, pushing paper, processing claims. The company sends 'em every week, and I have my seventy-two-hour consultant's turnaround. I handle overflow. Would you be surprised such a big-ass insurance conglomerate sends overflow claims to a guy at a sidewalk café? I read and process and approve and disapprove, this guy's disabled, this gal's not, this guy deserving, this gal not, all the while perched on a tall, wooden-armed stool, my feet up and pressed against another chair. Behind the ropes, the panhandlers can't get close. It's easier to work outdoors, and my kids scarf the raisin bagels. I pick them up here every other weekend, when it's my turn. They hate the back and forth, the running around, the two apartments, the different bedtime stories, the old, signed copy of *Cat in the Hat* you don't control anymore (you can never read enough to them). But they love the bagels. A half dozen is the best value, every other weekend.

I sip the coffee, watching the rain and thinking of the movie with his name. A great actor played him, the voice down cold, the timing perfecto. I understand the film portrays a childhood of discipline and awkward love. I have not seen it; is he worth the effort? As I guzzle my coffee and head to the john, I make the decision—I'll see the flick. It will be excellent research. In the stall, I wipe down the toilet seat and acknowledge to myself that I will experience the film despite the director's previous pretenses to factual history. Did he think his fiction was about himself? I crouch and sit and realize the metaphor of the film director and the prez is clear—Caught in the act, caught cold, caught with his pants down. Can we relate? Fiction is fiction; its creators should never pass it off as more. You can be faithful without being true (you know that). The director said, "He is us," but I never bought into that.

Leaving the bathroom, I order another cup, which comes this time from a fresh pot and with a patterned cardboard sleeve to prevent my fingers from burning. The franchises are threatening. Sipping anew, I scorch my tongue instead. Stirring, sipping more carefully, I meticulously focus on the rain outside, trying to spot the drops just before they hit the pavement. After several minutes, a bird with a black needlebeak flies into my view, alighting in a puddlet of rainwater that has gathered in an oval flaw in the sidewalk. The disturbance causes the bird and everything except the plummeting raindrops to leave my vision, and I epiphanize: Got to give Tricky this—He knew the best defense is a good offense. Why blame yourself when you can direct attention elsewhere? I will eschew research. I will make it up. No need to check quotes, to view film, to confirm socks. He and his voice are barnside targets—an entire family of opportunity. The truth is a trap.

Sipping, sipping, my decision down cold, I take up my pen and create my fiction—his final words, a tale from his childhood, a beach scene from his sorry little life, from all the awkward, complex damage he heaped on us. The coma before he died, a memory from his loving, disciplined childhood, his secret bitty cries for help, his cowardly masquerade of apology—it was all to be fiction. Fuck the shitty research; the double-crosser was never brave enough to offer the truth, why does he deserve it from us?

Yet the ending, it must be real (you know that). I slip the cardboard sleeve from my cardboard cup and finish the coffee and crumple the cup and make that one fiction decision. I prop my right leg on an oak-legged stool next to me, about six blocks from the big-columned house where he used to paper the shit from his ass, just like us, where he used to wash his ankles, just like us, and I decide the ending has to be genuine. In honorable irony, I will offer a dollop of what he never gave. I underhand both of my crumpled coffee cups into the trash and slip back into the pelting raindrops, away from the library in my town. What he deserves.

PART I: NIXON'S LAST WORDS

"Maria, Maria, Hola! Sorry, I need help. Hola!"

PART II: NIXON IN HIS COMA

When, August? No, it was after that August. Washington was gone by then. I was walking on the beach, back home, near San C, with the sandpipers running in the waves, running from me, their little beaks. Goddamned birds. It was September. Going back there was harder than anyone knew. The fuckers. They thought they knew what I was thinking, but they didn't have a clue. Thought I was brooding, made fun of me wearing my shoes in the sand. Of my shoes! They didn't know; they damned well didn't know. I was thinking of saying sorry, what I was thinking, saying sorry, walking on that beach.

Not for that, no. No way. Not then, anyway. It was for another reason, another time, long time before. Walking in the sand, in my fucking wingtips, I was remembering another beach, the one with the jetty, near Uncle Robert's house. Off Dana Point.

How old? Eleven? Yeah, eleven; not twelve, for sure. I remember now. Donald and I stayed with Uncle Robert for four months that time Mom was sick. We missed her nighttime stories the whole time. Even went to school there for a while. It was hard, a new school. We weren't there long enough to adjust, learn the ropes.

Eleven years old. The exact time, the exact afternoon I was remembering, Uncle Robert was already done for the day, sprawled on the blue-striped sofa with his head back on a pillow, eyes shut, arm dangling, his glass on the floor. He always used a glass. I remember the back of his hand resting on the floor, opening like an old flower. Those red calluses. I felt them when he shook my hand. I had given him my report card about an hour earlier.

It was a fucking school night. Wasn't supposed to go out at all, much less the beach. In fact, not the beach any day, any time, without Uncle Robert. His rules. But I made A's on that report card, straight A's. Except for phys ed. Always a B. That goddamned coach; I tried harder than anyone.

The beach was past Alameda, but Uncle Robert and Mom, on the phone, told us, "Never cross Alameda. Never cross Alameda." That was the boundary when Donald and I were staying at his house. "Don't cross Alameda and you'll do fine here," Uncle Robert said. I went anyway, that day. I left him sleeping it off on the blue stripes and went across Alameda where it hit Sepulveda, to the bus stop. Took what? The A-14? I remember perfectly; it was the A-14. My mind is fucking perfecto. I could go back today and do it—take the A-14, sit on the same bench, take the same bus. Ran every hour on the half hour; probably still does. Could do it today. Yeah and I can imagine what would happen. Fucking *People* magazine, a cover shot: "Sad Man on the A-14." Make fun of my shoes. Hah!

…The nurse. She's here, with the heavy perfume. Like the magnolia outside the Oval. I used to open the window, to hear the traffic, to hear something, anything. Drive the Service crazy. You would think you could open the fucking window in that house.

Can't see the nurse; can't see anybody. I smell her and hear her. But the sounds, they're goddamned muddled, like some familiar language you can't understand.

This nurse, she bathes me. Me! With a sponge.

Gentle. She talks to me and she washes everything. Once she told me about her children. Maybe grandchildren. Can't make out the words. She sounds older. Now she can tell her grandchildren she washed a fucking president.

I smell the alcohol when they change the IV. Can't feel the needle, but I know when they move me. Wish I could move myself. Just my eyes or my fingertips—anything. Would let them know I'm here. I'm fucking here!

Once I began to understand some words. It was a few hours ago, or a few days. They were talking like I wasn't there. Picked up a few—"the process" and something else. Then Trissie's voice. Telling them to stop. Couldn't make out what she said, but she was making them stop, stop talking in front of me. I felt it.

Trissie would be the one. Bet she was the first at the hospital. Felt her hand once. I knew it was hers from the smell. I can still fucking smell. She has used that soap since Washington. It was scorching that August. I remember it from the day we were packing. I remember smelling it and asking her about it. She said it was the soap. She started crying, with red eyes.

...Late. The A-14 was late that time, after I left Uncle Robert's. It took me within two blocks of the beach. Walked through the alley and right out onto the sand. Nobody much was there. It was supper time and everybody was inside. I headed right for the jetty. Can still picture it—big boulders, dark gray, and granite slabs all piled up and orderly in the middle but scattered on the sides. The slabs were the flattest right on top, so people could walk out on 'em from the beach, like a granite sidewalk. When you strolled out, the jetty got fairly high, especially past the breakers. Went out a quarter mile from the sand and curled around at the end, to protect the beach—a giant granite fishhook into the Pacific. From there, it was open water.

The pools. The pools formed all around the sides of the jetty, where the slabs were scattered. That biggest pool was at the end, where the jetty hooked back. That pool was about ten feet down from the sidewalk, like a rock theater in the round. Out there, the waves had nothing to stop 'em, and they came rushing in and rushing out at this sand-bottomed pool.

Timing was the key. If you didn't jump at the right time, you could hit when there was only a foot or two of water in the pool. It had to be full. I watched the other boys do it the week before. They told me to jump, too, but I decided not to. Called me chicken. Motherfuckers didn't know what I would become. Wanted to pin 'em to the sand, make 'em goddamned give. I remember thinking about that, how that would feel, pinning every one of them. Can still feel that, even now, all these years, I can still remember that feeling. They were all older.

...They're talking again, outside my room. Or maybe inside. Close. Wonder what goddamned hospital I'm in. Must be Manhattan somewhere, Mount Sinai maybe. Can't make it out, what they're saying. Too early for my bath. Is it every other day? I lose track. Maybe it's morning. Too much running around in my mind, back and forth, like those goddamned birds. Very tired.

I worry I might get hard when the nurse uses the sponge. She washes everything. Don't have the control. It would probably make the papers—"Thirty-Seventh President of the United Fucking States Achieves Erection." I must be careful. Wish I could move something. Why can't I understand what they're saying?

Spain. The time Ike sent me to Spain. VP. Convinced my Service guy to let me walk down this narrow street. Stone street. In Madrid? Yeah, Madrid. It was full of those shoe shops, where they have the good leather. I ducked into one. The agent must have lost me. Saw him running by, looking in all the shops. I hid from his ass.

In the shop, I turned to this Spaniard guy. Hola, I say. Hola! He starts blabbering in Spanish. It all sounded familiar, but I can't understand a word he says, not even numbers. And I know my fucking numbers in Spanish. I wanted the shoes, but he couldn't even communicate the numbers. Why can't people listen? I finally got what I wanted and got out of there.

…Clouds. There were clouds that day at the jetty, up and down the beach and scattered on the horizon. Didn't see much of the red sunset yet, which is the one faithful thing in that part of California. It was getting dark faster that day, with those clouds. There was already some pink in the sky, but only a little. I remember standing out on that jetty, thinking Uncle Robert would wake up soon. For his supper. He still had my report card on the couch. Rolled over on it.

On that end of the jetty, over the big pool, I stepped down onto the second layer of rock slabs so I wasn't on the top anymore, and I took off my shoes first. Sat on one of those lower rocks, and I lined up my shoes on a rock. Then my shirt. I folded it, put it under the shoes. Didn't want anything to blow away. I did the pants next, went right down to my underwear. No one could see. I was protected all around, the rocks and the sky. No one would find out, what secrets are for.

I watched the waves flow into the pool below. Every sixth or seventh was the big one. They filled it up, then went out. I remember one wave washed this dead sandpiper into the half-empty pool. Its eyes were open. It floated out in the backwash.

When the water was out, it was so shallow you could see the bottom. Brown sand. But right after the bigger waves swept in there was plenty of water, maybe seven, eight feet. Wondered for a second whether you were supposed to jump when the water was foamy or wait until it calmed down. The water was always quiet for a few seconds just before it went out.

I started counting the waves again, waiting for the seventh, telling myself, "Jump!" It was good practice. Your timing had to be perfect.

The sky was getting darker and redder at the same time and I was shivering, but it didn't matter. I ignored the cold. That was the key that day—ignoring it.

...The nurse. She's speaking to me. Can't make out the words, but they're soothing. She's taking off my gown. Her hands. They're strong. Warm. She lifts me and rolls me over by herself. Can't feel anyone else; she's talking to me. Tired.

She's giving me the bath. Must be careful. I must be careful. No one will find out. Don't cross me. Really careful and quiet (on the floor).

Wonder if Trissie is here today. She would take charge of this mess. She's like me—just handle it and keep going. Traps. She knows families can be traps. You see worthless shits, working in factories or insurance companies—all taking it on faith, convincing themselves their value is families. They never accomplish anything, then get burned or caught in the act or with their pants down and say their families are what's important. They're conning themselves, with their sorry little lives. It's a crock if you fall for it. I never did.

...I choose this big granite slab. It's nearly black and perfectly flat, but it's slick in the spray and when I crouch I almost slip off and I remember this big jolt of fear and I lose count. Hell, I'm only a kid.

I start over. Have to make sure it's the seventh. Counting each wave.

One, two. Crouching, ready. Three, Four. Legs cramping. Crouching. Have to stand up, wait for another cycle.

This time don't crouch until the sixth. Wait for the sixth to rush out.

Wait.

Wait. Seventh coming. It's in.

It's in. Not too big, but big enough. Go. Jump!

Only a little early, still crouching when I hit, flailing my arms. Underwater only for a few seconds. Very, very cold at first, then OK, fine. I don't even touch the sand. Come up before the foam is settled down, when the pool is calm. Those seconds before the water goes out. Did it. I did it! I'm up and treading and I did it.

Feel the pull at my feet first, the backwash slipping out to the ocean. I feel it pull me, so I make for the rocks, kicking hard. I had planned to walk. I didn't know how strong the pull would be. The other boys, they walked to the rocks. They fucked me somehow. Their fault (not mine).

Being pulled toward the opening. I can't get my damned feet down, fighting, kicking. The opening to the ocean is coming closer. I'm going out!

My feet suddenly dig into the bottom. The sand is hard, packed. The water's gone, and I'm on my hands and knees in the brown sand. I'm still in the pool. Only a little water. I stand up.

You can't imagine. Eleven years old! There's nobody around. It's better that way. No one needs to be here. I did it! The low clouds lift and the sky is bright red now up high, the rock all around, my stage, my granite theater.

Then behind me. I hear it and turn to see it behind me, this huge wave, coming toward the jetty, surprising me. Bigger than my wave. I scramble to the rocks, but they're too wet and I fall again, down on the sand. I get my right arm up, but it slips and wedges between two sharp boulders. Yank it out, scraping it, hearing the wave crash into the opening, closing in behind me, bracing for it, throwing me against the rocks. I'm caught on the sand and rocks, really caught. The wave hits.

Upside down. I bang my head. Underwater, but I'm against the rocks. Somehow I get my head up. Up! The foam is not settling down after this one. I hang on to a rock, breathing. Water's too deep to stand, much deeper this time. I look up, the red sky. I'm OK, OK. It takes a moment, my breath is OK. Tired.

Then the pull comes. It's tugging at my feet first. This big wave is going out.

It pulls me off the rocks, toward the opening, but I don't yell. I keep my head, kicking to make the rocks. I'm fighting like hell! Get one hand on a rock, then my other hand around it. Holding on. The water pulls me, but I hold on. My legs are straight out behind me in the water, suspended. I hold on.

The pool empties, but I'm still hanging on the rock over the brown sand. I don't wait; I climb as fast as I can. I remember feeling the spray on my back when I reached the top. Came out right where I left my clothes.

…What did I fucking say? Was it to Maria? Can't remember exactly. Very tired. My words. Was it the last time I spoke? Were those my last words? To Maria? I can't get anything out of my mouth here.

Why wouldn't she listen? If she just would have listened.

I know I didn't say anything in the ambulance. The lights passing by. I could feel the movement, when we took the corners. But I didn't say anything. Tired.

The words were to Maria, to her. I remember. But they were nothing. I remember looking up at her. I was on the floor beside my desk, really quiet on the floor. On the fucking floor, to Maria. Good thing she walked in on me.

Very, very tired.

On the fucking floor, with Maria. She caught me. Us. Looking up, seeing her eyes, very red eyes. Good thing she walked in on us. Red-handed, she caught us, me and Maria, every other weekend. With our pants down. (What she said: This looks familiar. What she said when I didn't answer: You know I'm leaving. You know that.)

What was I thinking, what I was thinking: What if I don't come out of this? I thought it was the heart. But this is different. This isn't the heart, believe me. A stroke? A stroke. Not my fault.

The words were fucked, horrid to say. Who would have guessed the maid? I thought no one would guess the maid, crouching on the floor. When I get out of here, I need to write something down, the right words, my final words. Even the papers will print them, fucking *People* magazine. Caught, by the maid, caught by the maid. With the maid. No more stories for me. The cat's hat is gone. The fiction's about ourselves, you know that.

...I ran all the way, from the jetty and the beach, ran, ran, ran all the way back to Uncle Robert's house. Took half an hour. Was so tired. My clothes dried on me. It was nearly dark. I opened the screen door, looked into the living room. The blue-striped couch was empty. Caught me cold.

Uncle Robert punished me later, said he phoned Mom about it. Made me stay in my room every day for a week, from after school 'til bedtime. Then I had to stay in every other weekend for the month, for chores. Couldn't go out except to the bathroom. It wasn't until the next month he told me why. I thought it was because I had crossed Alameda, went to the beach, but he said it was because I never said I was sorry. Tried to say it then, but he said it was too late, it didn't count anymore. Take what you deserve, he said. These are the consequences, every other weekend.

My teachers asked what happened—the scrapes on my arm, the bruises. You can still see the scar, on my right arm, if you get close enough. Made up a story, said I fell down the steps. The coach didn't want me to play softball in phys ed, but I did. Got damned right field.

My so-called friends didn't believe me when I told them the truth, what I did at the jetty. I was being faithful, I was, in my way, and it wasn't the heart. But no one believed me. I didn't care. They didn't fucking need to know.

That's what I was thinking, that September day on the beach, walking in the sand in my fucking wingtips, thinking of being sorry, of saying sorry, for the jetty thing. What I deserve.

PART III: NIXON REINCARNATED

run run, run run, run run,
peck, peck.
wave. run back, run back, run back.

run run, run run, run run,
peck. peck peck.
wave. run back, run back, run back.

run run, run run, run run,
peck, peck peck, peck.
big wave! help! run, run back. sorry! help! run back.

run run, run run, run run,
run run, run run, run run.

THE ENDING: NIXON'S FINAL THOUGHT

"One more story? Please, just one more?"

DAVID EVERETT directs and teaches in the Master of Arts in Writing Program at Johns Hopkins University. His recent publications include a chapter in A Field Guide for Science Writers. *His writing has been honored by the National Press Club and Society of Professional Journalists, among other organizations. He lives in northern Virginia.*

FROM "Your Mother Should Know"

MARK FARRINGTON

I was masturbating when my mother came home. I'd been lying in my childhood bed, talking long distance to my girlfriend Diana, late in the morning after her kids went off to the pool. Less than thirty hours ago, Diana and I had lain naked in bed together in Charlottesville, Virginia, but now, five hundred miles away in Vermont, I heard Diana say, "You bastard."

"What?"

"I'm lying on my bed, just talking, and the next thing I know, I've got my hand in my pants."

"Yeah?" I ventured. "What's it doing there?"

She told me, in graphic detail, and soon my own hand was busy, too. After we hung up, I finished, then curled up in bed, feeling a moment of soreness and a moment of shame. Then I heard the crunch of tires on gravel as a car pulled into the half-moon driveway in front of the house. The engine died; a door opened, slammed shut.

I bolted to my feet, yanked on my shorts, and raced downstairs. Hiding behind the curtain, I peered out the living room window at a woman bending into the open trunk of a big black car, a Lincoln Town Car. Although the trunk devoured the upper half of her, something about her struck me as familiar, and when she straightened, I understood why. The woman was my mother.

She tugged a giant suitcase out of the trunk, clutching it with both hands. It banged against her knees as she lugged it toward the steps and looked up to where I'd appeared in the doorway.

"Well," she said, "you could help."

95

My mother died seven years ago. On Mother's Day, if you can believe it. She'd gone to the hospital the previous December, saying she felt like someone was pile-driving a railroad spike into the back of her skull. For three days they did tests. My mother said they didn't know what was wrong, but they'd ruled out cancer. Then on the fourth day, her doctor asked me to take a walk with him. "I have bad news," he said. "I'm afraid we found the source. It's in her lung, and it's very serious."

The doctor was young, perhaps not yet thirty, with a soft-spoken voice and the trace of a British accent that didn't match his deep tan and bushy hair. "The source of what?" I asked.

"The cancer, of course."

The doctor ushered me into an examination room and closed the door. They'd known it was cancer since the second day, he explained, when the CT scan showed a half dozen tumors on her brain. All the subsequent tests had been to find the source, so they could determine treatment.

"I'm afraid it's too widespread for surgery," the doctor said. "I haven't spoken with your mother yet, not in these terms, but I have to tell you that the level of cancer your mother has is incurable. We can make her more comfortable, minimize her pain, but there is no cure."

"You said you told her?"

"No. I wanted to speak with you first. I thought perhaps we could tell her together."

"I don't think I—"

He laid a hand on my arm. "I'll do the talking. It would help if you were there."

The doctor reached for the door. "You said—how long does she have?"

"We try not to get into the business of predicting. Every disease develops differently. A lot will depend on how she takes to the treatment."

"Can you give me some idea?"

His dark eyes clouded. He'd begun the conversation saying how fond he'd grown of my mother, and at that moment, I believed him. "Patients with a condition as serious and advanced as your mother's usually survive an average of three to five months."

Months. I'd thought years. I recalled an old television show I'd watched in reruns, about a guy with a terminal illness who sold all his possessions to travel around the world. The doctors had given him a year to live, but the series lasted three or four seasons.

"We don't tell the patient that sort of information unless they specifically ask," the doctor said.

My mother never asked. She looked childlike lying there with the half-her-age doctor patting her hand. "I've got some news to tell you, and I'm afraid it's not as good as we've been hoping," he began.

I backed away. My mother took the news calmly, apologizing for putting the doctor to so much trouble. Later she apologized to the nurses for having a vein that was so hard to find.

At the time, I was teaching high school English at a private school in Connecticut. I arranged to take the semester off and moved back home to care for my mother. I drove her to the hospital for radiation treatments and took her shopping afterwards, or to lunch. When she started losing her hair, I helped her buy a wig. When her legs got so thin she had trouble walking, I rented a wheelchair and hired a carpenter to build a ramp over the front steps. I borrowed on my own life insurance policy because I wanted to have enough cash that whenever she asked for something, I could always say yes. Finally, when it was clear she'd have to stay in bed all the time, I rented a hospital bed I set up in the living room, making her the center of the house.

My father helped the best he could. He could never have cared for her the way I did. Regardless, we couldn't have afforded him taking the time off from work.

During my mother's final weeks, I gave her sponge baths as she lay in bed, carried her to the toilet and cleaned her when she was done. She'd lost all her hair except for little tufts scattered about her scalp like shrubs across a desert, and she never wore her glasses anymore, so the world must have seemed blurry to her. When she became incontinent, the doctors let the hospital admit her. She went into a coma two days later, and on Mother's Day she died.

Her death raised myriad feelings in me. I felt betrayed. I felt as if the earth had turned to quicksand beneath my feet. Like some medieval surgeon had carved a hole in my gut, reached in and grabbed the thing at the core of me, yanked it out and tossed it onto the scrap heap. And this: finally free.

Now she stood in the middle of the living room of the house I'd grown up in. I had no doubt it was her, although I can't say why, exactly. Her looks, of course. And something else that went deeper. She was my mother.

She wore a long coat, even though it was July. Her shoulders twitched, then shrugged, and the coat tumbled off like a waterfall to pool at her feet. Underneath she wore a plain green dress and flat shoes. Her body looked healthy, even a little plump in comparison to the cancer-ravaged image etched so thoroughly in the forefront of my mind. Her shoulder-length brown hair looked real, not a wig, styled in a familiar way.

She seemed only vaguely aware of me. Moving in front of the mirror above the couch, she knelt on the cushions and peered at her reflection. Before, my mother's face had always been pinched tight by tension, especially around the eyes and her perpetually down-turned mouth. Every breath had seemed a struggle, her every moment assaulted by worry and fear. Even her infrequent laughter had seemed guarded, like she was taking a risk.

The face I studied now in the glass looked relaxed, even peaceful. She raised a tentative hand to her face, her fingertips tracing her cheek, the line of her lips, the way one might caress a lover's face. She patted her hair, then bounced on both knees like a child and planted her palms flat against her reflection, as if she might feel her face's bumps and ridges in the glass. "Oh, Jay," she gasped, twisting toward me.

I stepped back. The shock on her face brought a fist to my gut, but before I could apologize she said, "Yes. Of course. I understand."

She climbed off the couch and tugged at her skirt. Seeming to notice the coat for the first time, she knelt and retrieved it, laying it neatly on the arm of a nearby chair. "There's another suitcase," she said, taking a step toward me, halting when I stiffened. "I can get it if—"

"I'll get it," I shouted and stumbled out the door.

Outside, I gulped the air. From the still-open trunk I hauled out a second large suitcase and a smaller canvas one. The car had New York plates, and nearly thirty thousand miles on the odometer. I leaned inside, pretending I was searching for more luggage, but I found nothing, not even an empty coffee cup or candy wrapper. The glove box was empty, too; no rental car agreement, no vehicle registration.

"Maybe we should have some coffee," she said when I returned.

She knew right where to find the coffee and filters. She'd always drunk instant coffee before, and I remember she got irritated the first time I brought home a Mr. Coffee from college. She'd seemed jealous of many things I learned in college: how to play chess and tennis, to identify and appreciate great art and music. "Don't forget where you came from," she'd warned me once, meaning I believe that I was still working class, despite my new upper crust interests. But jealous of Mr. Coffee?

Now, as the coffee dripped into the glass carafe, sunlight giving it a golden hue, she leaned back against the sink and folded her arms across her chest. "So," she said. "How about those Mets?"

It took a few seconds to realize she was joking. The mother I knew didn't joke.

And yet her standing there in the kitchen didn't feel as strange as it ought to. Her presence was almost a vindication to that part of me that had never fully believed she could die.

She awoke face down on top of a quilt on a still-made bed. Fully clothed, even her coat. The silky cover of the quilt beneath her cheek damp with drool. Looking around, her eyes burning from the daylight, she realized she was in a motel, along a busy road—she could hear the semis grinding past outside. Two suitcases and a bag sat beside the door. Otherwise the room was undisturbed; it was as if she'd flopped right onto the bed upon entering, or as if she'd been dropped from the sky.

Sitting up made her head spin, but eventually she swung her feet to the floor. On the night table sat a brochure: Elm Tree Motel, Poughkeepsie, New York. The suitcases were hers; she knew this, she said, without knowing how she knew. Finding car keys in her pocket also did not surprise her.

She had to pee. "That was the strangest feeling," she told me as we sat at the dining room table. "I hadn't peed in seven years." She laughed, while I blushed; this was not the sort of conversation I was used to having with my mother. "That feeling of having to give into the demands of a body, I'd forgotten what that was like. How a body is always screaming for attention."

"You didn't have a body, where you were?"

"Not a body like this one, that makes you feel like you're being tugged in a dozen directions at once. Your side aches when you twist, your nose clogs up, your stomach calls for food, your bladder demands to be emptied. It's like having a giant family of little children, each one full of demands."

She paused, as if giving me time to imagine it. "Anyway, that sensation passed. I'd forgotten that, too. How feelings are just sensations that pass with time."

She took a sip from her coffee. She, who had always preferred her coffee bitter and strong, had dumped in three lumpy spoonfuls of sugar after stabbing her spoon into the jar to break up the clumps. "So I'm outside and I see this black car and I know it's mine. I'd never seen it before but that didn't matter. I walked over, tried the key, and the door unlocked.

"Driving was OK as long as I didn't think about what I was doing. I let my hands and feet move of their own accord. It's like remembering phone numbers; if you just punch in the numbers you're fine, but stop and think what each number is and they're lost to you. I felt that way with everything, even walking. If I stopped to think how to walk, which foot to move when, I'd stumble like a drunk woman. But when I turned my mind off, my body knew what to do.

"I let my body drive the car. I didn't know where I was headed. Even when I got to Vermont, I didn't think about a destination."

"You must have known where you were," I said, "when you got here."

"I knew this was where I was supposed to be."

"You must have recognized the house. Did you know I'd be here?"

She yawned and rubbed her eyes. A gray hue now coated her face, and a puffiness had grown up around her eyes. "If you're tired—"

She shook her head. "I want to tell you everything I can. Everything I know." She took a breath and released it slowly. "When I arrived, I knew this was where I was supposed to be. I knew someone would be here. I didn't think it would be you—I didn't think it would be anyone, specifically—but when I saw you, it made perfect sense to me, and now, I can't think of anyone else it could have been."

That made me pause. Was she saying I was the reason she'd come back?

"I only got here yesterday," I told her. "I came up to clean out the house and put it up for sale. I live in Virginia now."

"I know."

"Dad—"

"I know about your father."

"You know," I started, then stopped. How far should I push this? Then something else snatched my attention. "Your glasses. You're not wearing them."

She raised a hand to her face as if checking. "I didn't find any glasses. I can see all right without them, I guess."

"Read that," I said, pointing toward the clock over the sink. She read it easily. As I was looking for something else to test her with, I noticed something else. "You're not wearing a wedding ring." She wasn't wearing any jewelry, no earrings or a watch.

"I don't know what to tell you. It's not as if I remember putting anything on, or taking it off. This is what I came in."

"What about when you left the motel? Did you talk to anyone? Did you check out? Did you pay?"

"I got in my car and drove away."

Great, I thought. The police could be after her for skipping out on her bill. "You must have left a credit card number when you checked in. They wouldn't have given you the room otherwise."

"I told you. I don't remember checking in."

"Do you have any credit cards?"

She got up and fished a wallet out of her coat pocket. There was nothing inside, no credit cards, no license, no cash.

"Good thing the car didn't need gas."

"Oh, I bought gas." She looked up, her brown eyes wide with innocence. "I put in ten dollars. It's funny, because I never thought to look and see if I had any money. I put in the gas and it stopped at ten dollars, and when I opened my wallet, there was a ten-dollar bill inside." She grinned. "Just lucky, I guess."

She rose and collected the two empty cups. "Do you want more?" I shook my head, and she put the cups in the sink. "Oh, my," slipped out of her when she opened the refrigerator door.

The fridge had been empty when I arrived last night. So far I'd restocked it with a quart of milk and some leftover Kung Pao chicken.

"Could you go to the store?" she asked. "Pick up a few things?"

I said "sure" the way I'd always said "sure," automatically, because that was what she wanted me to say. She started making a list that looked like Thanksgiving: a roasting chicken, potatoes, stuffing, cranberries, corn. I frowned, thinking about what these groceries would cost me. Then I flushed in shame. My mother had just come back from the dead, and here I was bemoaning the twenty bucks I'd have to lay out for a meal she wanted to cook.

When she put down her pen—left handed, as before—I stepped forward and hugged her. The move was awkward, since I'd caught her unawares, and I inadvertently pinned her arms at her sides, and then I jerked back quickly, as if her body were still sore and cancer ravaged, despite the strength and firmness I felt. "Oh, Jay," she whispered, and stepped forward again into my arms.

This time she laid her head on my shoulder, and my open palms settled on her back. My body remained stiff, my lower half arched back, and try as I might, I couldn't bring myself to rub her back; instead, my hands just sat there, the sweat from my palms making them stick to the material of her dress. But it was as close to a genuine hug as my mother and I had probably ever come, and when we finally extricated ourselves, I was glad I'd made the attempt.

At the door, she pushed a wad of bills into my hand. "I found a little money," she said. I shoved it into my pocket and stumbled outside.

It was hot in the car. My trembling hand struggled to fit the key into the ignition. A sudden urge to flee overcame me. I could head south, leave everything I'd brought, return to Virginia, crawl into Diana's arms, and forget this last hour had ever happened.

But too many questions remained. How could I leave now? And what if—like the story of Death seeking the man in Samarra—I drove to Virginia, only to find my mother waiting for me when I arrived?

You can always run, I promised. Things are not so desperate yet.

MARK FARRINGTON is fiction advisor in the Johns Hopkins Master of Arts in Writing Program. He has an MFA in fiction writing from George Mason University, where he also served as editor of Phoebe: The George Mason Review. *He has published short stories in the* Louisville Review, *the* Potomac Review, *the* New Virginia Review, *and other journals and anthologies; and has won a Virginia Commission on the Arts Individual Artists Award, the Dan Rudy Fiction Prize, and the Dame Alice Throckmorton Fiction Award. He is also a member of the board of the Northern Virginia Writing Project. He lives with his wife in Alexandria, Virginia.*

FROM "The Shelf Life of Secrets"

JUAN H. GADDIS

August 27, 1993

Like a summer thunderstorm, the night visitations began. The torrent of memories they uprooted left me spent. Bewildered.

It had been thirty years since my grandfather's death, perhaps half as many years since he last disturbed my sleep, but for twelve consecutive nights he visited me. Not once did he speak. He simply stood at the foot of my bed and beckoned. I had to heed his call.

I chose a time when Irene, my mother, who still lived in the family home, would most likely be out. She and I didn't like each other, but always played nice.

After dropping my daughters at daycare, I went to my old neighborhood and drove up one street and down another until my funeral-procession pace drew suspicious glances from porch dwellers. It hadn't been that long since I'd been to Carolina Corner, but on this visit I was acutely aware of changes.

Many of the houses that once echoed with children's laughter were now empty and dilapidated. Some homes were missing windows and doors, giving free access to the elements or an occasional errant junkie. Still others were shielded from the outside by bricks and plywood, their yards littered with remnants of a once-upon-a-time existence.

As I pulled up to the front of the house where I had spent the first twenty years of my life, it seemed as though I were viewing it through scrim; it appeared faded. I backed into the driveway, leaving my car positioned for a quick getaway.

Hoping the lock hadn't been changed, I inserted my key and turned it. I sighed at the familiar squeak of the hinges. I walked through the living room, through the dining room, and into the kitchen. Change, it seemed, had only occurred outside the house.

I climbed the stairs and paused at the top. My resolve wavered, so I sat and hugged my knees and rocked like I did when I was a child and watched the dust motes drifting from the skylight.

In the years since I had been up these stairs, been in that room, I had masked my feelings with indifference. The truth is I hated the room at the top of these stairs.

From this room I'd heard accusations of infidelity followed by retorts of "prove it." I was five years old before I learned "prove it" didn't mean someone was doing something forbidden. Often, my grandparents' voices started as muddled tones trapped inside their bedroom before escalating to shouts that spilled into the hallway and traveled the ten feet to my room.

I would hear an object crashing against a wall or a hand or fist striking flesh. This was often followed by his cries of "Dammit," or "You're trying to kill me." She would fiercely defend herself. My grandmother, at times, would use anything available—a brush, a shoe, a bottle—to quiet him.

From this room the whole house seemed to shake. He would stand on newspaper spread in front of the radiator, dressed only in a T-shirt, naked from the waist down, a rag in his hand as he cupped his penis and tried to urinate. Performing this simplest of bodily functions was such a painful process that he trembled uncontrollably. In an effort to relieve the pain, he would grip the elbow-shaped pipe leading from the radiator and stand on his right foot with his left foot waving behind him like a flag of surrender. His spasms were so violent that it caused the pipes to vibrate throughout the house, the resulting noise sounding as if someone were simultaneously knocking on the ceilings and floors.

Even back then the floor seemed unstable and sagged severely. I was fearful the floor would collapse and he would find himself sprawled on the living room rug amid fragments of plaster and splinters of wood, holding his thing, trying to pee.

Sometimes I watched his dance of pain from the doorway, transfixed, unable to enter, unable to step away. I would stare, confused, concerned, and saddened because I couldn't make it better. He would return my gaze with embarrassment and humiliation in his eyes.

On the rare occasions when his body did not betray him, the amber liquid would soak through the cloth, seep through his fingers, and snake down his left leg to dampen the newsprint underfoot. He would sniff, then search the rag through which his urine had been filtered, like a prospector looking for gold. I looked away as he clamped any found object between his teeth to see if he had rid himself of one of the many stones that formed in his kidneys.

Unwashed, he would return to his bed, pull up the covers, and beg some unseen father to help him, please.

From this room emanated a distinct odor. No matter how frequently it had been scrubbed with ammonia or pine oil disinfectant, the stink of unbrushed teeth, fever sweat, and stale urine suffused the room.

From this room came confirmation he would never return from the hospital. A classmate's delivery of the news had stunned me on the playground. He was only two years older than my seven; I couldn't believe news this shattering had been entrusted to him. I pushed him hard in his chest with both my hands and ran the eight blocks home.

I tiptoed up the stairs and paused on the landing to catch my breath before entering my grandparents' bedroom. My grandmother was sorting through papers and my grandfather's wallet was open on her lap. She looked up and with tear-swollen eyes confirmed what I had been told. I shook my head to erase the words she did not, and possibly could not, say: he was dead.

When I didn't move she said, "Why don't you go play."

Did she think I could *play*? At that moment, I hated my grandmother for what I would later decide was her insensitivity. I hated my mother for (once again) not being there. I was alone.

Years later I learned my grandfather had died with his lips wrapped firmly around my name. My grandmother thought he was asking for water that had been withheld due to an impending surgery. After her attempts to quench his thirst with a moistened towel failed to quiet him, she listened more intently. She could not give him what he wanted. His supplication had been for me.

And now, over a quarter of a century later, a silent dream had beckoned: I had heard his familiar cry for help. My grandfather had always been able to distinguish my footsteps from those of others and, upon hearing my footfall on the stairs, he, in a raspy voice, would strain to call my name. Then, he wanted water or food, the volume adjusted on the television, or piss-soaked newsprint removed. Today, unlike the day he died, I was here for him.

I stood and brushed off my pants. Ignoring my desire to flee, I took the last step to the landing. I entered the room and I gagged. The wallpaper and linoleum had been replaced but the stench remained.

I walked over to the chest of drawers; the middle drawer was where my grandmother's important papers and keepsakes were secreted away. Although she had not lived in this house since she remarried, all documentation that validated her existence, or linked her to life in Carolina Corner, was inside this drawer. Up until a few years ago, every month or so, when she had needed a respite from her new life, she would return for several days. Her past awaited, a shrine to what had been.

I wasn't searching for her social security card or her work identification with the picture that seemed to say hurry-up-and-take-the-damn-thing. Nor was I looking for the letter from the Veterans Administration that said she wasn't entitled to survivor's benefits; his death was not related to military service.

The object of my search was a three-by-five, black-and-white photograph. Although he'd looked different when he died, this cracked and fading photograph was the only tangible proof of his existence.

Most of those who knew him said he was hateful, ornery, and evil. For them, this represented truth. In their experience, he was all these things and less. Despite what others said, I loved him. I knew him in a way others, including my grandmother, did not. I may not have realized it when he was alive, but he had loved me without condition. I needed this picture.

I unfolded what turned out to be his birth certificate. I looked at the date on my watch, and a gasp caught in my throat. His visitations had begun on what would have been his seventy-third birthday. I hadn't known he was born on the fourteenth of August. I had never once wished him many happy returns. My tears fell on the page, blotting out the date. In that moment I felt the void his three-decade-long absence had created in my life.

Among the miscellany—old pay stubs, property tax receipts, mortgage stamped "paid"—was a document of particular interest. It was another piece to the story that had taken me most of my life to assemble.

No one had told me of the fire. No one had told me of the death. No one had told me the first event led to the latter. No one had told me I was the progeny of an arsonist and a murderer. Yet, I knew.

I had collected pieces of my family's story like a child snatches stars from the pavement during a game of jacks: one by one. I had gathered while playing under an opened window; while feigning sleep; while riding in the backseat of a car, my ears attuned to the whispers of the adults up front. My grandmother had said I could hear an ant piss on cotton.

I read the document twice to make certain I understood. It was consistent. Although only a double-spaced, legal-sized page in length, it spoke volumes. I lightly touched the seal and each rise and fall of my finger over the embossment raised another question.

Was this why my grandmother had lived as a recluse, only leaving the house for work and necessary errands? Was this why some of the neighbors had treated us as pariahs, speaking only when their silence would have been considered rude, and never including our family in neighborhood events or gatherings? Perhaps this was the reason our neighbor Mrs. Jones had asked her husband, "Why are you riding with that trash?" one Sunday evening as our car pulled to a stop at a corner where Mrs. Jones was standing. We were giving Mr. Jones a ride back to the tuberculosis treatment hospital where he was a patient. I watched, horrified, as my grandmother opened the door, jumped from the car, and attacked Mrs. Jones. In my five-year-old understanding, adults didn't fight—at least not in public. Mr. Jones, who was frail and cigarette thin, looked as if he wasn't sure whether he should get out of the car to assist his wife or stay in the car to avoid my grandmother's wrath. The two tussled, rolling over the hood before falling to the ground. By the time my grandfather separated them, Mrs. Jones was bleeding from the forehead, her lip was swollen, and her blouse was torn. My grandmother, on the other hand, looked no different than when she had gotten out of the car.

Now, two weeks after my grandfather's night visitations had begun, I stood in almost the exact spot he had stood trying to rid his body of pain. The understanding of what I had discovered washed over me like a fever and I, like him, whispered, "Father, help me, please." It seemed the stone of truth could be just as excruciating.

A car door slammed and I looked out the window. Irene was home. She rang the bell and knocked on the door, yelling, "Ron, open the door, I got to pee."

"Coming!"

Before closing the drawer, I folded together his birth and death certificates and my grandparents' marriage license and stuck them in my pocket. The cracked and fading photograph would have to wait. I grabbed a handful of LPs from a stack on the dresser, and went down the stairs. When I opened the door, Irene pushed past me. "Lord works in mysterious ways," she said. "I left my door key on the table."

When she came back downstairs I noticed how much she had aged since the last time I'd seen her. I thought it ironic that Irene finally looked old enough to be my mother when I no longer needed a mother. Motherhood was a role she had never fully grown into; I was born eleven days before her sixteenth birthday. Throughout my childhood and well into my early adult years, we looked more like siblings than mother and son.

"Ooo boy, you know, I hate to take my girdle down in public." She scratched her thigh through her dress and took a deep breath as if she'd suddenly realized she was no longer constricted. "I am surprised to see you," she said. "Looks like I was about to miss you...How you been?"

I almost asked why she hadn't gone to noonday prayer meeting as she usually did, but instead I said, "I am well. I just came by to get some Billie Holiday albums to put on tape."

I sounded too enthusiastic and hoped she hadn't noticed. She could always tell I was lying by the level of enthusiasm in my voice.

"That's fine, you need to come and get all of 'em...my turn-table don't work anymore...you know there's more outside in the shed...when did you grow a beard?"

She sounded a little winded, hesitant in her speech. She held her right hand at an odd angle and occasionally massaged the back of it with her left hand. I wondered if she had, at some point, suffered a stroke without knowing it; our family had a history of high blood pressure.

"Ma, you know I've had a beard since ninth grade."

I didn't mean to call her Ma; it somehow implied a closeness that didn't exist. Growing up, I had only called her that when I was trying to soften her up or lessen a punishment for something I had done. Most times she was Irene.

She responded with a grunt.

I went into the dining room to get a shopping bag, and when I came back she was flipping through the albums. "Boy, them some memories in here," she said.

"Yeah, I suppose so. I'll make you a copy of the tape if you like. Road House Oldies has turntables if you want one."

"I guess…but I probably wouldn't play many of them any-way…don't waste your money."

I felt guilty about leaving so soon after she had gotten home so I sat down to extend my visit. I asked where she had been.

"Oh, I had to go to the doctor…they trying to get my pressure medicine right. When you gonna bring my grandbabies by to see me…I suppose the next time I see them they'll be driving."

I couldn't argue this point. We lived in the same city after all, and perhaps it was a shame she didn't see her grandchildren more frequently than she did, but playing nice only extended so far.

Before I could respond, she added, "Noelle told me you brought them by for a visit."

I laughed. "Oh, really?" I said. "I haven't seen Aunt Noelle in nearly two years. Maybe she's confused. I think Caira may have given her a ride home when she saw her at the bus stop. The girls probably were in the car." I realized I was rambling and paused. "You know your sister."

"That lying heifer…she make me sick."

"You still letting her get to you? Listen, one question."

She continued going through the mail, but I could tell she was listening. I knew what I wanted to ask but wasn't sure how to pose the question.

"Were Bill and Pearl married when the fire happened?"

She didn't look up. Instead, she studied an oversized airmail envelope she was holding as if the answer might be inside. She flicked the envelope onto the coffee table and pushed up her glasses. "The fire didn't *happen*…that son-of-a-bitch tried to kill all of us…that was a long time ago…we hardly saw her…they were married…living together…something…I don't know…shit, ask Noelle."

I wondered if she already knew what I had just learned. I changed the subject. "So how is church going? You still on the Trustee Board?"

"Yeah, I have to finish my financial report…you should visit…people are always asking about you…I have your envelopes."

New Second Macedonia Baptist Church of Carolina Corner had been my family's place of worship for four generations. I hated that I had not allowed my daughters to attend Sunday school there, but I had grown tired of people treating me differently because I was now in what they perceived as a position of affluence. Members of the church who had changed my diapers or wiped my runny nose no longer called me by my first name; instead, they addressed me as if I were a visiting dignitary. Although I was sure there was no ill intent on their part, I no longer felt at home in my former church home.

Irene went to retrieve my envelopes. I noticed she was walking stiffly, and asked if her back was bothering her. Though she didn't answer, when Irene came back she had affected a pain-free gait. Pain, like emotion, was something she thought best concealed.

I put the albums and box of envelopes into the shopping bag and stood, preparing to leave. She braced her hands on the arms of the chair. "You want some macaroni salad?" she said. I made some yesterday…I think I have some saltines."

Macaroni salad with crackers was one of my favorite childhood summer treats. I smiled at the memory. "I'd like that," I said. "I'll put your car in the driveway."

As I was switching the cars I looked up at the window through which my great-grandmother had been pulled from the fire. I wondered what might have been going through her mind while she stood there, waiting.

Irene met me at the door with a small shopping bag. I took it from her and backed away before either one of us felt obliged to touch. I stepped off the porch and turned back to face my mother. "Another question," I said. "Are you sure of the date of the fire?"

My mother motioned with her finger for me to lean closer. "If the fifth of June 1950 was a Monday," she said, "then that's when it was...*that's* not something you forget."

I nodded, walked to my car, and when I was releasing the handbrake, I noticed the stiffness had returned to her gait as she walked out to the sidewalk. I waved in the rearview mirror and gave the car more gas.

IIII

When I got home with the twins, they were so exhausted that I ordered pizza instead of making the promised hamburgers. I ran their bath and put them to bed early. My wife's paralegal had left a message that she was tied up in a protracted negotiation and wouldn't be home until later, so I had time to reflect.

Sinking into my desk chair with a sigh, I gazed through the window at some deer that had ventured into my yard from nearby woods. I loved living in Rock Creek Park. I was minutes away from the hustle of downtown D.C. and close to nature at the same time. Sometimes too close.

I unfolded the documents and spread them on my desk. They were from left to right: certificate of birth registration, record of marriage, and certificate of death.

The record of marriage indicated that on the "*9th day of AUGUST one thousand nine hundred and FIFTY at TAKOMA PARK, MD. WIL-LIAM H. ADAMS and PEARL R. JACKSON were united in Marriage.*" This meant my grandmother had not *stayed* married to the man who was responsible for the death of her mother, as I had believed. Rather, she had, in fact, *married* that man. That man, who loved me and perhaps no one else, was my grandfather. I massaged the bridge of my nose trying to puzzle out why she would have still married him two months after her mother's death.

The marriage license, as it was positioned on my desk, reminded me of the dash on a tombstone bridging the beginning and ending of a life. This document represented much more than a span of time. Certainly, it meant much more than it revealed.

I picked up the certificate of death and tried to decipher what had been typed into the blank spaces. I recognized "edema" and "uremia" but the other word was foreign to me. I took a couple of reference books from the bookshelf in hopes of demystifying the word listed as the primary cause of my grandfather's demise. I wasn't exactly surprised by what I learned. My grandfather's body had poisoned itself because he was unable to urinate. I remembered a story I had overheard my grandmother telling a whist partner of hers, and I believed I knew the root of his ailments.

When my mother was seven months pregnant with me, my grandfather had pushed her during one of his tirades. He had often been verbally abusive but had never before put his hands on her. His shove unleashed six years of anger in Irene, who knew he was responsible for the death of her beloved grandmother. She hit him with a heavy glass horse head. When he stumbled, she continued to beat him with the statuette until her hands were covered in blood. After he had fallen to the floor, she kicked him repeatedly and promised to kill him if he ever touched her again.

Stitches and time healed the wounds to his head and face, but the damage to his lower body was more complicated. He had been released from the hospital with a drainage tube protruding from his pelvis. In fits of frustration he, on more than one occasion, pulled the tube out and ended up back in the hospital. Although scar tissue had formed on the surface, the wound never completely healed.

The word I didn't understand had proved fatal: *nephritis*. I had always known my grandfather had been severely hurt by my mother, but I hadn't known his death was inextricably linked to those injuries. My grandfather had died from injuries he received at the hands of my mother.

I jumped when the phone rang; Caller ID showed Caira's mobile number. She usually called when she was within a few minutes of home. The phone seemed to get louder with each ring. If I didn't answer, she would be concerned. But if I answered I was afraid I would blurt out what I had learned. I didn't answer. Caira and I didn't keep secrets anymore, but I wasn't sure how she would respond to my discoveries.

This was my fear: that Caira would back away from me as if I had been the one who had deliberately set the fire that killed my great-grandmother. Even worse, that Caira, with her left-brain way of analyzing things, would slowly deduce that I was the offspring of not one, but *two*, murderers, which meant that somewhere in my genetic makeup was the ability to kill. My wife knew I wasn't biologically related to the man I called my grandfather, but in her eyes I would be guilty by association.

Caira had insisted on full disclosure in our relationship. The first time she learned something troubling about my past that I had not told her prior to our marriage, she moved out of the house for two months and threatened to file for a divorce. The discovery that she was pregnant probably saved our marriage.

I had never mentioned the fire to Caira, nor had I told her that my grandfather had intentionally set the fire and my great-grandmother had died as a result of it. And now, I could add to my list of deceits the fact that my grandmother married the man who killed her mother, and that my mother, albeit delayed, had killed my grandfather. I envisioned her response: she would assume her courtroom demeanor, her words coming at me in a machine-gun patter as she pointed a professionally lacquered fingernail at me for emphasis. She would accuse me of nondisclosure in some Latin term that meant I had lied and therefore couldn't be trusted. I loved my wife. I loved my daughters. I loved the family we had created, my real family. If I told her this about my past, I would lose everything. She would leave. She would leave and take our daughters with her. The thought of being abandoned shook me to the core.

I looked at the silent truths of the documents spread on my desk. Information I had known for less than eight hours had confounded me. I wondered how long the documents, particularly the certificate of marriage, had been in that drawer, and how long they would have remained had I not gone in search of my grandfather's picture. I wondered if secrets had an expiration date, a period of time after which they lost their power and could no longer cause disruption or harm. What was the shelf life of a secret?

Caira came into my office and hugged me from behind as I watched the last of the deer hop over the fence and disappear into the dark, dense forest. I stood and returned her hug, holding on to her as if I feared I might fall. We kissed, and then I sandwiched her hands between mine and kissed them too before gesturing at my computer monitor to indicate I was in the middle of a writing project. She said she was going to make a cup of tea and, as she turned to leave, she drummed her fingernails along the top of one of the books on my desk. "Research?" she asked. "Need some help?"

I wanted to say I needed her to promise she would never leave me, but I didn't. I nervously folded the documents, put them in my desk drawer, and said "no." This journey of discovery and reconciliation was one I had to take alone.

JUAN H. GADDIS holds a master's degree in writing from Johns Hopkins University and has had stories published in Penn-Union *and* Metro Weekly. *He is a certified leader in the Amherst Writers and Artist Method and conducts writing workshops for special populations. Additionally, he is a Coaches Training Institute–trained life coach who specializes in coaching writers and other artists. He is enrolled in the Antioch University Los Angeles MFA program and is working on his first novel, "The Shelf Life of Secrets."*

FROM "High Desert Blues"

WILLIAM E. GARRISON

Leonard Balston lived and worked in a small stucco house in a nondescript neighborhood on the west side of Santa Fe. Nick and Gretchen went through an open gate in a low chain-link fence and in a side door beside the sign that said simply "Massage." Several quiet younger people wandered restlessly between the tiny waiting room and the narrow hallway, waiting for the session to start. Balston came into the room and Gretchen introduced Nick. Balston was somewhere in his late thirties, a thin and rumpled man in crumpled chinos and an unpressed white shirt. He seemed pale and unhealthy, even strangely dirty, to Nick. Balston appeared confused and distracted and didn't look at Nick's face when they shook hands. Balston's handshake was so limp as to be almost not there. He muttered "Welcome, be welcome, we'll start soon," and walked out of the waiting room.

Balston and his helpers had moved the furniture out of his massage studio and thrown various pillows and folded blankets around the edge of the small room. Half a dozen candles burned in dishes and saucers. The rug was worn, discolored, and spotted. As Nick and Gretchen took seats on pillows on the floor, Nick took care to keep his hands off the carpet.

The room filled. Balston turned off the ceiling light and the candles provided a dim illumination. Besides Balston and a man who seemed to be his slightly younger understudy, ten people crowded around the circumference of the room. One older woman had taken a lotus position and ignored everyone else. Two other couples were part of the group. The rest were single males, including one boy who didn't look old enough to buy a drink. Nick was a little surprised.

He'd expected most of the group to be the middle-aged women who seemed to be the main motor of Santa Fe spiritualism.

Balston quickly sketched the history of the sacred drink for the benefit of those who had come to the ceremony for the first time. He stuttered on about the native tribe down in Peru who had used the herbal potion for hundreds of years, their natural and peaceful life and how they struggled to hold onto their traditions and religion in the face of advancing commercialism and Christian missionaries.

Fred, the assistant, passed around the room with a collection of plastic and aluminum bowls and pots that could have come from the kitchen. "Everyone will expel the contents of their stomach," he said. "It's natural. It's part of the ceremony. Don't be shy or ashamed." He smiled. "You will want to keep the drink down long enough for it to take effect, but when you have to throw up, don't fight it. This is not about ego."

Leonard Balston stressed the sacredness of the ceremony, that it was religious, not recreational. He grew mildly enthusiastic while speaking of the natural nature of the herb drink, derived principally from a vine that grew in the region of the tribe, the secret other ingredients, and the special opportunity and privilege those in the room had that night to share it, the universality of it. Luckily, this was a fresh batch that had just arrived that day, brought into the country by one the Peruvian curanderos. He said that the curandero, a sort of medicine man, brought the herbal mixture into the United States at some personal risk. The drug was not illegal, not a designated controlled substance yet, but, since it could be considered hallucinogenic, wasn't exactly legal either. But the curanderos took the risk in order that more of the world could share their religious rites. They also believed that the herb provided protection for them in its transit.

Balston said the curanderos down in the Peruvian jungle knew those in the room would be joining them that night in the communion of the spirit through the herb. The members of the tribe would share the herb with them, would join their consciousness.

As Balston went on, Fred lit a Galois Bleu and slowly went around the perimeter of the room, kneeling and blowing smoke from the strong French cigarette into the face of every man and woman. Soon the air of the room was stuffy with cigarette smoke. Balston and Fred began singing in the tribal language and in Spanish, a song that gradually seemed to change into a chant and then animal and bird sounds, and seemed to have a chorus of repetitions of "curandero, curandero."

Balston continued the song by himself. Fred left the room then quickly returned with a large glass jug filled with a black, clotted liquid. Fred poured some of the potion into a Mason jar and gave the jar to Balston, who sang even louder while Fred moved around the room blowing smoke again.

Nick lost track of time. He had no idea how long he'd been in the room. Gretchen seemed a long distance from him even though their elbows sometimes touched as they shifted positions on their pillows. Every time Nick glanced at her she was sitting quietly with her head bowed, listening as if she understood the song. With all the waiting, the smoke in the small room, the ongoing chant and strange sounds from Balston, and the stress of maintaining his uncomfortable position on the floor, Nick felt half-mesmerized by the time Leonard began with the black liquid.

Fred took up the song. Balston stepped forward into the middle of the room and lifted the Mason jar. He slowly turned around with the jar high in his hands, the candle flames reflecting from the glass. He happened to be facing Nick when he took the jar to his lips and drank a large swallow. Nick thought he could see black chunks in the black fluid. Balston swallowed hard, wiped his mouth with the back of one hand, and gave the jar to Fred who drank and returned the jar.

Balston turned to his left and knelt before the woman in the lotus position. He sang on for another minute. She took the jar, took a big drink, and handed it back. She threw up in her bowl before Balston gave the jar to the next person.

Nick didn't like the looks of it. The drink resembled something out of a bad movie. And there were another six strangers who would suck the lip of the jar before it got around to him. Balston didn't look that healthy himself. Gretchen accepted the jar, lifted it to her lips, and swallowed her share of the drink as if the act were no more than taking a sip of tea.

Balston refilled the jar from the jug and gave it to Nick. Nick was ready to gag before his hands touched the jar, but he took it and drank. He felt several glutinous masses rumble over his tongue and down his throat. He immediately felt nauseous, but controlled the reflex, and sat on his squashed pillow with his head bowed and his eyes closed, wondering how and why he'd come to be in that room, and couldn't come up with a cogent answer.

The first wave of nausea passed. Nick sat as still and as self-contained and patient as he could. Time seemed a nonnegotiable quantity, a bad bet. He waited. Some spiritual ceremony, he thought. Almost everyone else seemed to be sick. The young kid had a really bad time of it. Leonard and Fred continued with the song. Nick appreciated their efforts. Got to be tough to keep at it that long, he thought. At one point Gretchen threw up into her plastic bowl with what seemed to Nick great discretion and style. He was amused by his own reaction, and after she seemed to have recovered, touched her elbow. She ignored his touch. He waited.

Balston, still standing, threw up in a bowl made from a dried gourd, and resumed the song. Fred was sitting on the floor, leaning back against the wall behind him, when he threw up. He didn't sing again for a long time, and Balston soloed a cycle of curandero chants and bird songs.

When Fred could sing again, Balston went around the room another time, very slowly, blowing more of the cigarette smoke and spraying cheap perfume on the participants. Balston knelt before each person, leaned so close his forehead almost touched the one he faced as he spoke words too low for anyone else to hear.

Nick did not feel very good. He wished he could breathe some fresh air, but he didn't feel particularly sick. His stomach was not enjoying its contents, but it had made no motion toward expelling the liquid, either. The sensation from his gut was more resentment than nausea. Nick wondered if anyone was experiencing a vision. He did not think he was going to be visited by the spirits. He wondered how long the ceremony was going to last. He hadn't asked Gretchen. He wondered how she was doing. She was so close and yet seemed very far away. He wanted to put his arm around her and have her sit close beside him for the duration, but it was against the rules. The restriction seemed unfair. Time was crawling, but he gradually became aware of some internal focus, as if he had to concentrate so as not to disturb his stomach or any other of the many delicate equilibriums of the balance that kept him upright and functioning. He began to feel weak and vulnerable, helpless in the grip of the ceremony.

Leonard seemed very tired when he knelt in front of Nick. Nick was shocked to realize that the Anglo shaman must have visited Gretchen before he'd appeared in front of his face, but the passage had gone unnoticed.

Balston sprayed perfume over Nick's head and blew more smoke in his face. Nick coughed.

"I'm sorry," said Leonard hoarsely, his pitted nose only a few inches from Nick's eyes, "but it's a required part of the ceremony. How do you feel?"

"I'm OK," said Nick.

"You haven't thrown up?" Balston touched the empty metal mixing bowl by Nick's crossed ankles.

"No."

"You're an imposing man, but don't fight it. Everyone throws up, especially the first time."

Nick slowly nodded. "I will," he muttered. "Whenever I have to."

"You have a strong spirit," Balston intoned. "I understand you're here for a special purpose."

"I guess so," said Nick, speaking each word individually.

"The herb does not necessarily answer any question. Do you know that?"

"I don't expect anything."

"Good," said Leonard. He blew more smoke in Nick's face and moved on.

Nick waited. He understood that the mixture of drugs, of the herbs, was infusing his thoughts. His stomach was beginning to complain that the load was too much. He could feel it grinding in a slow churn.

He remembered other confusing times. Lifting off in a helicopter from a destroyer escort off the South American coast in a driving rain in the middle of a night. Rolling in the belly of what was supposed to be a freighter in the Gulf Stream for days that turned into a stream of nights as what had been a late-in-the-season tropical depression turned into a hurricane that battered Cuba and trashed the mission. The question was still the same. What was he, why was he, here?

Time seemed a squiggle, a raindrop on a windshield. Nick waited. There seemed no end to it, the drop seemed to hesitate, grew, dribbled a millimeter to the left, and hesitated again. Leonard appeared in his face again, blowing yet more smoke in a room so full of rancid smoke that Nick could barely notice the new pollution.

"Don't fight it," Balston commanded. "Give in to the herb."

"Not fighting. Waiting."

"Strength is not in control. Strength is in accepting."

"I'm accepting."

"The spirit will speak with you."

"Good," Nick said.

"You are asking about Gail."

Nick couldn't think of an answer. If it were a question.

"I can't tell you anything about Gail. Do you understand?"

"No," Nick said, truthfully.

"I can't," Balston said. "There are many reasons. None of them important. None. The ceremony is important and you have become a participant. You chose."

Nick resisted that assertion. He didn't feel he'd chosen this. It, coming to the ceremony, seemed an accident. He couldn't remember how he'd happened to be there.

"Perhaps Gail will speak to you. From wherever she is. Not Gail as an individual. There are no individuals in the ceremony. But, just perhaps, Gail, as a member of the community, of the ceremony, will tell you something. Perhaps you will have a vision. Perhaps not. But don't fight the herb. Submit your strength to it."

Nick was alone again. He could have been anywhere in any dark, smoke-filled room. He could have been back to a time he'd been at a party in Washington and had casually accepted a toke from a passed-around pipe of hash that had turned out to have been laced with opium. He'd walked back to his apartment reeling down the center of a street at four o'clock in the morning afraid he was going to crash into the buildings on either side. He'd felt totally isolated from the world, and the only contained thought in his head had been the vague image of his bed and the wife who should be there wondering where he was.

The sickness rose from Nick's belly like some great demon that had only waited in order to grow stronger. Sweat dripped from his eyebrows into the bowl. His stomach was tied into knots and still he ejected bitter clots of bile. The muscles of his middle went into spasms and knotted into bundles of pain and still he retched. He felt his consciousness dwindle into a minute throbbing speck and he prayed to God, all the gods possible, any God, to allow him to get through this struggle to stay alive, to keep breathing, to avoid a slipping away into nothingness, an edge over a black void that invited him in.

Give me strength, he thought. His little aluminum bowl seemed to ring like a pandemonium of chimes and stank horribly of Baja Taco and the herb and Gaulois Bleu.

This better be worth it, he thought in a brief moment of lucidity. But he felt even more wracked and out of control and he only wished to survive. He was weak, sweat ran down his face and neck and armpits. Give me strength, he begged. Give me strength. This was no place to be. He braced himself to just survive. Everything, anything, had to pass in its time and place. Even this misery had to have an end. He held on to the slim and fragile idea that this had to have an end, that if he could just keep breathing and staying alive that sooner or later, more likely some long and distant later, the state of disequilibrium would dissolve and become another inexplicable bit of his history, that the sun would come up tomorrow and, somewhere, he would see light again.

He was out on the prairie, a great rolling plain where the distant horizon melded with the blackness of a moonless sky. The cold light of stars gave dim shapes to the landscape. Great dark shapes were around him. The night was cold and he shivered. One of the shapes was close to him and he saw that it was a buffalo. The creature approached a solitary man and, standing upright, put its arms or front legs on the shoulders of the man and brought its great muzzle close. The buffalo blew its breath in the face of the man.

What's that, Nick wondered. Then he realized that he was the man and the buffalo was blowing breath in his face, even as he remained off to the side and watching.

The image evaporated. Nick wondered if that was his vision. It made no more sense than anything else. He was still nauseous, his throat burned and his muscles ached, and he felt as exhausted as if he'd just finished a ten-mile run through the desert.

He waited for something from Gail Turner, tried to concentrate on Gail Turner. He remembered how delightful Gretchen had looked when he'd seen her at Ten Thousand Waves and the slanting sun had turned her nipples into rubies. He remembered Laura changing into her white dress in her bedroom when he'd come to find out why she needed him. He remembered Laura as she had been while they'd been lovers, willing but distant, even then expecting him to take care of her. Laura as a sort of Goddess in a nearly transparent white robe, Laura kissing him, Laura kissing other men, Laura kissing women, Laura on a dais smiling over a crowded hall. He tried to remember the photograph of Gail Turner, the beautiful dark-haired woman sitting on the stone wall at the edge of the great opening in the earth that was the Grand Canyon. He thought of himself holding the photograph in his hand when he'd found it at her casita in Tesuque. The photograph became a landscape he looked into in the night as the woman, still smiling, walked to him, pressed against him, and took his hand and put it under her dress and she wore no panties, and her hair was like some golden fire in his face.

He remembered a bar he had known in Washington. The One Step Down had a collection of good jazz on the jukebox and sometimes live music. He remembered being there late one night with a group of friends who'd come from an opera at the Kennedy Center, recalled sitting across a booth from a woman with long blonde hair whose face was obscured by her laughing. She'd been with someone else, but he remembered that she'd slipped off her shoe and smiled and lifted her foot and found his thigh and then his crotch and wiggled her toes and smiled and smiled. He remembered sliding out of the booth and going to the back of the long narrow bar to the restroom and that when he'd come out she'd been standing waiting for him. And they'd stepped out the back kitchen door into the alley and had coupled swiftly standing in a dark corner behind a dumpster while she moaned and laughed at the same time and refused to kiss him.

The dark room came back into focus with the participants sitting in silence as the candles burned down. Nick struggled to his feet and went looking for a bathroom. Balston had said they could use the bathroom down the hall whenever they had to, as long as they didn't throw up there. A light was on in the hallway. Someone else was in the bathroom. Nick leaned on the wall, laboriously considering the possibility of going outside and taking a leak in the bushes. One of the women came out of a door and left it open behind her as she returned to the ceremony. Nick could see into a dark bedroom with a lighted bathroom on the other side. He slowly and carefully made his way to this other bathroom and relieved himself, squinting in the light. After he zipped up his trousers, he staggered as he turned and put a hand out against the shower curtain as he caught his balance. He briefly saw packages in the bottom of the porcelain tub. Nick felt drained, barely able to stand up and walk, but he wanted another look. He pushed aside the shower curtain and looked down on three loaf-shaped bundles wrapped in foil and plastic. Bundles that once had been a familiar sight. He wondered if he was hallucinating or having another bit of a vision from his past. Unsteadily, he leaned over, his left hand on the edge of the tub for support, and picked up one of the packages. He recognized the weight—one kilo. Three bundles, three kilos. A bit much for religious use, he thought. He put the brick down, and closed the curtain. He heard noise outside. He quickly flushed the toilet and turned toward the open door with his head down while his hands fumbled at his zipper.

Balston was coming across the bedroom. "Please," he said. "We'd much prefer that our guests use the bathroom in the hall."

"OK, Sorry." Nick croaked, and shuffled back to his pillow in the other room.

Nick was no longer sick. He just waited in complete weariness, sitting on the floor, leaning on one arm or the other, no longer worried about the dirty carpet, no longer worried about anything except wanting for it to all be over. It seemed as if the movie was over but no one had turned on the lights. He didn't have the energy to get up and walk out of the theater.

"Poor Nick," she said. "It must have been awful for you."

"I've lived through worse," he said.

They were on Gretchen's bed where they'd fallen as soon as they shut her door. The clock said two in the morning, but Nick felt as if it must be much later.

"I can't imagine," she said. "You were more sick than anyone. You let out those terrible moans and kept shouting, 'Give me strength.'"

"I did?"

"Yes. For the longest time. I'm glad I didn't get sick."

"But you did," Nick said.

"No I didn't," she said.

"You were very discrete. Very polite."

"I don't remember being sick," she said.

With no more energy than that required to kick off their shoes, they fell back on the bed and slept side by side, the fingers of their adjacent hands interlocked.

WILLIAM E. GARRISON: Out of Ohio—never a question as a child as to escaping, just how soon. Married twice, two children from the first. Now in a great long and ongoing unmarried relationship with a talented and tolerant woman. Lived most of his adult life in the Washington area, but also years in New Hampshire, New Mexico, and the Florida Keys. U.S. Marine Corps, U.S. Merchant Marine, carpenter, picture framer, home builder, ski lift operator, U.S. Forest Service timber cruiser. Newspaper reporter/photographer; freelance writer; publisher of the The Circle, *a D.C. arts/literary magazine; writer and editor on* Mid-Atlantic Country *magazine; several unpublished novels. Breathes deeper hiking in the Rocky Mountains or sailing on any sea.*

Prole Art Nightmare

Sperma, the critic from the *Voice*, slumming in D.C., described my
    live installation
piece near the mouth of the Clarendon Metro station in arch pomo
    terms extruded from the bowels of
her leapfrogging mind as: "Like watching the slaughterhouse scene
    from Fassbinder's *In a Year of*
13 Moons reshot on a spotlit Lars von Trier soundstage with the iPod
    dialed in to the Arctic Monkeys
reinterpreting the muddiest deathdoor bipolar howl of Joy Division's
    Ian Curtis after a bonghit of
South Carolina ditchweed chased by Steel Reserve and Stoli straight
    from the freezer and burbled
down with a straw."
Constable Skrunk, 3rd in charge of of Arlington's new Clean Con-
    cepts Division, is
less understanding. His paisley codpiece in alarming overbulge, he
    menaces up to me mincingly,
fiery breath of squashed jalapeno codcake exhaling contempt, vomi-
    tous eyeballs draining hate
that palp into my own sight orbs with such virulence as to bring traces
    of Christ's blood squeaking
from my tear ducts, draw snotsickles from my horrified nostrils, and
    start the rectal mucous
churning near my furiously clenching anus. Fearing to snottify my
    crushed red velvet jacket,

recovered just hours ago from hock, I draw forth a noserag of quilt-
like proportions and blow so

copiously, so trumpetingly as to cyclone Skrunk back a pace or two,
attracting the attention of

my near-naked and bovine blood-soaked models as they execute
their Grotowski-imbued dance

movements to the saturnine skronk of two Strats reverbing out of
Fender Pignose amps.

The trapezists and fire-eaters continue unflapped.

A mixture of legalese and possible Sengalese pour from the florid-
faced functionary,

regarding my permit which I produce crushingly from my crushed
red, flashing him the Hugo Boss

label. He seethes faintly intelligible syllables about having it revoked,
and spins and sizzles away,

vectoring WNW across the park surrounding the Metro station and
across Wilson Blvd only to be

assbooted by the grinning barefoot proprietor of Orpheus Records,
which propels him past the

Clarendon Ballroom where he slouches around the corner of Irving
St. and is no more.

The trapezists flex trapezius and delts are dealt the glances of pass-
ersby and

standersbelow. Three of the dancers cavort in *Commes des Garcons*
couture rags, again the

Manhattan influence over a city a county a burb once called the
suburb of the week by

emmetswimming, peopled frighteningly by cells and domains of
intell and counterintell, by

espioneers official and self-appointed that look on the pustulating
populace as surfers look on

hodads splishing about in backyard or backward (gene) pools. *X-File*
style paranoia passes for

rationality on the streets, in bars, and especially among sequestered
cabals of eternal hipsters,

cyberpunks, veteran dopesters, desolation angels, tea leaf readers,
and coffee ground gazers who

infest Starbucks, their frontal lobes fucked to infinity on goddess
  caffeine, tapping on their iBooks,
flooding the internet with more and more plausible conspiracy
  theories based on Pythagorean
biorhythms, Mingus chord charts, Blavatskian arcana pirated from
  keystroke-tracers placed in the
Macs of cybernauts only twice removed from direct contact with Bill
  Gates or Bill Clinton.
Freed from the Sturm und Dreck and espionola of homespun word-
  sick coppers, we can
return by a commodious rictus of opportunity to the Holy Chilling
  Evening and sweet menses of
twilight fireworks, escapading dancers, arpeggiated guitar warble,
  a romilar-abetted buzz, and the
giant Mao-like posters of Twiggy Ramirez and Misty Mundae that
  catch the wind just so.

*FRANK GATLING served twenty-three years as a corporate slave, fuel-
ing, towing, and dumping the crappers of the private airplanes of the
rich, famous, and obscene. Also clerked euphorically for one of Arlington's
infamous Ricks (see also* Gargoyle *and* Rick's Tattoos*) at Orpheus Records.
Call him a cinephile, but only if you catch him sober. He is scheduled to
appear in the (in-production) indy film* Modern Love Is Automatic.
*Heroes: Godard, Lynch, Wong Kar-Wai, Tsukamoto, Robert Anton Wilson,
Pynchon, Joyce, Mark E. Smith, Bo Diddley, Lux & Ivy, Tura Satana,
Lennon, Jarmusch, Joe Strummer, Rockets Redglare, Basquiat, Almodovar,
Hanna Schygulla, and the fabulous Maggie Cheung.*

Money Jungle

Brian Gilmore

Funk Frazier, Attorney at Law, saw the busted window on his 1993 dark Green Alfa Romeo 147 as soon as he emerged from his law office. The car was one of his great joys, so his head, calm and clear only a moment ago, immediately seemed to fill up with cement rocks. It was six p.m. in Washington D.C. on a steaming hot Friday, and the muggy August air hit Funk's face hard like a wall of swamp water.

Cars were jammed bumper to bumper on Good Hope Road in the Southeast section of the city. The metal and aluminum heaps burping black smoke were full of slightly buzzed government workers, corporate clerks, and upscale professionals who had done their forty-hour weeks and had earned the red wine and cold beer they would drink tonight. All of the folks driving the cars were smiling too because it was the weekend. They were bopping their heads to the beat of whatever rhythm and blues song on the radio. They didn't know Funk's agony either. But they did see him scream at the top of his lungs like he had lost his mind.

Funk had only been in his law office five minutes. That was just enough for his car to get broken into again. He didn't even have to check. Fourth time in the last three months he had come out his office to a busted back driver side window and a ransacked automobile. Papers strewn about, glove compartment yanked open, glass everywhere.

First time Funk got hit, they stole his cell phone. Second time, they tried to take the radio and the speakers out of the car but failed. Third time, only a week ago, they didn't get anything because there wasn't anything to take. This time, some lucky soul hit the lottery: Thelonious Monk. Joe "King" Oliver. Edward Kennedy "Duke"

Ellington. Louis Armstrong. Compact discs freshly purchased still in the plastic and not once subjected to laser light. Classic jazz songs like "Round Midnight," "Canal Street Blues," "Mood Indigo," "Back O' Town Blues," "Ruby My Dear," "Cottontail," "Dippermouth Blues," and "Lazy River."

Funk had just come from purchasing the CDs at some chain store downtown. On the way home he remembered he had forgotten to fax a memorandum to an attorney that just had to go out tonight. He came back to his office just for a hot second. He left the bag of discs in the trunk. He didn't even think about it because he was going to be in and out. Five minutes tops.

But as usual, somebody found them anyway after busting the glass and then popping the trunk. In a hurry, the poor soul left all the books on the seat that Funk kept in his car. Funk always would laugh too because the thieves never took his books. Classics like Leroi Jones's *Blues People*, Herman Melville's *Moby Dick*, Booker T. Washington's *Up From Slavery*, Toni Morrison's *The Bluest Eye*, George Lamming's *In the Castle of My Skin*, Sonia Sanchez's *Under a Soprano Sky*, and James Joyce's *Dubliners*."

"Damn!" he shrieked again in the musky evening air, "got me again."

Funk hopped in his car, turned the ignition, floored it straight for his nearest ATM. Funk raced out of Southeast Washington up through the D Street tunnel, past the Mitch Snyder homeless shelter, the D.C. Superior Courthouse, cut up by Chinatown to hit the ATM he always used when he was coming from the courthouse. He could have found something closer or perhaps something across the bridge but this was the machine that came to mind and it was one of those ATMs where you only had to swipe your card and not have to risk having the machine eat your card up.

Before Funk knew it, he had a wad of cash in his hand and was hanging the left in front of the D.C. Superior Courthouse and heading back through the D Street tunnel to Southeast where he would do something he said he would never do: tap into the underground goods market where his office was located. The office that sat quietly at the intersection of Martin Luther King Jr. Avenue and Good Hope Road, Southeast. Right in probably one of the worst-looking intersections in urban America.

Here's what you're looking at: boarded up buildings. Half crazy people shuffling about panhandling for anything of value but not knowing why. Drunks asking you for fourteen cents when what they really needed was three dollars. Crack-addicted men trying to sell broken lawn mowers and stolen tire jacks. Heroin addicts fighting withdrawal and losing that battle like Jerry Quarry getting beat senseless by Muhammad Ali. And petty thieves who spent their days stealing anything and selling it for a markdown to anyone who didn't look like the man. Just the kind of wonderful people Funk needed to speak to if he wanted to buy his music back.

The neighborhood where Funk was going to try to recapture his wares wasn't totally hopeless. There were a few businesses that were sprouting up among the desolation where Funk worked kept his small law office. Soul food carry-outs like Nia's Chicken Cafe which had even recently gotten a positive review in the *Washington Post*'s dining section. The owner, Nia Briscoe, threw a party for the whole neighborhood the day the review came out. And there were other necessary businesses out here trying to make it work like Leroy's Shoe Repair, Efficient Copiers, Imani's Florist Shop, and numerous drug stores, wing joints, and automobile repair shops which doubled most days as car washes because business was so bad.

Funk pulled right back in front of his office and got out his car and didn't worry this time. There was absolutely nothing for anyone to take from his car but the books and he knew the criminals didn't want the books. Now they could only take the car itself and Funk had a club on the steering wheel like most of the other people around here whose car looked like anything.

He walked up Good Hope Road to Ike's Thriftshop. He knew Ike. Elderly black man who had fought in the Korean War. Ike had caught a bullet for his country and lived to tell the tale. Ike came back and told everyone that too many black men were dying over there. In fact, it got so bad and disproportionate over there President Harry "Give 'Em Hell" Truman stopped sending black troops to Korea due to pressure from civil rights organizations. But Ike knew why Harry did it. The bullet still inside him reminded him of those times.

Ike came back from Korea with his mind intact and opened a thrift shop at 1267 Good Hope Road. He had been there ever since the end of the war selling anything he got his hands on. Fishing rods.

Bookcases. Chairs. VCRs. CD players. Would always tell Funk how the neighborhood once was jumping when he saw him too. Clubs, businesses, furniture stores, black and white working and living near each other and no race riots broke out ever until Martin Luther King Jr. got killed in Memphis in 1968. That's when the white people left Southeast Washington fearing retribution. Most of the middle-class blacks moved out too and left behind the place where Funk kept his law office—a hell zone.

"What's up Ike?" Funk yelled, coming through Ike's door. Bells on the shop's door rang hard, letting Ike know someone was coming in. Ike had been robbed a few times over the years but only because he wasn't close enough to his .38 caliber snub nose when it happened. He kept it in his waistband too. Ike paid the local police who patrolled the neighborhood a small piece of change to let him do it.

"Hey, Counselor, you still out here, it's almost seven thirty. Weekend, man, I am about to pull out myself. Close up. You must have a big murder case. Anybody I know?"

"Not really, Ike, but I'm still here, I got a problem."

"What's that?"

Funk hesitated before he spoke and then moved closer to Ike. No one was in the store, but Funk thought someone could be in the back. Funk wanted to keep what he was trying to do quiet.

"They got me again, Ike, hit my car again."

"They got the car? They took that Italian sports car? I told you that car was too nice," Ike said, with his eyes rising in his head.

"No, man, same thing as before."

"Snatch robbery?"

"Yep."

"You got an alarm, man, I told you to get an alarm."

"I got an alarm. Got me for some CDs, Ike, the good stuff. Duke Ellington. Thelonious Monk. Louis Armstrong. King Oliver. Stuff I know they don't usually get out here. I want to buy them back. I'm sick of this. I know it isn't my style, but I work hard. I already spent about three hundred dollars on the CDs downtown; no sense in giving them another three hundred dollars. Makes more sense to me to just go to the people."

Ike burst out laughing. Funk laughed too but really wanted to get to the point. He knew Ike knew all the thieves out here. All the professionals who were moving valuables on a regular basis. Ike bought the stuff too. You could get any movie you wanted from Ike on VHS at anytime. In fact, Funk usually saw any movie he wanted before it even came out. Ike would give the crap to him. He saw *The Bodyguard* with Whitney Houston when it was still just being hyped on television commercials. Picked up a copy of Eddie Murphy in *The Nutty Professor,* and the movie still had the counting numbers on the bottom of the screen from whatever Hollywood movie house was finishing it. And Funk knew that *Godzilla* was going to be flop a month before the movie even hit the screen. That's how good it was out here once you came through the D Street tunnel over to Southeast Washington. Anything you wanted or needed you could get it. Maybe not from Ike, because he mostly ran a legal operation. But from somebody out here and that's what Funk knew.

Funk had kept his office out here for two years right in the community but never figured to tap into the underground market right at his doorstep which was always offering him watches and shoes and tennis rackets. But now he had to. He figured those CDs were worth it. He could go back down to that chain store and buy them again, but that was beside the point; he didn't want to buy them again. Ike kept laughing and looking at Funk. Funk wasn't laughing anymore. Ike pulled out a silver flask from under the counter of his store and took a shot of bourbon and gritted.

"You wanna hit, Counselor? George Dickel Sour Mash." Funk looked at Ike and got tempted. Ike's face showed years of hits like the massive swallow he just took. Wrinkles and lines. Eyes bloodshot with permanent brown stains covering the white.

"That's all right, Ike, just need to know where I can start looking to buy my stuff back."

"Man, you should let it go, man, those CDs probably in somebody disk player by now. People know where to buy stolen property. The people doin' the stealin' got contacts. Some white guy in the suburbs or over on Capitol Hill probably listenin' to Louis Armstrong singin' "Rockin' Chair" by now."

Ike smiled and took another hit of bourbon. Funk smiled back and looked Ike right in the face. His face exuded a plea. Funk was making his case. Ike didn't want to get into it, but he and Funk had become good friends. Now and then they hung out and went to jazz clubs. Ike could see he needed help. He was reluctant, but he was going to do it. Funk was all right as far as Ike was concerned. An attorney who could have put his office someplace else but instead he put it out here in an area of town where people didn't even walk around at night. Ike respected that. Funk represented a lot of people out here too. Would do cases for free on occasion if the right person asked him.

"All right, Funk, I'm gonna give you three spots. These are the hot spots. Police watch these, so you better not mess around too long tonight. But these spots is where the real petty thieves who come into the goods hang out and keep the stuff in their trunks and what not. Other than these three spots, you can just walk the block a little, see who's out, and just ask around. Don't be too loud, but drop a line here and there, and see what comes back. People hear what you lookin' for, they'll ask around. Sometimes they'll come up to you because they are trying to move the stuff fast. The stuff might be gone already but never hurts to try, right?"

"Thanks, Ike, I appreciate this."

So Ike put Funk down with the information he needed to get on the trail of his CDs out here. It was almost seven thirty p.m. He gave him three spots where some of the area's best fencers hung out and waited on customers. One spot was up on Morris Road by Mel's Liquor Store. The other was at Alabama Avenue and Stanton Road in a small mini-mall that was full of crack dealers. And the final one was right beside the Frederick Douglass home national historic site that sat up on the hill on W Street S.E. and overlooked the city.

"You better get going too, Funk, getting dark out, get crazy after a while. And take that tie off, man, you don't need to look too sharp. They know you ain't riffraff. But you wear a tie they gonna think you the black J. Edgar Hoover." Ike burst out laughing again. Funk smiled.

"Thanks Ike," he said as he left, bells ringing from the door flying open.

Funk hit the streets. He was going to do all three spots. Cruise pass in his car and look around then stroll through and try to get a feel for the movement of commerce. He hit Mel's Liquor Store first. He knew Mel anyway and could use that as a start to see what was happening out front. Everybody knew Mel too.

Funk rode pass the store once and then parked in the lot that was adjacent to the store. A mob of drunk panhandlers were out front as usual working their way towards a half pint of vodka or a forty-ounce bottle of malt liquor. If they had a good couple of hours, they would get both. They all converged on Funk too as he approached the store like he was water on the desert.

"Young fella, can I get twenty-seven cents?" an old skinny man asked Funk. He had on all gray. Slacks. Shoes. Shirt. Hat. His clothes were soiled. He looked wan and weak as if he had been out in front of the store for the last six months straight subsisting on a diet of cheap beer and whiskey. An impossible feat of human suffering perhaps, but something that probably could be true. Funk handed him a dollar. The old man smiled. His teeth were almost all missing. This could be his fatal drink, Funk thought as he walked on.

"God bless, young fella."

"Have a good day, man," Funk told him. Several more of the mob converged on Funk to see if it was Christmas for real. Funk moved quickly into the store and immediately saw Mel.

"What's up Mel?"

"Hey Funk, hanging out tonight, thought you would be gone back over the bridge by now, back over to the city." Mel laughed and slapped Funk in the back. Funk laughed too. He knew what Funk meant. There were a lot of people who didn't know about this part of Washington, D.C. Washington was the Capitol, the Monument, Howard University, Georgetown; no one had a vision that Washington D.C. had sections like this.

"Give me a cold Heineken to go, Mel, and a bag of hot peanuts."

"Coming right up, Funk."

While Mel bagged up Funk's order, Funk thought how he could break the ice. Ask Mel who the players were out here. Who were the cats who had the goods, or at least knew where the goods were.

"How's business, Mel?" Funk said, handing Mel two one-dollar bills.

"Same old same old, up and down, bad spot that's all, still a lot of numbers out here though, both inside and outside, you know what I mean." Funk smiled. He couldn't hide his urgency. He decided to just ask. He and Mel knew each other since he opened his office. He stopped by for a cold beer every now and then. Mel was a family man who ran his business within the law. He knew the neighborhood too. Funk knew that Mel knew he wasn't the man either and that Funk usually represented individuals who had been convicted of crimes.

"Looking for some CDs, Mel, anybody moving any these days?" Mel hesitated and looked at Funk seriously. In the five years they had known each other, Funk had purchased beer, wine, whiskey, and lottery numbers, but never had he asked about the goods that moved out front on the street. Mel looked him right in the eye.

"You serious, Funk, or just joking?"

"Serious, Mel, looking for some CDs. Jazz mostly. Duke Ellington. Thelonious Monk. People like that. King Oliver."

"King Oliver? Joe 'King' Oliver? You kidding, right? Ain't no King Oliver being sold on the streets."

"I got cash, Mel, I'm tired of buying for full price from the man." Mel looked Funk in the eyes again and smiled. Mel knew he was serious but figured this song and dance about tired of buying from the man was a put-on. He knew Funk didn't care; he made good money from his practice. He wasn't super rich but he wasn't poor either.

"I saw the busted window on your Alfa, Funk, they got you for this stuff, right? Today, few hours ago, I bet."

Funk looked at Mel and knew he couldn't lie to him. Mel was from this side of the city. He was almost clairvoyant when it came to things like this. "Yea, man, I jacked up Ike and he sent me up here, gave me three spots to check out. Yours was first on the list."

"What's the other two spots?"

"Alabama and Stanton Road in the mini-mall and by the little store up by the Frederick Douglass home."

"Yea, Ike is right, I know a little but I tell you, I wouldn't go up to that mini-mall. They cleaned that place up so much you can't sell stolen bubble gum up there without somebody reporting you to the police. Police run the whole neighborhood now. Not a crook or crack dealer within miles. Try up by the boarded-up Safeway grocery store in front of St. Elizabeth's Hospital. Look for a guy in a brown beat up van selling carpet and posters for the walls. His name is Disco. Used to be a disc jockey back in the '70s. Still wears some of the clothes so people know him when they see him. He knows where all the goods are. If somebody was trying to move it, he's got it or he knows who got it. Just go up to him and say Mel sent me or Ike sent me; he'll talk to you then. If nothing is up there, try the Shrimp Boat down on Benning Road. A lot of people moving all kinds of stolen goods up that way. Old cats selling stuff like sweat suits and cologne. Batteries and hand lotion."

"Hand lotion?"

"Yea, man, hand lotion. That's where I get mine all the time." Mel laughed.

"What about the Frederick Douglass home?" Funk asked.

"You can try up there too. It is kind of real low-key up there. If none of these don't pan out for you, come back, I'll ask around while you are gone. Maybe I'll have an answer for you." Funk looked at Mel and smiled. He picked up his cold beer and walked out.

When Funk finally made it up to the Safeway parking lot in front of the St. Elizabeth's Mental Hospital, he saw action everywhere. He was convinced that his CDs were here. There were people moving about like electricity in a circuit. He saw the brown van too that Mel told him about and he knew it had to be this cat Disco because there were carpets strewn over the side of the back doors of the van. Music was blaring out of speakers from inside the van. Disco music from the 1970s. Incense was burning. Disco was talking to everybody that went past as if he was a candidate running for office.

He was wearing a dark blue flare-collar silk shirt and wide-legged slacks. Had an afro too and was wearing dark shades even though night was falling. Funk parked his car right across the street from the mammoth St. Elizabeth's Mental Hospital complex. He turned and looked at the place. It was a horrific sight. Buildings were so old Funk felt like he had stepped through a time machine.

He thought about John Hinckley as he stared at the complex. Every time he was near the place he thought about John Hinckley. The same John Hinckley who shot President Ronald Reagan downtown at the Washington Hilton Hotel back in 1981 because Hinckley thought he was the taxi driver Travis in the movie *Taxi Driver*. He thought about Ezra Pound too. The poet Ezra Pound. In high school, Funk's English professor had been a huge fan of Ezra Pound and sang Pound's praises as a poet every chance he could get. Pound spent some time in St. Elizabeth's Mental Hospital too. Right after he told the world he was a fascist. Funk strutted over to Disco and didn't want to waste any more time.

"What's up, Disco," Funk said catching Disco off guard, "Mel and Ike sent me." Disco whipped his head around and looked Funk up and down. Nice boardroom slacks. Florsheims. Dress shirt. Must be a big spender.

"Cool, chief, what's your story?"

"Story?"

"Yea, what kind of sauce you want on your chicken wings?" Disco was obviously playing it close to the vest. Speaking in a code only he knew how to translate. That way he could always say later on that he didn't know what was going on. Funk picked up his melody quick.

"Armstrong," Funk said, "Louis Armstrong."

"Satchmo?"

"'Lazy River.' 'Black and Blue.' 'West End Blues.'"

"Vinyl? Eight-track? Cassette?"

"CD."

Disco had been folding carpet he was selling, but he stopped when he heard what Funk said. Disco realized that Funk wanted jazz. Disco reached under a pile of papers and pulled out a box and told Funk to go through the stack. Disco had been sitting on this all week. He didn't really have too many takers out here. Most of the CDs that were sold out here were rap stars. Jay-Z. The Notorious B.I.G. TuPac Shakur. Nasty Nas. "Check these out, main man."

Funk picked up the box to see if his journey was over. There was a stack of CDs in the box. He pulled the first disk out. White guy on front with frazzled hair and a beautiful smile. Well dressed, clean shaven, and playing a shiny soprano saxophone with his eyes closed. Funk looked at the title of the CD—*Kenny G. Live at the London Palladium.* Funk looked at Disco.

"I said I was serious, man, for real, I really am looking for some Louis Armstrong on CD. Duke Ellington."

"Check all of 'em out man, see what you like."

Funk reluctantly flipped through the entire box. Nothing but the same kind of stuff. Kenny G. Najee. Wayman Tisdale. The Yellowjackets. Funk looked back at Disco, who was folding his carpet again.

"Thanks man, but no thanks, not quite what I was looking for."

"How you figure?" Disco asked, "you lookin' for jazz, right, I gave you jazz."

"I said Louis Armstrong. Duke Ellington. King Oliver."

"So what's wrong with Kenny G and Najee and Wayman Tisdale? Tisdale was in the NBA, you know that right? All-American college basketball player."

Funk looked at Disco. He didn't even say a word. "I'll see you man." He could still hear him as he pulled off. Now he knew why they called him Disco. The music Disco was blasting faded out as Funk headed for the Frederick Douglass home in his car.

The Frederick Douglass home sat on the hill on W Street majestically. Clean, well-kept, white wood with beautifully kept trees and grounds that seemed to announce respect. The place had been declared a national historic site by the federal government, and now Douglass was property of the United States. At the top, if you had the right view, you could actually see parts of the rest of the city. In fact, you could see what was generally thought to be the most important aspects of the nation's capital. The White House. The U.S. Capitol. The Washington Monument. The Jefferson and Lincoln Memorials. Funk cruised slowly up W Street right by the home the great abolitionist used to keep but didn't see anyone but the police roughing up some young boys who had been standing on the corner. Three cops had about six young boys on the ground and were shaking them down from head to toe. Other than that there was no activity at all. Not a thief in sight. Funk looked at his watch. It was past eight thirty p.m. He was about to give up. Probably would have to go buy the CDs again from the chain store downtown. He had one more stop—the Shrimp Boat.

Nobody had really stressed the Shrimp Boat, but Funk had a feeling. Ever since he was a small child growing up in Washington, Funk remembered the Shrimp Boat. His aunt, uncle, and cousins lived right around the corner from the place and when his family visited, he and his cousins would go buy fried shrimp platters. Loads of cocktail sauce too because there was something about deep fried shrimp at the Shrimp Boat dipped in their hot cocktail sauce. Funk remembers all the other action too around the Shrimp Boat. In the summer days, hustlers would be selling bootleg eight-tracks and cassettes; old folks would be across the street moving bar-b-que rib platters and watermelons to cars that pulled up along the curb.

Funk came up on the Shrimp Boat in ten minutes. There were people moving in and out, getting that good shrimp with cocktail sauce and there was other activity too. Bar-b-que pits gasping clouds of hickory-coated smoke. Shady characters moving back and forth in front of the place whispering their hustles to customers. Panhandlers begging. This part of it was somewhat new. Funk got out of his car. He walked right up to the door. The panhandlers converged on him. Funk heard their pleas but ignored them and walked inside the Shrimp Boat and saw that the place hadn't changed much. He ordered a seafood platter and headed back outside. Where were the people out here who moved product?

He looked across at one of the bar-b-que pits which were blasting out clouds of smoke. An old black man and an old black woman dressed in farm clothes were selling ribs like they were gold to cars pulling up by the curb. Dinner platters with cole slaw and rolls to dip in the excess hickory sauce which smothered the ribs. They looked like they had just gotten up to the city from North Carolina or southern Virginia. They had been out here all day, so Funk figured, what the hell, ask them.

By the time Funk made it over to the bar-b-que pit, the couple was sitting. No customers were around. Their car was parked right behind them, and the trunk was popped. A rusted dark blue Cadillac with so much junk in the trunk the tailpipe was almost touching the ground. Funk heard the music that was blaring from their trunk as he got closer. It was gospel music. Music that could raise the dead, it was so emotional and strong. The music reminded Funk of Sunday mornings when his mother made breakfast for the family before or after church. The radio would be on and some music like this would be playing.

"How y'all doin'?" Funk asked them as he made it over to the old black man and woman.

"Pretty well," they both said in unison.

"Can I get one of those rib dinners?" Funk asked. "Haven't had one of those in years."

"Comin' right up," the old woman said. Funk watched her get up slowly from the lawn chair and reached for a Styrofoam carry-out plate. Funk looked at the old man sitting in the chair dressed in the farm clothes. He looked like he was a hundred.

"How are you, sir?" Funk asked him. "Anybody selling music out here?"

"What you lookin' fo'?" he asked Funk.

"Jazz."

"Lot of jazz, son, like who you lookin' fo', Miles? Billie Holiday?" Funk was impressed. Old man looked like he was more into the blues. Mississippi Delta blues. But he was in the ballpark.

"Duke, sir, Monk, Louis Armstrong, King Oliver."

"King Oliver?" the woman said from the bar-b-que pit, "what a young man like you know about King Oliver?"

"A little, ma'am," Funk told her as she handed him a steaming hot plate of ribs and he handed her five dollars, "just trying to find out some more, heard they sell a little hard jazz out here from time to time." The old man looked at Funk. The old woman sat back down in her lawn chair.

"Well, that's probably true," the old man told Funk. "Two guys been by here today looking for that same stuff, I think they both made a purchase too." Funk's eyes lit up.

"From who?"

"See the guy over there in that lime green Cadillac Eldorado with the television antenna on the back? His name is Cowboy. He's the music man. You name it, he's got it. Just go over and talk to him. He know you ain't the police." Funk turned around and looked. There was a man standing in front of a lime green Eldorado right behind the Shrimp Boat. He didn't look suspicious or anything; but he was there just like the old man said and people were coming up to him. Had on a cowboy hat too.

"Thanks a lot, sir, ma'am, and thanks for the ribs."

"You're welcome, son," they said in unison as the gospel music continued to pump.

Funk walked over to the man by the lime green Eldorado. He had a boom box beside his car. A blanket was spread out on the ground with cassettes and CDs for sale. Funk didn't speak to the man. A tall skinny black man with a ring on every finger shining in the street lights. He had on a jumpsuit all black and had a bald head that was covered by a cowboy hat which had an X on the front. Funk kept scanning his wares. None of the CDs he was looking for.

"Can I help you brother?" the man asked Funk.

"Your name's Cowboy, right?" Funk asked him.

"At your service, brother," Cowboy said, removing his hat as he spoke. "Something in particular your ears have a craving for? If it's not here, I can get it." Funk scanned the rows of tapes and CDs on the blanket again. Miles Davis's *Kind of Blue* was down there, Wynton Marsalis's *Live at Blues Alley*. Those were the only traditional jazz CDs Funk saw. All else was old rhythm and blues, Chicago blues, hard blues, gospel, funk, and hip-hop.

"You have any Ellington or Monk?" Cowboy looked at Funk.

"Man, what the hell is goin' on today, you the fourth person today looking for some Monk and some Ellington."

"The fourth person?"

"That's right, the fourth person begging me for some Monk or Ellington or Louis Armstrong and King Oliver. Now, I see Ellington CDs out here from time to time and Monk, and Louis Armstrong, he make it through here too, but King Oliver, I told them if there is some King Oliver out here on cassette, eight-track, vinyl or CD, Jesus was about to come back." Funk didn't understand. Why would anybody be out here looking for the same thing he was looking for?

"Did they buy any—I mean, did you find anything for them?" Funk asked Cowboy.

"Well, I made a couple calls and asked around, and then they asked around and in fact, we had some new arrivals in the area in fact, brand-new inside the plastic, and I would have sold them to the first two guys but they had left and before they could come back, a third guy came around looking like a fool asking for the same stuff. I thought he was the man at this point. But after I waited awhile, I sold him all of it for about seventy-five dollars."

Funk didn't hesitate. He thanked Cowboy. Dashed inside the Shrimp Boat, picked up his platter, and hopped in his car and headed back to his office. He must have gotten there in five minutes as fast as he drove. He parked out front and left his food on the seat. Probably wasn't going to eat it anyway. He walked up to Ike's. The store wasn't open, but Ike was inside. Funk knew it. Funk knocked on the door. Ike came to the door with his flask. He was still sipping. He opened the door and the bells he kept on the door chimed.

"What's up, Funk, any luck, man?"

"Yea, a whole lot."

"How much you want for the Monk and Ellington?"

"What you talkin' 'bout, Counselor? Ain't got no Monk or no Ellington."

"Whatever, man, I got the story from Cowboy."

"Cowboy?"

"Guy down by the Shrimp Boat."

"I don't know what you talkin' bout, Counselor." Funk looked at Ike hard this time and grinned.

"All right, I went down there looking around and asking around, I was gonna try to get 'em back fo' you, but Cowboy ain't deliver quickly enough. So I figured those CDs was in the 'burbs by that point, I let it go."

Funk looked at Ike. Ike wasn't a liar. He was telling the truth, Funk knew that. But Cowboy said there had been three visitors before him. Word had gotten around and somebody was trying to cut in on Funk's action. He left Ike's and headed for Mel's. Mel was just leaving for the night. But he told Funk the same story. As a friend he was going to try to get the CDs back for him through his own connections. Everybody Mel had talked to sent him to Cowboy. But Cowboy didn't deliver in time. Mel gave up. Mel gave Funk another cold beer and a half of Jack Daniels to take with him and drink away his frustrations. But Funk knew better. The CDs were here, he still felt. He took a hit of Jack Daniels and felt his esophagus burn. He chased it with the cold beer. Like Cowboy said, there had been three visitors. Funk had been the fourth person to ask about the classics. Funk just couldn't figure how things had moved so fast right in front of him.

When Funk pulled back in front of St. Elizabeth's Hospital about five minutes later and cut the engine to his car, Disco was still out there. Funk was walking over and he took all of his money out of his pocket. As Funk got closer, he saw Disco smiling and sitting down on the back of the van's open door area drinking a cold Pabst Blue Ribbon twelve ounce in the can. Music was blaring out onto Martin Luther King Jr. Avenue from the back of Disco's van. It sounded old, like it had been recorded seventy-five years ago. Funk made it out. It was the sound he wanted to hear. King Oliver and his Creole Orchestra which included Louis Armstrong on second cornet pumping out the sound of "Just Gone," one of their most famous recordings. Disco's head was bopping to the beat. Funk got over to Disco and looked at Disco smiling from ear to ear. Funk looked down and saw all the CDs in a stack. All the Ellingtons, the Monks, the Louis Armstrongs, and of course, the King Oliver, one of which was playing. Duke Ellington's *Money Jungle* was there as was Duke's *Live at Newport*. Thelonious Monk's *Criss Cross* and *Monk's Dream*. Louis Armstrong's *The Best of Louis Armstrong* and *Louis Armstrong Plays W.C. Handy*. Finally, King Oliver's *King Oliver and his Creole Orchestra, King Oliver and Louis Armstrong,* and *The Best of King Oliver.*

"Sho you don't want a Wayman Tisdale or a Kenny G to go wit' that, main man?" Disco asked Funk.

"Real sure," Funk told Disco, handing him all the money he had and picking up the CDs. Funk turned to walk to his car with the CDs.

"What about this one King Oliver in the box, man, you only got two of them?"

"Keep it Disco, you earned it."

Disco burst out laughing. Funk started his car and roared his engine. He paused for a second and listened again. King Oliver's band was still blasting up the avenue. Disco had started the record again and was still just sitting there bopping his head to the beat. King Oliver's instinctive nasty cornet was lighting up the avenue. Louis Armstrong was right behind him. Nobody knew that out here except the old folks. Funk just smiled as he looked back in the mirror and saw Disco waving CDs and jewelry in the air and calling out to customers as people kept coming up to him, looking at the good stuff he had. Funk hit the gas and headed back to the city.

Native Washingtonian BRIAN GILMORE is a public interest lawyer, poet, and writer. A columnist with the Progressive Media Project, he teaches in the Clinical Law Program at the Howard University School of Law. He is the author of two collections of poetry, elvis presley is alive and well and living in harlem *(Third World Press, 1993) and* Jungle Nights and Soda Fountain Rags: Poem for Duke Ellington *(Karibu Books, 2000). His poetry, essays, and reviews have been widely published and anthologized and can be found in such celebrated publications as* Voices of Dissent, In Search of Color Everywhere, Bum Rush the Page, Step Into a World, *the* Nation, *the* Progressive, *and* Callalloo. *His columns on current political and cultural topics have been featured in the* Baltimore Sun, Charlotte Observer, Miami Herald, Detroit Free Press, *and many other daily newspapers. Gilmore is also a contributing writer for* Jazz Times Magazine. *He lives in Takoma Park, Maryland, with his wife and three daughters.*

FROM *A February Song*

JOHN GUERNSEY

The alarm went off as usual at seven a.m. The only problem with that was that it wasn't my alarm, it was my neighbor's. She was a single mom with two young girls who needed to get to school and after they caught the bus she would always return and play the latest hip-hop record, take a shower, and then leave for work by eight thirty. Usually I could sleep through it but this particular Monday I couldn't. So at seven fifteen I got up to make some coffee. When I opened the refrigerator there was no milk and since I couldn't stomach black coffee I went out to TJ's market to get some. As I descended the stairs of the apartment building I ran into Deneen and her two girls.

"I hope we didn't wake you this morning Mr. Cowley."

"I didn't hear a thing."

She had enough to worry about without worrying about me.

When I got up to TJ's I bought a quart of milk and the *Washington Post*. The picture of Chevy Chase Circle on the front page immediately grabbed my attention. It was even more intriguing because it had been taken at the turn of the century. At the beginning of the article was an introduction in italics:

Another in a biweekly series of stories
about the people and events that shaped
Washington at the turn of the century.

There was a lone figure in the right-hand corner of the photo. I recognized the house immediately. It was the mansion where Sibylla made her home in the backyard! I hurried home to read the article.

Once upon a time Chevy Chase Circle wasn't such a busy place. It was at the outer fringe of Northwest Washington and few people had the means to live there. Today it is dominated by the upper middle class but in the early part of the 20th century it was dominated by one man and his mansion, John William Gardner. At the time of the photograph the mansion belonged to his immigrant parents from whom Gardner inherited the dwelling. Pictured with his back to the camera, Gardner was to become a prolific architect, building more than 6,000 houses during his lifetime. Indeed, he seems to be surveying the circle.

During his career Gardner was one of the few architects who successfully clung to the Victorian style throughout his life. While the Bauhaus and other forms of modern architecture changed the way Americans lived, Mr. Gardner happily went on building houses with huge decorative porches, ornate windows, attics as many as four stories off the ground, and roofs with diverse angles, all designed to specifications of those who could afford them.

In Takoma Park, Maryland, where nearly every house was created by Gardner, the landscape changed after World War Two when new, more economical houses were built in the large spaces between the Victorians. Many small towns up and down the east coast had similar fates and virtually all were first created by Mr. Gardner.

Frank Lloyd Wright once paid homage to Gardner in the form of a backhanded compliment saying "John William Gardner is the best architect of the 19th Century!" Gardner reportedly repaid the tribute by saying "It can be argued that all that is truly beautiful about designing buildings died on March 16, 1867" (Wright's birthday).

But Gardner was more than an architect. Friends with Franklin and Eleanor Roosevelt, he was also an inventor, philanthropist, coin collector, amateur actor, and the founder of the Alliance for a Better World. The latter was a curious group that believed that religion and science could commingle with beneficiary results.

Gardner was also a one-time colleague of Ron L. Hubbard, the founder of the Church of Scientology. Hubbard and Gardner had a bitter falling out over the use of technology. Both believed that science and religion could be combined in ways unimagined before but disagreed about its application. Hubbard believed in unrestricted experiments on individuals who were under his strict financial and intellectual control. Gardner called this approach "fascistic" and believed that all experiments should be done with full knowledge and cooperation of the individuals involved. He was also known to experiment on himself. In the early 1960s Gardner nearly blinded himself doing just that. After the life-threatening mishap he changed his approach to what he called "verbal experimentation," a sort of hit-and-run approach of Gestalt therapy, chance encounter, and unrestrained imagination. "I like to work with young people now, for they are the only ones open enough to fully embrace the future," Gardner said in 1965.

Shortly before his death in 1974, Mr. Gardner issued a statement on behalf of the Alliance for a Better World. "I have failed in my attempt to find a meaningful link between science and religion. And though this may sound self-serving, I feel like the 50 years I spent trying to establish this link was not unlike Albert Einstein spending so many years trying to find a unifying force in the universe. The philosopher Abelard said, 'By doubting we come to inquiry, by inquiry we come to truth.' With that in mind, I am directing the Alliance to turn its full attention to the more meaningful work of ending all wars and ridding the planet of hunger, poverty and disease. I bid you farewell."

It seemed like a sad comment from an extremely proud man. And sadness was not a stranger to John William Gardner. At the end of the 19th century he lost his wife of six months to anorexia and, by his own account, nearly committed suicide. It was architecture that pulled him back from the abyss.

In his will, he personally chose 20 delegates to continue the work of the Alliance and donated $50 million for them to do it with. The mansion was to be their headquarters. Almost immediately bickering broke out amongst the delegates as to what cause to support and what to do where. Within an astonishingly short period of time the Alliance was bankrupt. The mansion was put up for sale in 1977 and was purchased by a wealthy German businessman who still resides there today.

An interesting sidelight to this profile is a small booklet that one of the delegates wrote about the mansions surrounding Chevy Chase Circle. Amongst the descriptions of the interiors and landscaping, it was noted that Gardner was buried next to his wife, the former Mary Louise Crichton, near a Stonehenge-like semicircle of seven statues in a spectacular garden in the back of the mansion. The author of the book claimed the ghost of Mary Louise, who died in 1899, could be heard singing in the early morning hours, shortly before dawn.

I put the paper down. This was too much. My life was being choreographed by someone or something I didn't understand. But this was no time to panic and I went into the kitchen to make coffee. While it was perking I returned to the dining room and stared at the photograph. I thought I recognized something in the right hand corner but I had to be sure. So I calmly went over to my desk drawer and withdrew a pair of scissors and then neatly cut out the section of the photograph with William staring at his mansion in it. Then I got my car keys and drove to Kinko's at Colesville Road and East-West Highway, the place for computer nerds that is open seven days a week, twenty-four hours a day. There they had the best high-tech Xerox machines that could blow up or reduce a photograph in size without losing its original quality. It was eight forty-five in the morning but Kinko's was always busy and I had to wait fifteen minutes until a Xerox machine was free. When one opened up I put the photo on the glass face down and enlarged it twenty-five percent. Then another twenty-five percent. And finally another fifty percent.

I was right! Now I could see more clearly the outline of seven slabs of stone arranged in a semicircle, the first of which was obscured by a small tree and whom I believed would become Sibylla. If this picture was taken at the end of the nineteenth century there was plenty of time for the large trees that were there today to have been planted and grown thereby concealing the rest of the statues. Immediately I thought of the seven sister goddesses, all daughters of Zeus, who in classical mythology were given credit for creative thought and inspiration: Aoede for song, Calliope for poetry, Melpomene for tragedy, Polyhymnia for religion, Thalia for comedy, Melete for meditation, and Mneme for memory. But no Sibylla.

I paid for the use of the copier and went next door to the drug-store to purchase a roll of film.

"Can I get some black and white, ASP 400 please?"

"Will you be using a flash?"

"Yes."

"Twenty-four or thirty-six?"

"Thirty-six." Then I added: "The more I shoot the luckier I get."

"Don't we all!" responded the clerk.

Then I went home. I knew I was going to take some pictures of Sibylla and I knew it had to be at night. But that's about as much of a plan as I had. It was ten a.m. and I decided to lie down for a little nap, a nap that ended up being five hours long.

I never did drink that cup of coffee.

||||

I awoke at three in the afternoon and got up to take a shower. I was feeling guilty for wasting the day but I decided to make the most of what was left of it and gathered my dirty clothes together and took them down to the laundry room in the basement of the apartment building. Rather than sit and wait, I went back upstairs to practice piano until it was time to put the clothes in the dryer.

I was working on a Nat "King" Cole medley: "Paper Moon," "Unfor-gettable," "Straighten Up and Fly Right," "Sweet Lorraine," and the grand finale, "Route 66." I liked to string songs together that were identified with certain performers. For Sinatra I had: "Come Fly With Me," "That's Life," "Witchcraft," "It Was a Very Good Year," and of course "New York, New York." I even had a Beatles medley: "If I Fell," "Julia," "And I Love Her," "Michelle," and "Here There and Everywhere."

The ritual was I would practice for an hour, go put my clothes in the dryer and then practice for another hour, then sort my laun-dry. At six p.m. I drove over to my brother's house in Kensington, remembering to put his amp in the trunk of my car and my Pentax camera in the glove compartment. When I got to Connecticut and Knowles I pulled into the parking lot of Continental Pizza to get din-ner. It was the same pizza parlor that I had worked at as a teenager although the ownership had changed several times. Now it was owned by a Greek family and it had more things on the menu like gyros and shish kebab. I ordered a medium pizza, half with pepperoni for

Terry and half with green peppers and onions for me. (Adrienne wouldn't be home from work till about nine.)

When I arrived at Terry's Adrienne was home. She had left work early but said she had eaten a late lunch and wasn't hungry. She was sipping a glass of red wine and poured me one. Then she withdrew for the evening.

Terry and I chowed down on the pizza and then he lay down on the living room couch.

"Sorry, I'm not very good company tonight."

"No problem." And I got up to get my camera from the car.

"Where are you going?"

"I'll be right back," and I went to retrieve my camera and film. When I returned, Terry saw the camera.

"What's up?"

I opened the back of the camera and inserted the roll of film.

"Nothing much, I just feel like taking a few pictures."

"Of what?"

"A ghost."

Terry assumed I was kidding and we chatted about other things for a while. When we ran out of small talk he said, "Look, I'm gonna turn in. Thanks for coming over."

"Thanks for having me."

And without Terry noticing, I grabbed the bottle of wine and left. I didn't want to drink any more but I knew if I were going to follow through on my plan I would need some old-fashioned Dutch courage.

I hopped in my Dodge Dart and drove down Knowles Avenue to Connecticut and turned right towards Chevy Chase Circle. Just as the girls had done over thirty years ago, I rounded the circle into D.C. and came back down Connecticut into Maryland. As soon as I passed the mansion I turned down a side street and parked. It was eleven thirty and I uncorked the bottle of wine and took a swig. I quickly attached the flash to the camera and got out of the car, heading directly to where I remembered the statue to be. There were no voices in my head or anything.

When I got there I was in for a shock. Sibylla was there all right, standing behind the same tree, but there was no plaque. Not only that, I couldn't see her face. She had her back turned towards me. I looked from every possible angle but all I could see was her hind side. I wanted to scale the fence but it was too high and had pointed prongs on the top just to discourage that sort of thing. I followed the fence around past the iron gate to where it finally tuned into a stone wall at the front of the mansion. I tried to scale it but it was still too high.

"Shit! If only I had a step ladder," I said to myself. Then I remembered Terry's amp. I had forgotten to return it at dinner time. It was about two feet high and might give me just enough boost to get over the wall. I went back to the car, took a couple more sips of wine, and lifted the amp out of the trunk. It was a Fender twin reverb which weighed a ton and I lugged it to a secluded part of the wall. The street was deserted. It was now or never. I stepped up on the amp and hoisted myself to the top of the wall. I was obsessed with getting a picture of Sibylla. I would figure out a way to get out of there later and jumped into a thicket, falling on my ass. I found myself in the very front of the front yard of the mansion, at least a hundred yards from the statue. (Mansion isn't even the right word. It was a castle.) Floodlights were everywhere and a Rolls Royce was parked in the circular driveway. I could only hope whoever was inside had retired for the evening. There was only one light on in the lower level.

Then I began to think of that Japanese kid who had been shot and killed in New Orleans for mistakenly going to the wrong house for a Halloween party. I pushed it out of my mind and started sneaking along the shadows close to the fence as I edged towards the backyard. It took about three minutes but they might as well have been three years. Finally I reached my destination and I felt as if I had entered into a dream. The soft flood lights gave everything a surreal, pastel quality. It would have been the perfect setting for a Maxfield Parrish painting.

There was a beautifully manicured garden with a fountain and a reflecting pool in the middle surrounded by exotic-looking plants and trees. And then there were the seven statues, all of them women. The whole landscape was laid out with them in mind. The sympathetic interplay made for a mysterious, mystical setting. They were arranged around the reflecting pool and each one stood on a revolving stone pedestal that could be turned to different angles so they appeared to be conversing with each other. I recognized Sibylla immediately. She was different from the rest. She was the first of seven, and the sculptor had obviously spent the lion's share of time on her. Her lips were parted like before but her white gown had been worn by the weather and you could see through it, giving her tremendous erotic appeal. My first instinct was to walk up to her and place a wet kiss on her mouth. But when I got close enough to actually act out my desire I saw two things that stopped me cold. One was her hair. As it fell down her breasts it turned into snakes. Medusa! And the other was a black orchid. It was stuck in the cobwebs on the left side of her head. Someone must have placed it there and it looked fresh. I decided to take my photos and get the hell out!

As I snapped the first shot I was startled by a cat running across the lawn. The flash went off but my knee buckled and I dropped the camera against the stone base of the statue and ended up on my knees. There I was, at the feet of my muse. I quickly got up and tried for another shot but the camera jammed. It would flash but it wouldn't wind. I doubted if the first shot got anything and I stood there for a moment trying to finagle and then force the lever. It was no use. The only sensible thing to do was to admit defeat and come back another night. So I quietly retraced my steps back to where I had scaled the wall. Luckily the ground was higher on this side of the fence and I could just get over it without stepping on anything. I carried Terry's amp back to the car and started to drink the rest of the wine. I started shooting off the flash just for the hell of it when all of the sudden it started to wind again. I took three shots of my dashboard just to make sure and then grabbed Terry's amp and went back and scaled the stone wall once again. I knew I would never have the nerve to come back here again.

By this time I was drunk and I fell over the wall, scraping my back as I landed hard up against a tree. I could feel the burn on my skin and I thought I must be bleeding. I got up and ran towards Sibylla.

There I was greeted by another surprise. The black orchid was gone. It wasn't on the ground and it wasn't anywhere in sight. Someone had removed it. They must be watching my every move.

I was too drunk to care or be afraid. I took thirty-one shots in less than a minute, each flash lighting up the reflecting pool. Sibylla was resplendent in her pale beauty and when the last flash went off I didn't hesitate. I walked right up to her and kissed her parted lips, trying to force my tongue in between them. She was cold, lifeless, and I cut my lip on her marble smile.

"Say something!" I shouted.

A light went on in the mansion and I turned to run. Then lights started going on everywhere. Flood lights, sensor lights, the whole mansion was lit up now. I heard dogs barking, and they were coming my way. I got to the wall and scaled it, just barely in time to beat a snarling German shepherd from taking a bite out of my ass. I grabbed Terry's amp as I jumped into my unlocked car and sped down Brookville Road to East-West Highway and home.

I had made it.

||||

The next morning I woke up with a terrible hangover. I seriously thought I might have dreamt the whole thing. But when I got in the shower I knew it was real. The burning sensation on my back told me so. I turned off the shower and stepped out of the tub to get a look in the bathroom mirror. It hadn't fogged yet, but I still couldn't see anything since the pain was coming from right in the middle of my lower back. I got a hand mirror out of the hall closet so I could see. There was a huge welt going from the middle of my back down to my butt that was caked with dried blood and indented with lines as if someone had scraped me with a large fork. No doubt about it, last night's events had happened! There was nothing else to do but get back in the shower and rinse off. And though it stung pretty bad at first the throbbing became less painful and I realized the cut wasn't very deep. My head was hurting me more than my back so I decided to go to the YMCA for a swim. That usually helped with hangovers.

When I arrived there at about noon there was the usual crowd of old geezers taking their daily swims. I admired these guys. Seventy, eighty years old, still exercising—they were an inspiration. They could never figure out why I was always there in the daytime.

"You couldn't be retired, Cowley, what do you do for a living?"

"I'm a musician."

"A musician? But what do you do for a living?"

One of them saw the marks on my back and they all gathered around. "What happened to you, Cowley?"

"I got carried away."

"Looks more like someone carried you away! Does it hurt?"

"Only when I take pictures." Nobody laughed. "It's a private joke."

Half of the pool was being used for aerobic classes so there were only three lanes open for lap swimming. I picked the least crowded and swam my fifty laps. When I finished my hangover had lessened considerably and I returned home, ready to face the day. Or so I thought.

After eating a bowl of cereal with raisins and bananas I made a cup of coffee and sat down to unload the camera. As I had done hundreds of times before, I lifted up the rewind crank and depressed the release button. As I started to rewind there was a slight tension as there should be but then I heard a grinding sound and the tension increased significantly. I kept rewinding, using much more pressure than usual, until finally there was no more pull, which normally meant the film has rewound. I popped open the back of the camera and instantly had a sickening feeling in my stomach. There was the film and it wasn't on the take-up spool. Not only that, it was torn in half. I had exposed the film! I quickly shut the camera, hoping against hope that I might be able to salvage something. Then I grabbed my coat and headed out to Industrial Photo in Silver Spring.

Say what you want about Silver Spring (it's a dying town, too much crime, that it will never live up to its past glory), it has two institutions that Bethesda, with its trendy restaurants and high-priced real estate, can't touch: Industrial Photo, the greatest photography store in the Washington area, and Dale Music. Both have survived the sad decline of downtown Silver Spring and I predict that both will be there long into its renaissance that will include a renovated Silver Theatre which was recently purchased by the American Film Institute. If anyone could help me with my problem, it would be the pros behind the counter at Industrial Photo.

I came through the back entrance from the public parking lot in the rear. When you walk in you go up a ramp with award-winning photos on each side into the back of the store. It's huge, at least ten thousand square feet. There you might see a twenty-foot blowup of Marilyn Monroe or a thirty-foot mural of the Swiss Alps. There are backdrops of every kind to choose from. But this time I wasn't interested in any of that stuff and I marched straight for the development counter. There I saw Bobby, who had worked there for years with his ponytail and his ubiquitous package of Lucky Strikes in his front pocket.

"Hey Austin. Long time no see."

"Hi Bobby. Look, I got a problem." And I handed him the Pentax K 1000 camera.

"I used to own one of these. Boy she's a beaut, ain't she? Best camera you could buy for the money!"

"I think I exposed the film."

"The only way you could do that is to open it without rewinding the film."

I told him what happened and he gave a little grimace. "Let me take it in the dark room and see what I can do."

He was gone for at least ten minutes and when he retuned he wasn't smiling. "Better shoot another roll, Austin. You burnt this one real good. How the hell did you do that anyway? I've never seen the film ripped in half like that."

"Can you salvage anything?" I pleaded.

"Well it's a fool's errand, but I could send it out to Kodak with special instructions. All you're gonna get is a bunch of blurs, and that's if you're lucky. Besides, it'll cost you double just for them to look at it."

"Send it!"

"OK Austin, if you insist, if it's that important to you."

"It is. What's the time frame?"

"Give me a call in a week. I should know something by then."

"Thanks."

"Don't thank me. You're not gonna get anything."

Next Tuesday I called and got Bobby on the line. "Bad news, Austin. Kodak wouldn't even touch it. They took one look at my instructions and sent it right back. No charge though."

"Shit!"

"I did think of one other possibility. There's a place in Baltimore that does film restoration. Old silent movies and the like. I have a friend who works there. If you want, I could ask him to take look. He's somewhat of a magician when it comes to any kind of film."

"Any chance his name is Merlin?"

Bobby laughed. "Austin, you're a piece of work!"

"I owe you one, Bobby."

Two weeks went by and I hadn't heard anything from Bobby, so I called.

"Bobby's on vacation. This is Edna. How can I help you?"

"Did any prints come back for Cowley?"

"Hold on please."

I could hear her rustling through the orders.

"Mr. Cowley, there's a packet of negatives here…"

"Any prints?"

"No, but there's a note from Bobby. 'Tell Austin I did my best.'"

"I'll be right in," I said, and hung up the phone.

She looked like an Edna. Very austere and businesslike. Her hair was short and severe, and she wore a tight-fitting skirt which made her look even more overweight than she already was.

"Here they are, Mr. Cowley…Wow! Fifty-seven dollars for negatives that didn't print! I hope you're happy with them."

"Can I use the light table?"

"Right over here," and she led me to the table and went to help another customer.

I dumped them out on the translucent white table with a light bulb underneath. There were only four rows, much too few for a roll of thirty-six. It didn't matter. The ones that weren't totally blank had no image on them, only streaks of light and dark from when I opened the camera. Maybe Bobby's friend thought I was an abstract photographer. Then I realized I had only ten dollars with me and began to feel depressed. I started to insert the worthless negatives back in the envelope when I noticed there was a half a row still stuck down at the bottom. I pulled it out and placed it on the light table. There were just two frames and one was blank. The other had a blurred image on it. It was almost totally black but at least it was something. I wanted a print of it.

When Edna was free, I asked her to come over to the table.

"Can I get a print of this?"

She looked at the negative. "What on earth for? Bobby would have printed anything worth printing. You won't get anything."

Edna reached for a photo magnifier and placed it over the negative.

"Uh oh…We can't print this anyway. Nobody will print this for you."

I grabbed the magnifier from her and took a look. The image was seriously blurred but out of the darkness it appeared a breast was protruding from a pale, shadowy woman. I lifted up my head to see a disgusted expression on Edna's face.

"I swear to you it's only a statue!"

She relented slightly. "OK. But it better be. I could get in big trouble for printing pornography."

"I promise you it's a marble statue, nothing more."

She took me at my word and gave me a form to fill out for a five-by-seven print that would be ready by Friday at noon. Then I thanked her profusely and told her I would pay for everything then and left.

On Friday morning I got a call from my agent to play the afternoon tea at the Watergate Hotel from three to five. The pay was only fifty bucks, but a gig was a gig and I took it. At noon I went into Industrial Photo. Edna wasn't there, and there was a long line of people on their lunch hour waiting to pick up their photos. I had brought along the paper for just such a scenario.

Behind the counter an Asian woman was doing her best to take care of the ten or so customers in front of me who all seemed to be in a hurry. I felt sorry for her. "They should have at least two people behind the counter for lunch hour," I thought and began to read the paper. By the time I worked my way through to the style section, another employee from across the store came over to help out. As a group of customers shifted over to be helped by him, I became second in line. There was no one behind me and I began to take notice of the woman behind the counter.

She had black hair with thick bangs in front that covered her forehead. In the back it fell carelessly down on her shoulders while some of it spilled back over her ears. She was tall, maybe five eight, and had a graceful way of moving her slender body. I wondered if she was a dancer. Her loose-fitting black slacks were secured by a thin white belt around her waist. Over a purple blouse, she wore an embroidered jacket of green and gold. On it was a pattern of birds flying over mountains surrounded by clouds, and then the pattern would repeat until you felt like you were looking at a heavenly scene. She obviously spent a lot of time on her appearance. That's why I couldn't figure out why she choose to wear the glasses she wore. They were straight out of the fifties, with their catlike pointed frames, and seemed out of place with her other, tasteful attire. They made her look somewhat comical and I decided she wore them to keep men at a distance as much as anything else. I guessed she was in her late twenties or early thirties. After finishing with the customer in front of me, she looked up.

"What can I do for you today?" Her voice sounded musical and was accompanied by a warm smile.

"I'm surprised you're still smiling after dealing with that angry mob."

She laughed. "Oh, it goes with the territory...Besides, I kind of enjoy being the center of attention."

"Uh...I had a special print being made up...they were having all sorts of trouble with the film. It's black and white. Edna said it would be ready by noon today."

"What's your name?"

"Cowley."

"So you're the one that nobody wants to deal with. You don't look like the difficult type to me."

"Who said I was difficult?"

Again she laughed. "Well, since you asked, Bobby said you were somewhat of a charity case."

"He said that?"

"And Edna said you were a pain in the butt, that you insisted on printing one poorly lit negative out of thirty-six that Kodak wouldn't even process. She said it was a naked woman or something."

"No, no...it's a statue, just a statue."

"Don't get upset, I'll see if it came in. What's your first name?"

"Austin." And almost by reflex I asked, "What's yours?"

"Li."

"Really?"

"Don't you think I know my own name?"

"No, it's not that. It's just I used to know a woman named Li."

"Sometimes I think that half the women in China are named Li."

"So do I."

This amused her. "Oh you do, do you? And just tell me what you know about Chinese women?"

"Only that they're beautiful," I said in a momentary lapse of sanity.

I knew I had crossed over the line and for a second she flushed with embarrassment. She didn't know whether I was flirting with her or was just a nut case. But she decided to laugh it off and went to look through the packets of orders that were arranged alphabetically behind us. When she turned around I felt a twinge of eroticism as I couldn't help but notice how sexy her body was.

"Austin Cowley. One five-by-seven black-and-white print." And she brought the packet back to the counter. "Is your statue as beautiful as all the Chinese women you claim to have known?"

"Um...it's not like that...she's more like a muse."

"How sweet. I'm a filmmaker myself. The source of one's inspiration is always fascinating to me."

Just then, she accidentally dropped the packet and we both reached for it. Our hands touched and I noticed she wore no ring. I picked up the packet and gave it back to her. "Here, you open it."

"You trust me that much?"

"Yes, I do."

She opened the flap and took the photograph out of the envelope. All I could see was the back of the photo.

"How strange...she definitely has a unique kind of beauty. A face to launch a thousand ships. What kind of flower is that in her hair? Are those snakes?" And she handed me the photo. "My goodness, your hands are shaking!"

As I stared at the photo, I knew immediately it was the first shot I had taken when I fell to my knees. All the other pictures after that were without the orchid. How fitting. Sibylla would allow me to take her picture, but only on my knees.

"There's a long story behind this picture."

Li removed her glasses. "I'd love to hear it."

Now I had about as much luck at picking up women as I had in high school picking up girls, but I had to believe she removed her glasses just to show me how pretty she was.

The next move was up to me.

"Maybe I could tell it to you over dinner?" was the best I could muster.

"Maybe? Or are you asking me out?" She was toying with me.

"Um...I'd really like to take you out to dinner, Li."

"See, now that wasn't so hard, was it?"

"Then you'll go?"

"Sure! When?"

"How about tonight?"

I get off at seven. Meet me at the back entrance."

"It's a deal!" And I paid what I owed and walked out of the store supported by the clouds embroidered on her jacket.

I returned to my apartment and killed an hour before I left for my gig. Then I put on my tux and drove to the Takoma Park Metro.

If I had my druthers I would wear a coat and tie to all my gigs, but agency gigs always required a tuxedo. Since they took forty percent, I could make more money on gigs I found myself but they were few and far between. I needed the agency more than they needed me, given the number of piano players there were in the city.

When I arrived at the Watergate, they had moved the piano to the center of the lounge. Before, it was off to the side near the entrance of the hotel. The lounge is very elegant with fancy colonial furniture and old paintings on the walls. The bar is small and at the far end. From the piano I could see out the large windows across the Potomac River where Key Bridge crosses over from Georgetown into Rosslyn.

When I played the Watergate, I tried to play as elegantly as possible, if only to blend with the decorum. I opened with "Misty," playing rubato with lots of arpeggios and pretty riffs. As the set went on, I began to loosen up and swing more. There were about thirty well-dressed people there, a good crowd for an afternoon tea, and the groovier I got, they more they seemed to enjoy it. At the end of my set I played a very slow blues version of "Black Coffee." Then I broke into the bass line to the Erskine Hawkins classic "Tuxedo Junction." Before I even finished the intro, a young couple jumped up and started swing dancing right in front of the piano. Some customers started clapping in time and when I hit the plink, plink, plink, Count Basie ending there was a lot of applause and laughter.

Not everyone was happy, however. Out of nowhere, a rich old lady came storming up to the piano. She was covered with makeup and had jewelry everywhere. In her hair, around her neck, and on her arms and hands. And she was red in the face.

"You don't belong here! Your music belongs in a bar! This is the Watergate and don't you forget it mister! I'm going to have a talk with the manager!" As soon as she delivered her tirade, she was gone. It was break time anyway, and I tried to laugh if off but I really thought she was going to get me fired.

As I got up from the piano, the young couple who had been dancing came up to me and said, "She might not like it, but we thought it was terrific. We stay here every time we come to Washington, and we're going to have a talk with the manager too!"

I thanked them and then descended the stairs to the basement cafeteria. (Musicians weren't allowed to break in the lounge.)

After fifteen minutes I returned to the piano to play my second set. I toned it way down this time; after all, I did this for a living. I guess the young couple prevailed, for when I passed the manager on the way out, he said, "Thank you, see you next time," and I left the hotel, looking forward to my dinner date with Li.

When I got back to Takoma Park, I stopped at Mark's Kitchen and killed a half an hour with a cup of coffee. I thought about going home to change into something more casual but I thought Li might be impressed with my attire.

When I arrived at the back entrance of Industrial Photo, Li was waiting there and I pulled into the parking lot and got out of my car. She smiled at my appearance.

"Don't you look nice? But now I feel like I should go home and change!"

"Don't be silly. I'm a musician and I just came from a gig. Where shall we eat?"

"I'm tired from being on my feet all day. Let's go over to the Shanghai." And then she added, "You can meet my friend Chen."

The Shanghai was certainly convenient, being right across the street. It wasn't crowded and we got a table next to the window.

"What instrument do you play?"

"Piano." And I told her about the old lady and the swing dancers and how I thought I was going to get fired.

"What a strange profession. You have to worry about losing your job for making people feel happy."

"Well not all the time, but today I did."

Then I noticed a very old Chinese man off in the corner adjacent to the cash register. He was an artisan and had all sorts of sewing materials, threads, silks, buttons, but no machine. He was doing it all by hand. In his little cubicle, there were also some flowers and incense and small boxes of what I guessed to be herbal tea.

"Who is that?"

"That's Chen!"

"That's your friend?"

"He's more than a friend, he's also my spiritual advisor."

"Really? What kind of advice does he give you?"

"Mostly personal stuff. Affairs of the heart, who to trust…he made this jacket I'm wearing."

"Amazing!"

"Thank you." She paused. "He's taking a reading on you…"

"A reading?"

"He's sizing you up. If he approves of you he'll come over to our table shortly. If not…well you'll just have to meet him another time. But don't worry, eventually he accepts all of my friends."

"It's nice to be judged."

"Better to be judged by a wise man than a fool."

The waitress came and we ordered dinner. They had a brief conversation in Chinese and then laughed.

"What was that all about?"

"Oh nothing. Just girl talk."

It shouldn't have, but it hurt my feelings. I felt like she was keeping secrets from me. Li picked up on it.

"Don't act hurt. All she asked was if we were leaving in a limousine because of your tuxedo. Now tell me about this statue."

She had a way of moving the conversation right along and keeping things lively. It was fun trying to keep up with her.

"Her name is Sibylla and she can see into the future."

I expected her to laugh but she didn't. "Predict the future or just foresee it?"

Up until then I hadn't realized the difference. Sibylla hadn't predicted any specific events in my life but seemed to have an overall view of what lay ahead.

"No, I think she just foresees it."

"And what do you think she sees there for you?"

And then I heard Sibylla's voice for the first time in over a year.

"Be careful!" was all she said, quietly but firmly.

I got cold feet. "Uh...nothing really. You see I'm also an artist, so I took her picture to do a painting of her. I thought it might be interesting." It sounded flimsy, even hollow, and I was afraid she wouldn't believe me.

Li became thoughtful for a moment. "That's not a very long story."

That put me on the defensive. "No it isn't, is it? I'm sure I'll think of some more details but right now my mind seems to have gone blank."

I was saved by the food. Lemon chicken and shrimp fried rice. The two women carried on another brief conversation in Chinese, and this time I didn't dare ask what they were talking about. Now I felt as if Li knew I was hiding something, and I was feeling angry at Sibylla for butting in.

Li, however, acted as if nothing was wrong, and was as warm and friendly as ever. Then I saw the chopsticks. I marveled at how easily she got as much or as little fried rice as she wanted by manipulating them with her fingers.

"Li...I've never eaten with chopsticks before."

She gave me a brief lesson in how to use them but I was hopeless. The chicken would always fall back on my plate before it reached my mouth. Finally, out of frustration, I took one chopstick and speared a piece of chicken and put it in my mouth.

"That's how the cavemen used to do it!"

"Chen is watching you."

I looked over to see his eyes peering in my direction. "Does it mean he won't come over?"

"Why would it mean that?" and she signaled for our waitress. "Could we have some silverware please?" And once again they said something in Chinese and laughed.

"I feel like I've failed some kind of test."

"Don't be so self-conscious. All she said was that she doesn't like chopsticks either."

I was relieved, if not a little embarrassed, but Li seemed relaxed and began talking about an idea she had for a film.

"I want to interview Chinese citizens who supported the crackdown in Tiananmen Square. Ordinary citizens and perhaps some low-level army personnel. Everyone in the West has heard what the pro-democracy movement has to say. By acting under the pretext of making a pro-government film, I could move about freely. Then I would juxtapose those images with the actual footage of the students being killed by the army. I think it would have a more powerful effect than a strictly one-sided view of the dissidents. Hopefully, the message would be understood: that a slaughter like that cannot be justified."

All of a sudden I felt like I lived in a harmless world of little old ladies and swing dancers. "Wouldn't you have to go to China to make such a film?"

"Yes, of course. But I return there often." She paused for a moment. "I'm sorry, Austin. Let's forget about worldly matters and just enjoy ourselves tonight."

She said she loved jazz and would like to hear me play sometime. I told her if she ever made a film I would like to score it. When the waitress brought our check, I paid it and left a solid twenty percent tip.

And then Chen came over. By the way he shuffled his feet I thought he might have Parkinson's disease. He carried a flower in his left hand, and with his silk robe, long gray hair, and Fu Manchu mustache, he looked like he could have come from central casting.

"Just be yourself," whispered Li.

He greeted Li with a formal bow and then turned to me and held out the white chrysanthemum, saying something in Chinese.

Li interpreted. "A flower for the lady?"

"Yes, thank you!" and I instinctively reached for my wallet.

"No no! Don't offer him money! He'll be insulted. It's a gesture of friendship."

I reached out and took the flower. "Thank you." He gave me a little bow and shuffled back to his sewing cubicle.

Li smiled. "He likes you."

"How do you know?"

"Trust me, I know."

"I'm glad," I said and handed her the flower.

"He's a great judge of character."

"I hope I don't disappoint him."

Then we got up to leave.

When we arrived at my car, I said, "Now you can ride in my limo."

Li started waving the chrysanthemum as if it were a magic wand. "One, two, three, is that a limousine I see?"

When the car remained a Dodge Dart, she feigned disappointment. "I must be losing my magical powers."

"Don't worry, you haven't lived till you've ridden in a Dodge Dart!"

"No offense, Austin, but I live just a few blocks from here. Why don't we walk?"

It was fine with me. Spring was fast approaching, and it was a pleasant evening. "Your wish is my command."

So she waved the chrysanthemum again and in my mind's eye I saw fairy dust following the arc of the flower as Li said, "You must get me home by midnight, kind sir!"

We walked down Second Avenue to Colesville Road and one block north to East-West Highway where we took a right past the Kinko's where I had blown up the photographs. When we reached 16th Street we had to cross over East-West Highway and continue down the hill towards the District. It's one of the busiest intersections in Silver Spring. I pushed the button for pedestrians, but the signal was taking forever. There was a break in the traffic. Li said, "Let's make a run for it," and started to move. I clamped down hard on her forearm to hold her back.

"Ow! You're hurting me!"

"I'm sorry. I just didn't want you to get hit by a car!" And I loosened my grip and took her hand in mine.

"I didn't know you were so protective."

When the signal finally changed, we crossed East-West Highway, holding hands. As we were going across my hand started to perspire, so I let go once we reached the other side. We walked for about ten yards in silence and then she retook my hand.

"It's OK, Austin, sometimes I think I need some protection."

At the bottom of the hill, just before the circle that separates Maryland from the District, was her apartment.

"You live in the Falklands?"

"Yes, I enjoy it here, and I can walk to the Metro. Plus I have the top floor apartment."

I looked at the apartment building. There were three levels, and up top there was a small round tower with windows that reminded me of a mosque.

"Is that tower part of your apartment?"

"Um…yes! I use it as a studio. I keep my film equipment there."
It seemed as if she was searching for words.

"It looks like a mosque."

"Yes, it does, doesn't it. I'm Hindu though…I wish those two religions would stop fighting. It's enough to make one give up on religion…my God is greater than your God!"

I walked her to the doorstep.

"Austin, why did you wear a tuxedo tonight?"

"I told you, I was coming from a gig."

"You couldn't have gone home and changed? Were you trying to impress me?"

"Maybe a little. What are you getting at?"

"I'm just trying to find out what you want from me!"

"Well first and foremost I want to be your friend…maybe even your best friend…"

In mock broken English she interrupted me. "How you say in America, lovers no can be best friends."

"That's a song lyric…"

"Oooh! Number one son extremely bright detective! Make Charlie feel so proud!"

"You're crazy as a loon. Besides we aren't lovers."

"But we might be if we continue to see each other."

I was silent. Then I said, "I'd really like to see you again, Li."

She reached out and straightened my bow tie. "Austin, I've been a naughty girl tonight. I've failed to tell you I have a fiancé."

"You sure did!"

"Are you sorry you asked me to dinner?"

"No. I had a really nice time."

"And I haven't ruined it for you?"

"No, you didn't make any promises."

"Then I had a nice time too. And I'd like to see you again."

She leaned over and gave me the slightest kiss on the cheek and turned to enter her apartment. "Goodnight, Austin."

Either it happened so fast or I was too slow to respond, but she was gone before I could do or say anything. I almost ran after her but better judgment prevailed and I turned and started to walk back towards my car. "She said she wanted to see me again," I kept saying over and over to myself until I finally believed it. What I couldn't believe was that when I got back to my car it had been ransacked. I had forgotten to lock it again. As usual, there was nothing in it to steal, and this time it started right up.

I drove home feeling lucky. Not because my car was running but because I had a new friend. First of all I didn't believe Li had a fiancé. She wore no engagement ring, and I doubted she would go out with me if she were planning to marry someone else. There must be another reason, a self-protective reason, why she told me that. I would find out soon enough. Right now I wanted to dwell on the positive. I loved the sound of her voice. I loved her smile. And I even loved the funny glasses she wore. There was only one drawback. I was beginning to believe in reincarnation.

JOHN GUERNSEY was born in Washington, D.C., on November 16, 1945. In the late sixties and early seventies, he wrote songs and played keyboards for the counterculture band Claude Jones. This led him to writing poetry, then short stories, and finally a full-blown novel, of which three chapters are included in this collection. He teaches jazz and blues piano out of his apartment in Takoma Park and plays every Friday and Saturday night at the New Deal Cafe in Greenbelt, Maryland. He is also a visual artist working in etching and mixed media drawings and shows his work locally. If you would like to contact him, his email is jaguernsey@yahoo.com.

Just for One Day

James Harper

I've never used my daughter's name, not in calling her, not in addressing her, almost never in referring to her. Instinctively, it's more natural for me to call her by an affectation like sweetheart or honey. Sometimes, I call her Blondie for her hair that we've trimmed just once; her mother and I can't bear to cut it since its golden color distinguishes her beauty, especially her high-beam blue eyes. But, mostly, she responds best when I call her by the nickname I gave her within an hour of her birth—Button.

The Button's always loved David Bowie. After the first time I played "Changes" for her when she was fourteen months old, cranking up the car stereo to the line "Still don't know what I was waiting for," the word "Bowie" made it into her toddling lexicon by the second hundred words. You have no idea how thrilling it is for a father who traces his passion back to Ziggy Stardust to hear his barely walking daughter shout out the name. More, she loved the whole Bowie catalogue, assigning her own little titles to songs too elaborate for an Under Two to pronounce. She called "Fashion" "Beep-beep," "TVC15" the "Uh-oh" song, and of course, "Suffragette City" became "Wham Bam." But whenever we play Bowie for any length of time, we always play one particular song without fail.

Here's why.

Just a few months before introducing her to Bowie, I had lost my job, fired just after the Christmas holidays by the worst boss I've ever served under, a man whose style of management fell midway between Neanderthal and Cro-Magnon. I discovered I fit into the job as well as a grizzly in a fish market when, after four grueling months of antediluvian task-mastering, he put me out of that misery to propel me into unemployment when the Button turned seven months.

Few events in life equal the depression you feel in unemployment, especially if it's from a firing. Nothing deflates the ego so much as the rejection of being told your services are no longer required as you spend each day futilely dissecting the corpse of the job history, combing for clues that might have made for a different, better result. As every question piles one on top of the other, the stack of wasted, emotional agony serves to magnify a reflection of failure. It raked my soul, rankling me to the core. Days filled with resume dispatching did little to relieve the bleak void, the empty rote of cover letters cut and pasted in the email world provided scant creativity, and so, little engagement. The one saving grace from the emotional squalor was it launched me into life as a stay-at-home dad, allowing me to spend time with the Button, doing the job I loved best—cataloguing the encyclopedia of her smiles. But even the eagerness I felt in the prospect of spending days with her did little to prepare me for the bumps that inevitably come, like the day our license tags were stolen.

That day in July when it happened, my wife and I didn't even notice. In fact, we drove home about twenty miles without them, unperturbed by police. We had just done some shopping at a favorite store when, after I unpacked the Tundra, I went to get the mail. As I passed in front of the truck, I noticed our tag gone. Thinking it had merely fallen off, I fetched the mail to discover on returning that the back tag was gone too.

Calling the police, Officer I. Grimes of the Montgomery County Police Department soon responded. A fair-haired man in his early thirties, he dutifully took down all the details, asking the questions I expected: where did it happen, when, what were we doing, and the like. When we finished, I asked him how I could get a copy of the report.

"You don't need one," he said.

Taken aback, I protested. "Suppose I'm stopped? And, don't I need a copy of the report when I go to DMV to get new tags?" I asked.

Grimes shook his head. "You don't need any of that," he said, "Just show whoever stops you this." He handed me a three-by-five ruled notebook page. On it, he had written his name and precinct, the report and blotter number. "That's all you need," he said.

"You're joking."

"I'm serious. If anyone stops you, just have them refer to that number and your whole file'll come up."

He shrugged when I told him that it surprised me that we had not been stopped on the trip home. "Tags aren't high on our list," he said.

Officer Grimes recommended creating cardboard tags to replace our stolen ones until they could be replaced. "Don't worry," I said, "I'm getting them Monday. It's not like I have anything better to do."

That Monday, the Button and I headed off to the DMV for new tags. As usual, she charmed everyone who laid eyes on her, developing a whole new set of admirers. And, as usual, she was as good as gold. New tags in hand, we came home. I figured that would be the end it.

Until September.

Again retrieving the mail, I came across an envelope from the DMV. Had I blown a red light? Parking? Low-grade panic shot through my mind as I opened it. Sure enough, a citation, indicating time and date of commission, showed color photos of our tags in the act of passing through a red traffic light.

But not on our pickup.

Our stolen tags showed on the violator's truck.

The creep who had stolen our tags blew a red light at 11:27 p.m. on a Thursday night less than a mile from our house in early September driving an early '80s Toyota painted red.

I felt a cold rage sink through my gut as I stood there by my mailbox reading the citation that said the state of Maryland was fining me $70 for a crime I had not committed. Even more, as a good citizen, I had promptly and properly reported the theft so that they would have had the information that I no longer owned the tags used in the violation. By September, I had secured gainful employment so, while the money wasn't the same issue it might have been, the principle galled me.

Calling the 800 number listed on the citation, I reached Officer Simmons, who calmed me by explaining that I would not be held responsible for the violation if I completed a series of complicated steps, including obtaining a copy of the original report for $10, faxing it and a letter along with the receipt for my new tags to the central DMV in Laurel, an outer northern D.C. 'burb. As I described the truck that actually committed the violation to Officer Simmons, I noted that it had an ironic bumper sticker.

"What's it say?" he asked.

I told him it was one of those bumper stickers featuring an eagle and a flag that became popular after 9/11. "It says 'Proud To Be An American,'" I said.

The laughter from Officer Simmons forced me to hold the phone away from my ear. "Buddy, you just made my day," he said as he calmed.

I spent the next days chasing down the items I had foolishly believed the police department in one area, the traffic division, should have had from another, the robbery division. The nightmare of red tape I had to negotiate shouldn't have shocked me. After all, I lived just a few miles north of D.C., a place where Kafka would have thrown himself off a bridge in maddened frustration. It shouldn't have surprised me that one part of my county government had no communication from another. Still, I had to take comfort knowing I had all the documentation I needed to prove my case to the DMV, again. More than anything, I felt the sour, sickly taste you feel as a victim—not only had the bad guy stolen my tags but now the government sought to fine me for his further crimes.

Whatever considerable frustration I felt, I had the ticket which, in a very important way, gave me ammunition against my victimization. In fact, I had an opportunity that few victims enjoy. The citation provided me with knowledge I could utilize to actually catch the creep who stole the tags. It furnished me with something to pit against the wave of anxiety, arming me with a tool to use against the desperate sea of hopelessness.

First, from the photo of the incident, I knew he drove a early '80s pickup. That in itself was most telling since few can be found on the road anymore. In the region of the D.C. 'burbs, heavily populated by silver-slate-gunmetal-gray Acura-Lexus-Nissan-Toyota late model sedans and SUVs, this guy drove a refreshingly old pickup that stood out like a fly in the snow. I figured from this that the vehicle was a family/friend purchase, that he'd gotten the old-by-D.C.-standards truck as a fix-up and, as such, he had no title or ownership documents. He had no reason to steal tags if he had good paper.

Second, because the red light violation took place within a mile of me, I knew he lived in my neighborhood. In the D.C. 'burbs, especially in the wilds of Montgomery, no one has much business after eleven o'clock on a Thursday night unless it's with the television evening news. The time stamp on the ticket showed 11:27 p.m.

Finally, I knew the guy was an idiot: he stole tags in the county in which he lived. He didn't even have the grace or good sense to book up to Frederick or across to PG County—both fewer than twenty minutes from the parking lot of the grocery store where he stole our tags. Every thief knows you don't shit where you eat. Plus, he got careless at a red light with felonious material on his automobile. Obviously, he didn't boost my tags while taking a break from his string theory equation.

Over the next weeks, I spent nights staring at my sleepless ceiling, working the angles to convince myself I could find this creep in order to exact revenge. Some painstaking planning, coupled with some footwork, and I could cruise the neighborhoods in my area to locate the red pickup, find the bastard and...

What? What would I do once I found him? Smash his windshield? Sugarcoat his gas tank? Introduce his face to every inch of my Louisville Slugger? No ending to any of the scenarios I concocted seemed appealing—not just from the standpoint of getting caught, even if that remained remote. New fatherhood just doesn't offer the same thrills a Halloween mischief-maker enjoyed in his youth. This wasn't Hell Night anymore. Besides, they were, after all, only license tags. No manner of frustration I felt at my life nor the bureaucratic labyrinth I had to negotiate justified the acts my mind designed. Still, simply knowing I'd have the element of surprise, giving me a clear upper hand, made the thinking about it delicious.

So, while I put away dreams of exacting revenge, I never stopped looking for the red Toyota pickup. As I ran the errands suburban fathers run, I did double takes on every red pickup I passed. It got to the point where all it took was a red vehicle—pickup or sedan, coupe or wagon—to receive scrutiny for my tags.

Then one day, my vigilance paid off.

Driving the Button to daycare one morning, I passed a red pickup. As it was early morning, the coffee jolt to my synapses had yet to fully kick in as I glanced at the license, passing on the right. Suddenly, after my caffeine-deprived brain signaled "hey, wait a minute," my foot came off the gas pedal, I slowed and allowed the pickup to pass me.

Sure enough, my tags stared back at me.

We both pulled up to the next traffic light, a sizable mid-county intersection. Here, I got a good look at the driver of the long-sought red Toyota pickup as I dug into my wallet for my police report. The woman driving the truck looked middle–aged—mid-thirties to early forties—her dark blonde hair curled into a perm, the kind I had thought they didn't do anymore. As I studied the automobile, I saw its red paint faded, chipped in some spots, an age that reinforced my feeling that no one held paper on it. Her gaze seemed locked straight ahead as she waited for the long light to change. I dialed 911.

Dispatcher 1241, a woman, came on asking for my emergency. I told her who I was and said, "I reported my tags stolen July 10th to Officer I. Grimes who took my statement." I gave her the report number.

"So what's the emergency?" she asked.

"I'm behind those tags right now." I gave the location of the intersection.

"You're kidding," she said, "What're the odds of that?"

I didn't tell her that, considering I had been hunting this truck for months, knowing what to look for, the odds stood better than normal. I just gave her a description of the driver.

"I've got no one to send out to you right now," she said, "We're between shifts here. How long can you follow her?"

"I'm seeing this through to the end," I said. I figured Red was on her way to work. From what I could see, she dressed like a D.C. professional: suit jacket, silk blouse, probably a pair of high heels in her handbag to switch out of her sneaks when she arrived at work. "I'm going with her all the way. Wherever she goes, I go."

"Don't do anything dangerous," 1241 said, "I'm going to stay on the line with you."

I had expected that. "I wouldn't think of dangerous," I said, "I've got my eighteen-month-old daughter with me." The Button cooed an appropriate comment. "I'm not taking any chances."

"Oh my God," 1241 came back, taking a maternal tone, "you be careful now."

I told her I didn't think Red saw us but, even if she did, what of it? She probably didn't do the deed herself. I had figured that her husband or boyfriend committed the hands-on theft—she just happened to be driving the truck that morning.

The light finally changed. "Hold on, Button," I said, "We're going for a detour." Red sped off, causing me to step on it to keep up. She took an elaborate series of back roads in an obvious path avoiding

355, the main corridor bisecting the county north to south. Most Montgomery County residents go to great lengths to steer clear of that thoroughfare where waiting for red lights lasts longer than pachyderm gestation.

Finally, Red pulled into the parking lot of a large shopping mall, driving with assurance to a spot near the large department store anchor, a location directly across the street from where our tags were originally stolen. 1241 asked me to safely get a good look at her so I could identify her to the soon-to-be-arriving police officers. I parked ten spaces away, near enough to see her well but too far for her to spot us unless she looked hard. She got out of her truck, obligingly looked in our direction, then turned toward the department store employee's entrance. From the front, she looked nearly as I had imagined her, the puffy wear of middle age showed in her face as she cast a prework scowl around her. I almost ducked as she turned in our direction. She walked into the building at that clipped pace that most Washingtonians—especially women in high heels—adopt as they head to and from work, a kind of Washington prestissimo march, as if walking to a tune from Bizet's Carmen or Rimsky-Korsakov's "The Flight of the Bumblebee," staccato in stilettos.

As she went in, the dispatcher told me that patrol cars were seconds away. I drove closer to the entrance.

Then instantly I was surrounded by cops. From each of the cardinal points, four cruisers seemed to converge on me. The first disgorged a tall, well-built veteran in a crewcut who looked as if he could have just stepped off a military transport. I found out later, he had two days left in his last week. The watch commander, Lieutenant Acton, talked to me in brisk, clipped tones, reviewing the information related to him by the dispatcher, then outlining his plan for what came next. How I rated a watch commander was sheer luck. Since the entire shift was changing, he was simply on his way to work.

"We're going to need you to identify her," he said. "You think you got a good look at her?"

"No question," I said. "I saw her as she got out of her truck."

"OK, describe her for me."

I gave him a better description than I had to the dispatcher, then added, "She's about five-four." This I had judged when she stood next to the Toyota's cab.

As I said this, two other policemen entered the department store. A relay of walkie-talkie communications went back and forth from the commander to them as they located the woman. When they came out, Acton said, "All right, this officer," he indicated the cop in question, "will take you through the store. When you see the woman, indicate it to him."

"Got it."

While Acton watched the Button, the cop took me to the jewelry department of the store. He cautioned me about how to approach. "We don't want her to see you," he said as he led me to a spot where I could see her but remained out of her line of sight. There behind the counter, setting up for a day she'd never serve, was Red.

"That's her," I said.

"OK, you're done," the cop said. "Let's get you out of here."

Quickly, he escorted me out of the store, returning me to Lieutenant Acton who briefed me on what would happen next.

"We arrest her then book her," he explained. "There's no record of this truck—even existing anywhere—no title info, nothing."

I told him that fact confirmed my suspicions. Obviously, I said, a middle-aged woman living in the D.C. suburbs working at a major department store chain doesn't commit robbery. I gave him my theory of the no-paper truck and the husband/boyfriend. "He got it from a friend or relative or a friend of a friend who had it on some abandoned lot."

"Go on with this theory," Acton said, clearly indulging me.

I explained that I thought that, one day when he, the husband/boyfriend, took her to work in another car, she asked him again—for the hundredth time—to go to the DMV and get the tags she needed to drive the truck that they had parked at their house. Now he's stuck. The problem for hubby-boy lay in the fact that Red had no idea how he got the truck. He couldn't go to DMV without paper and now, of course, it's too late to admit that the vehicle was illegal.

So he drove across the street to the grocery store where I'd parked our truck to shop. He spotted our Tundra, and quickly and discreetly, removed our tags.

"Could be," Acton offered. Then he met my gaze. "You know, that's got to be it."

"Only I feel bad," I said. "I mean, it's not like this woman did it. She's almost as much a victim as we were—maybe more so. She's stuck with the creep who did it."

"Look, you got nothing to apologize for," Acton said curtly. "You did something we could never do. We don't have the resources to track down this kind of crime. But you found the people who did this to you. You took an illegal vehicle off the street. It's got no registration, no legal tags, and no insurance. God forbid if it was in an accident. How do you think she'd feel then? What if she hurt somebody in a wreck only to find out she's driving a truck she had no idea was illegal?"

"I never thought of it that way. I guess she'd feel worse." I glanced far across the lot as they led her out of the store in handcuffs.

The commander pointed his finger at me. "Right. You did the right thing."

As I got back in my car to drive the Button to school, I felt a strangely wonderful sensation. Not often in life do we get such an opportunity at vindication, at turning the tables on victimization. My dreams of revenge came to an end without my having exacted it. What I had accomplished felt more like retribution.

I remembered that they say revenge is a dish best served cold. But who "they" is can be called into question. No one seems to really know the source for the saying. I've heard it attributed to the Sicilians, the French, the Jews—even Native Americans. My feeling, however, is that no matter whether the dish is cold, warm or piping hot, the dish of retribution is best served with company, in the presence of family. When a witness is there to share your reward—even someone under the age of two like the Button—it's more than sweet; it's exquisite.

Driving out of the parking lot, I told her that she had done well, that she should be proud. After all, we had caught a criminal. Together, we were "Heroes."

Just for one day.

Just another transplanted native in a city full of them, JAMES HARPER found himself stranded in the District over twenty years ago. Four unpublished novels and unsold movie scripts later, he lives with his wife and daughter in the northern suburb of Rockville, Maryland, where tagless gunmetal trucks can travel with impunity.

Goliath

DAVE HOUSLEY

We are trapped in the old silver mine again. Everything is black and cold. It is different but not unfamiliar and I realize almost immediately that I am dreaming, that I am in the episode again. Fifteen minutes, I think. All I have to do is get through fifteen minutes. Soon, as always, the temperature will become unbearable. I will get hungry, desperate. My breath will grow short and the black void will seem insurmountable. Although I can't see a thing, I know that we are hunkered beneath a beam. In front of us, or behind, a mass of rock and dust from floor to ceiling. I can't hear the heavy dog breath, his playful and sincere voice, but I know that he is here, somewhere, waiting for my call, my touch, waiting for me to give up, lose faith, to reach the bottom of my capacity for belief. He is waiting so he can teach me the lesson.

"Davey!" a voice calls.

I fumble for my line, but I can't remember a thing. Again, this is the dream. In real life, I almost never forgot a line. If we had to do more than two takes, it was almost always his fault. Although I'm far removed from my acting days, I could still recite most of the scripts verbatim, both of our parts, all five seasons.

"Daaaa-viiiiiid." Wait. This voice is different, not the usual dream, not his voice at all. A woman's voice. Now she is grunting, sighing. She whistles. Whistles? "Daaaa-viiiiiid," she sings.

I wake up with a start. Drool is plastered down my chin. I reach for my glasses. "That took long enough," Sandy says. "The dream again, huh? The coal mine."

"Silver mine," I say.

"Like I said, I never really watched that too much," she says.

"No offense," I croak. And I really mean it. This is one of the things I love most about Sandy. Her parents were hippies who didn't own a television. Child star? She could care less.

She's dressed in her running stuff. The bedroom in the condo is little, and she barely has enough room for a hurdler's stretch between the bed and the TV. She stands, leans over and grabs her ankles, allows her head to fall almost down to her knees. The phone rings and she pops back up.

After three weeks, I still love watching these private moments, the arch of her back as she wipes sweat from her brow, the bounce of her ass as she walks toward the phone, leans over, and checks the Caller ID. "Your mom," she says.

I hold my hand over the receiver and clear my throat. "Hey," I say, trying not to sound too hungover. How did last night end?, I think. Did we drink all our housewarming presents?

"You sound terrible," Mother says. Even through the phone, her voice is clear as a church choir. "Shouldn't you be somewhere?"

"Late service."

Sandy rolls her eyes, leans over to stretch her calves.

"We need a favor," Mom says. "We're going on vacation and the dogsitter fell through. We need you to watch Goliath."

"When?"

"Next week."

Sandy is doing toe-touches. "I don't know Mom."

"He'll only be staying a week, David. For goodness sake, we thought you'd be excited about it."

"It's just, I don't know." How can I explain? She's never really understood what it was like between us. Not really.

"He's not what he used to be, I suppose," Mom says. "But I thought that after all your little adventures," she pauses and I can practically see the montage playing in her head—the soapbox derby, the time I fell through the ice at the old pond, the two of us trapped in the mine.

"After all our adventures what, Mom?" I wobble toward the living room. I smell coffee.

Sandy blows a kiss and heads out the door in a trot. I watch her bouncing gently down the street in her easy runner's gait. Sometimes I can't believe how lucky I am.

"I thought you'd be a little more sympathetic to an old friend is all," Mother says.

"Look, Mom." How to say this? "He's not like ordinary dogs."

"I don't know what you're talking about, David."

Of course, I remind myself. She never did know, not really, not the full extent of it, what happened when the cameras were off. "OK. We'll watch him."

"We?"

"I mean I'll watch him."

She pauses. Just long enough to let me know she knows something is off. Of course, she doesn't say anything, would never come out and actually *say* anything. This is the Lutheran way. "Fine," she says. "We'll be there Saturday morning. And it really would be nice to meet this *girlfriend* of yours."

||||

"You are a freak," Sandy says. We're sitting on the little balcony, watching the traffic move back and forth on the highway. We're drinking Mexican beer and listening to Etta James sing the blues. "I can't believe you still haven't told them we're living together."

"It's not that easy," I say. "He's…religious."

I swallow, trying to hide how worried I really am. I've been dreading this day, when I can't hide it any longer. Sandy is beautiful, the best-looking woman I've ever spoken to, much less dated. More than that, she is cool. She knows the right bands and the right clothes and her friends look like extras from a beer commercial.

I am not cool. Thankfully, we're at an age when coolness is starting to matter less. She knows nothing of my embarrassing elementary school years, the awkward Christian middle school, the disaster of trying to fit into public school after the show got canceled, and Father lost the pharmacy. All she knows is that I am solid and reliable. I express my feelings. I have a good job. I dress like a grown-up, I have a savings account, I am reserved enough to convey the spirit of still waters running deep.

"So are we just never going to tell your father, then? What about your mother?"

"That's not what I mean," I say. But of course I can't explain what I mean.

"I'm going to put up with this once," she says. "Next time your parents come down here, you go up there, you have to tell them."

I kiss her on the forehead.

"You're a freak," she says.

She has no idea.

||||

"How do I look?" Sandy says. She's dressed in a long white skirt with a light blue tank top. Her hair is still wet.

"Like Olivia Newton John in *Grease*," I say. "Before she got all whored up, that is."

The doorbell rings and I jump.

"Calm down," Sandy says. She squeezes my arm, kisses me on the cheek. "It's just your parents."

My mother breezes through the door, followed by my father, and then Goliath. I'm surprised at how old my parents look. How long has it been? Since Easter. Six months. Mother is the Iggy Pop of elderly housewives, all stringy muscles, nervous energy, and silent judgment. She scans the apartment, looking for weaknesses, like a dog exploring the perimeter of a fence. She shakes Sandy's hand. My father waves hello and makes his way to the bathroom.

Goliath looks the same as ever, like a cross between a great dane and a Chesapeake retriever, all head and paws and the big grin he wears most of the time. He bounds behind my father, leading with his big head. He jumps on me and whimpers.

"Oh my god," Sandy says. My mother flinches at the lord's name. "He is sooo cute! You didn't tell me he was so cute, David," she says. She holds her hand out and he sniffs.

Mother is rooting around in the kitchen. She finds a glass and fills it with orange juice. Goliath trots down the hallway.

"We'll be running along," Mother says, "just as soon as your father's out of the bathroom."

"Could be a while," I say to Sandy.

"Not funny," Mother says. "We brought you up to respect your elders."

"Does Goliath have to go to the bathroom?" Sandy asks. I can hear him breathing heavy in the bedroom, rooting through something.

"He'll be OK," I say. "We'll take him for a walk later."

My father emerges from the bathroom. "Hey Davey," he says. "Thanks so much for taking care of your old buddy there."

We exchange the usual pleasantries and they make to leave. Goliath runs in from the bedroom. He nuzzles my father's leg. Sandy rubs his head. "He is just adorable," she says.

"So are you over here…a lot?" Mother asks.

"We're dating, Mom," I say. "That's what people do when they date."

Mother packs her purse and my father stands by the door. While all this is going on, Goliath nudges my leg. He looks at Sandy and then back at me. He shakes his head. His mouth is set in a frown. The look in his eyes is something between anger and sadness.

"IN SIN?" he mouths.

||||

Goliath punishes me by cuddling up to Sandy. We take him for a walk and he stays by her side. She throws a stick and he retrieves it, tail wagging.

I know for a fact he hasn't retrieved a thing in at least five years.

When we make dinner he sits on her side of the table. She drops him scraps of tofu. He eats them, wags, and begs for more.

"Maybe he's a vegetarian," she says, rubbing his head.

He smiles and gives me the look.

Later, we're watching *The Godfather* on DVD and Goliath curls up with Sandy, lays his big head in her lap. She rubs his ears and he settles in.

When Sonny is driving across the Jersey wasteland, I look over. Sandy is asleep. Goliath is watching me. "Living in sin," he says. He tries to whisper but he can't. "For shame, Daaaavey."

Sandy wakes up. "What the fuck," she says. I point to the television. Sonny is getting whacked at the tollbooth.

Goliath jumps off the couch and lies down on the carpet. "Look at that," Sandy says, "Goliath doesn't like the shooting. It's OK, baby," she rubs his head and he wags. Soon, he is face down on the carpet, his paws in front of his snout.

"Awwww…so cute," Sandy whispers. She thinks he's sleeping off the walk, but I know what he's doing. He's praying. And not for a sunny day or a t-bone or a longer walk tomorrow, not the things a normal dog might pray for. He's praying for us. He's praying for our mortal souls.

||||

"Did you give me a, uh, *Creed* CD?" Sandy says.

"Creed? What are you talking about?"

She throws a CD case on the counter. Creed. *Human Clay.* "This was in my car," she says.

"Shit," I say.

||||

Sandy has had too much wine. She's wedged into a corner of the sofa, snoring lightly. She's wearing shorts and a tank top and I can't help but stare at her.

"We need to talk, Daaaavey," Goliath says.

This is what I was afraid of.

"It's David now," I say.

"You'll always be Daaaaavey to me, Daaaaavey," he says. It's been so long, I forgot how irritating that voice was, the way he pulls his syllables out so slowly, overpronounces everything, like a carnival barker on barbiturates.

"Things are different now. I'm different."

"I think you might be lost, Daaaavey," he says. His big face, square and earnest, looks up at me.

"I'm not lost. I'm happy. Finally. Look at that," I wave at Sandy, her shorts hiked up, her adorable face smushed into the sofa. Even her drool is cute.

"It's like the time we were lost in that silver mine, Daaaavey," he says. "You remember, Daaaavey?"

"That was a long time ago."

"And I told you that we didn't need a light. That god's light shone on us no matter where we were. Even in the deepest, darkest place, even when it seems like nobody cares."

Sandy rubs her eyes. "What's going on?" she says.

Goliath puts his head down and pretends to be sleeping.

I point to the TV. Jon Stewart makes a face and the studio audience roars.

Sandy rubs my leg. "Let's go to bed," she says.

||||

It was around puberty when I started to drift away from Goliath, away from the church. Before, I wanted to be with him all the time. But a thirteen-year-old boy wants to be alone in the bathroom, in the mall, on the bus to middle school.

When the show was finally over, all I wanted to do was distance myself from *Davey and Goliath,* from the church, the family, the whole thing. It's not easy growing up a child star. You add the church thing in there, even worse. The family thing, it's almost impossible to live a normal life.

I see that *Harry Potter* kid in the tabloids today—chasing women, appearing naked in some play—and I understand completely.

||||

I'm frying eggs when Sandy and Goliath get back from their walk. She hands him a treat, fills his water bowl. "Have you seen my birth control?" she says.

Goliath whines. I stare at him, trying to make eye contact.

"So have you seen it?" she says. "Weirdest thing, I can't find it anywhere."

"Must be up there somewhere," I say.

"Weird," she says.

Goliath walks into the living room and lies down.

"Fuck," I say.

She goes upstairs, comes back down a minute later. She throws a bible on the counter. "What are you trying to do here?" she says. "You wanna start going to church again just tell me. This is getting creepy, David."

"It's not me," I say. "You don't understand."

Goliath waddles up, rubs his head against her legs.

"Oh really. Who is it then?" she says.

I don't know what to say.

She walks back upstairs. Goliath follows.

||||

"Pray with me, Daaaavey," Goliath says.

Sandy is out shopping. Her sister, Allie, is coming for dinner, veggie burgers, corn, and beer. "I'm not going to pray with you, Goliath," I say. I open the bag and start shucking corn.

"You *are* lost, Daaaavey," he says.

"I am not. I'm home."

He lies down, puts his paws together over his nose. "Dear Jeeeee-sus," he says, "Daaaavey is lost again. Please help Daaaavey, Jeeeesus. Help him find the light. Like that time we were lost in the old silver mine and I said…"

"You gotta stop this," I say. "I can't have this shit going on much longer."

"What are you talking about?" he says. His eyes are so innocent, so sure.

"The whole thing. The praying, the birth control, the fucking Creed CD."

"You think I'm just going to sit here and let you commit these siiiiiins," he says. "I can't let you do that to yourself, Daaaaavey. I love you. God loves you."

I stand there for a moment. Our eyes are locked. I think about all we've been through, the little "adventures," as my mother calls them. But those weren't real, I remind myself. They were scripted, written by the Lutheran Church, for fuck's sake.

"It stops now," I say. Before he can respond, I go outside. I hose down the cooler and make sure we have enough gas in the grill. From the lawn, I can hear his mumbling, the rising and lowering of his voice, pleading for my soul.

||||

"And you won't believe what this one stuck in my car as a joke," Sandy says. She finishes her beer and throws the Creed CD onto the picnic table. Allie howls. She is, like her sister, not a Creed kind of girl.

"So seriously," Allie says. "I was half-thinking there might be some kind of announcement or whatever, you know…"

"What?" Sandy says.

Goliath's ears prick up. He sits, wags his tail. After a whole evening of moping, he is finally coming to life.

"You know," Allie says. "Like some kind of…ring…or whatever."

"Oh god," Sandy says. She laughs, quick, like a snort, and punches me in the knee. "Not yet. Nothing yet, Al. Premature. Just the sin. The living in sin is going nicely."

Goliath lies down again. He tucks his head between his paws.

"Bathroom," Sandy says. She finishes her beer, and goes into the house.

Goliath follows.

"You want it, you got it," Allie says. She pushes the Creed CD into the player. Soon enough, we're singing along: *"Can you take me Higher?"* we sing, each of us doing our drunk imitation of the singer's sober imitation of Eddie Vedder, *"to a place where blind men see? Can you take me Higher? To a place with golden streets."*

Something crashes and we turn off the music. Everything is quiet inside. "What was that?" I say, standing, already running into the house. Sandy is in a heap at the bottom of the stairs. Goliath sits next to her.

"Pray with me, Daaaavey," he says.

"I will not!" I say. There's something in his eyes. "You did this," I say.

"Who are you talking to?" Allie says.

Sandy is not moving. Goliath wags his tail once, looks me in the eye.

I get down on my knees. "What are you doing?" Allie says.

"I'm praying," I say.

DAVE HOUSLEY's work has appeared in Columbia, Gargoyle, Nerve, Sycamore Review, *and some other places. He's one of the editors of* Barrelhouse *magazine. His collection,* Ryan Seacrest Is Famous, *was published in 2007 by Impetus Press. You can check out more at ryanseacrestisfamous.com.*

Baptism

William Jackson

In October Julian knew that his class had begun a rebellion. A substitute, he did his best to project calm but a smell hung in the air: It pulled his students along, making them into wild animals. The department head couldn't be bothered with the class; these were quarantined students, after all. With the spirit of a crusader and nothing to lose, Julian abandoned required material and went further—he spoke out against his eighth graders so that he might rattle them into action.

It was the first cold day of the year and radiators pinged to life in the building. "Who is the Wild Man?" Julian asked the class.

Niles raised his hand. "The Wild Man? That's Rudy the Maintenance Man!" Niles assumed the character of the man who roamed the Bemis campus: he scowled.

"That's enough," Julian said, stopping the laughter. "Rudy's a good man."

Niles rose from his desk and bird-walked across the room, mouth shaped into a beak, eyes heavenward in a winged parody.

"Sit, Niles."

"Buk, buk."

"Catch him! Catch him!" someone yelled, and the class's laughter made Julian freeze. His uneasiness became a burn that moved down his throat and fastened in the lining of his stomach. He had the sensation of falling, even with his feet on the floor. Buk, buk, BUUUUK! Julian didn't have the strength to stop them. Beyond the classroom window, bright leaves twisted and swirled as though through stained glass. Niles began to gyrate, still in the maintenance man's body. "I feel the beat but I can't—wait, here it comes. Yes!"

"That's enough!" Julian shouted, and they came to attention, even Niles.

"Oh God, I can't take it," said Sarah, the well-behaved one. "I can't handle any more. My ribs ache."

"Niles," Julian said, "I don't mind your spirit, but the impersonation has holes. Maybe you'd like to practice with Rudy during free period."

Niles glared at him.

"The real Wild Man," Julian said, "has some polish. He's both rough and smooth. He can break things down, but he can build them up, too. Try to remember that."

When the classroom was empty Julian closed his eyes. He had red curly hair and a large wavy mouth that produced an apish look when he frowned. He thought of a painting of John the Baptist which hung in the school chapel. Julian had become interested in this picture of the man with long black hair and laserlike eyes. John ranted at onlookers, arms raised, face seething. As Julian thought of the picture, he was transported to a place that he imagined to be the Jordan River. John was talking to the crowd. Julian listened and took comfort.

He had been at Bemis for three weeks before he learned the harsh story of his English 8 class. The previous teacher, Mr. Heyerdahl, had raised a white flag after Labor Day. Julian was brought in because none of the other English teachers wanted them. No one had said a word of this to him when he was hired, although Ms. Thrush, the department head, emphasized that she expected him to finish the year.

Little by little, as he observed the grave nods and obligatory frowns of the other English teachers, Julian divined the truth. He was on his own.

Bemis had a reputation as a "good" private school where behavior issues tended to be small affairs—a late paper, a smug expression, too much exposed flesh at the midriff. The unspoken truth was that teachers were revered. The school had succeeded in making itself into a city on a hill, a society in which mentors walked with practiced dignity. Still, and this had to be admitted, even a veteran teacher could encounter a tough group, an unlucky preponderance of hard characters—hard being a troublesome quality in the young. Julian had walked into just such a class.

He hadn't expressed his feelings until a recent surprise meeting of the English Department. At the meeting, Julian learned that certain faculty, including a shadowy Dr. Fanshawe, had saddled him with their worst problems. With Heyerdahl's resignation, Bemis faculty had reassigned the class to Room 138, behind whose soundproofed walls shouting and mayhem would go unnoticed. Only now, as the class threatened to implode a second time in two months, did Fanshawe come forward.

"I should have thought it out," he said to all of them. "It was wrong to expect a newcomer to handle this class." He didn't address Julian but Ms. Thrush, the head of the department.

"Or even a veteran," Julian said, "I mean, to handle them." On the wall behind Fanshawe hung a photo of Mahatma Gandhi, the picture of magnanimity.

"Everyone makes mistakes," Fanshawe said.

"And who is everyone?" Julian asked. "Be specific."

"I don't see any need," Fanshawe said.

"But we are paid to be specific," Julian said, "and I'd like to be."

The other teachers looked away.

"There is hope for this class," Julian continued, "if we are forthcoming…"

The meeting ended soon after, at which point he found himself in Ms. Thrush's office for another impromptu meeting. She gave him a short speech on how to prepare for student evaluations. She told him he was doing a creditable job "given the situation." He was leaning against her office doorjamb.

"The situation?" he asked.

She paused to study him. "This is the toughest grade in the school," she said. "Every so often, a class comes along. When Mr. Heyerdahl resigned, we kicked around the problem. Everyone changing at once, sort of a crisis. Crazy eights! We picked you."

"But you didn't know me from the town preacher."

"Actually, I thought you might make them take notice."

He didn't want to explore that very much. She smiled, and he decided to take the high road. "I only wish someone had talked to me," he said. "I could have prepared."

"Prepared?" Ms. Thrush asked, her eyes widening.

"No one said a word to me about this class. It was a state secret."

"Aren't you being a little forward?"

"Why not?" he asked. "Do you want them yourself?"

She sat up straight. "For heaven's sake. We didn't want to scare you off." Ms. Thrush's eyes searched the office. "Honestly, we are grateful. I'm sorry."

This was better; the truth felt good. Julian studied the weave of his guayabera—the folksy note had pleased him this morning—and shrugged. "OK," he said.

She exhaled and shook her head a little too emphatically. Julian thought that Ms. Thrush was no different from some of his kids or their parents. If they had to be dressed down, so be it—to hell with their pride or standing.

Julian finds the life of John the Baptist instructive. John emerges from seclusion in the desert to preach to the people. He comes to baptize them in the Jordan. Dressed in haircloth, wrapped in a leather girdle, he has a strange, earnest manner that captures the attention of rich and poor alike. He lives a life of deprivation—neither meat nor wine, only locusts and wild honey—so his words carry authority. John is Christ's cousin, the son of Mary's cousin, Elisabeth. He is born in the same year as Christ. Before his birth, an angel heralds him the Precursor, the one who "paves the way"; now John heralds someone, he says, far greater than himself.

Julian found refuge from his troubles with the birds in his backyard. There was a competition for the feeder among cardinals, sparrows, and crows; the sparrows were winning if only because of numbers. One cardinal had been bumping into the back windows of the house. He would fly away when Julian came to the window, but as soon as he left, the bird tried again. Julian worried that the cardinal was hurt; perhaps genetics had been unkind and crossed wires. The bird might not survive the winter.

Julian found bird-watching a nice transition from school to his desk, where he was writing a book. Actually, he was finishing a rewrite. It was an expansion, a leafing out of his master's thesis on Edgar

Allan Poe in which he had argued that several of Poe's stories were not merely post-adolescent, drug-induced fantasy, but a culmination of the very same ideas explored by Hawthorne and Melville. In short, Poe was to be taken seriously. At one time Julian's ideas had to himself seemed rare and special, a collection of hothouse flowers that might wow the world. But recent literary criticism had turned back against Poe, and Julian's prospects didn't look as good anymore.

The Poe book had even become a sore spot in his love life. Julian's girlfriend of two years, Ariel, had moved in with him six months ago in what seemed to be a sign of better things ahead. Last week she had told him that the book was coming between them.

"It's not like I'm seeing someone," he said. "It's just a thesis that won't grow up."

"Substitute 'I' for the thesis, Julian."

Ariel was in the middle of two years of Freudian analysis, a prerequisite for being a practicing therapist, and often worked her skills at home. She paused, waiting for him to digest her statement. "Your struggle with Chapter Five is crowding out everyone else. It's the sucking baboon in the corner."

"The sucking baboon?"

"Yes."

"Which, the struggle, or Chapter Five?"

"Julian, it's sad and exhausting. If you don't finish this, and I mean the book, I'm going to leave."

It wasn't like Ariel to make declarations. In their two years together she had always been diplomatic. Now she looked at him with her steady brown eyes the way a child does, trusting completely. He was impressed. He asked if the Freudian therapist was behind this, and she said that he didn't make recommendations. So, it was a he.

No, Julian thought, the therapist nods and says, "Good girl." He envisioned an older man who threw out words like "anima" and "catharsis" as sexual foreplay.

"Is he good looking?" Julian asked.

"He's OK. A little Neanderthal-y. Big jaw and heavy brows."

Ariel called herself honest, liberated by the truth, but he'd have preferred more subtlety from her. He didn't care for the anthropological reference, either. She had once called Julian "Ape Man" and had found him attractive, so he didn't believe that she was turned off by a Neanderthal. That wasn't the only issue. It was dangerous to have a lover performing the role of his editor. Should they mix business and pleasure? Inevitably, he contemplated the next thought. He must finish Chapter Five quickly, and the others, or suffer the consequence of no sex. He knew Ariel well enough to know this. She wouldn't withhold sex per se but would become fixated on her ultimatum about his book. If he didn't write, she would not be in the mood, which amounted to the same thing. He wasn't sure he liked this kind of pressure.

At his writing table, he looked at Chapter Five. The last sentence read, "'The preoccupation with suffering in 'The Raven' is a precursor to Hawthorne's *The House of the Seven Gables*." Where to go from there? He started thinking about Ariel's "consequences" and got stuck—until he smelled lasagna coming from the kitchen. This he took to be a good sign. Ariel usually cooked when she was in the mood to fool around. Julian changed to a new poem, Poe's "Annabel Lee," and wrote in a white heat about sex and death.

Julian was right about Ariel's desire. That evening she served herself a large helping of lasagna and lit into a bottle of chianti. He didn't care for wine because it made him feel out of control, but when they were planning a night of it, why not? He had a glass, then another. Ariel licked her lips and stared at him with narrowed eyes.

"Let's go upstairs," he said, baring a tooth.

She changed into a black nightgown and unlike the Annabel Lee character was anything but dead; her skin glowed and flickered, her voice was breathy. In bed they wrapped around each other and rolled back and forth like cats. Ariel hissed and shrieked. Afterward there was no talk of his book, but he thought he detected a look of finality in her face. Would this be the last time with sweet cat woman?

Julian woke up to a horrible noise outside. Something was howling, perhaps a bird, as if it were being plucked alive. He hurried out of the bedroom past Ariel, whose arm draped off the bed. He turned on the outside light and searched the pachysandra, expecting to see the remains of an attack. But he found nothing. Perhaps the sound had been in his dream; still, a feeling persisted that one of his birds was gone.

On Saturday afternoon he stood in his backyard and watched the feeder. He told himself that he was planning his next paragraph, building toward a connection between Roderick Usher and Good-man Brown. He saw the idea more clearly of late—a glimmer that had begun to wink at him from a distance like an emerging train light. He was aware of these thoughts at the same time that he longed to see the cardinal.

"Hi Jules," Ariel said. "What's new?"

"I've got a line on Roderick Usher," he said. "I can't believe how long it's taken me—to see the house and the man."

"Seems like a good place to look," Ariel said. The squirrels had been busy in the woods. She tracked a flicker of movement among the trees.

"Looking into the woods is like looking into one's soul," he said, but Ariel was preoccupied.

"It's not the cardinal," Julian said. "He stands out in the open."

"He?" Ariel said. And after a pause, "Yes, of course. He's red."

Julian realized that he thought of the bird as a person. He was trying to say goodbye to him.

"You care about him, don't you?" she said.

"Yes."

On Monday morning in the faculty lounge, Julian stood next to the Latin teacher, Dr. Groshares. The man had immense feet for someone who was five-five. A long overcoat accentuated this fact.

"Good morning," Julian said.

"That's in doubt. *Deus* is dead."

Groshares plodded to the coffee machine and filled his mug; Julian could see his hand shaking as he brought the coffee to his mouth and burned his lips. Ach! Groshares reminded him of an old anxiousness; it came over Julian and he pushed it away, scat! It was a virus when it got started, everyone's self-consciousness joining in a web.

"Good afternoon, er, day," Groshares said.

The strangest thing—Dr. Groshares had made him notice the monster in the room. But this was no time, not now before English. Alas, there was the bell, nothing could be helped.

He leaned against the edge of his desk, arms folded, and watched the students file in: Niles with that ferrety look again, a fierce twinkle. The bell went off outside the open door, louder than a train whistle, making him flinch. The doctor is in.

The dog wants out. The wolf is at the door. What is his name, this thing that sits here looking at me. He is inside, outside, everywhere.

Julian laughed, yawned, then shivered.

"Hey. Mr. Ross. Hey."

"Niles?"

"I'm worried about you, Mr. Ross. Are you going to crack up?"

Gritty, rough-and-tumble John travels along the Jordan River preaching to anyone who will listen. His voice rings out, raps like a stick against a tree, seizes the collar. He's crazy, but crazy in such a way that people cannot leave. What is it, John? they seem to ask, what must we do?

John speaks about good works and charity. Everyone listens, hoping to be cleansed by the man "sent to baptize with water." He chastises them for coming to him in order to be validated. He tells them simply to give to others.

John's life ends in tragedy, as many of the lives of the prophets do. He denounces Herod Antipas for committing adultery with his own sister-in-law, Herodias. It is Herodias who plots revenge. When her daughter, Salome, pleases Herod with her dancing, he grants his niece one wish. Not knowing what to choose, she asks her mother. Herodias tells Salome to ask for the head of John the Baptist, in a dish. When Salome tells Herod of this wish, he is saddened because he knows he will fulfill it.

Soon after, John's head is carried in on a platter, his matted curls draped around in decoration. What does the prophet's face look like now? Still calm and sure?

Julian felt fine. He felt fine, really—until the nervous laughter started. The trouble was, he could never tell if a mighty act of nature were about to happen in his class.

The rest of that morning was hazy in his mind. As best Julian could recall, Niles had asked if he could perform a skit. Julian, who perhaps had a death wish, said, "Feel free."

"Guess who I am?" Niles stood up and began a routine that was half Rudy the Maintenance Man, half interpretive dance. This time no one laughed. You could hear the clock tick. Niles thrust his head forward, poised for the slightest sound or a shadow passing outside the window. Julian thought that Niles must be a cousin of the weasel: He could see him hunting rats, an expert rat catcher, a connoisseur of vermin.

Sarah-the-goody-goody looked as if she had just broken up with her boyfriend. In fact, everyone looked out of whack. Niles's head twitched, his chin jerked as though he were trying with difficulty to swallow. He began to act out the story of English 8: Mr. Heyerdahl's resignation, a parade of stand-ins, canceled classes. At last came Julian. Happy happy Julian, skipping in, full of fun and careless as the wind. Niles pointed to his shirt, to his heart. He skipped around the room, cupping his hands. Still no one laughed. But Sarah looked as though she would cry.

Julian felt a strange desire to see this through.

Niles made a soft cry and threw up his hands. Was this part of the skit? He searched the class for help but none came. His face contorted into a grimace, his body trembled, and Julian thought he heard a low moan coming from deep in the boy's throat, the noise of a predator in the woods.

Julian approached with his dusty chalk eraser. He told Niles to sit back down, then reached out to him; the boy slapped his hand away and kicked at him. Julian stepped behind Niles, seized him in a bear hug, and lifted him in the air. All Niles could do was swing his legs until Julian pressed him up to the teacher's desk and stopped that. Julian felt as if they were struggling on a small hot stage. There they remained in a suspension of time, a struggle without bodily pain, marked by grunts and cries. Julian let Niles down. He was aware that they were panting; beyond them, the class was as quiet as a congregation. Niles could join the flock now.

WILLIAM JACKSON has published short fiction and poetry in Word-smith *and* Helicon, *two Colorado magazines. A novel, unpublished, was named a finalist in competitions at Heekin Foundation and Ariadne Press. Jackson recently finished a new novel, "Grail Stories," which is a retelling of the Holy Grail myth. He is a full-time tutor in Montgomery County and D.C., and has taught at the Writer's Center. He lives with his wife and daughter in Bethesda, Maryland.*

Linens for Kandahar

Dennis Jones

1

She forgot to water the plants. That much she knew. To stop the mail, pick up Eddie's dry cleaning. A half dozen other things. The phone had rung at an odd hour, 2:47 to be precise, she had glanced at the winking clock in the microwave since nobody ever called in the afternoon and then she knew. The sudden uneasiness and cold flash of dreadful recognition—of what to call it exactly, she wasn't entirely sure—but she knew. She looked out of the window box in the kitchen above her sink. The violets in the small terra cotta pot needed watering, and she saw them coming up the drive. The black sedan pulled up slowly to the curb, and the two of them emerged from the car with their tightly pressed khakis, covers tucked smartly in their belts, then withdrawn swiftly and pushed neatly onto their heads, firmly—"Pisscutters" Eddie called them, she remembered that now. The phone stopped ringing. Then the doorbell and the long inevitable walk down the hall, past the framed pictures—of Halloweens past, of Russell as a ghost wearing a white bed sheet, of her second wedding, she and Eddie feeding each other cake without all the nonsense, of the official Marine Corps photo—and the lilies curling brown at their edges in the graying water in the vase on the side table where they placed the mail, the car keys, wallets, holding her breath with a tension like diving into the pool—the filter was broken, Eddie needed to fix that—and trying to reach the bottom but she couldn't hold her breath long enough, couldn't hold out, it was impossible. She had been a good swimmer once, her long pale arms pulling her through the water,

194

firm legs kicking in tight splashes, but that was long ago; it seemed like another time altogether, another woman. She opened the door and the two handsome men, babies really they were so young and keen eyed, began to speak, asking her name, although they knew, they had checked and rechecked, they had done this deal enough to get it right, because they had to, and told her about her son, what she already knew the moment she raised the watering can in the kitchen and the phone started ringing. They plunged ahead with the spare details from the cable, the handwritten letter from Russell's CO, telling her what she already knew but what she really didn't want to hear. In the morning, she would pull a fraying sweater over her head and she and Eddie would make the long trip to Dover.

||||

The Sergeant gave her a footlocker with Russell's belongings. It had a plastic bag in it. "With his personal effects," he said. Such a bland meaningless term. Personal Effects. A contradiction, she recognized now. There were his dog tags, some pictures of him and his buddies, with a brilliant mountain range filling the entire length of the picture. The one like she had sent to Abby. Sunglasses to protect from snow glare. Thumbs-up, shit-eating grins. Russell always had the Good Boy smile. It could break your heart with its earnestness. At the bottom of the bag were bed linens, a pillowcase, wrinkled and a bit dirty. The one Abby had made him. With the word HERO in glittering capital letters. And We Miss You in large magic marker script. And THANK YOU on the back. She brought the pillowcase to her nose and breathed it in. She thought she could smell the sweat from his hair still in it, the faint sweet scent of his skin, a burning smell lingering there as well, deep in the cotton, the dullness of dust from a far-away place. Could she smell his fear, or was it her own worry that he knew she carried? Impossible, of course but the thoughts persisted. The Sergeant shuffled his feet for a second bringing her out of it, but suddenly she remembered changing Russell's diaper for the first time, or what seemed like the first time, she couldn't really be sure. Overcome with pain from his delivery, delirious with fear over what she would do, how she would care for him, trying to unhook the safety pin from the cloth, she pierced her thumb and it started to bleed. She stuck her finger in her mouth as Russell wailed on the changing table, his legs straining, turning a splotchy red, and she was simply too tired, too overwhelmed to cry.

||||

She thought of the cliché of it, looking into the misting Delaware countryside, Eddie driving them home, the wiper blades dragging loudly against the windshield. How it would be when they took him from the metal box. The playing of Taps. Sitting dumbly, mute between her second husband and the honor guard, her two stepkids behind her from Eddie's First Go Round, as she called it, whispering to each other, as the bereavement escort comes forward with the folded flag, the cloth feeling rough, raised where the white stars laid across the blue, a quick precise turn on his heels and her thinking as if this flag could make any kind of difference now. Her hair had gone crazy in the rain, Bev had such beautiful dark hair, down to the middle of her back when she was young, and slowly, those gathered, family friends, Russell's buddies from high school, others from town with nothing better to do, this casual pattern of grief, and they would nod grimly at her, a sniff from somewhere behind the tented gravesite and tears, streaming down her cheeks, down Eddie's cheeks—he was always such an easy crier for a tough guy—and it would all be over except for the sound of handfuls of dirt dropping onto the casket from the palms of the people filing out.

2

Russell kept them hidden at first, until Mathison caught him smelling them, the fuck. The First Sergeant couldn't keep his mouth shut about the pillowcases and sheets sent by his niece and her friends in her third-grade class from the Jersey Shore. His squad leader, Menedez, took to calling him Downey after the fabric softener, a real smart guy, but Russell knew that secretly they were all a little envious and wanted new sheets for themselves, the selfish lowlifes that they were. Only a few months ago, he didn't even know these guys. And now they gave him shit about bedsheets. As though it were life and death. In high school he had not even thought of traveling to *Europe*, let alone Afghanistan. Despite 9/11, the thought of Arabic, the Taliban, al Qaeda was so foreign it was unthinkable. Now he woke in a bunk room to the call of the muezzin from a mosque a few miles off, bombed during the first few days of the war. When he had thought of the Marines before he joined, he thought mostly of the uniform, the tall white hat, the dress blues, of firing guns maybe, of new friends he might make. High school hadn't exactly worked out the way he had thought it would, so mostly he thought it would be *something, anything* to do to get him out of New Jersey. The idea of actually fighting somewhere, of killing someone was as distant as the horizon over the ocean. Still, he should have been more careful with the sheets. When he went to sleep he was; at night he would take the pillowcase out of his rucksack and place it over his pillow. When he lay down, he would bury his face in it and breath it all in as deeply as possible. An occasional mortar would fall into the base at night and he'd sleep straight through it, certain he was immortal. In the morning he would carefully fold the linens into a tight square and stick them back in his rucksack. He enjoyed the ritual of it, the special act of doing it every morning. It kept him calm, though he would never admit to anyone that he needed to be calmed. There was no telling when they'd get their orders and would scramble out of the airfield and head out. So he folded his pillowcases, the baby blue sheets, and hid them away.

||||

"Them little girls sending you any more sheets?" Jimmy Ha Ha and Stone Cold sat on their bunks, eyeing him. They called Russell "Automatic" because his last name was Browning. "Haven't heard," Russell said. "No telling." "Send her an email, Automatic," Ha Ha said. "We are fucking *networked* out here, man." Stone Cold sat next to him, stripping and cleaning his weapon. He wasn't looking at the two talking on the bunks, but he was listening. Stone Cold was tired of the rough sheets he was sleeping on. Felt like shit and god damn it was cold in Kandahar. Why the Taliban dudes wanted this place was way beyond him. But he wouldn't have minded some new sheets to sleep on his rack. "I'll give it another day," Russell said. "Heard we're moving soon." "We move when we move," Ha Ha said. "They'll send us the sheets wherever we go. Timbuk Fucking Tu, Tora Bora. Wherever. Those sheets will make it there before we do. Most likely heading into the Province anyway. They'll be back here when we get back." Total optimism, unconcern. It was funny how totally mundane things could overwhelm the situation, as if they weren't at war. Russell looked at the two guys and felt satisfied. Sometimes he felt a strange kinship to them, as though these were the boys he had been born with and these most certainly were the boys he would die with. That final thought wasn't always there, but it came on him sometimes like a swift cloud that covers the sun, then passes. He didn't know if any more were coming, but he wasn't giving his sheets up for anything. At night he laid his head on the pillow and in the dull tang of the fabric Russell thought he could smell the sea spray from home. And in that scent he thought again—for how many nights now he could not count—of Melissa and that time on the beach before he left. He had built a small bonfire off in the dunes. The chill of the late summer came on fast after sundown and the embers from the driftwood kicked up in the ocean breeze and spiraled upwards like the petals from a blooming clematis vine. Cord grass rubbed behind them, as they talked haltingly of their lives after high school. She had wanted to design dresses. Russell had been to see the recruiter, sitting with such casual authority behind a card table draped with velvet fabric and the Marine Corps symbol on a red flag. And then she stiffened and started to cry. Russell touched her hand, gently, then turned her face, her makeup smudging beneath her pretty eyes. And then the slow terrible slide in his stomach and it was happening, all things falling away as if this was the last moment between them—its awkwardness, its tenderness, its desperation in the sweaty rush, the grit of sand rubbing between their stomachs, caking their ankles, then the chill of the beach and the snap and pop of the fire and the smoldering smell filling his nose again. Lying there in the dark of the airbase, the heavy breathing of his comrades in the darkened bunk, it was as if that time and that moment, the tangle of Melissa's hair between his clutching fingers, never existed. Kandahar and all the space between that moment and this made it like that. His days were consumed with the monotony of waiting, cleaning gear, packing kit. General fucking around. A game of pickup basketball in the heated dust. Kandahar was so bright a spot now in his mind that nothing else could enter its light. Melissa and that night were more gone than real. He knew now what he didn't know then: that he could either live or he could die and that the line of work he had chosen, this Marine's life, could give him either without any concern for his preference. The next morning the orders were given. They were off to resupply the fire teams in the south, heading towards the Pak border. Russell stowed his sheets, packed the rest of his gear, and loaded onto the Hummers, then ran onto the Chinook. The helicopter lifted away, sending sand and rocks in a great circled blast and they were flying, banking over the river. They were gone, these boys, lost in their thoughts, staring at their hands, at their dirty boots, ahead into the too-bright sun. Gone, into the dust and towards the mountains, they seemed to be everywhere, Russell marveled. Death was always straightforward.

3

Why her mother didn't tell her Russell was coming home was beyond her. She heard her on the phone with Aunt Bev. Abby thought of her church dress she would wear the night he would come to the house for a visit. She had sent him the sheets as a Christmas gift. She thought Russell would like something soft and nice to sleep on. She thought she and her friends from school could make them in the basement, and then hang them on the clothesline so the fresh air could blow into them and make them smell nice. Russell had been gone for so long now she sometimes couldn't remember what he looked like. Her Aunt Bev had emailed a picture of him and two buddies, standing before a brilliant snowcapped mountain range, the sky so blue it seemed almost impossible, and she printed it out and kept it in the corner of the mirror in her room. She thought it would be fun to draw on the pillowcases with her friends, write notes to the boys who would get them and that Russell would like it and it would smell like home and she wouldn't feel so sad about him being gone and not know why she felt so sad. Russell was so far away that it didn't make any sense. The pillowcases and the sheets made sense. The pretty writing she drew on them made sense. They were there, in her basement, smooth to her touch, stretched tight beneath the palms of her hands. So she took the markers to them, took sequins and lined the edges, took glitter and glue and wrote her messages on the linens telling Russell they missed him, that he was a hero, though she wasn't exactly sure what she meant by that, and that they all wanted him home soon. She thought of the previous Thanksgiving, before Russell went away. He was so big, she remembered. Russell seemed quiet, but he picked her up anyway and kissed her on her cheek and her stomach turned over, she wasn't sure why. He smelled sweaty, she remembered and sweet from some cologne he must have put on before he came over. She remembered waiting for him to arrive, she always loved Russell, how he filled the room. She loved him in a way she couldn't quite describe and it made her uncertain. She was anxious for him to come to the house, anxious for him to hold her hand, it wasn't like anything she really could name, but she knew it wasn't bad or anything, it was just a slow jumpy feeling that made her skin feel prickly and cool. He didn't say much during that dinner, just forked at his food, but smiled at her mother when she said something, put his arm lazily around her shoulder and read her a story from her Madeleine books, kissed them all good night and gave them hugs that lasted longer than most before he walked down the sidewalk with Aunt Bev and Uncle Eddie to his car and drove off into the night. Why her mother didn't say anything about Russell coming back was puzzling to her, she heard her on the phone and then later whispering about it with her father. But still they didn't say anything. She thought the dress would be nice. She thought she would look great. Abby loved to dress up with her girlfriends, loved to tell them how beautiful they looked and if they would only try this scarf or this blouse they would look so great. Her sweetness was unblemished and the idea of the sheets just came to her. So she did it, patiently working the paints and the markers into the fabric until she was satisfied it looked right and that Russell would be pleased. Blue was his favorite color. She wanted him to be happy and would ask him again when he came back if he liked the sheets and if he would still use them when he settled back in. Abby thought of how excited she was about the project, eager to get them into the mail—it could take weeks, she would have to ask the postman how long. But she wanted it to be right. Before she folded the cases, before she wrapped them in Christmas paper and packed them in freezer bags to preserve their smell, she hung them on the line so the sea spray would fill them with their saltiness. A heavy wind came out of the northeast and blew the linens straight out and stiffened them like flags snapping in that crazy breeze, and as she watched them flutter on the line, all she could think was come home, Russell, come home, where you know us and you know how the wind here feels.

DENNIS JONES has had short stories published in the Crescent Review, Gargoyle, *and* Georgetown Review. *He lives in Falls Church, Virginia.*

Metal Church

Matthew Kirkpatrick

We worship power chords. On Sunday morning we fill the pews of Metal Church, sing hymns to the Metal Gods, throw our goats in the air and shake them, as if to say that we no longer care, and listen to the Hessians in the guitar choir with their axes tuned to drop-D thrashing in their ragged leather robes until way past brunch. And, if we don't have to be home with our wives or have gotten all of our chores done on Saturday, we will stay and listen well into the afternoon.

Those of us who still have long hair throw it around as we used to; some of us (myself included, I would like you to note) cut our hair to hide among the non-Metallic as if to say that we have forgotten our roots, forsaken our black Metal God; that we now cringe at the sound of a distorted barre E on the twelfth fret, when in fact the sound makes us shiver as the chord rings out and breaks up into a long feedback whine. We pretend and deny that tweaked-out Locrian scales fill our heads during the workday when we should be reading emails or paying attention to conference calls. They believe that our black clothes are merely a fashion statement and that we have packed up or sold our black B.C. Rich "Bitch" electric guitars. I will tell you this—we still have them, and they are tuned.

You thought it was something nice in my headphones at work, didn't you? A little R.E.M., perhaps, or maybe some Phish? We hate that shit.

Each Friday as I scrambled to bullshit my way through another timesheet, you leaned against the fabric wall of my cube and smiled. I eyed you suspiciously at first, thinking that you pretty much had me figured out—that you knew I sat in my cube and did a total of thirty minutes of actual work most days and spent the rest surfing the net for free pornography or MP3s by bands like Iron Maiden or Confessor.

Man, I love Confessor.

Anyway, you stood there and waited patiently for me to fill out my form and email it off to you each week an hour or two late, and you smiled and thanked me. Even though I figured you would have me fired for being such a waste of company money, you were hot so I didn't mind; I knew that the longer it took to make up things I did that week, the longer you would stand there. Did you notice how I mimicked heavy, double drumming with my typing? You wouldn't.

Once, you asked me what I did in a way that sounded like you might be suggesting I didn't do anything at all. I told you I programmed things. This and that. You know, "Special Projects." You nodded and asked me if I wanted to go get coffee.

Now? During work?

Yes, during work. Come on, we'll be fine. Don't be such a pussy.

I almost invited you to Metal Church right then.

I'm no pussy, I said. Have you seen my guitar? I wanted to ask. If you had seen it, you would know; I am no pussy. It's shaped like lightning.

Then come on, let's go, you said.

Outside on a workday, the sunlight seemed brighter and the air had a strange heat to it as people bustled about on the street. During the weekends, when I roamed around these deserted neighborhoods, I tried to imagine what it was like on the "outside" during the week because it was my own strict policy not to leave the office during work for fear that it would needlessly draw attention to my lack of productivity. With you, the outside seemed like a new, beautiful, and urgent world and I could not imagine having to ever go back inside, away from all of it. Things were happening out here, and I was missing it.

We made it a ritual, you and I. You'd show up and playfully scold me for bullshitting on my timesheets, and then we'd go get coffee. Once, we didn't make it back to the office and went back to your place and screwed on the floor. OK, you are right. I am making that up. It was after work, not during (we were afraid we would get caught) and we didn't screw the first time, only kissed and petted each other in a heavy way.

Again, I considered asking you to Metal Church, but didn't. Even though I am no pussy, I did not want to ruin a good thing by telling you about Metal Church. At work, you wrote a computer program that took all of my accumulated bullshit and generated new, random bullshit and put it on timesheets, so instead of you standing there over me while I tried to recycle my own new bullshit, it was taken care of by the computer. I had no idea that you even knew how to do that. I don't even think I knew how to do it, and programming was supposed to be my job.

Now that we had more time to get coffee, we tried doing it in the supply closet, to which you had a key, but the shelves of paper got in the way and we ended up frustrated and just went for coffee like we had planned in the first place.

Soon, you figured out a way to submit our timesheets automatically using a feature of the system that had always been there, but that nobody seemed to know about. It was no longer necessary for you to come by my cube anymore, or for me to email you anything, which at first made me sad, but you told me we could just meet at one of our apartments and go in late instead of going for coffee.

That's when we started to screw in earnest, on the floor. OK, you are right, it was in bed. The floor would be uncomfortable, you said.

But we most certainly did it, and when we did, I heard Bon Scott singing down from Metal Heaven. We were that good.

Before you came to my apartment, I hid my Metal, which was easy, because it was all on cassette tapes in milk crates. I put them down in the basement in the storage unit and all you saw were fifteen compact discs that had been given to me as gifts. They were not cool, that is for sure, but they were normal stuff that people thought I would like. Jazz, for example—there was some of that, and if I had to, I would put it on. In preparation, I took these discs out of their wrappers and arranged them alphabetically.

My Metal clothes were not so easy. My concert T-shirts I could tell you were some sort of ironic joke on the '80s, but there were so many of them that you would probably not believe it. You were pretty sharp. So, I put them in trash bags and hung them in the back of my closet behind my Eddie Bauer khakis and polo shirts that I wore to work. And the framed Eddie poster from Iron Maiden's *Seventh Son* tour—a prized possession—I donated to the Metal Church for the rummage sale.

The black candles, leather jackets, incense holders, bongs, black lights, and high tops went, too. These things were merely relics, not my Metal identity, not my Metal future, only symbols of my glorious Metal youth. I told myself that you were worth it, and that these things could be thrown away because I loved you and it was the right thing to do.

I told myself that these actions did not forsake the Metal Church. But they did.

Soon, you figured out that since everybody's timesheets were being collected automatically now, and that since your job was to collect timesheets, and my "Special Projects" existed only in the timesheet system, which seemed good enough for management, we no longer needed to show up for work at all. You circulated a memo that said we had been sent on Special Assignment at our company's office in North Carolina, so even if somebody noticed that we were gone and bothered to look into things, our asses would be covered.

Again, I thought of telling you about Metal Church, but I waited. Now, without jobs, at least in the sense that we no longer had to go to a place and appear to be working to collect a paycheck, we were 24-7. I had missed a lot of Metal Church and knew that they would wonder where I'd been, so I snuck out and visited the Metal Priest late on Sunday afternoon while you slept.

After services had ended, in the Metal Church office among Metal relics like a set of mint-in-the-box KISS dolls and a framed Sabbath set list from '75, I explained the situation to the Priest and promised that I would tell you soon, and that we'd have a new convert.

He warned me not to be so sure, that new converts were rare these days and even then they were rarely pure. If you didn't know of my Metal worship already, once informed, you might form a different opinion of me, one that I would not like.

Why not court one of our Metal women?

From Church? One of the Metalheads from church?

Yes, some are very beautiful, and they all love Heavy Metal. They do not forsake it. They would not shun a Hessian, no matter how long his hair or dirty his high tops.

You are wise, Father, and while I agree that they are beautiful, their hair is very large.

Wouldn't a large-haired Metal girl complement the long hair and chain wallet that you wish you could have? Instead, you let the desire for these things fester inside you like some Metal disease. It's unhealthy.

You have a point, Father, but I feel that I must pursue my current woman.

It will be your undoing.

While she may not love Metal, she's rigged the work computers so we don't have to go in anymore.

While that is indeed sweet, remember your roots, and remember who loves you.

He formed his fingers into a goat and touched my head with his index finger and pinky. I heard the choir practicing in the background and understood the Heaviness of the situation and thanked the Priest for his guidance.

So, while standing in the middle of Banana Republic looking at pants, I told you that I was a Metalhead. At first you didn't believe me and continued to look, but I unbuttoned my shirt and revealed my Megadeth shirt.

Megadeth, you said.

Yes, I said.

That's serious, you said.

Very.

You cried into the cardigan you were about to buy. I probably should have waited.

From my head, where long golden locks once did flow, to the tip of my feet, once protected by steel-toed work boots in the pit, or white high top sneakers for more formal occasions, I am a Metalhead.

Where now are Dockers, once were torn, acid-washed jeans adorned with bandanas, and where now I wear a fitted baseball cap when out on the golf course to protect my bald spot from sunburn, once was a terry cloth sweatband. I am a Metalhead. I have a selection of guitar picks in my pocket.

After I told you these things, you said you were confused. The Banana Republic shoppers looked confused too, but I felt that I had made my position clear. You did not understand Metal, or the Church that I attended every Sunday.

Couldn't I just listen to the music once in a while? Couldn't I wear the sweatband when exercising? Couldn't a bandana be replaced with a stylish handkerchief?

It would not be the same.

Back at my apartment, I showed you the shirts, my Bitch, my high top Ponies. Down in the storage unit, I showed you the crates of cassettes and my bong. I told you about the Maiden poster. You told me that you could not deal.

When my timesheets stopped appearing in the system, my boss must have gone over to my cube and when nobody in North Carolina knew who I was, he told his boss, the head of our department, and he had no idea what I had been working on, either. He must have asked my supervisor exactly what "Special Projects" meant, and when he didn't know, I was fired. They made you a manager.

Things have been heating up at Metal Church. The solos on Sunday have smoked and attendance has been huge. People can't sit down while the Metal Priest wails the Metal Sermon, so we mosh while Metal Gods possess us.

You could have been there.

I'm a Metal Deacon at Church now, and counsel young Metal couples about to be married in the Metal Church. Even though it hurts, I tell them our story and warn them never to hide their Heavy Metal worship. I give them mix tapes of the classics so these young Metalheads understand their roots. I believe that with my help, these couples have stronger marriages. I took the Priest's advice and started to date a pretty girl from Metal Church. We're not as passionate, and her hair is much larger than yours, but I can be myself around her. She likes headbands and bandanas, and we trade cassettes. I got a new job too, and have grown my hair out around my bald spot and no longer care about wearing torn jeans to the office.

One thing I can't stand, though—at this job, my supervisor reads the timesheets and yells at me when it's pretty obvious I've only been working a half hour a day, so I've been picking it up a bit. As long as they don't make me put my hair in a ponytail or tell me to turn my music down, things will be OK.

After living in Alexandria, Virginia, for nearly a decade, MATTHEW KIRKPATRICK is now a doctoral candidate in literature and creative writing at the University of Utah in Salt Lake City where he holds the FC2 Fellowship. His fiction has appeared in numerous journals, including Hobart *and* Gargoyle. *He was recently awarded a fellowship to the Virginia Center for Creative Arts and coedits* Barrelhouse *magazine.*

Watermark

Len Kruger

It is not difficult to learn the identities of the richest men in America. Your names appear on bottles of shampoo, jars of pickles, on candy bar wrappers that stick to the bottom of my shoe. I write to you, today, with one simple request. Would you please send me one million dollars?

Let me step back for a moment, sir, and assure you that this not a threat, not an extortion, not a violation of any legal code of the fifty states, territories, or the District of Columbia. You may stop reading this letter at any time. I will not send a follow-up, nor do I enclose a self-addressed stamped envelope as a monetary incentive for your reply. Nevertheless, I believe that by the time you finish this letter, you *will* send me one million dollars, not grudgingly, not with reluctance or fear or dread, but with a tingle in your extremities and love in your heart.

Allow me to introduce myself. My name is James X. Radecky. The "X" stands for nothing, but in an abstract way it stands for everything, like how the Lincoln Memorial stands for liberty and freedom. And like the Lincoln Memorial, I was conceived, created, and constructed in our Nation's capital, born in my parents' bedroom despite a robust network of health care facilities adorning the Washington Metropolitan Area.

Why the home birth? My father was a very frugal man. Ironically, he worked for the Bureau of Engraving and Printing—sadly, in the personnel office, not where those sheets of money roll over the presses like fast-flowing rivers. His goal in life was to be a "millionaire," as if that sanctified word would someday appear in big bold letters on his business card and follow him until it was chiseled in big block letters on his grave.

Permit me to give you an example of my father's thrift. After my mother left us, we went to restaurants often—diners, cafeterias, early-bird specials. Because of the cost, I was forbidden from ordering a soft drink with my meal. Water would do just fine, thank you. But my father didn't want the waitress to think he was cheap. I was required to agonize over my choice. *Let's see now, what do I want to drink?* I was supposed to wonder out loud. *Um, um, um. You know, I think I'll just have a glass of water, if that's all right.*

June 22, 1967. The Summer of Love. I was ten years old and I didn't want a glass of water! *I'll have a Coke,* I said, smiling at the waitress. She smiled back, brushing strands of red hair from her eyes. She looked like Jill St. John in my favorite episode of *Batman,* the one where she discovers Batman's secret identity before plunging into the Batmobile's atomic pile. I felt stirrings. *A Coke please,* I said. *Please? A Coke?* And then—KICK!—from under the table, the square tip of my father's mail-order penny loafers plunged into my calf. I looked into his eyes. Fury. Reproach. Betrayal.

I grew up. I got a good-paying government job. I was well off but I lived poor. My apartment was infested with moths, their husks dripping off the ceiling like miniature stalactites. I wore shirts so threadbare I could see my chest hairs in the mirror. I collected pennies in a brown paper shopping bag, anchored by its slowly increasing weight to the corner of my bedroom floor.

I was afraid of investment, terrified of loss, mortified by needless expenditure. When I turned thirty-five, I had $175,000 in my checking account. I did the calculations. By age sixty-seven, I would have a million dollars. That was my goal.

Then everything changed. It always does, doesn't it? My father passed away, dead of a stroke at age fifty-seven. He left me all his money. When I tallied his assets, I found he had fallen just short of a million dollars. I deposited the amount, in full, to my checking account. It was as if he had poured his brimming shopping bag of pennies into my own half-empty collection, the pennies cascading over the sides, the coins bouncing and rolling on my hardwood floor.

I had a million dollars. I, James X. Radecky, was a millionaire!

At first, I basked in the concept. Thinking about those six decimal places put a spring in my step as I walked to the bus stop in the morning. But soon that spring became a glide, the glide became a shuffle, the shuffle a drab listless trudge over cracked sidewalks and dirt lots.

I needed to enjoy the money in a more direct way. I went to the bank and withdrew a fresh new one-hundred-dollar bill. I held the C-note in my hand, swept it against my face, sniffed it. I studied the oval portrait of Ben Franklin, long haired, fat jowled, his lips pursed with contentment. *Congratulations,* he's saying, *you have a hundred dollars!* I held the bill up to the sunlight. A ghostly figure hovered to the right of the Treasury Department seal. It was the ghost of Ben Franklin, eyes troubled, brow furrowed. He is contemplating the abyss. *So…you have a hundred dollars,* he's saying. *Now what?*

Shaken, I returned to the bank and withdrew $100,000 in cash, one thousand hundred-dollar bills. I sorted them in ascending order by serial number, wrote down the serial numbers on a piece of notebook paper, and stuffed the cash into a shoebox, sealed tightly with rubber bands.

I put the shoebox under my bed. Sleeping over the money was nice for a while—but the magic soon wore off. Back to the bank I went. I made the necessary arrangements—a withdrawal of nine hundred thousand dollars in cash, a lengthy and unpleasant process. My banker pleaded with me. "As your financial advisor…" he said, voice shaking, "I advise against this. You're committing financial suicide."

"I am not jumping into the abyss," I replied. "I am catapulting out."

I took the money home, feeling like an excited parent taking home a newborn. "Boys?" I said, opening the shoebox, "come meet your brothers!" My $100K reunited with my $900K in one big pile on the kitchen table. I had a plan. No longer would the money reside under my bed. I sorted my big pile into one hundred piles of one hundred hundred-dollar bills, wrapping each packet in cellophane and a rubber band. I washed the bed linens, flipped the mattress.

I labeled the one hundred packets, each as a major city of the world, and placed each packet into different geographical locations of my bed. There I lay, Atlas-like across the planet, reclining and stretching over my global domain. I could feel Tokyo with my right foot, New York with my left hand, London with my stomach. Charlotte, North Carolina, center of banking and financial services for the New South, pressed into my loins, the hard rectangular bulge, the plastic sticking like a pinprick, clammy and clinging against my skin.

My salvation began on the day of my thirty-sixth birthday. I awoke late on a Sunday morning. Sunlight streamed into my room, illuminating the motes of dust floating in the air like clouds of smoke. I was hot, sweaty, lethargic. I felt sticky plastic packets of money on my skin. I felt despair.

We all get to this point, don't we? I sat at my kitchen table reading an article on volunteerism in *Parade* magazine. The article said that volunteerism and helping the less fortunate provide fulfillment and satisfaction that money can't buy. They interviewed a pretty young woman wearing a University of Wisconsin sweatshirt. The picture showed her talking on the phone and looking concerned. She told the *Parade* reporter, and I quote: "giving is more fun than receiving."

I, of course, had never believed this. Was black white? Was pain pleasure? Was up down, in out, love hate? How could giving *possibly* be more fun than receiving? But then I thought about my million dollars. Was fortune, indeed, misfortune? Could it be?

I decided to volunteer. The following Sunday, I prepared myself for a fundraising telethon being held at a local community center. I excavated a stack of C-notes from my bedclothes and taped it to my thigh with surgical tape. This would keep me grounded, give me confidence in my dealings with the world. I drove to the telethon. I walked into the lobby, feeling the packet of hundreds tickling my thighs, rubbing and chafing my skin. A woman at the front desk greeted me.

"Thank you so much for helping us out," she said. "And your name is?"

"James X. Radecky," I said, fingering the wad of cash through my pocket. Perhaps I would develop a skin condition and go to a dermatologist, and what does it say in the medical literature about hundred-dollar bills against the skin, the ink, the sharply defined edges, all that money flush against human flesh?

I was ushered into a short orientation session. Joseph Franklin, a professional fundraiser, told me it was more effective to ask for a specific amount. "It's about control," he said. "You have to set the tone."

Ensconced at my post, pencils sharpened, notepad at the ready, I called the first person on my list. I said, "I'd like to ask you, sir, *today*, for one hundred dollars."

"ZERO! ZERO! That's how much I'm giving you!" yelled the elderly man at the other end of the line.

Oh, the venom, the hatred!

"Did you know, sir, that I'm wearing hundred-dollar bills in my pants?" I said. "I'm putting my hand down my pants, I'm fingering the sharp edge of this nice thick stack of fresh newly minted hundred-dollar bills. I'm lifting the top bill, gently sliding it from beneath the rubber band."

The man hung up. I heard the click, the dead air. All around me, volunteers talked excitedly on their phones, pencils squeaking with delight as they wrote enormous sums on pledge sheets. They ripped the sheets from gummed pads, stacking them on piles so mountainous they would have to be shoveled into giant bags and fork lifted to the needy.

I put my head down on the table and thought about the shoebox of cash under my bed, the bundles of benjamins embraced by my bedclothes. What was I thinking? What if someone broke into my apartment and robbed me while I slept at night? Maybe I should learn how to sleep with my eyes open. I once read about ancient desert wanderers who slept with eyes open to guard against robbers slipping into the tent and slitting their throats. I tried to practice right there, at the telethon, but my eyelids got heavy, my mind went scrambling in crazy directions. I wondered. Did their exposed eyeballs move while they dreamt? Did their eyes roll in circles, dart back and forth? Or perhaps they gleamed with a sudden and unexpected realization?

I felt a gentle nudge on my shoulder. It was Mr. Franklin, smiling sympathetically. His tie was loose around the collar, his shirtsleeves rolled up on hairy forearms. He carried a clipboard. "James, I'm afraid you're not cut out for telephone solicitation," he said, escorting me out of the room. I felt Mr. Franklin's hand tighten around my shoulder.

On my way out, I stopped in the hospitality "suite," a lunchroom smelling of disinfectant. Bright plastic cartons of orange juice and packages of vanilla wafers were stacked on a long table surrounded by metal chairs. A woman with red frizzy hair sat at the table, pouring orange juice into a paper cup. She wore a gray sweatshirt that bunched up around her elbows. She drank down the juice in one quick gulp, took a deep breath, then poured herself some more, a thick tumbling stream of juice that almost capsized the cup.

I looked at her hands. The nails were painted bright red, her fingers long and thin, like fingers you see opening bottles of perfume on television commercials. On her left wrist was a small tattoo—it looked like a jagged mountain rising from a body of water.

"That's an interesting tattoo," I said.

"It's the iceberg in *Titanic*," she said, ripping open a package of cookies, not across the top where the instructions specify, but down along its flank, longitudinally. The cellophane was shredded, the wound gaping. She grabbed a fistful of vanilla wafers from the middle of the package, like entrails from a body.

"Pretty humiliating to get fired from a volunteer job, wouldn't you say?" she said, looking at the vanilla wafer, almost addressing it.

"I don't care about that," I said, shrugging. Suddenly, I had a revelation. *I had something else they might like!* I loosened my belt.

"Why did they fire you?" she asked.

"I have a hard time asking for money." I dug into my shorts and yanked out the packet of hundreds, wincing at the sharp pain of surgical tape shearing skin.

"I have the opposite problem," she said, watching me, eyes widening. "Um, what are you doing?"

"Committing an act of senseless generosity," I said, wrapping the money in a paper napkin. I fished a pen out of my pants pocket and wrote on the napkin: *One hundred Franklins for Mr. Franklin—here's a little something for the cause.—James X. Radecky*

"Good God. How much money is that?"

"One hundred hundreds. Equivalent to ten thousand-dollar bills or one one-hundred-thousand-dollar bill." I bit into a vanilla wafer. "Of course those denominations no longer exist. Although...there *was* a one-hundred-thousand-dollar bill in the Game of Life by Milton Bradley. And do you know whose face was on that bill? Mr. Art Linkletter."

She made a whistling sound through her teeth. "Very cool. And what's *your* name?"

"James X. Radecky." I felt confident, strong, desirable.

"My name is Barbara," she said.

"Bar-ba-ra," I said slowly, drawing out the syllables. "That was my mother's name."

"*Was?*" she said. "I'm sorry." I shrugged and snapped another vanilla wafer in half.

A few volunteers wandered into the room. Barbara popped out of her chair and grabbed a knapsack behind her. "Hey James," she said, wiping the crumbs from her mouth, "there's a blood drive this afternoon in Rockville. Wanna come?"

"Absolutely."

"Don't you want to make sure that gets to the right person?" she said, pointing at the napkin-covered bundle sitting on the table.

"I don't care," I said. "It's not mine anymore."

Thirty minutes later, I lay on a cot, veins hooked to a plastic bag draining my blood. I stared at the ceiling, a vast plain of grayness, unpopulated, desolate. Barbara's face hovered over me, smiling, beckoning, ghostly. Hundred-dollar bills revolved around her head, like planets orbiting a big red sun. I wondered. Was this a dream? Was I sleeping with my eyes open? Would I be able to recognize what was happening to me?

"That'll do it," said a nurse, pulling the needle out of my arm. She guided me toward the food table, where Barbara was sitting. Barbara jumped up and took over, grabbing my arm, patting me on the head. "How do you feel, James?" she asked.

"A bit light headed. I've lost a lot of bodily fluid."

"Relax," she said. "Have some juice and cookies." She held me by the shoulders and gently guided me into a chair.

"Didn't they want your blood?" I asked.

She laughed. "I told them I have bad blood. But that's not true, James. I was just saying that." Barbara sat next to me, her knees up against mine. "We have to talk, James. You carry around some serious cash. Why don't you tell me about yourself?"

And so…I did just that. I told her about my father and his legacy of thrift. I told her that pleasure always fades, that you can crank the knob and get more power, but that it always dwindles to a disappointing trickle. I told her about sleeping in my bed with one million dollars, about my vision of Ben Franklin floating in the ether. I told her my discovery that money is not everything, that it's not even anything.

I showed Barbara the bank statement certifying my million, the document I kept with me always, those zeroes strung together like a caravan to oblivion. "You probably think this is all very strange, very distasteful," I said.

"I think it's beautiful," she said. There were tears in her eyes. She stroked the bandage on my left forearm, caressed my wound, lovingly.

She leaned close. "Let's do something James," she whispered. "Something crazy." I closed my eyes. I saw Jill St. John plunging into the Batmobile's atomic pile, heard the whoosh of the fireball, felt the tears running down the cheeks of millionaire Bruce Wayne. *Now what*, he's asking himself. *Now what?*

We went to my shambles of an apartment, all dust, decomposition, and squalor. Barbara didn't seem to mind. She kissed me, passionately, under the hanging moth husks I brushed a few strands of red hair from her eyes.

"Your bed," she said. "I want to see your bed."

I ushered her into my bedroom and pointed to the proud array of cellophane packets adorning my mattress. She gasped, awestruck at my handiwork.

"I have a surprise for you," she said, kicking off her shoes. "Something to show you."

"Um. OK."

"First we have to get rid of this cellophane."

"And why is that?" I inquired.

"I don't lie on top of plastic. It's like being in the hospital."

"But—the bills'll get wrinkled."

"Don't worry," she said, winking "I'll be gentle."

Barbara undressed the hundreds from their plastic sheaths as I teased off the rubber bands from each neat crisp stack. Cellophane gently fluttered to the floor, the labels still affixed—Singapore, Brussels, Houston. I thought of Atlantis, El Dorado, Babylonia—once gleaming cities of wealth and prosperity, now lost forever.

"Why don't you take your shoes off?" Barbara said. She had spread the hundreds over my bed, like thick icing on a cake. She lay down on her back, wriggling. The C-notes crinkled and crunched, like brittle leaves rustling.

"Now," said she, queen to my king, stretching and reclining over our royal domain. "Ready for your surprise, James?" She laughed and slowly lifted her dress.

And there, on her stomach, was another tattoo! A ghostly head, balding on top, hair flowing from the sides. (*Odd*, I thought, *this tattoo looks familiar.*) Hair flowing from the sides of the head down to its shoulders. Fat jowled, lips pursed, contemplating the abyss! *It was Ben Franklin!*

I reached for her.

KICK! KICK! KICK! I stopped short, feeling that square-toed penny loafer going into my thigh. It was my dear departed father, shadowing me like an avenging watermark haunting Federal Reserve notes of the most exalted denomination. And don't you realize, my father was telling me—kick, kick, kick—counterfeiters cannot duplicate haunted hundred-dollar bills. Only the Bureau of Engraving and Printing can infuse C-notes with restless and discontented souls, phantoms that roam the earth seeking an elusive peace.

"Problem?" Barbara said, lying there. I imagined my eyes gleaming with a sudden and unexpected realization. I loomed over Barbara, suddenly exhilarated, aroused. I was contemplating an act of sheer senselessness, reconnoitering that thin line separating sanity from insanity, reality from fantasy, shame from satisfaction. I felt a rush of adrenalin. Could I? Should I? Did I dare?

"Please leave now…" I said.

"But…"

"…and take it all!"

"You mean…"

"I GIVE YOU THE WORLD!" I cried, sweeping my arm across the bed, knocking at least $450K onto the floor. "But beware! Beware this burden you now bear!"

"I'll bear it! I'll bear it!" Barbara shouted. She sat up and put her dress back on.

"Do you have a bag?" she asked. "A big one?"

I had just the thing. I walked to the corner of the room, where my grocery bag of pennies sat. I lifted the bag and poured it all on the floor, thousands of rolling bouncing gyrating Abraham Lincolns and Lincoln Memorials, liberated after years of stagnation and inertia, after years of feeling that red metal heaviness pressing down as they sunk lower and lower into the pile. I helped her fill the bag—handfuls of hundreds stuffed to the brim. She staggered to the door, straining under its awful weight.

"You're not going to call the cops or anything, right?" she said.

"Why should I?" I said, giddy with happiness, "it's not mine anymore."

I closed my eyes. I heard the soft rustling of the paper bag, my apartment door slamming, her footsteps skipping down the stairwell. I felt a shimmering joy, an unparalleled ecstasy, the peace which passeth understanding, the pause that refreshes! My father's kicks grew softer. One last loafer-toed poke and he was gone, I knew, forever.

OK. Enough about me. Let's talk about you, shall we?

I offer you, today, that same unspeakable joy, that same guilty pleasure that I have experienced. Think of it. *Imagine it.* Soon it will be autumn. Outside, you will hear the rustling of leaves, a brittle stirring and sifting, a swirling cloud of crisp one-hundred-dollar bills taking flight. You will hear the wind, a long building sigh. You will take out your checkbook. You will write my name on the check (James X. Radecky), and fill in the amount: one million dollars and no cents. You will sign the check and find an envelope, the kind that is lined, with no window. Rummage through your desk drawer and find a stamp, the Love stamp with the little angel pondering, dreamy, his head on open palm. What could he possibly be thinking? Reflect on the irony—chuckle softly to yourself—that it takes forty-two cents to send one million dollars through the mail. All envelopes are beggars without that stamp, with it, all kings! Imagine the envelope going through the mail system, mixing with lowly supermarket flyers, jostling elbows with fundraising pleas printed on both sides of the paper. "Over, please" they all say at the bottom of page one, that shuddering comma between command and entreaty, between certainty and doubt. I thank you for reading this letter. Rest assured that you are not the sole target of my solicitation. I have constructed a mailing list, using addresses supplied by *Who's Who in Finance and Industry,* available in the reference room of any public library in the land. The directory yields tens of thousands of names and occupations. Investment banker. Software company CEO. Shipping magnate. *Haynes, Edward Allen. Brown, William Samuel. Morrison, David Fulton.* Good solid American names, last, first, middle, like the interchangeable blocks of a Rubik's Cube. Shuddering, I click through the combinations and permutations.

Over, please.

I await your reply.

LEN KRUGER was born at the George Washington University Hospital. His stories have appeared in Zoetrope: All-Story, Barcelona Review, Blue Moon Review, CrossConnect, Bound Off, WordWrights, *and others. He can be reached at lenkruger@comcast.net.*

Leaving Prison

Robert Lang

The Buddhist monk closed his eyes and allowed the journalist's agitation to wash over him.

"In a stretch," Rick said, "and I mean a lo-ong stretch, I might be able to understand how the foot soldiers back there in prison could be forgiven—they were just following orders, they didn't know what they were doing, all they knew was war—but Sok Cham, the commander and mastermind behind all the death and violence of the Khmer Rouge? How could you forgive him?"

"He needed to be shown that there is a way to let go of the hate," the old monk replied. "The Buddha said that the unwholesome-minded people need loving kindness more—"

"But this isn't some kind of abstract forgiveness. We're talking about forgiving one of the most evil people in Cambodia. I seriously doubt that millions of people throughout the country will ever forgive the Khmer Rouge for murdering their families."

"I know, and if they learned how to forgive, they would also learn how to heal themselves."

"It's one thing to forgive someone who has remorse, because then there's a little bit of hope that he might change and go on to live a productive life. But Sok Cham: he doesn't get it. He's still evil, and I got the feeling, while you were up there chanting and sprinkling water on everybody during your ceremony, that if he were released tomorrow he'd go out there and commit the same kind of atrocities."

"Anger is like picking up a red-hot charcoal to throw at your enemy. Hatred is never appeased by hatred."

Rick halted the thirty-year-old Lada before an unavoidable stretch of vast water-filled potholes, then put the car in first gear and drove slowly through the middle. The monk pondered the driver who was kind enough to give him a ride home from the ceremony at Wat Lanka, Phnom Penh's largest temple. The Western journalist seemed to be in his late twenties, and he had short black hair, lightly speckled with gray. Water from the puddle splashed around the doors, brown water spattered the front fender, but the bottom didn't scrape, and the car plodded forward.

"I see your point," Rick said once they reached dry land, "but some may respond that while Sok Cham was burning his hand on your red-hot charcoal, he was killing a hundred thousand or so people by shooting or starving them. Long after the war was over, he split peoples' heads open with axes—and those Western tourists!" He turned right. "Oh, shit," he said unhappily. "I shouldn't have gone this way." The street, rather a trail of mud with cratered islands of asphalt, ran between two buildings, two four-story apartment blocks. The east side of the street was shady and contained all the activity. The left side was deserted; a few shop doors were ajar, but the rest were closed tight against the sun.

The building on the right, a tired gray and sun-bleached yellow apartment building, was splattered with patches of black and white mildew; one section towards the top was an unstained rich lemon-yellow. Small balconies, demarcated by cement walls and wire fences, lined the building. To the right of the door that entered upon a balcony were Palladian windows. A faded turquoise shutter filled one arched window, while clothes hung on a pole in another. A pair of cyclo drivers were sleeping in their shaded cyclos in front of the building.

"Let's take this street as an example," Rick waved expansively, suddenly animated with a new idea. "This won't be in my article but it illustrates my point. I wrote a piece on this street about six months ago. Tim Sokha, the businessman/drug smuggler/arms dealer/logger who is closely connected with the prime minister, bought all the land in this block from the government, and plans to tear it down to build office and residential buildings, and the residents can't do a thing about it! They can't claim they own the property even though they've been living here since 1980 when they returned from the Killing Fields. They have no property rights because there's no property law, and even if there were, it wouldn't be enforced. Now, you tell me that this guy is not evil for making two thousand people suffer to satisfy his own greed? And he doesn't even compare to the evil of Sok Cham and his ilk." Rick regarded the monk defiantly. "And they're all like this: politicians, businessmen, that jerk in the Mercedes back there who made me yield when it was he who was breaking the rules. You may forgive them, but what difference does it make? They keep doing evil."

A woman in a white blouse and red-checkered scarf appeared on a second-floor terrace. She shook a heavy scarlet sheet, then draped it over the railing. "We condemn the act, but we cannot hate the actor."

"Hmm…"

The monk gently ran his hands along the building's cragged cement and damp mold. The tender *tch* as a crisp yellow chip flaked off.

"…I can see that…"

Several people, indistinct forms submerged in the brown shade of a Mild Seven cigarette promotional umbrella and strung-up blue tarps, squatted on low red-plastic stools. One hand cradled a bowl close to a mouth, while the other worked noodle-shoveling chopsticks like a lever.

"…hmm…theoretically…but can a person really be separated from his actions? What is a person if not the sum total of his acts? And there's always an infinite number of excuses. The evil person says, 'Oh, back then I believed in communism,' or 'I believed in Maoism'—like Pol Pot in the beginning—'so at least my intentions were good; I was thinking about a common good, I wasn't power hungry; and it's not my fault the economics part didn't work out.' Or, the evil person was elected by the people, which makes the entire population guilty. But these are only excuses. Sok Cham murdered people to increase his own power, not because he believed in anything. Don't let anyone tell you differently. If there's only one thing I've learned in my three years working as a journalist in Cambodia, it's that nobody does anything in this country unless it will make them more powerful."

"He may still be ignorant of many things, as we are still ignorant of many things," the monk replied in his unhurried intonation. "There's good within everybody; and if we acknowledge that, the good may grow."

"Maybe…" Rick rubbed his chin stubble. "…Maybe…" The car crept up behind a woman who was stepping among the dry patches. The contrast between the red in her scarf and her mud-streaked black hair. "But that's assuming that the forgiving Buddhists are stronger than the people who do evil. Otherwise, as we've seen, it's like lambs going to the slaughter. Buddhism barely survived the Khmer Rouge. They executed ninety-five percent of all monks, remember—twenty-five thousand people."

"Yes. Cambodia has suffered deeply."

"I heard of several incidents when the Khmer Rouge executed monks for refusing to kill a chicken."

"They do not know the truth. They destroy Buddhism, they destroy themselves."

"Recent reports say that the Khmer Rouge killed two million people—out of a population of ten million."

The monk didn't respond, for there was nothing to say that would satisfy Rick. The journalist knew the facts, but he was struggling against them. If he were groping for deeper answers, he would have to look within; the monk only iterated words, fleeting and wafting, often coming to rest on infertile soil. Perhaps his gentleness would show Rick a way to escape his anxiety; however, that, too, was beyond his control.

Rick lit another cigarette and tossed the match out the window. A young woman, dressed in white, her blouse split stylishly up the sides, tiptoed gingerly through the mud. She looks so anxious, the monk thought. How she should laugh, tomorrow, if not today— right now—at her exaggerated concern, especially if she fell. Rick drummed the steering wheel.

A woman squatting by the curb submerged a bowl into a tub of water. The monk felt the wetness on her hands and heard the sleepy spli-unk of the soapy water tumbling. Hanging from a terrace:

Clinic Tito
→150m

painted in red, decades ago, on blue chick-blinds.

The monk felt the tearing, gliding, as effortlessly as his own breathing, as a cigarette vendor tore cellophane from a new pack and withdrew three papery cylinders for a motorcycle driver. The monk smiled and let the moment wash over him: although she would undoubtedly sell thousands of cigarettes in the future, this one was infinitely precious, never to be repeated.

Steam was rising, and he followed its trail to a pot of boiling liquid. Next to the pot, a thin man in a white singlet washed pots in a tin bucket by the curb. His skeletal legs straightened to stir the pot, then he added several spoonfuls of something, covered it with a lid, and resumed squatting.

Above: a trio of open arched windows. Behind one opening, a burgundy shadow rolled and sank into the dark. Inside, cigarette smoke mingled with the smells of sour body odor, frying fish, and the starchiness of cooked rice. Crude, impenetrable walls encased the darkness, but inside the window's vacant frame, suspended in the palpable air, undefined grays and blues undulated distractedly. From the window the elliptical street was available, unfiltered, and the colors and vibrations converged on the monk's aged, hairless head in the decrepit Lada inching along through the mud and forging the potholes, eventually disappearing from sight.

A young monk, his head shaved, his oversized saffron robe threatening to engulf him, stood outside a stereo shop-house. He carried a dirty yellow, nearly gray, parasol to protect him from the sun.

"Hey, did you use to beg like that?" Rick asked.

"Of course," the old monk answered smiling. "Asking for alms is an important part of—"

"I can't even imagine…"

The ride became smoother once they reached the constant pavement around the New Market. Green and yellow bunches of bananas dangled on the outer fence of the Market.

"Jesus, it's hot," Rick complained. "It feels like an unrelenting bludgeon," he swung an invisible club, "at the back of my head."

Dozens of people examined and negotiated and carried ingredients for their next meal. The sound of shooting and machine "wheees" and "clings" from an arcade.

"Venerable," Rick said, "how do you respond to critics who say that your forgiveness of Sok Cham and the other Khmer Rouge soldiers could backfire on Buddhism?" The corners of dusty blue tarps, clouded plastic sheets, and desiccated Siam Cement bags were tied together to shelter the venders and parked motorcycles. "I mean, it seems to me as though Buddhism is on the ropes in this country—OK, that's an exaggeration—but you've got to admit that Buddhism failed to protect people from the war, and it can't explain how Cambodians could kill fellow Cambodians on such an enormous scale. Plus, now you've got tons of Christian missionaries running around the country offering a picture or explanation that people can at least grasp and understand."

"There is no conflict between Christianity and Buddhism."

Rick rushed on. "I work with some of the victims' families. The Khmer Rouge starved to death the two children of one my colleagues. Can you imagine seeing your own children wither away in front of your eyes, and there's nothing you can do about it?!" Slowing, but not stopping, Rick crossed the busy intersection.

The monk suffused, evenly and smoothly like benign flood waters, down the length of the street. He and the bisecting and interlocking planes, rectangles, and spheres were constructed of the same, unchanging material—where everything was there, outside the car—waiting to be heard and seen and felt, though indifferent to the depth of sensitivity and detection.

Rick drove slowly through the crowded street. "Another colleague was forced to watch while they shot his parents; they left their corpses right there in the field to rot. And those are just two of my friends! What about these people?" he waved at the passing motorcycles and cyclos. "Three decades later and they're still carrying it around with them. They're all victims. Every single person." Two blinding flashes of silvery white: someone was soldering. "By forgiving people who murdered their entire families, what are you telling them about the state of the world today, about justice, and some sense of higher being? About what kind of answers lie out there? Don't you think that people will begin to wonder, if they haven't already, about the purpose of life? What is their incentive to act morally? Apparently none in Cambodia. If people don't believe that justice will eventually be served, that there will be some kind of righting of wrongs, either now or in the hereafter, well…what will people believe in anymore? Why should not," he struck his palm angrily against the steering wheel, "self-aggrandizement be the law of the land?"

The monk caressed the back of Rick's head, particularly the gray hairs, and embraced his unshaven cheeks, worn shirt, and expensive foreign-made sandals. "One shouldn't be moral out of fear," he said, "but because it connects him with himself and with the rest of the world."

"I'm sorry, but I don't think that will hold society together. That may be fine for me, but what about the other guy?"

"If that's fine for you, then you don't need to worry anymore."

"For me? But that seems so selfish."

"It is the least selfish thing you can do," the monk smiled brilliantly. The shop-houses—a succession of encounters—passed by without interruption, yet each was unique: two-story simple dusty structures ending at unadorned square angles, outstretched TV antennas—spindly heron legs—impaling the chalky clouds that were pastelled in the blue sky, while the discordant wind and horns and engines hummed and reverberated through iron balustrades on terraces, and dust settled on blazing roofs.

A pair of young girls held books up to their temples to shield their faces from the sun.

Unimpeded by the presence of a traffic light, two cars slowly cut across the intersection. "Jesus, I feel like I'm an ant and someone's holding a magnifying glass over me," Rick said, driving slowly as they descended into a wide pothole, crawled out, then prepared for the next crater…"You certainly went through a lot of red tape to get into prison. The warden changed his mind and wouldn't let you speak to everyone at the same time, and then he said you couldn't sit close to the prisoners."

"So I moved the table closer," the monk laughed.

"Yeah," Rick laughed. "They didn't know how—" the high-pitched noise of a metal-grinding lathe forced him to start over. "The guards didn't dare confront you. But don't you think what happened underscores the political nature of the event: that no matter how much you would like to operate independently in your own spiritual realm, that whatever you do has political consequences?"

"That is not my concern."

"And that's precisely the point. Because even if you don't want to be political, others will exploit you to serve their own purpose. Everything in this country is political."

"I'm not." A boy carrying a small pot of yellow and white flowers bounced on the back of a motorcycle.

"Hmm…" Rick wagged his head from side to side. "You are, and you're not. You're not a member of any political party, though many people think you are, but I mean 'politics' in a broader sense. Your marches against corruption; when you fast; and when you feed the poor squatters—that's why you're famous, that's why you're loved—at least among the common people. All that's political, even if you don't mean it to be."

"Yes," the monk replied, and he heard Rick exhale.

The center of the street crumbled into gravel and Rick concentrated on locating a relatively smooth route. He swerved far to the right, almost on the curb. Hammering, and a baby wailing…and they passed.

Two vertical advertisements in Chinese and English:

Eating	Blessing
Staying	You
Only	To
One	Get
Lido	Lucky

"Earlier, you said it took over six months for the government to approve your visit to the prison." "Eight," the monk laughed. Rick frowned at his passenger. "I don't get it, Venerable. You lead marches against corruption, you forgive murderers…I'm sorry to be so blunt, but how can you be so gullible? They allowed you to visit the prison because it served the political agenda of the prime minister."

The monk was silent for a moment as the Lada fought another pothole. He focused on the disagreeable, inescapable heat and he seeped into the cracked asphalt and scaling buildings. The violent sun overpowered the colors and dried up their depths. The air was steeped in a dusty glare; it glinted off the white hood of the Lada, the olive painter's caps of the motorcycle drivers, and the blue- and white-wedged Mild Seven umbrellas.

Nothing was out of place, each upturned rock and engine-drone seemed correct: perfectly placed randomness. He savored the distraction, even the unpleasantness: the ephemeral, albeit potentially lethal, layer over the stillness—over the being

it was the cadence, and its imminent resolution

the cacophony imbued the moment with purity and serenity,

and he smiled at its passing—for its own beauty, and for another of equal beauty would follow.

"It doesn't matter who is in power," the monk said. "If politics are based on hate, the rulers are all the same. That is what needs to be changed."

Rick laughed and shook his head. The monk stopped inhaling. Was this all an illusion? He suddenly wondered. Was he forcing beauty?

"That may be true over the long term, but there's never a long term. Life is only a series of short terms—"

"Yes."

"—and therefore it's not realistic to hope we can live in a world without egos or hate. It's not" CLACKETY! "natural." CLACKETY! from a motorized cart, overloaded with terra cotta bricks.

But no: for it came from within him.

Rick pulled to the left to avoid a short, stocky woman—a fireplug of a woman—who was pushing a cart towards them—her age could have been anywhere from forty to seventy; her eyes were narrowed, her lips pursed. The monk lightly brushed his fingertips against her leathery face. The crevices were deep, he discovered, and he caressed their callused folds, seeping into the arid estuaries. He burrowed inside,

melting over their numbness—the woman's, the cyclo driver's, the journalist's—gently soaking in deeper until he reached their individuality, that impenetrable kernel, sculpted from lifetimes of striving—and he delicately rolled the stony kernel under his tongue,

cold, sour, metallic vapors instantly permeated his sinuses: the taste of insecurity, and of indignation violently repressed;

because the frenetic present, experience, and the future,

by decreeing the ineluctability and the sanctity of the walls—walls constructed with mortar of fear, walls that claim that only predominance can ensure attainments and survival, survival by preempting—

assault and splinter us

who can remain intact,

without the fortifications of self-deceptions and exaggerated worries therefore, we are convinced, force-fed and gagging on the coping, seeking refuge in the one-dimensional life of tangibles, unquestioningly obeying convention, not only that the search for an alternative will fail or more likely be somehow cursed, but also that we are undeserving—guilty—and to ask for more would expose the arrogance of our species,

so the kernel willfully hardens with each day, each encounter, each conversation and thought, as we labor under the fantasy of autonomy, certain that there are no options—that life was meant to be, not an iota more than, a succession of struggles: an often loathsome degrading road, but secure at least, approved and well trodden, which holds out the promise of control—that illusory way to evade terror and deny desperation,

for what wasn't clung to would slip away or be stolen, while the implications of feeling fortunate and inexpressibly grateful cannot be grasped

let alone borne—

and, loving them for their weaknesses,

the monk swallowed the kernel and closed his eyes and exhaled noiselessly through his nostrils,

and felt himself grow thin, translucent as he flowed into them— through the broken-off door handle, the roof, the rear windshield, and the holes in the floorboard, until he was waferlike, a shapeless bundle of four square meters of cloth, a saffron glow smoothing their jagged cleavages and eroding their boundaries, their lifetime strivings; for yes, yes, it was a struggle—inescapable suffering—but they didn't have to cede their essence

rather, it was out of struggle, from inside the woman's wrinkles and the cyclo driver's ropy hamstrings, out of the tips of their fingertips and the crook of their arms, that their potential radiated, and

it is not arrogant it is not arrogant:

it is the only way out.

"Listen." Rick spoke urgently. "I've written articles proving that the Minister of Industry is corrupt, I've shown that the largest garment company in Cambodia abuses its employees, I've uncovered enormous waste and greed at the UN, and received praise for my profiles of the victims of so-called economic development. As a result, many things have changed, they've improved. If I don't do it, who else is going to reign them in? Who else is going to fight The Evil?"

The old monk contemplated the journalist before saying: "The Buddha struggled with similar problems twenty-five hundred years ago."

"But what's changed?! What's changed?! Ach. It's this one, isn't it?"

"Yes."

"Oh, what's the point," he said with disgust through his locked jaw as he maneuvered the Lada through the gates of the pagoda. The familiar faces of the ancient nuns, heads shaved and dressed in white robes. A dog with swinging teats trotted nervously out of the way.

The car came to an abrupt halt. The monk waited for him to continue speaking, but Rick, after baldly pondering his passenger for a long moment, said tautly, "Never mind. It's no use."

"Just have compassion for yourself," the monk said. With the help of his assistant, he stepped out of the car.

"Thanks for your time," Rick called.

The assistant slammed the door twice before it finally shut. The old monk felt the hands of his assistant steadying his step as he ascended the stairs.

ROBERT LANG has traveled through Africa and lived in Cambodia, Indonesia, China, New York, and Washington, D.C. He is married and the father of two children. Of four completed manuscripts and a dozen short stories, this is his first work to be published.

Floaters

Charles R. Larson

And my brother drags on: "When I was a kid, I can remember closing my eyes in bed, holding them so tight that a pinpoint of light would slash through the darkness like an eruption in the night. Now it's just the opposite. I look at you, or anything else, and a dark spot obliterates part of my vision. It's as if someone's taken scissors and cut away a part of what's in front of me. Something's missing. Sometimes I think I see the scissors digging around the edges, ripping the piece out."

"But you won't go to a doctor?" I ask him, already knowing the answer. It's difficult to get medical help when you don't stay at one address for very long. He's come to the beach where Susan and I and the kids always spend the summer, once I'm through teaching and Tommy and Sarah are out of school. He's promised that he won't stay more than two weeks.

"Doctors? I've been to doctors. They've already told me. My eyes are falling apart."

"This is a little more serious than hemorrhoids, Freddy. Not something you can cure with over-the-counter medicine." I take a swallow of my beer and listen to the silences of the old house. The kids are finally asleep, and Susan—who's annoyed that my brother has come to visit us—is reading in bed upstairs. It's even quiet outside, because it's too early in the season and a weeknight.

"You're just like Dad and Mom. Always got the answer, always telling me what to do."

"We're talking about your eyes, Freddy. Something you need to take care of, if you want to continue to function."

"And if I don't?" he shoots back at me.

"That's up to you. All I'm saying is that if you can't talk about anything else, maybe you'd better do something about it."

"I will—after I have my vacation, if you don't mind."

We leave it at that.

"His vacation?" Susan asks twenty minutes later, after I've showered the beach off my skin and climbed in the four-poster bed. "What about our vacation? Does he ever think about anything like that?"

"Shhhh," I tell her, which gets her more upset.

"How can you have a vacation, if you don't do anything anytime else?"—her reference to the fact that a year ago, Freddy cashed out, quit his brokerage job, and hasn't done a thing since. Nor remained in any one place for more than a couple of weeks, though he's kept his apartment in Philadelphia.

She's been in a funk since Sunday afternoon when Freddy got here, all smiles, talking about getting a little R&R. It's Thursday night, and she's trying to read herself into oblivion after missing sleep the four nights my brother's been with us. "He gets up too many times in the night. I hear him every time," she informed me the second morning.

"I haven't heard a thing," I told her.

"You've never heard a thing. Ever since the kids were born," she added, defending her territory and her responsibilities. When I didn't reply: "How long's he going to stay?"

"I don't know. I haven't asked him. I didn't think I had the right."

What neither of us mentioned was that the house is half Freddy's, though he's never come here by himself. After Mom and Dad died, everything was split fifty-fifty.

I put my hand on her thigh, but she pokes her head closer to her book. "I'm always horny at the beach," I remind her.

"Not with your brother in the next room."

"For Christ's sake," I tell her. "By the time he leaves, you'll have your period."

"He's staying two weeks?"

"He always stays two weeks. I don't suppose this is different than any other year."

"You're right. I'll have my period," and she turns a page of her novel.

"What's happened to the kids?" Freddy asks me the next afternoon, moving a little forward in his chair.

"They're right in front of you. Don't you see them?"

"I can't see them," he replies, tilting his head at a forty-five degree angle. "Oh, now I do," leaning back again.

We're on the beach, sprawled on wooden chairs under the family umbrella. The canvas is so faded you can barely tell that it once had red stripes. Mom and Dad must have got it the year they bought the house, back in 1956.

"You drove down here from Philly, right?"

"Lucky I didn't cause an accident," Freddy replies, taking a puff on his cigar. He smokes on the beach but not in the house because Susan gets upset. Tommy and Sarah are playing in the water fifty feet in front of us. Susan's in the house sleeping. I've been trying for an hour and a half to determine how serious Freddy's problem is. Susan's already told me it's nothing to worry about. "Lots of old people get spots in their eyes," she told me when I was painting the back of the house in the morning.

"He's not old. Fifty-seven," I reminded her, afraid that Freddy might hear our conversation.

The truth is that my brother reminds me of an old man. Even the way he dresses for the beach: floppy hat, striped shirt with long sleeves, and white trousers with rolled cuffs covering so much of his body you'd think he'd been invited to afternoon tea. Everybody else is down to the absolute minimum. I can't keep my eyes off the girls in those v-crotch bathing suits, especially the ones who've been a little careless shaving. Freddy's twelve years older than I am, but acts as if it might be twenty. I excuse his fuddy-duddy ways because he never remarried after he and Joyce split, and that was ten or eleven years ago. When I glance at him on the chair next to me, I can't help thinking of J. Alfred Prufrock. I wish I could offer him a peach.

"If you can drive your car and read the newspaper, and do every-thing else you do every day—" I ask him, "then what's the problem with your eyes? You've obviously learned to compensate for what's happened."

"Easy as turning my head," he answers, through a breath of thick smoke. "Long as I remember to turn my head."

I look at the newspaper in his lap. "You've been reading that for an hour."

"It used to take me twenty minutes."

"So you've slowed down a bit."

"I can't read the market quotes any longer."

"Maybe you need new glasses. Trifocals."

"Yesterday you said I needed to see a doctor. Today you tell me to live with it."

"I think you were the one who brought this up, Fred."

"I'm just telling you what it's like. So you'll know."

"Know what?" For the life of me, I don't know what he's talking about. He's worn glasses since middle school. I didn't start until a few years ago when I hit forty. Although we never talk about it, he was adopted ten years before Mom and Dad had me. We don't have the same genes. We don't even have any of the same mannerisms. All we are is brothers who didn't get along when we were growing up, who hardly communicated with each other until Freddy's divorce.

We don't talk for a few minutes. I watch my kids playing happily in the sand. Tommy's building a castle city with some other boys he's befriended. Sarah's a few feet away from them, digging on her own. Some of the crowd's already left the beach for the day, though there's still quite a show if I keep my eyes on the strollers walking along in the salty foam. There's enough of a breeze that it's not as hot as it's been the last few days. Susan will be upset when I tell her that she's missed a perfect afternoon in the sun.

When I look at my brother, he's folded up the newspaper and closed his eyes. I start to get up to check on the kids when he asks, "They still out there?"

"Where else?"

"Drowned maybe."

"I suppose that's your idea of a joke. Or are you trying to tell me that you can't see them?"

"I can't see anything."

"What do you mean?"

"There's a large spot in front of everything. All I can see are the peripherals."

"You mean you can't even see me?"

"I can see you because you're at my side, not in front of me."

"I thought you said they're only spots—not whole gobs. What happens if you turn your head?"

"They'll probably go away. Or change shape."

"What do they look like?"

"Black holes."

"Black holes? You mean those things astronomers—"

"Yah, the same thing. Space. Nothingness."

"They still there?"

"Only one of them, as if a chunk of the water's missing."

"You're telling me this is worse than usual. Is that what you mean?"

"Not really. Most of the time they're small, only part of the picture. Maybe it's something about the sun on the beach. It's bright out here, and I—"

I look at his face but it's difficult to see his eyes because of the hat and his sunglasses.

"Is it still there?"

"What?"

"The spot."

"Floating right out there." He's looking in front of us, directly at the ocean.

"Floating? You mean it moves?"

"A little. It kind of shimmers as if it's alive. Mostly it's just there in the same space, filling up everything in front of me."

"Does it have a shape? What's it look like?"

"A footprint, without the heel. Or a claw. More like an animal footprint. A bear. But now it's changing a little."

"What do you mean?"

"The edges are rounded a little more. Looks like a large boulder crushing everything."

I can feel sweat running down my arms. I'm more in the shade than Freddy, but I'm so upset about what he's telling me that I feel as if I'm directly in the sun. I'm about to tell him that we'd better get to a doctor when Tommy comes over and whispers that he needs to pee. "Can we go home?" he asks, fidgeting so noticeably I realize he's about to burst.

"Can't you do it in the water?" I ask him, annoyed that he's interrupted the conversation with my brother.

"I don't like to do that, Daddy," he replies. He's standing on one foot as if he's a bird. "Can't you take me back to the house?"

I start to get up from my chair when Freddy interrupts me. "I'll take him."

"Susan's asleep—"

"I'll take him up the boardwalk to the public john," and he stands up, stretching his frame.

"I thought you couldn't see?" I ask him, getting up and looking at his face.

"It's gone. I'm fine. Give me some exercise. Here, Tommy," he says, extending his hand so my son can take hold of him.

When they come back half an hour later, Tommy's got a Coke in one hand and cotton candy in the other. He's smeared so much of it around his mouth, it looks as if he's bleeding. I tell him to wash off his mouth in the ocean but encounter the same resistance I got when I told him to pee. "I can use this," he tells me, wiping the sticky goo on my towel before I stop him. Then he puts the Coke on the sand and thrusts the cotton candy at me, expecting that I'll hold it for him.

"I don't want it, Tommy. Take it to the trash, or ask Sarah if she wants to finish it." He walks toward the water and his sister, and I watch the encounter between the two of them. Sarah shakes her head and points toward the trash container behind us. When Tommy realizes that she doesn't want it, he drops it on the sand. I'm about to get up from my chair and lay into him when Sarah picks it up and heads toward the trash receptacle.

"Great kids," Freddy tells me, breaking in on my anger.

"Some of the time." I regret the remark as soon as I've made it.

Freddy's relit his cigar. I can smell the sour odor even through the salty afternoon breeze. I wonder why he continues smoking those damn things. Everyone else we know got the message years ago.

When Sarah returns to her digging on the beach, I glance at my watch and wonder if it's time for us to return to the house. I've slathered the kids with sun protection, but fear they'll still get burned. I'm about to move my chair so it's back in the shade when I realize that Freddy may have the right idea: you dress the way he does and you're sure not going to end up with skin cancer. Then I think about his eyes and wonder what the hell, what's he got to lose?

And my brother starts talking again. "You know, I never told you something about Joyce."

"James Joyce or your ex?"

"Who's James Joyce?"

"A writer."

"Never heard of him."

"Didn't think you had." My response kills our conversation. It's two or three minutes before he continues.

"You know what I learned after the divorce was final?" He doesn't look in my direction but towards the water in front of us.

"What? That you'd made a mistake?"

"Sort of, but not the way you suspect."

"What?"

"She was pregnant."

"By you?"

"That's what she said." He's still looking directly in front of him.

"She told you that?"

"Not at the time, no. Months later, after she had an abortion."

"But how do you know it wasn't someone else's?"

"I believe her."

"And that means that you were still doing it until the divorce was final."

"Does that sound crazy?"

"Then why the hell get a divorce?"

"It was never sex."

"And she told you afterwards that she'd had an abortion?"

"Because she knew if she'd told me before, I'd try to prevent her."

"Jesus." I don't know what else to say. I never particularly liked Joyce, but didn't care much for my brother in those days either.

"If the kid was alive, he wouldn't be that much older than Sarah."

"I'm sorry it didn't turn out that way." I've been facing him ever since we started talking, but Freddy's still looking at the sea.

"Sometimes I think about it—especially when I'm around Tommy and Sarah. At the very least, she could have put the kid up for adoption."

So it's adoption he's really talking about as much as anything else: the cruel joke he believes that life has played on him. We've gone over this terrain too many times, especially when I was at the university. I used to visit him on weekends, because he wasn't so far away, until those visits became too painful. The litany was always the same: once I was born, Mom and Dad forgot about him. I don't know whether it's true or something he made up. By the time I was seven, he was already away at college. When he came home for vacations, I thought of him as a visiting relative.

"I didn't know you liked kids that much."

"I don't know whether I do. It's hard to know about something when you haven't tried it. Joyce and me, we never really talked about kids. We were too busy to think about anything besides ourselves."

"That's true of everybody, Freddy. Nobody knows anything about kids until they've got them, and then it's too late."

"It might have been nice to try."

I glance uncomfortably toward the water at my own children and wonder how to change the topic. I'm not used to talking about anything of substance with my brother—certainly nothing this emotional—yet it seems that's all we've done since he came here. His eyesight, the kids. What's next, life and death? Mostly we've concealed our true feelings from one another, avoided the raw nerves that got pinched so often in the conversations after he got divorced. Or Mom and then Dad's death.

"You have any problem if I stay a little longer this summer?" he asks me. Before I can respond, he continues: "It'd give me a chance to get to know my niece and nephew a little better."

Now he's trapped me in a way I didn't anticipate. It's no big deal for me, and probably not for the kids, either, but Susan's something else. Already she's been asking when he's going to leave, and it hasn't even been a week. I mumble something noncommittal and suggest we gather our belongings and head back to the house.

"He won't look at me when he talks to me," Susan says late that night when we're alone in the bedroom.

It's been a busy evening. We walked down the boardwalk for pizza and then afterwards over to the arcade where the kids enjoyed the rides and tried every game of chance suitable for their ages. They didn't want to leave—as long as Uncle Freddy was indulging their wishes. I practically had to carry Tommy home.

"It's the stuff in his eyes. While we were at the beach, I realized that sometimes he has to look away from you so he can see you in his peripheral vision."

"Well, it's very off putting to carry on a conversation with someone looking somewhere else."

She's reading another novel. All I can do is catch up with the semester of magazines I brought from home. I'm afraid she's going to ask when Freddy's going to leave, so I try to get a jump on her and put him in a better light. "He told me something at the beach today I never heard before."

"What was that?" she asks, without looking up.

"Joyce was pregnant when they got divorced." The information takes her away from her novel, which she stands on the bed between us, spine up as if she's constructed the first section of a wall.

"How does he know?"

"She told him—months after she had an abortion. When he told me, he was all choked up. He said he wishes he'd had the chance to have kids."

"Huh!"

"What's that supposed to mean?"

"I can't see that in a million lifetimes."

"I think we used to say something like that about ourselves."

"It isn't the same thing. There are some people who are fundamentally—"

I interrupt her sentence: "He wants to stay a little longer."

"Then I'm going back home."

"It's his house—as much as ours," I remind her.

"But we're the ones who have to take care of it. He's not helping you paint when he's down here, is he? Or worried that the house needs new screens—let alone a new roof."

"I know, but it's really ours. He's told us that every summer. Christ, we don't even see him the rest of the year. All he wants to do is visit us for a few weeks each summer. The house is ours the rest of the time."

"Nice, convenient arrangement. He gets a vacation and we do all the work. I cook, wash his clothes, while you do all the repairs."

"He took us out to dinner tonight."

"Once a week so he won't feel so guilty."

"He wants to be with the kids. Can you deny him that? Jesus, what's he got to give him any pleasure? No wife, no kids. He's going blind."

"You don't go blind with floaters," she throws back at me.

"How do you know?"

"Somebody told me."

"Who?"

"A woman I talked to at the beauty parlor."

"Quite a source for medical information."

"She's got a brother with the same problem. He's learned to live with it, even plays tennis, while your brother toddles along the beach as if he's walking on eggs."

There's no point arguing any longer. I take the sheet and pull it over me, knocking the book over in the process. She picks it up as I turn on my side to get away from the light. It's been a heavy enough day that I can feel the sleep hitting me as soon as I close my eyes. Susan, I know, will be awake until she finishes her romance. It was not for nothing that she took a nap in the afternoon.

Over the weekend, he doesn't seem to have any problems with his eyes, or maybe they're so minor that he doesn't mention them. Even better, the tensions of the earlier days of his visit seem to disappear. Susan spends her time shopping with Sarah, doing a thousand-piece puzzle, and bicycling on the boardwalk. Tommy and his newfound friends shatter their own time together, running from house to house. I keep plugging away on house repairs, though Freddy doesn't offer to help. He spends a good bit of time on the phone talking to some guy about a hot business deal, and the rest of the time shuffling the weekend papers. It's Tuesday, right after lunch, before I hear anything more about his eyes.

"You want to take the kids to the beach?" I ask him, since he's made the suggestion several times over the weekend. If Susan and I can have a little privacy, maybe we can get back into the routine of things. Throughout the school year, sex gets put on the back burner, though sometimes we discover that the pilot light's also gone out.

"I'm having a lot of trouble today, Michael," he replies, immediately lowering my expectations.

"You mean your eyes? You haven't mentioned them in several days."

"I didn't want to bother you."

"I thought that since you hadn't talked about them you weren't having any trouble."

"The spots come and go, because they're always moving around, but they're there most of the time."

"What do you mean by 'moving'?"

"Sometimes I think there's an inchworm inside my eye."

"An inchworm?"

"Slowly crossing my pupil. I don't know how to describe it, but—"

"Hey, I've read about that. There's an African worm of some kind that gets into your system and migrates to the eyes. Maybe you really do have something—"

"You think I've been making this all up?"

"I didn't mean that. Maybe there's a physiological explanation for what's been happening."

"Of course there is. It's called bad eyes. My eyes are shot to pieces. Since I can't control what's happening to me, I'm trying to save the images that are still there: you, Tommy, and Sarah." And then he adds, "Susan." He continues a moment later, "I wasn't going to drive down here this summer, didn't think I should risk it until I realized it's the images that I'm losing."

"How can that be?" I ask him. "If I close my eyes, I can still see what you look like."

"You've still got your sight. For me it's like a picture with some parts missing. People's faces are beginning to have holes in them, missing places, and I don't seem to be able to fill them in."

"This is impossible. You're talking about memory, which is different from sight. I can remember faces I haven't seen for years. If I close my eyes, I can see the first house we lived in—before the place on Indiana Avenue."

"It's what I'm losing, Michael. Every day. Like brain cells being destroyed by alcohol or something."

"Well, that's possible, too—all of us—"

"You're not hearing what I'm saying. I can't see Dad and Mom's faces any longer—I mean their entire faces. They're full of holes, as if someone's taken a machine gun and blown them all to bits. Even Joyce. Every time I try to remember what she looks like, the image is full of holes. What's killing me is that the gaps seem to be multiplying. How long is it going to be before there's nothing there but space itself?"

"Freddy, this is pretty awful stuff. I didn't know it was so bad. I don't think I understood."

"I don't understand it most of the time either. It's not the way the doctor said it would be. The memory's supposed to be able to put everything back together."

"What happens with things immediately around you?"

"Holes, of course. I've already told you."

"I know that. I mean, if you look at me, can you still see all of me when you turn your head, or are the holes always in the same place?"

"They shift. The gaps can be filled back in as long as I can keep close to the source." He doesn't say anything for a few seconds but then continues, "That's why I wanted to stay here a little longer, before I go back to Philadelphia. Once I leave, I don't know what's going to happen, what I'm going to remember."

I'm overcome by a burst of emotion. If he weren't my brother, I'd grab hold of him and hold him tightly, but there was never much touching in our family, and I feel uncomfortable starting now.

"Well, stay longer. Stay as long as you want. Stay the whole summer."

"He's making it up. I know he's making it up. There are people who've lost their sight who have incredible memories. They claim they can even see colors. I've read about it. He's got to be making this up. The mind doesn't do things like that."

"I agree that what he's said probably's distorted, maybe worse than it really is, but this is something I have to take seriously, Susan. You can respond in any way you want, but he's asking for help, and I can't let him down."

Lately I've thought that the gap between us in the bed is getting wider. The book that separated us the other night was only the bottommost of a growing pile of books. I can't see them any better than my brother sees the faces he's trying to remember, but I know they're there, stacking up between us.

"This is a case of panic, of fear. I've never seen him like this. It's a little as if we've reversed roles. I thought I was the mildly hysterical one."

She puts her hand across the invisible barrier and runs her finger along my rib cage, tickling the skin. It's her attempt to make up for the past few nights, but it's too late. I'm no longer interested; there are more important things on my mind. When she sees my chest contract, she pulls her hand back across the center of the bed and waits for me to make the next move.

"He wants to stay with us a little longer."

"How much longer?" Her voice is hollow, as if something inside her has dried up.

"The whole summer maybe. What's—"

"Not the whole summer, Michael. Not the whole summer."

"Why not, if it'll help him?"

"But it won't help you, *us*, don't you see? We come down here every summer to get away from the city. You can hardly wait. You're shot by the end of the semester, or have you already forgotten? If he's here the whole time, you'll start teaching the same way you ended the semester; and I'm not willing to go through that again. Have you already forgotten?"

"This isn't the same thing. I don't have to mark papers. I don't have 125 high-IQ morons swarming around me. Only one more person than the four of us."

"It can't be good for any of us—especially the kids. Things aren't the same with someone else invading the house. The kids deserve more than that."

"I haven't heard any complaining."

"It's not something you want to hear."

"I can't throw him out at the end of the week, Susan. He needs help. I don't even know how the hell he drove down here, and I certainly don't want him going back by himself."

"Maybe you should drive him home."

"And leave the three of you in peace?"

He's beginning to do things I've never noticed before, or maybe I simply ignored them. Yesterday there was a cut on his chin, where he'd nicked himself when he shaved. When he walks any distance beyond his room, he has trouble navigating a straight line. When he toddled on the beach last week, it wasn't because of the sand. He can't see where he's going like he used to. He's all right with most activities: cutting his food, getting up from a chair, but I've watched him put his hand out in front of him when he's walked through a door and didn't realize that anyone was watching. The spots have taken over so much that he's going blind.

"What do they look like today?" I ask him at the end of the third week. Susan and I have barely spoken to one another for three days. The only voices you hear in the house are Tommy's and Sarah's. When they're gone, it's like a crypt.

"My eyes?" he asks me.

"The spots."

"What is this, a Rorschach test?

"I'm concerned about what's happening to you."

"Not much is going on at the moment. Earlier in the day there was this funny little shape. I though it was a squashed tennis ball, except that it had little protuberances growing out of it. Like arms or feet, swimming in the sea."

I'm about to respond that it sounds like a fetus, but I keep silent because of the implications.

"How did you get down here?" I ask him a little later. We've been sitting on the porch to get more of the breeze. Susan's taken the kids to a movie, and we've stayed home.

"I don't know what you mean." He doesn't turn in my direction, so I figure he's trying to see me in his peripheral vision.

"How did you get down here? I know you didn't drive the car yourself."

"I don't know what you mean, Michael."

"Look, Fred, your car. You haven't moved it since you've been here. It's stayed in the same place, and that's not exactly your style. You're always on the run, shopping for things you don't need. You haven't left the house except to go to the beach. You don't read the papers any longer, though you pretend to. You may have fooled me the first week, but now I know what's going on."

He doesn't say anything.

"So how did you get down here, Freddy?"

"A college kid drove me. I put an ad in the paper and this undergraduate answered. He needed to get down here for a job. You'd like him; he's majoring in English. Talked my—"

"So what can you see these days, Freddy?"

"Not much." There's an incredible sadness in his voice. It's as if he's confessed some terrible sin.

"What are we going to do, Fred?"

"I don't know. This is not the way I planned it. I thought there'd be more time than this. They told me it wouldn't happen so quickly."

"Who?"

"The doctors, the specialists."

"When did it begin?"

"Years ago, apparently."

"But when did it get this bad?"

"Months ago—years. That's why I cashed in everything, though everybody's called me a fool. I thought I really had it made, that money somehow—and modern technology—would make it all right, but I guess it's caught up with me."

"What do you want me to do? What can I do to help?"

"Nothing."

"You can stay here the rest of the summer."

"It's no good. You've got your family. You need a vacation without someone else busting it up for you." He's careful enough that he doesn't mention Susan, though I know he's picked up on her moods.

"Nonsense. You sound like somebody I bumped into on the street—not my brother, for Christ's sake."

I talked him into staying a fourth week and then a fifth. More importantly, I convinced Susan that his visit was necessary, which is not to say that the situation between the two of us was any improved. I'd call it resigned more than anything else: to her fate. Our summer was not going as she had planned it. During the third week, she dropped a few hints that after he left we could still have a "normal" family vacation—whatever that was. During the fourth week her comments were less frequent.

What impressed me more than anything else about my brother was that he made a concerted effort to get to know his niece and nephew. He tried to do things with them, spend some time with each of them, every day.

What I remember today are the oddities that mirrored Freddy's own deteriorating condition. As his physical state worsened, his mood seemed to soar. When I got the call in late October informing me that he'd killed himself, I felt relieved—almost elated—as if he'd conquered something. He kept his blindness from Tommy and Sarah to the last moment—until late in July—when I drove him back to Philadelphia. In one particularly painful moment, Sarah asked him to help her start another thousand-piece puzzle. He didn't decline but tried valiantly to help. Instead of identifying the pieces by looking at them, he did it by touch, gathering together as many of the straight edges as he could, and then giving them to Sarah and letting her put them together. He even found two of the corners, which seemed to please him.

Our conversations? There was one that sticks in my mind. I've almost become fixated on it. After I pried all the details out of him, what struck me was the way he first realized that something was wrong.

"I thought it was psychological. It took me years to work out the fallout from Joyce, all the time paying the shrink. Then one day I had trouble reading the quotes in the *Wall Street Journal*. I thought it was some kind of mental block. I'm getting pretty good at this, I thought. I can figure it out myself, without spending thousands of dollars for therapy. We'd spent two years going over my self-image, and I determined that I didn't like my job. So what did I think was going on? It's very simple. I couldn't read the financial pages because I didn't want to be a broker any longer."

"When was this?"

"Three, four years ago. I tell you, Michael, I seriously thought about quitting my job and getting out of the market right then. I even began to feel nausea some mornings when I drove to work. It's very logical. I couldn't read the figures because I hated what I was doing."

"What changed?"

"You're not going to believe this."

It didn't matter whether I believed it or not. What I was seeing was that Freddy's depression had lifted. He could almost make a joke out of what he was telling me.

"What happened?"

"I started having trouble with the faces of the people I worked with. They didn't look the way they used to. Especially Ben Summers, the guy who was at the next desk. I couldn't stand him because he made twice as much as I did, when all at once I realized I didn't have to look at him any longer. It was as if he wasn't there. It was absolutely fantastic. I could hear his voice yakking away on the phone, making deals, but I didn't have to look at the son-of-a-bitch any longer."

He stopped talking and I watched him try to light a cigar. We were outside on the porch where we had begun spending the evenings. I refrained from helping him, even though I was afraid he was going to burn himself; but he managed it, as he'd begun to conquer so many other things the last few days he stayed with us.

"Then it all stopped a couple of weeks later. I was buying groceries on the way home from work, and when I got to the head of the line, I couldn't see the checker's face, even though I was standing two feet away from her. And I knew it wasn't psychological." Then he added, "How stupid of me—I thought I'd developed a system where I no longer had to look at what I didn't want to see."

Now it's summer again and we're back at the beach. It's the middle of July, so the place is really hopping with people. If you don't stake out a place on the sand first thing in the morning, forget it. It's only a problem because of the kids. Tommy's seven; Sarah's nine. When it's windy and the waves are rough, they're not exactly safe. In all the years we've been coming here, I've been knocked over enough to know that the undertow can be pretty brutal. What it means is that the kids have to be watched more carefully than when they were younger and frightened by the waves—especially Tommy, who's become fearless.

I've told Susan that it's her responsibility to get to the beach early enough to stake out a place for the day. The trouble is that she's not very good at getting up in the mornings.

"What are we here for, if we can't sleep late? Can't you go to the beach with the chairs and the umbrella and get a place for us before we get up? How long would that take you—thirty minutes?"

It's late at night and she's reading in bed. "It's not the time," I tell her. "It's the coolest part of the day for me to work on the house.

I don't want to lose the time before it gets so hot. You go with the kids in the mornings. I'm perfectly willing to take the afternoon shift after I've finished my work. But if they want to be on the beach, one of us has to watch them."

"You worry too much," she replies. "What do you think lifeguards are for?"

"Lifeguards can't watch everyone."

"Maybe you need new glasses—" and her voice drones on.

I blink my eyes, wondering why I need to see her so clearly.

CHARLES R. LARSON is the author of a number of works of literary criticism and fiction. His scholarly books include The Emergence of African Fiction, American Indian Fiction, The Novel in the Third World, The Ordeal of the African Writer, *and a biography,* Invisible Darkness: Jean Toomer and Nella Larsen. *His novels include* The Insect Colony, Arthur Dimmesdale, *and a collection of satirical sketches called* Academia Nuts. *He recently edited* Under African Skies: Modern African Stories *and* The Complete Fiction of Nella Larsen, *and coedited (with Roberta Rubenstein, who is also a professor of literature at American University) an anthology of short stories,* Worlds of Fiction. *In 1991, he received the American University Faculty Award for Outstanding Teacher. For ten years, he was the fiction and book review editor of* Worldview.

Joy Pasture

Nathan Leslie

Man, I finally find the place and pull into the drive at maybe two in the morning. No lights or anything. I mean, the place is dark. All I want is some sack time, you know? The thing is though, when I walk up to the front door I can hear that Ravi Shankar sitar radiating from the walls like some kind of gas, and some dude firing double speed about how he's down on Erich Fromm, how all that esoteric crap about love can now just go fly a kite. I hear a woman's voice asking if anybody else wants another hit from the meerschaum pipe. The speed demon says the French Blue has him elevated fantabulous. Oh yeah. Hands are clapping and slapping along to the raga. That tabla hits me in the gut and the beat rises, stretches, soars, sings, gallops, hammers, drips, and floats on back to me. I'm dogged, man, but who can miss out on such a ginchy entrance?

I knock on the door and a great applause bursts from the room. Someone turns up the music, and the door lurches open, and I do a swirling, stamping dance into the room. No slouch for a zoid, I think. Glancing about, I'm not sure who Cricket is. All I've got is a sleeping bag, a duffle, and a thin old pillow that smells like cheeba, b.o., and jism. Then a short girl catapults over the back of the sofa and sways to the music in front of me: cropped pixie do, squirrel cheeks, aquamarine hoop earrings down to her shoulders. She asks if I'm Ike, and I nod in the affirmative. The group clappity-claps along to the escalating rhythm.

"Man, we need a nickname or something," she says. "All I can think of is Eisenhower, and that's a mondo downer, man."

"OK, what about Peanut?"

Cricket grins, claps my back, and spins me around like a ballerina. She gestures to one of the guys to turn the music down a notch
or two. I see a mesh of wide eyes and grins. Nobody moves.

"Everybody, I'd like to introduce you to Peanut," Cricket says,
circulating her neck in concentric circles.

Cheers and salutations: "Welcome Peanut!"; "Hey Peanut!";
"Howdy Peanut"; "How's it hanging there, Peanut?"

Cricket shows me a corner where I can lay my stuff, and I do. She
tells me if I need to catch some zees now I can crash in her rack and
if not I could come down and get blissed out with the rest of them.
My eyes felt like two lead balloons, but it was a clear choice. I've never
been one to pass up on a choice buzz.

"What's your fave?" she says, flicking her right earring. She gives
her tongue a kittenish little nip.

"Oh, I don't know," I say. "Can't go wrong with a doobie, I guess.
Good old standard."

Suddenly she leans both hands against my chest, licks my neck,
and melds into me. "Welcome to Joy Pasture."

"Thanks," I say. But before the final S even slithers out of my pie
hole, her tongue is performing a dental inspection, and her other
hand is caressing my intimates.

"That's just an appetizer," she murmurs. Then she bounds down
the stairs, like some hyped-up psychedelic hare. That's when I notice
the candles. Man, there's a huge torch candle in the hall, candles
splayed all over the furniture and over the floor in Cricket's room,
and candles following me as I walk downstairs all the way down the
stairs and into the living room. Bet they don't actually have power
in this joint. Battery operated everything, man.

So I'm down there squatting on the floor with all of them.
Almost as soon as I sit Cricket hands me a roach. All the psychic
energy shifts: they all want to hear from me. Why have I come to
Joy Pasture? Where am I from? Who have I fucked and who haven't
I fucked? What drugs have I *not* done? What is my stance on Jimmy
Carter? Have I ever read the Egyptian *Book of the Dead*? Do I dig the
blues? Am I into holistics? Do I do macrobiotics? It's dizzying, but
dizzying is good. People care. Curiosity reigns.

When that cools down I end up talking gestalt theory and Maoism with this guy called Hyena, which is a strange name to pick for

yourself. I wonder what the dude is on for half the time; for the other half he just seems to be pissing in the wind. Man, Hyena goes on about hiking up Machu Picchu, only he says it was in China not that other place. Then he tries to tell me that the only way to purify your system is with bean sprouts and acid.

All I want to do is grok. Life seemed to be getting massive stale recently, like everybody is turning flunky paper-pusher. Maybe I'm paranoid, but the grooviness of things seemed to be fading. So there I am trying to do a one-eighty from that, putz around those with these sweet, low-down, cosmic types.

"That's all I eat. Bean sprouts," he says.

"Really?" I ask.

"Absofuckinglutely," he says. "It's the only way to go. Bean sprouts is where it's at, man."

I'm not browned off or anything though. He's got his right. Then Hyena starts into this thing about how hippies are the niggers of the '70s. Time for an uprising. He says the CIA has executed twenty thousand hippies Chilean-style, and that we are just now finding out about it.

"They take us down to Oklahoma, to those old Indian reservations, man. That's where they get us. They have pits filled with dead hippies out there. All over the place. It's a fucking My Lai Massacre all over. Only this time it's a slow seep," he says. "Like air from a balloon, so nobody fucking notices. You know?"

"Are you sure about that?" I ask.

"Natch. Natch," he says.

The more I talk to Hyena the more he starts repeating himself in abbreviations. White niggers become "wigs." Bean sprouts become "brouts." Machu Pichu becomes "Mich."

Luckily Cricket snags me by the wrist and guides me back through a dark hallway before this whiz totally kills my rush, and she takes me through two more candled rooms, and onto the back porch. I can hear the door clack behind us. Then it opens again and clacks again. A tall stud with hair down to his ass carries a long, blood-red candle, dripping red wax here and there. He's holding a topless woman by the hand, and even in the candlelight I can see the guy has an erection. Man, they all reek of patchouli oil and sweat and pot and sex.

"Hey, Peanut," the guy says, coming from underneath with his hand. I shake it. He hands me the meerschaum pipe, asking me if I want some more hay. "The elixir of life," he says. He says his name is Kitty and that the fine young dame on his arm is Snowbird. "Like it goes," Kitty says. I'm not sure what that means at all, so I'm smiling dumbly and just nodding.

"Like it goes," I repeat dumbly.

I take a few hits from the pipe and pass her on. Cricket has a bottle of Mazola in her right hand and her left hand is unbuckling my cutoffs. My head floats from the weed and the weird blips from the trippy music they have going on now. I close my eyes to let it all sink in. I blink my eyes open and realize Kitty, Cricket, and Snowbird are all naked, dousing me with Mazola.

"Ritual," Kitty whispers in my ear. Suddenly I realize I have six hands going, rubbing, caressing, and smearing. Snowbird's pubic hair grinds into my leg, and her legs slip and wrap around my legs. She begins licking my thighs and shins. Cricket's hands stroke me, and she presses her breasts into my mouth, and wraps her neck around mine. Kitty holds me from behind, and I can feel him pressing against me. They lay me on my back on the picnic table, and my head goes into orbit. As if I'm looking down on myself I can see Cricket, my member in her mouth, and Snowbird rubbing her oily body against me, pressing herself into my face, and Kitty behind me, head back, sweaty stream of hair thumping, thumping, thumping, in the candlelight flicker.

So the only reason I'm down to Joy Pasture in August is some palooka started rolling then lighting up a doobie on the boardwalk thirty seconds after I sold him the bundle of hay. Man, all I did was go to the can, and as I sauntered back to my spot I ran into the blue cuffs. They nabbed Palooka Joe, and I was toast too. I was shitting my pants since I'm only twenty-one and I'd already been busted outside a head shop for possession. Man, I didn't want to be laid up in a cell getting my gourd knocked in.

I've always been lucky though. My parental units let me slide in high school, even when I boosted the second Led. Even when I stumbled in stinking from a major grog jag, they copped me a break. My rents are cool beans. Into the whole macrobiotic thing.

Health nuts. Hippies themselves. As long as I put forth my best, they figured I could just hang loose the rest of the time. They were loosey-goosey. Of recent, they've been wiring me boo-koo green, just walking around money. I told them I'd get with the program by '78, but I still have two years to freewheel. I call them every week as a kind of thank you.

I guess Sergeant Blowhard could see that I wasn't some weed fiend out to detonate the morals of the good old U.S. of A. I guess he could see I was just a bit player trying to get his rocks off. Man, I lucked out: instead of sending me down to the clink, he set up a harsh dealio: man, he made me a damn stoolie.

"There's this Goddamn filthy pinko hippie commune," he said. The guy was popping lifesavers like popcorn and crunching them with his molars. I could see the neon colors glomming to his teeth as he talked, and I had the munchies something terrible. Guy was chewing like a cow with its cud. He had this baby face with gray hair—probably forty, but his face read eighteen. He leaned toward me and winked. I could smell the candy-coated stink of his breath. "What you're going to do is go stay there for a month or two," he said. "Scout things out for us."

I asked him the obvious question: why? I wasn't trying to be dingy, I just didn't get it.

"I'll tell you, guy. You're going to call us as soon as you hear a woman who goes by Peacock is coming around the bend. Got it? You find out when she's coming and you let us know ASAP. That's it. I want all the names of the others, but she's your target, buster. That's why."

"Who's Peacock?"

"You'll find out, smartass. Our sources tell us she'll be making a call at this Joy Pasture commune in the next few days, but we simply don't have the manpower right now to track it. Wish we could just abolish all those piece-of-shit joints. This is where you enter the picture. And by the way, if you split town, I'm sure we could just let the full effect of the judicial process run its course from there."

"Yeah right," I said.

Then Blowhard leaned to me. I could hear the bones in his back adjust to the movement. "Asshole, ten pounds of marijuana would net you a good vacation. Believe you me."

Driving out to Joy Pasture took a good two hours. I was listening to Canned Heat on the radio, one foot out the window of my sky blue Pinto. I was trying to flush that uptight square voice out of my ears. I guess I could've been uptight about all the ego games, but for some reason I wasn't. I was feeling too dogged for stress. I also knew I was damn lucky. The whole time I was driving I scratched my head over this Peacock lady. I couldn't wrap my brain around it.

But even more than that, I actually looked forward to going M.I.A. with some funked-up megafamily. Yeah, it felt good to be a pilgrim again. I'd spent some ultracool times at hippie houses, and even if I was a stoolie, I could still have a blast. What would they care? In the end I thought I could let everyone down easy. I thought I could choose for myself.

The sun is smearing up the horizon, then I pass out. When I come to it's three in the afternoon, and I'm sweating bullets. My head feels like Sugar Ray used it as a punching bag, and I'm famished and parched. As I limp down the stairs, the house is silent. I step over more naked bodies sprawled in every position.

In the kitchen, I lower my head and drink straight from the tap, and I find a Baggie of aspirin, or what looks to be aspirin. The floor is covered with a coat of sticky gray scum, and littered with rasty beer cans, airplane glue, cigarette butts, spoons, cloves, empty aluminum foil pipes, T-shirts, panties, paper plates, forks, spent matches, and banana peels. The counter is piled with plastic bags filled with brown rice and gorp. Pots and pans are precariously stacked by the stove, and piles of white trash bags slump on the kitchen table and chairs. The air smells like panther piss. For a moment the whole vibe in this room gives me the heebie-jeebies.

Tapped on the fridge are Polaroids of the Joy Pasture group swimming, and planting, and carrying basketfuls of tofu, and tossing a Frisbee around a muddy field. I'm rubbing the hangover out of my face with the back of my hands, and trying to regain my balance in this helter-skelter room. Directly beneath the pictures is an orange piece of paper with "House Rules" written at the top in black ink. Underneath, the paper reads: "By staying at Joy Pasture you implicitly agree to the following joyful restrictions:

1. No violence.
2. No children.
3. No hate.
4. No flesh eating.
5. No energy grid.
6. No possessions.
7. No pets.
8. No stress.
9. No unresolved conflicts.
10. You must contribute."

"Hey there," a voice says behind me.

A heavyset paper-bag job dressed in a loose maroon robe stands behind me, smiling rim to rim. Her hair is up in two pigtails, and her desiccated-looking love beads dangle down to her belly. Man, she's wearing sandals, and her toenails are gnarled and yellow.

"Nice to meet you," she says. "You're Peanut, right?" I bob my head, and she tells me that it's her turn to cook for the house, and she asks if I want some gorp to tide me over, or maybe a peanut butter and banana sandwich.

"OK," I say, and back out of her way. In five minutes she has the table and stove cleared, and I'm noshing gorp and drinking ginseng tea while she boils a tub of water and chops vegetables and tofu on a large wooden platter.

"These days most of us are macro," she says. "But if you want eggs I could scramble some for us as well. I'm not morally opposed."

I tell her I'm so hungry I'll eat whatever, and that I'm used to macro from my parents and all.

"I just hope you're not a flesh eater. I thought for a second I could smell animal blood on your breath."

I thought this was an odd thing to say, but I sit down at the newly cleared table anyway.

"I've eaten beef and chicken before, but not for years." A lie. She nods her head and says that they usually consider her the weaver of the house—she makes clothes for everybody.

"What's your talent?" she asks.

"Bird-dogging," I say. "But don't tell the others."

She bends her head down and turns back to her chopping. I can tell she didn't like that answer, but then I wonder if she's ever been in the saddle. She turns her back to me and sprinkles the water with salt.

"Have you met Kitty?" she asks, craning her neck behind her to see me.

I nod, and she turns to see it.

"His goal is to fuck everyone that comes into Joy Pasture. You should know. It's no secret." Still, I look out into the living room to see if anyone heard. Lowering my voice, I ask her if he's had everyone currently here. She shakes her head.

"But I'm the only hold-out," she says. "My name's Plum, by the way."

By four, the Joy Pasture crew is seated around the picnic table on the porch, drinking ice water and eating brown rice and vegetables with tamari sauce, bean sprout sandwiches on wheat bread, and grabbing handfuls of gorp. I meet the rest of the house: a black guy who goes by Lizard and his perky girlfriend Skink; Slim, a fat moody acid freak; Wisp, a rail-thin spiritualist dude in a ratty white robe; Chola, a sexy music lover, and Sunbeam, a hard-core druggie who says he will try anything in the book, you name it.

They tell me about their crops (tomatoes, peppers, melons, potatoes, cucumbers—all planted on top of the hill) and they rhapsodize about the chicken coop, and the tofu hut, and how in the summer they are usually self-sustaining.

"Especially with the money crop out back," Sunbeam says. Man, they tell me about the hate mail that tells the "fucking faggot hippie commie fucks," that the Klan is coming to burn their "Jew-house" to the ground. They tell me about the bullets lodged in the door, about the townies circling the Joy Pasture with shotguns and dusters.

"We've been here six years now, and believe me we can take the heat," Cricket says. "Some fossils just don't know what's the sauce."

Wisp and Snowbird stay back to clean up the kitchen, and Chola tells the rest of us we should go tend to business. She asks me if I'd rather help Cricket, Hyena, and Plum with the tofu hut, or help her, Sunbeam, Lizard, and Skink out in the garden. My kismet always takes me outside, so I tell Chola I'll take what's behind door number two. Sunbeam pops a square of some yellow sunshine and asks if I want one.

"Absofuckinglutely," I tell him.

Within half an hour Papa Time is truckin'. We must be out there four five hours weeding, picking vegetables, restaking tomatoes, spraying natural insecticide everywhere. My thoughts are flying at a hundred miles an hour back to last night, to my old squeeze Rosa who dumped me for some stockbroker sellout flavor of the month. Then my mind whizzes to which one of these fantabulous flakes will end up leaving this place with me. The Joy Pasture feels just right. For once in my life I don't have the meemies in the back nook of my brain. My mom always said, "Don't push the river," and for once I get it.

As the sun grates down the sky, Sunbeam and I are in plot seven, spraying for aphids in the watermelons, looped and giggly like little girls at a birthday party. I look down at my waffle stompers. The melon leaves curl around the laces, and around the base. I can hear the ants and worms tunneling through the soil. The air smells like the seed of Dionysus, and the sky is the eye of Ganesha. I sit in the dirt and watch my fingers leg it down into the soil. I can feel the rot and life in it. I can taste the shit of a million years in it, and the Cosmic Dharma in it, and the nights of ice and snow and death.

Sunbeam sits next to me, and collapses behind a melon plant in laughter. We kick open a melon and dig out the meat and seeds with our hands, eating soil and seeds and juice as the sun screams my name and pants into the slate. I'm ready to fuck the universe. Instead I find union with Sunbeam's holy member. I don't care who can see. When he explodes my heart bursts into a million shards that encircle the fields and bring me the bounty of life, and the wisdom of a thousand prophets.

Man, the acid won't let me have any sack time. It's six in the morning and I haven't lost a second of consciousness. I've cut some dark meat with Skink and Sunbeam and God knows who else, and smoked a hookah for what felt like five hours, but while everyone else (even Sunbeam) dozes, I'm sitting at the picnic table, pasted with Mazola oil, saliva, semen, and sweat.

A blonde head of hair is what I see first—a girl carrying a white cat. Behind her, holding the door, is another woman, straw boater hat, long red hair and skin the exact color of eggshells. Even in the thin porch light I can see the freckles that dot her arms and face and the painted peacock on her left cheek. She opens her mouth as if to say something, and the girl squeezes the cat to her chest. The woman's tongue curls behind a wall of teeth: is this the final wave of my comedown? Is this some vision of the collective Joy Pasture unconscious, some damp DayGlo vixen along to layer icing on my cake?

"I didn't expect anyone to be awake," the woman says. She runs a finger along the outer ridge of her flowered dress, smoothing a rumple. Her voice is ripe and thick with existence.

"Me neither," I say. I think it's the bicentennial, why shouldn't my luck blossom? Why shouldn't this be the year when my fate harvests?

"Do you speak Esperanto?" she asks. I notice her cat is missing one leg, and man, the girl hasn't blinked once. She wears green fruit boots and a red T-shirt that reads "Burn Baby Burn."

"No," I say. My thoughts dangle, and at this moment the woman can do anything she wants with me as far as I'm concerned.

"Too bad," she says. "My name is Deborah. This is Sophie."

I introduce myself and rest my chin in my hands. Deborah tells me she is Cricket's sister.

"Do you know of a place we can crash? We drove all night from Cleveland," she says.

I couldn't imagine this beauty in a dump like Cleveland. In fact, at that moment I can't imagine Deborah anywhere other than where she is.

"Well, it's pretty packed in there," I say. "And it's sweltering. I was going to sleep out here." I point to a blanket on the floor of the porch. "It's cooler."

"That sounds good to me then," she says. She turns to Sophie and Sophie nods. Deborah opens the porch door and grabs three bags, and pillows, and without speaking I collapse on the blanket, and Deborah and Sophie lay next to me, curled on top of a sleeping bag together, the cat purring in the crook of Sophie's arm. I close my eyes and the swirling slows, and I can hear the sweet breath next to me, the purring of the cat, and I can smell lilac and the nutty scent of Deborah's hair.

I wake up with the sun blaring in my face, and my brow sweating, and the sounds of laughter from the kitchen. I ease my body up, and then I stand.

"For sure," I hear Cricket laugh from the kitchen. "Great to see you, Sis. For sure."

I feel like a Dudley stumbling into the kitchen like I do, but my mouth is parched, and I'm ravenous. When I enter the room, Cricket and Deborah lean against the counter. Sophie hides behind her mother's legs. Cricket is topless, and for a moment her apple-sized breasts look like shrunken heads. Cricket kisses my cheek, and asks if I've meet her sister Peacock, blah, blah, blah. As soon as she says "Peacock" I just about fall backwards. But at the same time I know I can't reveal my shock, so I tighten my stomach and grin.

"Oh, what a cool nickname," I say, and ask for some water. Cricket pours me a glass, and she pulls a chair out for me, and I sit on it.

"Yeah, take a load off," Cricket says. "Cool it Jack. Want an Alice B. Toklas brownie?"

I shake my head, but Cricket says she'll make some eggs for me. That's the cure for the blahs, she says. "Got to get the juices flowing back into your system. Elevate you with some protein. That's the downside of a macro diet. For sure."

Peacock pats her daughter's back and says Sophie is shy around guys.

"That's what happens when a girl doesn't get to know her daddy," Peacock says.

Man, I don't want to harp on that, so I bury my face in the glass of water. I wonder where Peacock is stowing the Mexican mud, and when she plans on making her exchange. I think about crafting some excuse, hopping in my Pinto, and calling Sergeant Blowhard from town, as instructed. But then Peacock turns around, picks Sophie up by the armpits, carries her over to the table across from me, and plops her down on her lap. Sophie smiles slyly and nestles her head in her mother's chest. Cricket is breaking eggs into a bowl, and stirring them with a fork. Something holds me back.

"Where is everybody?" I ask.

"Man, they're all with Plum in the tofu hut. The guy comes this evening, so they're finishing off a batch." Cricket must still be buzzed from last night because then she starts rattling on and on about the bean-soaking process, and how Kitty is usually the kettle operator, pushing the soybean slurry until it reaches its critical temperature. She talks about soymilk and nigari and how Slim and Wisp usually remove the whey from the curd with strainers and a vacuum pump, and Chola seals them in their "Joy of Soy" packaging. "It's the whole sustainable living thing at its best," she says. Like I give a rat's ass.

Cricket turns back to the scrambled eggs, and I look at Peacock, and she investigates my face, bouncing Sophie on her lap. Then suddenly, Peacock rolls her eyes, and I almost fume my water in surprise.

"Get a grip," she says. "Ain't no great shakes to make a bunch of shitty tofu."

Man, I lean back in my chair and grin, and she smirks back, and Cricket brings me the plate of eggs with a spoon, and two slices of bread, and she apologizes that nobody's done the dishes from last night yet.

"No problem," I say, and I begin shoveling the eggs into my mouth. The eggs are crusty and dry and burnt in parts, but it's better than nothing.

Cricket sits down at the table with us and I ask them about growing up together. Cricket sighs and says she loves her parents and all, but that her childhood wasn't at all biblical or anything.

"They were my meal ticket and all, and I thank them for that, but they're big-time whodos," Cricket says. "Man, they got suckered into believing the scam. They're way too sosh, trying to keep up with the Joneses, all that."

Peacock sighs and crosses her legs. Something about the way she moves seems glamorous, or powerful, like she's above all the rinky-dink moaning that most people take as their ordinary lot. She seems to float above the concerns of the Joy Pasture. There is something different about her.

"Oh save it," Peacock says. "They raised us right. They gave us a roof over our heads. They're still together and relatively happy. What more can you ask? Do you want them to be your buddies?"

"That's pretty chilly, Sis," Cricket says, slumping forward. She bites her fingernail and rips it off. "I mean, I'm just saying—"

"Yeah," Peacock says. "I know exactly what you're saying. Forget it." Then she turns to me and snaps her fingers. "You want to go for a walk around here or something? I want to be outside."

I watch Cricket's face drop, and I nod and scoop the rest of the eggs into my mouth. Cricket shakes her head and mumbles, and I try to pat her shoulder, but she withdraws from my touch. Man, I think I should say something to her, even if it's only to ask who's cooking tonight, but I don't. I feel a compulsion to follow Peacock and Sophie right out the door. Then I do it.

The three of us walk down the east side of the house and past the chicken coops and yellow and orange outbuildings. I wave to Sunbeam, who is out there smoking some Lebanese blonde from an aluminum foil pipe, and painting red and purple tulips on the face of one of the sheds. I watch her face drop when she sees who I'm with. Peacock slides a pair of sunglasses on, and tightens a sunhat on Sophie's head. We walk past the steam-pumping-Paul-Butterfield-blaring tofu hut and we climb the rise to the vegetables.

Peacock grabs my shoulder, opens her arms toward Joy Pasture, and turns to look back at the house. "Do you see anything wrong with this equation?" she asks.

Man, I think of Cricket telling me how Joy Pasture shares its environment with our animal friends: the deer, fox, rabbits, skunks, hawks, songbirds, owls, eagles, and bats that live in this neck of the woods. I look down at the pond and the blips in the water, and the sun shining upon it. "We honor the spark of the divine in all beings," Cricket told me last night. She took a hit from the hookah and kissed my neck. "We reach through our hurts and fears to find and share our deepest truths." I can't imagine two sisters who are more different.

"Not really," I say. "It seems like a beautiful place to me."

"Look past that for a moment," Peacock says. Sophie watches a dragonfly dart towards her, veer, and then make a beeline back down the hill to the pond. "The house is built on a floodplain. This is my sixth time dropping by, and each time I try to tell my sister and her bozo friends, but they don't listen. Then every year the basement floods. The house is slowly sinking into the swamp."

I nod. Peacock doesn't seem to be the kind of person I want to get on my bad side. The way she coldcocked her sister showed me that to be in like Flynn with Peacock I'd have to just go along for the ride.

"I mean, don't get me wrong," Peacock says. "Joy Pasture is a beautiful place with beautiful people. But if you're not into drugs or group sex, what is there? They're not changing anything here.

What are they actually doing? I mean, let's get real. Drive around the country a bit, you'll see."

"Good point," I say. I'm about to tell her that I have driven around the country, but instead of taking the bait, or seeing all this as a personal chop, somehow I'm stirred. I don't know if it's my post-high state, the eggs, or what, but this blint is getting under my skin.

"Come on," she says, taking Sophie's hand. "Let's walk up to the road."

Peacock walks in front, and Sophie swings her mother's arm. I follow behind, scratching my head over all this. When we reach the edge of the road, Peacock points in both directions. I know I should hop in my Pinto, that the reason why I'm here is to fulfill a duty—or else. But for some reason I just can't pull the trigger.

"Look out there," she says to Sophie, then turns to me to punctuate her point. "*That* is America."

When I find out Snowbird and Kitty are on dinner detail, I'm worried they're going to spike the salad with mescaline and Spanish fly. But it turns out to be a great spread: a giant tub of pasta salad (with tofu of course), fresh watermelon, corn bread, and fried squash. The Joy Pasture clan sits out on the porch picnic table, candles all around, and wine and beer flowing freely. Though it is raining and muggy as hell, everybody compliments the good eats.

The conversation ranges from bubbas to communards to DDT to geodesic domes and back to John and Yoko, but throughout the meal Peacock eats silently, smiling here and there, but mostly seeing to Sophie, making sure she gets enough to eat. The tension is palpable the whole time, as if at any point someone is going to jump all over Peacock. Watching the faces, I can tell they all know why she's there, and they are just choosing to lump it until the deal is over and done with. But they all seem to be holding back, and I'm not sure what it is.

Man, the tension mounts when Hyena asks Peacock what she thinks of *The Little Red Book*. Peacock nods and says she's not really interested in Mao, thank you very much.

"You're not interested? How can you not be down with The Red Book? It's where it's at, man. I mean, if you're not down with Mao, you're not interested in humanity."

Peacock shrugs, and sips her wine: "Well, I guess I'm not interested in humanity then."

Hyena winces, and stabs into a piece of squash. He turns to Cricket: "Hey what's the lowdown with the kid? What the fuck happened to rule two? This is bullshit, man."

"My sister and her daughter are only here for tonight, and then they leave in the morning," she says, pointing at Peacock. "Right?"

"That's right," Peacock says. Then she stands up, and says family time is over. She'd like to do the deal right now. "Nice to see you, Sis. But let's get it over with." She says she'll be right back. Sophie sits across from me and blinks. Hyena mumbles. Chola coughs. Otherwise we listen to the cicadas and the hiss of the candles.

Peacock bangs through the screen door, and tosses a paper bag on the table. Skink's wine jostles and sloshes over the lip of the glass. Skink passes the bag down the row, to Cricket. I'm watching Cricket open the bag, peer inside, and dip her fingers into the opening. Then I hear the click behind me. Peacock has a pistol pointed at her sister's hand, and as Cricket lifts it from the bag Peacock follows the hand.

"Wise up. It's good," Peacock says. "All of you just rest and recline right where you are."

Heads go down. Plum hides her face with her hands. Snowbird ducks as if Peacock just blew somebody away. Wisp bows her head. Plates crash to the floor. Glasses break.

"Now where's the money for this joy pop?" Peacock reaches out for Sophie, and Sophie stands next to her mother, holding her leg casually as if this has happened a thousand times before.

"I have it in the kitchen," Cricket says. "In the large sugar bowl."

Peacock points to me, and I push myself from the table and go for the sugar bowl. I open the top, dive my hand down into the granules, and withdraw a stack of bills. When I open the door, Peacock's hand is stretched in front of her, and I hand the bills to her.

"I think it's about time for me to leave," Peacock says, then points to the bags behind her. Sophie runs and picks them up, and Peacock sticks the pistol in her duffle bag. "Thanks for the hospitality. Peace people."

Man, I stand there watching Peacock and Sophie evaporate into the shadows. I watched Joy Pasture watch me. I had helped Peacock, dug my hands in the sugar. While the rest of them quivered in the candlelight I stood there like a flunky. This was one of those moments my mother used to talk to me about. She'd say there are pivots in your life that change everything, and that sometimes you don't have a choice. She always told me if you do the right thing at those pivots, you get ahead. If you don't, you're stuck wallowing in the mud.

Man, I didn't know for sure, but I had a feeling in my gut, and I had to follow it. As I watch those eyes, I could see into the future somehow. There was something suddenly decrepit and frail and out of date about these people, about Joy Pasture. It was as if a barrier suddenly separated us.

I know then what I would do. I would follow Peacock in my Pinto. It wasn't a meat wagon, but then when you're in love it wouldn't matter. I would sit across from her and Sophie at a diner, buy them both a slice of good old apple pie. Peacock would order coffee and tell me the history of communes, about the masons, and the Mormons, about the shakers, and the Moravians, and the Anabaptists. All that. She would speak and it would all make sense. In the back of my mind I would think again about stopping to call Sergeant Blowhard, but in the end, I wouldn't. Instead, we would pull over to a quaint inn nestled into the foothills, and Sophie would sleep in a heart-shaped bed as Peacock and I nested under the white blankets in the adjacent room. In the morning Peacock would wash her hair in Vidal Sassoon, and I would shower and shave, and comb my hair until it looked like a wheat field in September, and we would drive, and drive, and drive, and drive until we found a brick colonial for the three of us, right off Main Street somewhere, a dog yipping in the backyard, maples growing in the front, the general store a block away.

They would wonder about me back at Joy Pasture. They would call me a sellout, a bozo, a cave-in, an AC/DC who let himself have the short end of the stick. As the frost set in they would pull their ponchos on, smoke their Afghani black, and initiate the latest newbie with a Mazola party. And when the spring came around, the house would flood, and they would come to see I was right. They would shake their heads, and wonder what ever happened to Peacock and Sophie and Peanut. Then they would stick out their thumbs, hoping and praying for a guy in a VW bus. But by then it would be too late.

The party will be over. It will be 1977, the two hundred and first year of the U.S. of A., the dawning of a new age.

"Yeah," I say to all of them. "Thank you all for the hospitality." Man, I can feel them watching me with shock, with scorn, but I don't care. I turn around and follow the sounds whispering through the grass darkness, circling Joy Pasture, following her, heading to the driveway and beyond.

NATHAN LESLIE's five collections of short fiction include Believers *(Pocol Press, 2006) and* Reverse Negative *(Ravenna Press, 2006). Leslie's work has appeared in over a hundred literary magazines including* Boulevard, Shenandoah, *and* North American Review. *He is fiction editor for* The Pedestal Magazine *and* The Potomac. *His website is www.nathanleslie.com.*

This Great White Absurdity

PETER LEVINE

In addition to the blood tests, the EKG, the MRI, the gallium scan, the bone marrow biopsy (medieval), it is recommended, if you are a man, that you freeze your sperm. Because the treatment kills fast-growing cells.

Like cancer, like hair, like sperm.

For this adventure you go with your father, him being a man, him having been around the block, your mother having gone to pieces but still enough of her old self to say that she doesn't want you to be alone for any part of this. Your dad: stoic, or simply unfazed, you can't tell—says *Yeah, let's do it, and be sure to give them a good one. Give 'em a tug for me.* You say, on the ride to the lab in the city, you're not sure that's going to help things out, and he says *Right, OK, don't think about me. Think about whatever it is you think about.*

The lab. Looks like any regular waiting room, and there's a receptionist, wearing a ton of makeup, too much makeup, but not bad looking. Certainly not your type, and maybe not anybody's type—this wavy red hair, creamy, even skin, middle aged, glasses, looks like she's in disguise. But she's a really nice lady, she says your name in an awfully sweet voice and you say that's me, that's I. She knows why you're there—the diagnosis and the whole bit, what brand of lymphoma you have—she got the order from the oncologist's office, and she says *OK, I have everything ready, why don't you have a seat and we'll have a room ready for you in a minute.*

You go to sit down. Your father is reading a magazine and looks up.

I have to wait for a room to open up.

Fine, he says.

The office: neutral-colored with a giant ficus plant in the corner. On some kind of steel barrel.

The door to a room opens. A guy comes out. Looks like a guitarist. Black hair, black jeans, black shirt, boots, even. He talks for a minute to the receptionist—you can't hear what she's saying, but she sounds really friendly. And you wonder if she was hired *because* she is really friendly, and also because someone thought she might be nice to look at before you went in and jerked off into a cup. Not in any kind of conventional sense, on account of that disguise look she has on, but maybe she's got a good figure, you can't really tell. You wonder if a patient was having a really hard time, like really couldn't pull it out—if she would come in and help. Of course not, of course, but it's sort of funny to think about that, waiting in the office of this sperm bank facility with your father, sick but not feeling sick, about to jerk off into a cup so that they can freeze it and use it, your come frozen for a decade, more or less, and then unfrozen, swimming around like mad, anxious sperm, hoping like hell to tear through the skin of the egg of a woman you haven't met yet but will likely.

Hopefully.

The doctor, a giant Indian guy, about six feet tall and two hundred and fifty pounds, hardly looks like the type of man to deal in sperm. He comes out and shakes your father's hand and then shakes your hand and explains the whole process. His accent is very heavy. His eyes are like fat marbles—they don't seem human. He tells you all about cryopreservation and how long the sperm will last (indefinitely) and then he points to the giant steel barrel, on which the fichus plant is resting, and says *Here, this is where we keep it. This is an older model.* He taps the steel barrel with the fichus plant on it. It makes an old, hollow sound. It's pretty funny that this Indian guy thought it would be decorative to rest his plant on an obsolete sperm storage unit.

He asks if you are ready and you say *Yeah,* look at your father, he's not saying much, and the doctor leads you into the room the guitarist just came out of. Which is a little creepy, or rather, a lot creepy—the notion that some guy just jerked off in this room that you now have to jerk off in. There's just one lamp on, in the corner, and a medical examining table, if someone wanted to lie down and do it. There's a chair, if you want to do it like that.

The Indian doctor isn't bashful about touching stuff. First he gives you this plastic cup and tells you to get it all in the cup, if you can. Then you put the cup through the little metal door, about a foot wide and long. His lab is on the other side. And you say *So, you're just sitting on the other side?* and he says *Yes, but of course I can't see or hear you, you have total privacy.* And you say *You can't open this little door?* and he looks at you and says *No, it's one-way.* He says they've got a couple videos which you can use, and a couple of magazines and you say *OK, thanks.* He says when you're finished, stay in the room, and he'll come in and let you know everything is good. But then you can go.

He recites these instructions like a flight attendant.

He says sometimes people need to come back for a couple more donations, because what they give is not enough. *But we'll see,* he says.

The Indian doctor leaves.

Since you're practically a professional jerk-off, do it all the time, ever since you were a kid and even when you are sleeping with someone, you figure it's going to be no problem. You're not sure if you should get totally naked for it, but then you decide against that, just take down your pants and boxer shorts and start playing with your dick, tell it to wake up. You open up the drawer where the magazines are. There are a couple issues of *Penthouse.* You leaf through them. Aside from lots of labium and one woman peeing on another woman, and one guy with a dick like a dirigible, about to screw a blonde secretary (or assistant, or business partner—you cannot tell), it's not really doing the trick. So the video. It's a small television they have, mounted on the ceiling, and so you push the Power button and then you push Play and then you think that the guitarist and a million other guys probably pushed the Power button right before and after they jerked off, and this is sort of disgusting to think about. There is a small sink and you wash your hands.

A movie starts and it's some movie with Mike Horner and a woman. It's from the eighties, you can tell by this woman's feathered hair and all the blush and the texture of the video. Now, you know Mike Horner, you know his work, even have a couple of his videos. He's sort of a skinny guy, looks like some kind of pervert, gets a lousy, fiendish look on his face when he's doing it, but you know that there's only a handful of guys in the business who can get it up and come on command, he's one of them, so good for him. He's really skinny in this video. He's doing it with this eighties-looking woman. His dick looks like an uncooked polish sausage. He's got his own rhythm, too. It's like his signature rhythm. You could probably tell it's him without even seeing his face.

You watch this for a little bit. You have a hard-on. You're not worried about the Indian doctor in the other room. Maybe he's waiting for your sample. Or, maybe he's just doing paperwork. Maybe looking at the guitarist's sample. But, who cares? If you have to do it, then you're going to take your sweet time. And you don't care and aren't embarrassed about your father sitting out in the lobby of this place. Fuck it. You used to steal all of his porno materials, books, and videos from back in the day, and he's no stranger to it.

His gear is your gear, his father's gear your gear, and on and on until Adam.

It's OK watching Mike Horner, but not the best. You lie down on the medical examining bed thing they have. The lousy paper on it is terrible, it always is, and these days you've had to familiarize yourself with examining tables. In fact, this scenario has become familiar: your pants off, on an examining table—all you need is some doctor to come in and roll your nuts around in his hand to check for lumps.

Luckily, no lumps. Lumps are not uncommon in men your age and lumps mean you're in for a long haul.

The scene in the movie is really decadent—some castle or something, baroque, Mike Horner doing it with this woman on a bed of red silk sheets and her wearing red stockings. He's got that lousy look on his face. They have close-ups and wide angles. The director must've really put some time into this one. There's music and the music is relaxing and involves a whole orchestra. You figure they got the entire San Fernando Valley Orchestra to play. You think of something like *Jane Eyre*. Something like that. But, for some reason, the video is not getting you where you need to be. It's just this guy, going in and out of this woman, and it's one of the times you wonder why guys, or women, even, get off to porn. What the hell is so great about watching other people do it? You're not doing it. Someone else is.

You turn off the TV. You have a good hard-on going, but there's room for improvement. You're only about two-thirds engorged. The third tube in your dick, the bottom one, is still waffling, not sure it's ready to do its business. You sit in the chair. You hold the cup in front of you. The cup smells like latex or something—terrible. How can they expect you to do it in a cup that smells that awful? And further, it takes you about three strokes to realize that you can't get any kind of good arm movement in this chair. It's just a regular chair. But it's not a good jerk-off chair. If you wanted to run from the tip of your dick down to the base, or even your balls, you couldn't do it in this chair. You wonder if the Indian doctor tried to rub one out in this chair and are sure he didn't. Probably just thought about the lighting. Put a plant in the room. That was it.

At this point you've been in this room five minutes. You don't know what the regular amount of time is for guys trying to jerk off into cups just having found out they have cancer, freezing their sperm so that they can have kids. How long was that guitarist in there for? Who knows? Maybe an hour? There was the other room, and that room never even opened up. There could still be a guy in there, the sides of his dick raw, about to weep because he can't get it done. It would be really shitty, you think, if you couldn't get off. They should let you bring someone in with you. And then, you remember reading in some of the literature you were provided (one of the side benefits of this—you have all the pamphlets and brochures you could ever want), that sometimes you *can* go home and have your partner jerk you off. As long as she doesn't use any lotion, or get the lotion in the sample. And then you'd have to run the sample back over to the lab right away. But, you're on your own for this one.

Concentrate. Think about the best sex you ever had (and you've had a lot, with many, you don't even really know the number), which was the first time you had sex, this girl so wet your dick came out dripping, your almost having come inside her but not, because you weren't wearing anything and she wasn't on the pill yet, and when she jerked you off at the end, you shot this load straight across the basement in her parents' home. You could hear it hit the wood paneling. You were like one of those high-powered sprinklers. You were like an irrigation spout across a field of wheat. You looked at each other like *Oh. My. God. What the hell was that?*

Couldn't find it later. Might have gone straight through the wall.

But concentrating is difficult. A few days ago you had to do this scan where you laid down on a flat, square table and this scanner, also flat and square and fucking huge, came down right in front of your face. Like you were in a hydraulic press. There was a technician, a woman, and she said the scan took forty-five minutes and you had to lie still and you thought *Are you fucking kidding me? I'm going to fucking lose it. I have to sit here under this giant square thing, and can't fucking move? I'm going to get claustrophobic. I'm going to piss myself.*

You didn't say any of this. But thought it.

So, for forty-five minutes you had to lie there. She turned off most all the lights. There was the glow from a computer screen in the corner of the room, imaging your body. And what you thought about was not the Olympic-distance load that you shot with your first girlfriend who's now gone and gone, but about the technician. About her being outside, right outside the door, and how maybe she would come in and ask you how you were doing and you would say that you were having trouble sitting still, you were nervous, right, and she would say I know how to make you not nervous. And then she would push some button and the scanner would lift up, it would elevate, and she would start taking off her blue hospital gear. Top. Off. Pants. Off. Clogs. Off.

Because it's a fantasy, so who cares, right?

She had short, blonde hair. Really cute. Seemed really Midwestern and wholesome, and that was part of what made her attractive to you in the fantasy. So maybe she would undo your pants and start blowing you. Like in the movies. Not amateur blowjob stuff, either. But professional-ball-grabbing-shaft-massaging blowjob. Playing-with-your-asshole blowjob. And then all your clothes off, you two doing it, her on top.

You fell asleep thinking about this.

You woke up to the sound of the scanner being reelevated, and she came back in and asked if you wanted to look at your scan. You said sure. You said you'd fallen asleep and she said many people do. You stood next to her. She smelled like Dove. The room was still dark. On this computer screen, there was a picture of a man's body. A white outline and a black body, like a crime scene, except for the malignancy they'd discovered, which was a glowing white circle.

White against the blackness on your phantom head; this great, white absurdity.

She said the scan looked good, no other growths, tumors, except for the one your oncologist already found.

So, the receptionist. Her high, sweet voice. That red hair that must have been a wig, didn't look real, but for purposes of this, it is. She's just a redhead. She knocks on the door and asks you if everything is OK and you say *Yeah*, but she doesn't hear you and comes in and sees you with your dick out, jerking off. But she doesn't say that she's sorry or anything. She takes off those crazy glasses that she has on.

It's your fantasy, it's your life, you can do with it what you want.

And what she does, rather than give you some kind of blowjob or anything like that, is she takes off her slacks. You don't remember if she was even wearing slacks. But let's say she was. She smells really good. She smells like rosewater, whatever that smells like, if even there is such a thing, but say there is, she smells like it. Takes off her panties. The panties are black and lace. It turns out this secretary has got great legs—perfectly smooth; you never would have guessed it to look at her.

She gets on you and says *Fuck* and *God* and *Sweet Jesus*. Her hands find themselves in her hair, her flushed face, the lower curve of her breasts, her nipples, which are out like they too are players in the event. She is slick, viscous, spilling out around your scrotum, thighs, knees, ankles, toes. Pools on the floor. She says that she loves you—of course—loves you, wants to live inside your skin, blood, marrow, in the lining of your belly, your lungs. And you say *They could be infected* and she says, sweat breaking out on the tiny lines in her forehead— that disease or nondisease, alive, dead—it is of little matter to her.

You say that you're sick and she says that she can't tell—you seem fine to her, perfect, even. *Can you feel that?* and you say *What is it?*, and she says *It's the bottom.* You say *I think I'm going to come* and she says *Please wait* and grabs your nuts. You say *You too?* and she says *What?* and you say everybody's grabbing your nuts, looking for lumps. She says *They feel big and good to me*; her stomach so tight that as she lurches forward it makes only very small wrinkles. Her back strong and full of delicate muscle, veins in her thin arms and hands which have rested on your shoulders.

She kisses the scar; she kisses the scar.

You say *I think I'm going to come now—I can feel it*, and she says *No, if you hold onto it, you'll be around forever* and you say *What?* and she says *You hold onto life, you hold onto life, get it? That's the great secret.*

And you tell her you're wicked and full of sin and she says *Oh, you're young. Do you feel that?* she asks. You say you brought this on and she says *That's not how it works* and you say *I drank from a cistern which wasn't mine to drink from; the lips of the women were like honey, their mouths like oil.* You've eaten, you explain, from the bread of wickedness. You drank, you explain, from the wine of violence. And to your mouth she brings her breasts and she says *Taste.* And from her middle she swipes her hand and puts it into your mouth, and she says *Drink.* She says *You will be ransomed and a fugitive made of your disease and highways made from which infirmity will depart. You will obtain only gladness and joy.* She says *You're a fine young man, it's just a few rotten cells,* and you say *But will I live?*

And she puts her lips on your lips, her tongue on your tongue, her breath passes into your lungs and she says *Before your bones cleaved to your flesh, your days were lengthening, and you were withered like grass.* And you say *Now?* She says *Now your heart will be the well, your eyes will see across the desert, your hand will work the soil as long as the soil will give of itself; your feet will walk for miles, your blood will be the blood of your children and grandchildren and for generations down. Touch here and here and here.* And you do and she says *You will be increased mightily* and you say *Now?* and she says *Now.*

Aim for the center of the cup and all in it goes. Squeeze off the rest, and put the blue cap back on. Put your pants on, wash your hands, pass it through the little metal door to the Indian doctor.

Sit there and try not to look creeped out. A knock on the door, which comes quickly, is startling in spite of the fact you knew it was going to happen. The Indian doctor comes in. He's got the sample with him. There's the lid on it. He's got a funny look on his face.

Is there something wrong? you say. He's probably going to tell you your come is infected, like the rest of you.

Well, he says, looking at the cup. Inside it is your sample, or specimen, or whatever they call it. Thick and heavy looking. This plastic fucking cup, all white with you in it. A damned good thing he's got that cap on—the cup is so full if he even moved it a little, he'd be spilling you out.

Is this all one ejaculate? he asks.

What do you mean?

You masturbated only once, correct?

Right.

You didn't put soap in here, or anything like that? None of this lotion, he gestures to the lotion.

No, you say, *is something wrong with my sperm?*

No, he says. He looks puzzled. *I have to confess though—I've been doing this for a long time. Thirty years. And I've never seen...well,* he says shaking his head and lowering his eyelids. *So much. In one ejaculation.*

And you don't reply, but would like to: *You people said you were going to take it out of me? Start with this.*

PETER LEVINE earned his MFA from Johns Hopkins University. His stories have appeared, or are forthcoming, in The Cincinnati Review, The Missouri Review, The Hopkins Review, Storyquarterly, *and* Arts & Letters, *as well as other literary magazines. He was a Tennessee Williams Scholar at the Sewanee Writers Conference and is originally from Chicago's northern suburbs.*

I've Come to Shallow Waters

GREG LIPSCOMB

In 1965 the sole secretarial school in Columbus, Georgia, was an upstairs affair, a converted dance studio, with the studio's mirrors still on the wall, so that the tiny secretarial classrooms seemed large to Delia. Delia and her friend, Darlene, were evening students at the school. In the midst of the classes on typing and shorthand and accounting Delia wondered about the ghostly shuffle of feet that had once slipped across those floors, the men tall and elegant, the women as curved and white as swans, wondered what had happened to all that grace.

Columbus was a service town to Fort Benning, and Fort Benning, in 1965, was the army's principal staging ground for the war in Vietnam. The town and the military post were filled with troops, and during breaks from their secretarial classes that spring Delia and Darlene leaned out of a second floor window and watched the trains bring in the boys from a thousand towns, boys with tattered bags, boys with unkempt hair, boys who joshed and kidded as they stood on the station platform. Across from the station, just down from the secretarial school, was the USO, and there stood all that these boys would become, solemn clusters of orderly men in uniforms.

"Would you marry a serviceman?" Darlene said. Darlene was tall and lean to Delia's roundness, and the daughter of an in-town merchant. Her face was a set of soft planes and generous lips that gave her a French look. A swirl of impractical hair fell down across her ears, so that she constantly looped her hair back with her fingers.

"I don't think so," said Delia, which she pronounced "Dee-ya," short for Cordelia. Her hair was more chopped than cut into a page

273

boy, but her cheeks rose toward her eyes like two soft suns. During the day she ran a highway vegetable stand.

"I would," Darlene said.

"Why?"

"You live everywhere."

"And then what?"

"Then you have babies."

"I dunno."

Darlene had the idea for the secretarial school, after she and Delia graduated from high school. Darlene had pressed Delia's arm and repeated the secretarial school's slogan, "Learn to type and see the world."

"Maybe Atlanta," Delia said.

When Delia was a child her father fished for a living off of the Georgia banks. He was a lean jowly man with hands the size of lobsters, and when she was six he said, "Take the bow, Delia." He held the tiller, that big hand upon it, his face fold upon fold of sea-seasoned skin, and as they came through the evening fog Delia shouted back her sightings in the words her father had taught her. "Sandbar starboard" and "green buoy port." Her father's boat was a flat-bottomed skiff that plowed stubbornly across sand and sea, like a stage at sea, a school play come to life, Delia thought, and so she was stunned when her father decided to sell it. "Banks' all fished out," he said, and so with her mother the three of them moved up river to the Georgia piedmont, to become poor whites, which they always had been, but the sea somehow shielded that, with its fog and expanse.

The piedmont was her mother's idea. She grew up on a farm, and was as steady and stable as the land itself. She was a short, stout woman, with square blocked features that moved jointlessly and with great strength. She could heft a bale of hay as well as any man, and she canned and cooked and ran a strict household. She also spouted little limericks, like "idle spine, idle mind," and she was a keeper of animals: ducks and turtles, chickens, Arabian goats, bees, anything that yielded eggs or milk or honey. When Delia and her father came in from the fields, they had to wade through a menagerie of load-bearing creatures that seemed to have free range. Goats bleated to be milked, chickens flapped across the lawn, and Delia had to be careful not to step on randomly laid eggs. "Gold yoke, gold folk," her mother said.

The piedmont, near Columbus, Georgia, was not so much a place as a state of mind, red clay determined not to yield, as though it begrudged a crop, as though there had to be a real wanting for it to stir. I am no farmer, Delia thought, because her father said that too. "This earth's too much for me," were his words. Delia's hands were raw from root and weed, and she squatted and bent and was burnt by the sun, her daddy down the row upon row of corn and whiskey oats, cotton and cane, until one day he lumped over swollen and dead in the heat. Delia was ten and for a long time dwelt in disbelief, for every morning her father had stood up and growled, and he fixed the kitchen windows, and he knew how to run a tractor. By the time Delia was fifteen her mother grew quiet too, gave up on all the milk and eggs and honey, and slowly slipped away, "came to rest," the minister said at her mother's graveside.

Delia felt orphaned and that she, too, had come to rest, that great forces had moved her up out of the sea and dropped her on a plateau cut by gullies and vines that whistled in the wind. After school she picked up with the highway vegetable stand her mother had started, where she mainly sold the neighbors' produce, and she read paperbacks, stacks of them, thick pulpy sagas with raised lettering on bright covers. She spent her days in knighted kingdoms or on Mediterranean yachts, a relief from her fly-swatting world along a hot stretch of Georgia macadam.

One evening, as Delia and Darlene leaned out of the window of the secretarial school, Darlene said, "There's a dance this Saturday. At the USO."

"You're not saying."

"I'll go if you will."

"I dunno."

"We can always leave."

"I dunno," Delia said.

They arrived at the USO on time, which was too early. A gravel-voiced sergeant, his face wrinkled as a walnut, greeted them and said the buses from Fort Benning had not yet arrived. Delia was dressed in white and looked like bridesmaid. Darlene wore a floral bouquet of a dress.

"What shall we do?" Delia said.

"Wait, I guess," Darlene said.

"Any minute, girls," the sergeant said. He sat behind a counter of candy and cigarettes and beer.

The lobby was so bright that it hurt Delia's eyes, and a sign, "USO Social Tonight," seemed to scream at them. She peered into a vast, dark dance hall off the lobby. A band was setting up in a cone of light. She heard the tinkle and trill of the musicians as they tuned their instruments. The rest of the hall looked dark, with threads of crepe paper and balloons that struggled against the gloom. Here and there small groups of women, women older than Delia and Darlene, sat in tight high-cut skirts and talked and sipped beers.

"They don't look like us," Delia said.

Darlene peered over Delia's shoulder. "Good."

Suddenly the sergeant straightened up and the doors of the USO exploded with men in uniforms. They pushed in and tripped over each other, muscular, tight skinned, hairless, loud voiced, and they stormed the sergeant's counter and ordered beers and whole cartons of cigarettes and pockets full of candy. They waved crisp bills and coins that shined like gems in the bright florescent light. Another wave arrived and pushed past the first and Delia and Darlene got caught in the flow, and suddenly they were in the dance hall, which lit up like a circus arena, and the band blared out a fast-moving number so that the men grabbed the women at the tables and the dance floor rumbled as the dancers swayed and waltzed and jitterbugged, and the women looked colorful as exotic birds pursued by the muscular uniformed roosters.

"They look hungry," Darlene said.

"Yeah. Hungry." They sat at a small table, the two of them, just out of the dance floor light, with nothing but their small purses on their table, so Delia's hands fidgeted from her face to the table to her lap, and Darlene leaned forward and slapped her hands against her thighs to the music.

"What's the deal?" Darlene leaned over and yelled. "Are we too weird?"

Just then a lanky soldier, as tall as Darlene, swaggered up to her, palm out, and Darlene turned to Delia, her brow pinched, but Delia waved her on, and Darlene and the soldier disappeared into the dance floor.

Delia sat and folded her arms. Couples jostled past and bumped her chair. Darlene popped up and down a few more times, and gushed and grabbed Delia's forearm. "Are you OK?"

"I'm fine," Delia said, and Darlene was gone again. Delia felt her skin flush, and she felt an isolation from the world that swirled around her, the kind of aloneness she felt at the roadway vegetable stand, only then she could disappear into her paperbacks. She turned her head and stared in the direction of the lobby door, and she imagined a man who leans toward her, square faced and taller than Delia, dark haired, teeth bright as pearls, sharp in his crisp uniform, and he extends a hand to her, a beckoning, a wanting. Then the image went away, and she turned her head back toward the dance floor, and between her and the dance floor stood a fellow with a puffed face and a shaved head, about her height, round in his middle, a little frumpy in his uniform. His lips moved, but whatever he said did not make it through the noise. She stood up and said, "Hi."

He did not exactly ask her for a dance, but stepped aside for her to pass to the dance floor, which she did, and he followed. The tune was mournful, something from the fifties, about teen dreams gone bad, and they danced stiffly to it, one round hand holding another, and each stared blank faced past the ear of the other. His legs seemed to move like tree stumps, and she could not determine who was leading whom, but he managed to say that he was from New Jersey, and that his name was Gerard, Gerard Dupree. "They call me Gerry," he said. "With a G."

"Oh. My friend's name is French." He pulled his head back and looked at her, wordless as a post. "Danielle. Her name is Danielle." She felt the heat of his face, and saw the rasp of a razor on his chin, as though he had been through pain to come here, and she smelled the starch of his uniform and the musk of his cologne. When the dance ended they continued to move, tuneless and stiff, and the next dance was slow too, for the hour was getting on. At ten o'clock the wrinkled-face sergeant announced that the buses were back, and in the garish lobby lights "Gerry" Dupree pulled out a candy wrapper, and on the back of it took down her phone number, and said he would call the following week. She waited for two weeks, and then he did call.

During May and June and July of that year the two of them tangled in the sheets of every cheap motel that lined the entrance road to Fort Benning. Delia tried to slow the moment, tried to take the hour, and in her wish she saw the two of them in a graceful waltz of white sheets, like those vaporous dancers on the dance school floor, or the sheets became sails on an open bay, but time would not wait. The two of them were in a desperate sizzle, flush against Gerry's training schedule, Delia hot and pink from the Georgia sun, shy in her whiteness elsewhere, and Gerry gray-faced from night maneuvers. But he grinned when he saw her, and he hugged her tightly in his short thick arms. "When I get out, we'll get a regular place," he said.

"A house?"

"You have houses in Georgia, don't you?"

"What else?"

"In Bayonne we have apartments."

"Bayonne?"

"It's a town in New Jersey. Across from Staten Island."

"I've heard of that," she said.

"Bayonne?"

"Staten Island."

"That's just across the Van Kill."

"The Van Kill?"

"Kill Van Kull. We call it Van Kill. It's a body of water," he said.

"Can you sail on it?"

"In a steel boat."

He looked like an ill-fitted potato in his uniform, the collar too tight, the belt askew. "What do they feed you?" she asked.

He stood before a motel mirror splotched from the flaked silver coating on its back, and he worked at his collar button. "Step-and-thrust," he said, "that's what they feed us, step-and-thrust, step-and-thrust. It's what you do with a bayonet."

In bed he seemed baffled by the speed of things, but he went where Delia led. Afterwards, one evening, he said his father ran an upholstery shop, and that he had trained to take it over when the Army drafted him. "Would you go there with me after I get out?"

"Yes. Yes I would."

By July Delia was nauseous. An army doctor confirmed her pregnancy, and an Army chaplain counseled marriage. "The Army encourages marriage," he told Delia and Gerry. He was an older man, lean and solemn, with a voice that sounded like a shovel against sand. "It settles the men down."

The Army made it easy, a chapel of brick and wood perched like a fast-food outlet in the patch of parking lot, the chapel's interior white, an ecumenical white that extended to the starch in the chaplain's vestments. "In the eyes of God," the chaplain said, but Delia saw her father's eyes, wide to the morning and evening sea fog.

Darlene was the maid of honor. She giggled and said "Yes" to Delia, yes it was the right thing to do, and she said who would have thought Delia would be the first to marry a military man? "The world," Darlene said.

Delia laughed and looked up from her bouquet. "New Jersey."

Gerry shipped out to Vietnam the next week, as part of a unit called the First Calvary, which Delia thought sounded strangely like a church. The horses of First Calvary had become the flying kind, big Huey helicopters that whacked the wetness out of the summer air, a sound Delia heard from the tiny off-post apartment Gerry rented for her. The apartment was in a hot box of brick and tired wood, one of a cluster of hundreds of buildings that hovered at the edge of Fort Benning, packed with wives and lovers, and all of them alive on rumors and bad coffee. "Be careful, Gerry," she said.

"I will," he wrote from San Diego, "If it's a boy, let's call him Henry. My favorite uncle."

"OK," she said to herself, looking at the postmark, "San Diego," which seemed full of sea-dreams, California, the pounding Pacific. She felt, once again, like a great sweep of life had passed around her and through her, and left her to deal with the remains.

She finished secretarial school, and as an Army wife she had priority in hiring as a clerk-typist at Fort Benning. The typing pool was an acre of Underwood manual typewriters, row upon row of Army wives and Army girlfriends, dressed as grayly as their Underwoods. Delia's fingers moved liquidly across the keyboard, like the legs of a sand crab, the Underwood her instrument, playing it for Gerry, whose orders for Vietnam must have come through that mill, for she typed the orders for many more. Each name a boy, a son, a husband, a father, a Gerry. Thinking so kept her job human, that and the swell in her middle, her stomach piled in a hunger on top of whatever was blooming inside of her. She could not keep up with the food, the bananas, the pickles, the candy, three donuts at a sitting. An oven within, and baby fat blossomed all over her. "Aren't you the pretty one," Darlene teased, as Delia's stretched clothes fell to the floor in a pile. The Army, good to its clumsy word, gave Delia green fatigues to wear, and as she put them on she thought of Gerry, dressed in fatigues as he might be dressed, out there somewhere.

In the typing pool, Delia sat next to Sheila. Sheila was a Negro and told Delia all about birth and New Jersey. Delia never knew a Negro office worker before. Sheila was sleek and she dressed brightly against the grays, her lipstick a deep red, and when she walked she sauntered as gracefully as one of the panthers in Delia's paperbacks. "You're gonna feel like one of your watermelons," Sheila said, and she leaned close to Delia, and placed a hand on Delia's arm. "Don't look for comfort anytime soon."

Gerry said in his letter from San Diego that he had been assigned as a radioman, part of a headquarters, so he should be safe. But by fall, by November, 1965, rumors came in that even field headquarters in Vietnam were being overrun. Delia saw the rumors sweep the acre of typewriters, as the work slowed in one corner of the pool, slowed to a halt, quietened against the rattle elsewhere. Whispers slithered in waves across the vast room. After a big battle, long before the newspapers had it, the entire room came to quietness, the stillness of a shared uncertainty. A gray-haired colonel came out of his office and waved the whole room, a couple hundred women, to take a break. "This happens, honey," Sheila said, "and there ain't nothin' you can do about it. Just don't answer your doorbell."

Delia's doorbell rang a week later. It was the same chaplain. The two of them sat down inside. "He's missing in action," he said. "MIA."

Delia stared at him. When Delia first moved with her parents to the piedmont, they lived in a trailer park. "Trailer trash," the children at school called her, but that did not bother her so much, because the schoolyard had a swing, and in the evening her parents took her there, and traded pushing her higher and higher in the swing. At the very tip of the arc she could see over the school, and she saw how small the school was against the great Georgia sky. What they called her at school did not matter against that sky, and as she fell back to earth her parents were there to catch her, only this time they were not there, no one was there, not even the chaplain, who looked away in her silence, and then back at her. "There was a battle," he said, or his lips moved, Delia was not sure, "but there were no remains."

When Delia and Gerry were first counseled by the chaplain, Delia thought he was too grim faced for a marrying man, stiff in his gestures, his cheeks lined with gravity, but that night she saw a man of many callings, a man who had to mask according to the hour, while yet one mask bore true above the others, the mask he called upon that night when he said, "All we know is that it happened at a place called Ia Drang."

Delia's ears followed her eyes into sea fog, the sound of the chaplain's voice muffled by a haze, a miasma of land and sea and sky, and after the chaplain left she was not sure what else he said, or when he left. All night long she lumbered back and forth across the floor, so that it creaked and the neighbors downstairs pounded from below. "M-I-A, M-I-A," she wailed and held a towel to her sad green eyes against the flood. Sometimes her cry came as one long word, "missingingaction," and sometimes just one word, "missing."

By late November things were not going well inside Delia. "Something's twisted," the doctor said. "You may have twins, but they're fighting off the same umbilical."

"What's that mean?"

"One of them will wash out," he said. "The stronger will prevail."

She spotted for the next month, and then the weaker embryo miscarried. She ran from the living room and squatted in the chipped porcelain bathtub, her large belly between her large legs. And she caught whatever she could in a pan, a bloodied mass, but still, a plasmic child, the arms, the legs, and the nub of genitals in between. A boy. She held the beginnings of a boy in a saucepan.

She did not know what to do with it. Was anything left inside her? Did the doctor need to see it? The doctor had left for Vietnam. Sheila was in New Jersey, visiting her family. Delia called the hospital but the orderly who answered had no idea what to do. Finally she just flushed it, and then she sat alone in the living room of the small apartment and she moaned to herself, for the deep loss of yet another link with Gerry.

The new doctor said she was still pregnant, and in December she took leave from her job. She caught glimpses of Gerry everywhere, at the grocery store, pumping gas, walking along the road to Fort Benning. All soldiers wore green, and many of them looked to her round and distressed. She even went by the USO, as though going back to the source could undo events. The sign over the secretarial school still read, "Learn To Type And See The World." In the fading winter light, the second-story window where she and Darlene took their breaks looked bleak and untended. Inside the USO a different sergeant sat behind the counter. "Help you, ma'am?"

"No, thank you." she said. What a sight she must be, she thought, pregnant and wandering around the USO. The dance hall was empty. A glittery sign announced a dance for the coming Saturday night. What had it been, six months? It looked so innocent, and it had passed on to a whole new crowd of sergeants and corporals and country girls who had no idea of what they were headed for.

Every day she drove to Fort Benning. She hoisted herself out of the car with a grunt and waddled, ducklike, up the steps of the public information office. Her hips had loosened, so that, as she pulled herself up the office steps she thought each hip might walk off in a different direction. The straps of her bra dug into her shoulders, holding her heavy, painful breasts. She oozed wetness all over, milk, eggs, honey, her mother's whole menagerie in one walking aching barnyard of agony.

And every day, as she held on to the counter with one hand, and she signed her name on the visitor list with the other, her question was the same. "Gerard Dupree. Do you have any information about Gerard Dupree?" Once a week she had to break in a new clerk about the MIA list, where it was and what it meant, for the clerks kept getting shipped to Vietnam. She felt she was fighting a huge beast across the

Pacific that sucked up all of the blood and knowledge and money and men of America, and that everything disappeared beyond the rim of the horizon.

And every day the answer was the same. "No information, ma'am."

Then one day she said to the clerk, a pimply faced kid with no hair, "Can I go to Vietnam? Airlines still fly there, don't they?" The clerk's mouth was half open and she continued. "Why can't I get a ticket and go there and get a bus to Ia Drang?

"I don't think so, ma'am."

"Do you even know where Ia Drang is, sonny?"

"No ma'am."

"Have you even heard of Ia Drang?"

"Yes ma'am."

And she slammed the counter with her free hand and screamed, "You took my husband and you have no information? You misplaced him and you have no information, no remains? No remains whatsoever?"

Colonels and matrons in WAC uniforms sprang from offices and rounded the counter and converged on Delia as she crumpled and almost fell to the floor, "No remains," and they held her as she wept, "no remains."

Darlene and Sheila traded off and stayed over and slept on the couch. Sheila put Delia through a bracing set of exercises, down on all fours, back against the wall, the bends and squats of birthing. "My guy's over there," Sheila said, as she worked Delia's legs. "Maybe your guy is too."

In January Delia went into labor. On the way to the post hospital, the ambulance attendants gave her a mild anesthesia. As she drifted off, barely able to see over the huge ball of her belly, the attendants moved dreamily in and out of her sight, smooth dancers in a play of light. Delia remembered the time she and her father followed a female manatee off the coast of Georgia.

"She's about to calf," her father said, and the manatee rolled, and Delia saw the enormous distended swell of the manatee's middle, wildly out of proportion with the rest of the creature. "And see beneath her flippers," and Delia saw the puffed pink teats, fat with milk, and Delia thought of the animal's sheer generosity, the grace of it, the morning light rare upon such a thing, and she felt her own blood rush, and she was wild with admiration, wild with envy. "That's why she's come to shallow waters," her father said, and in the ambulance that night, as the siren wailed in her ears, Delia closed her eyes against the sound and brightness and she said to herself, "I've come to shallow waters."

GREG LIPSCOMB lives among the libraries at George Washington University. He has a master's degree in writing from Johns Hopkins and is a frequent student of Robert Bausch at the Writer's Center in Bethesda.

Life Time Trouble

ERIC LOTKE

Five past seven in the evening and it's nearly dark outside. John had promised to leave the office by 7:10 so he could reach his daughter's school play by 8:00. He's right on schedule.

The phone rings. He makes a quick calculation. If he answers he might not get out on time; if he doesn't, he might miss something important or delay a colleague's race for deadline.

He presses the button for speaker phone while he puts on his coat. "John Blake," he says. His secretary left two hours ago.

"This is Jen in Stu Nelson's office," says the voice on the other end. "I'm calling to say that Stu can't make your meeting tomorrow morning at nine. He's very sorry. Can we reschedule? Ten would work."

John sits down and opens his calendar. He'd set nine aside for Stu but the rest of his morning was jammed. "How's two?"

"Sorry but Stu's afternoon is full. How's Friday?"

"No good." Friday he had a 10:00 staff meeting and a 5:00 filing deadline in court. "Maybe next week. Can you email me some possibilities?" He reaches towards the button to disconnect.

"Sure. How's Tuesday at two?"

He looks back at his calendar. "I can probably do Tuesday at two. I might run late, though. I have a lunch across town. Call it 2:30 to be safe."

"Deal. I'll email confirmation."

"Thanks. Good night." He disconnects and loads papers into his briefcase, then realizes he needs hard copy of a memo to review on the train, part of the calculation that had him out by 7:10 and at school on time. The memo needs to be finished by tomorrow close-of-business. But he forgot to print it.

He returns to his desk, his computer still running. He is smart enough by now never to turn it off.

But where's the file? He hasn't worked on it lately so it's not in the recent documents tab, and his secretary is long gone. He hunts through well-organized folders, finds the memo, opens it, presses the print icon and closes without saving. He figures it will take about sixty seconds to print and thirty seconds to walk to the printer. He'll be OK.

He cuts through the empty conference room to shorten the walk. Nobody is in the hallways but several colleagues are visible in their offices, pressed low over keyboards, coffee and paper cluttering their desks.

The printer light is glowing red. Out of paper. Ugh! He looks around but sees no support staff. He checks his watch and gets some paper. He's done this many times before. He knows exactly where the paper is and how to load the machine, but it costs precious time. He closes the door and listens as the paper tray rises. The print roller starts to whir.

He pulls the first page off when it comes out. Might as well start reading. But it's not his document. The printer's been out of paper for a while and there's a print queue. Should he leave now or wait for his to come? He figures it can't be long. He returns the first page to the printer as the second page rolls out. Not his.

He stands and watches the printer run. Several pages roll out fast but his memo hasn't started yet. He checks his watch and does math in his head. It's worth waiting.

A tiny pause indicates that a new print job has started. He looks at the first page. It still isn't his. Should he keep waiting? He takes the gamble.

The new document is only two pages long but the next document isn't his either. Now the time is starting to add up. He can forget about dinner, even fast food over the memo. But still he figures it's worth it. Hard copy to read on the train is worth twenty minutes right there. Plus he'll have intermission, bedtime, and other opportunities to read without wasting time logging in.

The next document rolls on, page after page. A PDF report, he can tell, not regular word processing. He just stands there at the printer thinking that surely it can't be long now, that surely his eight-page memo will come out soon. Pages keep rolling without the telltale pause.

Finally his document arrives. By now he is plenty late. He staples it and dashes for the exit, runs down four flights of stairs to avoid the risk of a slow elevator.

He hits the street and walks as quickly as is dignified for the Metro. It's early spring and warm. The school year is coming to an end, his older daughter's first year in middle school. Heather is one of the maidens in *Camelot*. She has solo lines, rare for a newcomer.

He sprints for a yellow light and he's not alone. People in D.C. always race to beat the red.

When he reaches the Metro platform he learns that the dash made the difference. A red line train going his direction is arriving as he reaches the top of the escalator. He maintains his stride down the escalator and the doors open as he reaches the platform.

Rush hour is ending and his good luck holds. He finds a seat. He pulls his cell phone from his pocket and dials home for a status check. The phone warns him that he'll have to pay roaming charges but he decides it's worth a few seconds on the line. He presses the call button.

His wife, Nancy, picks up on the second ring. "Where are you?" They have Caller ID.

"I'm on the train. I'll make it. I'm running a little late but I'll see you at the school."

"What about dinner?"

"I'll grab takeout while I walk to school."

"No, what about *our* dinner. We were going to have a family meal before the show."

Ouch. He forgot all about that. His careful calculations brought him to the show on time. But he needed to be home a whole hour earlier, before he'd even left the office.

"I'm sorry. It didn't work out that way. I'll make it to the play. That's what matters."

"You won't be able to wish Heather luck before the show."

"I'll take her to ice cream after the show."

"She's going to the cast party after the show."

He's paying roaming fees for this conversation and people are starting to look at him, but he goes the next step. "Put her on."

He hears random sounds on the other end of the line, then "Hello?"

"Hi, Heather. It's Daddy."

"I know."

"I just wanted to wish you good luck tonight."

"OK."

"I'm proud of you."

"OK."

"You'll be great. Can you put your mom back on?"

But Heather hangs up on him or he loses connection in the tunnel because the line goes dead. He studies the display until he confirms that it disconnected, then decides not to call back. Roaming fees and nothing else really to say.

He reads the memo and is careful not to miss his stop. It's in pretty good shape. His last comments were put to work by his team, and few modifications will be needed before they can use it. He puts a check mark next to some lines that need attention. If he were at a desk he'd write comments in the margin but writing is hard on a moving train. The check mark will tell him where to look and he'll remember to add his comments later.

He grabs dinner at Quiznos. The memo needs more time but it's too late to sit and eat. He orders to go and eats while he walks. He'll buy soda from the machine at school. The proceeds go to the school, too.

His wife and younger daughter, Emma, are sitting on the school steps as he arrives, a few minutes before curtain. "I'm here," John says.

"Can we go in now?" says Emma. "I'm tired of sitting on the steps. My butt hurts."

"Let's go," says Nancy.

Nancy has already bought tickets and left their coats across three good seats. Emma wants to sit next to Mom and not next to a stranger. That puts her in the middle between them.

John sits down, wipes the Quiznos on his pants, and pulls the memo out of his pocket. He reads a paragraph and returns to his briefcase for a pen.

"No you don't," says Nancy. "We're here for the play. Look, there's Catherine from the PTA. She's so grateful for your help on the by-laws committee."

But Catherine doesn't see them, racing for her own seat as the lights dim.

John leans towards Emma. "How was school today?"

"Shh! Dad. It's starting!"

He packs his memo into his briefcase as the curtain rises. The kids are dressed as knights and princesses. He doesn't recognize any of them. Maybe because his daughter is relatively new to the school and the stars are in higher grades.

He realizes that part three of the memo needs clarification. It makes sense if the reader knows the property is zoned under section 11(a), but 11(a) is unusual for a property of that type. The introduction needs to explain that the property is 11(a) and why. An easy thing to do but also an easy thing to forget. He reaches into his briefcase for pen and paper.

"No, Dad!" Emma exclaims. She's young and talks too loud. People behind them chuckle.

The show goes on and on. Kids singing and talking. Eventually Nancy grabs Emma and says, "There she is. In yellow."

Emma doesn't seem to see her. Nancy leans in and points. "Over there."

"Right," says Emma. A careful whisper.

John still doesn't see her. She isn't the only girl in yellow.

Finally she steps to the front. It's a choral number so her voice is lost but she's standing in the front of the crowd, beautiful in a long blue dress. The yellow is in her scarf, which drapes across her shoulders, and a ribbon behind. She's curled her hair.

He thinks of more problems with the memo that he wishes he'd considered earlier. Tomorrow's deadline seems much closer than it did this afternoon.

At intermission the lines are long at both the soda machine and the concession stand. John feels a surge of pride that he doesn't consider himself above drinking out of the water fountain. He makes a minute to scribble notes in the margin of the memo.

At the curtain call the children all bow in unison. Heather is beautiful. Her shawl flips awkwardly over her face but she stands up glowing.

John is in a hurry to return to the memo but Emma has heard of the ice cream possibility. "That was for Heather," John says.

"I didn't know it was a secret," Nancy replies. "I thought it was a nice idea."

Emma picks Ben & Jerry's. "I like the cow," she explains. She chooses peppermint in a dish with M&Ms on top. Nancy has coffee in a cone and John has Cherry Garcia. Emma picks a table near the door.

As they sit down, Nancy says, "Tomorrow is Thursday."

John looks up without understanding.

"That's why I'm reminding you. Tomorrow I have an 8:00 a.m. meeting. You'll be on the kids in the morning."

He'd forgotten! She'd reminded him plenty. In person and by email, but the implications hadn't fully registered. He was lucky that Stu Nelson canceled that 9:00. John needed the change anyway. He never should have made the date…but Stu gets the blame for the change. Score one for the good guys.

Nancy continues. "And it's a Thursday. That means Emma has Brownies and Heather has judo after school. Make sure Emma wears her Brownie uniform. She usually remembers but it doesn't hurt to remind her—before she gets dressed, not as you run out the door late for the bus.

"The Carters will bring Heather to judo. It's best to lay out her judogi in the morning because the bus gets her home at 4:15 and she has to leave at 4:30. She lets herself in but she needs time to snack and change. Not hunting for her judogi helps.

"And we both need to remember Emma's reading certificate. She did today's twenty minutes of daily reading but I forgot to sign the form. We need to sign it before school tomorrow.

"And the kids go to different schools now. Heather's bus comes at 7:50 and Emma's at 8:25. It's the same bus stop. You can go to work after Emma's pickup.

"I made lunch for Emma. It's in the fridge. Heather buys her own lunch and she's in charge of her own money. If she forgets, it's a lesson in remembering."

He's listening carefully but not taking notes. He'll need the kids to help. "Do you have to go to the 8:00 meeting?"

"I can bill the entire day."

Six months ago Nancy's company had reorganized and she lost her full-time job. They told her she could stay but she'd change to hourly and lose her benefits. She took the deal and started job hunting, feeling shrewd. John added her to his own health plan—though it cost some money—and helped with her resume.

Six months later she is still job hunting and the company is cutting back her hours. She enjoys the extra time with the kids but the missing dollars are starting to hurt. Losing the job entirely would be a disaster. He says, "You should go early. There might be networking time over coffee."

"Planning on it," she replies. "Coffee and lunch breaks, too. I have targets in mind if I can get a minute." She'd researched the targets during an earlier phase of the project, and even billed the time.

Emma has been fully engaged in her ice cream. Now she looks up. "Daddy, can I sit on your lap?"

"What?! Sit in my lap while you eat an ice cream sundae and I eat an ice cream cone? What a mess!" He makes a yucky face and she giggles. "Maybe if there's time after we finish."

He turns to Nancy. "How's Heather getting home from the cast party?"

"The Hobsons are giving her a ride. They said she'd be home by eleven."

"Eleven? That's late."

"The show went from 8:00 to 9:30. The party won't start until ten. She gets an hour with her friends."

"Eleven is late."

"She'll be grumpy tomorrow morning. Have fun with her. And don't forget her judogi."

Emma is chasing the last M&Ms around the bottom of her bowl. John asks, "Are you ready to roll?"

Both parents stand. "Wipe your face," Nancy adds.

Fifteen minutes later they are home. Emma asks if she can take a bath and her parents figure it's a good way to cool down. She's still excited from the evening—and sticky with ice cream—and it's a late night for her too. She puts herself in the bath while John changes out of his work clothes.

Nancy says, "How long will it take me to get to L'Enfant Plaza in the morning? That's where the meeting is."

"Ten minutes to walk to Metro, three minutes to wait for a train—none, if you're lucky." He estimates the length of the ride to Fort

Totten, the time to change to a green line train, and the green line time to L'Enfant Plaza. "Forty minutes," he concludes. "Plus however long it will take from Metro to the meeting.."

"Ten minutes on foot. Fifty minutes total. So I'll leave the house at 7:00, a few minutes earlier if I'm lucky."

"Why's it called L'Enfant Plaza, anyway? Doesn't that mean child or something in French? As if it's a playground or an amusement park."

"It's named after Pierre L'Enfant, the guy who designed the city. He was French."

"No wonder it doesn't work."

"I'm setting the alarm for 6:00. You can get up with me or grab maybe thirty more minutes of sleep. The kids need to be out of bed by 6:40 to eat breakfast and catch the bus without screaming."

They hear the front door open. It's Heather. She walks up the stairs and sees Emma getting out of the bath. "Is there any hot water left? I need a shower."

Her parents greet her and manage the transition of Emma into bed and Heather into the shower. "Dad's in charge tomorrow morning," Nancy says. "Everyone be good. Heather, we'll be in bed by the time you finish in the shower. So good night."

"Nighty-night, mom. I love you."

"I love you too."

Heather and John undress and lie down in bed. She double checks the alarm once more. "The Hobsons are getting a divorce," she says.

John lifts his head from his pillow. He likes the Hobsons, and their kids too. "Why?"

"I haven't spoken to them. I just heard through the grapevine. Not spending enough time together. Growing apart. The usual stuff."

He checks the clock on his own side of the bed. It's too late to talk about this. "That's a shame," he says.

"Good night."

"Good night."

ERIC LOTKE is research director at the Campaign for America's Future. He lives in Arlington, Virginia, with his wife and two children.

Touching the Pole

Alex MacLennan

Darren steps onto the grooved plastic floor of the Muni train's third car and dances awkwardly backwards to avoid a fat woman with an oversized purple sweater and frizzing, snapping hair. He plants his feet widely, feeling for his own weight. His feet are encased in modern, moisture-wicking socks and shoes that are made of thick, black rubber. *I will not touch the pole,* he tells himself, holding himself doggedly upright. He looks to the grooves on the floor and mouths: *I will not react to her hair.* Darren is going to the library today.

Darren sways with the first lurching movement of the train, the late-morning light striking his eyes, the dread mounting. In moments, the train will carry him underground. He manages his balance, carefully. He watches the big woman, warily. Darren tries to pin down each yellow-gray curl of her discolored, smoke-gray hair as if to ensure that no small strand will escape his notice and float toward him like some gossamer emissary of doom.

He hasn't ridden the Muni in years, but is determined to survive this first, terrifying voyage through the public underground. He is going to the library, the new library at Civic Center. It will be brilliant—sleek and shimmering, a magical land of order rising out of San Francisco's dirtiest, most dangerous streets. It will be clean.

Years ago, when Darren still worked as a librarian in West Portal, he had read, wide eyed, over the plans for sweeping metal stairs and railings, private offices for the librarians, a soaring, airy atrium, modern ventilation, and a full-time custodial staff. Civic Center is almost unbearably dirty, Darren knows, but the library with its perfect rows of books and blue-faced computers will be very, very clean. And now he is invited, they had invited all the current and former librarians, for a private tour. Despite everything, despite the impossible terror of this trip, he knows he has to try. Dr. Rowe has told him so.

Darren surveys the other passengers, assessing them for danger, but since he has waited well past rush hour the train is almost empty and people are very still. *Do not make eye contact with strangers. I will not make others feel uncomfortable today.* Darren notices a younger couple, maybe in their twenties, sitting close together in a cramped, backwards-facing double seat. Her knit green hat belts her head and squeezes a confusion of black curly hair into her eyes. His hand, as he reaches to brush the hair from her eyes, is small and hairy like a subterranean rat, and intermittently covered to the knuckles with a scuffed orange leather coat. His coat matches the seats of the Muni. *I will not tell him not to touch her,* Darren promises himself. *I will not tell him about the germs.*

Darren has been in trouble in the past for telling people about germs, for approaching them, goggle-eyed and insistent, with urgent warnings about their doom. He stands perfectly rigid with the motion of the train and imagines himself as a surfer in a movie, closing his eyes in order to breathe, trying to ride the nauseating swells. He can't keep his eyes closed too long for fear someone might approach. He can only shut out the world, expelling his breath harshly through his nose, and settle into his own pumping inner warmth for seconds at a time. He has to breathe in the world and its germs. He has to look it in the face.

At least that's what Dr. Rowe had said, and he wants to believe it is true. *I will not be afraid of the world,* Dr. Rowe had made him repeat. Sitting in the therapist's office, cheap pillows and wan plants struggling against the free clinic's blue linoleum swell, Darren had heard Dr. Rowe's admonition, and chanted his new mantra over and over, and over again. His shoes arranged on six squares of toilet paper, the toilet paper arranged in two neat strips of three next to three, protecting his feet from the sparse, stubbled rug. *I will not be afraid of this world. I am of it and can breathe it in. I will not be afraid of this world. I am of it and can breathe it in.* I am *not afraid of this world,* he repeats to himself conspicuously, realizing suddenly that he is speaking out loud.

Holding his lips very still he repeats, *I am of it, and can breathe it in.*

A sudden stop forces his hand, yanking him by the back of his neck like his mother used to, and throws him into that purple swathed woman, that fleshy monster with too many bags and spittle in her pink-drawn lips. He presses against her briefly, her rough baggage and potato-sack flesh, and then rights himself and steps away. He leans back away from her as she tromps down the two steps to the street, smiling. Darren does not quite manage to smile back, though he comforts himself that the corners of his mouth, spittle-free, turned upwards when she said "goodbye." *I will not judge her without reason.* This is a new one, he realizes, as two more people exit the train. He even came up with it himself.

The couple sprawl across the seat, one of her legs up over his lap, and they are both wearing leather pants that Darren doesn't think people really wear anymore. He'd certainly never had a pair—and hers, which are bloody red, have shining, faded stretches where her legs fill and rub against them. *I will not think about her skin.* One very large man gets on at the sliding doors nearest him. Another, small and blond, boards farther down.

The man stands in his black suit in the center of the aisle, right next to Darren, and breathes huge breaths through a mouth that pants like a dog. Darren imagines the man's muggy breath, and it is almost as if he can actually see the flecks of hot dog and bun, the tiny bits of white onion and green relish trapped between his teeth. He imagines the fat pink tongue and saliva bulging behind the thin lips and black mustache of this huge man named... *I will not make assumptions about people I do not know. I will not imagine germs where I cannot see them. I will not be afraid of this world. I am of this world and...*The man coughs. A thick, wet cough that fills all the air in the car with noise and horrible droplets that catch the yellow light. The man chuckles and wipes his hand on his arm, leaving a slick of something on his black sleeve. Darren puts his head down, fumbles into his pocket for the chalky surgical glove he had promised himself he wouldn't use, struggles it onto his left hand, and snaps it at his wrist. It is as if ants are crawling over his skin, their sharp toes leaving tiny spikes in his cheeks, the edges of his eyes. His eyes are watering. He is sweating. He grabs the pole so that he can close his eyes and disappear.

*I will not touch the...*he wants to begin.

Instead, *I will not be afraid of the world.*

He stands there, head down, holding the pole through the Muni's waves and currents, looking up only to gauge the movements of the other riders on the train. The huge man disembarks and, at first glance, the train seems emptier. Darren quickly realizes, however, that the train is no emptier, that its passengers have simply parted in two ellipses around him where he stands with his chalky glove and mutterings, and around the small blond man who had boarded one stop before.

This new man is wearing a brown corduroy jacket with sleeves that don't cover his narrow, knobby wrists. His hands are curled inward; his chin is tucked into his chest. Soft, downy hair rests on his head, or floats upward with the static of the dry air around him, and his eyes are small and puffy like a newborn gerbil in a cage. Head down, he is shuffling up to and into different passengers, attempting a kind of coddled hug, and causing person after person to back away with soft, uncomfortable looks in their eyes. He might be twenty-three.

Darren can't help watching him, this opposite entity who needs and craves touch as strongly as Darren shuns it. *I will not run away,* he tells himself sternly, from this little man with his scruffy yellow whiskers who looks like a child or cherub in dirty jeans. He is wearing soft-looking green sneakers with yellow stripes. Darren watches with mounting anxiety as the man moves his way through the train, the savvier passengers having already moved out of his range and into full seats, taking refuge in the company of less disturbing strangers whom minutes before they had purposefully ignored. No one appears to be malicious. This person is clearly an innocent and almost filled with light, but no one wants him to touch them, no one wants to be asked to connect. Darren has begun to sweat—something he hates to do—and can feel the warm damp of his armpits, his underwear, the arches of his feet. He will have to shower at least three times when he gets home.

This ride isn't working. It isn't getting better, he thinks as the shuffling, childlike man comes closer. He wants to back away but can't bear to remove his gloved hand from the pole, his tenuous, prophylactic hold on safety. The library feels impossible, and, impossibly far away. The small man never looks up, just steps sideways into each person's radius, trying to fold himself into their chest and rest his head on their shoulders. Each person steps away. Darren watches it all with a detached fear, the man's soft ricochet toward him. He has totally left himself behind, is watching the unacceptable, inconceivable insertion of another human being into his immediate proximity, watching through his own reflection in the blackened windows of the train.

Suddenly, the man is in front of him, and the train, the whole glittering, fractured world is pulled off its track. Suddenly, the man is there.

Darren feels his arms lift as if he had been pushing them against a door, or as if they are being pulled open by an invisible puppeteer's strings. He tries to resist, denies the enfolding movement of his arms. Feels this thin blond bird of a man curl himself into his own barren chest. Feels his heart speed to a place where he thinks it might explode. Feels the man's soft hair brush his chin like feathers and imagines he can see a golden shimmering of light. He has lost all connection to the pole.

Darren wants to shout or to push the man away: *Don't touch me!* His mind screams but it does not reach his mouth. His eyes, he is sure, are screaming uselessly for help. The leather man and his girlfriend, an older Chinese man with paper blotting a cut on his chin, two dark-skinned children with a shopping bag as tall as they are—all studiously ignore his silent plea.

Then, an utterly new voice inside him speaks. *I will not be afraid.* It is a softer voice, and he can hear the echo in his young man's head. He is as afraid as I am, Darren thinks, and realizes that his arms have curled around the young man's back, this young man's back that feels like a starving dog's. He is shocked to find his own chin dipping and sweeping across the cool, thin hair. The pale corduroy feels right under his fingers, and realizing this, he lets himself gently stroke the man's ribbed back. He realizes that the corduroy is just a fabric that *looks* dirty, that he can't actually feel any germs. He settles his back against the pole.

Darren leans into the boy's head and breathes in one deep, fresh-washed-blond-hair breath. The hair smells like being a child. The young man just smells so good.

They ride like that, hugging, through four more stops, passing Darren's stop at Civic Center, riding until every other passenger leaves the train and new, outbound passengers begin to board. Darren feels frozen in a transparent crystal, safe and entirely removed from time. He can't look at himself too closely, or he knows the illusion will pass. The new passengers make wary circles around them until the man shifts for the first time since Darren began to hold him, turns in his space, and walks off the train.

Slowly, Darren follows, stepping at the last possible moment through the quiet shushing of the doors. He enters the pale light of the underground platform like a blind man testing a new cane, and finally, tenderly, pulls off the glove. He doesn't know what has just happened, or who the man was. With great care, he tosses the spent glove into a battered green trashcan, from what he hopes is a distance of precisely three feet away.

ALEX MacLENNAN is a former fiction editor of American University's literary journal Folio *and a contributing writer/reviewer for* Hill Rag *and* DC North *magazines. He holds an MFA in creative writing from American University and a bachelor's in English literature from the University of Maryland, College Park. His debut novel,* The Zookeeper, *was named a finalist for the Violet Quill, Edmund White, and Lambda Literary Foundation Debut Fiction awards. "Touching the Pole" received a Larry Neal Writer's Award in 2004.*

Death at the Tavern

Joe Martin

One day I will tell my son the story of how I came to work in my present vocation. I have reflected on it through the years. Now I am trying to figure out how to find a happy ending in it. How else can I tell it to a child? Let us try.

It starts with my first artistic career, it ends in Tall Timbers Tavern where my band played its last set, its last song, and I was liberated. The key, my son, is what led to the fatal outcome of that job. What had brought dyed-in-the-wool, soft-headed rockers to the brink of despair? What made one sign up for the army, another become a shoe salesman, another become a common thief, and myself to lose my perspective enough to stay in the arts for the rest of my life? Let's set the scene. I'll start with our twenty-four-hour studio session.

We had gone straight through the night in the studio to make sure we had the material down and mixed, because we had to burn the demo the next morning. We were going to flog our stuff in New York, and the stakes were high. The band had reached its limit. A decade of ups and downs had left our brains singed like the inside of a Barracuda muffler. One week we were sleeping under a bridge in Atlantic City while engaged at the tawdry Chez Paris in Atlantic City. Another we would open for Fleetwood Mac in concert. The next we'd be playing in an American Legion hall just off a military base somewhere, looking at a wall of gold trophies.

We were known, in a way. I was doubling in a career that I felt worked well with rock music: as a counselor for in-patients who were hospitalized with acute psychotic episodes. Once I noticed that a certain young patient had been looking at me with curiosity and fear for days, before he confessed that he was imagining I was someone he had seen jumping up and down at the keyboards singing post-Morrison poetry with a look in my eye like Rasputin. I was, happily, able to reassure him that it was not any hallucination, it was me. Perhaps he was not actually reassured. At least he could know that he had passed a key reality test. He didn't consult with me after that.

So among certain circles, we were known.

We were not just any old band playing the circuit. Our sets were always full of original material. We didn't compromise with anybody, because we were artists. But we did have to take whatever jobs were offered to us, as a result. Imagine the confused couples at a senior prom, or the Sons of Norway benefit ball, trying to dance through a rock opera, which switched to three-four and then to seven-four time. Those who were not musicians could not grasp why their bodies were not moving properly.

It was an era when country-rock fusion was coming in, and we tried to integrate some socking numbers into our sets. Perversely, however, we did our own arrangements of little-known tunes by Woody Guthrie and Leadbelly-inspired tunes, and this undermined still more our commercial viability.

We were originals, goddamit. From high school through college we played on, waiting to be discovered like a silver lining inside a cloud—of alcohol and beng—and it hadn't hit pay dirt. We resolved that if the recording companies were not going to come to us, we would get our stuff to them. Remember (son), these were times before do-it-yourself compact discs were happening. Then, no records were produced outside of the big companies. It was before indie producing in the music industry. (In fact, CDs were only being hatched inside technology institutes and laboratories.) This is a story of trying to do it the old-fashioned way.

I was given the assignment of taking our demo with four tracks to New York. I dutifully researched the addresses of the major recording studios. I sent copies of the tape to reputable agents. That is, I supposed people I found in the Yellow Pages like "International Creative Management" would be reputable. That particular agency had an agent by the name of Mitch who told me on the phone that he had listened already to our demo, a week after I sent it, and that it had impressed him very much.

See me when you get to New York, he had said.

I was encouraged.

My ex-girlfriend, also a songwriter and dedicated to the cause, agreed to supply the wheels, so that we could both check out the New York machine. It is not really worth describing the visits with every agent or record company. They were similar to the point of blandness. It's enough to briefly describe two visits. The first record company we visited was Warner Brothers. As we passed through the glass doors with a six-by-ten-foot color display case portrait of a blue Bugs Bunny, I suffered a shock of what we used to call, in those times past, "alienation." Today we might call it gas pains. After a wait of an hour or so, I was finally seen. I walked into the designated office past a fair-sized picture of Bob Dylan—not quite on par with the blue bunny—which took away my stomach pains, but raised my anxiety level a bit past the top of my cerebellum. The long and short of my meeting at Warner Brothers, with a tan lady in a tan suit on a tan swivel chair in beige lipstick and with long legs reminiscent of the ears of a hare, was that the Company could not seriously entertain (nor be entertained by) the offer of our demo tape unless it was advanced to them through an agent.

Get an agent first. Then we'll be glad to listen.

I tried to show her some press. To no avail.

Get it to an agent first. That's always the route. Then have them give it to us, and I guarantee, we'll give it a listen.

This message was repeated at the other studios. Which brings us then to the agents themselves. Here again, one example will suffice.

In this case I was one step ahead. The demo had been sent weeks before to International Creative Management, I had followed up, the agent Mitch had listened to it, given me a nibble, and I had a one o'clock appointment. We made it up to the twentieth something floor with ten minutes to spare. (You must never be late when doing business, my son.)

The wallpaper was a grainy and glittering metallic silver. The art was original, and there was a Manhattan mixture of people dressed to kill, talking with people who looked like they killed to dress. I approached the well-cleaved woman at the reception desk to state that

I had an appointment with Mitch so-and-so at one o'clock, assuming it would work more or less like a dental appointment. He would run a bit late, but then you just read the *New Yorker* or *Vanity Fair* or *Cosmo* until he comes to the entrance and calls you in. Once the receptionist had given him a call, she disconnected and reported:

OK. He knows you're here.

Two hours later, I asked if she could buzz him again. I had made the appointment with Mitch himself. He had our demo. Without showing signs of displeasure or resistance or of any humanity (you see, this is what we call "professional," remember that) she called Mitch again.

He apologizes, she said, but asks if you could wait another fifteen minutes.

Sure.

I started reading *Cosmopolitan.* After another half an hour, noticing that the receptionist was engrossed in conversations with all the insider males who were drawn to her web—I slipped through the glittering doorway past her and turned a quick right into the corridor. I was relieved to see that all the relevant people had their names shingled onto their doors. I walked two hundred feet. No Mitch. I turned down another silver-papered hallway, blinded for a moment by all the track lighting that was bouncing off of it. There, at the end of this corridor, I saw the open door of the elusive Mitch. His shingle was lit up.

I stood in his door.

He had a beard and a corona of curly brown hair in a bowl around his head. His mouth opened for a moment, in the manner of the housewife in the horror movie who answers the door only to find whatever-it-is standing there. Mitch, unlike the housewife in the movie, recovered quickly. There was no one in his office. Though he was perplexed that I had made it to his door, he asked me to sit down.

It's been very busy here today. Horrible.

Oh, that's OK. I knew that might be the case. The demo got to you in good shape?

Oh yes. Oh yes. Like I told you.

Did you get to listen to all four tracks?

Yes. And I must say, I like it very much.

All four tracks? Because each one is really different. The different styles that we go for.

Was it four? Oh yes, that's right, four.

I was pleased. The ice was broken. I mean the big thick ice between the marine life forms below, the people playing music, and the cruisers floating on top of the music business. (That's how it was in those days, you see.)

There's one issue here, Mitch said.

Yes?

You don't have a recording contract, do you.

Well, that's why we have come to you. You're the agent. We need someone to get us a contract.

Well, let me explain. These days, there's so much good stuff out there, you really need to have a contract to get an agent. Then your agent's job is to lead you onto better deals, better contracts, promote your records with touring, and so forth.

But I've been visiting the recording studios. They say they will only evaluate tapes supplied by an agent.

Listen, it's this way all over town, all the time.

In the end I stood up, I took his hand when he offered it. I walked out to meet my ex. It was dinner time. We went back down the avenue to find a deli. A truck went by throwing up a rain of ashes, one of which got under her contact lens. I thought she was weeping. But it was my frame of mind.

I'm telling you all this—about how we in the band resolved to sell ourselves in New York, how I met Mitch—because this sets the scene for Tall Timbers Tavern, where the roof fell in on us. Because I hold Mitch responsible for everything that subsequently happened in my life. I hold him responsible for my switch from one tormenting art form to another. I hold him responsible, along with Bugs Bunny, for the destruction of a good ensemble; I hold Mitch responsible for my giving up existentialism and finding religion, my waiting till my forties to have a kid (you); I hold Mitch responsible for the brutality of the bar scenes where unknown bands rev up to feed late-night idiocy all across this great country; I hold him responsible for the loss of my song-writing muse; and I hold Mitch responsible for the death of the club owner at Tall Timbers Tavern somewhere in the south of the great state of Maryland.

I returned from New York with copies of our well-packaged demo, with failure on my face. I had no encouragement to give Rich, Rob, and Dave. Life had to go on. We played for a time in a small place, Mr. Henry's, where we kept getting messages passed up to us to turn our amplifiers down. Talk about getting feedback. Our next engagement in a space larger than a dog coffin was at the aforementioned Tall Timbers Tavern. Actually, we were told it was quite spacious and always full. The pay was adequate. We were told there was a motel attached to it, so that covered lodgings. We all enjoyed a little down-home Americana, and we looked forward to a setting out of a Hopper painting.

It was freezing, and the parking lot outside Tall Timbers Tavern was out in the trees somewhere. We couldn't make out the motel we had been told about. All we could see at the street address was one house with a bare light bulb over the front porch. Our headlights caught the tavern, a dark wood building, looking like something the park service might construct. We could see through the windows that it was open, but it was just a regular bar night, with no acts on stage. We went into the tavern. It was spacious enough, all wood. The bartender showed us where we could store our instruments offstage. Our drummer, Dave, worked with Peach, our imposing and sullen road master, to get the equipment locked away, while the bartender took the rest of us across the drive to the owner's house. The one with the naked bulb over the porch. At that point, Rich, our bass player, pointed:

That's the motel?

We were now able to see the darkened eaves of the "motel" adjacent to the owner's house. It had no lights on, inside or out. An old Motel sign stood above the roof like a hopeless banner planted on a hill by a long-gone horde defeated in battle. The owner himself was so huge that it looked like his body was permanently locked in his rocker. His suspenders might just as well have been straps tying him to the chair rather than to his pants. The chair hovered backwards because of his impressive weight. His home was itself little more than a salvaged motel room, or perhaps the old motel front office. Food was stored on wood shelves and on step ladders. His television was left on, seemingly perpetually. I sat with Rob, the guitarist, and Rich and talked about money with the owner.

If we like you this week, we'll have you back often as you like, he said.

That would be great, I said. An image of Bugs Bunny was still playing in my head, and came back to me at that moment. (I used to have these problems when I played rock 'n' roll, lad, but it's all cleared up now.) Here I was in the woods of Maryland, and I still hadn't gotten over New York.

Where's the motel? asked Rob. He was sagging.

That's it. Right next door.

Is that where we stay? Rob sagged even more.

That's it. Like I say. Right 'cher. You can come over here for your water. We've got running tapwater here.

Like...

Rich was not always in his right mind after long drives. Like... where do we go when we get up. It's getting cold out here. Is there breakfast?

Oh, when you get up, you go on over to the bar. You can set up in there. Make yourselves some coffee.

Can we jam tomorrow?

Sure, you go ahead. No customers during the day.

We were indeed relieved that we wouldn't have to wander the woods and dirt roads of early winter Maryland looking for sassafras roots for tea in the morning.

Do you get many people down here? I asked.

Oh, well, yeah! Fills up full on the weekends. Just fills up.

Where do they come from?

All around. All around.—He turned his eyes to the TV now as he spoke, sparingly, to us. Then he said:

Rooms four and five.

And so we got ready to retire for the night. The motel room had no lights. The faucets were rusted shut. The wall-to-wall carpeting was partly pulled up, partly disintegrating. There was, of course, no heat at all, just dead old heating vents that stayed as cold as the porcelain sink. We had blankets and sleeping bags in the vans, and situated ourselves as far as we could from the exposed pipes in the room where insects might be lurking. Beetles on their last autumn legs crawled slowly over the planks during the night contemplating their mortality and coming closer to their God.

The next evening, our first set started at eight. We decided to do one of our fifty-minute operas then, before the folks got too bois-terous. Kids from local farms and nearby suburban sprawl built around a strip mall came in first. They had an innocent good old time. I don't know if they felt they could dance to us, but they tried, and wouldn't have cared one way or the other. By the end of that set the bar had filled. For a wood-and-rafters sort of a place, it had a rather distinguished, polished wood bar, with the requisite mirrors hovering between its liquor racks. The tables too were all wood. The sense that the whole structure was surrounded by trees gave it a feel of something between the old West and a Canadian loggers' pub.

During the first set the crowd lubricated itself and got set into motion, dancing, joking, telling loud stories. The floor vibrations from the bass and drums mixed with the motor roar of the parking bikes outside and the shuffling and thumping of feet in the wood. When you play music in a dance bar, actually the cosmic music comes not just from the instruments, but from the whole space. That night, the high tones of the music came from the laughter of the young squeegee dolls in jeans and the clatter of glasses in the sink. The lows came from those motors outside and the percussion of feet on the floor. Then there was us, living in the illusion that we were the only music in the room. The bikers were loping around looking for ways to mix and mingle, but most people weren't asking them to dance—women or men. The band was cooking more as the room filled, which was always the case. We reached the end of our abridged opera, and Rob took a couple of minutes to retune. A biker out in front of me, a sort of iconic figure, in fact a sort of biker Father icon out of a biker basilica which exists probably under a speed ramp outside of Cleveland, with his beard and barrel chest and leather paraphernalia, this Biker Icon stepped up on the stage and approached the keyboards.

Is that your sets? he asked, pointing to the pad on top of the electric piano.

That's right.

Let me see it.

With no reason to object, I prepared to turn it around and let him peruse it. Instead, he just took it. As he scanned the list his face revealed the analytic concern of a professor reading a poorly reasoned essay. He shook his head almost forlornly.

You're not going to play this. You're going to have to play what we want you to play.

Not only was he rejecting the original work, but our reserve of country rock tunes and blues, some of it even recognizable.

This is all we've got for tonight, I offered with a tinge of apology.— But there's four sets of material there.

The same sorrowful nod of the head:

No. We'll tell you what to play...

The Father Icon's beard reminded me of the beard on Mitch in Manhattan. Without the cologne scent. Even his lack of appreciation of what we had to offer resonated in my obsessive brain of Mitch, though he expressed himself somewhat differently. I might have replied: If we show you our record contract, can we keep our list? Rob had long been ready to start, and the people who had been dancing were chilling a bit too long out on the dance floor. So I pulled my set list back and gave a silent but terse nod of acknowledgment to the opinion of this Iconic Biker. He looked at me, turned, and disappeared, I hoped for the rest of the evening, into the crowd.

The next upbeat tune featured a keyboard solo from my end. I first sensed, then perceived, hovering over my shoulder in the dark, a long thin morose-looking representative of the biker delegation. He was watching my fingers go. The fact is I never was a highly evolved keyboard player, and his presence was ruining my focus. In the back of my mind perhaps I was wondering if any of my fast-moving fingers were about to be broken by some steel implement employed by the Angels and their ilk on the knuckles of errant keyboardists, saxophonists, and bass and conga players. He then stuck out his forefinger, selected one of the highest keys, and began tapping away on it. He tapped in a rhythm all his own, unrelated to anything we were playing at the moment. Not to mention it had no relation to the key we were playing in. As I had cranked the volume for the solo, his high-pitched key pierced the surface of our music like an ice pick. He didn't stop until the song was over. By that time my nausea was making me turn colors. Rich and Rob looked kind of pale themselves. Dave, who kept telling me I ought to give up keyboards, was looking at me as if I were responsible. I signaled for the others to come over and have a huddle.

Was it cool to keep playing?

If we do, there might be trouble.

Somebody here has got to take responsibility for this.

The owner.

He's in his apartment, the light's on.

I was elected to go see. So I crossed out of the tavern across the dirt drive and knocked on the owner's door. He was seated in front of the TV, his eggplant-shaped body wedged between suspenders and the arms of his rocker.

There are bikers in there, and they are giving us trouble.

What're they doing?

They're messing with our instruments while we are playing. They told us they're going to tell us what to play.

So what do you want from me?

Should we keep playing? With this going on? The band is about ready to stop playing, but if we stop we still need to get paid. So you tell us what you want.

Then the owner came up with the following common-sense idea.

Well, you just make an announcement to the people. Just get on the microphone and tell them that if everyone can just relax and have a good time you will keep playing.

A brilliant idea. Why hadn't I thought of it? I went back in.

What did he say?—Dave, the drummer, his eyes always wide, on the alert. Rich and Rob were tuning.

Rich: What'd he say?

He said we should make an announcement. We don't have to keep playing if there are more problems.

So we got our situation in tune. We were ready to start, but I went first to the front microphone and summoned up my best Woodstock Hog-Farmer voice.

OK, people. We're hoping everyone can relax and have a good time tonight. If everyone can stay cool and enjoy themselves we'll keep playing all night. So we hope...

Who the hell are you referring to!—A voice jumped out from the center of the room. The Biker Icon was pointing his beard up at me on the stage. People moved away from him. I put up both my hands in the gesture of: Look, it's all fine, and began to speak...

Who the hell are you talking to us about keeping cool. Who the hell do you think you are!

The Icon was heading toward the stage fast. Just before he got there I saw Peach appear from nowhere, grab him, and pull him back from me. Peach was a big guy; unintimidated, however, the Icon pulled back his fist and planted a crushing blow to Peach's mandible and as they both went to the floor the hands of many people went toward them like filings to a magnet. The heap of interventionists went to the floor with the first two. As bikers and partiers tried to free or attack various people in the growing pile, others jumped on *them* to pull them away. Thus several new lines of people erupted from the first pile and fell into three or four other pile-ups around the room. Of course at the bar, all the bartenders went down, which is apparently deep in the blood of American bartenders going back centuries. Either that, or they were conditioned by Westerns. Whatever the case, it was not too soon because smashing sounds were starting up, which seem to have been the beer and liquor bottles of legend being thrown at the mirrors.

I had gone out on the floor to look for Peach, but someone pushed me back away from the tumult. I looked to the stage. Dave had already cleared his drums off the stage and placed them in a dark corner out of the light right behind where I was standing. On stage, he was busy taking the amplifiers off into the wings left and right so no one with ideas of trashing our technology would see it and act on the impulse. Rich and Rob were not to be seen, but they too had taken their instruments out. I turned back to the melee. Of course, what else. Standing right before me was the Biker Icon, looking round at the progress of the destruction, not two feet away. He was turning to scan the room. My sense of time has always entered a new zone in crisis situations. Everything appears to slow down, which means my mind is working at double or triple its normal speed. It was no different this time. His turn toward me was in slow motion, and as my inner predictor told me they would, his eyes fell on me. My speeding brain was calculating directions of escape. It had to take into account, however, that my body speed had not increased at all. The Father Icon's wrathful fist came laterally toward my face. My inner calculator predicted the second of impact and the force behind it. I fell backwards in accordance with this reading. Booming thunder, clashing sounds of lightning, unknown objects dropping on my skull, hardware and—yes—bells, falling on the ground around me. I had fallen into the midst of Dave's piled-up drums, which fell in on me, cymbals, tom toms, cowbells, and all, and the bastard hadn't touched me. I lay there like a dead man. The Icon flew off to another part of the room, thinking he had done me tremendous damage.

From where I lay I could watch the finale. The bartenders had finally gotten their local boys in, on-call bouncers. They were forcing the fighters out the door (Some of the clientele, dazed, of course got it together to escape on their own steam.) People grabbing onto each other were forced out the door. A bouncer shoved two people out onto the stoop, one of them had another man by the hair and his leather jacket, and his victim was squirming on the floor, only to find himself bouncing down the steps with his attacker rolling over top of him. The sirens of police cars were very close outside, moving our Suzuki critics to disperse more quickly. Suddenly the floor was clear. The furniture was everywhere. A shimmering bar mirror was broken and I looked back at myself in that mirror from a broken utopia. Then I saw Peach staggering out on the floor, looking right, looking left. His T-shirt was ripped to shreds that hung in a few strands around his neck and one shoulder, his shoes were off, his glasses gone. He looked up and was visibly relieved to see me.

It's you. Look. I'm trying to remember. My house. The car. My girlfriend…

Someone had taken it upon themselves to ram Peach's head into the floor a few too many times. I was not happy, since it had all begun when Peach had inserted himself between the Biker Icon's first blow and myself. Peach was taken to the emergency room, a mere forty-five minutes away in the woodlands of southern Maryland. He was treated for a concussion. Our equipment suffered little damage. We rockers had hid ourselves away better than the clientele had. We certainly were better off than the owner: We were told later that the biker club came back the following weekend with knives, perhaps expecting us to be there. (Did they think we were extended at the tavern?) The result was worse. The owner died the following week of a heart attack, though no one could pin it down to the trouble started by our attempts to do original work in rock clubs. But our egos were battered by the poor understanding of our unique work, the poor reception—the lack of reception altogether.

In this regard, Mitch was as bad as the bikers. From our point of view, if he and his colleagues had opened their ears, it would not have mattered what happened in the tavern. No, he and the group he represented were worse. They were the great demoralizers. Our Harley critics were just the coup de grâce. The band folded, though three of us had been working our act for a decade. Undoubtedly, Mitch went on to be a very rich man, agenting preprocessed music made in the maws of the entertainment machine, all sounding the same, and designed to numb minds and condition them to formulas that could quickly churn out mass market music like cheese food. My artistic path changed. I moved from there into the world of theatre, to which I committed my life. It is a world where people help one another, where good work is appreciated, where even critics are helpful and write you personal letters of thanks. Where people love to work together, and leave their egos back home behind them, and everyone loves animals, talks to their plants, and where the innovative, thinking artists do public service work in grateful thanks for the recognition they have received throughout their country.

And so my son, that is how I put my past behind me, and came to be in my marvelous line of work. Good night. Sleep tight. Don't let the bedbugs bite.

JOE MARTIN is a playwright, theatre director, and author of nine books including the fiction works Foreigners *and* Parabola: Tales of the Wise and the Idiots. *His stage adaptation of Rumi's* Mathnavi *was issued by Asylum Arts/Leapring Dog Press in February 2008. He lives in Washington, D.C. His website is www.joemartin.us.*

First Day

James Mathews

The job advertisement assured me that no experience was required. You wouldn't know it from the size of the machine I had been hired to operate. Hank and Eli Oglesby, the machine's owners, led me into their basement, for what was to be my first and last day on the job.

The machine filled the room. Centered immensely on a concrete slab, it was an industrial accident waiting to happen, a sheer menace of oily pistons and vents. I couldn't imagine what purpose it could possibly serve, and I certainly didn't ask.

Hank gestured to a long lever jutting from the machine, its handle painted lipstick red. "All you got to do," Hank said, "is pull this here lever and watch she don't get overheated. Go on and give her a pull."

I did as he said. The machine roared to life. Tiny needles on the nearby gauges flickered and twirled. Steam whistled through an array of pipes running along the ceiling. It reminded me of the inside of a World War II submarine.

Eli rolled his eyes and spat on the floor, seemingly unhappy with my performance.

"Don't mind him!" Hank shouted over the noise. "His girlfriend run out on him."

"That's your opinion!" Eli yelled back. "Thanks for sharing it with the help!"

I scanned the panel of gauges, none of which were labeled. "So how do I know if it's overheating?"

"Not to worry," Hank said with a reassuring wink. "She'll behave herself. This baby is 99.9 percent guaranteed safe." Then he grinned and gave me an enthusiastic thumbs-up.

Ten minutes later, we were in Hank's pickup truck, racing to find the nearest emergency room. Hank was driving. His eyebrows and mustache were burnt off. "She blew," he kept saying over and over. "I can't believe the mother blew!"

Eli sat in the passenger seat. Except for the twelve-inch metal rod sticking out of his eye socket, he looked to be in perfect health. Every now and then, he would vaguely point down a side street, indicating the direction Hank should be taking.

"What the hell happened?" I said, wedged between the two men, a muffled ringing in my ears. "I did exactly what you told me to do."

"Now don't go blaming yourself," Hank said. "First things first."

"I wasn't blaming myself," I said. "I was blaming you."

As we sped down the highway, Eli examined his ghastly wound in the side-view mirror.

"Does it hurt?" I asked him.

He shrugged, reached over, and turned on the radio.

"Damn," Hank said, swerving onto the shoulder of the road to turn around. "Gotta backtrack."

"Told you to go right on Montana," Eli said.

"Which I damn sure did."

"Sailed right past it far as I could tell."

"You couldn't tell the time with that thing sticking out of your face."

"I can tell we ain't at the hospital yet!"

"We should stop and call an ambulance," I suggested. "He could lose his eye."

Hank scoffed. "Hell, it's already a goner. Who's kidding who."

I stared back at him, shocked. "How can you say that? Isn't that for the doctors to decide?!"

"They already decided it. Six months ago."

"Five," Eli said, his fingertips probing at the corner of the wound. "This one's glass."

"*Glass?*" I said. "You have a glass eye?"

He nodded. "I punched some feller in a bar and he stabbed me with a fork. He was making a move on my fiancée."

"Is that what you call it?" Hank said. "A move?"

"Shut up and drive."

"Everybody else called it marriage."

Eli gritted his teeth. "I'll bust your goddamn lip."

"What for?" Hank snapped back defiantly. "It wasn't me that married her!"

With all the grace of a drunken sailor, Eli lunged for his brother, driving his elbow into my chest in the process. The metal rod in his fake eye quivered up and down like a diving board. He managed to snatch the collar of Hank's bloody shirt. The truck swerved again skidding on and off the gravel shoulder, kicking up a chalky mix of dirt and roadside litter.

"Guys! Guys! Guys!" I yelled, struggling to separate the two hulking men. "For God's sake!"

Finally, Eli's body grew slack and he leaned back against the door. "Bastard," he hissed, out of breath. "You don't understand the pain. You don't understand nothin'." Then he sighed mightily and passed out.

Hank fussed with the stretched collar of his T-shirt and said nothing.

At the corner of next intersection, I noticed the blue hospital sign complete with large white arrow that pointed in the opposite direction we were heading.

Before I could say anything, Hank cut me off. "I saw it. This way's quicker."

Actually, it wasn't quicker. In fact, it took us another half hour of backtracking before we finally reached the hospital. Soon after, Hank and I were sitting together in the waiting room, me with a mild concussion, Hank with a broken wrist that the emergency room doctors had hastily reset and wrapped in a cast. There was no word yet on Eli's condition. They had wheeled him away on a gurney through a pair of automatic doors under a sign that read, *EMERGENCY PERSONNEL ONLY BEYOND THIS POINT!* Taped over the small glass window was another sign that asked, *Did We Remember To Wash Our Hands?*

With what sounded like a heavy heart, Hank fumbled through a short speech. He was halfway through before I even realized he was talking to me. The bottom line was that he had no choice but to let me go. He hoped I understood. "Probably never find that damn lever again anyway," he said.

"What did it do?" I asked him.

"What did what do?"

"It. The machine."

Hank plucked a tuft of cotton from the lining of his new plaster cast. "Fool thing was Eli's idea," he said. "If you ask me, he was just trying to impress his girlfriend. Lot of good it did."

JAMES MATHEWS was raised in El Paso, Texas, and now lives in Maryland. His stories have appeared in numerous literary magazines, including the Florida Review, *the* Wisconsin Review, *the* Pacific Review, Carolina Quarterly, *the* Northwest Review, *the* Greensboro Review, *and others. His first collection of stories,* Last Known Position, *will be published in the fall by the University of North Texas Press.*

Closing Time

Richard McCann

After you died, I lay on a chaise lounge each afternoon at the pool club, listening to the same song over and over through my headphones. I knew there was work to do, like disposing of the medicines that littered your nightstand and packing your suits into boxes for Goodwill. But I was trying to figure where your dying had taken me. *I'm lying by the pool,* I kept telling myself. *I'm lying by the pool.* Did I imagine that if I lay there long enough I'd be returned to the afternoons I'd spent there long ago, in the years before I met you?

It was almost midnight the first time I saw you in the downstairs bar of the Lost & Found, where you were leaning against the pool table in a black T-shirt and a pair of faded Levis that hung low on your hips. The place was packed with men, some in leather pants, others in polo shirts and chinos.

"Want to play?" you said, hoisting your beer bottle toward me, a small salute.

I just stood there. I was like that in those days, nervous and shy, held tight within my own body. I could hear Donna Summer's "Love to Love You Baby" pulsing through the ceiling from the disco upstairs.

You bought me a beer. We talked awhile. "OK," I said when you asked me to go home with you. I remember what I was thinking: *It's happening, it's happening, my life's about to start.* Back then, I still knew what I wanted: a boyfriend, and then a condo with nice furniture. A coffee table made of chrome and glass. Some Breuer chairs.

Of course, that was before everyone started dying. First there was Paul. Then Larry. And then Edward and Tom and Victor and Darnell and Dario. By then, we were living in a small apartment, where you sat on the sofa at night, fingering the swollen lymph glands in your neck. *Don't do that,* I wanted to tell you.

But that came later. That first night, I waited outside the bar, as you'd instructed, while you went to get your car. As I waited, I kept studying the pink neon sign—*Lost & Found*—that hung above the door. I remember thinking it was almost funny, the way someone had rigged it so that the words blinked on and off in alternate succession, first one and then the other. When you pulled up, I was still watching it: Lost. Found. Lost. Found. Lost. Found.

RICHARD McCANN is the author, most recently, of Mother of Sorrows *(Pantheon Books, 2005), a collection of linked stories. He is also the author of* Ghost Letters *(Alice James Books, 1994), a collection of poems, and the editor of* Things Shaped in Passing: More "Poets for Life" Writing From the AIDS Pandemic *(Persea Books, 1997). His work has appeared in such magazines as the* Atlantic, Esquire, *and* Ms., *and in numerous anthologies, including* The O. Henry Prize Stories 2007 *and* Best American Essays 2000. *He has received grants and awards from the Guggenheim Foundation, the National Endowment for the Arts, the Christopher Isherwood Foundation, and the Fine Arts Work Center in Provincetown. He is a professor in the graduate program in creative writing at American University.*

The Scent of Memory

Matthew L. Moffett

The sign outside the Romper Commercial Gallery exclaims in bright red letters, "Aaron Tzara: Old Works and New Directions." Inside, the second floor containing Tzara's most recent work sits closed until the unveiling ceremony in a few minutes. The typical crowd for an art opening in Dupont Circle—the odd mixture of critics, collectors, and hangers-on—drifts amidst one another on the first floor, each pretending to look at the early paintings and sculptures while they grab food off the serving trays of passing caterers and scan the room to see who managed to come.

Peter Dhalgren stands in the middle of this mild chaos, shaking and itching in his tight, rented tuxedo with the crowd pressing him against the museum-white walls. A caterer offers him a small shrimp stuffed with crabmeat, but his stomach churns too much from nervousness to eat. He calms himself by playing with his ponytail and by humming the twisted melody to "All These Governors" by the Evens.

Peter arrived a few minutes before with Professor Childers, his art instructor at James Madison University. Childers knew Tzara from when they both lived in New York City and was able to get a pair of invitations to the opening based on their past relationship. Peter and Childers made the two-hour drive together from Harrisonburg to D.C. with Childers constantly trying to change Peter's mind about going, but as soon as they got there, Childers made himself at home by chasing every caterer with a wine tray.

Peter waits patiently, holding a small portfolio of his own work. Although he would never admit it, Peter dreams of Tzara smiling on him, taking him under his wing and carrying him to a point where people will crowd together to see his own works.

Squeezing in between two large people smelling of cheap white wine, Peter finally makes it over to a faux-marble display pedestal with a pool of silly putty gelled on the top and sides. The title plaque underneath names the piece *Time Slips Away #37*. He picks up a brochure from the nearby stand and reads the description:

> *This particular piece is a rare work from Tzara's silly putty period that occurred between 1978 and 1980 while he was living in Berlin. Tzara quickly yet distinctly constructed over 100 busts of people he knew out of giant masses of the popular toy; as days went by, the putty would slowly metamorphose into a simple pool of gray plastic, completely indistinct from the form Tzara created with his own hands just days before. The exact image Tzara chose to represent in this sculpture is no longer known.*

Price: $32,000

Peter reaches out and strokes the melted, formless mass. Although he thinks he understands Tzara's pointed joke on form and imagery, knowing he will never see the form Tzara created with his own hands fills him with a sadness that feels like tiny pieces of ice lodged in his chest refusing to melt.

A heavy hand grabs Peter by the shoulder, jarring him out of his thoughts. Peter turns to see Childers, a large glass of white wine in hand. Peter and his classmates all call him The Walrus, and it never seemed more appropriate than tonight. Rotund with a scraggly beard and thin glasses, Childers not only looks the part but also carries every bit of the lack of subtlety of the large animal. While some professors take the approach of kind encouragement, Childers never backs down from telling his students which he sees as "artists" and which he finds as "fakers." Somehow Peter managed to get into his good graces and they developed a relationship like that between a father whose son is just entering adolescence: admiration and respect heavily tinged with embarrassment.

"Your hero's just across the room," Childers says. "Why don't we get the introductions over with?"

"He's here?" Peter exclaims. "Where?"

Childers points across the room with one hand and slops half the contents of his wineglass into his mouth with the other. The imaginary line from Childers's meaty finger aims at a shambling tree-trunk of a man dressed in a white suit over a teal low-neck T-shirt. The large man stands gesticulating in front of an early Tzara painting Peter immediately recognizes as *Faster, Pussycat*: a bizarre collage of hair, leopard skin bikinis, movie reviews, and blood-red paint done over a photograph of a race car as a tribute to the Russ Meyer film. Peter gasps when he sees to whom the large man is talking. The figure is unmistakable; with his fluorescent white hair combed straight back, the steeply angled nose, and his trademark black leather jacket and chrome chain belt. It's Tzara.

Peter's heart jackhammers inside him; while he's hoped for this moment for months, an innate fear creeps in. What if Tzara doesn't like him? Or even worse, doesn't like his work?

"Come on," Childers says. "Let's get this over with."

Childers takes Peter by the elbow and walks him across the room, zigzagging between clusters of people. A tiny bit of blood flows into Peter's mouth, making him realize he's so tense he was biting his own tongue. They get there to hear the tail end of a conversation between Tzara and the large man.

"You obviously possess a discriminating eye," Tzara says to the large man. "No other piece in this room displays the full diaspora of my soul from this period of my life. I certainly must not allow you to leave without this creation. My typical price for work from this time runs at $200 per square inch, making this run at $96,000. But for you, Willard, for you I'll let it go for $75,000."

A snort escapes the large man's nose as he thinks about the price. "I'm guessin' I can afford that. Sure will look nice above the fireplace. Where do I drop my ducats?"

A sly smile spreads across Tzara's face as he points towards a desk near the front door. "They'll have it wrapped up and ready for you when you leave, Willard."

"Always the salesman, aren't you, Aaron?" Childers says.

Tzara turns with a look of blue fire in his eyes. When his gaze catches Childers, his features soften slightly.

"Tommy? Tommy Childers? It's been a long time, my boy. But my sales technique? It's really more what I would call Business Art."

Amused at seeing his professor rebuked by his hero, Peter snickers.

"Isn't that what Warhol called it, Aaron?" Childers retorts.

"He may have said it before me. I don't really remember. Even if he did, I'm the one who made his concept a reality." Tzara reaches out and shakes Childers' thicker hand. "What has it been, eight years now?"

"At least," Childers responds.

"Come to see an old classmate at work?" asks Tzara.

"Actually, I only came to introduce you to Peter here," Childers says. "He's one of my best students, and he fancies you as a hero of sorts."

Tzara turns and looks Peter over for the first time. Peter feels trapped in that gaze, but not altogether too uncomfortable for being trapped in it.

"So you're his student?" Tzara asks. "What do you think about old Tommy? What kind of teacher is he?"

Peter almost laughs at Childers being called Tommy; he's always thought of him as Professor Childers, or, at the very least, Thomas. Never anything so informal as Tommy.

"All right, I guess," Peter responds. "He's, you know, a teacher. Always pushing the basics like still life studies and anatomy. Sometimes I get a little bored. I want to try new things." Peter shrugs.

Tzara shakes his head. "Tommy, sounds like you haven't changed a bit." Tzara returns his eyes to Peter. "We went to school together, Tommy and I. While I was busy bronzing lumps of my own feces, he stayed focused on the basics. His still lifes are more for himself than for any audience. His paintings have, what is it they say about your paintings, Tommy? Yes. They have a *quiet poetry* about them." Tzara points at the portfolio in Peter's hands. "Now, you're bringing some work of your own for me to see?"

Peter nods and hands him the slim portfolio of drawings and watercolors; he trembles watching Tzara open it. Tzara flips through them quickly, almost haphazardly: *Still Life with Headless Hobbit, The Corpse in the Copse, The Transmigration of Timothy's Fist.*

"Who do you like?" Tzara says, looking dead at Peter.

"Excuse me?"

"Which artists do you like? Besides me, I mean?" he says with a laugh.

"Oh, I dunno. Basquiat, Dali before he went all religious, Jeff Rowe. Mostly, though, I love Duchamp."

"It shows. Especially with this one." Tzara holds up a collage titled "Bemused Mask Beneath the Waves," a new one Peter still struggles with that mixes collage with faux-cubist drawings. "What is it you like about Duchamp?"

Peter shrugs. "He makes me laugh, I guess. I mean, a moustache on the Mona Lisa, and then writing *her ass is hot...*"

"And that's what you want to do?" Tzara asks. "Make people laugh? If that's all you want to do, you should try comedy."

Embarrassed by the unexpected criticism, Peter blushes and turns his eyes to the floor.

"Peter, I think," Childers interjects, "enjoys the attention work like this gets. Just recently, he spent several weeks painting very detailed images on the insides of television sets, only to throw them out the third-floor window of the art building at the opening for the student show."

"So, you like the attention art can bring, do you?" Tzara asks.

Peter shrinks back a bit, unsure of how to answer this.

"Now, now. Don't worry," Tzara says, extending an open hand. "No need for you to get defensive. It's just you'll need to answer to these things as you go. You're going for shock, for the quick effect, but critics will want you to explain it. Make it convoluted and full of nihilism and they will eat it up. The hard part is moving on to the next big thing. You come up with something fresh, but it's not long before the public gets tired of it and starts saying, "OK, but now what?" The only way to sell and keep selling is to outdo yourself every time." He looks at Peter more intently and then says, "Every time."

Tzara stops speaking and looks across the room. "Uh oh. I'm being gestured."

A middle-aged woman with jet-black Prince Valiant hair in a dark suit and electric purple makeup comes towards the three. She grabs Tzara by the arm and starts to pull him away.

"Well now," Tzara starts, "I guess that means it's time to start the next phase of this affair. Time to put my public face into high gear. We'll talk more later."

The two walk over to a small podium positioned at the base of the spiral staircase. The woman turns on a cordless microphone with a loud click and she clears her throat a few times to get everyone's attention.

"Good evening," the woman says in a very nasal tone. "I am Julia Romper, and I am very pleased to have you all here this night. This is not an ordinary opening. Tonight is very special, in that this is Aaron's first exhibition in almost eight years. After claiming to have abandoned art altogether, he has pulled together something new for us. Based on his past work, I think we can all agree that the only thing we can expect is to be surprised. So, without further delay, I give you Aaron Tzara."

"What a pompous ass he is," Childers whispers to Peter, shaking his head. "Aaron hasn't changed a lick. Always thinking about the dollar value and not about the quality of what he creates. I'm ready to go if you are."

Peter clenches his fists and closes his eyes, trying to hold something back out of respect for Childers. The feelings boil and finally overflow with a life of their own. "You could learn a thing or two from him. When's the last time anyone paid any attention to your artwork, to your carefully rendered, carefully realized still lifes? He's doing something new, shaking things up, and I'm going to be part of it."

"OK, Peter. If that's the way you want it. We'll go upstairs and see what Aaron has for us. Just promise me you won't get your hopes up too much."

Childers reaches out to take Peter's arm again; Peter shrugs away from him and makes his own way by merging with the crowd as it scurries towards the narrow spiral staircase rising to the second floor. He finds himself behind the large man and an elderly woman with frizzy hair dyed fire-engine red. Snippets of conversation surround him, each one trying to guess what Tzara's newest work might entail.

"I bet he's gone back to painting. All the great ones return to painting"

"I bet it's a whole video thing…"

"He knows how to stay current…"

All the lights are off when Peter reaches the gallery on the second floor. People cram and push into a tight space of complete blackness. They mutter and breathe and Peter smells the thick stench of their bodies as they begin to perspire. He thinks of a womb and wonders what thing will be born once the lights come aglow. Tzara must have taken the microphone, because his voice suddenly fills the room.

"All visual art," Tzara begins "has digressed to the point that we always know what to expect. Sculpture, video, collage, film, painting. Painting especially. So now it's time to throw it out the window and search for new surprises, new horizons of expression."

The lights click on, stabbing knives of brightness into Peter's eyes. He blinks a few times to adjust and finally sees Tzara's next step in art. The walls, floor and ceiling are all painted in flat gray. Lined down on the left and right sides of the room are gas masks plugged into a black panel attached to the wall. Each set of gas masks is labeled with a few short words like "My First Time" and "A Sunny Day at the Ballpark." The crowd mumbles, confused but still hopeful.

"This, my new phase that I call Olfactrism, is about scent, about memory. By strapping on these masks, your olfactory senses will be inundated…quite safely I assure…with scents designed to create a specific reaction. Tonight is quite a pleasure for me in that a student of an old colleague is with me, and I would like to invite him to be the first here to experience this next great art form."

Tzara holds out his hand to Peter. Childers shakes his head at him, but the glow of Tzara's welcoming smile draws Peter away. Sucking in his lower lip and holding his breath, he walks towards Tzara, meeting him by the mask labeled "One Lost Summer." Peter sits down in a small chair as Tzara places the mask over Peter's face and ties the straps around the back of his head. The straps fit snugly, but not too tightly. Peter peers out through eyeholes of black tinted glass, seeing everyone in the crowd watching for his reaction. Not knowing what to expect, thoughts of electric chairs and gas chambers leap into Peter's head.

A hissing like a basketful of snakes blows out behind Peter as the tint of the glass darkens further, making it impossible to see. The air inside the mask changes; he picks up the subtle scents of leaves, moist trees, a trace of mildew. He closes his eyes and soaks deeply into the pools of memory hidden in the back of his mind.

Peter floats, confused at first by his surroundings. He sees a lake with soft wisps of clinging morning fog surrounded by rings and rings of tall trees and thick shrubs. A few feet away from the lake, a small squirrel that almost dances as it ran between a pair of bushes and into a hole in a tree. At the top of the very same tree a fly entangles itself in the threads of a spider and cringes as it senses the spider flick towards it, ready to eat. Peter sees all this simultaneously; the mask transformed him into the air itself, cradling the surrounding environment and knowing everything about it.

One thing in particular takes Peter's notice: a small boy hidden under a tree, hunched over a pad of paper. The boy breathes in and out, and Peter feels each breath as it pushes against him. Peter suddenly slips inside the boy, sucked in through the mouth, zipping down the windpipe and into the lungs. His essence floats to the bloodstream and pumps up and out, spreading to the heart, the fingertips and, finally, the brain. Peter realizes this small boy is himself, his old self at age nine. With that realization comes the full memory of this almost forgotten moment.

It was the third year in a row his parents sent him to Camp Wiccamaw. The camp's landscape stretched out like a dream for most young boys: full fields and woods for hiking, a lake for swimming and canoeing, an archery range, and even a soccer field. But Peter was small, always made fun of and beat up, so the dream scarred like a nightmare. This third year he faked an illness and spent the whole week in his tent or off in the woods alone, closed off in his own private citadel of green trees.

Out of boredom he picked up a pencil and paper and just drew what he saw. He'd always been able to draw, but had only tried cartoons; little scenes of Mighty Mouse and He-Man caught in compromising circumstances. But this was different. Something incredible lay hidden within the simple, subtle lines of a leaf stretched on the ground, something he couldn't describe or explain through words but only through drawing it on paper. When he got home, he told his mom he wanted to be "an artist, because it made me feel real." Peter's heart swelled with that forgotten joy; he knew then that, no matter what he had to hold onto that joy, to possess it for a lifetime. He needed it like a drug, and it wanted to stay within him as long as possible.

Peter sets down the pencil and sighs; he knew as soon as the gas within the mask ended and the scents subsided, the dream would end and the feeling would fade with it. That couldn't happen, not now that he had this back. Peter stands and walks into the forest, faster and faster, praying to be swallowed by the sweet fog that surrounds him. A bright blinding light chases him, cutting through the fog. Peter tries to run, but it catches him, obliterating everything in its violent wake.

||||

The hissing stops and the powerful scents subside. Peter takes the gas mask off his face and sees Tzara standing over him, a razor thin smile splitting his face. Still off balance by the memories and feelings warming his insides, Peter stumbles while he gets up.

"And he's OK!" Tzara shouts in a dramatic manner. "Tell us, what was it like?" The crowd's eyes focus on Peter, still unsure what to think about this new form of art. "I've never experienced anything like it. It was like…"

"Never experienced anything like it!" Tzara interrupts loudly as he prances across the floor. "Now who else is ready to experience something new, to experience the beauty, the majesty, the mystery of Olfactrism?"

Several others move in to become encased in the other masks, and even more line up to be next for the experience. Tzara overlooks the scene, a slightly bemused look on his face as if he enjoys seeing the various critics, collectors, and hangers-on strapped into gas masks.

"Mr. Tzara? Mr. Tzara, I've never experienced anything like that in my life. I…"

"What? Oh, it's you again," Tzara says, taking a quick look at Peter. He looks up, and then scans all the other faces in the room. "You want an autograph, do you?"

Tzara grabs Peter's portfolio and signs it with a flashing silver pen.

"That's great, Mr. Tzara. Thanks. But I have to tell you…"

Tzara shoves the portfolio back into Peter's hands. "There you are. Sorry I can't talk, but I see a sale over there."

Tzara walks away, heading towards a young man in a well-fitting tuxedo. Peter looks down at his portfolio folder and sees the telltale A. T. that makes up Tzara's signature. He looks up and hears Tzara barking like a carny to anyone who will hear. "All right, all right! Who's next for the greatest adventure in art?"

The words fill Peter with a cooling dissatisfaction. He watches Tzara a few moments, listens to him as he pushes sale after sale more like a carnival barker than an artist, and realizes Tzara has no idea what he's created. While some fragment of genius may sit inside Tzara, it lay deep and buried beneath miles of commercialism and well-rehearsed drama. The warmth reclaimed in that mask threatens to slip away as Peter looks on Tzara with both pity and revulsion.

Peter turns away and walks back down the staircase to the first floor. The caterers are there, cleaning up after the guests. Sitting down cross legged on the floor, he begins sketching on the back of the brochure, struggling to hold onto the warm memory before it fades away like a soft scent on a winter breeze. It flows out of him, a rough, sketchy picture of a small boy huddled under a tree, clutching a pad of paper tight to his chest. He sketches the overhanging limbs of the tress, limbs that were both comforting and restricting in their protection, and barely notices as Childers walks up behind him and sets a warm hand on his shoulder.

"I'm sorry, Peter. He's always been an asshole. He…"

"Don't worry," Peter interrupts, not bothering to look up from his drawing. "I don't want to be him anymore."

"I'm glad to hear that."

Peter stays seated on the floor for several minutes more, continuing to draw, as Childers stands behind him looking down at his student's work. The drawing grows with a life of its own, expanding beyond the boundaries of a single sheet of paper. Peter tears a second sheet out and places it next to the first and continues his drawing, creating a larger and more detailed scene with every passing second. But then, suddenly, Peter stands up and looks Childers directly in the eye.

"But I'm not going to be you, either."

The current version of MATTHEW L. MOFFETT lives and works in the Virginia suburbs of Washington, D.C. He's currently pursuing a master's degree in library science at the Catholic University of America.

FROM *Cologne No. 10 for Men*

RICHARD MORRIS

They sat in the twilight watching wisps of fog rising from the glassy lake. "It's becoming clearer to me now, Robbie. What we need to create is the functional equivalent of war: everything except the killing."

"You mean the illusion of war."

"Yes," Wilfred said, astounded at Reckert's clarity. "But I'm not sure I should've used that old man's body. The look in that woman's eyes. I don't think I could do that again."

"You'll think of something else. There are bodies all over Nam. That's what someone told me, anyway."

"It's not the bodies that worry me. It's the guns. Where will we get enough of them?"

That night Can came to Wilfred in his sleep. She snuggled up and forgave him. "Wilfed love Vietnamese. Wilfed no kill Vietnamese. Wilfed numbah one. Can love Wilfed." He felt her hands caressing him. He felt her slip down her pajama bottoms and unbutton her top. He felt her warm breasts press against him and felt her hands unbuckle his belt and pants and reach inside. He pulled her close and felt her hand grip his penis. She was on top of him now, guiding him into her. He groaned and felt the rising and falling. He heard the sweet smack of flesh on flesh. He wanted to be closer and he thrust upward and gave her all he could. In and out, up and down. The dance of the gods. He rolled over on top of her and the beat grew stronger and louder and more insistent, demanding, obligatory, imperious, and virulent until he could no longer withstand it and his mind succumbed in toto and let his body have its way. It grabbed and held and crushed and shouted, "Oh…oh…oooooooooh!"

"Sir. Sir! Really, sir! I-I...Will you please get off of me, sir. Please!" Wilfred was all over Welbourne. He awoke embarrassed and wet and cursing the war that made him sleep with men, squeezed together in a hole under a net and rubberized canvas, and he vowed that as long as he was changing other aspects of the war, he would change this too.

"Robbie! Robbie! I figured it out," Wilfred cried. The sun was flooding the plain, and Reckert had toothbrush in foaming mouth and canteen cup in hand.

"Bwoo?" Reckert asked, lips closed to hold in the froth.

"I couldn't sleep last night, and I lay awake and figured out why we have to have a war every ten or twenty years."

Reckert spat onto the ground. "Why?"

"Two reasons. First, so we don't have to fight a war without veterans. Can you imagine fighting without veterans?" He held an imaginary microphone to his mouth. "'This is Daniel Dud at the Pentagon. I'm talking to General Malaise. Sir, can you beat the Russians?' 'Gee, Ah don't know. Ah've never fought anyone before, and neither has anyone else in the armed forces. We haven't had a war in fifty years, you know.'"

"'Don't you think that's a little...dicey?'"

"'Oh, Ah don't know. Ah'm sure we can beat 'em at war games and maneuvers. Ah always beats the Red Team at them.'"

"'Good, sir. We'll all sleep better knowing that.'"

"I get it. We have to fight a war every ten years or we won't know if our personnel are good enough to win. What's the other reason?"

"Back to Daniel Dud. 'I'm talking with Howard Lose, CEO of General Munitions and Armaments Corpse. Mr. Lose, sir. Can your new F3001 fighter beat the Ruskies' new MIG 2973?'"

"'I've got to hand it to you, Dud. You really know how to ask the hard ones. The truth is, I don't know. They've never been in a dogfight before. All I can say is that the F3001 exceeds all possible specifications. It's even blown away our new MEF2538, the most advanced mock enemy fighter we've ever developed.' 'Thank you, sir. That's comforting. This is Daniel Dud, returning you now to ABM Central.'"

"So the only foolproof way we can test our weapons systems is to use them in a real war. Everything else is conjecture."

"That's it, Robbie. For reasons of personnel and ordnance, war is essential to our national security. The only way we can be sure we can keep the peace is to remain at war."

"A sobering thought, Will. But we need a better war than this one if it's going to do the job. We can't test nukes or gas or chemicals or missiles or anything good in this dumb war."

"We need to attack Russia real bad, Robbie."

"You bet. And here I thought we had wars to win presidential reelection campaigns."

"To have streams we can't change horses in the middle of?"

The company cordoned yet another village this day. The operation was a replica of the day before except that Wilfred couldn't find a body. Undeterred, he went to Trinh, who was sitting with detainees at another interrogation point.

"Hey, Charlie," he said. "Come here."

Trinh reluctantly complied.

"Today you die twice." Trinh shuddered. "But not for long,"

It was an easier operation than the day before, since Trinh was self-mobile and Wilfred had the foresight to steal the gallon can of ketchup from the mess line the night before.

"Hey! Where's the ketchup?" growled the soldier, his franks nestled in their buns like fresh bodies in caskets.

Wilfred and Henry led Trinh and two old Vietnamese men wearing shorts and shirts to a secluded part of the village, ordered them to disrobe, fired a burst into their shirts, and soddened them with ketchup. He dressed Trinh in one shirt, ordered him onto his belly, hid the amazed old men, and called in Captain Simms and Colonel Clary.

"Now this one looks more like a Charlie," Clary said as he kicked Trinh in the ribs. Trinh quaked, let out a grunt, and stiffened in pain. "He's not dead!"

"I can assure you he is quite dead, sir," Wilfred said. "Haven't you ever seen a chicken run around with his head chopped off? It's the same sort of thing. Involuntary reflexes."

"Every time I come to this company, I learn more about bodies," Clary marveled.

Shots rang out again, and this time Henry led Simms and Clary through a maze. Wilfred ordered Trinh up and ran him to Reckert, the Kit Carson clutching his bruised ribs all the way. Wilfred dressed him in the other clothes, had him lie on his back, laid the rifle beside him, poured ketchup on his wounds, and instructed him on how to stare away with his mouth open.

"Move a muscle and you're a dead man," he said in encouragement.

Clary and Simms arrived, and Clary commented on the amazing resemblance between the dead VC and the company's interrogator.

"Sir. I'm surprised at you," Wilfred said. "I mean I would expect a racial bigot to see similarities between Vietnamese that don't exist. But not you. You can see the differences, can't you? Surely. I mean they don't really look anything alike. Trinh is much taller—" Wilfred noticed a fly land on Trinh's cheek and begin marching toward his open mouth. "Get down!" he shouted and dove to the ground and fired six rounds into a nearby bush. Reckert and Henry also began firing, the captain and colonel hitting the turf a second later.

"Did you see that?" Wilfred asked Reckert.

"Those pith helmets in the bushes? I sure did."

"They's still in there, sir," Henry said.

Simms wasn't sure if it was a hoax or not, but Clary was shaken. It had been more than a decade since he'd seen combat.

"Captain Simms. You better get Colonel Clary out of here. We'll clear the area. There's no sense you risking your life along with ours. You're too important, sir."

Reckert and Henry opened up while Wilfred crawled forward almost as quickly as the two senior officers crawled backward.

Wilfred tossed two grenades for effect and when he was sure Clary was gone, said, "OK. Get Trinh dressed. On the double!"

By the time Clary reached the interrogation area, Trinh was sitting, in full uniform, sweat dripping from his brow, talking to a prisoner, the faint taste of fly flesh bitter in his mouth.

"Oooh, that was close," Wilfred said to Reckert that night.

"I almost died when I saw that fly land."

"Clary might have died if he'd seen Trinh come to life."

"And we'd have been next."

"Yep. Well. Our score's improving," Wilfred said proudly. "That's four-zip now."

"That's not bad, but you're really gonna have to make a killing if you want to be best in the division."

"I know," Wilfred said, raising his canteen cup full of coffee to his lips. Then the cup was in the air, a finger-size stream of black gushing from each side. Wilfred hit the ground before the cup did, and this time the perimeter opened up. Thunks of grenade launchers sounded followed by distant explosions, all amid the steady chug-chug of a machine gun and random splatters of rifle fire. By then, however, Colonel Dai was well along his escape route, crawling behind a dike, through bamboo and high grass, down a stream bank, and away.

"The rat," Reckert said.

"It was nearly four to one," Wilfred said.

The next few days were discouraging. "We don't have any weapons. How can we get any kills if we don't have any weapons?"

Their frustration peaked the day they found the three old fishermen who had drowned in the lake during a sudden storm and washed up bloated onto the shore.

"Three perfectly good bodies," Wilfred wailed. "And we can't even use them."

"Hey, man," Henry said. "You couldn't pass them off as no Charlies. They're all puffed up."

"Man, all you have to do is poke holes in 'em to let out the gas and cover 'em with blood. They'd be great!"

"Sheeit. They'd fall to pieces before you even got 'em where you wanted 'em."

"That's better yet. The worse they look, the less chance Clary'll look at 'em."

Wilfred began pressing his men to search the villages more carefully and promised a three-day trip to Vassar to any man who found a weapon. The new bonus system paid off at a fishing village on the South China Sea. The cluster of huts clung to a finger of sand three miles long with the sea on one side and a bay on the other. A Company marched toward the objective between dunes twelve feet high covered with waving grass.

He decided that the company was moving too secretively, so he paused for a bit of target practice at some Viet Cong mirages, enlisting the aid of a large portion of his platoon. He would have been pleased had he seen the result: five enemy soldiers racing toward a sampan on the other side of the village, pushing off the sand into the surf, leaping over the side, sculling madly, and raising the sail.

When the company reached the village, the men quickly executed their nine to five cordon, and Wilfred's platoon went in for the search. They were unusually thorough—tapping, thumping, jabbing, sweeping away the sand, touching, looking.

While searching the hut of a young, tough-looking mother, Sergeant Matfield made a discovery—a glint of defiance in her eyes. He turned the two-room house upside down, personally tapping every square inch of floor, moving the furniture and a large crock full of rice. He thrust his bayonette into the walls in a hundred places but found nothing. Still, he remembered the woman's eyes, and he looked around again. Then he noticed, from inside, that the rear wall, where it met the slope of the roof, was more than a foot higher than the front wall. He walked behind the house and saw what he had expected to see: outside, the front and back walls were the same height. Double wall, he concluded, feeling stupid to have nearly missed it. Back inside, he pulled two beds away from the high wall, drew his machete and chopped a hole in it. There it was: a cavity between the walls, a foot and a half deep. He called for his men and shined a flashlight inside.

In his peripheral vision, he noticed that the woman was edging toward the door. "Grab her," he said. "She goes first."

They brought her to the hole, struggling and shaking, and Matfield pointed at it and pushed her toward it. She resisted and began crying and talking rapidly in Vietnamese.

Wilfred came in first, smiling. "Good going, Sarge." He went to the hole, but Matfield blocked it with his arm.

"Hold on," he said. "I figger it's booby-trapped." Wilfred stopped short and stepped back. "The woman wouldn't go in. Get Trinh to tell us what she says."

Trinh came and Wilfred told him, "We want in. Ask her how to get in. Ask her where the booby traps are. Oh, and Trinh. If one of us dies, you die."

Trinh questioned the woman. She showed him a place where the side of the wall could be lifted out. She said it was booby-trapped, but she didn't know how because she didn't do it. "Ask her if there's anyone in there," Wilfred told Trinh. He did so and told Wilfred there were none. "OK. Let's clear everybody out and frag the hell out of it."

They threw in eight grenades, one at a time. On the second try, they heard two explosions. The other grenades blew apart much of the thatch but caused no secondary blasts.

Matfield and his squad went back in, removed the rest of the wall and found a stack of ammunition cases in the corner.

"Eureka!" Wilfred said. "We have found it."

Henry came in and disarmed another booby trap from one of the boxes, and they brought them out and looked inside. There were fifty-eight rifles, two machine guns, three pistols, ammunition, twenty-five sets of NVA uniforms, a mortar, radio, and several inches of documents. Wilfred had Matfield's troops hide the rifles, pistols and uniforms, then called for Charlie Charlie. Clary flew in and viewed the cache with mixed feelings. "No small arms," he said. "Strange."

When Simms begin a sparkling rendition of how he, the captain, had led the operation, Wilfred cut him off.

"Let me tell it, sir," he said, and as Simms cringed and Clary waited in sadistic good humor for Wilfred to reduce the captain to the sniveling coward he was, Wilfred proceeded to describe how Simms had personally discovered the double wall and disconnected four other booby traps. "We'll write up the request for his Distinguished Service Cross tonight. There's no telling how many lives he's saved by his courageous action in capturing these munitions." He turned and whipped a salute on Simms. "Sir. I want you to know how proud I am to have had the privilege of serving in your command. Congratulations, sir."

"Thank you, Lieutenant," Simms said, returning the gesture with the total sobriety the occasion deserved.

Clary's eyes were popping. "C-congratulations, Captain Simms," he managed to utter. "Ou-outstanding!"

That night a band of thugs led by Henry, Matfield, and Rodriguez roamed the camp spreading the gospel, threatening potential snitches with horrible deaths, and getting every man's signature on the request for Simms's medal. Later that night Wilfred presented it to the ecstatic captain. "Just remember to keep your end of the deal. Don't forget your mother."

The next morning Matfield, who'd discovered the cache, left for Vassar—his reward for finding the weapons.

RICHARD MORRIS was born in 1943 in Pittsburgh into a steel family and lived for many years in Cleveland. He graduated from Haverford College and Harvard University. He was a rifle platoon leader with the First Cavalry Division (Airmobile) in 1967. As a second lieutenant in Vietnam, he learned first hand about the startling tactics, spit-shined jungle boots, and fight songs of the Vietnam War. There, as battalion songwriter, he wrote twenty-five songs, which can be found at www.vietwarsongs.com. In 2007 he recorded nineteen of the songs on a CD, Skytroopers, *available at www. cdbaby/cd/richardmorris. One of them—"Diggin a Hole"—was a finalist in the vocal jazz and blues category in the 23rd Annual Mid-Atlantic Song Contest (2006). With his wife of forty-one years, Morris lives in Bowie, Maryland, where he writes fiction and enjoys his three children and four grandchildren.* Cologne No. 10 for Men, *his first novel, is available at barnesandnoble.com and amazon.com.*

Working the Changes

KERMIT MOYER

I had never actually heard of Carolyn Conestoga, despite her memorably alliterative name, until my daughter Sophie began singing her praises, and I might never have met her at all if Sophie hadn't invited Nancy and me to a reading Carolyn gave as the new writer-in-residence at the university. Although only in her early thirties, Carolyn had already published two collections of poetry—*Smoke and Mirrors* and *The Apple Tree*—and each had gone on to win one or two prestigious, if somewhat esoteric, prizes. Sophie was hoping to be a poet herself someday, and not only was Carolyn Conestoga her teacher, she also seemed to embody virtually everything else that—with uncharacteristic boldness but without much confidence, I'm afraid—Sophie was in graduate school trying to become.

What struck me most about Carolyn's reading that evening was the way she had of reciting her poems in an intense and intimate *whisper*, as if what she was telling us were highly confidential and, at the same time, a matter of life and death. The poems themselves felt burnished and filigreed and intricate, full of surprising images and turns of phrase, and it didn't seem to matter in the least that they were as impossible to make literal sense of as a David Lynch film. The audience couldn't have been more pleased by her performance. I know I was spellbound. It didn't hurt, either, that she so perfectly looked the part: flyaway wisps of ash-blonde hair floating halo-like around a flushed and luminous face and an impression, even from behind the lectern, that she had just stepped out of the shower. She seemed to glisten. There was a certain athleticism, too. She was boyishly slender and small breasted but also long limbed and loose jointed, and she sported, like the fulcrum on which everything else turned, what you might call a *retroussé* rear end. It was hard not to be smitten. Even my wife, an Upper East Side New York City girl with an Ivy League education, was suitably impressed. "Floats like a butterfly, stings like a bee," Nancy said when the performance was over, nodding her head with what turned out to be a heavily ironic seal of approval. Sophie, for her part, was vibrating like a struck tuning fork.

At the wine and cheese reception, Sophie seemed less self-deprecating and looser than usual, as if the pink zinfandel she'd been compulsively sipping while we hovered about waiting for the perfect moment to be introduced to the eminent poet had gone straight to her beautiful, hero-worshiping head. "This is my mother, Nancy Stein Baker," Sophie said with an uncharacteristically breezy sweep of her hand. "She's a very fine numbers-cruncher should you ever need your very fine numbers crunched, and this is my dad, Lon Baker, a very fine jazz pianist and composer should you ever need your very fine...your very fine..." She'd been showing off, but now she was apparently stumped. "Jazz composed or knuckles cracked," I finished, coming happily to her rescue. After laughter all around and some shaking of hands, Carolyn turned to me and said, "But jazz piano? I love jazz piano...Oscar Peterson, Ahmad Jamal..." She put her hand on my arm and then took it back again. "I've always envied musicians," she said. "It must be like knowing how to fly. That immediacy of feeling you get..." She spoke with the self-conscious earnestness of a bookish girl who has been made shy by the pressure of her own good looks. Nevertheless, her eyes continued to hold mine while she half turned toward Nancy and said, "It must be great having your own personal jazz pianist in the house." "Yes," Nancy agreed, "it is great," and Sophie said, "Except for when he gets stuck in the middle of something and starts plunking out variation after variation of the same phrase ad infinitum." I put on a mock-sheepish grin, we all laughed some more, and Carolyn—she was Carolyn by then—said it sounded a lot like working on a poem—maybe our kinds of composition weren't so different. Her hand reached out again to touch my sleeve, her eyes locked on mine, and, although my wife and daughter were standing on either side of us like sentinels, there was the nearly audible sizzle of an electrical connection. Carolyn said she'd been looking for a way to cross-pollinate her work, open it up to a new range of possibilities, and studying jazz piano might just do the trick. Did I give lessons, she wanted to know. Did I give lessons? I said. You bet I did.

Which is how it happened that only a week after our first meeting, Carolyn Conestoga and I were seated thigh to thigh (mine in jeans, hers in what looked like seersucker pajama bottoms with a drawstring at the waist) on the piano bench in front of my vintage Steinway baby grand. We were in the middle of my free introductory lecture on the basic theory of jazz improvisation. Doing my best to ignore the question of whether or not those were actually pajama bottoms she was wearing, I was explaining how you could take a standard like "As Time Goes By" and, while staying in the same time signature and following the same pattern of chord changes, make different melodic choices, modulating the musical mood and filling in the shell of the old chord structure with a whole new tune virtually on the spot. I played a few bars of the tune as written—immediately evoking images of Ingrid Bergman, eyes brimming, and sad-eyed Bogie cradling his bottle of scotch (it's Sophie's and my favorite movie; optimistic Nancy prefers movies with happy endings)—and then I began playing around inside the changes, working them until there was only a smoky trace of the original melody left and giving the whole thing a slight blues inflection with a few flatted thirds and minor sevenths.

"I knew you'd be good," Carolyn said, intently watching my hands, "but you're fucking amazing."

Child of the '50s that I am, I can never get used to the casual way women of my daughter's generation use that word. "Most people don't realize how structured jazz improvisation really is," I said, feeling a familiar flush of pride at my own skill. "Even though I'm improvising, I'm still following the same chord pattern, so if I were playing with a bass or a sax or whatever, we'd be in harmonic sync. Working the changes is what lets you play freely with other people."

"But the piano does seem like such a great solo instrument," she said. "I think that's what really attracts me to it, loner that I am. It's like an orchestra all by itself." Her voice had a shy, slightly breathless quality, but then she laughed and her shyness seemed to disappear. "Don't get me wrong," she said, and she flashed me a look from under her eyebrows. "I'm all in favor of playing freely with other people."

It was a warm afternoon early in the new millennium, and the light diffused its way through the room's expanse of louvered windows and made a bright corona of her artfully disheveled hair, which was pulled back and held loosely by a blue ribbon. Her eyes were pale gray and long lashed, and her mouth was wide with a parenthetical dimple at either end. Just looking at her filled me with a deep tidal swell of longing. "Good," I said. "Because playing with other people is like taking a bath in feedback sometimes. It can get so intimate it's spooky."

"Speaking of intimate," she said, "here's one for you," and lightly touching my leg (she did a lot of touching), she looked at me sideways with an exaggeratedly cocked eyebrow, cupped her hand mock confidentially to her mouth, and, giving her delivery a slight faux alcoholic slur as if she were some guy in a bar, stage whispered in my ear, "Know what the difference is between a piano and a pussy?"

There was a pause while I absorbed what she'd said. To her credit, she was blushing again—she had the kind of delicate complexion that seemed to take the temperature of every passing fluctuation in her emotional weather. At the same time, I could feel some sort of fundamental shift going on—as if the ground were tilting beneath us and I were sliding in her direction. Or if it wasn't exactly like an earthquake, then it was like being drunk. "I guess I can't think of any," I finally said, feeling foolish. But then I had an inspiration. Before she could deliver the actual punch line (which to this day I don't know), I deadpanned, "Except maybe for a slight difference in the fingering technique."

She gave a surprised sputter of laughter and in the next instant she was laughing like I'd said the funniest thing she'd ever heard, rocking back and forth with the palm of one hand pressed against her chest and the other hand clutching my thigh to keep from falling off the piano bench. Passion aside, there's nothing more satisfying that making a beautiful woman laugh, and Carolyn's laughter was like drinking flute after flute of ice-cold champagne on a hot summer's day. I felt deliciously besotted with it and at the same time supremely conscious, especially of that hand on my thigh.

While Carolyn and I were laughing together on my piano bench—a few moments before our lips touched and our mouths opened and our tongues greedily met (everything happening much faster than seems possible even now)—my wife Nancy was also sitting at a keyboard—in her case, at a keyboard in front of a computer terminal in her office a whole universe away. It being April, she was no doubt going over a corporate tax return, blithely unaware that the train she was on had just gone off a cliff. In an instant, I'd convinced myself that so long as Nancy didn't know what was happening, she'd be like one of those cartoon characters who can walk on thin air as long as they don't look down. Nancy herself has a saying—she's an epigram collector, and this one, which is one of her favorites, she ascribes to a philosophy professor of hers when she was at Barnard: "Things are not as they appear," the saying goes, "nor are they otherwise."

The truth was that Nancy was more strikingly beautiful now than at any time in the thirty years we'd been together, as if time had done nothing but reveal the perfection of her bone structure, and I loved her truly, loved her the way you might love your own best virtue or the good and healthy habit on which your very survival depends. That part of my life, the core of it, still felt intact to me, although I did have a gambler's exciting, panicky sensation of putting it all at risk. As if all those years of fidelity were a kind of investment of capital against which I was now going to make a temporary cash withdrawal—what made the withdrawal possible was the size of the investment—you could think of it as a kind of dividend. It occurs to me now that it's proof of what I'm trying to explain that, in the process of explaining it, I've ended up citing one of Nancy's adages and using a financial metaphor.

And even at the time I knew that Nancy wasn't the only one to take into account—there was also my daughter Sophie to consider. She and I have always been unusually attuned to each other—close the way counter melodies are close, each defining itself harmonically against the other. Sophie is almost telepathically sensitive, unerring about other people and yet stubbornly committed to self-doubt, tentative to the point of exasperation and yet, once decided, completely beyond the reach of reason or persuasion. Sophie, I knew, could be unforgiving. At the age of twenty-eight, when her life should already have begun to define itself, she had quit a good job with a catering business and enrolled in a graduate program in creative writing. I admired her courage and I was proud of her talent, which I believed was real, but I didn't want her to be disappointed, and I knew first hand that for an artist disappointment was inevitable, even if she turned out to be…what? Sylvia Plath? Carolyn Conestoga?

IIII

That afternoon and after each of her next two lessons, I followed Carolyn back to the summer cottage she'd rented out by the state park. There was no plan—each time felt separate and unique, uncontrollable fits of passion rather than an "affair." Lovemaking with Carolyn was a kind of slithery delectation, with lots of verbalizing (as opposed to Nancy, who was generally silent until the moment of crisis) and a kind of isometric intensity where I had expected double-jointed gymnastics. It was after our third encounter that I happened to come across a folder full of the poems Sophie had been turning in to Carolyn's workshop. The folder was lying on top of a pile of similar folders on a drafting table with an adjustable lamp in the corner of Carolyn's bedroom, clearly her work space, where I had no business sticking my nose. But in a state of post-coital elation, I'd been wandering naked around the room, examining every personal object and knickknack as if it might offer a clue to the mystery of what had drawn this lovely and accomplished young woman to a middle-aged musician like me—moving from the encoded eroticism of Balthus's *Solitaire* on the wall (the deciphering of which had amounted to a kind of foreplay) to a shiny pair of what she assured me were authentic Ben Wa balls in a little velvet-lined bird's nest basket on her dresser to the Pinocchio puppet slouched phallic nosed and open eyed on the bookshelf next to the CD player, where Keith Jarrett's incomparable *Koln Concert*, a recent gift from me, was just beginning the galloping A section of Part II.

"I think maybe you shouldn't be reading those," Carolyn said. She had just come out of the shower—not merely figuratively but in actual fact—and was standing in the doorway to the bathroom rubbing and patting at her flushed and glistening skin with a fluffy white towel, tilting her head and shaking out the fine blonde tangle of her hair. When she looked up at me, there were two vertical frown lines between her eyebrows, but otherwise she didn't seem overly concerned.

"Why not?" I said, and then, deepening my voice in an automatic parody of the concerned parent, "I'm her father, for Christ's sake."

"Exactly," Carolyn said. "The very person guaranteed to take her stuff much too personally."

"'*You are the silhouette of my desire,*'" I read. "'*As well as the light that casts the shadow.*' That's not half bad, is it? Or is it? How do you judge poetry? It's like abstract art—what standard are you supposed to apply?" There were several copies in the folder of each individual poem, the copies marked with marginalia, each scrawled in a different hand—checks and question marks and cryptic exclamatory comments. Then I came to a sheet of paper I recognized immediately as an email letter.

"It's like life, I suppose," Carolyn was saying. "What you want in a poem is energy, excitement, surprise. In the end, it's all about getting off, isn't it?"

Smiling, she gave a little bump and grind, and when I looked back at the file, the words "*You must know by now how crazy in love with you I am,*" seemed to leap out at me. This wasn't a line in a poem, it was an email letter written in straightforward prose, a letter from my daughter to this naked woman standing before me, and it was dated over a month before Carolyn and I had met.

"Good God," I said, reading on. "You didn't tell me about this." The fact that Sophie preferred women to men wasn't a discovery. She'd come to Nancy and me with her tearful confession five years before, after she broke up with a guy she was just three weeks away from marrying. I remember taking a secret satisfaction in the announcement, as though it were a guarantee that from then on I would be the only man in Sophie's life. What hit me now, though, was the odd feeling of being in a kind of ménage à trois with my own daughter.

"Didn't tell you what?" Carolyn said.

"About Sophie being crazy in love with you—" Sophie is dark haired and hollow eyed and much too thin but with a certain fawn-like quality, like Audrey Hepburn if Audrey Hepburn had moved less like a model and more like a modern dancer. It may seem an odd perspective for me to take, but I had no trouble seeing Sophie's physical appeal, and a flash of jealousy ricocheted from Carolyn to Sophie and back again.

Carolyn was towel drying her hair now. I could see the auburn tuft of her pubic bush and, when she half turned, the miraculous curve of a dimpled hip and the Y-shaped cleft of her buttocks, and the sight of her nakedness in the context of what I had just been thinking made my chest tighten with feelings too confused to decipher.

"I told you not to read that stuff," she said.

"You could have said something—"

"But it's private, Lon. Just like we are. And just like you and Nancy. Separate universes, remember?" After the first time, we'd made what I assume are the usual rationalizations, and this had been chief among them. "It's just that now the bedroom slipper's on the other foot," she said. "Share and share alike."

"Whoa," I said. "Wait a minute. Adultery's one thing, but it feels like we're getting into some other kind of territory here." Because, despite all the rhetoric about separate universes, I could easily imagine Carolyn reciprocating Sophie's interest and then coming on to me just for the sheer hell of it. Despite the delicacy of her temperament—which was really a kind of preternatural sensitivity to her own moods—Carolyn had the mind of a lapsed Catholic schoolgirl with a particularly prurient imagination. In fact, in combination with her angelic good looks, that prurience was precisely what had captured my attention in the first place, some quality of innocence begging to be defiled. I'd found out that, among other things, she was a lover of Victorian pornography. She told me she liked to spend whole rainy days lying in bed holding a book from her collection of erotica in one hand while she leisurely masturbated with the other, occasionally looking up to watch herself in a mirror, an image that had precisely the effect on me it was designed to have. The idea of sharing Carolyn's hot-house brand of sexuality with my own daughter boggled my mind. As love triangles went, it put the other one, the more conventional marital one I was already trying to negotiate, in the shade. I knew that sex could be merely sport for Carolyn, motivated in part by pure and simple narcissism and in part—and maybe it's the same thing—by her writer's appetite for emotional material. But I didn't like to think that sex could be merely sport for me, and I was certain that it wouldn't be merely sport for Sophie, who took everything much too seriously and who was not only easily wounded but easily wounded to the bone.

"I don't see what's so strange, Lon," Carolyn was saying. "It's not unheard of for a student to get a crush on her teacher. Take me and you, for instance." She had wrapped the towel around her breasts and tucked it in so it covered her vial parts, but just barely, like a short sarong.

"Come on, Carolyn, we're talking about"—but for some reason I didn't want to say her name—"my daughter," I said. And all at once, I was uncomfortably conscious of being naked, as sometimes happens in a dream when you suddenly realize you aren't wearing any clothes. "And what about the university?" I said. I set the folder back on its pile. "Aren't relations with students strictly forbidden?" My clothes were draped over the chair beside the drafting table, and I bent down and stepped into my briefs, then slipped into my shirt and began buckling up my jeans like I was girding myself for battle.

"I guess people just naturally want whatever they're not supposed to have," Carolyn said. "I know I do. Don't you? I mean really and truly. I've always thought it was one of the more endearing traits of the human species. We just won't take no for an answer." And she laughed.

"Does that go for you and my daughter," I said, "or just for the human species?"

"Sophie and I are…" she began, but she was having trouble finding the words. "We're another universe too, and not merely a sexual one either, although it's true that things sometimes lead to other things in intimate relationships, and then sometimes there's an intersection, or more like a fusion really, like something nuclear, and *that* can be terrifically exciting, of course." She paused and looked at me as if to gauge whether or not I was cracking the code. Maybe what I was listening to was the first draft of a new poem. "But we're not quite up to that point yet—"

"Who's not?" I said. "And up to what point yet?"

"Lonnie, my love, I'm sorry…I thought…surely you knew…"

"No," I said. "I had no idea." Which seemed like the simple truth, although a moment later I found myself wondering. "Tell me something," I said. "Does Sophie know about us? About you and me?"

Carolyn shrugged. "Not unless she's a mind reader—which I sometimes think she may be. But, really, I think that if she knew, if she found out somehow, she might actually, you know, be cool with it—"

"Be cool with it," I repeated, feeling like a stranger to the language.

"You know, nonjudgmental—" She giggled. "Cool but also maybe sort of hot…"

But a thick curtain, transparent to sight and sound but impermeable to sense, seemed to have come down between us, blocking all further communication. Carolyn was twenty years younger than I was—young enough, yes, it had occasionally occurred to me, to be my daughter. She and Sophie could have been sisters. But this was cutting it too close. "That's enough," I said, holding up one hand. And then, biting off the words as a wave of panic began to rise inside of me, I said, "I think I'd better be going." Like I'd just dropped by for afternoon tea.

And that was it. In another moment, I was gone.

||||

What happened next was almost like one of those Biblical occasions when God communicated via some unlikely but natural phenomenon, a burning bush or a pillar of cloud. In more secular terms, it was like a waking dream. I had just pulled out of Carolyn's gravel driveway and turned onto the main road that runs down along the tree line by the entrance to the state park, the road hypnotically dappled with moving shadows from the new spring foliage, when, in my already dazed state, I noticed that one of the shadows down by the windshield wiper on the passenger's side of the car was moving in a slightly different rhythm. And then I saw that it wasn't a shadow at all but some sort of branch, not unusual since Carolyn's house backed onto a state forest. But it only stayed a branch for a moment or two on its way to becoming something else, something I finally saw that it actually was. Which, coiling and uncoiling there on the glass down by the windshield wiper, was a large and sinewy *snake*. Hoping that the wipers might dislodge it and fling it off the car, I turned them on, but the snake was too long and too heavy for that. Heavy and thick and, for all I knew, poisonous. Ironically, the true dream part of the experience was the dawning realization of the snake's *reality*, of it's actually being there—the dream part was that morphing moment when everything you think is true begins to change into something else—until suddenly there the snake *is*, right there on the windshield in front of you, slowly writhing, part of its tail disappearing down the windshield wiper well into the crevice and under the car hood—a tight squeeze that I soon discovered it had used (in fact, was probably using at that very moment) to shed its winter skin. Thinking that another one could be inside the car with me, maybe coiled under the front seat (I'd heard they traveled in pairs), I pulled to the side of the road, glanced down at the ignition, and flinched at the sight of the coiled black cord of the cell phone plugged into the dash. The rest was a slapstick pantomime as I got out of the car, took a long rolled umbrella from the backseat, and proceeded to fence with the thing for a minute or two, its blunt, diamond-shaped head weaving from side to side, its forked tongue darting back and forth, until I was able to work the umbrella under the thick, iridescent body of the creature and finally lever it more than flip it off the car hood into the tall grass. Where it slithered away with a liquid, dreamlike motion, as if it were somehow moving and at the same time standing absolutely still.

"Man!" a voice called out. "I never saw a snake on a car windshield before!"

I looked up to see a young guy in a gravel truck who had evidently pulled over to watch the fun. And fun was exactly what if felt like. I was grinning so hard my face ached, and I shouted, "Me neither, pardner!" Pardner! Like we were cowboys out on the Western plains. "I guess I'd better check under the hood," I called out. "There might be more." And when I popped the hood open, I saw the long papery tube of skin, like a pale blue ghost of itself the snake had left behind. Gingerly, I worked at it with the metal tip of my umbrella, uncoiling it from the carburetor and hoisting it into the air like some kind of battle trophy before tossing it into the weeds. I tell you I couldn't have felt more elated at that moment if all the perplexities of my situation had somehow suddenly resolved themselves—and all because a snake had shown up on my windshield and I'd managed to send it packing.

But it also felt like Fate, or my unconscious, or *something* was sending me a message. But what did the message mean? How did it translate? That evening, I was still puzzling over this question as I sat at the piano idly noodling around inside the changes of a loose twelve-bar blues structure that left plenty of room for meandering. Carolyn had made me an unwitting agent in her betrayal of Sophie.

We'd also betrayed Nancy, of course, but I'd gone into that with eyes open, if glazed. Which was about as far as my thinking had gotten me when Sophie came in and dropped down on the old leather sofa that Nancy's always threatening to replace. Wearing her baggy sweat pants over a black leotard, Sophie was eating an apple, that's all, but she was giving it her full attention, as if she'd never eaten an apple before. But despite that, and despite everything else, her mere presence was enough to perk me up.

"How's tricks?" I said. My standard opening.

"No tricks," she said. "Just magic." Her standard reply. It was a reassuring exchange of passwords, but the meaning is always in the tone, and Sophie's tone definitely sounded preoccupied. She took a chomp out of her apple and, with her mouth full, unexpectedly said, "That was nice, what you were playing. What's it called?"

"This?" I said, striking a minor chord and playing a bluesy glissando with my right hand. "Nothing. Just the basic blues."

"Than which," she said, "nothing could be basic-er."

"Feeling kind of blue, are we?" It was a reference to one of our favorite albums, but kind of blue wasn't exactly how she sounded.

"More like mood indigo," she said.

"You and the Duke, huh?" I nodded sagely. "Well, you're in good company."

And then, without warning, she said, "Daddy, have you been seeing Carolyn Conestoga?"

"Sure," I automatically replied, as if butter wouldn't melt in my mouth. "She's taking lessons with me. You know that—"

"But I mean have you been *seeing* her?" She was studying her half-eaten apple as if she'd discovered a suspicious hole.

"Yes," I said. "I have." I sat back and lowered my hands to my sides, ready to take my punishment. "But I'm not anymore." And as soon as I said it, I knew it was true. It was a fact, not a promise.

She took another bite of her apple and in the silence I could hear her chewing. I was waiting for her to say something, but she didn't speak and the silence went on like a held note, an endless fermata. Then she abruptly sat up straight and tossed the remainder of her apple into the wastebasket by my bench, the wastebasket where I filed my penciled compositions. And then, "That was nice," she said. "You ought to write it down before you forget it."

"I was just noodling around," I said.

"No, you ought to write it down." She was up from the sofa now, brushing her hands against her thighs, on her way out, but as she passed my bench, she stopped and touched my arm, exactly the way Carolyn liked to do. "Really," she said, and she held my eyes for an extra beat.

"I won't," I said. "I mean, I *will*...I'll write it down. I won't forget—" but I knew it was really another vow I was promising to remember.

Sophie nodded and continued on her way, leaving me sitting there like a condemned man whose execution has just been miraculously commuted. Or rather—and this connection dawned on me with the hair-prickling sensation of a true awakening—like I had just sloughed off my old skin.

CODA

Now, in a little while, Nancy and I will have our ritual evening cocktail (Dewar's and soda for her; Jack Daniels on the rocks for me), and I'll tell her a funny story about how I found a live snake on my windshield. Then maybe I'll play the piece for her that Sophie told me I ought to write down, the piece that will eventually become the central theme of my best-known concerto for solo piano, *Blue Serpentine*, which will become Nancy's favorite among my compositions. Carolyn, as we'll later learn, will have already started the sequence of poems that will become her third book, the award-winning *Jazz Improvisations*, inspired in part by her piano lessons with me. And Sophie, that very evening, will begin writing what will become her controversial first novel, *Working the Changes*, about a girl whose father shares the bed of the girl's female lover, who also happens to be the girl's art teacher as well as her father's piano student, a novel that, much to her publisher's surprise and Sophie's own confused delight, will become a national bestseller and a National Book Award winner as well as an Academy Award-nominated film, lifting Sophie to a level of literary recognition and financial success beyond her wildest dreams. (Unlikely, I'll admit, but possible nonetheless.) As for Nancy—and here comes the resolving home chord (say, a C-major seventh)—she'll smile enigmatically, and wisely keep her own council, demonstrating that the greatest gift of all, and by far the most generous to other people, is the gift for hope—which is all that makes this forecast of a happy ending possible.

An emeritus professor of literature and creative writing at American University, KERMIT MOYER is the author of Tumbling *(University of Illinois Press, 1988), a collection of short stories. His stories have also appeared in such literary journals as* The Georgia Review, The Southern Review, The Sewanee Review, *and* The Hudson Review. *His collection of linked stories,* The Chester Chronicles, *is scheduled to be published by The Permanent Press early in 2010.*

Babysitting

TERENCE M. MULLIGAN

Laurie shook Tanner awake to say the babysitter called in sick. "So could you watch the kid for the day? It's not like you've got something better to do." She said there was coffee and grape juice and Froot Loops in the kitchen. So now he was stuck trying to figure out how to spend a whole day with an eight-year-old girl.

Tanner was between jobs. He'd only been going with Laurie for three months, and he'd never been left alone with the kid for more than a few minutes. He'd planned on heading up to the Chi Chi Club later, where the beer was pretty cheap if you didn't mind Coors or Miller on tap. Not a great place for a kid, but maybe he could drag her along anyway, watch her from the bar stool, make sure she stayed out of trouble. Tanner checked his wallet: twelve dollars. He scratched his beard, poked his head into the fridge—one beer, a Coors Light. Laurie's. Like I really need to go on a diet, he thought. He popped the tab.

Tasha came out of her bedroom rubbing her eyes. Laurie had already warned her about the babysitter before she left for work at the diner. Tasha's dirty-blonde hair stuck out from her ponytail, and she wore a faded Denver Gym Kids T-shirt that hung to her knees.

"Um, you want some cereal or something?" said Tanner. "Some Froot Loops?" He stood up to fetch it, but she was already climbing the kitchen counter.

"I can get it myself," she said, standing on the sink and reaching for the cabinet. "I'm not a lame-o."

Tasha set up a bowl on the table and poured milk from the half-gallon jug. Her hair hung over her face as she slurped her breakfast, and her eyes were puffy from just waking up. She looked at Tanner from across the table, then at his beer. Tasha pointed at him, her face suddenly animated. "Hey, what's that on your face? It looks like—is that an 'L' on your forehead?"

Tanner rubbed the spot, puzzled, then looked at his hand. Nothing.

"Loser!" shouted Tasha, and she started laughing.

Third grade humor, thought Tanner. Ha-ha. Fucking hilarious. "Shut up and eat your cereal," he said, instead of slapping her.

After breakfast he said, "Don't you usually take a bath? You oughta take a bath. You smell like stale milk."

The kid whined. "Mom never makes me wash in the morning, stupid," stretching out "morning" to punctuate his obvious ignorance on the matter. No one, as far as she knew, took baths in the morning.

Tanner decided to be generous. This would go over a lot better if they learned to like each other. "Well, brush your teeth anyway. We're going for a ride. Maybe blow off some of that stink."

"Whatever," she said with an exaggerated sigh she must've learned in school. "You're the babysitter."

The Oldsmobile still had enough gas to get up to the Chi Chi on the north side of town. They opened at noon, and Tanner liked it lots better than the downtown spots like Cheerleaders, with their overpriced drinks and greedy dancers begging you for tips all the time. Plus, who ever heard of a strip joint with a nonsmoking section anyway? Pretty soon they'd be selling hummus and cappuccino. A tourist trap as far as Tanner was concerned.

Tasha sat quietly in the passenger seat. The late morning sun highlighted the mountains to the west, visible between the factories and barbecue joints on Washington Street. They drove through the auto repair district, where he used to work in a transmission shop. He used to go to the Chi Chi almost every night before he got canned. Now it was more like once a month if he could stretch out the unemployment check.

Tanner liked this part of town. Industrial, gritty, it was far removed from downtown Denver or the pretentious residential districts that anywhere else in the country would be called suburbs. It had a plain simplicity that was calming, a straightforwardness. It made him miss those days before he got fired for excessive absence and lateness. Not that Mac, the shop foreman, explained it in so many words; he just told him to take a hike. But the work had been easy, the money tolerable.

At thirty-six, Tanner's greatest pride was that he'd never owned a credit card in his life. He always paid his rent, and the phone bill and utilities were easy. The car was paid for, a 1979 Olds with over 150,000 miles on it. But he was a pretty good mechanic, and he kept it in good shape. There was comfort in knowing there would always be beer money after paying the bills. Sometimes he'd play blackjack with the guys over at Freebird's shack. Sometimes he'd even win.

But things were different with Laurie. Not harder, just less comfortable. She took care of him, bought food, let him sleep over without paying rent. He'd toss in a few bucks for groceries when he could. But it wasn't the same as the easy self-sufficiency. He always felt like he was walking on glass, waiting for the whole situation to collapse, just like the job. Laurie didn't pester him, not much, anyway, but he imagined some unspoken guilt trip in the air whenever she came home from work. He'd have to get his act together soon.

Tasha yawned, stretched her legs up onto the dashboard, straight and firm, and started touching her toes. Tanner was so wrapped up in his thoughts he'd forgotten she was even there.

"Hey, aren't you supposed to be wearing a seat belt?" said Tanner.

"I'm stretching," she said. "For gym class."

Tanner vaguely remembered that she'd won some sort of tumbling award that summer, something Laurie had mentioned when he was half-asleep one day. Maybe this was the thing to break the ice with the kid. "Gymnastics, right? Yeah, I used to do gymnastics. Great sport," he said knowingly. It was true, too. Although he didn't mention that it was in high school, almost twenty years ago, before he dropped out to get his G.E.D. "Used to do the rings, you know."

Tasha frowned. "Girls don't do rings, Tanner. That's only for boys."

Tanner wasn't much for patience. In his mind, he'd just made a pretty major effort at being friendly to the brat. He pulled over, raised his left hand, and pointed his finger straight at her nose. "Listen!" he shouted. "I'm trying to make conversation—trying to be nice. So quit being such a little snot for a change, OK?"

Tasha shut up, and she sat up straight in the passenger seat. "Sor-ry," she grumbled, stretching out both the syllables the way kids do when they're forced to make an apology under duress. She fastened her seat belt.

A few minutes later, Tanner said, "So I hear you won an award for the gym thing, huh? Tumbling?" Again, he was trying to get the kid to like him, but with even less enthusiasm than before.

"Floor exercise," she muttered. After a pause, she said, "They don't call it tumbling anymore—only in kindergarten. I won a ribbon," she added.

They parked in the gravel driveway of the Chi Chi Club and walked to the door, where Smitty stood in his denim jacket with his beer gut hanging out from under his T-shirt.

"Tanner," he said. His yellowed teeth showed from behind his frizzy red beard. "Long time." Then Smitty looked at the kid. "You're not planning to go inside or anything stupid like that, are you, Tanner?"

"No, I just drove ten miles to look at your belly button. Whadda ya think I'm doin' here?"

"You can't bring a kid in a place like this! What the hell's wrong with you, Tanner, you got no brains?"

"Right, and who's gonna stop me? Sure the fuck isn't you. Molly!" Tanner yelled inside towards the bartender. "Hey, Molly, can you tell Smitty here to give me a break? I'm babysitting here; can't a guy come in for a beer without the good citizen rap?"

Molly looked over from the bar beneath the Kronenbourg clock. "Aw, hell, Tanner, why'd you have to bring a kid here? You tryin' to get us in trouble?"

"Come on, Molly. Cut me some slack, OK? You want me to leave her out in the car so she can boil to death like some dog in a shopping mall parking lot?"

"Let 'em in, Smitty," she said in her hoarse, cigarette-scarred voice. "What the hell—good a day as any to lose my license." Molly wiped the bar with a dish towel.

Tanner led Tasha into the dark room. "Thanks, Molly." He looked back at Smitty, grinning.

"Asshole," said Smitty.

Tasha propped herself up on her knees on the stool next to Tanner, leaning over the bar on her elbows. They had one of those old spinning disco balls shooting dots of light through the room and a blacklight over the clock behind Molly. "Nice place," said Tasha.

Molly lit up a Newport. Tanner remembered her fortieth birthday last year, when he gave her some carnations after winning a hundred bucks in the lottery, but she looked ten years older. Her hair was still black, although Tanner figured she must dye it some to keep out the gray.

"So what's the deal, Tanner?" said Molly. "Paternity suit, or is this just the best you can do for a date?"

"Funny, Molly. A regular clown, you oughta be on cable TV."

Molly poured him a Coors from the tap. He laid out two bucks on the bar, one and half for the beer plus a fifty-cent tip. Always smart to tip good on the first one, Tanner figured—that way she won't get pissed off when he's spent his cash and weasels out on the last one.

"What about the kid?" said Molly. "Or are you guys goin' dutch?"

Tasha looked up at Tanner and said, "Grape."

"Grape?"

"Grape soda," said Tasha. "Like, you know, the purple stuff?"

"Right. A grape soda for Tasha," said Tanner. He thought maybe he could win a few bonus points with the girl. After all, his honor was at stake, what with being called a loser just an hour ago. "That's her name, Molly. Not 'the kid.'"

"Sorry, no grape. No orange either. We got Coke, Diet Coke, and 7 Up."

Tasha frowned. "Nice place," she said again.

Tanner lit up a smoke and sipped the foam off his beer. "Helluva joint, can't even give you a fucking grape soda." Then he said to Tasha, "How about it?"

"7 Up," said Tasha. "With extra ice."

Tanner laughed. "You heard the lady, Molly. Make it a double." The kid smiled. Tanner figured she was impressed with the novelty— this was special, a grown-up place with grown-up talk, forbidden. Maybe she'd learn to like him after all.

Tasha went to the bathroom while Tanner watched the lunch crowd come in. The Garcia brothers wore their baseball caps and matching greasy uniforms from Alvin's, the factory up the street that made steel springs for trucks. Freebird came in from the optical plant over on Quincy, always too cool to wear a smock or shop jacket outside of work—he wore his old pot plant T-shirt that was too tight so he could show off his muscles and the tiger rose tattoo on his biceps to the dancers. He nodded to Tanner from across the room and pulled up a chair in front of the stage, right under the disco ball. A couple of longhairs with Harley jackets went straight to the pool tables in the back room: Rick Lupis, who Tanner still owed twenty bucks from a pool game he'd lost over a month ago, and some other guy Tanner didn't recognize.

"There's no toilet paper," he heard Tasha say. He looked down at the girl, who'd appeared almost magically like an elf at the foot of his barstool. She just stood there, gaping at him like he was supposed to do something about it.

"Aw, Christ," he said. "Molly?" He turned around towards the bar, but she was gone, taking orders around the room.

"I hafta go," said Tasha. She raised up two fingers to specify. "Number two."

Smitty dropped some quarters into the jukebox near the front door. The first dancer was about to come out.

"All right, wait a minute," said Tanner.

Tasha started twitching, doing a little ballerina dance on her tiptoes. "Hurry!"

Tanner ran to the men's room past the pool tables in the back. Rick Lupis looked at him with a raised eyebrow from behind his pool cue. "—the fuck's wrong with that dude?" he heard the other one say.

He came back out with a handful of toilet paper and circled around the stage back to Tasha. Freebird stared at him too as he hustled past, looking amused. Freebird had two kids of his own. "Emergency," said Tanner.

Tasha took the tissue and went back to the ladies' room behind the bar. Victor and Sergio Garcia followed Tanner's moves, then looked back at the stage, pretending not to notice him. They just snickered to each other.

Jasmine came out to the stage from the other side of the bar, all done up in her white bikini with the silver glitter dots on the nips. It was one of those string-type suits, tied loosely in the back, and the bottom piece was so tight it could've split her in half. Tanner smiled as she wagged her ass towards the stage, kicking her auburn hair aside while ZZ Top cranked out from the jukebox.

The stage was just a wooden circle in the middle of the room, stacked on two-by-fours with a fireman's pole stuck up through to the ceiling. Jasmine rubbed her legs against it, stamped her white platform heels onto the floor to the drumbeat, and shook her boobs to the melody. Freebird just sat there with his beer in his lap, not even smiling, while Sergio walked over with his greasy shop jacket on and stuffed a dollar into the thin strand of bikini against her thigh. For a reward, Jasmine leaned into his face with her cleavage, played with the glitter dots on her tits, and quick as a bunny turned away, aloof, eager for another buck from somewhere else. She raised her right leg high above her head, taut and firm like a ballerina's, propping it against the fireman's pole. But Freebird was too cool, thought Tanner. Freebird looked straight up her crotch and didn't even flinch, just sipped his beer again.

Jasmine swung around towards the bikers in the pool room, who weren't even paying attention. She untied the string of her top behind her back, let it drop to the floor in front of her. She arched backwards like a gymnast, doing a slow bend as she raised one leg to the sky and let her head lean back towards the floor, pointing her nipples to the ceiling, pursing her lips straight at the bar. Then, with her false eyelashes opening wide, she looked towards Tanner with the big come-on smile, the "c'mon baby, don't ya wanna give me a dollar" look, when suddenly her mouth fell open, upside down no less, as if she'd just snapped out of a sleepwalking episode and found herself buck naked in the middle of Main Street on a Saturday afternoon.

"That's the worst backbend I've ever seen," said Tasha. She was standing next to Tanner, pointing at Jasmine with the leftover toilet paper carefully wrapped around her fingers. "And why's that lady naked?"

Tanner looked down from his stool, then back at Jasmine, who was trying to gather her composure, pretend like nothing was wrong. Freebird was laughing like crazy, even spilled some beer on his lap. Victor choked on his beer after some snide remark from Sergio on the other side of the stage.

The ZZ Top song came to an end, and everyone heard Jasmine bitching out loud to herself, "Can't believe he brought a fuckin' kid in here. Smitty! I'm takin' a break!"

Silence was never a good thing in a place like this—no pool balls knocking around, no tunes from the jukebox. Everybody just stood there for a minute, all eyes on Tanner and his eight-year-old sidekick who'd suddenly ruined the atmosphere. Molly opened her mouth. "Uh, Tanner..."

"He's outa here," said Smitty. He heaved his fat bulk towards the bar.

"This is kinda bad for business," said Molly. "Know what I mean?"

Freebird and the Garcia brothers didn't appear to mind, even though Jasmine was one of the favorite dancers for the lunch crowd. It seemed like they got a kick out of the break in their routine.

Tanner grabbed Tasha gently by the shoulders, holding her in front of him like a shield. Smitty stopped in his tracks about two feet away, barking in his face. "You're history," he said. His hands were trembling, like he was barely holding back from smashing Tanner's nose.

"What did I do?" said Tasha.

"Yeah, what did she do?" Tanner parroted.

"Easy," said Molly. "Easy does it."

"You?! You?" bellowed Smitty. "You didn't do nothing! Yer friend here, though—aw, what the fuck am I talking to you for? Tanner, get your ass outa here before I drag it across the parking lot!"

"Customers," said Molly. "Ya gotta think of the customers. Right, Tanner?"

"OK, OK," said Tanner. "I get it. I get it. Can't even buy a grape soda here anyway. I can take a hint. We'll do our drinking elsewhere. Right, Tasha?"

Rick Lupis by this time had walked towards the bar from the pool tables. "Wait a minute, Smitty. This guy owes me twenty bucks. No point kicking him out until he squares up, don't ya think?"

Tanner gulped down the last of his Coors. He held onto Tasha with his free hand.

"Hey, no, Rick, save it for later," said Molly. "For cryin' out loud, there's a kid—"

"Cough up, Tanner," said Lupis. "C'mon, first you shut down Jasmine, then you think you can walk out without paying what you owe?"

"Leave Tanner alone, you meanie!" said Tasha. She put both her hands on her hips, as if she could stave off the biker with a stare. "He's just a loser, like you!"

"Oh shit," said Tanner.

He heard Tasha scream. Lupis decked him with one punch, right over Tasha's head. Tanner found himself on the floor, his nose bleeding all over Tasha's tennis shoes. The cowboy boots were next—the first thing he saw when he opened his eyes. I'm dead, he figured. But suddenly the boots turned point-side up, with Lupis falling backwards. Tasha was crying.

He looked up to see Freebird pulling Lupis by the hair, then grinding his nose into the sawdust floor. Freebird's knee was pinned into Lupis's back while he yanked at the ponytail. The Garcia brothers blocked the other biker guy from getting into the fight.

Freebird made a deal with Lupis. "Some choices, Rick: collect it later, call it a bad debt, or I break all your fingers. You're cool with that, right?"

Lupis grunted. "Sure, man. Fuckin' A."

"And no more cussing!" said Freebird. "There's a kid in here!"

"OK, OK!" Lupis got up, dusted himself off, and signaled his buddy to go with him. They went outside, and the sound of their kick-starting bikes was a welcome relief to Tanner.

"What'd ya do that for, Freebird?" said Smitty. "He's just a loser!"

Tanner wiped the blood from his face with Molly's dust rag on the bar.

"Wow," said Tasha. "That Freebird guy is awesome!" Then, as an afterthought, she said, "Are you OK, Tanner?"

"Sure, Tasha, sure," he said, thinking 'since when did you start giving a damn?'

"Go home, Tanner," said Freebird. "You're a mess. Look at yourself in the mirror, OK? Will you do that when you get home?"

"Thanks, Freebird. I owe you big time."

"You got that right."

Victor Garcia snickered, but his brother Sergio jammed his elbow into his side to make him stop.

Molly grabbed a fresh towel for Tanner to clean up with. While they were standing by the bar, Jasmine came out, covered in an oversized men's shirt. She watched, along with Freebird, Tanner, and the Garcia brothers, as Tasha spun around the dance stage, twirling on the acrobat bar like an Olympic trainee before executing a picture-perfect backbend.

"Sugar rush," said Molly. "Too much 7 Up."

"Strangest thing I ever saw," said Jasmine.

"Me too," said Tanner, as he held his nose up to stop the blood flow, awed by the flexibility of the kid's spine and baffled at how she could possibly care whether he was all right or not.

TERENCE MULLIGAN lives in Arlington, Virginia. His fiction has appeared in the Washington Review, The Baltimore Review, Word-Wrights, Catalyst, Bee Zine, *and the* Anathema Review. *He's also published nonfiction articles in* Maryland Musician, *the* Takoma Voice, Northern Virginia Rhythm, Pitch Magazine, Alive, *and* Amazing Heroes. *He is the publisher and fiction editor for the literary journal* Minimus. *He plays guitar with the rock band Craig's Basement and the acoustic-oriented Terry Mulligan Troupe. His collection of short stories,* Children of the West, *was published in 2000.* Washington City Paper *admired the artful use of cuss words and described the work as "hard-core drifter fiction."*

Bread and Other Distant Memories

Andrew Nachison

1

It was sweet, yeasty warm bread fresh out of the oven in the kitchen just behind the swinging door and it filled the entire house with its moist perfume late on a wintry Saturday afternoon just after sunset. The dog, Spot, had settled into his tartan cedar doggie bed near the fire that crackled in the stone fireplace, Vivaldi whispered out of speakers up on tall stuffed cherry bookshelves, and Jackson, stretched in the black leather lounge chair, struggled to keep his eyes open. The comfort of a perfect existence lulled him deeper and deeper into a contented doze, and his eyes fluttered, the book dropped gently from his hands to his lap, and he began to drift…But no. Forget it. It was just before noon on a hot spring Wednesday and Jackson was dozing and dreaming and stuck in gridlock on his way home from the post office and behind him a Toyota pickup with giant tires and a chrome roll bar and fog lights loomed over his creaking old Datsun B-210 and the pickup honked and Jackson's eyes shot open and without thinking he shouted fuck you asshole and it was a stupid mistake, a really stupid groggy mistake, because the good old pioneer boys are armed, really armed, and ready like hell for that papa elk that wanders down the wrong path, and the guy in the pickup had a Skoal baseball cap and sunglasses and good lord, he probably had snakeskin cowboy boots poised over the clutch and he was shouting something, mouthing something, and waving his hands and oh lord he was reaching for his Glock semiautomatic, the good old boys love the German semiautomatics, and the cops love them, seems everybody loves the German semiautomatics, and everybody out West wants to shoot, and ya shoot ta kill, ain't no such thing as shoot to wound, and Jackson was stuck, stuck at a red light in front of a killer Toyota next to a city-block-sized commercial bakery that churned out hundreds upon thousands of loaves of sawdust white bread for the soldiers in the war in the desert, day and night it filled the neighborhood with the humid scent of white bread lighter than air.

The light turned green and Jackson pulled forward and the pickup changed lanes and sped by and Jackson let his left arm hang out the open window to feel the bugs frolicking in the heat. Spring had arrived and the cherry and apple blossoms and robin redbreasts were resplendent in life so radiant and sweet with red convertibles polished brighter than the western sun and the ground nearly dry after months of rain, rain that should have driven normal human beings away. But some stayed. They built a city on two rivers and the rivers flooded the docks and streets and homes and normal families should have packed and gone south, but these families, these pioneer families stayed and they rebuilt and the government built dams to stop the floods and to power the trolleys and the factories that spread out from the rivers and some women baked bread and tried to keep their men and their children warm and dry, others worked in chaingang brothels and were sold as concubines to passing cargo ships, and some of the folk moved south to California but some held on, and still more came and ignored the rain, ignored the mildew and the frost, they stayed and they killed the fish and the trees and the Indians, and they had children, and the children stayed, and still more came, and they killed the fish and the trees and dismantled the tribes, and the newcomers still arrive, in airplanes, in U-Haul vans and sun-baked moving vans in the summer when it makes sense to stay because the air is hot and dry and the snow-capped mountains are lush with Douglas fir and western hemlock and red cedar and Pacific yew and ferns and mushrooms, and who could guess what the winter holds? And when the soil finally begins to dry, not only the birds and the trees are thankful. The people who stayed behind are thankful, because like the plants and animals, they too have survived a dark winter.

And they dry out, and they stay. They buy guns and pickups and baseball caps and chewing tobacco and they chop down trees and fish for salmon and bake bread for the soldiers in the desert and they pull their pickups right up to your bumper and sometimes you wonder, has something gone wrong, genetically speaking, is something messed up here, are these people messed up, or is it me?

Shirley Barrett seemed original stock, genes that went way back to the wagon trains of desperate failures and their progeny, and that cold almost stupid sincerity as she explained, "We're very impressed with your resume, Albert, but I'm afraid we just don't have a place for you at this time. We just don't mesh."

As if mesh ever had anything to do with it, as if all of a sudden getting a job is like being a peg in an IQ test and Shirley Barrett can't fit the plugs in the holes, and the personnel script says, they just don't mesh.

Jackson drove slowly and tried to stay out of the way of all the impatient drivers who just had to get where they were going faster, before the light changed, before it was too late. The Datsun could go faster, not too much faster, but faster, and he could have made the next light, sped up to hit the intersection at the yellow light and clear the other side as the light turned red. A Cadillac that started out several car-lengths back had made it through the light and was now stopped at the next intersection.

Jackson didn't bother. He rolled to a halt at the red light next to the McDonald's and on a whim he turned right.

Not really a whim, because it was just an alternate route back to the apartment. It just wasn't the planned route. But at the light, sitting in the right lane in front of a long line of cars, Jackson wanted to turn and get out of the way because he felt like he was holding up the traffic, that he was the cause of this enormous impatience behind him, building quickly in anticipation of the green light, and he didn't want to be there when the light turned green and the engines behind him roared and everyone cocked their Glocks. So he made the right on red.

It was all a preoccupation with safety and a distrust of fellow human beings, who after all had caused all the misery in the world and were constantly scheming new means of waste and destruction. And they were unreliable. That was the trouble. If a smile and a handshake meant something, if a friendly face was truly friendly, then perhaps it all wouldn't be so dangerous, so utterly unpredictable and nerve wracking. If you aren't making money and the car has got to last, how on earth can you trust anyone in a fifty-thousand-dollar car that doesn't have a speck of dirt anywhere, even in the wheel wells?

At the third intersection Jackson came to, at the corner with the twenty-four-hour gas station and convenience store on one side and the pasta pizza pistachio bar next door, a midnight blue Mercedes convertible sped through a stop sign and hit Jackson's Datsun broadside. The impact pushed his car into the oncoming lane, which thank god was empty. As the two lines of cars on either side of the accident began to build, and as she approached, her loose silk skirt blowing in the gentle wind, and as the first horns began to honk, Jackson remained speechless, his hands frozen to the wheel of his beloved dearest Datsun that had served so valiantly and selflessly in times of bitter cold and sweltering drought, and now, to take this blow, a random shot from nowhere, it was all too much to process, just a swirl of crunching metal on metal and screeching brakes and the Datsun's feeble little horn, oh shit...

"Are you all right?"

She leaned against his open window and placed her hand on his shoulder. Her hand squeezed his shoulder.

"Are you all right?" she asked again, now rubbing his shoulder and bending down to see his face.

"I'm so sorry," she said. "It's all my fault. I don't know what I was thinking. I saw the stop sign, I saw it staring at me saying stop, hey Jean, stop your car, and I understood, but I couldn't stop, I just went straight through. I'm so sorry."

Jackson released the steering wheel and looked up at this woman stroking his shoulder and the first thing he noticed was the loose expensive fabric of her dress and then he saw the long bleached blonde hair falling below the scoop of her open-necked dress front, which plunged down onto a tan flat breast, no cleavage, just brown smooth skin far below her neck, and purple and pink blowing gently around it and round shoulders and blonde hair that must have been bleached because its blondeness was so unreal, like her blue eyes and her pearl earrings and her smell, like a rose, as close as a rose, as delicate, and like a rose, you want to kiss it.

"Your brakes failed?" Jackson asked.

"No, they're fine. I didn't use them."

"You said you couldn't stop."

"I know. I couldn't. I couldn't put my foot on the brake."

She was rambling on and it was difficult to follow.

"...I don't know what it was, but something forced me to roll through that stop sign, and I knew I was going to hit something, the first car I saw, I knew I was going to hit it, and there was nothing I could do and you know what I thought?"

"What?"

"I thought, I hope I don't go through the window. I never thought about that before, but now I realize that the thought of going through a windshield terrifies me. Have you ever thought about it? I mean, I use my seat belt..."

Her hand was still squeezing his shoulder.

"...and Mercedes makes pretty tough cars..."

Gently she brushed his shoulder, as if she knew it and knew that it wanted to be squeezed, to be told that this, like the Shirley Barretts and the killer Toyota pickups of the world, is OK, it is all OK...

"...and I figured well, if I ever get a new one I'll make sure it has air bags, because you might as well get them, but I never really thought about sailing through glass. I could see it happen, right before we hit..."

...it is all just funny and beautiful and above it all, beneath it all, illusions of something greater, feel it, something greater...

"...I saw my body fly through my windshield and the windshield shattered into tiny square pieces and it was like popping out of a giant birthday cake in a bathing suit, it was absurd, and terrifying, and terribly embarrassing, but until I hit the ground, it was pain- less, almost fun, like a roller coaster. And then I hit the ground and I was dead."

Her voice fell silent just as it had exploded out of nowhere and now she stood there, caressing his shoulder gently, cars all around them honking. Jackson put his hands back on the wheel.

"I think we better move our cars," he said.

"You're right," she said, and she pulled her hand from his shoul- der and walked back to her car, the skirt floating around her ankles like mist.

Jackson pressed his left foot on the clutch and turned the igni- tion key and the Datsun started up without a pause.

"Yes," he whispered to himself. He made sure he was in first gear and rolled forward and up to the cross street that the Mercedes had been on. The two spaces nearest to the intersection were empty and he pulled into the first. The Mercedes rolled in behind him.

As he turned off the engine Jackson realized that he hadn't even bothered to inspect his car and that he shouldn't have driven without inspecting for damage. If the axle was broken he could have caused even more damage and he knew he should have inspected the car, but he didn't, and it felt fine, it rolled forward as it always had and the tires weren't flat and the hand brake worked, so maybe he got lucky, but he knew he should have checked.

The traffic had resumed its normal hurried pace and they were now just two people chatting on the sidewalk as life resumed where it had stopped briefly for a small traffic jam and a brief moment of magic that began and ended with her touch. Jackson walked around his car and she followed, looking where he looked and touching the spots he touched.

"Just that scratch," he said. "I can't believe it."

He circled the car again, looking for the broken pieces that must have been hanging somewhere. She hit him solidly. Her own car had only a scratch, but that was to be expected because her car weighed at least twice as much as his, and hers was steel while his was thin filmy sheet metal that a small man could dent with a fist.

"That's it," he said. "Incredible."

"Should we exchange insurance information?" she asked.

"Yes, I guess so. Just in case I missed something."

"What about the cops?"

"I'm surprised they're not here," Jackson said. "They always show up. Keeps them away from crime."

"Should we call them?"

"I guess not."

"Good," she said. "Then we can forget about insurance information. You need a police report to file a claim. How about I give you my number, and if there's a problem with your car, I'll pay for it."

There was no problem with the car. Jackson knew his car, and it was fine but for a new scratch that blended in with the old, so he agreed.

"Come have something to eat and I'll give you my number," she said. "My treat."

Jackson never actually agreed but she walked away from him to lock her car and he locked his and they walked across the street to the pizza pasta pistachio bar. They sat in a booth by a window.

"Let's share a pizza," she said. "I'm starved. How about pepperoni pistachio?"

She closed her menu and laid it down on the table and waved for the waiter. Pepperoni pistachio. She ordered a large, with two large glasses of seltzer with lime. She did not ask if he liked seltzer, or lime, or pepperoni, or pistachios, all of which he did like very much.

"So anyway," she continued, "my name is Jean LeGene and my number is two-two-eight, six-six-oh-four."

"Wait a minute," Jackson said. "Let me find a pencil."

She pulled a pen from her pocketbook lying next to her chair and wrote the number on a paper napkin.

"Now what's yours?" she asked.

"Here, I'll write it," he said. He took the pen and scribbled his name and number on the bottom half of the napkin and tore it in half, handing the half with his name and number across the table and folding the other half neatly and placing it in his shirt pocket.

"You don't talk very much do you?" she said.

"Actually, I talk quite a bit."

"Oh really."

"No, really. I just can't keep up."

"I know, you can't keep up with me. My ex-husband said the same thing. Are you married?"

The waiter arrived with the seltzers and they both squeezed the lime into the carbonated water.

"Well?" she peppered.

"No," he answered. "But I'm living with someone."

"Good for you," she said. "I should never have gotten married. I mean, when you're twenty-two and in love, it seems like a natural. But when you're twenty-five and he's metamorphosed into this, well, this complete asshole. What is it with men, Albert? I mean, you're like insects. And I don't just mean completely disgusting. You've got this mating program and you can't think about anything else, and then you get married and curl up in a cocoon, and two years later you're completely different. And believe me, you don't come out butterflies. More like cockroaches, or giant carpenter ants. Am I wrong?"

She put her glass down and leaned forward and stared into his eyes, smiling, waiting for an answer, and all Jackson could muster was "Yes."

"Uh huh," she said. "So anyway, how's your car?" She sat back in her chair and stretched her legs beneath the table.

"Fine," he said. "Perfectly fine."

"Mine too. Isn't that strange. It's like, maybe it was supposed to happen. Maybe we were supposed to meet and that was the only way it could happen. I don't know, but there should have been more damage. Are you blessed? I'm not. I don't know. Maybe we are together."

She was blessed, there was no doubt about it, her genes were not of wagon train stock, they were perfect, improved, not of this planet, she moved slowly before him to show every angle, all her unearthly smiles, frowns, giggles, and sniffles as she explained the cost of repairs is what kills with a Mercedes, the mechanics eat you alive, and damn it Jean LeGene in the blue Mercedes, don't talk like that, don't.

"So Jean LeGene," he said.

"I know, isn't it awful. My mother was a real nut. She said she almost named me Le. Is that sick or what?"

"Right. Look, Jean LeGene. What do you do for a living?"

"My my, Mr. Jackson, aren't we getting a little personal? I mean, we hardly know each other."

"I know you're divorced and you drive a beautiful very expensive Mercedes and whatever you do you don't have to be at work this afternoon."

"How do you know that?"

"Because it's been about an hour since you smacked into me and you haven't once glanced at your watch. And you just don't seem to be thinking about work."

"So maybe I work at night."

"Do you?"

"No. Since you must know, Albert Jackson, I don't have to work. He was very rich. He gave me a lot of money. I'm lucky."

The pizza arrived and it was far too much for two people. It filled most of the table and left barely enough room for their two small plates and the glasses of seltzer.

"Yum," she said. "Pepperoni pistachio. Do you like pepperoni pistachio?"

"I've never had it," he said.

"Really? Me neither."

"You haven't?"

"No."

"Then why did you order it?"

"Excuse me, but have you ever seen pepperoni pistachio on any other menu? No, I don't think so. Albert, you have to take some chances in life."

She smiled and bit into the end of her slice and a small droplet of orange grease rolled down her manicured pointer finger to her wrist.

"Not bad," she said as she chewed and rubbed her wrist on the napkin in her lap.

It was better than not bad. It was sublime. Maybe it was the pistachios. It had been so long since he had sifted through a bag hunting for that one last uneaten green nut hiding inside a shell. That sweet, tropical flavor, combined with the salt and pepper of the red sausage, with cheese and tomato sauce, dripping down her hand toward her wrist, smiling, staring, chewing, licking her fingers and her lips, and brushing away the crumbs from her upper lip. Pizza had never tasted more perfect.

Jackson slipped a second slice onto his plate and he was just about to take a bite when she said, "Well listen, I'm afraid I've got to run."

He put the slice back down on his plate.

"Really, but you hardly ate."

"Oh no, I had enough. I never eat more than a slice. Take the extra home."

The waiter placed most of the large pepperoni pistachio pizza in a white pizza box and Jean LeGene paid the bill and the tip and drank a final mouthful of seltzer and they walked back to their cars and she said, "Well, it was nice to meet you, Albert, and I'm sorry about the car, and if you need anything fixed or you want to sue me or whatever, call me," and she hopped into her Mercedes and drove away.

2

Jackson drove straight home. It was barely four and Lucy wouldn't be home until after five, but he felt the need to get home immediately, to be certain he was there before her.

He carried the pizza up to the door. In the mailbox he found a letter from his brother and a telephone bill. He opened the bill, which was for $27.62, and he scanned the typically short note from Jeffrey.

Dear Albert: It was good to talk with you on the phone after so long. We really should do better. Mom seems very worried about your plans, and she seems to want you to move back to the city. I told her it takes you less time to get home than me, but that didn't seem to calm her. She doesn't like her son living on the West Coast. I told her not to worry. Work here is progressing. I'm hoping to graduate this year. I've finished the first four chapters and have four more to go. The writing is speeding up now because I have a pretty good idea of what I want to say. The first chapter was the slowest—it took me nearly a year to write. Don't tell Mom or Dad that. I've also written an article for a small philosophy magazine, so that took up more of my time, and I've been teaching night classes, which pays the bills. I'm not sure if I'm ready to face the world anyhow. Life here has suited me just fine so far, although I am dirt poor and living in a closet. Will you be getting home at all this summer? I'm hoping to be home in August. It would be nice to see you then. Well, we'll talk. Good luck finding work, and say hi to Lucy. Love, Jeff."

Jackson stepped into the apartment and tossed the bill and the letter onto his desk, with the other bills and his typewriter and Lucy's paints and calligraphy pens. She would have to pay the bill.

Then he walked to the kitchen to put the pizza into the refrigerator. He opened the door and pushed the ketchup and mustard out of the way and he was about to slide the box into the fridge when something changed his mind and he closed the refrigerator and walked out back behind the building. He tossed the pizza in the dumpster.

He came back inside and took off his shoes and scanned the classifieds, in case he had missed something good. But there was nothing. Waiters. Nurse practitioners. Dental assistants, electricians, car salesmen. If nothing good came up by the end of the month, then he would get a grunt job, maybe a waiter in a brew pub or a job in an espresso bar.

So much beer and coffee. It wouldn't be bad, but the money would stink. Lucy had said wait a year before taking something like that, but the money was running out and six months seemed long enough. When the job came along, Jackson would see it and apply and wait. She had said make job hunting your job. You'll get a good one. Knock on doors. Call people. I can support us for now. Don't worry.

Lucy moved for a job with her bank. Jackson moved for Lucy.

There was a knock at the door. Jackson ran to the door and peered through the spy hole. He hoped it was Jean LeGene, but through the tiny glass he saw a tiny old woman clutching a book.

"Yes," Jackson shouted through the door.

"I'm here to offer a prayer for the Lord," the squeaky voice said. "Have you prayed for the Lord today?"

"No, not today. Sorry."

"It's not too late."

"Sorry. I've decided not to pray today."

There was silence on the other side of the door and Jackson saw he had confused her.

"Well how about tomorrow?" she asked.

"Tomorrow's Wednesday," Jackson said.

"Yes?"

"No prayers on Wednesday. Sorry, it's a rule."

"Thursday?"

"Sorry, same rule. I think you'd better try somebody else."

This she recognized. Just another sinner trying to get rid of her.

"You know the Lord has done some wonderful things lately. He deserves our prayers."

"What's he done?" Jackson asked.

"The flood in Bangladesh..."

"That's impressive."

"No, no. Listen. One of the little islands in the middle of the sea. All the others got swept away. But he saved one island, because a saint once visited the island and the islanders prayed at the shrine of the saint, and they were saved. The Lord saves."

"Which saint?" Jackson asked.

"Saint Ignatious, I think," she answered.

"Yes, well, sell that in Bangladesh. Goodbye, ma'am."

He watched her turn calmly and walk down the sidewalk and out onto the street. From a window in the living room he saw her join a small army of little old ladies that had fanned out across the neighborhood. Beneath the cherry and apple trees they looked like an Easter parade without the children. Smartly dressed, proud, God-fearing ladies, at least for a day, their mission made for a perfect promenade and constitutional. They seemed so happy, busy little beavers looking for believers, out in the warm city air clutching each other's arms, pointing to houses and apartments that showed promise, studying the flowers in the gardens. Jackson's old lady was at the house across the street ringing the doorbell. No one was home. He turned on the television and watched the local news of shootings and factory closings.

"Well those bathing suits came out in force today," the weatherman said. "I think we'll see more of the same tomorrow, but change is on the way. Look for clouds by the end of the week."

Lucy arrived home shortly before six.

"Hello darling," he said as he opened the door for her and planted a kiss on her lips. She lowered her head and walked into the apartment. He closed the door and asked, "So how was your day?"

"Not bad," she answered as she pulled off her high heels. "Jack Halliday is a real prick. I don't know if I'm going to be able to stand working for him."

"You better," Jackson said. "What did he do?"

"Oh nothing. He's just a sexist jerk and I don't like him. How was your day?"

"OK. Nothing good in the paper. I sent out some resumes, took a walk in the park. An old lady tried to get me to pray."

"Me too, just a minute ago."

"I told mine to shove it."

"You didn't."

"No, but she didn't get a prayer out of me. How about you?"

"I told her I prayed this morning. She was very pleased."

"Did you?"

"Of course not. Anything to eat? I'm starved."

Lucy tossed off her shoes and walked barefoot into the kitchen, where she found a piece of a chocolate bar and a glass of milk.

"I may get a trip to Tokyo next month," Lucy shouted from the kitchen.

"Tokyo?"

"Yeah, I may go with Jack to meet a big client."

"No expense too great for the great bank?"

"I guess not."

"I thought Jack was a prick."

"He is. He's also my boss."

"Uh huh."

Lucy sat down at the dining table and leafed through the catalogues that arrived in the mail the day before. Jackson watched the national news.

"Trouble in Kenya," he shouted to her.

"Oh yeah."

"Yeah."

"That's too bad."

"I know. I hope things don't get too bad. Something is going to have to change there. I hope it doesn't get bloody."

"Can we go for a walk?" she asked. "To the park? I've been inside all day."

"Sure."

Lucy changed out of her navy blue business suit and into blue jeans and a white T-shirt and sneakers and she was again Lucy, the real Lucy, not the bank Lucy, and together, hand in hand, they walked out past the small park around the corner to the forest half a mile away. It was much cooler and wetter in the woods, dank with decay. The trail followed a small brook that was running high with runoff from the rain earlier in the week. They stopped at a small wooden bridge that crossed the brook and they looked for fish, but didn't see any. The water had a slightly foul smell.

"I bet the piss and crap from all the houses around here flows in there," Jackson said.

"It does not," Lucy said. "They've got sewers."

"So why does it stink?"

"I don't know."

They walked on and turned to climb another trail that reached above the tops of some Douglas fir and big leaf maple, and this trail was still partially lit by the sun low in the western sky but still an hour away from setting.

Jackson slowed but Lucy pushed ahead at full speed.

"Come on slowpoke," she said. "You don't get enough exercise."

Jackson didn't answer but he tried to keep up with her. Again he slowed, and this time she slowed too. They stopped, panting, sweating, at the top of the hill in a patch of sun.

"I got into an accident today," he said out of breath.

"You mean with the car?"

"Yes."

"What happened?"

"I was driving down 21st and at Flanders a Mercedes went right through the stop sign and hit me in the side."

"A Mercedes?"

"Yes."

"Is your car OK?"

"Yes, it's fine."

"What did you do?"

"We exchanged phone numbers, just in case something turns up."

"Did the police come?"

"No, they never showed up."

"God, a Mercedes. Was it damaged?"

"No, just a scratch."

"I bet that's an expensive scratch."

"Maybe."

Lucy stretched her arms and then bent to retie her shoe laces. Her dark brown hair fell over her head so that for a few moments there was no head, just a mop of chocolate hair flopping at the end of her neck.

"Are you OK?" she asked.

"Yes, I'm fine."

They walked on listening to the crunch of twigs and leaves. The walk home was mostly down hill.

Jackson cooked hamburgers and string beans and salad and they drank red wine with dinner in front of the television. Jackson finished his first hamburger before Lucy had eaten half of hers. She was transfixed by the color television screen and she only picked at her food.

"Don't you like it?" Jackson asked.

"It's good," she said. "I'm not hungry."

After dinner they watched more television and read magazines and Jackson reread the letter from his brother.

He folded the letter and put it back into the envelope and tossed it on the floor and he sighed.

"What's the matter?" Lucy asked.

"Nothing," he said.

"How is your brother?"

"He's fine. He said to say hello."

"That's nice. Is he finished yet?"

"No."

"God."

Lucy turned off the television before the eleven o'clock news and they brushed their teeth and crawled into the futon on the bedroom floor and Jackson turned out the lamp on the floor and Lucy squeezed next to him and they kissed.

"How long will you be in Japan?" Jackson asked.

"A week."

"Maybe I'll have a job by then."

"Maybe. You'll get one."

"I wish I could go with you," he said.

"Me too. We'll take a nice trip for our honeymoon."

"Maybe Egypt, or Greece."

"Yes," she said. "Egypt or Greece."

They rolled onto their stomachs and tried to sleep in the soft blue glow of the clock radio and the dancing shadows cast by the young maple outside the window and as Lucy's breath slowed and steadied cool evening air saturated with the scent of fresh-baked bread sifted into the bedroom through the screen window behind Jackson's head and he breathed the sweet air in deeply and listened to the crickets and the leaves that rustled in the wind, he heard the honk of cars, the crash of metal, the click of heels, a gunshot, and he tasted salt, and pistachios. He pulled a long hair from his head and it smelled like a rose, delicate, sweet, close enough to kiss on its soft round loving brown shoulder. He did not know whose head the hair came from.

"How about Italy?" Jackson whispered.

Lucy didn't answer.

"Good night," Jackson said, to himself. He held the mysterious hair to his nose.

ANDREW NACHISON is cofounder of the We Media conference and community (www.wemedia.com) and a partner in The 726 Group, a media consulting firm. He is a writer and online publishing veteran who learned from remarkable teachers: the art of fiction from novelist Frank McCourt, computer programming from BASIC creator John Kemeney, and social activism from Pacific island nuclear testing witness and author David Bradley. He has reported and edited for the Associated Press; written for the New York Times, Infoworld, Audubon, and other magazines; managed one of the world's most ambitious small-market newspaper websites, lawrence. com; played clarinet at Tanglewood and Carnegie Hall; studied wildlife, development, and environmental policy in Kenya; and spoken on media convergence and business strategies in Asia and Europe. He has published one piece of short fiction, written many others (at nach.com), and swears there's more to come. He earned a BA in philosophy at Dartmouth College and lives with his wife and two sons in Reston, Virginia.

A Few Good Men

DAVID NICHOLSON

The way the men in the shop start talking about women that Saturday night is this: The telephone rings once more for Speed, and Lamarr Jenkins, whose shop it is, heaves a heavy sigh of exasperation. Even if Speed were not the newest barber, it would still make sense for his chair to be near the pay telephone and the back room. Since Speed came to work at the shop three weeks before, the telephone has rung for him with the regularity of a factory whistle or the landlord's knock. Always, it is some young girl, a different sweet young voice each time, asking tentatively for Speed. Always, Speed talks to her, his back to his customer, his own voice pitched low and soothing. This time, when Speed finally returns to the head he has been cutting, Jenkins scans the line of men waiting in the chairs underneath the mirrors against the wall. And then, without looking at Speed, Jenkins asks if Speed thinks about cutting hair when he is getting pussy. Speed says no—a man ought to keep his mind on the task at hand. Jenkins says fine—from now on, stop thinking about pussy when you in here supposed to be cutting hair.

After the laughter dies down, old Mr. Perkins, over whose half-bald head Jenkins has been aimlessly wielding his clippers, rouses himself long enough to say, "Boy must be working two or three jobs. Got to be, all them women he got."

Speed grins. A razor-thin man, he has a wicked Ike Turner goatee and a sleek otter's head of slicked-back hair.

"Who you think I am?" Speed asks. "Hubble?"

Hubble, the second barber, ignores it and continues placidly grooming his customer. Hubble is a big man. Though he does not drink, there is a whiskey sadness about him, an amiable alcoholic diffidence. Speed snorts and shakes his head.

"I got one rule," he says, "and one rule only. I live by it. If they don't pay, I don't play."

"Shee-it," says A. B. Prudhomme, a Louisianan known for obvious reasons as Seventh Street Red. "You pay. We all do. One way or another, you pay. Don't nobody give up nothing for nothing. Especially these black gals out here."

"Thass right," Mr. Perkins says over the chorus of assents from the men waiting. Speed says, "You right. Somea these young girls they got out here, you got to be careful. They'll try to game you in a minute."

Doc, an English teacher at the high school, looks up from the newspaper he is reading. "Now wait a minute," he says, taking off his glasses. "What is it you are trying to say? As far as I can see, there is no difference between men and women at all."

"How many men you know got a pussy?" Speed asks.

Doc folds his glasses and puts them in his shirt pocket. He smiles. When the men finish laughing Doc says, "Now you know that is not what I meant. But since you do not seem to understand, I will break it down for you. What I am saying is that there is no *essential* difference between men and women. There are just as many men as there are women out there who are not to be trusted."

Jenkins looks at Doc from underneath his green eyeshade. "Doc," he says, "you wrong when you say there ain't no difference. It's a whole lotta men I wouldn't turn my back on. But I'll tell you one thing—a man might dog a woman, but a woman will give a man the blues for life."

"That may be true," Doc says. "But even if it is, none of it is any worse than what black men have always done to black women."

Hubble lowers his clippers and looks over at Jenkins. "All this y'all talking about got me thinking," he says. "Know who I ain't seen in a long time?"

Speed says, "Your daddy?" and a ripple of appreciative laughter runs down the line of waiting men.

Hubble frowns.

"Speed, I done told you," he says. "I do not play that mess. Now come on now, boy—you might get hurt."

"Hurt?" Speed looked sideways at Hubble. "*Hurt?* Man, you better think twice before you mess with me. I'm the one that whipped lightning's ass and put thunder in jail, drunk all the water out the ocean, and tied a knot in the whale's tail."

Hubble tilts his customer's head.

"Uh huh," he says. "Uh huh."

Prudhomme snickers, and Hubble stands back from his customer, his face a mask of blank disdain. Underneath his blue barber's smock he wears a long-sleeved shirt, the same kind he wears every day, always buttoned at the wrist and the collar no matter how hot it is. For the past twenty-four years, Hubble has worked in a hotel restaurant downtown, first as a cook's assistant, then second cook, then head cook. Two years ago, he became manager. One night every two weeks and one weekend a month, Hubble is absent from Jenkins's shop—those times are reserved for his service in the National Guard. In a year, Hubble will retire from the guard. Five years after that, he will leave the restaurant. He will collect two pensions and still be young enough to cut hair. If he wishes, he can also take another day job. In the fifteen years that he has worked for Jenkins, Hubble has always been on time and seldom sick. He is a good barber. Because of this, he has Jenkins's respect and his own key to the shop.

"You couldn't park in front today, Omar?" Jenkins says. "I didn't see your car."

"Didn't drive. Man didn't have the car ready when I went to get it yesterday."

"You need a ride? Won't be no trouble to drop you off."

Hubble shakes his head.

"Earline picking it up. She'll come for me after nine."

For a few moments the only sound in the shop is the hum of the clippers and the rattle of the old Coke machine. Then Speed says, "Hey, I didn't mean nothing, awright?" He exchanges glances with Prudhomme. "Awright? 'Cause Hubble, I don't know nothing about your daddy—just ask your momma."

"Well, it seemed peculiar to me," Jenkins says, before the laughter can encourage further impudence from Speed. "'Cause I know you can usually find a place in front of the shop."

"Yeah," Hubble says absently, "that's true," and then, "Carver. That's who I was thinking about. What works down at the post office. He still with that young girl?"

"Carver? Lloyd Carver?" Jenkins looks at Hubble and shakes his head. "Omar, where you been, man? They buried Lloyd Carver two weeks ago Friday."

"You got to be kidding me." Hubble considers it. "Come to think of it, last time I seen him Carver look like he'd been sick. But I didn't think he was doing that bad."

"And I'll tell you something else," Jenkins says. "By the time it was over, if it wasn't for the VA, Lloyd Carver woulda been in the street. Yeah, that's right." Sweeping the cloth from Perkin's lap, Jenkins looks to see who is next. Prudhomme rises. Despite his appreciation of Speed's gift for insult and exaggeration, he trusts only Jenkins to cut his hair.

"Now, see, that's just what I been saying," Jenkins says, pinning the cloth around Prudhomme's neck and then leveling his clippers at Doc. "That girl had Carver's nose wide enough open to drive a Mack truck through. And all the time she was fattening him, fattening him just like you fatten a hog for slaughter."

Doc smiles. Like the best bartenders and cabdrivers, men whose chosen profession also requires them to come daily into contact with members of the public, Jenkins is both a storyteller and a philosopher. Doc knows this, and so do the rest of the men present. Whether this is part of Jenkins's temperament and always has been, or whether it is something Jenkins has learned in his years behind his chair of white enamel, overseeing the heads of men, boys, and the occasional woman, Doc neither knows nor cares. He, and the rest of the men, have long been connoisseurs of Jenkins's stories and those that are told in his shop.

"Well, I did not know Lloyd Carver," Doc says. "So I guess you will have to tell me what happened."

"Doc," Jenkins says, as he begins to work the comb through Prudhomme's hair, "what that woman did to Lloyd Carver was a shame. Took everything he had and after she was finished, she just stepped over where he was laying and kept on going. But man, she musta had some good stuff, because as soon as he met her Carver start to act like he in junior high school, and here he was a grown man with more'n forty years at the post office.

"How it started was Carver met the broad in onea them little joints up on Georgia Avenue. Wasn't too long before he ask her to quit her job and come stay in the house his momma left him. Now, it was two things that girl could do, and one of them was cook. Every night Carver come home she got the food on the table, cooked just the way he like it. So when he come home one night and dinner ain't ready and she just sitting there with a long face, Carver know something ain't right. He say, 'What's wrong, darling?' The broad say she want to know do Carver love her.

"Carver say, 'Love you? Of course I love you.' So she say, 'Well, I hope so, because you all I got. And if something was to happen to you, I don't know what I'd do.' Carver say, 'Ain't nothing going to happen to me,' but she keep on, till finally he say, 'Darlin', what you want me to do to set your mind at rest?' And she say, 'Lloyd, honey, would you put your car in my name? That way, if something happen to you, I'd at least have me something to ride around in.' Now Carver had him a Park Avenue didn't have but twenty-eight thousand miles on it. But he just laugh and say, 'Is that all you want, honey? Shoot, I'll do it tomorrow.'

"Few weeks later him and the broad sitting in the living room watching the Redskins and the broad say something, but Carver too busy watching—you remember that game where they kick Dallas ass? That's how come the broad got mad, 'cause Carver wasn't listening. So she got up and turned off the TV and run upstairs crying."

Speed says, "*Turned off the TV?* In the man's own house? Turned off the TV? Shee-it. I'da kicked the bitch's ass in a red-hot minit."

Jenkins lifts the clippers from Prudhomme's head and looks over at Speed.

"Yeah," he says, "I believe you would have. But all Lloyd Carver done was go upstairs asking himself what the hell was wrong. Get in the bedroom, the broad say, 'Lloyd, I quit working 'cause you asked me, and now I ain't got nothing of my own. And I coulda gone back and finished school and had me a good job working for the government.' Carver say, 'Baby, you ain't got to worry about no job. I'ma take care of you.' Broad say, 'But we got to face facts. I know we got us a good long time left together, but you ain't gon' be here to take care of me forever. What am I gon' do after you gone?'

"Carver say, 'Whatchu want me to do?' Broad look at him. Broad say, 'I'm gon' need something to get by. Will you go in tomorrow and make over your insurance to me?' Now Lloyd been paying into that policy the whole time he been at the post office, and you *know* the post office got them a good retirement plan—"

"Wait a minute," Doc says. "Wait just a minute. Do you expect me to believe this? That a man, a grown man, would sign away his car *and* his insurance policy to a woman he met in a nightclub? I'm sorry, but I just cannot believe such a thing would happen."

"You ain't as sorry as Lloyd Carver was, once it was all over," Jenkins says, "and I don't care whether you believe or disbelieve. These are true facts I'm telling you. True facts. The next day Carver went in and changed over his policy. Now, once he did that, you'da thought she'd be real nice to him so she could get the rest of what she wanted. But next time Carver try to get him some, the broad say she feeling sick and ask would he mind sleeping on the couch.

"'Nother few weeks go by and Carver still sleeping on that couch. But what shoulda tipped him off is they been living in that house three, four, maybe five months, and the whole time he ain't never seen her nekkid. Now all of a sudden she wearing these little old shortie nightgowns, leave the bedroom door open and he walk past and she laying there ain't wearing nothing but panties. After a while, Carver start to feel like he gon' go crazy he don't get him some.

"One night, she come downstairs wearing one of them old shortie nightgowns. Come in the living room and say, 'Lloyd, we got some stuff we got to talk about.' Carver say, 'What's on your mind, sugar?' Broad say, 'It's more than thirty years difference between us. Now I know you don't like for me to talk like this, but I got to. You ain't gon' be here for me forever, and it's a mean old world for a woman ain't got no man. You got to do something to make it easier for me if you pass.'

"Carver ain't say nothing for a long time. Then he say, 'Woman— you asked me to put my car in your name. I did it. You asked me to make over my insurance to you. I did that too. What you want me to do for you now?' And the broad, she say, 'Lloyd, it ain't for me. It's for the baby.' Carver say, 'Woman, how come you ain't tell me?' She say, 'I just now found out.' The two of them sit there grinning at each other, and then she say, "Now come on upstairs with me, Lloyd. I ain't been as good to you as I should.'

"Afterwards, Carver about to fall asleep, and she say, 'Do it for me Lloyd. Please.' Carver say, 'Do what?' Broad say, 'Put the house in my name. So me and Lloyd Junior can have us a roof over our heads if you pass.'"

"Goddamn," Prudhomme says, and the laughter that follows is rueful and mocking all at the same time, a taunt and an elegy celebrating the recklessness of the late Lloyd Carver and his imprudence in the face of love. Only Speed's laughter is entirely without sympathy. Hubble does not laugh. He frowns, the whiskey sadness heavy on his face. "Shee-it," Speed says again, and Jenkins unpins the cloth from Prudhomme's neck. He snaps it to shake off the hair.

"And then?" Doc says as he approaches the chair. "What happened next?"

"Whatchu mean, 'What happened'?"

"I mean what happened? It didn't just end that way. What happened?"

"Whatchu think happened? Wasn't but a couplea days after he put the house in her name, Carver come home and found two suitcases on the porch. Key didn't work 'cause she'd done had the lock changed. Rung the bell, and she come to the door, didn't even open it. Told him to get his ass off her porch before she call the *po*-lice. And when Carver went to see a lawyer the next day, the man said there wasn't a damned thing he could do."

"He brought it on himself," Speed says, "letting the bitch game him like that. First time she asked for something, he shoulda told her, 'I give you a roof to sleep under, and a bed to sleep in. You want anything else, go get you a job.'"

"That's right," Prudhomme says. "It's all a game, and the sooner you learn that, the better. See, it's like that old man was trying to get next to this young girl, promised her a whole lotta stuff if she just give him some. Girl finally gave him some leg and he putting his clothes on and she say, 'Now, Daddy, don't forget all them things you said you was gon' do for me.' And he just buttoned his shirt and said, 'Baby, lemme tell you something—when I'm hard, I'm soft. But when I'm soft, baby, I'm hard.'"

Speed laughs and takes a cigarette, a Kool, from the pack on the counter behind his chair. He lights it.

"You got to be that way," he says. "Somea these no-good black bitches they got out here will take a man for everything he got, if he let 'em. And it ain't about color. Somea these high-yella and brownskin gals ain't shit neither." Speed blows a jet of smoke out the side of his mouth. "But I still say a real man wouldn't let nothing like that go down. A real man is gon' take charge, a real man know he stronger than a woman."

"Uh huh," Hubble says. "Well, I can see you ain't never been married, son," and Jenkins says, "Doc, what you think?"

"Frankly," Doc says, "I still do not see how a man could be so foolish as your friend to sign away his car, his insurance, *and* his home." Before Jenkins can reply, Doc says, "Also, I prefer to believe black women are not that greedy, at least no more so than any other women."

"Well, that's a true story," Jenkins says, lowering the clippers. "Lloyd Carver told it to me while I was cutting his hair, down to the VA hospital the week before he died."

The telephone rings. Speed picks it up. A moment later he hangs up and, turning to the counter behind his chair, searches for a new blade for his clippers. Catching sight of himself in the mirror, he leans closer, fingering a blemish on his chin.

"Doc," Jenkins says, "you may have plenty of book learning, but you and Speed might as well be twins because the two of you are still as ignorant about some things as the day you were born. Lloyd Carver just couldn't help himself—that little girl's stuff was too good and her game was just too strong."

"Well," Doc says, when he has finished laughing, "all that may be true. And it may be true that I am ignorant. But there is one significant difference between Speed and me—I respect black women. At least I try to."

Speed turns away from the mirror, one fist on his hip. The ash from his cigarette dribbles onto the front of his smock. "Who don't respect black women? I respect all womens. Long as they respect me."

"All right," Doc says, holding up his hands under the cloth in mock surrender. "But that must be a lot of respect, because we all know you have a lot of women. Mr. Jenkins, for the sake of argument, let us say your story is true. Even so, I still say what happened to your friend is no more than what some black women complain black men have always done to them. And you could even argue that she deserved some compensation for taking care of him."

Jenkins says, "You believe that shit?"

"I certainly do. *I* read. You should too, and not just the sports pages. You might learn something. Or watch TV. Like that talk show in the afternoons."

"Which show? One got that great big old fat broad?"

"She is not fat. Not anymore."

"Huh. Just wait. You'll see—she gon' put it all back on."

"That may be true," Doc says. "But it is neither here nor there as far as what we are talking about."

Jenkins looks at the clock. It is nine, closing time.

"Say, Omar," Jenkins says, "close the door, before some fool can't read come in here. And turn off the sign."

Hubble goes to do it. When he comes back, he says, "I been standing here listening, and I got to say it's been a long time since I heard Negroes this full of shit." He unpins the cloth and dusts the back of his customer's neck with talcum. Sweeping the cloth from his customer's lap, Hubble says, "Speed think Carver shoulda smacked the broad, and I can understand that, 'cause Speed's brains in his dick, if he got any. Jenkins, you think it's all about the woman had a better game than Carver. And you, Doc, you can't understand how a man could let something like that happen. But don't nonea y'all know what the hell you talking about. Y'all ever consider the possibility that Lloyd Carver was in love?"

Prudhomme says, "*Love*? Ain't nobody said nothing about love," and Jenkins says, "Omar, whatchu know about a old man and a young girl? You been married to the same woman twenty-seven years. And I know you don't do no running around on the side."

"Ain't got to. I love my wife. And I got what I need right at home."

"Shee-it," says Speed. "Don't lie. You be too tired. Working as many jobs as you got."

The men laugh, but Hubble says nothing. The chairs against the wall are almost empty now; only Prudhomme, Doc, and one or two stragglers are left. Hubble folds his cloth, hangs up clippers and scissors. He discards an empty bottle of hair tonic, tosses towels and the folded cloth in an orange nylon bag to go to the laundry on Monday. He counts the money he has taken in, counts out the share that is due Jenkins, and counts it again before giving it to him. Finished, Hubble takes a pair of clippers and a small wire brush. He sits down in his chair. He sits for a long time cleaning the clippers, brow furrowed and his mouth pursed, as if closing in on something he does not yet know if he wants to say. Finally, Hubble says, "Long as y'all telling stories, I got me one."

"Go on," Jenkins says, "you think we can understand it," and Hubble says, "It was this man one time loved his wife. Loved her more than he did his momma and his daddy, which is only right, because that's what the Good Book say you supposed to do. Every Friday night this man come home with his money and give it to his baby. She didn't even have to ask.

"Now one day him and his wife decide to get them a little house. He didn't want her working, and the only way they could do it was if he went out and got himself another job. Wasn't like it is now—colored man could only find certain types of work. And times was hard, so hard they was a lot of men couldn't even find *one* job. But this man found him some work washing dishes at night in a restaurant.

"Every morning he get up and go work his regular job. Get off and go wash them dishes till midnight six days a week. Was a whole lotta times he'd come home at night and his baby be sleeping when he get in. A man shouldn't be outside his house like that, not as much as this man was. See, by him being away from home like that, he wasn't able to take care of business. And it was plenty of other men just waiting to take care of it for him.

"One Friday morning, this man getting ready to leave out the house. His wife say, 'What time you comin' home?' He say regular time. And she say she been thinking—bank they been keeping their money in, she been reading the papers, and the money ain't safe no more. She say, 'I want us to take it out. Monday morning we'll find ourselves a good, safe place to put it.'

"He been working himself like a dog for two, almost three years. Had more than five hundred dollars saved up. He say, 'Sugar, you think it's the right thing? I don't like to think about carrying around that kind of money all day like that.' And his wife, she just throw back her head and laugh, say, 'Big as you is, who gon' mess with you?'

"Come lunch time he take all their money out the bank. Walk around all day with them bills folded over in his pocket. Every once in a while reach in his pocket and touch that money, thinking about how he could work so hard and so long and still have so little. Come midnight, he finish washing dishes in the restaurant and get on the streetcar, thinking how he just want to get home and put that money someplace safe.

"Man get off the streetcar and start walking. Almost to his house when he hear somebody say, 'There he is!' and two men jump out the alley. One got a knife. And it's a little man got a handkerchief over his face. One carry the knife say, 'I'ma have to cut you, you don't give it up.' Little one say, 'Yeah, we know you got it.' This man I'm talking about don't even stop to think about what he doing—he knock down the little man closest to him, kick him. Little one yelling, 'Cut him! Cut him!' and the man with the knife bring it down. Man do like this"—Hubble sets the clippers in his lap and raises his arms to cover his face—"and he don't even feel it when the knife cut the back of his arms from his wrist to his elbows. All he thinking about is how he gots to keep that money.

"Knife come down one more time and he grab the man's arm. Knife fall out the man's hand and he pick it up, turn on the little one. Hit him across the face, raise the knife. And hear the little man say, 'Naw, naw, don't do it. Don't you know who I is? It's me. It's me.'

"Man pull down the scarf, and you know what? It was his wife. It was his wife."

No one says anything, and for a moment the men in the shop can hear all the sounds from outside—footsteps on the sidewalk, laughter from the corner by the liquor store, the cars idling at the stoplight on the Avenue. Finally, Prudhomme whistles.

"Damn," Speed says, "that's some terrible shit. What he do, Hubble? Kick the bitch's ass and leave her in the street?"

"Naw. It didn't go like that. This man, he just left and went on home. Couldn't think of nowhere else to go. Got there and the *po*-lice was waiting. She told 'em he beat her. Judge give him six months."

Jenkins turns the chair so that Doc faces the mirror. Their eyes meet, and then both Doc and Jenkins turn to look at Hubble. Neither says anything. Speed says, "*Shee*-it," and puts down his clippers, disgusted. "Now that's what I been telling you. Man let a bitch run a game on him like that, he gon' get what he deserves. He shoulda smacked her a few times, let her know who was in control."

Hubble laughs.

"Speed, trying to tell you something is like trying to preach the Bible to a cat. Yeah, this man I'm talking about, he coulda beat her—he was twice her size, but see, he loved his woman. And while he was in jail, the woman searched her heart and come to understand how wrong she'd been. When he got out she came to find him. They been together ever since."

The telephone rings. Speed hesitates, unable to decide. He wants to set Hubble straight, but there is a little girl waiting. In the end he goes to answer the telephone. Jenkins, still looking curiously at Hubble, says, "Omar, long as you been working in my shop, I ain't never heard you tell no story. Least not like that. Now lookahere—"

Before Jenkins can finish, a car horn sounds outside and Hubble goes to the window. He waves, then turns. "Gentlemen," Hubble says, "y'all gon' have to excuse me, but that's my wife."

As the door closes after him Prudhomme says, "I don't know about y'all, but I don't believe a word..." and then he makes the connection, the same connection Doc and Jenkins have already made.

A man can learn many things in Lamarr Jenkins's shop—what to put into a transmission or a motor to keep a vehicle running long past its time; where to get the freshest fish, the cheapest television, the best suit; how to slaughter a hog or raise a sagging roof. And, sometimes, what a man learns may remind him of the true facts— that he can work alongside another man for fifteen years, can know him for that time and more, and still not know all there is to know about him. Prudhomme joins Doc and Jenkins at the window.

The big-bodied Chevrolet is double parked. Hubble walks to the driver's side while his wife slides over. There is nothing remarkable about her—she is a plump, brown-skinned woman with graying hair and a sweet, dimpled face. Hubble gets in and puts the Chevrolet in gear. Doc, Prudhomme, and Jenkins stand watching, long after Hubble has driven off.

Leaning against the wall with the telephone against his ear, Speed shifts the cigarette dangling from his lips and squints past the smoke. "Hey," Speed calls, "whatch'all looking at?"

Jenkins turns, motioning for Doc to sit down so that he can finish and they can all go home. "Never mind," Jenkins says. "Never mind. It ain't got a thing to do with you."

Formerly of Washington, D.C., DAVID NICHOLSON now lives in Virginia, where he is completing the final draft of "The House of Eli," a novel about black men, fatherhood, and violence.

The Conjecture Chamber

 Jim Patterson

Amanda Gay is dead.

I don't like to muse about death. As a reference point for the varying propositions regarding life it can be useful but I have never entertained the fascination that seems to obsess many. I will be forced to deal with its many aspects soon enough.

I'm standing on the Metro platform in The Capital of the Empire, Washington, D.C. I'm waiting for the subway far beneath the business district. I'm trying not to think about Amanda Gay when suddenly I notice that the fellow standing next to me seems very uncomfortable. Curious, because he's got to be wearing five thousand dollars' worth of clothes. A camel hair coat. Italian loafers with tassels. He's carrying an umbrella and briefcase. Beneath the coat is a blue suit, white shirt, red tie. The Kakistocracy Uniform. He appears about twenty-five pounds overweight. His hair is professionally coiffured. He is approximately my age, that is to say, nearing forty. He is perfect. A perfect example of the white-collar class of fatuous, self-absorbed, self-important, ill-informed, unread, culturally inert pigs that you find lurking around centers of money and power.

I am a working musician playing two hundred nights a year. Just one other musician and I tour together, write all our material and book and promote the gigs as well. I've lost my patience with people who don't support the arts, never go out, read crap, and presume their financial status to be the sum and substance of their societal prerequisites. I've had a thousand and one encounters with arseholes like him. Pick a topic and he'll spit back some arbitrary gibberish he's heard shouted from his TV, or hit you with his who cares, so what, kind of apolitical cynicism that prides itself on looking out for number one yet denudes his personality of any individually inspired content whatsoever. The reactionary expressions he shares when with his peers will vary, but the overall smug, peevish sentiments are the same with all these guys. I used to indulge these fellows. I used to give them the benefit of the doubt. I used to have a do unto others as you would have them do unto you attitude. But no more. They've done unto me enough. They've taken over. They are the enemy. Now, I openly challenge them every chance I get. Lead Belly was right, I think to myself as I click my teeth with disgust, this is a bourgeois town.

Single women outnumber single men here in The Capital of the Empire. An intriguing statistic. When I hear these women bemoan the fact that "all the good ones are taken," I think it's absurd until I catch a glimpse of guys like this. He's a good one. I'm sure he's taken. I look for his ring finger but he is wearing gloves. I am about to turn away in search of some more pleasant preoccupation when I think of other empire capitals throughout history and wonder what the merchant classes of those eras were like. I wonder how similar or different this son-of-a-bitch is from them. How does he stack up? I try to imagine myself standing on a London railway platform, circa 1890, or in Constantinople, or Rome, Paris, Tokyo, Berlin, Athens, Ayodhya, Beijing, all at the height of empire. Now, this specimen seems quite interesting. A real live artifact. On another day, in a better mood, I might have tried to strike up a conversation with him. I could go into my affable kook routine I use on stage to disarm him and draw him out. Maybe see if I could come away with some identifying quotes. Some kind of watermark I could then cut and paste into something useful. A caricature of our times. Then I suddenly know why he's uncomfortable. He's afraid that is exactly what I am about to do.

As soon as I get on the train my mind is on something else. Seven stops later I exit the subway, pick up my car, and arrive at the Royal Mile Bar early, so I must wait for my friends. The Royal Mile isn't my idea of the perfect bar. The tables are too big and too close together. The lights are always bright and there is no place to hide. Nor am I impressed by their infinite selection of beer. I would never come here on my own with a good book and my journal. I feel conspicuous and the short wait is excruciating.

Amanda Gay was a beauty, but I didn't lust after her as did every other male in her immediate orbit. On the contrary, I've always found giant breasts humorous in the extreme. Some women don't like being made love to by a fellow who can't stop giggling. She was a musical stylist, had a unique way of rearranging popular songs in their flat or sharp keys. Whenever we were playing in the same burg she would seek me out and we would sneak off for a quiet drink and a chat. She would hold my hand. We were at a hotel bar during a convention of college booking agents once when some kid wearing his ball cap backwards, knee-length shorts, and sneakers that didn't match, approached her drunkenly and without once making eye contact with her said in a loud voice, "Hellacious tits!" I put down my drink and was reaching for his throat when she stood up majestically, pulled back her shoulders, and raised his chin to meet his poor vapid gaze, and without a trace of gratitude said, "Thank you."

My friends arrive and the frenzy begins. These are tough-nosed, school of hard knocks, self-employed people who see the world differently than most corporate or government employees. Most people have to do the job hunt boogie half a dozen times in their lives. Self-employed individuals essentially have to look for work every day. Jaded, edgy, and angry, they have a very practical appreciation of how things do and do not work; of whom they can and cannot trust. They also have a deep and abiding loyalty to anyone who ever got them a gig, made them a sale, or sent a hot prospect their way. We have all met through our various professions. We enjoy each other's company but we will never be what you might call "close." That's fine with us. Somewhere deep down we all know that before long we will disperse, life's imperatives will carry us away from one another. We've also reached an age where death is more and more likely. So we know how to savor the moment.

Cid is a real estate agent. Divorced. Unlike most real estate scum, he's a real bright guy, but he just walks around enraged all the time. He blows up at stupid and inept retail clerks. Warm beer makes him furious. During the first Gulf War those "We Support Our Troops" banners would make him go berserk. "How many people are you willing to kill to remain dependent on foreign oil? You! I mean you, personally, how many?" he would accost some unsuspecting patriot. Everywhere Cid looks he sees inanity and stupidity closing in all around him. His healthy reflex is to lash out to create neutral space for himself. As soon as he sits down he's at it again, red-faced over some idiot in the parking lot. I order a half-and-half and make an attempt to alter the course of his harangue. What's the use of challenging every damn fool in your path? I argue, forgetting the fight I was dying to pick with the dweeb on the Metro platform. Cid has been practicing Zen for a while. He says it's to calm him down, but I feel it has contributed to his frustrations. I'm not sure it's wise to integrate universes, metaphysically, I mean. Being Aware is one thing, but trying to bring that Other, whose existence is a surmise at best, to some intersection with the corporeal is potentially dangerous, if you ask me. It certainly hasn't calmed Cid down any.

Earl Riles is another one. Another musician. A perfectionist. He gets in these incredible funks. Hates everybody. He wears black all the time, and, although several people at the bar have recognized him, he is oblivious. Tonight we'll all troop back to his place and sit up drinking Pernod and he'll just let it all out. The world, according to Earl, is a place without love. He believes romance is pathetic. This belief renders him hopelessly romantic to his dark legion of followers. He, too, sees uselessness and dreck everywhere he looks. All Earl wants is a little recognition and respect. When he gets it, he finds it to be hideous and deformed. He wants to lash out as well. But at what? I've been hearing these laments all my life and I wonder about the syndrome at large.

As this familiar rant reaches its apogee, I'm trying to remember a passage from Henry Miller's *The Air-Conditioned Nightmare*, penned in 1944,

> *As to whether I have been deceived, disillusioned... The answer is yes, I suppose. I had the misfortune to be nourished by the dreams and visions of great Americans—the poets and seers. Some other breed of man has won out. This world which is in the making fills me with dread. I have seen it germinate; I can read it like a blue-print. It is not a world I want to live in. It is a world suited for monomaniacs obsessed with the idea of progress—but a false progress, a progress which stinks. It is a world cluttered with useless objects which men and women, in order to be exploited and degraded, are taught to regard as useful. The dreamer whose dreams are not utilitarian has no place in this world. Whatever does not lend itself to being bought and sold, whether in the realm of things, ideas, principles, dreams or hopes, is debarred. In this world*

the poet is anathema, the thinker a fool, the artist an escapist, the man of vision a criminal.

I perceive the same sense of abandonment in Cid and Earl. I feel it too, somewhat. Cid, Earl, and myself are lucky in that we are able to stay mobile. I am always on the road. Cid likes to travel and Earl gets gigs twice a year in Europe, where they treat him like an artist rather than an ornament or an afterthought as they do here in the States.

Agnes has joined us and is taking us all in with a grain of salt and a shot of tequila. She waits to get a word in edgewise and then informs us that she has problems too. Her boyfriend has dumped her. "Good riddance!" we all agree, then vote to move on to another topic. Not good enough. Agnes wants a pound of male flesh, but she's come to the wrong place. We're only willing to cough up an ounce apiece. Why are men like this? Where is he? Have we seen him? He must have another girl. That's it, isn't it? You guys are protecting him! What an asshole thing to do!

"The problem we have here," I interrupt, "is that you're the dump-ee and he is the dump-er."

"I've been dumped on all right!"

"Well, yes, but you see, in this situation, when you are the dump-ee, all you are left holding onto are a lot of worthless conjectures. Where is he? Where did you go wrong?, etc. It's like this big iron door slams shut on you, and you're locked in this deep dark Conjecture Chamber where the most complicated personal questions are posed, and, since you are suddenly cut off from the data flow, out of the loop, those questions can only be answered hypothetically by your deepest fears and insecurities. These horrific negative scenarios are displayed over and over as if on a big-screen TV for your own private torment. No good can come from spending time in the conjecture chamber. What's worse is, the longer you stay in there, the farther from reality you stray. So, when and if you do emerge, the farther you have to go to make it back."

"OK, that's exactly where I am. Now how do I get out?"

"You have to change the subject, but it doesn't occur to you to change the subject when you're in the Conjecture Chamber because that's not the Conjecture Chamber's function. So something has to be randomly introduced that changes the subject naturally."

"Like getting rid of the hiccups," Cid says to Earl, tossing him a wink.

"It's pitiful being the dump-ee. I wish he would take me back just so I could dump him and see how he likes it in there," she scowls. Now she's slid from anger to depression. She turns to Cid for some positive reenforcement, but his divorce has left him cynical and broke all the time. When he realizes it's his turn to speak, he shrugs and says, "Look, you're in love. You thought he would be different."

A heavy silence descends.

Agnes watches that weight settle on our brows, then lets us know she isn't finished. Cid's last remark has pissed her off again. She is dangerously close to tossing the lot of us in the same boat with her despised lost love. "Men, you're all brain damaged at birth. It's a scientific fact. Did you know that?"

She's got our attention.

"I've always suspected it was something like that," I say, trying to humor her but a little afraid that she might be onto us.

"It's true. In the womb we all begin as females, then, when the first jolt of testosterone gushes through the forming corpus callosum, it turns you into males and turns your brains to shit. All of you. Shit for brains. That's what I'm going to call him from now on. Shit for Brains." That said, she looks at us defiantly, awaiting rebuttal. We look at each other stupidly and launch into a discussion of contemporary films.

Cid quit going to the movies years ago. Can't remember the last film he went to see. "They're all made for adolescents. Super heros, pirates, cartoons, and TV sitcoms pretending to be movies. Films made for people my age are about depraved serial killers or drug addicts. I have zero interest or empathy for either."

Amanda Gay's death has jerked my mind around in another direction. I'm thinking of a worrisome spate of films to come out in the past decade also aimed at teenagers. Films like *Mr. Destiny*, *Ghost*, *Ghost Dad*, *Weekend at Bernie's*, *Weekend at Bernie's II*, and a whole bunch more, all with this cavalier, sophomoric, thoughtless attitude toward death. It's healthy, I think, to whistle past the graveyard, but these films take us somewhere else. Death as adolescent situation comedy. Death as cartoon. Death as just another bogus adventure in our frivolous and bogus lives. No discovered nugget of wisdom;

no mirrored image of obvious truth revealed. It's a classic bait and switch, a quest for frivolous sex is interrupted by an equally frivolous death. As superficial and interchangeable as shopping and fucking. Love and death. Shopping and fucking. And where do young people go to see these films? Shopping malls.

Agnes comes bursting out of the Conjecture Chamber with a vengeance. Her expertise is in urban planning, and if there's one thing that can set her blood to boiling, it's shopping malls. She sees them as the perfect link between corporate television advertising and consumers without the disturbing notion of community and social responsibility interfering with the exchange of funds from lower class to higher. You needn't feel responsible for buying your shoes from the local retailer who is also your neighbor because there is no longer a local shoe retailer. And your neighbor? Screw him. You've never even met.

Cid unexpectedly takes a turn in the Conjecture Chamber wondering why it is so. Why do people frown on the solid urban brick dwellings built to last a century, downtown, where everything is convenient and you don't even need a car, to the prefab claptrap pasteboard houses that cost twice as much.

Earl is eating it up. He launches a rant of his own. The opposite of love is not hate, but death. And into this loveless void, the one Agnes's ex-boyfriend has jettisoned her, and now all of us, into, the anxious citizens of the world will live in the music-less hateful ugly void that they so richly deserve.

I abandon them to their joyous nihilism to watch a hockey game on the bar's television, keeping one ear on the conversation lest it turn carnivorous.

"Yes, you *can* take it with you!" is the subliminal corporate message being insidiously injected into our doped-up psyches. Alone and unloved, our culture has been driven to the edge of an abyss we are only dimly aware of. Why? Because the consciousness of the hive is stupefied and two dimensional.

Don't tell Mom, the babysitter is dead.

Miller was right, we were nourished by great American poets and seers. He was one himself. But as I look around the room all I see are Earl, Agnes, Cid, and myself among the automatons. Earlier post–World War II eras had their intellectual heros. Ginsberg and

Kerouac, Adlai Stevenson, Bob Dylan, Gene McCarthy, Hunter Thompson, Rock'n'Roll. Now we look around and realize we have only each other. The field is barren. We have, for tonight at any rate, formed an inebriationed Star Chamber in which Amanda would have felt right at home. We have broken on the wheel of our mutual anxieties the poor, guilty, overpaid slob from the Metro platform, who is just one of the many co-conspirators threatening to bring darkness down upon our life and times. For the remainder of the night the Conjecture Chamber door will remain open, and we enter and exit at will. Politics, mysticism, and human relations are played out upon its grand screen. We agree to recognize the possibility that a new dark age may well be upon us but at least we'll not have to face it alone.

We break it up at five a.m. I stumble out of Earl's place as delightfully pickled as a fellow can be. I remove the T-top from my Oldsmobile, fire up a cigar, pop a fresh brewski, and cruise home through the park. The tall lush trees of the Empire Capital undulate luxuriously in the cool springtime air. Amanda loved the T-top. She would designate me her charioteer, undo our seat belts, and cuddle next to me on the bench seat, knees drawn up, her crazy hair whipping my face as we blazed through the summer night. Now, the angst, hubris, and delirium of the evening have already fallen from me like old skin. Amanda was killed four months ago, a few days after the new year. She was jogging, wearing headphones. Got struck by a car. Two thousand admirers and fans went to her funeral. I only heard of it the other day when asking an agent from her hometown Chicago what she was up to. I had sent her a card saying, "Have A Hellacious Holiday."

I blow her a kiss from my dark and happy night.

JIM PATTERSON, AKA Jimmy Pheromone, crisscrossed North America for fifteen years in the 1980s and 1990s as a member of the satirical pop music duet, The Pheromones. He was born in Washington, D.C., and has spent his life sipping beverages with the drones who turn the wheels and wheel the deals in The Capital of the Empire. He is the publisher of SportsFan Magazine *and the author of* "Bermuda Shorts" *and* "Roughnecks." *Find him at www.jamesjpatterson.com.*

FROM *The Only American Waiter*

Michael arrived at the Rio around six to get prepped for the seven o'clock first feature. That required rewinding the last two reels from the night before. Adam had left him a note that he had had three splices to make and couldn't do the rewind. If Michael had just run the reels as they were expecting them to be in order, they would have appeared backwards on the screen. The kids would have loved that, but there were enough natural disasters with the old equipment and abused reels that came to them in metal canisters week after week. Miguel Fernandez, the part-time usher, was waiting for Michael when he arrived with word that a tall Rastaman named Freddie had been by looking for him. Fernandez and the other ushers showed up early to stock the candy counter and get the popcorn machine up to speed. The appearance of Rasta Freddie in the hood was great news to Michael. He asked Fernandez into the booth to query him further and asked him to send the Rastaman straight up when he returned. Rastaman Freddie was a D.C. native who earned his dreads in Negril with his band, Free Hawks. They were an excellent mix of reggae, rock, and what the D.C. kids called Go-go music. He also had the line on good Jamaican smoke. It looked as if Michael's prayers were being answered. Soon he would be rich again.

High Plains Drifter was the first feature. Michael had seen it a hundred times, but he always loved to watch the midget, Billy Curtis, in what he consider the best performance in the film—other than Clint's, of course. Everybody in the hood loved Clint, even if he was a white muthafucka. He was a man, true to his word. He was a man who never took advantage of lesser men. That code was integral

396

to the way of life in the hood. The strong protected the weak, and everybody protected each other from the cops. Only outsiders broke the code. Michael was cueing up the first reel of the second feature, when Fernandez banged loudly on the metal door to the booth. "Hold yur fuckin' horses!" Michael shouted, with his head buried in the film gate. He was looping the film through its series of sprockets that eventually led it to the light. "All right all ready, I'm coming," he yelled when he had everything under control. He always got a little nervous just before a reel change, as he was new to the film thing. Albums and 45s he could cue with his eyes closed. When he heard the sound was on track, for the second reel, he opened the door, and there was tall, thin Fernandez in his Sergeant Pepper coat. Standing next to him was the even taller Rasta Freddie. Michael yelled, "Hey man!" and invited them both in. He thanked Fernandez, who pulled out a sketch from his ever-present art pad. It was a cartoon-like characterization of Rasta Freddie in colored charcoal. Michael and Freddie both praised Fernandez, who shyly accepted. Fernandez was going to be a famous comic book illustrator someday. He was young and full of dreams. The two old friends, Michael and Freddie, began to rap about old times and the music biz and eventually about the subject of herb. Freddie told Michael he should come down to Kilamanjaro where his band was opening for King Sunny Ade. He said he'd get him backstage and introduce him to a brother that was lookin' to off-load some weight. He said he could get a front, if he was sure he could turn it in a hurry. Michael assured him he could turn a half over by Sunday noon. They decided to burn a spliff and then watched the second reel together. Freddie had to get to his gig, so he split, saying, "Later man." Michael responded, and Fernandez gave Freddie the cartoon of him playing guitar amid some palm trees and a Rasta lion he had added to the picture while he listened to the brothers rap. Freddie was thrilled with it and invited Fernandez along to the show.

At the end of the third film, Michael gave Fernandez the bad news, that he was not going along to Kilamanjaro. He was a little young for such an adventure, and there was the additional business of coppin' a front that made it awkward for anyone to be along. Michael knew he would have to rap to the dude, with the Jamaican, and having a long-hair college kid along would only mess up the deal.

Michael was all business about the business of herb. He finished all the rewinding and cleaned the booth of the leftover beer bottles and carry-out containers, then hustled off to meet Freddie. It was almost midnight and Freddie's band would be going on soon for the final set of the night.

He was walking as fast as he could through the pitch-black streets. It was just on the edge of cold. He folded his scarf tightly around his neck, and looked in all directions, as he turned down the empty side street that led to the rear of Kilamanjaro. The stage door was open, and he could hear a band tuning up; each instrument was racing through its favorite riffs, making final adjustments. He spoke to the guy sitting on a bar stool at the entrance, telling him he was a friend of the bass player. Rasta Freddie noticed him and waved him in. Freddie was on stage checking his amp and he motioned to Michael to join him. Under the cloud of warm-up sounds, Freddie introduced Michael to a big Jamaican dude named Clive. They spoke freely on the stage, with the drummer creating perfect cover as he pounded out the basic rhythm that moved the crowd of happy reggae fans. Michael offered to get them a couple of Red Stripes and agreed to meet with Clive outside, in the bus with the pastoral landscape of Negril painted on its sides. Freddie took his beer and signaled to the drummer to start the show. The snare rang out with a rim shot that sounded like a .30-30. At once, the crowd was on its feet and the music swallowed up the house like a Caribbean heat wave. Michael stood by the side of the stage, grooving to the music and watching Freddie sing and strum his songs of love and revolution. Michael was feeling great. Many women, white and black, suburban and urban, swayed to the hypnotic beat of the Free Hawks. After the last song, Clive signaled Michael to join him in the bus. Now that he had been sanctified, he could come and go through the stage door at will.

"Freddie says you're cool, mon. Can ya turn a half? Have to be quick, mon." Clive reached into an empty drum case at the back of the bus and pulled out a half pound of sweet Jamaican in a large zip lock. "If I front ya mon, I got to have the green by Sunday noon. We be pulling out for Philly then. Can ya make me proud, mon?"

"Yeah, man I'm working at the Cafe Dog on Saturday, a double shift. I'll see everybody there and I'm sure I'll have your money by closing time."

Clive was very laid-back, very Rasta, and he seemed pleased, though he felt it necessary to lay down the heavy line so there would be no misunderstanding. "Cool runnin's man, I got ya down for four hundred American. Take the knapsack and bring it back on Sunday, with the money in an envelope inside. No fuckin' up mon. And don't say nothin'. Just ask for me. I'll be loadin' out the gear. If the door's locked, pound on it! Ya dig me mon?"

"Yeah Clive, I got ya. And thanks a lot man, really. I won't let ya down."

"Of course you won't, mon. Now I gotta catch the rest of the show. Ya comin' back in mon?"

"No thanks Clive, I'm gonna get to work, I can probably sell some tonight if I hurry over to Slaggers and see who's about. I'll catch ya on Sunday unless you wanna come by the Dog for a beer Saturday afternoon. You know where it is, right across from the Rio Theater?"

"Maybe so mon, maybe so. Make me proud White Boy."

"For sure man, for sure. I'll see ya later. OK?"

Clive returned to the music and Michael headed for the 7-Eleven to get some sandwich Baggies. There was a cop in the joint so Michael bought a loaf of Wonder Bread and a small French's mustard plus a package of sliced bologna, for cover. He stood at the cash register with the knapsack over one shoulder while the cop looked at the magazine rack. He didn't let on anything. He was sure the cop couldn't smell a thing where he was. Michael politely said thanks to the Bangladeshi guy behind the counter and headed out without ever acknowledging the cop. Outside, he breathed a bit easier, as he moved quickly towards the Dungeon. He had to find his hang scale and get to work making up half Zs and ounces. No nickel-bag bullshit for Michael. That was all too much chase, too little play. Besides, he had learned over the years it doesn't pay to mess with cheapskates. They always complain. No, it was ounces or half ounces only and cash up always. He looked through his dresser, tossing socks and T-shirts over his shoulder, as his eyes and brain worked feverishly together to locate the Middle-Eastern-style hang scale. It was lying under some audio-cassettes of antinuclear demonstrations he had recorded in Malcolm X Park. He stretched the string out on the round Formica table and Scotch Taped it into place, so that the scale hung over the edge without slipping. It twisted and finally settled into a stable, balanced position. Now he was ready to begin the fine art of product packaging. Happily, the buds were big and fresh, so there wouldn't be a need to select and arrange, as was usually the case with Mexican.

In about twenty minutes, Michael had made up two ounces and four halfs. He figured that was enough to get started with. He placed them in a large manila envelope and tossed it in his knapsack along with a towel he used to flesh out the sack a little. He also twisted up three joints for the bartenders as samples, then he looked in the fridge and pulled out the only remaining beer, popped the top, and headed off to Slaggers to find some late-night customers.

Slaggers was rockin' when he arrived, but it wasn't really a great marketplace for pot. It was more of a coke bar. Michael did pass out a couple of the joints to his friendly bartenders and asked them, in turn, to pass on the word that he'd be at the Dog all day and night on Saturday. While there, he did manage to sell one half Z to one of the waitresses who loved good Jamaican. He had a beer at the bar, and stood for a while listening to Mike Cotter's Band. Then he headed up to the Dog to look for more customers and check in with Abe, the Afghan owner. He wanted to let him know, for sure, that he would be on the floor Saturday. The neighborhood was jammin', and Michael felt he was right with the world. He moved as if guided by a cosmic force. He gave his favorite bartender, Khan, his last joint and had a couple beers with him, talking big bullshit about the filthy Russian invaders. The Soviet occupation of Afghanistan was a constant topic at the Dog. Khan held a particular hatred for President Babrak Karmal, having gone to college with him and having played soccer with him in the streets of Kabul. He always said, "I kicked his fuckin' ass when we were kids, and someday I'll kick his communist ass out of office too." Khan always finished his speech with a European version of the finger. Khan was an international man, smooth, educated, thin, and handsome. Everybody loved him. He was as American as anybody, but he had an eternal presence, like he'd been reincarnated many times over. You got the feeling he had ridden with Genghis Khan. He was swift, like the Hashishins, but he had the nonviolent exterior manners of Gandhi.

It was almost one thirty in the morning when the owner, Abe, Khan's uncle, came in. He had been in the U.S. for over twenty years, and he had worked his ass off to bring his family over to a better life. He was a jovial man and was always helping out fellow Afghans as well as his American patrons. He cashed checks for them when the banks were closed, helped them fix cars or move furniture, or whatever else they needed. It was like his patrons were an extension of his Persian family. Michael had been befriended by him when Abe offered him a part-time job waiting tables on the sidewalk. He knew Michael knew nothing of the restaurant business, but Abe liked him, and he knew Michael knew everybody in the neighborhood. It was good business and good citizenship to offer Michael a few days a week, until he got his rock 'n' roll feet back on the ground. Michael would always be grateful to Abe, and he admired him for his leadership role in the Afghan community in exile. Michael had been the only American to protest with the exiles in front of the Soviet embassy. He had helped them burn the Soviet flag, and he gave a speech through the bullhorn in front of the State Department. They were always happy to see each other.

Abe had come in to close up and count the money. He had a kabob carry-out restaurant in Virginia that he closed at eleven, then he headed into the city to finish up his usual sixteen-hour day. He had the stamina of an Afghan warrior. Michael loved and respected him, as he did all the exiles. He wondered why his own people had become so lazy and self-centered. It was a sad thing that had happened to America since World War II. A generation of self-righteous whiners had sprung up to take over the culture. Michael was so glad he had left all that behind in some bullshit top-forty radio studio. All that was part of an ugly America he didn't want anything to do with. This world of immigrants, offbeat rock 'n' rollers, and poor people was his America. Abe greeted him with a slap on the back, as he sat talking to Khan.

"Hey boss, how's it goin'?" Michael responded with a laugh and a hug.

"Are you working Saturday?"

"Yeah, if you need me. Will the patio be open?"

"If weather is good, we open sidewalk. If weather is bad, we put you inside."

"OK. Great, I can always use the money."

Peg called Khan down to the service bar with the familiar plea. "Order up!"

Michael finished his beer and said good night to Khan, then he spotted a couple of potential customers in the back booth sitting with Blade Sylvester. He waved, and they motioned him over. The juke was blasting "New York, New York" by Sinatra. The room was filled with conversation and laughter. It was after two a.m. when Michael finally headed out the door to get some sleep.

Saturday was going to be a successful day; all he needed was to sell a couple Zs and make a decent amount on the tables, and he'd have Clive's dough. It would be easy. Then he could sell the rest of the half at his leisure and make his profit. He showed up at the Dog just before noon to set up for the sidewalk, but it was too cold. So he sat inside and drank coffee and helped get the dining room set. The place was dead and so was Michael. The stuffed Great Dane above the transom was livelier. The original owner had been a hunter, and the walls were decorated with his trophies in glass cases. All beautifully mounted, with background rocks and brush. There was a wild goose, a fox, an otter, even a seven-foot diamondback, coiled and ready to strike at any worthless drunk who might try to peer in. The art of taxidermy was a lost art, and these highly unusual and tacky examples of it were the source of numerous culinary jokes. The Great Dane had been the owners' beloved pet, also the source of the bar's nickname. The real name on the license was Café Don, after the owner. People in the hood had taken to calling it "the Dog" after the original owner had passed away. He had had the Great Dane mounted a long time ago in the mid-fifties. The current crowd had no knowledge of him, except for his stuffed animals. Abe had added a slogan to the menu, right below the AKA. It read, "Style but no Class!" He was proud of that little bit of humor. The cook was a woman named Bizzle, and the Saturday bartender was one of her friends, a woman named Sheila. They were raucous and humorous women, both capable of wisecracks or come-ons, whichever was in order.

Michael hated waiting for business, and it seem like forever before a couple of regulars came in to take a seat at the bar. They gave him two quarters and asked him to punch up B17 and P31. Joni Mitchell livened the joint up with "Free Man in Paris" and Sheila sang along. Michael paced near the front door, looking out the window, hoping for customers with double interests. The day strained along until around three when Michael got the first of the customers he was hoping for. He managed to sneak a transaction in while serving a burger and a couple of beers to a pair of regulars, and then around six o'clock he sold an ounce to a guy he knew from a poetry reading at Slaggers. In between tables, he read the paper. He was worried about Reagan gaining ground on the campaign trail, but, like most of his friends, he thought it would be a cold day in hell before the country went back to Nixon-style government. The hostage issue dominated the news, and it was generally accepted wisdom that the country wouldn't change presidents in the middle of this stream.

As the evening wore on, it became clear he would have enough special customers. At seven, Khan came back on duty and said a guy he knew was interested. By ten, Michael was nearing his goal. He sold an ounce standing on the empty patio, using the bus station as a counter. It was easy; all his customers knew how to lay their money down out of plain view. They knew to carry on a pretend conversation while he placed their Z in a carry-out box, which he then placed in a white paper bag. Michael calmly counted out their money and pretended it was an official restaurant order. The customers would make a big thank you and goodbye gesture, then go on their merry way to a waiting car or walk off down the street. They would carry the order flat, as if it were the real thing. Nobody was ever the wiser. Michael believed the best way to handle things was to do them in the open. Nonchalance in the restaurant. Nobody gave a damn anyway. Michael stood on the patio, looking at the passing street scene and smoking a Marlboro. The tables inside were all covered by his coworker, Sandy. His pockets were starting to bulge, and he patted them lovingly. He returned to the tables inside after his cigarette and finally took off his apron at two in the morning. He had managed to sell everything he had brought to work and picked up almost sixty bucks after tipping out. He had a couple of drinks after closing with the crew and then walked Sandy down the street to her building. He turned left on 18th, headed to the Dungeon for a few hours sleep before he was to open the Spanish movies at one o'clock. He was dead-dog tired and drunk to boot.

At noon, Michael woke up like a scared cat and realized he was going to be late to meet Clive. He threw on the nearest things that appeared to be clothing, and then—without shower, shave, or the brushing of

teeth—he ran the three blocks to Kilimanjaro and started pounding on the locked stage door. No answer. More pounding, still no
answer. He had forgotten to strap on his watch, so he wasn't sure
how much time he had. He went around to the front entrance and
pounded, but no answer. Then he scanned the area for something
to write on. Michael always had a pen with him. Seeing nothing to
write on, he peeled a poster off the wall and dashed back around
to the stage door. He wrote to Clive, telling him he had gone to the
Rio Theater and that Joe would let him into the booth, if he asked.
He ended the note with the phrase "cool runnin's" and hoped Clive
would find it, as he folded it in half, and stuck it in the crevice of the
stage door, with about a third of it protruding.

The Spanish movies were mostly from Mexico and mostly ran-
chero-type Mexican Westerns, with some detective movies, plus old-
fashioned comedies starring Cantinflas. The Spanish movies drew
several hundred people every Sunday and were far more successful
than the regular shows that ran Monday through Saturday nights.
Sunday night was usually dead for the Anglo movies too, dead as a
doorknob. Michael wondered, why not just run Spanish movies all the
time. The owners of the theater didn't really care, they just wanted
to meet payroll while they held onto the property. They, like other
landlords, were stuck, waiting for things to improve. Waiting for that
mystery buyer, or waiting for the neighborhood to change back to
the white-middle-class bastion it had been prior to the late sixties.
That was not going to happen, and that was fine with Michael. He
loved seeing all the Latin families with their children, all dressed
up in traditional costume. All of them were proud to be living in
El Norte. They were raising their *niños y niñas* away from the problems of home and still being true to their culture. The theater was
filled with screaming children still dressed up from church. Proud
parents beamed, even though they held the lowest level jobs in the
Washington food chain. They didn't waste money on superfluous
self-aggrandizement. They toiled day and night and sent money
home. They were all proud to be able to send U.S. postal money
orders home, week after week. They ensured a better life for their
loved ones, south of the border. These people, these illegals, were
true Americans in spirit, and Michael loved working for them. He
also enjoyed watching the movies from his window high above the

audience. It didn't matter that he couldn't speak the language; the plots were simple and the women all had mucho cleavage. He could have been a projectionist in any language, because of the little cue dots in the upper right-hand corner of the screen. The system was the same in French, Spanish, or Italian. He was watching a chase scene on horseback through the Sierra Madras when the knock came at the door. It was Joe ushering in Rasta Freddie and Clive. Obviously they had gotten the note and seemed pleased to be in the unusual world of a projectionist's booth. Michael locked the door after Joe left and proceeded to count out Clive's money. Clive was happy that Michael had lived up to his billing, and they vowed to get together next trip to D.C. They had no time to waste, and both Rastas left together for a club date in Philly. Michael thanked Freddie as he shut the door behind them. Then he attended to hand cranking the rewind of reel number one of the first Spanish feature.

JIM REED was a radio disc jockey in the Washington market at several stations, but his radio career ended abruptly when he refused to play the Bee Gees on a progressive station. He started as a sound effects man and announcer on The Bozo Show *in Orlando. He was a founding committee member and stage manager of Adams Morgan Day, and was stage manager of the Ontario Theater during the early days of the New Wave/ Punk invasion. Reed has had one-man shows at D.C. Space, Washington Project for the Arts, and the 9:30 Club. His TV documentary writing credits include* The Making of a Holiday, *hosted by Lavar Burton on NBC, and* The Dream Today: Hodding Carter Reports *on PBS. Currently, he produces the radio documentary,* Downing Street/Layfayette Park, *available on the website AfterDowningStreet.org. Novel #2 is in the oven; it's called "Grain of Truth."*

Where I Want

JEFF RICHARDS

I decided a long time ago that if I couldn't have what I want, I could at least live where I want. That would be Verde, New Mexico. If you're driving north in the mountains on State Highway 33 a mile before the *Welcome to Santa Fe National Park* sign, you come to a bend in the road. In front of you, you'll see a sturdy red wood bridge over a burbling, rock-strewn creek, next to it a small adirondack made out of the same wood, where the students huddle in the wintertime waiting for the Mora School District bus.

On the other side of the bridge is a dirt road that cuts through an aspen grove before it disappears into a dark forest of hemlocks, much like a dark forest in a child's fairy tale where the wolves are waiting to grab anyone who wanders off the path. It's a gauntlet you have to fly through before you wind up the mountain to Baldy Pass, a bare patch of land that gives you a 360-degree view. The edge of the world. All you can see are the mountains rising in the distance like humpback whales in a blue sea. Or sometimes you can see a black cloud in the distance and a jagged streak of lightning followed by a clap of thunder that bounces from one mountain to another until you are surrounded by thunderclaps. It's an exhilarating feeling to stand on this mountain, which I do about every morning after I run. I'm in the most god-awful wonderful shape.

Below me in the valley is the Rio Verde. It winds its way through the green fields and the town before it disappears in Baldy Canyon. I've run that canyon a half dozen times in a kayak and nearly killed myself every time. Once I broke my leg and the wife dragged me out of the kayak screaming. She fashioned a splint out of a couple pieces

406

of wood, slung me over her shoulder, and hauled me up a rocky path to an outcropping halfway up the canyon. It took her about an hour. Then she lay me down gently and scurried up the rest of the path to find Ed, her lover at the time.

My life's been pretty rotten up to now and that's why I want to live where I want. The reason it's so rotten is that I've been married too many times, two to be exact, less by one than my mother. I'll tell you the places I've lived growing up. Vernal, Utah. Winnemucca, Nevada. San Francisco. Seattle. Cleveland. Philadelphia. I even lived in Germany. Mom's second husband was in the armed services. I have one sister. She's lived with a man, but she's never married. She doesn't have children and does not understand why I do.

"What?" She ponders. "You want to ruin another generation?"

I think the best wife I ever had was Verna. But I didn't trust her. I trust the woods. I trust the sky. I trust the mountains. I even trust the weather because when you see dark clouds in the distance, you know that bad weather is headed in your direction. You never know with humans.

When I moved from Winnemucca to San Francisco after my mom divorced my dad, her first husband, Miss O'Grady, my teacher, took pity on me. She was a petite Irish lady with red hair, freckles, and a radiant smile that lit up the classroom. For the first time ever I didn't mind going to school until one day she asked me to stay after class. She was disturbed by my interaction with the other students, especially Freddy Pesky, one of the more popular kids I was trying to impress. Freddy asked me where my father was. I told him that he was a spy for the CIA. He could be in Moscow trying to infiltrate the KGB or he could be running guns to the rebel forces in Nicaragua.

"David, you're a very good boy," said Miss O'Grady. She patted my hand. "I consider you my friend, and, as your friend, I want to tell you that you're making a mistake."

"I am?" I scraped my chair closer to her. She smelled fresh like the clover in Vernal, Utah.

"Yes, darling," she said, in a tender voice that made my legs weak. "I know you're the new boy. You want everyone to like you, but they won't if you tell lies."

That night I dreamed the Russians dive bombed our school. I rescued Miss O'Grady and held her in my arms.

Two days later she caught me telling Freddy that there was a black car outside my house 24-7 with a man in it whose job was to make sure that me, my mom, and sister weren't kidnapped by the KGB.

"David," said Miss O'Grady. "You know what we talked about when I kept you after school."

"Yes, ma'am."

"Then why are you telling stories to Freddy Pesky?" she asked, in a scolding voice.

I turned three shades of red and muttered under my breath that I didn't know why, all the time watching Freddy's face light up in a smirk. I was found out. Freddy pushed me to the ground. He told all the classmates I was a liar. They laughed at me. I hated him. I hated them, but most of all, I hated Miss O'Grady and I swore to God that I'd have nothing to do with another human being as long as I lived.

There were other times I felt this way. With my dad who sent me birthday and Christmas presents for a couple of years after we left him in Winnemucca but never visited. I haven't seen him in thirty years. Or my mother who swore we'd never leave any of the places we left. But she was always kind to me. Or any other number of classmates and teachers in these places. Or my first wife. I don't want to talk about her.

But Verna was different, I thought. She had my mother's kindness without her wandering eye. Then she met Ed.

If you go down the other side of Baldy Pass on the dirt road, you pass through another dark forest of hemlock before you come to a clearing at the edge of town. In the middle of the clearing is a small hill on the top of which is a two-room hut. It reminds me of the woodsman's hut in *The Wizard of Oz*. That's where Ed lives. But he isn't a woodsman. He's a wolf.

Verde has two streets, Main which starts at Ed's hut and ends at a bend of the Rio Verde where the Cattleman's Bar is located, and Water. That's where I live. I have two willows in my yard, two dogs, and six cats. In the winter, the cats sleep in the mudroom in a box on top of each other to keep warm. I love animals.

In the middle of town on the corner of Water and Main is the Baptist Church. We all go there on Sunday mornings even though we aren't all Baptists. It's something to do. On Thursdays, the church turns into a movie theater and once a month it's the town hall. Most of the time though, for entertainment, we go to the Cattleman's. That's where we first saw Ed eleven years ago when Verna and I were freshly married. She was six months pregnant and looked like a barrel, but that didn't bother Ed. He asked her to dance.

One of the things I thought after I broke my leg and Verna hauled me up a rocky path to an outcropping halfway up the canyon was that I was going to die and not from natural causes. I believed that at last they got me where they want me out here in the wilderness three miles from town. Verna and Ed would sneak back several hours later and roll me off the outcropping. I'd dash my brains against the rocks below or drown in the water. My body'd shoot down the rapids to Angel Falls where it would catch up in the hydraulics and spin like a top around and around for an eternity.

I was so frightened of this thought that I tried to think of anything else that would put my mind at ease and what I thought was that maybe I was wrong. What proof did I have that Verna and Ed were lovers? He called her up at all hours and visited our house. They'd sit on the porch and talk nonsense. Sometimes he asked her to dance at the Cattleman's. I saw them kiss but that was under the mistletoe. Is this a love affair? Once I caught her sneaking home at one a.m. She said she lost track of time. She was talking with Ed and a friend, Molly, at his hut. I got mad. I grabbed our wedding picture and broke it against the corner of our fireplace.

"Stop with the drama," she said. "I love you, not Ed."

I tried to keep this in my mind like a mantra. She loves me. She loves me. The funny thing about Verna is that she has red hair and freckles. She reminds me of Miss O'Grady so it was hard for me not to view her with suspicion.

When I heard her and Ed clomping down the trail to rescue me, my heart climbed into my throat. They lifted me onto a canvas stretcher.

"Be careful," I whimpered. I closed my eyes, held tightly to the wooden bars as they inched up the trail. I decided to accept my fate whatever it was. It took another hour, but finally we reached the top. They lowered me down gently on a soft spot of ground covered with pine boughs near the canyon lip. I leaned up on my elbow and stared down at the Rio Verde roiling through the canyon a few hundred feet below. A clean fall. I looked up at Ed and Verna. They both smiled.

"How you feeling, honey?" asked Verna.

They got at either end of the stretcher and lifted up. I could feel myself rolling from side to side. I could feel the pain in my leg where it was broken. I held to the wooden bars. This is it, I was thinking. I closed my eyes and waited, but nothing happened. They turned away from the canyon and headed over the ridge to the town below.

It took Verna a year to gather up the nerve, but finally she and the kids moved to Las Vegas, forty miles southeast in the desert.

"You're the jealous type," she told me.

Ed didn't move with her. That was three years ago, and, as far as I know, Verna's a single mom who works the day shift at the Wonder Bread factory. I signed the divorce papers, but I'm not like my father. I visit the kids all the time. The girl's nine, the boy's eleven. He spends all his time at the local skate park. I tell him to keep his helmet on or he'll break his head. The girl, Lisa, looks like her mom. The same red head. The same freckles. She breaks my heart.

Sometimes I don't want to stop when I make it up to Baldy Pass in the morning. I blow down the dirt road like the wind through the hemlock forest and the aspens. I pull up at the red wooden bridge. I lean against the rail. I look at the license plates of the cars as they round the bend. The cars could be from anywhere. Texas, Louisiana, Pennsylvania, Saskatchewan. I've been to all of those places and more. I like to travel, but right now I need to catch my breath. Marriage is hard. You can't trust it. But living in one place where you want to live is easy. All you got to do is stay put.

JEFF RICHARDS's fiction has appeared in more than two dozen publications including Gargoyle, River City, Southern Humanities Review, *and* Weber Studies, *and forthcoming in* Zone 3 *and* Karamu. *His essays have appeared in* Tales Out of School *(Beacon Press) and* Letters to Salinger *(University of Wisconsin Press). He is a contributing writer to* Blueswax, *the online blues magazine, a native Washingtonian who grew up on Macomb Street, and a present resident of Takoma Park.*

The Mad Mad Magical Misery Tour
B. B. RIEFNER

They spent October in Poland chasing art, amber, and angst. It took two visits to former Nazi extermination camps before Kate Norris labeled it OUR MAD MAD MAGICAL MISERY TOUR. This label certainly applied once Kate and her husband, Street Norris, had visited Auschwitz with its two million or so ghosts eternally pleading for remembrance. Their anger at what they could find no adjectives to describe what was wrought upon these innocents cemented the title. Auschwitz compelled them to continue visiting one extermination facility after another. They traversed Poland, then Hungary with neither really understanding why. After a dozen of the camps, each with bin after bin, even at times whole barracks, filled with eyeglasses, shoes, canes, umbrellas, luggage, human hair, clothes all categorized by sex, size, seasons, and signs of wear, her husband, Street, made some wry comment that they were becoming Misery Junkies. At their final stop, Terezin, Czechoslovakia, they met Henry Geuritz, and that chance encounter cast a completely different light on their collective WHERES.

He came upon them as either the Voice of the Turtle or the Thunder from Mount Sinai as Street and Kate were staring at a plain stone wall pockmarked with hundreds of bullet scars. They were both wondering if children had stood in this place. If each bullet hole represent one child? If they were slaughtered by single shots to the back of their ringlet heads?

"I have only this morning. I wanted to avoid these places, but I find I cannot. Would you help me? Would you show me what is most important for me to see and remember?" Later Street knew that

411

Henry understood what he had to see and why. He simply could not trust himself to go alone. He wanted people, sympathetic people, people who spoke his language, to go with him.

Street's inner voice asked how Henry could assume they were veterans. And what would Henry say if Street were to tell him all his German relatives had been Nazis and that some of them had stuffed Jews into Polish and Russian wooden synagogues, nailed the doors, and set them on fire?

Street Norris was tall, so he was unaccustomed to looking up into faces. It usually disturbed him when he had to raise his focus and communicate with mostly younger beards since his dated back to 1967. However, it took only a few exchanges, a small warm wave of trust washed over him, the type of trust you had in combat for your comrades. A total acceptance without reservations and without regrets.

Terezin is not very large. It consists of just three segments. The school and its dormitories, the guards' barracks, and the crematorium with graveyard attached. Henry bid his farewells an hour later, as they exited the barracks.

As they sat, not certain if they wanted or needed to inspect the final area, Kate mentioned the extermination camp outside of Lodz, Poland, where they had experienced first hand the everlasting shock, sadness, and terror, realizing just how insignificantly small an area it took to contain the ashes of 300,000 or so corpses. As the number sank into his memory slots, Street revisited Majdenek and its ravens.

||||

Majdenek appeared to be just another rerun of barracks filled with mute demands to remember what inhuman events took place there. They were on their way out when they passed a uniformed guard who asked what their thoughts were about the shrine.

The shrine was a huge cement mushroom squatting on the crest of a slight ridge. It was surrounded by a waist-high concrete wall. Its solemn sadness was why they had avoided it.

"You should go there. The entire world should be forced to go up there," the guard muttered as she walked away.

Guilt ridden, Street tried to offer one last excuse. "It's really late and it's going to rain, Kate." She shrugged and set out. He almost told her he would wait for her in their truck.

When they were near enough, they saw a large flock of ravens sitting on the wall. The birds seemed to be perfectly spaced, like a guard of honor, or at least a choir of monks. The damp chill engulfed them as they stepped under the dome.

As Street waited for his eyes to adjust, a raven gave a cry that resembled a punctured bugle trying to sound Taps. Kate had already reached a second lower wall on the inside of the dome, and her hand was pressed to her mouth as if she were smothering a scream.

When his eyes grew accustomed, he stepped up just as a huge raven landed on the wall to his left and glared at him before it gave a very long loud squawk. The bird seemed alien. Street almost swatted at it, but the unblinking eyes fixed on him and the raven's cry seemed to say, *"We are here not as guards, nor as monuments, but as guides. Our duty is to constantly shock anyone who is about to look into this circle. If you dare. If you dare."*

"Bear!" Street knew Kate was in dire straights whenever she used his nickname. "Oh God. Have you looked in here?" Her tone seemed to mimic the raven's. He knew that was outrageous. Then his eyes fully adjusted to the dim fall twilight, and forced him to look.

All that covered the floor was a pool of grayish powder like ash, about four feet high at its center and less than half that at its outer edges. Then his mind joined his eyes and bits of jawbones and charred elbows and knee joints slowly appeared. Perhaps the bits of dental braces and false teeth won the horror award. The nearest ravens glared at him, daring him to look deeper. He knew he was going to fail that test.

||||

"Street? Where the hell are you, my Bear?"

"Back at Lodz and that pile of ashes. Every time I think about it, I just wonder."

"How can that little pile be 300,000 human beings?"

"I guess it's because they were subhuman."

"That's terrible, Bear."

"As terrible as I can get it."

There was a long pause and then she rose and motioned, "Come on. We've got to go all the way again."

Terezin's burial area was bare except for a huge white cross and a Star of David. Below them stood Henry Geuritz, and, even though they were at least eighteen feet high, Henry dwarfed them and drove them from Street's focus. Henry stood directly between them, a blue-striped white prayer shawl draped over his shoulders and a black yarmulke fastened to the crown of his large head as if held there by a driven nail. They waited while he bobbed back and forth, chanting Kaddish, the Jewish prayer for the dead, in an operatic baritone. His wondrous voice resonated across the clean unmarked graves. It passed over the cross and caressed the star. Its echoes flew over the low stone walls like a group of bombers streaking through the ash gray sky as if they would seek out and destroy forever and ever. Street heard Kate's sobs as he cursed his Nazi relatives in tempo with Henry's lament.

When he was done, Henry was so physically and emotionally exhausted, he staggered for balance. So Street rushed across the short space between them and embraced him. It seemed that he had to support Henry's entire weight for hours before he could help him back to the stone bench. There they all sat, completely mute.

"That was your prayer for the dead, wasn't it?" Street lamely offered, trying to end the numbing silence.

"Yes, but this time I was really only praying for the dead. Not to God as I am obligated." He whispered this as if God could hear. "God was never here," he sobbed. "These children never believed God would come to protect them." He shook his head so that the two sets of tears would leave his cheeks without scars. He had better control when he continued. "Which is why today we Jews have no choice. We are alone. We are our only source of love and comfort and protection. From here on, only we are responsible for our future." Then Henry rose and kissed each of them on the cheek before marching off, cleaving a great wake between the anguish of the past and the potential for its eventual rebirth.

"That's exactly what the world has become," Kate pronounced when she finally broke the silence and blotted the tears with her woolen mittens.

"Tell me exactly what you felt."

"I know that he cut right through all the middle men. All of them. Buddha, Allah, Mohammed, the Son, the Holy Ghost, even Mary. Henry swept away all the layers of middle management." She shook her head as if silently trying to offer an argument, then added very forcefully, "Somehow he's allowed to. No Maybe entitled to is better. I just don't know. But what I do know is when he was out there, he cut right through to the CEO. I'm sure if there is a God or a Divine Designer for all of this, Henry got The Boss's attention. And for a change The Boss heard nothing but the truth."

"And what did Henry tell The Boss?"

"Oh, Bear! I'm too emotionally drained for pop quizzes."

"Please try."

She frowned, glanced at him, her eyes searching him to be sure he really wanted to hear her thoughts before she growled, "That we've had enough tests to see how strong our love for Whomever is."

"Whew."

"Well, you asked for it," she spat as she rose and started for the twin smoke stacks of this manmade Hades. Street followed at a respectful distance. It was at that instant he felt the layers of horrors past, present, and future, part for Kate, then crash back on him, forming a wave demanding that he ride it toward WHERE or drown. And as he did, he marveled at how dramatically his insights into his beloved expanded as this wave of rationality grew.

B. B. RIEFNER has retired from being a jazz musician, football jock, Marine, life and body guard, educator, athletic coach, and long-distance hiker. He is still a world traveler, wildlife photographer, multimedia creator, published author, and in love with his wife. His writings center on Who We Are, Where We Are, Our Relationships With Our Fellow Man, and The Universe. His most recent publication is found in Iconoclast *93.*

The Deer

Lewis K. Schrager

Marilyn Shaw found the deer down in the lowest corner of her property, where the stone bridge on Old Glen Road crosses the spring-fed stream that marks the boundary of her land with the Reynolds' to the south. The deer lay on its right side, head and forelegs toward her, hind parts awash in the gentle, pure water, its right, hind leg bent beneath it in some crazy, impossible angle, the hoof protruding out and forward from beneath the girth of the animal along the ridge of its spine. Across its flank and down its back to the level of the water, blood matted its short, brown-gold hairs.

She approached the animal slowly, coming toward it with tentative, muffled steps on the soggy gravel. The cool April air, still belonging more to the night than the new day, carried the scents of earth and water that drew her back here each morning; pure, natural, life-affirming scents that, as if charged with some magical life-giving essence, somehow cleansed from her the despair that came upon her in the dark, quiet hours of the night. The actual touch of the water upon her face completed the cleansing; water scooped in her small but still-strong hands, cold against the ring she wore on her left thumb against the wishes of her husband not as jewelry but as a sign, a token of remembrance (as if forgetting ever was a possibility), a silent reminder to herself and all who knew and understood (and the others who cared to ask) of her pain, her loss, her fury. And now, in the midst of the waters far holier to her than those of the Jordan would ever be, this.

She came closer. Two small bony nubs protruded from the top of the young buck's skull. She crouched down before it, steadying herself with outstretched fingers pressed into the moist silt. Her gaze met the eye of the fallen animal, large and brown and frozen open in the stunned ignominy of sudden, unexpected death. The empty glaze of the great open eye reflected the branches of a brook-side poplar dense with buds, a lightening sky beyond, and then a fleeting vision of herself, barely recognizable in the concave distortion of the liquid lens. "I am so sorry," she whispered to the fallen animal. "At least you do not suffer." It's only the living who suffer, she thought. Only the living, left behind to bear the pain.

And then it moved. It snorted once, then lifted its head, flailing out with its front legs, spraying sand and stone in a desperate attempt to rise up. The sudden evidence of frantic life sent her backwards upon the stream bank; the hoof of the upper leg barely missed her shins as she scrambled out of the animal's reach.

As abruptly as the thrashing began, it ended; the head of the animal collapsed back on the bank, its mouth half open, its tongue and snout covered with grit. She stood and wiped her hands upon her pants. Please be dead, she thought. Please, now, be dead. But the quick, small puffs of its steaming breath, the occasional shudder that swept across the animal's hide, gave ample evidence that her plea remained unanswered. "Oh God," she whispered. "What do I do now?"

She headed back down the path past the spring, then out of the cover of the trees. She climbed the hill, ran past her terraced garden, across the broad lawn alongside the house and up the stairs, slammed open the screen door to the porch, then hurried inside. A golden shaft from the rising sun burst in through a side window, illuminating the top of the hutch upon which rested the tightly folded triangle of flag that never had and never would fly free, the portrait, framed in simple black: David Shaw in full Marine uniform, the medallion on his white-banded hat and the medals pinned to his dark dress jacket alive in the day's new light. She glanced at him as she did every time she passed, as she had ever since clearing off David's old (but never dusty) baseball and basketball and football trophies, after boxing up the small, framed pictures of him and Richard (never including herself as she willingly carried the burden of family photographer and documentarian) fly fishing on the upper Potomac, posing with wild ponies at Assateague, hiking through the blue mist of the Smokies, and creating this simple shrine nearly two years before. Often she lingered, to brush her fingers across the folded flag, to whisper something or other; a concern, an observation, a message of regret or love or frustration or, sometimes, anger at his stubbornness, his sense of responsibility and duty and sacrifice unrequited (in her view) by those ultimately responsible for putting him in harm's way. Now she hesitated for only a moment, pausing directly in the path of the light, eclipsing with her own small shadow the single photograph she had of David that had not been taken by her own hand, the proud, hated photograph that had replaced all the others for the simple reason that this was how Richard wanted to remember his—their—son: David the Marine.

She kept a cordless phone in the kitchen. She thought about calling Richard, but called information for the number of the local SPCA instead. She paced the kitchen floor, the telephone held tight to her ear, as the woman's calm voice on the SPCA recording told her to call back during regular office hours or, in case of an injured or threatening animal, to call the county police.

She looked up the number on the scrap of paper pinned to the corkboard above the phone. "EMERGENCY NUMBERS"—written in her own handwriting, in big, block letters across the top, how long ago? Police and fire, the dentist, Dr. Sandra Meyers, her ob-gyn, first to see and touch David, this when her labor proved fruitless despite all her preparation and the dreaded C-section became necessary (after twenty-seven hours of labor Dr. Meyers insisted on the procedure, as much for the baby's well-being as for her own). Dr. Emily Wilcox, David's pediatrician, who thankfully had little to do except chart David's growth, emphasizing the importance of eating right and getting enough sleep and, when the time came, avoiding smoking and drugs and unprotected casual sex (nothing David hadn't heard from her), vaccinating him against measles, mumps, rubella, diphtheria, pertussis, tetanus, meningitis, pneumonia, hepatitis, and who knows how many other of the ancient infectious scourges against which modern medical science had so ingeniously devised protection. Later, there were more vaccinations; cholera, yellow fever, anthrax, among others, administered to him by some anonymous doctor in camouflage dress in a barracks a few hundred miles from here (none too bad except for anthrax, according to David; it swelled his arm three times its size, but got him out of a few days of basic training).

There were the numbers of the neighbors, the Smithsons (long gone after selling their property to developers for an obscene profit); the Reynolds (one heavy line through their name and number, Richard's doing after the county court refused to halt their clearing of a patch of trees on the property just south of the stream). And then, further down, the number for Camp Lejeune, followed by an emergency number that families of Marines sent to Iraq could call, just in case. Just in case. Like the others, these were numbers written in her own hand. Unlike the others, these were numbers she wrote against her will, numbers written with a foreboding so strong as to cause an ache in her chest. Where the other numbers had faded with time, these stood out boldly, mocking her with each grammar-school-perfect flow and curve. Finally, a number for Dr. Dana Simmons, the marriage counselor who told them that the blame that she and Richard shot at each other, like high-caliber bullets at insanely close range, was a common, but misplaced, reaction; who said that it was all-too-usual to have a marriage fall apart after the death of a child, particularly an only child; who emphasized that any decision about the marriage might best be delayed until the shock waves of David's death had passed. As if—.

"County police, Sergeant Henderson." A beep on the line, the call being recorded.

"Marilyn Shaw, 1805 Farmland Road, Damascus. There's a deer down on my property. It looks like it was hit by a car or truck or something. It's hurt bad."

"It's still alive?"

"Yes, Officer."

"Have you called the SPCA?"

"Yes, Officer. Their offices aren't open. The message said to call you."

A pause. "How badly is it hurt?"

"Very. It's back leg is shattered."

A pause. "It's not threatening anyone?"

Marilyn squeezed the phone. "It can't move, Officer. It's lying half in my stream. It's suffering, I know it's suffering." She swallowed hard against the tightness squeezing her throat. "Someone's got to do something."

"Where is it, exactly?"

"Old Glen Road, about three-quarters of a mile south of Farmland, down the hill. It's right there, just below the bridge, on the north bank of the stream."

"Give me your name again."

"Marilyn Shaw. 1805 Farmland Road."

A pause. Clicking sounds of fingers on a computer keyboard in the background. "Richard and Marilyn Shaw?"

"Correct."

A pause. His voice suddenly different, a hint of recognition and, perhaps, sympathy. "David Shaw was your son?"

She closed her eyes. Not was. Is. Is my son. Will always be my son. "Yes," she said.

"He was in school with my Tommy. Tommy used to go over to your house to play football. He said you had a great field."

She looked out the kitchen window to the broad lawn atop the hill. The field. That's what David called it, that's what all the kids called it. She and Richard would watch them out on the field, running, passing, tackling. Rainy-day games were the best, they would slide for ten feet after a tackle. Sometimes they would slide right down the hill toward the woods, clear out of sight. David's clothes would be a mess afterwards, but it was worth it. The way he would smell, of wet grass and earth and cold. Boy smells. She would watch them through this window, through this very window. Tommy Henderson was out there, too. Which one was he? The boy with the white blond hair that flowed behind him like a pony's mane? The boy with the tight, dark curls? The tall boy with the glasses who didn't run much but could throw the ball farther than anyone? Tommy Henderson, right there, out on the lawn, still alive somewhere, still alive to play, to work, to love.

"We were all sorry to hear."

"Thank you."

And then: "What was it? An IED?"

The question, asked as easily as you might ask someone for the time, landed like a sucker punch. An IED? Who are these people? WHO ARE THESE PEOPLE? An IED? As if two vowels and a goddamned consonant could somehow blow a Humvee and three Marines a hundred feet in the air. As if it made any fucking difference to you, Sergeant Henderson, what "it" was.

"Not too many heroes in this town," he said. "He was one of them."

She fought the tears but they came anyway. "Officer, right now there's a deer down on my property. Can you please send someone over? Please? Now?"

"Hold on for a minute." The line went quiet. She searched her pockets for a tissue. Finding none, she wiped a stray tear from her cheek with her finger, then walked back into the family room. The clock on the wall by the window ticked off the seconds like a bomb. A click and he was back. "Ms. Shaw, hate to say it but we can't help you. If the animal's not a threat—"

"Jesus Christ, that animal's out there suffering and you can't do anything?"

"Please try to calm down, ma'am. There's no point in yelling."

She took a deep breath, tried to gather her thoughts. "Listen, what I want to know is whether you can send someone out to help this animal. Yes or no?"

"Ma'am, it's like I told you, we can't unless the animal is threatening—"

She hung up. I'm calling Richard, she thought. I've got to call Richard. She checked the calendar push-pinned into the wall below the clock. Today he's in Singapore, tomorrow Shanghai. She punched the number to Richard's mobile phone into her own, then glanced up at the clock. Ten after six here; what time will it be in Singapore? This is a mistake, she thought as the line buzzed. He hates when I call him when he's on business. Only for emergencies, he says. Well, goddammit, this is an emergency. She paced the floor, her hand sweeping back loose strands of her graying brown hair. Answer the phone, damn it. Please just answer the phone.

He did, on the seventh ring. "What is it?" he whispered.

It was as she feared. "Please, Richard, not like that."

"I'm in the middle of a meeting." In the silence after his sharply whispered reply, in the few quiet moments when her words again stuck in her throat, a woman speaking in the background, her Oriental-accented English distant and tinny. Something about profit margins under pressure.

"There's a deer, Richard."

"A what?"

"A deer. In the stream, by the bridge. It's hurt, badly. Probably hit by a car or truck or something." Silence. In the background, the woman's voice speaking of inventory buildup, projections of demand slowing in the third and fourth quarter. "It's suffering," Marilyn said.

She was looking at David's picture. Even her mother said there was nothing of her in him, he was all Richard. She would often search his face, looking for some sign of herself; her eyes, perhaps, or cheeks or chin. It was true, what her mother said, what everyone said; looking at a picture of him, watching him as he sat down for dinner or did his homework or rode his bicycle or played football on the lawn outside the house with Tommy Henderson and the other boys, he was all Richard. Only when he was frightened, when his brow lowered and eyes narrowed, when his lips tightened down into each other, only then did she see a glimmer of herself in him. Like Richard, he was not one who frightened easily. You don't drop out of college to join the Marines if you frighten easily. And yet, and yet—when he shipped out, she saw, in his face, herself, and wished to God she hadn't.

They would not let her see his face afterwards, they would not let either of them see his face. She had read about what the heat does, how sometimes the goggles melt through the skin right onto the bone, if there is any bone left at all. They were told that he had died instantly, that he did not suffer. DOA—three more letters that seem to roll off the tongue, letters she wanted to believe in, needed to believe in. DOA—an almost magical incantation. DOA. No suffering. There was no suffering. But with all the lies, how could she believe anything they told her?

"It's suffering, Richard. I don't know what to do. What should I do?"

"Call the SPCA."

"I already did."

"And?"

"No one's in. The voicemail message said to call the police."

"And?"

"They weren't any help."

"Then just leave it be."

"I told you—"

"I heard. It's suffering. Get something straight. Animals don't suffer, humans suffer."

"You really believe that?" She rested her head upon crossed arms cradling the folded flag. Tears fell onto the dark blue of the fabric, fanning out like fireworks exploding in the night sky.

"You don't?"

"No, Richard, I don't. I definitely don't."

"Then kill it yourself," he said. "You don't want it to suffer? Go kill it yourself. Put it out of its misery."

"How—how am I supposed to do that?"

"You said it's in the stream. Drown it. Drop a rock on its head. Use your imagination."

"Richard—"

"Listen, I'm sorry. I've got to go."

She put the phone down, then rested her cheek on the flag. The fabric smelled like summertime, like the camping tents she remembered as a girl. With her eyes closed she saw the fallen deer, its hind parts awash in the gentle flow of the water. When the crying stopped she wiped her eyes with her sleeves, then headed into the kitchen. For the first time in her life she found herself wishing that she had a gun. She searched through the black handles of the knives in the butcher block alongside the stove, pulled out her big, broad-bladed chopping knife, and headed back out the door.

It was still alive when she reached it, its side rising and falling with each panting breath. The sun was well up now, brilliant in a sapphire sky. Rays of golden light reached through the tangle of branches from the budding trees, dappling the fallen animal. From somewhere across the stream a cardinal sang out its mating call— *come-to-me, come-to-me, come-now-come-now-come-now*—echoed a few seconds later by a competing suitor in a tree alongside the road.

She removed her shoes and socks, rolled up her pants legs to her knees, and waded out into the stream. The cold water rushing by her feet and ankles, the feel of the smooth, hard knife handle in her hands, the smells of water and woods, earth and animal, awakened her past any awakening she had known since as long as she could remember. She approached the deer slowly, circling it, coming at it from behind so as not to startle it as before. All the while she spoke to it, using a soft, gentle voice she had last used when David was but a small child. "It's all right, it's all right," she said. "There's nothing to be afraid of." The animal fidgeted, pawing the ground once with a front hoof at her soft, gentle sounds. Again it made an effort to raise its head off the bank, but it had weakened, and now could drag its snout barely an inch through the soft silt.

"It's all right, it's all right," she said. She circled past the injured flank, and when she saw the full extent of the damage, a deep, visceral ache ran through her as if the injuries somehow were her own. She stopped, put a cupped hand into the stream and brought the cold water to her face, slapping her cheeks and brow until she felt her breath return. "It's all right, it's all right. It's going to be all right."

She was close enough to touch it. She crouched behind the deer, reached out and laid a fingertip upon the nape of it's neck. The unknown, forbidden touch of skin upon hide sent a wave of panic through the animal, a spasm of nerve and muscle that seemed, for barely an instant, to lift its entire body off the ground and out of the water. And then it was down again, flat and motionless on the soggy ground. A sharp, hard breath scattered the sand by its snout, a final acquiescence. "It's all right," Marilyn whispered. "It's going to be all right."

She crouched low over the animal, first laying three fingers upon it, then five. She stroked the head of the deer, her fingers running down the narrow space between the two bony nubs, the ring she wore on her thumb, David's ring, clicking up against one of the nubs as if in a quiet, final kiss. She stroked the side of its head then gently around the base of its ears, petting it as if it were a cat she had befriended. Finally, when she convinced herself that the animal had become used to her touch, she moved her hand to its neck. She inched closer now, kneeling full in the stream so that the water covered her legs below her knees, soaking her rolled-up pants nearly to the level of her waist. She slid her hand across and beneath the deer's neck as her other hand tightened around the handle of the knife. The neck felt soft, smooth, warm with life's blood. And then the hard pulse hammering through the heavy animal musculature against her hand, the arterial spring that she must sever, that her blade must find with her first thrust.

"I will not let you die alone," she whispered. She petted the neck gently, lovingly, easing the head back. The animal did not fight. She anchored her knees in the stream bed. "No one should die alone. No one should suffer." She leaned forward, her knife hand dripping, the image of herself filling the great glassy convexity of the deer's unblinking eye. "You need not suffer any longer. You need not suffer—"

From somewhere across the stream a cardinal called—*come-to-me, come-to-me, come-now-come-now -come-now*—. A pickup bumped over the bridge and disappeared down Old Glen Road. The cold, fresh water sang its song as it splashed upon the rocks, as it washed over Marilyn, and the deer, and made its way downstream to the great river beyond, and out into the boundless sea.

LEWIS K. SCHRAGER is a writer and physician from North Bethesda, Maryland. He received a BA from Johns Hopkins University, an MD from the Vanderbilt School of Medicine, and an MA in writing from Johns Hopkins. His work has appeared, or will be appearing, in the South Dakota Review, Southwestern American Literature, Epiphany, *the* South Carolina Review, Colere, Windhover, *the* Bryant Literary Review, Talking River, *and* Workers Write. *Produced dramatic works include* Levy's Ghost, *the story of Uriah P. Levy, the Jewish naval officer who saved Thomas Jefferson's Monticello; and* Shadow of the Valley, *a story of a friendship between an Israeli and a Palestinian in a time of hate. His most recent play,* "Chekhov of Sakhalin," *explores Anton Chekhov's 1890 journey to the Russian penal colony on Sakhalin Island.*

New to the Neighborhood

MATTHEW SUMMERS-SPARKS

Dick Vermeil is at the frozen custard stand, John says, and this is my chance to see what kind of frozen custard he eats, the way he eats it, and whether he cries while doing so.

My ear presses against the phone. I recognize the name Vermeil but I'm not sure why. "Who's Dick Vermeil?"

"He's a genius," John gushes. "He's one of the great coaches of the NFL, having led teams to two Super Bowls, combining hyper offenses and austere defenses."

I vaguely remember Vermeil—tight-cropped gray hair, always sporting puffy jackets with his team's logo, often cries during press conferences.

"He's the coach who's famous for crying during his interviews," I say.

"I knew you'd love that about him, you pansy."

I throw on my running shoes, then slip out the door, unbothered—evidently I didn't wake Steve, my sister's lover, whose attic I'm sleeping in—and limber up on the porch.

I've been here for a week and it still seems strange. I grew up about two blocks from here. Shortly after we moved away—this was about eighteen years ago, when I was fourteen—the new owners remade the property. They cut down the old elm tree in the front yard (the state once labeled it the second oldest elm in Virginia) and changed the shrubs. They dug up the pool in back, and I bet they painted over the murals my mom painted above the fireplace and in the dining room.

I'm running on the sidewalk, shaking rust from my legs. The custard shop is only half a mile from here. I should be there in five minutes. As I ease into my stride, I spot something curious about fifty feet ahead. There's this kid, about twelve, who just dropped into a relay runner's position. His head is turned, watching me as the rest of his body faces forward. I approach and he stretches his arm back in a relay runner form, waiting for the baton.

Why not? All I have are my keys, five bucks, and my cell phone—which still has my Brooklyn prefix, which I'm not ready to give up, lose, endanger, or let anyone else use. I decide to go with my keys—the boy is chubby and I gauge that I can catch him if he tries to take off with them. And I have a couple minutes to spare—Dick Vermeil probably hasn't ordered, and all of the tasty options probably brought him to tears.

From my pocket I fish my key ring, which is really just Steve's spare set—it's the two front door keys on a ring with the tiny, one-inch-long Dutch clog he got during a visit to Amsterdam. About fifteen feet in front of me, the kid breaks his pose and gingerly runs, his arm trailing. I continue, and in a perfectly executed exchange, he accepts the keys I pass to him.

The kid huffs as he chugs forward. He's pretty slow and I have to slow down as we run neck and neck for thirty then fifty then eighty feet.

"I need to make it to the finish line alone," he tells me.

I glance ahead: a white wood fence, a row of shrubs, a drainage ditch, driveways, several parked cars, a lamppost, a busy intersection. It's tough to tell what the finish line could be.

I fall from the pace, let him take a five-, then ten-foot lead. As he approaches a mailbox with cardinals designed into its fiberglass hull, the kid lunges with a triumphant stride, chin inching forward, arms swept back, breaking the imaginary ribbon that marks the finish line.

"The winner!" he shouts, pumping his arms in triumph. "The world record is shattered!"

"Congratulations," I tell him, applauding. I pretend to hold a microphone and recount the story to a TV audience. "Today we're in Arlington, Virginia, at the site of a truly remarkable running achievement. A young man has single-handedly broken the relay race world record. Tell the American people: what's it like to be so awesome?"

I hold the mock microphone to the boy, who begins spinning in a quick circle, arms extended to his sides. "It's awesome being awesome!"

"The new American hero is truly awesome."

The kid keeps spinning.

"He's dizzy with excitement," I tell the audience.

He stops. He swoons. His dizzy momentum draws him to the lawn. As he rests on the ground, he presses his hands over his eyes.

"You live down the street, right?" he asks, lifting a hand and pointing vaguely in the direction I came from. "In Steve's house."

I ask why he wants to know.

"Steve said you're the guy with the little wiener."

There's no way I'm talking about that with a kid. (I'm an actor who was in a nationally broadcast commercial, cast as a man with a miniscule appendage.) "You're, what, eleven?"

"I'm twelve, I've hit puberty. I know all about it."

"Look, I have to be somewhere. Give me my keys."

"OK." He sits up in the lawn. "Just ask me one more question with the microphone." He stands and places his hands on his knees.

"Fine," I tell him. "What's your name?"

"Terry."

I position the imagined microphone and clear my throat.

"Terry, America wants to know what's next. Now that you've broken the relay race world record as a twelve-year-old, what's next? Ski jump? Motocross? Bicycle championships? Hopscotch?"

The little boy begins to spin again, faster then before, then raises his arm into shot-put thrower position. "I'm running a marathon!" he shouts and, with all his might, he shot-puts my keys. I lunge for his hand but I'm too slow. I stumble to the ground then hear my keys land on the roof of the ranch home in front of us, sliding across shingles before plunking into the aluminum gutter.

I hop from the ground and try to figure out where, precisely, my keys landed but they're a good eight feet above the ground and it's impossible to tell. Behind me Terry moans, clearly dizzy.

"Tell my mom I'm sick again."

"You're not sick."

He moans, loudly. "I'm gonna barf."

I assure him that he is not going to barf.

A compact glob of yellowed mush glumps from his mouth. "See?" he says, holding it for inspection. "Cap'n Crunch and Cocoa Puffs and Fruit Loops."

"You brought this on yourself."

"Tell my mom I'm sick."

"Look, I gotta go," I tell him. "I gotta meet my coach."

"Just knock on my door and tell her," he says as he rolls on his back and puts both hands on his head.

I walk up the lawn to the house's front door and, just as I'm about to knock, I glance to the window beside the door. I spot the profile of a woman, shirtless and low, near the floor. I glance again, and see that she is naked, talking while straddling a man with incredibly hairy legs. I press myself against the house, hoping they don't see me. My heart pounds and adrenaline is running through my veins. I've never seen two people have sex. I caught Jack, an old roommate in New York, jacking off but that was different. He was sitting on our couch and pulled a blanket over himself and pretended nothing was out of the ordinary. I saw an old, kind-of-girlfriend when another actor—actually the lead from *The Blue Lagoon*, who was the visiting thespian one season in college—had his hand up her shirt, but this is different.

It's strange, like it's something that should be studied. Perhaps I can learn something valuable from watching these naked strangers. Right now, nothing else matters. Dick Vermeil and the barfing kid on the lawn are just gnats on my windshield and it's time to clean the windshield so I can see the world clearly, so I can study these two people who are naked. Maybe this is the feeling people get when they have their first child. Suddenly priorities shift and what's truly important in life reveals itself.

I ease away from the wall and around the corner and spot the couple. They must not have seen me a moment ago because now they're clearly having sex. She's trim and slim, about thirty, black haired and olive skinned. Maybe she's Italian or Greek or Hispanic or Spanish. She has a lot of control to her lovemaking, easing up and sliding back down. Hairy-knuckled hands grab her hips and follow her thighs to her knees then trace back to her hips, up to her torso to her shoulders, then knead her breasts. A thick gold wedding band is on his ring finger. It's fascinating and worthy of extended study.

But everything starts to be tinted by shame. As I watch his hands lead to her hair and she bends toward him for, I presume, a kiss, I'm increasingly afraid of the embarrassment that would come from being spotted—what if someone from a house across the street sees me? Plus, there's the whole uncomfortable fact that as I study this and get all the educational value I possibly can, Terry is barfing on the lawn.

The kid runs to the porch and slams into the wall beside the storm door. "No, no, no!" he says, pointing a woozy, still-dizzy hand across the street. "My house is over there."

I move clear away from eyesight of the window and an instant later I hear scurrying sounds, like they're getting away from the window.

"Your house is over there? Why'd you run to the finish line in this house's driveway?" I ask Terry.

"Mom doesn't want me barfing in our yard." He's swooning from the dizziness.

"Which house is yours?"

"The white one."

A string of some five white houses line the opposite side of the street. "Which one?"

The boy points a woozy finger that slides from one house to another to another, to the cloudless sky, a mailbox, a passing truck, his barf, a powder-blue house on the horizon, two blocks away, then settles to a loose focus on three of the five white homes across the street.

"That one," he says.

I pat my pockets and locate my cell phone. "What's your phone number?"

"555-F-A-R-T."

"What's your real number?"

"My mom said not to give my number to strangers."

"You really listen to your mom, don't you?"

He says he does. "She's cool. She plays violin in a country band and works in a bank."

The door opens behind us and a man about my height stands in jeans and a hooded gray sweatshirt that reads *Property of Stanford*

University. "Can I help you?" he asks me, then glances at the kid. "Ah, Gary. How're you doing, my man?" The little boy—Gary or Terry—is still swooning from the dizziness. He says he just won a race. The man gives him a high-five that the dizzy boy miraculously completes.

As I begin to explain the situation to him about the keys—while trying to remain calm, not letting on that I got a very informative and educational eyeful of him and the woman in the house having sex, I recognize the guy. It's Jim, Jim Fassen, a guy I kind of knew in high school. He was a big nerd back then, all gawky and his face seasoned with acne.

"You're Jim," I say. "Jim Fassen."

He says he is, then asks who I am.

I explain that we went to Arlington High School, and we had advanced algebra class together. He doesn't remember me. I love that he doesn't remember me. I'm an actor, have played several roles in TV commercials. I've gotten fairly recognizable, which was nice at times but became a burden when I became super-popular for playing a man with a very tiny penis. I'm thrilled that he doesn't recognize me.

"I'm sorry, I don't remember you," Jim says as the cream-coffee-skinned woman eases beside Jim in a Philadelphia Eagles sweatshirt and a pair of jeans. He introduces her as his wife, Sandra. Sandra speaks with a slight Spanish accent while meeting me, then smiles in a very controlled way, like she knows, maybe, that I had a very educational experience today, watching her and Jim having sex. She snuggles up to Jim and tells me hello.

"I haven't seen you since graduation," I say. "Have you been here all along?"

"No, no, we just moved back last week," Jim says. "You want to come in, have a glass of water?"

It's strange to see my former high school acquaintance and his wife, who is beautiful and seems to care for Jim. I'm alone, living in my sister's lover's attic, having trouble landing roles. I explain that I need to go—I'm actually on my way to see Dick Vermeil.

"*The* Dick Vermeil?!" Sandra says. "The crying, Super Bowl-winning football coach?"

"The very one," I say.

Sandra grins at Jim, then pokes him in the ribs.

"This is amazing," Jim says. "I wrote my thesis on Dick Vermeil. Where is he?"

"He's up at the frozen custard stand," I say.

"Let's go, let's hop in the car," Jim says.

"There are a couple of other things to take care of," I say. "Terry or Gary needs to get home." I motion toward the boy, whose eyes look a little unfocused, like he's coping with the last stages of dizziness.

"Gary, go home," Jim says.

"See ya," the boy says, then shakes his head, like he's shaking off the dizziness. He walks toward the street.

"Long story," I say. "But my keys are in your gutter." I point to the general area, which is right above the front door.

"Does this involve Gary?" Sandra says.

I say that it does.

"Was it a relay race that ended with a baseball game?" Jim asks.

"It ended with a shot put."

"That's a new one. I don't know what he gets out of those games, but he must like them," Jim says. "We've been here six days and this is the third time already. I'll get the ladder and get them down."

"He threw up on your lawn."

"Again, it's not the first time," Sandra says.

I ask Jim if we can just get the keys when we get back? I'd like to see Vermeil. They invite me in, and we snake through a hallway packed with boxes, and a large, fully stocked kitchen, completely unpacked.

"I cook a lot," Sandra says. "Flautas, papusas, burritos."

We make our way to the garage, also packed with boxes, and hop into Jim's car, a charcoal sedan. The garage door opens. Gary stands across the street, doing jumping jacks.

On the ride, Jim and I talk about life since high school. We both moved away—he to San Francisco, me to New York—and moved back within the past couple weeks. He for a job with a high-tech company, me because casting directors are persuaded that I have a tiny penis. He and Sandra were married two years ago. They both want to have a kid soon, now that they're back near Jim's family—his parents are retired and would love to see grandkids. I haven't had a steady relationship for about a year now, some of which I attribute to my reputation for a tiny penis, but I also suspect that it has something to do with my general feeling that I'm unsure of what I want to do with my life. Really, I started out as a stage actor and have worked almost exclusively in commercial roles—first on a soap opera and then more and more in commercials since the pay is good. But what sort of career is that, selling Red Lobster and Midas and Budweiser in thirty-second snippets?

It feels good to discuss my life. I get little chance to do so with Steve, who mainly prefers to talk about his kitchen renovation or what is off limits in his fridge.

We drive past the frozen custard stand and spot Dick Vermeil. He's holding court near a Toyota Prius or a Ford Fusion—some hybrid car. Tight-cropped gray hair, sporting a red puffy jacket with a large Kansas City Chiefs logo, a tiny tear catches the sunlight as it runs down his cheek.

We park and Sandra, clutching her autograph book (I meant to ask if that was one of the first things she unpacked), runs to Vermeil.

Jim and I stand in one of the five lines, among about forty people. This place is a local institution. Steve, my sister's boyfriend, bought his house, he claims, because of its proximity to the frozen custard stand.

"Tell me about your infamous commercial."

I recount, briefly, the story of me getting the role. It was a Budweiser ad, which is tough to land. But I've been typecast and have had trouble landing new parts. I haven't been able to get new roles since the ad aired seven months ago. "Everyone associates me with a small penis," I say.

Jim nods.

"Speaking of," he says, "did you see anything at our house today?"

"I saw a bunch of boxes."

"I'm talking about right by the front door. This is embarrassing, but I feel like I have to ask. My wife and I were having sex just inside the window near the door. I know you were standing near the window. Did you by chance see us?"

I was trained as a stage actor. In times like this, when things get tough, I often try to pull lessons from famous works. *How would*

Shakespeare handle a situation like this? I ask. *What would Arthur Miller do?* I try to not lie or embarrass my new friend.

"No. No, no. No, no, no. I mean, I didn't see your genitals. But I did see two people naked, making love. Was that you and Sandra? When I saw you a couple minutes later, you were dressed. I never assumed that the naked man who answered the front door could be you."

"We don't live in a duplex or have roommates."

"It must have been you, then," I say. "You and Sandra. You looked very loving. It was very educational."

"OK," Jim says. "But I don't want you to come back in our house today. It feels all strange."

I tell him that I can understand that.

"It's good seeing you again, but this is a bad way to kick off a friendship, you know?"

I do.

Sandra returns with the autograph book. She waves it and has a huge smile. She shows us the autograph and gushes about how nice he is. We order, and a couple minutes later, Jim says they need to leave.

"I'll get your keys," he tells me. "I have the routine down by now. I'll leave them on the porch, by the front door. Just stop by on your way back through."

We wave goodbye.

I meet John and stand and listen to Dick Vermeil tell stories about going to the Super Bowl, first with the Philadelphia Eagles (which the team lost), then winning the game with the St. Louis Rams. Tears roll down his face a couple times and his wife hands him Kleenex. It looks like nothing out of the ordinary for her.

About half an hour later, I jog away. I return to Jim and Sandra's home and look on their front stoop for my keys. I don't see them. Even though I probably shouldn't, I peek through their front window. I think, *Wouldn't it be funny and educational if they were naked and having sex?* But no one is there, only unpacked moving boxes and a sofa are visible. A room away, I spot someone leaning over a packing box. I squint for a second, then recognize that it's Sandra. I rap on the window. She turns, looks shocked, then stands. She yells, "Jim put the keys behind the flower pot."

I wave. I sense that I'm never going to see her or Jim again. Nothing is behind or around the flower pot. The keys aren't here. Across the street, a door opens. I turn and Terry/Gary exits one of the five white houses.

He dangles my keys in his hand, then takes off, running away, away from Steve's house, toward the frozen custard stand. I kick into gear and run after him. That stupid kid.

MATTHEW SUMMERS-SPARKS's writing has appeared in the New York Times, Mississippi Review, Gargoyle, McSweeney's, *and the* Morning News.

Wash 'N Wag

D. A. TAYLOR

Ford saw the van painted in dalmatian spots resting near the curb. It stuck out from the rest of the cul de sac scene, but he couldn't assume anything. "Is that it?" he said.

"That's it," Christine said. "Pull over."

The name on the van was in bold serifs: Wash 'N Wag. "Cute."

"Don't let the spots fool you," Christine said. "Adele's a killer. She'll chisel your margin right out from under you. I'll do the talking."

"Right, chief."

He locked their car—a brown Nova with "We R Pets" in blocky letters on the door below the dog-dish globe logo—and they walked toward the spotted van. *Like two TV detectives*, he thought. As they got closer, Ford looked in the window near the back of the van. An inside light revealed a woman with her back to him, using a hose attachment on a small white dog on a counter. A little clinic. He heard a vacuum whine. The scene struck him like something out of Kubrick: the pristine white counter, the modern attachments built into the van.

Ford was fifteen years older than Christine and three days into his job as her chauffeur apprentice. A mid-life career change sucked on the ego, big time. He knew it shouldn't, but it got to him. He felt confidence draining out of him when he needed it desperately.

Christine said, "But I guess you had some tough customers in the livestock supply biz, huh?"

He glanced over to check for sarcasm. "We didn't call them customers. And I wasn't in livestock supply," he said. "In ag extension we called 'em clients." He had told her this before.

436

Which meant, *In my previous life I wasn't a salesman.* But he didn't want to sound all high and noble. Six months' severance and six on unemployment had wiped out his past life in agriculture, which now looked like a nineteenth century vocation. How coddled he'd been! He had commiserated with farmers as they filed their inventories for bankruptcy, but he'd never felt their pain. Comes a new decade, and what do you know? With fewer farms, the Extension Service needed fewer farm agents. Guess where that left Ford?

Out of work and moping around his girlfriend's apartment in D.C. Delores lived just an hour from his Pennsylvania farm country and disgruntled clients like Jason Finster, but a world away. Delores's job at the zoo, even when it was horrible, always meant a story. Her eyes half closed with glee when she described the crowd around the new orangutan center, or what made school groups bark with delight. Ford couldn't manage his story yet. He could see her face settle into a calm (bored?) mask—a beautiful one, with that Debi Thomas nose and narrow Egyptian forehead—when he started in on his unemployed despair.

For months he shuffled around the neighborhood, retrieving her laundry from the cleaners, shopping for groceries, reworking his resumé in his slippers. It wore on Delores, he could see that, but she got him to the point of looking at the We R Pets announcement. She helped him look at the new economy of pet products and see himself.

"Clients, sure," Christine said. She crinkled her eyes. "Adele is one of our best clients. She can be a royal pain in the ass."

Christine was We R Pets' wundergal for the Mid-Atlantic region.

"When you ride with Christine, you ride with the best," Ford's supervisor told him the first day as he walked Ford down to the lot. "You're lucky. She's going international in a few weeks."

Ford had met her that first morning standing by the Nova. She was slim, early thirties, dark brown hair in a businesslike bob, attractive but no stunner. She reminded Ford of his niece at Hunter College, with the Sandra Bullock-like way she squinted when she first talked. "So you're the new kid," she said. They both burst out laughing.

In three days, he'd gotten used to visiting customers at fixed-location stores. He'd learned pet supply jargon, and Christine quizzed him on changes in the human-animal bond, their impacts

on market trends, whether they were confirmed by surveys. Ford had
barely cracked the stack of reading assignments on the dining table.
Now this mobile stuff.

"Will I have to track Adele down like this every time?" Ford said.
"Just from knowing her route? Christ!" He twisted his neck to free it
from the collar. "She's had this business how long?" he said.

"Started three years ago," Christine said.

"Fuckin' A," Ford said. "I'm a fucking idiot that I didn't do that.
All these rich schmucks with dirty dogs. Meanwhile I was patting the
backs of slow-footed farmers. Dinosaurs blinking up at the meteor
as it comes down."

"She's got franchises in twelve states."

"Get out."

"The market for these mobile wash-a-pet services has no ceiling.
She keeps this little operation for herself," Christine said, nodding
to the van. "She's sentimental that way." She knocked on the glass.

The woman vacuuming the pomeranian turned and eyed them,
then holstered the wand against the van's wall. The vacuum whine
spun down. The pomeranian looked up, expectant.

"Smile," Christine reminded Ford. "Hey Adele," she said brightly
as the cargo door slid open.

"Hi Christine," Adele mock-lilted. "Who's Goober?"

"Adele, this is Ford Bain. He's following me on my route for a
few days, learning the ropes."

"Good to meet you, Ford." Adele grinned and shook his hand,
a solid handshake. She had a round face poised on the verge of an
Aunt Bea smile or a wrestler's scowl.

"Likewise," Ford said. "Christine's been going on and on about
your operation."

"So it's true you're leaving us?" Adele said to Christine.

Christine pulled her lower lip down. "Not yet. You'll have to put
up with me for another month. What'll it be today?"

"What are you charging for that anti-scabies shampoo?" Adele lit
a cigarette. "If you've come down to a reasonable price, we can talk."

Christine laughed fetchingly. "It's an excellent product. I don't
need to tell you the test results show how much glossier it makes
pomeranians. Quality costs."

"An arm and a—"

"We have other shampoos that would cost you less. The problem, Adele—"

"So Ford—it's Ford, right?" Adele turned abruptly to him. "Ford, what did you do before you joined these shylocks?"

Taken off guard and immediately resentful of any diversionary role, Ford flinched. "Nothing," he said, "you'd be caught dead doing. I tried to help people."

Christine's head jerked. Adele seemed to straighten up. "No, really," she said.

"I was in livestock," he said, avoiding Christine's eyes. "Farm animals."

"Chickenshit!" Adele said happily. "My brother-in-law's a chickenshit. That's great. Why don't you tell Christine what kind of break you livestock folks cut for good customers. Think of me like Frank Perdue. Meanwhile I'll take Peaches back to her owner." Adele bent down and scooped up the pomeranian.

"So Ford, how *would* you handle a customer like Adele, in livestock?" Christine smiled as Adele walked away.

Ford shook his head. "I never dealt with that asshole Perdue," he said.

"First of all, does she trust us?" Christine said.

"No."

"So what do you do?"

Ford sighed. Catechism. He was too old for rhetorical bullshit.

"Bite the pomeranian," he said.

Christine shook her head. "You acknowledge her volume position and you bargain."

"Bargain?" Ford said. "What's my leeway?"

"You have five percent wiggle room. Confirm that with Dan, but that's what I've worked out with him. Here she comes."

Adele crossed the street toward them. She cracked a smile when she saw them. "So Ford, what do you tell Frank Perdue?"

Ford turned his head to loosen his collar. "First off, Adele, you gotta know that Frank treats his suppliers well. Real well. He puts on shindigs twice a year and we all get rooms at Ocean City, lobster dinners, the works. He knows who gives him his margin."

He'd been staring at the van's black Holstein-sized splotches near the rear wheel. He ventured a glance at Adele.

"You're shitting me," she said.

"Nope. Frankly I've been surprised at the chickenshit that Christine has been taking on her beat—"

"Adele," Christine broke in, "let's focus on the product. We don't want—"

"No," Adele said, "I want to hear Ford spin this one out."

"Hey, I'm the new kid," Ford said, hands spread. "Just answering the question."

Adele dropped her cigarette and stomped it out near the curb. "Christine, I'm going to miss you more than I realized."

Christine laughed and said, "You know we really don't have much room on the shampoo. How can we make this work?"

Adele lit another cigarette, sucked a drag off it, and exhaled. "Sixty gross for two K," she said. "You do that, we got a deal."

Christine smiled. "How about sixty gross for two and a half? That knocks out our margin completely, you know."

"OK. Deliver by Friday?"

"You got it."

Adele smiled and turned to Ford. "See? I'm not hard to do business with. You follow Christine's lead, we'll get along fine."

Ford forced a smile.

"You take care." Adele leaned forward and hugged Christine. "Don't be a stranger." She winked, took a last drag, and smashed the butt into the street.

"You're not rid of me yet," Christine said.

They got back in the car and as they strapped in, Ford mimicked, "Christine, I'm gonna miss you more than I realized."

That weekend he and Delores went to the Eastern Shore. It was their first vacation since he had started the job. It was a celebration, a new life, even if We R Pets felt strange. It was early enough in the spring that he found several decent weekend rentals, including a dowdy motel they'd visited when they first got involved. (Their mattress was so spongy that two springs poked lethally into kidneys and other vital organs. In the throes of new love, the deadly springs shot them with laughter.) He chose instead a little hotel near Chincoteague.

The legend of wild ponies was an aphrodisiac, part fantasy of a life of *amour fou* or *idiot savant* or some other wild *je ne sais quoi*. That and the seagrasses and the quiet of the park and their own brief history of love made it a place that refreshed Ford's spirit. They left D.C. late Friday night and by lunch on Saturday their spirits were high. They packed a lunch of deli cold cuts in the daypack for a hike through the park. The light was flat and white, like late winter, and the breeze off the water was bitter cold. The grasses sprang underfoot. A squadron of ducks held the inlet and refused to budge when Ford and Delores approached.

"It's freezing!" Delores said, laughing.

Ford raised his arms toward the ducks. "This is the best I've felt in months."

Suddenly Ford felt he had experienced that moment before: Delores's smile and comment about the cold, the ducks, the angle of the path. And something else, almost a foreboding, maybe a good one.

"So, when are we getting married?" he said, to feel bold.

Her eyes widened and she took the line just as he'd hoped.

"Next week, I guess," she deadpanned. "What's your schedule like?"

"I've got to tag along with Christine for rounds of retailers on Monday and Tuesday. Otherwise, clear."

"I'll pencil you in for Thursday."

"Thursday? Why not Wednesday?"

She laughed. "Careful, Mr. Bain. It's not good to toy with a woman. She might call your bluff."

The water glimmered in the low sun. He hugged her close around her waist, inhaled, paused to consider her warning. Then said, "Please do."

She grimaced. "What kind of proposal is that?"

"A heartfelt one," he said. He wanted to tackle her, tumble with her behind the dune. He tasted her hair.

"I'm serious, Ford," she said. "I don't want you waking up tonight in a cold sweat and having it fall on me."

"OK. I'll change the subject. For now. But watch out! I love you. So. They call those 'fossil dunes' up there. Want to walk over behind that one? The woodland path is supposed to be nice."

"Are the ponies making you horny?" She studied him.

"They are wild companions to my soul," he said in a posh accent, "urging me, Away! Away!"

"Well then, let's away down the woodland path." She giggled and seemed happy, and free from the monotone she used at the zoo. They rounded a bend that revealed a wide strip of dune, and a flush of quail flapped past them.

Ford knew she was right. He was just getting out of a bad stretch and felt flushed. Swayed by any uptick in his life. He needed to see his situation with Delores clearly. She was a creature of rare understanding, he knew that. Best to wait and see, he thought. Best to keep loving her.

"So," said Christine during lunch, "pop quiz. Which regional market will grow the fastest?" They were between stops on her route. Christine looked like she might have had a rough night last night.

Ford looked from his chipotle wrap out the window, as if the traffic on Connecticut Avenue offered a clue.

"This is a trick question, isn't it?" he said.

"They're all trick questions," she said. "This is practice."

D. A. TAYLOR's work has appeared in numerous reviews and anthologies, including Prairie Schooner, The Baltimore Review, Potomac Review, Zone 3, Rio Grande Review, Jabberwock Review, *and* Eclectica's Best Fiction. *His nonfiction has appeared in* Outside *and the* Village Voice, *and his book* Ginseng, the Divine Root *was published by Algonquin Books in 2006. His collection* Success: Stories *won the 2008 Washington Writers' Publishing House fiction award.*

Five Unrelated People Eating a Meal at the Good Hotel on Thanksgiving

Ross Taylor

Ham

Linda, Fred, Alyson, and Ward

Well, since we're all in more or less the same situation, let's all eat at the Good Hotel tonight—it doesn't have to be Thanksgiving dinner exactly.

"Alyson keeps looking over at the waiter. Does he look like an interesting person Alyson?"

"I think I still see two microscopic bits of hors d'oeuvres on her plate."

"See that! Just now when you said that and she looked at her plate she reached for her fork, like 'Oh, there's still some food left!'"

"Maybe I'll ask the waiter to come over and help me beat you guys up."

"See! She is hungry—she's getting feisty."

"Is your ham good, Fred?"

"Yes and I was planning on eating all of it, Alyson."

"You're so mean! I ask politely how his meal is and he starts giving me grief about being hungry all the time. I haven't insulted you once ever since I got here."

"And it's pretty much the first thing we've heard you say tonight."

"She was kinda busy eating. It's not nice to even pretend to throw things Alyson. Mr. Shankly will be stopping by your cubicle just "seeing how you are doing." Doesn't Mr. Shankly remind you of your third or whatever grade principle? And third grade is kind of what throwing things at the table is like—I know you didn't—OR insulting people at the table. Fred. I'm going to tell on Fred to the monitor. Did you guys have monitors in third grade? Alyson how do keep such a good figure *when you're always munching!* Ha! No, I mean it you look great."

"See, Fred, some people appreciate me."

"Ladies and gentlemen, welcome to the Linda, Fred, and Alyson Show! I love it when you guys get going. Alyson, when you're home, does your family eat Chinese food much?"

"Every night."

"Oh sorry didn't mean to touch a sore spot."

"The excuse is always my Buddhist Grandma, 'Lemmy doesn't like Mexican' or 'Lemmy doesn't eat this or that' but everyone always caves too fast, I don't believe it. They're just not adventurous."

"Like you."

"Like me."

WATER

Ward

We're all in the same boat. Let's have dinner at the Good Hotel. It doesn't always have to be family.

"I told you about how my brother lost his mind when they gave him the sedative he was allergic to—started calling the doctors nurses and interns Nazis and Klansmen when they were—well, I won't say again what they were doing because—Dinner. But it wasn't that he objected to the procedure, he really thought they were interrogating him, yes and it was even on his chart that he was allergic to amylo-whatever. Thank God Dr. Spies got there or I might have punched that so-called Doctor Beauregard who gave him the amylo-stuff—incredibly careless and arrogant. Dr. Spies was like the return of reason, obviously had lots of authority, and anyhow my damn sister

got there and yes I told you all that. So when that was under control
it had been about five hours of crisis, and I realized I hadn't noticed
suppertime. So I went walking through the hospital to find food
and to calm down.

"I had no idea where the cafeteria was—it's a huge place—and
there were signs, but they were cryptic. And there would be some
busy area I would hope was the cafeteria and it would be something
very different. Ugh. But hunger got the better of my squeamishness
and I persevered. One nurse had a hyacinth growing in a vial taped
to the glass of her station and I watched her water it with a syringe.

"But the cafeteria was closed. Coming back, there was a Middle
Eastern intern filling out a chart at some station and there was, I
swear, a huge platter of bacon-cheese hors d'oeuvres just like these.
I said those look good, mind if I? And he gave me a grin and said
he didn't eat pork, help yourself. A friend had brought them in. I
gobbled a few and made small talk and gobbled again. His name on
his tag—Atagun—was the same as my old astronomy teacher, who
after all was at the same University so I asked him if he knew him.
He didn't, but we talked about Astronomy and Turkey and Musicians
(the friend who brought the noshes) and I ate every nosh. Then I
went back to my brother's room and slept in a chair."

WINE

Marcia, Plus Linda, Fred, Alyson, and Ward

So here we are, castaways in the Good Hotel, eating our not-neces-
sarily-Thanksgiving-dinner.

"There you all are. Sorry I'm late. Listen, I hope this isn't a problem but
my parents wanted to send this bottle of wine. You know, they do their
wine thing, and this is from a friend of Mom's who's a major grower.
Have a look. It's 1967. Ward, do you think the waiter will mind? Perhaps
you should say something to him when he comes by. I brought my own
corkscrew. Actually, do you think he would give us glasses?"

"Here he comes. Ward, please could you talk to him?"

"He's a very solemn fellow, Marcia. I think he spent his morning
torturing veal calves."

"Excuse me?"

"You know, they put them in very small pens where…"

"Ward, please, don't tell me that, just talk to him."

"But he is stern. *Ah, of course, a very jolly joke. For the love of God, Montressor! For the love of God!*"

"I've got what I ordered, Fred and Alyson are—fine, Ward and Marcia are happy and he's bringing the cheese. Shall I say grace? Bless us, oh Lord for these thy gifts which we are about to receive in thy name. And we thank you for the chance to be with good friends and for blessings upon our families and friends and loved ones. Please help Ward and his sister with their recent loss and we pray for the spirit of Ward's brother. And we pray for the flood victims and everyone around the world who has trouble. And—in the name of the Father, the Son and the Holy Ghost, amen."

POTATOES
Mostly Fred

Since our schedules are all clear this Thursday evening, I've booked us a table at the Good Hotel and it can be Thanksgiving or not, depending on what we order.

"How's your end of the table, Fred?"

"Excellent. I can't even tell the potatoes were microwaved."

"What makes you think they were?"

"When the kitchen door swung open a few minutes ago I heard someone holler 'Oh no, we're dragging spuds!' 'Dragging' was what we used to say meaning something wasn't ready when I worked at Eleanor Rigby's. Then when the waiter brought them, I could see him poking the potatoes as you do to make sure they're not so hot they'll burn the customer. Just now a cook looked out and the waiter nodded back at him like 'Everything's OK.'"

"I thought you were just pausing for emphasis in your jokes, but you were really monitoring the restaurant."

"I was doing both."

"When were you a waiter at ER's?"

"Many moons ago, when I was still in college. I started as a cook and moved up."

"Do you still go there to eat?"

"Yes I do. The same chef is still there—they call him Tweety. Oh, once in a while we'd cheat on things, but we worked hard. Man, we worked hard. The owner, Lance, is Swedish, sometimes he'd mop the floors himself, just like swabbing the deck of a ship he'd say. Actually he'd start mopping then hand the mop to somebody after a bit. He's old you know. He'd get really mad if we went to the bathroom and came out too fast—would say we hadn't washed our hands. He also got mad if we didn't take a meal break—would say we were eating the merchandise. What that meant was we could actually pause from time to time. When you worked you were fast and furious, like in a basketball game, but when you stopped you washed your hands s-l-o-w-l-y, you sat down to eat, and you went outside to smoke. It wasn't too bad. Waiting was harder. You didn't get burned or cut or steam in your face but you got dirty looks. I think most people go out to eat mostly to have a waiter to beat up on. And if you didn't get a good tip you felt you'd let the team down. We shared our tips."

Fish
Linda

The Good Hotel is great, Thanksgiving is perfect, and the five of us are like family.

"My cousin Chantal really needs to move, just somewhere. The place where she is, her boyfriend's two buddies and their whole posse have practically moved in and they're pretty much totally bad news. I'm really not sure why she stays there, she's smart, and she looks to the future, and she's got really useful skills unlike all the men, or boys, around that apartment. She knows French, she's fluent in Spanish, and she kinda is the interpreter for them and this, well, gang they sorta do business with. Are you much of a fish-eater? This is really good. I love fish but I never had any that even *might* have had bones in it until I was a teenager. I mean I had fish sticks. The bones still seem weird—like it's more like an animal than most stuff we eat. I guess fish aren't as smart as, say, cows, so eating fish is better, and it's got less fat. I used to think vegetarians were weird, but then I'd never really seen an animal. Since Mom and Dad had so many of us it seemed like too much to also have pets, especially since we all wanted our own. A lady down the street had a German Shepherd she walked and we'd always go out to pet him. Chantal has Maynard, but he's mean, he's the meanest cat I've ever known. She thinks he was a lab cat, he's neutered and declawed and when she found him he had all sorts of weird habits. Then there's all those so-called men around the place teasing him and feeding him marijuana for jokes and I don't know what. He's part long-hair and part short-hair so it's always in clumps. Under the clumps it gets sore so if you touch him in the wrong place he attacks you like wild. He can't scratch so he bites hard, it's scary. And he's big so he packs a heavy punch. He hates Chantal's boyfriend and whenever Dennis is sitting in a chair or something he comes up behind him and *whammo*—punches hard with a paw. Dennis practically cried once. I think one reason Chantal's been slow to move is she can't find a place that'll take Maynard. She loves her cat."

VODKA
Mostly Marcia Plus Comments from the Peanut Gallery

We'll be at the Good Hotel, probably until late. Sort of Thanksgiving. I don't know whose name—Fred, Linda, Alyson, Ward, any one of us. My beeper is 223-9878-1-marcia*5.

"This was at my parents'. That's Bob and little Bob, and that's my brother Adam and two of his boys. This is Mom and Dad looking cute on a couch. They got it in Mexico. I think this looks like an illustration for preschoolers—one of those Mr. Rogers books that uses photos. Here's some wackiness by the pool. More pool shots—sorry, I didn't have to bring all these. At least I didn't turn off the lights and make you watch slides."

"I wouldn't mind. You wouldn't mind if some of us slept would you? Then we could rouse ourselves and continue the festivities."

"I don't mind a party, but Ward are you proposing we all sleep together?"

"We're all friends and don't go there Fred. And we love the pictures Marcia."

"Don't mind me. It's the white Russians talking, Linda."

"Oh, don't worry, I've got other copies, Alyson."

"I was trying to wipe it off before you saw, Marcie."

"This is all three boys being the Cure. Don't ask me how they heard about the Cure. Travis just turned eight but he's got the moves and he's kind of got the hair. And—Mom can still look beautiful if she doesn't overdo it. I think she was going to a party. Bob can still look beautiful too. There's kind of a lot of Bob here. And more pool stuff. There are some beautiful beach shots somewhere. Oh and this is the vineyard. Mom and Dad getting mushy. Mom and Dad—I suppose you would call that grab-assing…"

"Hoo mmm."

"I can't see…"

"Let me—hold on…"

"Alyson!"

"Ward, your sleeve went in the whatcha-call-it."

"Oh, that's just a blur, perhaps that's what makes it look provocative. Anyway, in a similar vein, this is a photograph of a glass of wine—I don't know. These are the two guys that own the farm next to my folks. They're very sweet and Dad has gotten used to them. Here are the beach shots—pretty much postcard city. Here is a beautiful old Ford. And here it was so foggy you couldn't see anything but I thought it was lovely."

CAKE

All

Five unrelated people at the Good Hotel eating a meal on Thanksgiving.

"Sometimes it would be so foggy you couldn't see it was the school bus until it was close enough to get on."

"I always switch my silverware around—I'm that left-handed."

"My great-grandparents all came to Hawaii around the turn of the century."

"I find this much less stressful than a big meal with my family."

"One bite of my chicken is the least I can give you Fred. You once pulled me out of the path of a raging Metro bus."

"Dad always wanted Mom to set out water with every meal."

"The living room turned the corner like this. The porch went around the corner too and joined the kitchen porch, but I don't have enough room on the deposit slip to show that."

"I learned my spaghetti technique from a cool rabbi I had in Junior High. Rabbi Dan, the Jewish man, everything he says has rhythm."

"Everybody always thinks of the aptly named slimy okra, but fried okra is excellent."

"What a hell of a century. Perhaps Somebody bellied up to the bar and said "Pour me a brace of annihilation wars. Just keep pouring them until I tell you to stop. Ah. That's one, says Somebody, hit me again. Ah. That's two. You can stop now. I don't think I want anymore.""

"Do you recognize what they're playing? Do you remember?"

"I found my father on the Internet the other day. An automobile advertisement he posed for, for a friend, in the sixties. Somebody scanned it in at a Classic Cars site. Hey Dad, how's tricks?"

"The chicken was highly spiced. I am experiencing underground nuclear testing."

"Hundreds of miles from here a small boy is wishing he could have this cake."

"Isn't there some medical thing where if you eat a big meal it makes the night seem darker?"

GRAVY
Waiter

Meet and Eat on Dupont Street—in The Dinner Bell, at the Good Hotel.

ASK ABOUT OUR THANKSGIVING SPECIAL! (minimum 4 persons)

Table five is a bunch of friends having T-day din., probably stay long, but laid-back, jokey, I should get out of my mood. 2 KINDS GRAVY.

Chef Barkling fought w/ his wife again, he's getting picky about the vegetables. It's the SAUCES he should watch.

Carpet bunched up by kitchen door, somebody's going to get hurt tonite, if it's me I am going to SAY SOMETHING at tomorrow's briefing.

Colonel Dupont's eyes are following me from his portrait again. Not enuf sleep. In picture he wears a vest like one I saw in Re-Threads shop Sat. Could work for 19th cent. as well as Shakespearean stuff. Buy it for the workshop tryouts.

No one will miss this piece of broccoli. Fruits and weggibobbles. Can be a drawback, between the teeth, if one has to smile. IF one HAS TO smile.

New kid on the line, no idea how many potatoes to put in for a room like this. Ah, youth. If he's a goof-off, OK. If he's forgetful, watch out sonny. More broccoli. Green that drags minerals out of the earth, scatters them through your body. Didn't know that, did you Colonel Dupont?

Little Inez always gets the biggest load on her bus trays. Looks like a huge tray of dishes being transported by a gnat. Looks like a piled tray moving itself. Barkling thinks Portuguese is same as Spanish. I hereby mentally COMMAND those people not to sit at that table.

Man saws steak slowly, slowly, slowly, separating tissue with serrated strokes. Stealthy steak stabber. Stop. Second start. Skewering; speaking. Table five sinks into the bowels of the earth.

RETURN to a vision of a face that has forgotten long division. Twenty percent is EASIER than fifteen percent.

Oh, God, I'm in their photograph. I am now in some permanent way associated with five other people. The hippie woman won't notice that I am missing a bottom jacket button, but the tall thin man with graying hair may.

If you miskey too many times Visa thinks you're trying to hack it and locks you out so please allow me. The code is ***-****-**.

ROSS TAYLOR has recently had poems in Virginia Quarterly Review, Seneca Review, Poet Lore, Blackbird, *and other small magazines. A story of his was included in* Alice Redux *(Paycock Press 2006), an anthology dealing with the creation of Lewis Carroll, and he has a story forthcoming in the* Texas Review. *He can be seen playing guitar and singing with a friend at Virginia farmers markets most Saturday mornings. He lives in Falls Church with his wife and daughter.*

The Gun

Robichaud S. Thorstensen

A man named Peter woke one morning and descended the stairs to the living room to find a gun—a rifle to be more exact—with an attached spotting scope, lying on the coffee table. It was a dark cherry coffee table, and the stock of the gun—the rifle—was of a similar color. In fact, now that he looked at it, the rifle stock almost appeared to have grown from the table, for how else could it have gotten there? He pondered this for a moment, a gun—a rifle—having grown from his coffee table, before he called his wife.

"Carol?" he called. "Could you come here for a minute?"

Carol, who had been in the kitchen, walked into the living room wearing her pajamas and robe. "What is it?"

He pointed at the gun since this was all the explanation needed.

"I was going to ask you where you got that gun," she said. "Why did you get it?"

"I? Me?" He then thought to add, "It's a rifle." And that's as far as the conversation went. He knew it wasn't he who brought a rifle into their marriage.

They stared at the rifle for a moment, and then retired to the kitchen where Peter ate breakfast and Carol chopped vegetables—onions and peppers—which she was to freeze for later use. They didn't speak of the rifle while Peter ate. Peter spoke to Carol's back of problems in the newspaper, as Carol filled plastic bags of chopped vegetables. Her pajamas were creamy and silky, and the sleeves, where she stored tissues, were just a little longer than the sleeves of her coral robe. She often said, "Hmmm," to Peter's remarks, but she said little more. After he stood to leave, he stopped for just a moment to look at the gun from the doorway of the kitchen. Behind him, Carol wiped the detritus of the morning meal from the table and dropped it into the garbage. Peter then walked into the living room to look more closely at the rifle. He touched the stock without picking it up and then pushed it a little, and the gun rotated on the tabletop; he pushed it back into place. He grimaced at the thought that he may have scratched the table top, even slightly, by moving the gun without picking it up, for dust rubbed into the finish would scratch it. At this thought, he grew annoyed with Carol for having left the gun there, on a dusty surface. His brow furrowed before he left for his basement workshop.

Stacks of lumber, buckets of scrap metal and rough stock, spare parts, and broken machines filled and overcrowded the space between the tools. He had wood and metal lathes, a table saw, a bench grinder. There were shelves with buckets containing ball bearings and brass bearings, or small electric motors, or gauges and valves, forty-pound boxes of nails and screws. There were compression tanks and gas tanks. Parts of lathes and large milling machines, band-less metal band saws and working wood ones, fans and hair dryers that could be repaired, ancient electric drills with burned-out motors, *Popular Mechanics* and *National Geographic* magazines, broken lamps, and unusable sporting equipment—old skis and an unstrung tennis racket—outlined the catwalks through the basement.

Although Peter entered through a doorway inside the house, he could also enter the basement through a Bilco door that led to the outside. It was through this door that he went outside with a ring of keys hanging, and lightly clinking, from his pointer finger. He unlocked the small outbuilding on his property. This outbuilding—the small one—held the lawn mowers and roto-tiller. On the walls hung rakes and shovels, scythes and posthole diggers. The building was full because it also held the lawn mower housings, the broken shovels. It held the electric hedge trimmer with a burned-out motor. It held metal snow shovels that, from use, were bent into scoops, a chainless chainsaw, bicycle tires and bent rims. All of these parts were inside, stacked against the back wall, or they filled deep shelves that hung over the working machinery along the left and back walls. All were parts to be saved, projects he would get to.

He considered all of this and yet still had no idea where the gun may have come from.

He turned and faced the other outbuilding—the large one, the size of a single-car garage—across the large lawn about forty yards away, and pondered it for a moment. Inside it, he knew without looking, was a motorless boat, the deck disconnected from the hull. It had no trailer and sat on sawhorses. There was a boat motor, for a boat larger than the one in the shed, it ran, though it needed work. Everything needed work. Surrounding the boat was a disassembled picnic table, two gas grills—one working, one not—a small, glass-topped frame to protect seedlings from squirrels and late spring frost, a collapsible screen gazebo, and the lawn tractor and trailer. There were bicycles, all of them working, some for adults and some from when his children were kids. They were good for the grandkids now. In the rafters of that building he would find sheets of plastic and tarps—both canvas and plastic—and long strips of wooden molding for different rooms. There wasn't a gun there, nor had there been. There was no gun there, or in the basement or in his two-car garage attached to the house (he knew this without looking). He would remember a gun.

Yet there was the gun in the house.

Carol considered this as she dusted. She had finished chopping vegetables and putting them in the freezer, and now was standing in the living room with the can of polish in one hand and a darkened rag in the other. She had dusted the rest of the room, the home-built bookshelves, the piano, the desk and television. She had dusted the photo frames of their now-grown children, two of them, one nearby, one in New York City. She had dusted the fireplace mantle. Now she stood next to the coffee table and stared at the gun. How long had it been here? She knew, actually, that it had been a long time because there was a faint coating of dust on it equal to that of the table. She was curious more how they had missed the gun all this time, not as much how it got there, or where it came from. Certainly if it had been there on the table they would have seen it. But when she dusted the table around the gun, and then pushed the stock of the gun, she found little dust had collected beneath it. She rubbed the stock, finally, with the dusting cloth, then picked the gun up by the barrel. It was lighter than she'd expected. A small scratch was left on the table top, the sort of scratch visible only in glancing light.

When Peter walked into the living room for lunch, he was relieved to see that Carol had done whatever it was she did with the gun. He sat in his large recliner, slid the TV tray close into him, and dug into the sandwich Carol had made. Peter, who was born just before the start of the Great Depression, ate his entire sandwich and licked his finger, then dabbed up the crumbs on his plate. He flipped between the local news and a national business news show on cable. Had she done something with it in the past? Maybe. The business show reported advancements in the pharmaceutical industry's pursuit of Alzheimer's cures, and Peter told himself that getting old was terrible. The show then slid into a feature about a company he didn't know, and he slipped into a nap in his recliner.

Carol stood in the kitchen, flipping between the same TV shows when her hands were clean. Mainly they were slimy with the grease from the boiled chicken she rendered, pulling the thighs from the drumsticks, then the flesh from the bones, and then shredding the dark chicken into small pieces with her fingers; chicken flesh remained under her nails. She dropped the pieces back into the strained chicken stock, which simmered with chopped vegetables on the stove. The television stayed mainly on the national business news show. Stock prices trailed along the bottom of the screen. The bones she tossed heavily into the garbage container under the sink, opening the cabinet door with the pinky she wiped on a dish towel.

As she held the parts of the chicken—the drumstick and thigh, and now the two halves of breast—she couldn't help but feel the gun in her hand, its surprising lightness, and the surprise of having held it before. She could feel it in the pressure on her palm. The gun—and now the chicken believe it or not—touched memories she hadn't brought to the surface in years.

No, not memories, but emotions, the shadows of memories. Her grandmother, the stern woman who raised Carol in the '30s and '40s while Carol's single mother worked, was there, or, more precisely, the feeling of worthlessness she gave Carol, was there. Foolish, illogical, a disappointment since five years old. She thought of the letter she had written to her grandmother, who was long dead at the time. It was an assignment a therapist gave her after their second meeting, a few years ago, to get down to some basic issues.

"Nanna: Why is it that everything I did was wrong?" it began and went on for pages. She hadn't finished the letter, nor had she returned to therapy. She felt exhausted and on the verge of crying.

Peter was there a while later, placing his dirty dishes on the counter near the sink.

"G.E. is up fifty cents or so," she said.

"What?" he asked.

"G.E. stock, it's up fifty cents."

"No, not that much," he said. "It was up forty-five cents." He paused before asking in a cheery voice, "So, what did you do with your rifle?"

"Nothing. It's still in the living room."

"No it's not."

"I moved it into the corner."

"Oh, I knew you'd done something."

Peter left and returned with it. He held it by the stock, his fingers through the cocking lever, and the barrel pointed toward the floor.

"Don't you think it's best to move it someplace else?"

"I don't know the first thing to do with it, Peter," Carol said.

He chuffed. "You could lock it someplace safely, wherever it is that you put it," he said to her back. He lifted it so that now he held it across his body in both hands.

"You know that's not mine. I don't know what to do with it."

"Don't you remember where it came from, because I'm sure I didn't bring it."

"Where would I get a gun?"

"It's a rifle," Peter said, flatly.

"Where would I get a rifle?"

"You could have picked it up on one of your trips."

"Trips?" Carol asked. "What trips?"

Exasperated, Peter said, "What do you mean? Your shopping trips."

Carol turned away from the counter, where the exposed breast bones and deboned breast meat lay bare on the chopping board, to stare at Peter. She asked, "When have I ever gone on a shopping trip?"

"What do you mean?" He sounded genuinely surprised. "Every couple of days. You're always going out for something."

"To the grocery store?" She held her hands open in front of her to show her disbelief.

"Not just the grocery store. You go down to Albany sometimes." The anger crept into his voice.

"Not to buy *guns*."

"Well, I didn't bring this gun to the house!" Peter was shouting now and shaking the gun in front of him. "I did not bring this into our marriage!"

"Well neither did I," Carol said, her voice rising, but not shrill.

"Then where did it come from?" Peter demanded. He held it out in front of him, between them, tightly clenched in his fists. He might have been offering it to her, or asking her to examine it to see that it was hers.

"Maybe it grew from all the junk in this house!"

"What junk?" Peter asked, incredulous. Carol sighed, heavily. "Tell me what's junk."

She turned back to the chicken breasts. She picked small pieces of flesh from the bones, threw them in the pot with the rest of the chicken pieces. "All of it," she said.

"No it's not. Junk would mean that it had no purpose. Parts have purpose. If I fix it up, I can sell it."

"Well then sell it, Peter," she said. One hand held the edge of the counter, the other, a knife.

"The rifle?"

"Everything. Peter, you need to empty this house," Carol said, turning to him, and she would have crossed her arms in front of her to show her resolution if her hands hadn't been covered in chicken grease. As they were, she could do nothing with them but wave them ineffectually and let them drop to her sides.

"I can, once I get the shop built. What I need to do is get the shop built in the back building so that I can get some of the larger pieces out."

"Well then, get that done so that you can get the house cleaned out. You've got to clean out this house," she said again.

"Now look who's talking. Look at all the stuff you have around." Her shoulders sank. "Where?"

"Judy's room is full of stuff," he said. "Your stuff."

"You know what I mean."

"What?"

"Look at the garage, look at the basement."

"What about them?" he asked, shaking his head just slightly, a disbelieving frown on his face. "I just said that first I need to get the shop working in the back building. Then most of what's in the garage can be fixed and sold. And, yes, some of that will be junk, and at that point I can throw it away."

"Are you working on that?"

He looked at her for a moment.

"On what, the junk?"

"No," she sighed. "On the shop. On whatever your plan is."

He looked at her for a moment. "No, of course not. I can't start that right now. I've got to get these small machines prepared before the summer's over. And since I'll need to build a shed roof off the side of the building, I won't want to start that in the late summer. I'll need to wait until spring at the earliest. I've told you this before."

Carol shook her head for a moment and then turned her attention back to the soup.

"I have told you this before," he said. "You fight me every time I explain this to you. If you have a better idea, explain it to me."

She used her knife to chop breast meat into cubes. Peter looked at her back while she did this before shaking his head and walking to his recliner where he frowned at the television and glanced at the newspapers, before falling asleep.

The next day, Peter stood at his lathe in his workshop, turning a brass bearing to the correct diameter for a lawn mower engine. He had gotten the lawn mower a couple years before from his neighbor Larry. This one was a nice little machine, an older model walk-behind with power wheels and electric start. It worked fine, Larry assured Peter, except for the drive wheels which cut in and out and then finally didn't work. He had bought a newer model and gave the old one to Peter. That's how Peter got much of his stuff. People gave it to him, or he found it, ready for the trash. Before he retired, he was an engineer, and the factory where he worked often threw out working machines rather than maintain them if they were older than a certain age; so long as he got permission from the department in charge of trash, he could have those too.

Although he found a malfunctioning switch that controlled the wheels' operation, he had dismembered the entire mower anyway. That's when he found a worn bearing on the blade's drive shaft that would give him all sorts of trouble in a couple years, if he didn't take care of it now. He liked to have the machinery working in fine order. In the disassembly, he could always find parts that were worn and that could be fixed. He could always get down to the bottom of a problem in a machine.

With the new bearing in hand, Peter realized he had felt the rifle in his hands before. Although he was sure he hadn't picked up a rifle since high school when he borrowed a friend's to go hunting, when he picked this one up in the living room, he was amazed by how easy it rested in his hands. It felt natural to him, and he thought that must be the feeling of carrying all rifles, that they were made this way, to feel natural. The companies, certainly, would design them to feel like an extension of the arm, a sixth finger. But once he shook the rifle in front of Carol, he had the distinct impression that he'd done this before; the grooves in the barrel stock bit his hands in such a way that he was sure he'd felt it before. This only confused him, played with his emotions.

It brought to mind how he and Carol made up just after the fight that had ended their engagement for the second time, how Carol had said, "My grandmother told me to come back to you." Carol was in her mid-twenties at the time while Peter pushed thirty. "I guess I'm just nervous," she said.

"You'll be fine. I'll take care of you," Peter said. When she didn't respond, he added, "We're not getting younger."

"That's just what my grandmother said," Carol told him.

Could the gun have been there, even then?

He turned and looked at it. He had brought it to the basement workshop with him after breakfast and leaned it against the parts of an old, disassembled metal desk on the floor behind his stool.

When he was younger, Peter always waited until Carol called him to lunch, and Carol always made sure lunch was on the table when she called him because he grew angry if he was called away from his work in the basement even five minutes too soon. She still found it odd, though it had been happening for years, that Peter would come up twenty minutes, sometimes a half hour, before lunch to wait in his chair, watching cable news, where he would stay sometimes long after lunch. More often than not, she had to wake him. And so it was when she brought his lunch to him as he snored lightly, the gun across his lap. The noise she made placing the plate on the tin TV tray woke him, and he said, "Don't put this on the coffee table anymore because you scratched it."

She left the table and sandwich in front of him and walked back to the kitchen. "Did you hear me?" he called.

She stepped back into the living room. "What are you talking about?"

"Come here and look," he said, and he moved the TV tray, then slid from his chair, placing the rifle on the floor while he squatted near the coffee table. The piano's lamp gave the sort of glancing light that showed off the scratches, a small star burst of them where the gun had been. Carol bent over to see them.

"Why is it always my fault, Peter? How come you didn't do it?"

"I didn't touch the gun." They were standing now, Peter with the gun in one hand.

"Yes you did. I saw you from the kitchen doorway. You pushed it."

"No, that's not the reason. It's the dust you left on the table. Scratches in the finish come from rubbing dust into it. If there wasn't dust on the table, there'd be no scratch."

On the third morning of the gun, Peter woke very early, long before Carol, and took the gun to his basement workshop. He plugged in the florescent light over the workbench, pushed away parts to the unfinished lawn mower, and then spread a couple rags over one end of the bench. As he removed the rounds then pieces from the rifle, he placed them on the rags. As the first parts came off, he felt a sort of happiness, or pride maybe, at the fact that they were clean and had obviously been cared for despite the fact that it had never been used. Loaded, but never used. If it had never been used, why did he know its feel in his hands?

Soon he had all the parts laid out before him. The feeling of pride had left him with disappointment. The parts didn't tell him anything. He didn't know what he had hoped to find. Maybe where it came from, why it was here. The parts lay there, spread out on the rag, near the parts from the lawn mower. He examined them, slid his glasses down his nose, and looked over the rims, closely, at the firing pin, the chamber.

Exhausted, he cleaned and oiled the rifle, then put it back together. When finished, he leaned the rifle against his workbench with the stock on the basement floor, near parts to another lawn mower tucked under the bench.

Behind him—he knew without looking—sat that large, industrial gray metal desk, disassembled. He looked up from the bench then and saw nearby a metal-cutting band saw that needed a new motor; it was a classic from the '50s he'd gotten from the trash at work. And then he saw an old record player that probably needed a new needle, maybe a new resistor in the volume control, but then the grandkids could use it. From where he was standing, he could see over alleyways of parts and machines to the fireplace he'd built in the basement when he'd built the house. He thought of his original plan to finish off half the basement with a rec room and bar, and the other half would be his shop. Sleds, broken or not he didn't know anymore, covered the mouth of the fireplace. The sleds could be fixed if needed, and the other sports equipment, too. And when the shop in the back building was finished, he could move much of the stuff out of the basement. The basement, though, was probably twice—make that three times—the floor space of the back building, even after he expanded it. He was exhausted when he returned upstairs with the rifle in hand.

The barrel of the gun in hand, he stepped into the kitchen, silently, and looked around. "There you are," Carol said. "I wondered where you'd gotten off to so early. You're never up this early—"

"Sure I am. What are you talking about?"

"Forget it."

"Where'd you put the paper?"

"I didn't put it anywhere. It's still on the porch," she said and turned from him to prepare breakfast. She heard him walk into the living room instead of toward the porch as she'd expected. The tinny sound of the TV reached her a few seconds later.

She poured him a cup of coffee and brought it to the TV tray. Peter stared blankly at the screen. "There's your coffee," she said. He loosely held the gun across his lap.

"You'd have me sell all of this," he said, almost under his breath.

"What are you talking about?"

"You'll never understand." He sighed heavily.

"You can't get it all done," she said. "Peter, there's just too much."

"You brought this into our marriage," he said as Carol slipped into a seat on the couch. He raised the gun toward her. "Admit it, this is your responsibility. Don't try to get out of this."

She drew a sharp breath, but then let it out in a sigh. "I'm not trying to get out of anything. I've never tried to get out." The rims of her eyelids turned red, nearly crying.

She could see the depression and disappointment in his face as he drew her into the sights. But suddenly she wasn't afraid because she knew they'd been through this before. She'd seen him make these same motions before, and she leaned forward.

She leaned forward as she knew the time for shooting the gun had long passed, and that Peter wouldn't pull the trigger when she grabbed the barrel and felt the familiar stiffness and weight in her hand.

He let her have the gun then as she stood and walked with it to the kitchen. He found her but not the gun in the kitchen ten minutes later chopping onions and mushrooms next to a bowl of cracked and beaten eggs.

ROCHIBAUD S. THORSTENSEN received his master of fine arts from Wichita State University in 1993. His stories have appeared in various magazines and journals including the North Atlantic Review *and* Aura: Literary Arts Review. *A journalist and writer, Thorstensen teaches news writing and fiction at Montgomery College in Rockville, Maryland. He lives in Arlington, Virginia, with his wife and children.*

FROM "Over the Falls"

Tim Wendel

As soon as we come through the garage, Deb-Deb, their daughter, shouts out from upstairs—"Russell!"

For some reason she calls after him like you would a dog. No daddy or anything like that. Just Russell. Here boy.

"Where you at, kid?" he says as he begins to climb the staircase. He pauses and turns back toward me. Russell holds out his hand and we shake. "Catch you later, Garrett. Have a good flight back to New York."

Then he adds, "Shelby's around someplace. She wanted to see you before you left."

Left on my own, I look around the house, wishing that my parents had stayed in Briarwood instead of moving closer to Lake Ontario. The houses in this subdivision were built right. All out of the same kit with hardwood floors split into several levels that give the illusion of more space than the structures actually afford. I walk through the living room and peer into the kitchen. It has been remodeled with mud-brown tiles and lighter cabinets. The oven is set to 350 degrees and something is in there, cooking away. It's going on three o'clock and I need to be getting to the airport.

Down in the family room I hear the dull hum of a motor coming from somewhere out back.

"Shelby," I say.

I open the screen door that leads out onto a new wooden deck, and there she is. The cover to the hot tub has been pulled back and its jets cranked up high. A lazy mist rises in the heavy afternoon air and there, riding the surface like a misguided angel, is Shelby. For a moment, I linger in the shadows, watching as she lies back in the water, with her eyes closed. The throbbing, mechanical current carries her up to the surface, where her slender arms, palms out, then her collarbone, and now her breasts, and finally the top of her thighs break through. For a few seconds she rides the bubbling froth like a goddess before pulling herself back under. Mesmerized, I stare as she arches slightly backward one last time. That raven-haired head briefly rests on the surface of the fast-moving water. Her pink nipples again break the surface. She's as beautiful as she was ten years ago when we graduated from high school. When she was the homecoming queen and I the king, and we rode in that convertible from Murphy's Cadillac around the black cinder track that encircled the football field as the bleachers packed with people applauded. Before everything in my old world fell apart.

The breeze in the treetops whispers of such occasions and for the first time in years I pause to listen. Another man, maybe a more prudent one, would have turned away. But I walk out onto the wooden deck, and Shelby hears the vibrations of somebody approaching and dips down deeper in those warm waters before opening her eyes. Those hazel orbs hold a measure of alarm, but mostly they are angry and defiant and I admire them so.

"Garrett," she says. "Russell was supposed to call."

"I'm glad he forgot."

She refuses to smile at my compliment.

"Be a gentleman," she says, "and fetch me my robe, will you?"

She raises one hand toward the pink terry cloth draped over a nearby deck chair.

I hold out the robe with one hand and Shelby lifts it from my fingertips as she steps out. In only a beat or two, she has it wrapped around her, tying the sash, leaving my one hand to rest on her shoulder. Her eyes peer up at me. She's warm to the touch and smells of steam and lotion. It flashes through my mind that if I kiss her now, right away, the years will roll back. Dissolve just like that. But as with too many things, I'm not as quick as I need to be. Too soon, from far back in the house, comes the cry of her daughter.

"Mom, where are you?"

"Coming, honey," Shelby says and pulls away from me.

I trail her into the house. Their back room, which I remember as a dark place, with brown paneling, has been repainted with the light hues of clover and off-white. Even the beams have been highlighted, giving the family room a light, airy feel.

"I'm here, Deb-Deb. Did you say hello to Uncle Garrett?"

We find the girl in the front foyer. With both hands, she holds up a stack of magazines and letters held together by a thick rubber band.

"You still haven't looked at the mail from the other day, Mom," Deb-Deb says. "The mailman told me to take it right inside."

"That's because he knows he can trust you," Shelby says and gathers up the stack from her. "You're a very responsible girl."

Deb-Deb beams at her mother's praise. Shelby flips quickly through the stack and pulls out a single postcard.

"They are going to do it," she says and holds up the correspondence. "That crazy Swany. He screwed up the tenth-year reunion so bad, he's going to give it another shot. The Encore Reunion, he's calling it. Scheduled it for next month. Molly Jackson's the new co-chair."

"That means it'll be top drawer," I reply.

"Are you coming back for that, Garrett?" Shelby asks.

"I don't know, Shel."

"You should," she says.

Her eyes settle upon me, and there's something in the tone of her voice, some small reassurance, that I haven't heard in years.

"You were always a big schemer," Shelby teases. "You can make time for this, can't you?"

I don't know what to say or what to think about the way she's looking at me: a smile bordering upon a smirk, a proud tilt of the head.

"Maybe," I reply. "Maybe so."

TIM WENDEL's books include Castro's Curveball *(University of Nebraska Press),* The New Face of Baseball *(HarperCollins), and* Red Rain *(to be published in 2008 by Writer's Lair). His stories have appeared in the* Potomac Review *and* Gargoyle, *and his articles in the* New York Times, Washington Post, USA Weekend, Esquire, Washingtonian, *and* GQ. *A professor of nonfiction and fiction writing at Johns Hopkins University, he is a Walter Dakin Fellow and Tennessee Williams Scholar to the Sewanee Writing Conference and a PEN/Faulkner visiting writer to the Washington, D.C., public schools.*

Murder Ballad

Jim Williamson

It was the kind of suburban street where it wouldn't do to park your car in plain sight unless you lived there. These were people who paid attention to their neighbors and their manifest arrivals and departures. Every pizza delivery was quietly logged in and checked off against the number of empty boxes stacked curbside on trash day. Every case of empties counted. A strange car would draw attention.

An old man on an afternoon stroll would be nearly invisible.

I parked at the public library lot, some half dozen blocks away, next to a police car, and walked to a certain house with a gun tucked into my trousers. The house was where my son lived, and I was going to kill him. Afterward, maybe I'd read the local papers, or check out some DVDs under an assumed name.

There were no sidewalks on these side streets. I walked in the shade of tall trees and waved openly at the few drivers going by. From the top of the block I could see him in his yard, looking dumpy in polo shirt and khaki shorts, rake in hand, a pile of lawn clippings at his feet. There was an electric lawn mower, its orange power cable snaking into the backyard.

He had gone to fat, of course, twenty-five to thirty pounds overweight, mostly in the gut. Christ, I thought, I bet he has tits. Somehow taller with all the bulk, or maybe I was just shrinking into my old age. His hair had a lot of gray. A bald spot shone out from the crown of his big head, a gift from his mother's father. The hairline in front had also retreated, drawn back to the same wolfish contour as his grandfather's but mostly unseen due to hair length, which was honestly just too long for a man in his late forties. But there was the eyebrow ridge, and the cheekbones. I'd recognize my face anywhere.

I counted the fifteen years that had elapsed since we last spoke. Fifteen years of willful silence. I was never a sentimental man—when you make the kind of decision I've made, you don't want any second guessing disguised as compassion. When fortune provides the chance to correct our mistakes, we should take it.

Time jerked forward in short steps as I got closer. There was a quick swerve of his head as he saw me. A spin take to make certain his vision wasn't tricking him. A scan cast to the paved horizon of driveway and doorstep to gauge what gawking neighbors offered witness to his panic. Less than a second had elapsed. A blink.

I smiled and asked if he had forgotten how to answer his telephone.

He looked at me hard, his knuckles white on the rake handle. He asked if I was familiar with this new invention called voicemail. His voice was high and peevish.

I held my smile, and gave half a shrug.

He lowered his gaze, dropped the rake, and said we'd better go inside.

It was my turn for an anxious glimpse to the neighbors. Every case counts.

The house was a brick Cape Cod, unpainted except for the black shutters. Faded pink clay and black with gray shingles were the highlights of the palette, with accents of dull matte green provided by the lawn and a few sparse bushes. Shade was cast by tall oaks and maples in the front and back, ill tended and tangled with dead branches above the roof line, scrabbled bark shrouded with ivy closer to the ground. Patchy grass with moss growing in the gaps.

I couldn't see why he was bothering with the ruined lawn.

Inside, I smelled home cooking and air conditioning. He led me through the barely furnished living room to an elaborate kitchen, where something brown with onions and mushrooms was simmering in a red enamel-clad cast-iron skillet. Judging from the the matching stainless steel–fronted refrigerator, stove, and dishwasher, a lot of money had been put into the room. The walls were the color of rust. Above the butcher block there was an iron pot rack attached to the wall, from which was suspended more red cookware. There was an expensive set of knives pretentiously displayed in a huge knife block.

He filled a tall glass with tap water and, offering me nothing, drank till the glass was empty. "OK," he said. "You gonna tell me exactly what you want?"

I rolled back on my heels and felt the gun shift in my waistband. I said, "Just wanted to see what life is like in old False Church." He didn't laugh, and I continued, "So, where's the brood?" I looked past the kitchen and into a family room that had been taken over by children's toys. "You've got, I'm guessing, girls, right? I mean, there are the doll houses and dolls and such. Although, these days, I guess I shouldn't assume."

He glared. "I asked you a question. Don't you—don't worry about where my family is." He stepped back and braced his hands on the edge of a marble counter strewn with cooking utensils I couldn't iden-tify. "And *please* don't bullshit me about making up for lost time."

Marble really is such an extravagance.

"No. Just wondering if I could meet them. But they're not here."

"You stop by unannounced, what do you expect?"

I looked at the skillet on the stove top. "Your wife leave in the middle of fixing your supper? Forget a key ingredient?"

"I'm cooking dinner. You stay on your good behavior, you just might get to meet everyone. I'll even feed you."

I could barely stand to look at him. "So, your wife doesn't like to cook?"

"It's my kitchen. I do the cooking."

Then he raised an eyebrow, which, when he was a teenager, would have earned him a beating. Maybe he was recalling past instances of kitchen stand-offs, or maybe just one in particular.

Years ago, when he was in his teens, I used to draw a rectangle in the air during arguments with my son, which was the sign I made to inform him that he was an asshole. The two index fingers together at eye level, drawn out sharply right and left, then down, and back together. I always imagined it in flashing neon. When I wasn't also informing him that he was about as worthless as tits on a boar hog,

I would often employ this bit of semaphore, sometimes saying the words aloud in singsong iambic: "*Jimmy is an asshole.*"

Sometimes I'd make him say it with me.

Once, in his late teens, well after his mother had left me, and when he had perfected his natural talent for provoking me to a bloody-eyed rage, my son and some of his friends were eating and carousing in our dining room. I was in the kitchen getting a soda and listening in on their idiotic teenage tripe, the same from all teenagers everywhere, when something my son said, I can't remember exactly what, ticked me off royally. So I leaned into the room, caught their attention, and made the asshole sign. One of his friends said, "Did your dad just call us *squares?*" and I laughed. My son pushed back from the dining-room table and came after me into the kitchen with a steak knife in his hand. When he got close enough that I thought we were going to tangle, he brushed past me, threw the knife into the sink and left the room.

This was the first time I was aware of any violent impulse on his part, and it gave me hope. Straight to action, no sarcasm, no condescension, no raised eyebrows. Maybe he wasn't going to turn out to be the worthless sissy I always feared he would be.

But I was wrong. This kitchen was evidence of that.

I saw a cookbook on the counter, and I found myself thinking about my first wife, the mother of my son and his sisters. That was several lifetimes ago. I stopped myself from counting the years and forced the smile back onto my face.

"Hey, it's the good old blue book." I pointed to *The Joy of Cooking.*

"Yeah, it's Mom's. Was Mom's. Still has the book jacket, although it's pretty shredded."

"Let's see," I said. "'*That which thy fathers have bequeathed to thee, earn it anew if thou wouldst possess it.*'"

"What?"

"The dedication. It's Goethe, I believe."

He flipped the book open and found the quote on the dedication page. He looked back at me.

I said, "Who do you think bought it for her?"

There was a window above the kitchen sink that looked on a brick patio in the tree-shaded backyard. The bricks were filmed with greenish black. Not much sunlight got back there, apparently. I began counting them.

He carried the cookbook to the kitchen table and sat on one of the chairs. "So, do you think she liked using it? I mean, she only check marked about seven or eight recipes."

"I think it's fair to say your mother wasn't a skilled cook."

"Please. Do you remember her liver and onions? The fried bacon, the onions sautéed in bacon fat. Then she'd add the calf's liver, parsley, salt and pepper. It was the most amazing smell."

"But it tasted like dirt."

"Well, liver is an acquired taste."

"You kids never ate any."

"Not true. She fooled me more than a few times. Wasn't till recently I discovered I like it."

I repressed a shudder. On the outside windowsill a dead fly had decomposed to a small cloud of black fur. I was up to seventy bricks when I said, "Are you going to offer me anything to drink?"

"Sure. Iced tea?" He got up from the table and got a glass from a cabinet by the stove.

"Iced tea's fine."

"Sweet?" He was at the refrigerator, pulling out the tea pitcher along with some salad greens.

"You know I don't like it sweet."

"Uh, well, it's gonna be sweet, that's all I have."

"Then why did you ask?"

He stopped in mid-pour. "Ice?"

I looked away, and after a second I heard cubes hit glass.

"So, how's your wife?"

"She's fine. Why wouldn't she be?"

"I'm just asking." He placed the glass on the counter.

"Why do you ask?"

"Just making conversation."

"Well, don't."

"OK."

I didn't like this turn. It still rankled me that none of my children had ever respected or accepted their stepmother enough to show the common courtesy of addressing her as "Mom." Bad enough that he had just invoked the *spiritus matri.*

"How's your, as long as we're just making conversation, how's your *ex?*"

"*My* ex? Uh, Dad, you don't want to do this, you know?"

"No, tell me, how is the former Mrs. Williamson?"

His breathing tensed. "Not that that was ever her name, and you know it, but she's doing well. Happy and remarried and doing just fine. No bad blood there."

"So you say."

"So I say, and so it is." He was looking at his feet. "I happen to be doing fine as well, thanks for asking."

"She was a lively one, wasn't she?"

"What does that mean?"

I sipped my tea. Too sweet by far.

"We were out to dinner, the four of us. You and I got into a tiff because I said you should go back to school and finish your degree. Of course you had something smart to say. So I said I'd be only too happy to kick your ass up between your ears if you didn't grow up fast. Damned if your wife didn't just about jump over the table at me."

He raised his eyes. "That's almost twenty years ago."

"So?"

"You and I remember things a little differently, you know?"

"I know I always thought that she was just a little too much woman for you to handle."

"And you'd be the expert in that department. A shining example."

"You never listened, but I always said: son, you have got to box your weight."

"You know what? We are not doing this."

"And then there's the new wife."

"We are not. Really."

He had started chopping the greens when he broke silence. "So, are you going to tell me what you want? Why you're here?"

If I didn't know how dick-fingered he really was, I would have had to admit that he was showing some skill with the knife.

There was a radio on the table. I turned it on. Johnny Cash was singing.

"I'm here to correct a mistake."

"What's that?"

"I want you to come home."

He looked up from the butcher block. "What are you talking about?"

"I think you should come home. You gave this life a shot, and you bitched it up royally. Look at how you live."

He turned his back to me, his shoulders squared. "Look, your opinion of how I make my way in the world is of absolutely no god-damn interest to me. Now it's time for you to leave."

"No," I said, and reached for the gun in the back of my trousers.

He was laughing. "Seriously. You have got to be kidding me. This is what you came for?"

Not exactly. I pulled the gun out into the open.

I aimed and pulled the trigger. Wood splintered, and the cabinet door behind his head jumped on its hinges. But it had been years since I had fired a weapon indoors. I had forgotten the intensity of the sound pressure, like a hammer blow to the head. My son doubled over, hands over ears. Then he snapped upright, grabbed the skillet handle, and swung at my head, screaming.

I aimed the gun, but before I could fire, my son had grabbed the hot skillet handle in his bare right hand, bringing the skillet up to block the shot and also dump its hot, greasy contents down my front before clubbing my skull to paste.

I aimed, but the gun slipped from my hand and fell to the floor. My son picked up the chef's knife and plunged it into my chest.

Does it matter which one happened? My favorite was the knife.

I was on the floor, covered in blood and slop, and he was raging, towering above me, arms flailing, taking wild glancing kicks at my smashed skull, my sucking chest wounds, my scalded torso. Floating above me, screaming *This is what you came for,* his giant head wreathed in blue and red rotating police lights.

Black fur clouded my vision, closing in on the color of rust. Sirens and other voices cut through the receding chug and wail of the Johnny Cash tune, and these were the last sounds I heard in this rotten bitch of a world.

Eventually he'll wake up and I'll be gone. But memory is a sticky thing. My presence will linger well beyond his daylight hours and the days that follow; whether coursing and dissolving along those psychic crevices that memory provides and dreams reveal; or held in ready suspension, as the oceans hold sheer metric tons of invisible minerals and vile, shadowy life. He will hold these thoughts of me like he'll hold his last sour breath, past the point of necessary and inevitable expulsion.

Like a cloud holds water, or a bruise holds blood.

JIM WILLIAMSON last appeared in Gargoyle *in issue #46 (spoken word/music CD), and before that in issue #42. Since 1993, he has been introducing music audiences to hearing loss as one of the composers and guitar players in the instrumental band Tone. The most recent Tone CD is* Solidarity, *on Neurot and available on iTunes. (Visit at www.tone-dc. com.) Williamson has been a resident of the Washington, D.C., area since 1965. Does this make him a D.C. native? Are you kidding? An introduction to his music can be found on the afore-mentioned* Gargoyle *#46 CD, or at www.myspace.com/jlwilliamson.*

The Treatment

Terence Winch

1

On the way home from campus there was a Chock full o'Nuts. The donuts were crunchy and the coffee was excellent. Sitting at the counter, I would light up a Kent. Kent was a beautiful fat white cigarette. They were the favorite cigarettes of intellectuals, a friend had told me. I liked the Micronite filter too—so much more scientific than the filter of a Marlboro, say, or a Winston.

I lived in a nice cheap apartment. Once when I was typing, my next-door neighbors started banging on the wall. I wasn't sure what that meant and continued typing. Then finally they started banging on my door. I answered the door and this old man who lived next door with a big family—I guess he was the grandfather—started complaining to me.

"Jesus Christ, mister, what ya got, a printing press in there?"

"No, it's just a typewriter," I said.

From then on I felt very uncomfortable typing. I like to be alone. I don't like the idea that I can be overheard. I don't like the thought of people looking at me without my knowing it. For that reason I always have curtains or shades on my windows.

It was a pretty good neighborhood, but a friend of mine, a fellow grad student, who lived a few blocks away was raped one night. She and her roommate were sleeping. It was four a.m. They were awakened by a man with an ice pick. He raped both of them. I was surprised that he was white. When I first got the news, I just figured he was black. That hard-wired racism. But he turned out to be Italian. If he were smart, he probably would've gotten away with it. But he tried to break in again, unsuccessfully. After that, the cops were really after his ass. The two women kept their eyes open too. They were both terrified.

I was with Sheila, my friend, one day on the street when she spotted the rapist going into Sears. She froze in her tracks as we were walking along Fordham Road, her mouth open in surprise, or maybe fear. I never even caught a glimpse of the guy. We headed after him into Sears. I wanted to help her capture him. I wanted to walk up to him and put him away with an unexpected right hook. But I was also afraid. I didn't want to fuck with some crazed criminal who just might have the famous ice pick under his shirt.

It didn't matter. The store was packed with weekend shoppers, and we lost track of him. I felt almost sick at the thought of what happened to Sheila and her roommate. I'm not very forgiving—I wanted the guy to be locked up forever and raped every night himself. I had no idea how the experience affected Sheila and her friend. I was too young then to know how damaging and long lasting are the effects of something like that.

Eventually the rapist was caught by the police. He lived in the neighborhood. In fact, from his apartment he could see Sheila and her roommate coming and going. He knew their routines inside out. His attacks were carefully scheduled. The case attracted a lot of attention in New York back then. It is very hard to convict a rapist without corroborating witnesses. And almost all rapes are one-on-one situations. But in this case each victim was the other's witness and the scumbag was convicted. I lost track of Sheila after the rape. The two girls didn't stay very long in that apartment, understandably, and Sheila dropped out of school next semester.

Sheila's roommate was an attractive blonde named Christine. A few months before the rape I ran into her one day at a second-hand bookstore and she invited me back to the place she shared with Sheila for lunch. I said sure. The girls' apartment was the first floor of a private house. I always need to pee, and as soon as we got to the apartment, I asked Christine where the bathroom was. The bathroom was off the bedroom, and she led me to it. I relieved myself, flushed, and came back out into the bedroom. There, with her back to me, was blonde Christine unsnapping her bra, her bare back in full view.

Was this a sexual signal? I didn't know what to think. I thought, well maybe she's just uninhibited and free-spirited and it never occurred to her that what she was doing was sexually provocative. On the other hand this is New York City and it's the twentieth century and she's not stupid so she must know what's up. I mean, she could have waited till I finished in the bathroom and was safely back in the front room before changing her clothes. The timing seemed deliberate. But uncertainty got the better of me and I did not act. I awkwardly, but quickly, slid past her and made my way to the front room.

All through lunch we talked about her fucked-up, miserable past, her divorced parents, and her horrible brothers and sisters. And all that kept running through my head was shit, what if she wanted me to put the make on her back in the bedroom and I blew it! She might even think I was a real jerk, not smart enough to figure out the obvious. Neither of us made a move. But before I left, she invited herself to my place later in the week to borrow some notes for a class she was taking.

On the appointed day, at exactly the agreed-upon time, she knocked on my door. I thought to myself that her promptness was a good sign. I am always punctual, and appreciate the quality in others. Then I opened the door and there she stood, looking really fine. All spruced up. From the way she looked I knew she wasn't treating this as a casual visit. She had on a short, sexy black skirt and a tight white blouse that called attention to her alluring, curvy figure. In my kitchen, we made conversation, while I cooked up a couple of grilled cheese sandwiches, for which I am famous.

After we ate I suggested that we smoke a joint of some very heavy dope I happened to have on hand, and listen to *Blonde on Blonde*. She thought that would be cool. We were stoned in a flash and, overcome I guess by drugs and music, Christine stretched out on her back on the floor, her short skirt riding up, almost exposing her panties. She was writhing around in response to the music. I looked at those smooth tan legs on display and thought there could be no mistake this time: she was definitely looking for a little action. I got up to flip the record, but instead of returning to my seat on the beat-up couch I sat down next to her. I figured I had it in the bag. I put a hand on her leg and tentatively began to touch her thigh. Abruptly, she bolted up to sitting position.

"What do you think you're doing?" she shrieked at me.

"I, uh, I didn't think…I figured…" I stammered in stoned confusion. It was a quick switch from offense to defense.

"Is that why you invited me up here?" she demanded. What bullshit, I thought. This girl is playing some game whose rules I just don't get. All of a sudden she was a victim. I felt led on. I told her to relax, that I was sorry if I misinterpreted her desires, and I resumed my seat on the couch. Now I felt bad about myself and extremely disappointed in human nature.

Sometimes the very notion of sex can seem so alien. What was it exactly that I wanted to do with this person? Remove all her clothing and insert parts of me into her various orifices? Too strange. What could I have been thinking? Now I just wanted to be alone. She, on the other hand, apparently wanted me to be the villain, preying on poor innocents. The fucking lights were all green and that's why I hit the gas. She knew that and so did I.

But apparently my apology and resumption of formality was not what she wanted either. She wanted drama and conflict. Maybe she was afraid I'd think her an easy lay.

It was very tense for a moment, with me on the couch and Christine still sitting on the floor. She knew I was pissed off and I knew that she didn't expect that reaction. I was direct with her. I told her not to worry, I wouldn't try anything with her again, and I suggested that I walk her home right away. She got up and went into the bathroom. I sat there waiting for her to reemerge so I could escort her home and be done with the whole transaction.

The water was running in the bathroom. After a while it occurred to me: the water has been running for a long time. I walked over to the bathroom door and listened for some sound. Nothing. Just the water running.

"Christine, are you all right?" I asked. I knocked on the door, first softly, then with a hard fist. There was no response. I tried to open the door, but found myself pushing against something. With the door a little ajar, I realized the resistance I was meeting was her body on the bathroom floor. I panicked. O Christ, she's killed herself! The water running, the silence, her body on the floor—it all added up. She slit her wrists with my razor. Committed suicide over nothing, over an imagined assault on her purity. I was able to push the door open enough to get in, dreading the sight I would encounter.

She was not dead. She was lying on the floor sucking her thumb. Staring off into space. What the fuck is going on? I wondered. I got her up, turned off the water, and led her out of the bathroom. She offered no explanations. But she asked if it would be all right if she lay down for a few minutes before I took her home. With definite reservations—I wanted her gone, the sooner the better—I said OK. After all, she was in bad shape, self-induced or not. I was pretty shook up. I am not good at dealing with the craziness and desperation of others.

As soon as she lay down on my bed her mood changed. I brought her a glass of water. She had been molested in her imagination, and had then traveled to oblivion on the bathroom floor, and I guess the experience left her relieved. In any case, she was back to being sweet and attractive. She had whizzed quickly through my apartment—kitchen first for grilled cheese, living room for sexual harassment, freak-out in bathroom—and now here she was in my bed sending out sexual messages, practically cooing to me. In my mind I said no. I will not make the same mistake with the same person. Certainly not on the same night. After a few minutes of recuperation, I suggested that she would be more comfortable at her own place and that we should leave. Now I had the upper hand in whatever warped power struggle was going on.

Instead of walking her home—their place was about ten blocks from mine—I hailed a cab and put her in it. I gave her a few bucks and told the cab driver where to go. She was surprised—she had thought I was going to go all the way with her. Just before getting in the taxi, she asked me, "Can we get together again?" I said, "No, I don't think that would be such a great idea." That was the last I saw of her.

After the rape, Sheila and Christine were very close for a while, but then the differences between them outdid the bonds and they went their separate ways. I felt terrible for both of them after the rape, and even a little guilty, as though our encounter was some kind of adumbration of the crime. But Sheila told me later, after I had published an article in the *Village Voice*, that Christine was very impressed and was convinced that I would one day be famous. Christine, according to Sheila, was annoyed with herself that she hadn't played her cards right with me.

2

I was very fond of that apartment where Christine and I acted out our evening of drama. It was the first time I had ever lived on my own. I grew up in an apartment with seven other people and grew to dislike crowds. When I was little, we could barely squeeze in around the kitchen table. I remember the almost uncontrollable frustration I felt as a kid when I would be jumping up and down in front of the locked bathroom door waiting desperately to take that first crucial piss of the day while one of my sisters finished putting on her makeup in the bathroom. "Why don't you put your makeup on in your room?" I would plead. I was the baby of the family, and my sisters did not answer such questions.

My mother did not like cats, but my father did. After the family disintegrated, through death and marriage, my father lived for a while in a basement apartment with two young Irish drunks. I was very worried about him, since he was sick and the place had no heat, but he seemed to get by all right. He had an electric blanket. He also took care of thirteen stray cats that lived in the basement. He fed them every day and gave them all descriptive names like "Blackie" and "Whiskers." They loved him. Cats can tell when a human is a sucker for them. I asked him why we didn't have any cats when I was growing up. "Because your mother didn't want any animals in the house," he said. I felt bad that he was denied cats for such a long time, but glad he could finally enjoy them in abundance.

It was while he was staying in that apartment that he advised me to make sure I washed my sheets at least every few weeks. He claimed that dirty sheets encouraged bed bugs. My mother changed all the sheets in the house every Thursday morning. She also turned the mattresses. She waxed the linoleum floors and would always ask me to polish them. It was ball-breaking work. I would get down on my hands and knees and rub the linoleum till it gleamed like ice. When she came home from the supermarket, she would ring the downstairs bell to get one of us to come down from our apartment on the second floor and carry the many bags of groceries necessary to feed us for a few days.

Before I moved into my place and my father moved to his cat-filled basement, we spent three years together in the old apartment where I grew up, which by then was definitely haunted. There was a long hall that ran through the place. The rooms were all off the hall, which made a ninety-degree turn in the middle of the apartment. After my mother died, I would still catch glimpses of her walking slowly down the hall, holding onto the walls to support herself, which is what she had to do when she was sick. The place had gotten too spooky for me.

I was twenty-one years old when I moved away from the haunted house my father and I shared, where I had lived my whole life. I looked at my new apartment at the end of July, and I liked it so much—it was big and cheap—that I rented it right then and there, even though I wasn't going to move till the fall. I had this grant that started in September and no other money, so to pay the rent for August I sold my beautiful black mother-of-pearl set of Slingerland drums for $160. Some chubby boy from the suburbs bought them and was very pleased with the sale. My brother, who was a much better drummer than me (actually, it is presumptuous to even call myself a drummer), was very annoyed that I would sell my beautiful set of drums. I even threw into the deal my forty-inch Zildjin cymbal.

I like things in their place. I like a bit of order to my life. I spent that August trying to put my apartment in some kind of shape. First thing I did was set up the bathroom. I had a lifelong yearning for a bathroom I could call my own, so concentrating on the bathroom was entirely in character for me. I bought an ugly black shower curtain, which at the time I thought was hip. My taste was not as highly evolved as it is now. Someone gave me a bathmat, and one of my sisters sent me some old towels and an ice bucket. I was all set. In the afternoons, I would take a bus over to my new place, sometimes lugging boxes of my belongings with me (once the bus driver wouldn't let me on with this old end table I was carting—I warned him that this would cost him his job), and when I arrived the first thing I would do was take a shower. Actually, that was about all I could do since the rest of the apartment was empty.

I was brought up to bathe at least once a week, and I grew older I increased the frequency of my baths (later, showers). I was, however, nowhere along the line encouraged to wash my hair more than once a month or so. My parents were immigrants, with different standards than those of middle-class Americans, and I inherited some of their attitudes. I would brush my hair out in the morning and sometimes I'd rub a little Listerine into my scalp for the dandruff. In fact, I paid very little attention to my hair. I did not even own a comb.

One day, about a year before I moved to my apartment, I was brushing my hair. At that particular time I was working as a construction laborer for the summer. As usual, bits of rubble were disentangled from my dirty hair as I brushed. But then something else began to happen as well—numerous hairs started falling out with the rubble. My brush was thickly webbed with my fallen hairs. I panicked. I never before in my life could recall losing a single hair and now they were tumbling out of my scalp with a vengeance. I calmed myself down, cleaned out my brush, and gave the matter some thought. Finally I decided this was just a fluke. So I lost a little hair. Big deal. It probably wouldn't happen again.

But my consolation was short lived. From that morning on the hairs fell like confetti in a ticker tape parade. And they didn't just fall out when I brushed my hair. It became an almost continuous occurrence. I would be reading, and all of a sudden several hairs would appear on the white page, like some horrible one-celled creatures under a microscope. I would blow them away, but before long others appeared to take their place. Hairs got caught in the hinges of my glasses. There would be hairs on my clothes, in my toothbrush (how? I don't know), hairs everywhere.

I became a man obsessed. From never caring about hair, I went to the opposite extreme. It was all I could think about. The panicky voice inside me couldn't stop—only twenty years old and losing his hair! No! Impossible! He'll be bald by the time he's twenty-two! But what could be done? Loss of hair seemed like something a real man wouldn't care much about. A real man would be too embarrassed to allow himself to think of something as vain as his hair. But I was no real man. I told myself I wouldn't mind if I was forty and started losing my hair, but I'm only twenty fucking years old! I felt fate was being very cruel to me.

But I decided that even if it meant acknowledging to the world my concern, my vain concern, for the future of my hairline, I simply had to do something about it.

In the *Daily News* was an ad for Bryant Hair Specialists. Bryant Hair Specialists were located right near my new apartment, but I didn't know that at the time since I was still living at home with my father and the summer of that beautiful empty apartment with the fully equipped bathroom—my Utopia!—was still a year away. The ad said that if you clipped it out and brought it with you, you would qualify for a special discount rate of four dollars on your first "treatment."

For about a week, I mulled it all over in my mind. I had clipped the ad and was carrying it around with me. Every once in a while I would take it out and examine it, trying to decide if I should risk a visit to Mr. Bryant and his team of Specialists. Usually I rejected the idea—what if someone should see me going into the place? What if someone I knew was being "treated" there? What if, God forbid, someone who knew me worked there? I didn't know what to do.

My father, forty years older than me, had a pretty good head of hair. It was still mostly dark and pretty thick. He had a little bald spot, barely noticeable, on his crown and a slightly recessive hairline. All in all, as much hair as any reasonable sixty-year-old man could hope for. In fact, I began to feel that if I had as much at twenty-five I'd be happy.

So far, I had mentioned my hair problems to no one. I hoped fervently that no one would notice the hair crisis I was going through. But I began to be keenly observant of people's hair, a complete switch for me, who never focused on the stuff before. Now when I looked at a person, I started with their hair and worked down to their face. I decided I had to break my silence on the matter and talk to someone.

My father was sitting at the kitchen table, reading the *News*. "Dad, I think I'm going bald," I said. I was very serious. I might just as well have been saying, "Dad, I think I have cancer." My father's response was very generous. "I started losing my hair when I was about your age. It kept on falling out for a few years, till I was about twenty-five, then it just stopped," he told me. The fact that my father, not at all a vain man, would even seriously address the problem of losing hair gave me hope. He was very sympathetic, at the same time cautioning me about being too concerned about hair. My father was the type of man who had learned to accept life. Or maybe he was always that way. I don't know. There was nothing you could do about most things that happened, he felt, except live with it.

I decided to research my father's claims—not because I didn't believe, but just to reassure myself. There was an old suitcase jammed with family photographs in one of the closets. I fished out photographs of my father from when he was a very young man right up to recent times and, sure enough, the photographs bore him out. He had pretty much the same head of hair at twenty-five or thirty as he did at present. So, hope at last! Maybe it would stop for me too, before I wound up looking like Yul Brynner.

In the meantime, however, it was still happening, and one day I summoned up my courage to pay a visit to Bryant Hair Specialists.

They were located on the ninth floor of a big office building in the Fordham section. I told the elevator man, "Eighth floor, please," since I didn't want anyone to know, including the elevator man, and walked the one flight from eighth to ninth. I walked briskly into the waiting room trying to stay in command of myself, wanting to seem relaxed. Only one other man was in the waiting room. He looked scared for his life. He sat forward in his chair, head bowed. He might have been a refugee trying to secure papers from hostile authorities at the border. He was at least twice my age.

All the personnel were Puerto Rican. That was a good sign. None of them would know me. There would be ethnic detachment between us. No familiarity, just businesslike anonymity—that was how I wanted it. I gave them a phony name. I saw no reason why they had to know who I was. If I decided to continue with them, I would pay in cash each visit.

But I knew, not too deep down, that this would be a one-shot deal. I am in the habit of "testing" things out before I plunge into them, if I plunge in at all. I just wanted to see what it looked like, and felt like, inside the hidden world of the hair-obsessed. I knew myself well enough to know that I really didn't want to stay long in the Hair Treatment universe.

The first thing the Puerto Rican ladies had me do was take off my shirt. I had not doped the situation out enough to expect this. It immediately injected an erotic note into the proceedings. Being a construction laborer and twenty years old, I was looking good, even if I did feel a little self-conscious. I was wearing my green chinos. They were old, but they fit me well, and I thought they looked sexy on me. An older lady had me sit in a big chair, like the kind in a dentist's office or barber shop. The chair reclined back, so that I was almost lying flat on my back. Before washing my hair, she began massaging my scalp.

The massage felt very good. In fact, the whole experience was turning into a sensual kick, and who's above a harmless, passive thrill once in a while? I felt embarrassed, helpless, literally in their hands. They had secret, private knowledge of me—that I was there because I was concerned about my hair—and this gave them power over me. What did I know about this Puerto Rican lady massaging me? Absolutely nothing, except where she worked.

After she washed my hair, she raised the chair up and maneuvered a dryer over my hair, the kind of contraptions found in ladies' beauty salons. Now I really felt silly. And they knew it.

When they finished washing and drying my hair, I went into a little room behind a curtain to comb it. I looked like a frightened Stan Laurel with my bone-dry hair reaching for the skies. The refugee was in the room too, combing his almost nonexistent hair. I think he, and the ladies who worked there, thought I was a little crazy, since it certainly didn't look as though I were going bald. I looked like a young man with a full head of very clean, dry, upright hair. What brought me there was the panic going on inside my head and not so much as what was happening on it.

On the bus back home to the apartment where my father and I lived, I thought everybody was staring at me, wondering—why is that guy's hair so dry and sticking up in the air like he's seen a ghost? He must have been to a hair treatment place, the sissy. But I think I only imagined that anyone noticed.

I never went back to Bryant Hair Specialists. But about a month after my treatment there I went downtown to another, fancier hair hospital, the Devon Hair Works. Another one-shot exploration. A very serious man with wavy blond hair and glasses, wearing a white smock, looked me over. The importance he seemed to attach to my "problem" outdid even my own frantic concern. It was as though I were a victim of a unique and terrible disease for which he had the only known cure.

"I think we can help you," he said very seriously as I sat in yet another huge dentist's chair feeling ridiculous but determined. He poured some caramel-colored goo onto my scalp that felt wonderful. It was freezing cold and shocked and invigorated my faltering follicles. "How does that feel?" he asked, knowing full well that it felt terrific. "OK," I replied indifferently, not wanting to give him too much of an edge and having already decided that this place was not my style.

We had a talk in his office after the goo treatment. I was just going through the motions, asking about prices, how long it would take, things like that. He was very evasive. But I think he sensed I wasn't going to bite. After a few minutes of pompous beating around the bush, he said it would cost me five hundred dollars for them to take on my case. This was 1967, and that was a lot of money. "I'll think about it," I said. He made a face that made it clear he knew I would not sign up. He made me feel so guilty, in fact, for wasting his time that before I left his office I would up giving him eight dollars for three bottles of special shampoo. Each bottle had a specific function. One was full of some thick green fluid that you washed your hair with. The second contained a thinner, blue liquid that you used after the green stuff. The third fluid was the color of coffee and you were supposed to use it at different times during the day.

I threw all three bottles away the next day after a lengthy session in the bathroom during which I applied the magic fluids to my beleaguered scalp with religious attention to the instructions, finally deciding that it was too much trouble and bullshit.

Thanks be to God, as my mother used to say, I stopped going bald. By the time I moved to my new apartment, a year after my encounters with Bryant and Devon, my condition had stabilized.

I met my friend Sheila one afternoon during the summer I moved into my apartment. Sheila knew I had a crush on her roommate, Christine. Christine was a little crazy, but very attractive. I pumped Sheila for information on what Christine thought of me. "Christine thinks you have nice eyes and beautiful hair," Sheila told me.

TERENCE WINCH's latest book is a collection of poems called Boy Drinkers *(Hanging Loose, 2007). His previous books include* Irish Musicians/ American Friends, *which won an American Book Award;* The Great Indoors, *winner of the Columbia Book Award;* The Drift of Things; *and a short-story collection called* Contenders. *His last book,* That Special Place: New World Irish Stories *draws on his experiences as a founding member of the highly regarded Irish band Celtic Thunder. His work is included in the* Oxford Book of American Poetry, *three* Best American Poetry *collections, and* Poetry 180, *and in other journals and anthologies. Winch, whose work has been featured on the* Poetry Daily *website, the* Writers Almanac, *and NPR's* All Things Considered, *received an NEA fellowship in poetry and a Fund for Poetry grant, among other awards. See www.terencewinch.com.*

The Definition of Man

I was young and living in Adams Morgan. My girlfriend and I broke up late in the winter. She was a bony, dirty blonde. She had tiny breasts with dark, plum-colored nipples and an archipelago of freckles around her belly button. She came from California. She tossed her hair to the side, unless she got drunk, when she threw every word at me like it was a stone coming over a barricade.

Spring came. We stopped talking. One Wednesday she left me a note saying she was spending the night at a friend's house—the friend's parents were out of town. That night I steeled myself with a few quarts of ale and went to get my bike which had rusticated in the basement all winter. While on my way to the basement I passed my friend PJ's apartment. Everyone called him Jommies.

"Where are you going?" He had Widespread Panic on, Letterman on mute, and the shades drawn.

"Gaby's. Well, sort of, she's at Melinda's parents' place. Little house. Near the Watergate." I was explaining too much.

His hair cowled his eyes. He spoke in staccato sentences. "Good. Dude. Listen. Beer ball or cases for tomorrow night?" Jommies asked as if this was some physics theorem, with just one correct proof that centuries of scientists had been unable to unravel. A ball of string. He was the cat.

"Beer ball."

"Right, dude. It makes good financial sense."

I wheeled my red Schwinn Traveler III out of the basement. It was a ten-speed. They didn't make them anymore. Its tires were flaccid, deflated from its winter nap. I walked down 16th to the old gas station on Irving. No one was there. Past midnight. I put a quarter in the air dispenser, which whirred to life with a bad cough. I wrestled the hose over to my front tire. In the half-light, it took eons to untwist the black lid off the prong, couple the hose and the prong, and start pumping air in. Just as I finished the front tire and was lurching in great haste towards the back, the machine went clunk-clunk and died. I reached into my pockets—no more quarters.

I rode into the dark night. Insistent stars blinked over the rooftops. The rim of the back tire scrapped with an ugly crunch. I biked down Columbia and onto Connecticut. It was downhill. They lived on Eye Street. I met Melinda's parents once, at a graduation party a couple of years earlier. The mother, smelling of coconuts, had told me that it was Eye not I. There was no J Street in the District. No one knew why.

They lived between 18th and 19th. Nowhere near the Watergate. Gray, empty wastescape, office towers and Starbucks. And one little house, red brick, three stories, hemmed in like a book on a shelf. It was a relic. Melinda's grandmother had been born there, when there was a school across the street, when the black-garbed Quakers walked in silence to their meetinghouse.

I was late. Gaby flipped her blonde hair over her shoulders and turned away, a slish of stockinged feet on the stair. Wordlessly, I followed.

In the morning, in the master bedroom, we heard the deadening rumble of the front door opening and Melinda's parents arriving home.

I swore off backsliding. Never again.

I fell in love. Shirley was working as a cashier at an obscure second-hand bookstore in Takoma Park. She asked about the book I was buying. She had pale green, mountain lion eyes. She had a ring on every toe. Within days we were traveling together, first to old mill towns in Maryland. She had dated a guy from Ellicott City, so she knew the bars there, a place to crash that was not near the railroad tracks.

She smiled a lot. She read novels at breakfast. She called me "Frankly." Within weeks, we found ourselves overseas.

We ended up in a cottage outside a fishing village on the Indian Ocean. It was on a part of the African coast where a war had just ended. We lived as if we were in a cave. We swam when the tide was high and then dried ourselves in the sun, the salt pebbling and stinging our skin. We listened to water meeting the sand, the earth's heartbeat. We listened to the radio. We loved the BBC game show in which you had to bullshit on a subject for sixty seconds, without pausing or repeating yourself. No one could do it. Dissembling is like breathing: you can't do it well on purpose.

We watched the rain dapple the sea. We ate meals at midnight, candles at the window. We grew food in the abandoned garden terracing the hill. Shirley stopped shaving. I stopped shaving. Our hair grew down our backs in ropey hunks. Barefoot. We were cavemen.

"What is this?" she said one afternoon, the rain pattering the broken windows. "I can't get enough of you. I hope you are bottomless."

"I hope you are topless," I said.

"No, I am serious. Where does this love come from? Where does it lodge?"

"Do you really want to know?"

"Yes," she said and she pulled at her hair from underneath the pillow. "Self-hatred? Self-love? An old mill town? The sea?"

"Have you heard this story? In 1863 in Paris, René Sully-Prudhomme bumps into a childhood friend on the Boulevard des Italiens. The friend, short and fat as a boy, is now tall and thin. All successful. Proud. Runs a drapery firm. Sully-Prudhomme says he looks like a little elastic man who had been stretched. They chat about a school friend in common. They run out of things to say. The elastic friend hands over his card. Sully-Prudhomme has no card. He is perpetually unemployed. Sully-Prudhomme has nothing to say about draperies. The friend asks him what he is doing: 'My dear fellow, I am looking for a definition of man.'"

Our little world was not enough. It spun us out of the cave. We met other people. We had affairs, excuses, girls from Reunion Island, a fisherman with a glass eye who spoke Spanish. Rain dripped off the mossy wooden roof with despair.

The rainy season never ended. "What is the rain for?" she moaned, unable to get out of bed.

"To remember love," I said. Her eyes crawled away.

She got malaria. We went inland. We stopped at a hotel. The train ran twice a week. I cooked lentils on a camping stove in our room. She wrung sweat out of her body. The clinic was empty. I read her "The Cat in the Rain." She loathed Hemingway, but she liked cats and she loved the feel of raindrops on her aching head.

The train came at five in the morning. We rumbled inland. We reached the city. She flew home.

Years later, Shirley was visiting a small town in western Pennsylvania. I had been working on a story about Groundhog Day which coincidentally was held each winter in a small town in western Pennsylvania. I drove out and met her by Lake Erie. We had lunch.

Shirley was still a sunny person, but more fine-grained, fragile. She and I, pushing our salads around our chipped plates, strained to talk about anything besides ourselves or the world. There was no middle ground. The coffee smelled of the jungle.

We drove to Punxsutawney. Within a few minutes of arriving in town, we were sitting in the living room of the official handler of Punxsutawney Phil, "the Seer of Seers, the Prognosticator of Prognosticators." The handler complained that farmers digging up groundhogs while doing their spring plowing brought him groundhogs by the dozens. He had three or four young groundhogs running around in his living room while we sat on a sofa sheathed in plastic. His wife brought us warm cans of beer. They lived above a funeral home.

Like George Foreman and his sons, the handler named all the groundhogs Phil. The real Phil was kept in a little zoo on the town square. They kept the lights and heat on all winter. "We don't want him to start hibernating," the handler told us, furry black beasts ravaging under his couch. "If he hibernates like a normal groundhog, when we wake him up on the second of February, he's going to have a heart attack."

We got a motel room on the outskirts of town. We did not leave the room for two days. We emerged. It was snowing and our car made a soft, cobblestoned spoor as we drove away.

JAMES ZUG is the author of five books, including Squash: A History of the Game *(Scribner, 2003),* American Traveler: The Life & Adventures of John Ledyard *(Basic, 2005) and* The Guardian: The History of South Africa's Extraordinary Anti-Apartheid Newspaper *(Michigan State, 2007). He has a master's in nonfiction writing from Columbia and has written for the* Atlantic Monthly, Outside, *and* Fast Company. *He can be contacted at www.jameszug.com.*

RICHARD PEABODY *is a native Washingtonian who now lives in Arlington, Virginia, with his wife and two daughters. Read more at www.wikipedia.com.*

G. BYRON PECK *lives in Washington, D.C., and has created over eighty murals throughout the United States and abroad. He has won four grant awards from the D.C. Arts and Humanities Commission (1987, 1995, 1997, 1999) and two Fellowships for Painting from the Virginia Museum of Fine Art (1977, 1979) and was given the Mayor's Art Award for Excellence in an Artistic Discipline in 2000. Mural commissions have included the John F. Kennedy Center for the Performing Arts, the American embassy in Santiago, Chile, Mount Vernon, Virginia, and the U.S. Nuclear Energy Commission headquarters.*